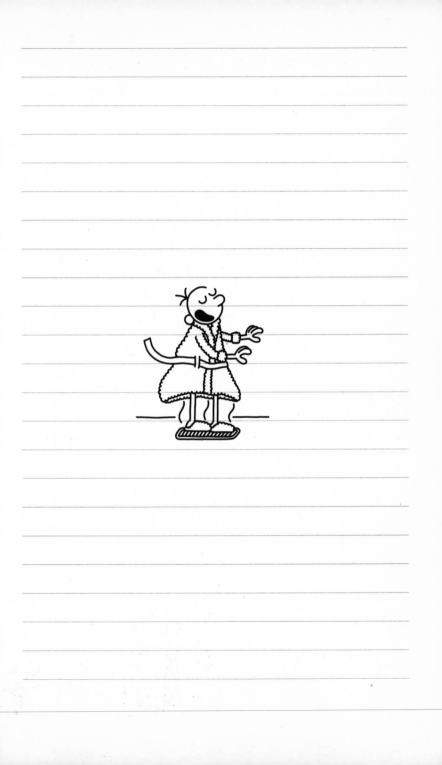

OTROS LIBROS DE JEFF KINNEY:

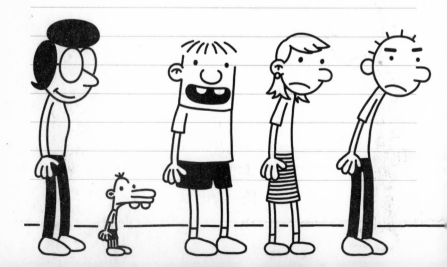

DIARIO
de
Greg

¡ESTO ES EL COLMO!

Jeff Kinney

MOLINO

LECTORUM

DIARIO DE GREG 3. ¡ESTO ES EL COLMO!

Originally published in English under the title DIARY OF A WIMPY KID: THE LAST STRAW

This edition published by agreement with Amulet Books, a division of Harry N. Abrams, Inc

Spanish edition copyright © 2010 by RBA LIBROS, S.A.

Lectorum ISBN: 978-1-933032-63-4
Printed in Spain
10 9
Legal deposit: B-14185-2017

A TIM

ENERO

Día de Año Nuevo

Se supone que al empezar cada año todo el mundo hace una lista de "buenos propósitos" con el fin de mejorar como personas.

El caso es que me resulta difícil pensar en alguna forma de mejorar, porque de hecho ya soy una de las mejores personas que conozco.

Así que mi buen propósito de este año es tratar de ayudar a que otras personas mejoren. Pero me estoy dando cuenta de que hay gente que no aprecia demasiado cuando intentas ayudarles.

Una de las cosas que he notado enseguida es que mi familia no se toma demasiado en serio lo de los buenos propósitos para el Año Nuevo.

Mamá dijo que hoy mismo iba a empezar a ir al gimnasio, pero se pasó toda la tarde viendo la televisión.

Y Papá dijo que iba a empezar a hacer una dieta estricta, pero después de la cena le pillé en el garaje, atracándose de bizcochos de chocolate.

Incluso mi hermano pequeño Manny ha sido incapaz de seguir adelante con sus propósitos.

Esta misma mañana le dijo a todo el mundo que él ya es un "chico mayor" y que iba a dejar para siempre sus hábitos de niño pequeño. Y tiró al cubo de basura su chupete favorito.

Fue un propósito de Año Nuevo que ni siquiera duró un minuto.

La única persona de mi familia que no ha hecho ningún propósito para el Año Nuevo es mi hermano mayor, Rodrick, y es una lástima porque su lista podría llegar hasta el infinito.

Así que decidí poner en marcha un programa para ayudar a Rodrick a ser mejor persona. Lo llamé "A la tercera va la vencida". La idea básica era que cada vez que pillara a Rodrick en un lío le apuntaría una X en su tarjeta.

Pero Rodrick consiguió las tres X incluso antes de que yo tuviera claro qué quería decir eso de "va la vencida".

PAF
PAF
PAF

En fin, que me estoy planteando olvidar yo también MI buen propósito. Supone un montón de trabajo y la verdad es que hasta ahora no he progresado nada.

Es más, después de recordarle a Mamá por millonésima vez que no debía hacer tanto ruido al masticar las papitas fritas, ella hizo un comentario interesante. Dijo: "No todo el mundo puede ser tan perfecto como tú, Gregory". Y hasta donde he podido comprobarlo, tiene toda la razón.

Papá ha vuelto a intentarlo con su dieta, y eso no es bueno para mí. Lleva casi tres días sin probar el chocolate y está SÚPER irritado.

El otro día, cuando me despertó y me dijo que me arreglara para ir al colegio, accidentalmente me volví a dormir. De veras que no pienso volver a cometer ESE error.

Parte del problema es que Papá siempre me despierta antes de que Mamá salga de la ducha y sé que todavía puedo aprovechar unos diez minutos hasta que sea realmente necesario salir de la cama.

Ayer se me ocurrió una idea estupenda para poder dormir un poco más sin que Papá montase en cólera. Después de que me desperté, me llevé conmigo la manta al piso de abajo para esperar ante la puerta del cuarto de baño mi turno en la ducha.

Allí me tumbé sobre la rejilla del calentador de aire, cosa que resultó todavía MÁS AGRADABLE que estar en la cama.

Lo malo es que el calentador sólo funciona durante cinco minutos y luego se apaga. Cuando paró el aire caliente, sentí debajo de mí el frío de la rejilla metálica.

Esta mañana, mientras esperaba a que Mamá terminara de ducharse, recordé que alguien le había regalado un albornoz en Navidad. Así que fui al armario y lo cogí.

Fue una de las mejores ideas que he tenido nunca. Llevar eso puesto era como ir envuelto en una toalla grande y mullida, recién salida de la secadora.

Me gustó tanto el albornoz que lo conservé puesto también DESPUÉS de ducharme. Creo que Papá sintió envidia por no haber tenido él antes la idea de la bata, porque cuando me presenté en la cocina para desayunar me miró con mala cara.

Ya te digo. Las mujeres acertaron sin duda con este invento de la bata de baño. Me pregunto qué OTRAS COSAS me estaré perdiendo.

Tan sólo desearía haber pedido un albornoz para mí como regalo de Navidad, porque seguro que Mamá me va a hacer devolverle el suyo.

Volví a recordar los regalos de este año. La mañana de Navidad supe que iba a ser un día duro tan pronto como bajé las escaleras y los únicos regalos que había en mi calcetín eran una barra de desodorante y un "diccionario de viaje".

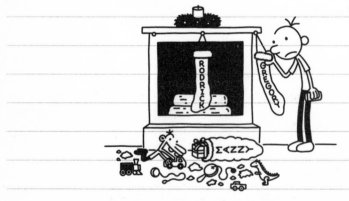

Supongo que cuando ya vas a la escuela intermedia, los adultos consideran que eres demasiado mayor para recibir juguetes o cualquier otra cosa divertida.

Sin embargo, todavía esperan que te emociones cuando abres los regalos chungos que te hacen.

Casi todos mis regalos de este año fueron libros o prendas de vestir. Lo más parecido a un juguete que tuve fue un regalo de tío Charlie.

Cuando lo desenvolví, ni siquiera supe qué se suponía que era aquello. Era una arandela de plástico unida a una especie de malla.

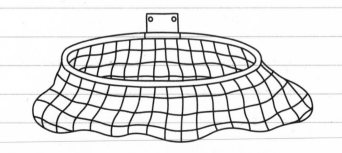

Tío Charlie me explicó que se trataba de una canasta de ropa sucia para mi dormitorio. Dijo que era para colgar en la parte de atrás de la puerta y encestar la ropa sucia de una manera divertida,

Al principio creí que se trataba de una broma, pero entonces me di cuenta de que tío Charlie hablaba en serio. Así que tuve que explicarle que yo NO me lavo mi propia ropa.

Le expliqué que yo tan sólo me limito a tirar al suelo la ropa sucia y Mamá se encarga de recogerla y bajarla al lavadero.

Luego, pocos días después, la ropa vuelve a mí cuidadosamente doblada y apilada.

Así que le dije a tío Charlie que podía devolver la canasta a la tienda y simplemente darme dinero, para que yo pudiera comprar algo que de verdad me resultara ÚTIL.

Entonces fue cuando habló Mamá y le dijo a tío Charlie que a ella le parecía que lo de la canasta había sido una idea FORMIDABLE.

Y dijo que desde ahora yo iba a ser responsable de lavar mi ROPA. Al final, tío Charlie me regaló una tarea más por Navidad.

Es horrible que este año recibiera unos regalos tan miserables. Yo me había dedicado a ganarme a la gente durante los meses anteriores y esperaba que para Navidad mi esfuerzo diera sus frutos.

Ahora que tengo que lavarme mi ropa, me ALEGRO de haber recibido tanta ropa. Puede que pase todo el curso antes de que me quede sin nada limpio que ponerme.

Lunes

Esta mañana, cuando Rowley y yo llegamos a la parada del autobús, nos llevamos una sorpresa desagradable. Había, pegada a la señal, una hoja de papel informando que la ruta se había "cambiado" con efectividad inmediata. Significa que desde ahora tenemos que ANDAR hasta el colegio.

Me gustaría tener una conversación con la persona que ha tenido ESA luminosa idea, porque nuestra calle se encuentra casi a un cuarto de milla del colegio.

Rowley y yo tuvimos que correr hoy para llegar a tiempo. Lo peor de todo fue cuando el autobús de siempre pasó por delante de nuestras narices, lleno de chicos de Whirley Street, el barrio colindante con el nuestro.

Los de Whirley Street nos hicieron gestos de mono cuando nos pasaron, cosa que nos molestó de veras, porque era exactamente lo mismo que NOSOTROS solíamos hacerles a ellos.

He aquí una buena razón para no hacer andar a los chicos hasta el colegio. Resulta que está de moda que los maestros pongan muchas tareas para casa, y con tantos libros y cuadernos, la mochila acaba pesando cientos de libras.

Para comprobar los efectos de tanto peso a lo largo del tiempo basta con ver a Rodrick y a algunos de sus amigos.

Hablando de adolescentes, Papá se ha marcado una victoria en el día de hoy. Resulta que el mayor gamberro del barrio, un tal Lenwood Heath, es su máximo archienemigo. Papá ha llamado unas cincuenta veces a la policía para quejarse de Lenwood Heath.

Los padres de Lenwood debían estar hartos de sus actuaciones, porque lo han enviado a un colegio militar.

15

Quizá piensen que con eso Papá se quedaría contento, pero creo que no va a darse por satisfecho hasta que todos los adolescentes del planeta se encuentren en un correccional o en Alcatraz o algo por el estilo. Y eso incluye a mi hermano Rodrick.

Ayer Mamá y Papá le dieron a Rodrick dinero para comprar los libros que necesitaba para estudiar sus exámenes de evaluación, pero él se lo gastó en hacerse un tatuaje.

A mí todavía me queda algún tiempo antes de entrar en la adolescencia. Pero en el mismo minuto en que eso ocurra, estoy seguro de que Papá estará aguardando la primera oportunidad que se le presente para enviarme fuera.

Lunes

Casi toda la semana pasada Manny estuvo levantándose de la cama por las noches y bajando al salón.

En lugar de enviarlo de nuevo a su cuarto, Mamá le
permitió sentarse con nosotros y quedarse a ver la tele.

No es justo, porque cuando Manny está con nosotros
no me dejan ver los programas que me gustan.

Recuerdo que cuando yo era pequeño las cosas eran
distintas. Nada de eso de "levantarse de la cama".
Cuando lo intenté hacer una o dos veces, Papá cortó
mis intentos en seco.

Recuerdo también que Papá solía leerme por las
noches un libro titulado "El árbol generoso". Era un
libro estupendo, pero la contraportada tenía una
foto del autor, un tal Shel Silverstein.

La cara de Shel Silverstein parecía más la de un ban-
dido o un pirata que la de un tipo que escribe libros
para chicos.

Papá seguramente se dio cuenta de que me asustaba
aquella foto, porque una noche que me levanté de la cama
me dijo:

Aquello tuvo un efecto mágico. Desde entonces, sigo TODAVÍA sin levantarme de la cama por las noches, incluso si tengo ganas de ir al cuarto de baño.

No creo que Papá y Mamá le lean a Manny libros de Shel Silverstein y eso explica por qué se sigue levantando de la cama después de acostarlo.

He oído algunas de las historias que Papá y Mamá leen a Manny, y permitan que les diga que la gente que escribe esos libros se ha montado un buen chanchullo. Para empezar, apenas tienen texto, así que debe llevarles tan sólo cinco minutos escribir uno.

Le dije a Mamá lo que opinaba sobre los libros de Manny y ella me contestó que si tan fácil me parecía escribirlos, entonces yo debería probar a escribir uno.

Y eso fue lo que hice. De veras, tampoco resultó tan difícil. Todo lo que tienes que hacer es inventarte un personaje, ponerle un nombre fácil de recordar y asegurarte de que aprende alguna lección al final de la historia.

Después hay que enviarlo a un editor y esperar a que el dinero llueva sobre tu cabeza.

¡ESPABILE, SR. SHROPSHARP!

Por Greg Heffley

Érase una vez un hombre llamado Sr. Shropsharp que tenía la cabeza llena de ideas absurdas,

Un día el Sr. Shropsharp fue a dar un paseo en su coche.

Y entonces,,,

¿Ven lo que quiero decir? Sólo que después de haber terminado el libro me di cuenta de que se me había olvidado hacer que las frases rimaran. Pero el editor va a tener que pagarme un extra si quiere ESO.

Sábado

En fin. Después de las dos últimas semanas yendo al colegio a pie, estaba deseando llegar a casa y no hacer nada durante dos días.

Lo malo de quedarse viendo la tele un sábado es que no ponen nada más que juegos de bolos y golf. Encima, el sol entra por el ventanal de la sala y apenas se puede ver la pantalla de la tele.

Hoy quise cambiar el canal de la tele, pero el mando a distancia estaba encima de la mesita de café. Yo me encontraba tan cómodo, con mi bol de cereales sobre las rodillas, que no me apetecía nada incorporarme.

Intenté usar la Fuerza para que el mando de la tele levitara hacia mí, a pesar de que ya lo había intentado un montón de veces en otras ocasiones y nunca había funcionado. Hoy lo intenté durante quince minutos concentrándome de manera REALMENTE intensa, pero tampoco hubo suerte. Ojalá me hubiese dado cuenta de que Papá estaba detrás de mí todo el tiempo.

¡UNG!... ¡OMMMM!,... ¡OIGGGG!... ¡MMMM!...

Papá me dijo que me convenía salir fuera y hacer ejercicio. Le dije a Papá que SIEMPRE estoy haciendo ejercicio y que precisamente esta mañana había usado el banco de musculación que él me había regalado.

Pero debería haberme inventado algo más creíble, porque saltaba a la vista que era mentira.

A Papá le ha dado por decirme que tengo que hacer
ejercicio y todo eso porque tiene como jefe a un tal
Sr. Warren, y el señor Warren tiene tres chicos que
son de esos forofos que se pasan el día haciendo
deporte. Papá los ve todos los días en el jardín al
pasar por delante de su casa, cuando hace el trayecto al
trabajo en coche.

Así que me parece que Papá debe sentirse decepcionado cada vez que regresa a casa y comprueba en qué andan ocupados sus hijos.

De todos modos, como dije antes, Papá me hizo salir al exterior de la casa hoy. No se me ocurría nada que me apeteciera hacer, pero entonces tuve una idea genial.

Ayer durante el almuerzo, Albert Sandy le estaba contando a todo el mundo acerca de ese tipo de China o Taiwán o de donde sea, que es capaz de saltar seis pies hacia arriba, de veras. La forma en que consiguió esto consiste en cavar un hoyo de tres pulgadas de profundidad y saltar dentro y fuera un centenar de veces. Al día siguiente, duplicó la profundidad del hoyo y de nuevo se dedicó a saltar dentro y fuera. Al quinto día, casi se había convertido en un canguro.

Algunos chicos de la mesa le dijeron a Albert que eso eran chorradas, pero lo que estaba diciendo tenía mucho sentido para MÍ. Es más, supuse que si hiciera lo que Albert había dicho y además pudiera AÑADIR algunos días al programa, todos mis problemas con los matones del colegio podrían quedar resueltos.

¿BUSCAN A ALGUIEN, CHICOS?

Agarré una pala del garaje y elegí un sitio en el patio que me pareció un buen punto para cavar. Pero antes de que hubiera empezado, salió Mamá y me preguntó qué estaba haciendo.

Le dije a Mamá que sólo iba a cavar un agujero y, claro, ESA idea no la convenció en absoluto. Y me dio veintitantas razones por las que no me permitía hacerlo.

Mamá me dijo lo "peligroso" que era cavar en el patio, debido a las líneas eléctricas subterráneas y a las conducciones de aguas residuales y todo ese rollo. Entonces me hizo prometer que no iba a cavar un agujero en nuestro patio. Tuve que prometerlo.

Mamá se fue al interior de la casa, pero siguió
vigilándome desde la ventana. Supe que iba a tener
que irme con la pala a cavar el hoyo a otra parte,
así que me dirigí a casa de Rowley.

No he ido mucho últimamente por casa de Rowley,
principalmente por causa de Fregley. Fregley pasa
mucho tiempo en el patio en frente de la casa y, por
supuesto, ahí es donde estaba hoy.

Mi nueva estrategia con Fregley se limita a evitar el
contacto visual y seguir caminando. Y al menos por
hoy parece que ha funcionado.

Cuando llegué a casa de Rowley, le conté mi idea y le dije que prácticamente podíamos convertirnos en ninjas si éramos capaces de soportar el programa de saltar dentro y fuera del hoyo que yo había concebido.

Pero Rowley no pareció entusiasmarse demasiado con el proyecto. Dijo que sus padres se enfadarían mucho si cavábamos un mega hoyo en el patio en frente de la casa sin preguntarles antes, así que iba a tener que pedirles permiso.

Si hay algo que tengo claro sobre los padres de Rowley es que NUNCA les gustan mis ideas. Le dije a Rowley que podíamos cubrir el hoyo con una lona o una manta y poner encima algunas hojas como camuflaje, de modo que nunca se iban a enterar. Esto pareció convencerle.

Está bien, admito que los padres de Rowley podían descubrirlo EVENTUALMENTE. Pero eso no iba a ocurrir al menos hasta dentro de tres o cuatro meses.

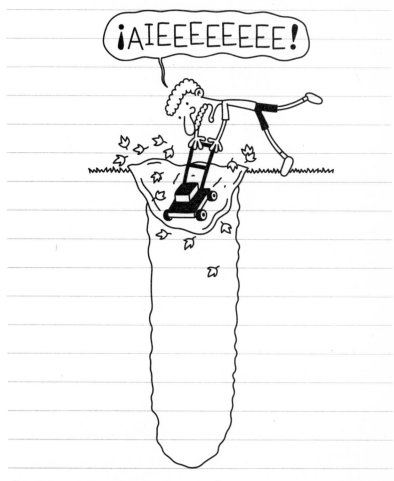

Rowley y yo encontramos un buen sitio en el patio para empezar a cavar, pero entonces surgió otro problema.

El suelo estaba totalmente helado, y durísimo, así que apenas pudimos hacer una muesca en él.

Pasé unos minutos intentando cavar, hasta que le pasé la pala a Rowley. Él tampoco consiguió hacer ningún progreso, a pesar de que le concedí un turno extra-largo para que pudiera sentirse como si estuviera contribuyendo al proyecto.

Rowley consiguió profundizar un poquito más que yo, pero lo dejó cuando empezó a oscurecer.

Me parece que vamos a tener que hacer otro intento mañana.

Domingo
Anoche lo estuve reconsiderando y me di cuenta de que, al ritmo que llevamos, Rowley y yo estaremos en la universidad antes de que nuestro hoyo llegue a tener una profundidad considerable.

Así que se me ocurrió otra idea totalmente DISTINTA acerca de lo que podíamos hacer. Recordé una serie de TV en la que unos científicos construían una "cápsula de tiempo" y la llenaban con una serie de objetos como un periódico, un DVD y cosas así. Luego, enterraban la cápsula de tiempo. La idea era que unos cuantos cientos de años más tarde llegaría alguien y desenterraría la cápsula, y así podría saber cómo era la vida en nuestra época.

CÁPSULA
DE TIEMPO

NO ABRIR HASTA
EL AÑO 2300 D.C.

Le conté mi idea a Rowley y pareció muy entusiasmado. Más que nada, me parece que estaba contento porque no íbamos a pasarnos los próximos años intentando cavar un agujero.

Le dije a Rowley que tendría que donar algunos objetos para ponerlos en la cápsula de tiempo, y ahí es donde empezó a enfriarse su entusiasmo.

Le expliqué que si ponía algunos de sus regalos de Navidad en la cápsula de tiempo, entonces la gente del futuro dispondría de buen material cuando abriera la caja. Rowley dijo que no le parecía justo que yo no pusiera ninguno de mis regalos en la cápsula. Tuve que explicarle que la gente del futuro iba a pensar que éramos unos cutres, si al abrir la caja la encontraban llena de libros y prendas de ropa.

Entonces le dije a Rowley que dejaría en la cápsula de tiempo tres dólares de MI propio dinero, para demostrar que yo también estaba dispuesto a hacer sacrificios. Esto fue suficiente para convencerle de que se desprendiera de uno de sus videojuegos nuevos y un par de cosas más.

Pero yo tenía un plan secreto del que Rowley no formaba parte. Y es que sabía que poner dinero en metálico en la cápsula de tiempo era una buena inversión, porque ese dinero iba a valer muchísimo más que tres dólares en el futuro.

Así que es de esperar que quienes encuentren la cápsula viajarán hacia atrás en el tiempo y me recompensarán por haberlos hecho ricos.

ESTO PARA USTED, AMABLE SEÑOR.

Escribí una breve nota y la introduje en la caja,
para asegurarme de que la persona que la encuentre
sepa exactamente a quién tiene que estar agradecida.

A quien pueda interesar.
El dinero procede de
Greg Heffley
12 Surrey Street

Rowley y yo nos hicimos con una caja de zapatos y
pusimos todas las cosas dentro. Luego sellamos la caja
con cinta adhesiva.

En la parte exterior de la caja escribí un mensaje
para que no fuera abierta antes de tiempo.

Después pusimos la caja en el hoyo que cavamos ayer y la enterramos lo mejor que pudimos.

Ojalá Rowley se hubiera esforzado más en cavar el hoyo, porque en realidad la cápsula de tiempo no está totalmente cubierta de tierra. Esperemos que nadie tropiece con ella, porque tiene que permanecer ahí por lo menos unos cuantos cientos de años.

Lunes

Pues ya empiezo mal la semana. Al levantarme esta mañana, el albornoz de Mamá no se encontraba en su sitio habitual, colgado del picaporte de la puerta.

Le pregunté a Mamá si me había cogido el albornoz, pero dijo que no había sido ella. Me temo que Papá tiene algo que ver con todo esto.

Hace un par de días se me ocurrió una manera de combinar la experiencia del albornoz y la de la rejilla de aire caliente, pero no creo que a Papá le hiciera mucha gracia la idea.

Me imagino que ha escondido el albornoz o se ha deshecho de él. Ahora que lo pienso, Papá hizo un viaje hasta el cubo de basura anoche después de cenar, y eso no es buena señal.

En cualquier caso, si Papá se ha deshecho de la bata, no sería la primera vez que tira a la basura cosas que son propiedad personal de alguien. ¿Recuerdan cómo Manny ha intentado dejar de usar el chupete?

Ayer Papá tiró a la basura todos y cada uno de los chupetes de Manny.

Bueno, pues Manny se puso por completo fuera de sí. Sólo se tranquilizó cuando Mamá sacó su vieja manta, ese trapo que él llama "Pringui".

Pringui comenzó sus días como una mantita azul que Mamá tejió para Manny por su primer cumpleaños y fue un caso de amor a primera vista.

A cualquier parte que fuera, Manny llevaba la manta consigo. Ni siquiera permitía que Mamá la lavara.

Poco a poco fue haciéndose más pequeña y para cuando Manny cumplió dos años, su manta apenas eran unos cuantos hilos que se mantenían unidos con pasas y mocos.

Creo que fue por aquel entonces cuando Manny empezó a llamar "Pringui" a su manta.

Durante los dos últimos días, Manny ha estado arrastrando su Pringui por toda la casa, tal y como solía hacer cuando era un bebé, y he tratado de mantenerme apartado de su camino todo lo posible.

Miércoles

Me estoy cansando de andar hasta el colegio todos los días y esta mañana le he preguntando a Mamá si nos podía llevar en coche a mí y a Rowley. Si no se lo he pedido antes es porque su coche está todo lleno de pegatinas de lo más embarazoso, de esas que los chicos del colegio no perdonan.

He estado tratando de quitar las pegatinas, pero da la impresión de que llevan un pegamento hecho para durar hasta el fin de los tiempos.

Mi niño se ha graduado en la **Guardería Mimitos**

Así que cuando Mamá nos llevó hoy en el coche, le dije que nos dejara DETRÁS del colegio.

¿SEGURO QUE SE BAJAN AQUÍ?

SÍ, MAMÁ. GRACIAS POR TRAERNOS.

Cometí el error de olvidarme la mochila en el coche, de modo que Mamá me la trajo durante la cuarta clase. Y tenía que ser precisamente HOY el día que ha elegido para empezar a ir al gimnasio.

También es mala suerte, porque la cuarta clase es la única que tengo con Holly Hills, y llevo todo el curso intentando causarle una buena impresión. Este incidente me va a hacer retroceder al menos tres semanas.

Además no soy el único que está tratando de impresionar a Holly Hills. Me parece que todos los demás chicos de la clase andan locos por ella.

En realidad Holly es la cuarta chica más guapa de la clase, pero las tres primeras ya tienen novio. Así que hay un montón de tíos como yo intentando ligársela.

He buscado la manera de diferenciarme del resto de los chicos que van detrás de Holly. Y creo que al fin tengo la solución: sentido del humor.

Resulta que en mi curso parecen de Neanderthal cuando se trata de chistes. Para haceros una idea de lo que quiero decir, esto es lo que entienden en mi colegio como "actuación":

Siempre que Holly está presente, utilizo mis mejores recursos.

o usando a Rowley como compañero y le he

para representar un par de chistes estu-

pendos.

El único problema es que Rowley está empezando a cues-
tionar qué parte debe representar cada uno, así que
seguramente no vamos a durar mucho tiempo juntos.

<u>Viernes</u>

Ya he aprendido la lección de lo que me puede costar pedirle a Mamá que me lleve en coche, y he vuelto a ir caminando al colegio. Pero esta tarde, cuando volvía a casa con Rowley, realmente no tenía energía para subir la cuesta hasta mi casa y le he pedido que me llevara montado a caballito sobre su espalda.

A Rowley la idea no pareció convencerle y tuve que recordarle que somos estupendos amigos y que entre los buenos amigos se hacen este tipo de favores. Al final cedió cuando le dije que yo me ocuparía de llevarle la mochila.

Pero tengo la sensación de que esto no va a repe-
tirse, porque Rowley estaba totalmente exhausto
cuando me dejó en casa. Si el colegio suprime el
servicio de autobuses para regresar a nuestros domicilios,
lo menos que podrían hacer es instalar un teleférico
para subir la cuesta.

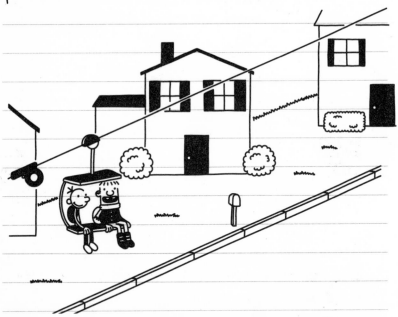

Ya le he enviado al director cinco mensajes de correo
electrónico con esta sugerencia, pero todavía no se ha
dignado a contestarme.

Al llegar a casa, yo también me sentía muy cansado. Y
ahora me ha dado por dormir la siesta todos los días
al volver del colegio.

La verdad es que VIVO para mis siestas. Dormir después del colegio es lo único que me recarga las pilas y la mayor parte de los días me meto en la cama tan pronto como llego a casa.

Me estoy convirtiendo en todo un experto en el arte de dormir. Una vez que me pongo, soy capaz de dormir sin límites.

El único que me supera en esto de dormir es RODRICK. Lo digo porque hace un par de semanas Mamá encargó una cama nueva para él, porque la suya ya estaba hecha cisco.

Cuando llegaron los empleados de la tienda de muebles para llevarse el viejo colchón, Rodrick se encontraba en mitad de su siesta. Pues cuando le quitaron la cama, siguió durmiendo en el mismo sitio, pero encima del suelo.

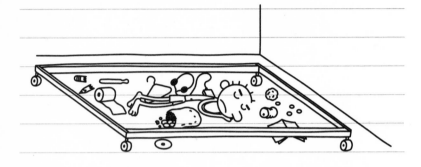

Me preocupa que Papá pueda prohibirnos dormir la siesta al volver del colegio. Empiezo a tener la sensación de que está harto de tener que despertarnos para cenar todos los días.

Martes
En fin, me revienta tener que reconocerlo pero me parece que las siestas están afectando mi rendimiento escolar.

48

Resulta que antes hacía los deberes al volver a casa y luego por la noche veía la televisión. Últimamente he intentado hacer los deberes MIENTRAS veo la tele, pero a veces no resulta.

Para hoy tenía un trabajo de Biología de cuatro páginas de extensión, pero anoche me quedé viendo el programa que estaban poniendo y hoy he tenido que escribirlo todo en la computadora durante el recreo.

Pero, claro, no me ha dado tiempo de hacer búsquedas ni de documentarme, así que he tenido que ajustar los márgenes y el tamaño de la letra para estirar todo lo que tenía hasta que ocupase cuatro páginas. Pero algo me parece que no va a colar y que la señorita Nolan me va a decir algo.

LOS CHIMPAN

Un trabajo de cuatro páginas
escrito por

GREG
HEFFLEY

Esto es un chimpancé
o si se prefiere,
un "chimpan",
para abreviar.

Los chimpan son
la materia del
trabajo que tiene
usted en sus manos.

Ayer saqué un cero en un examen de Geografía.
También hay que decir a mi favor que resultaba
difícil de veras estudiar para el examen al mismo
tiempo que veía el fútbol.

Para ser sincero, me parece que los maestros no
deberían hacernos aprender todos estos rollos, ya
que en el futuro todos tendremos un robot personal
que nos dirá todo aquello que necesitemos saber.

Y hablando de maestros, la Sra. Craig no ha tenido hoy un buen día, porque el enorme diccionario que siempre tiene encima de la mesa ha desaparecido.

Seguro que alguien simplemente lo tomó prestado y ha olvidado devolverlo, pero la Sra. Craig habló todo el tiempo de "robo".

La Sra. Craig dijo que si el diccionario no aparecía sobre su mesa antes de terminar la clase, nos íbamos a quedar todos castigados sin recreo.

Luego dijo que iba a salir de la habitación y que si el "culpable" dejaba el diccionario sobre la mesa, entonces el asunto no tendría consecuencias y no haría preguntas.

La Sra. Craig dejó a Patty Farrell como encargada del orden y salió de la clase. Patty se toma verdaderamente en serio su papel, así que cuando es ella quien se queda de vigilante nadie osa pasarse de la raya.

Yo esperaba que quien hubiera agarrado el diccionario se diera prisa en devolverlo y resolver el asunto, porque tenía dos batidos de chocolate para el almuerzo.

Pero nadie salió a devolver el libro. Y, por supuesto, la Sra. Craig mantuvo su promesa y nos dejó a todos sin recreo. Además dijo que iba a ser así todos los días hasta que apareciera el diccionario.

Viernes

La Sra. Craig nos tiene castigados sin recreo desde hace tres días y seguimos sin noticias del diccionario. Hoy Patty Farrell estaba enferma, así que la Sra. Craig puso a Alex Aruda para mantener el orden en la clase mientras ella se ausentaba.

Alex es un buen estudiante, pero la gente no le tiene el respeto que le tiene a Patty Farrell. Tan pronto como la Sra. Craig salió del aula, se montó un alboroto generalizado.

Un par de chicos que estaban cansados de quedarse todos los días sin recreo decidieron averiguar por su cuenta quién había cogido el diccionario.

Al primero que interrogaron fue a un chico llamado Corey Lamb. Creo que Corey encabezaba la lista de sospechosos porque es un chico listo que usa un vocabulario muy amplio.

Corey confesó ser el autor del delito en un santiamén. Pero resulta que lo hizo abrumado por la presión.

El siguiente de la lista fue Peter Lynn, que también confesó casi antes de preguntarle.

Me di cuenta de que tan sólo era cuestión de tiempo que aquellos tíos la tomaran CONMIGO. Tenía que pensar en algo rápido.

He leído suficientes libros de Sherlock Sammy como para saber que a veces hace falta un idiota que te saque de apuros. Y me di cuenta de que, si alguien podía solucionar este caso, ése era Alex Aruda.

Así que junto a otros dos compañeros que también estaban preocupados por la posibilidad de que fueran a buscarlos a ellos, me dirigí a Alex en busca de ayuda.

Le dijimos a Alex que lo necesitábamos para resolver el misterio de quién se había llevado el diccionario de la Sra. Craig, pero resulta que él ni siquiera sabía de QUÉ estábamos hablando. Creo que Alex estaba tan absorto en la lectura de su libro que no se había dado cuenta de lo que había sucedido a su alrededor durante los últimos dos días.

Además, Alex siempre se queda en clase leyendo durante el recreo, de manera que el castigo de la Sra. Craig en nada afectaba a su vida normal.

Por desgracia, Alex también ha debido leer unos cuantos libros de Sherlock Sammy, porque dijo que nos ayudaría si le pagábamos cinco dólares. No me pareció justo, porque Sherlock Sammy sólo cobra cinco centavos. Pero los otros chicos y yo estuvimos de acuerdo en que merecía la pena, y entre todos reunimos los cinco dólares.

Le expusimos a Alex todos los detalles del caso, pero no teníamos muchos datos. Le preguntamos si podía orientarnos en la dirección correcta.

Yo esperaba que Alex empezara a tomar notas y soltara algunas frases incomprensibles en jerga científica, pero todo lo que hizo fue cerrar el libro que estaba leyendo y enseñarnos la portada. Por INCREÍBLE que pueda parecer, se trataba del diccionario de la Sra. Craig.

Alex dijo que había estado estudiando el diccionario para el concurso estatal de ortografía que se celebra el mes que viene. Hubiera sido bueno SABERLO ANTES de darle los cinco dólares. De todas maneras, no había tiempo para discusiones, porque la Sra. Craig podía regresar a la clase en cualquier momento.

Corey Lamb tomó el libro de las manos de Alex y lo puso encima de la mesa de la Sra. Craig. Pero ella entró en el aula en ese mismo momento.

Al final la Sra. Craig se echó atrás respecto a su promesa de que "no habría consecuencias" y Corey Lamb va a quedarse sin recreo durante las tres próximas semanas. Al menos, tendrá a su lado a Alex Aruda haciéndole compañía.

FEBRERO

Martes

Cuando ayer vacié en la cafetería la bolsa de mi almuerzo sólo había DOS PIEZAS DE FRUTA y nada de snacks de chocolate, ni de galletas de nata.

Eso sí que era un problema. Mamá siempre me pone snacks de chocolate o dulces o alguna cosa rica en mi bolsa del almuerzo, y normalmente es lo único que como, de manera que me quedé sin energías para el resto del día.

Al volver a casa, le pregunté a Mamá qué era eso de la fruta. Me contestó que ella siempre compra galletas de nata y snacks de chocolate para que duren toda la semana y que por tanto alguno de nosotros tiene que haberlos cogido de la lata que se guarda en la despensa.

Seguro que Mamá piensa que soy yo el que roba los dulces, pero de veras que ya aprendí la lección.

El año pasado solía cogerlos de la lata, pero me costó caro cuando abrí la bolsa del almuerzo y vi lo que Mamá me había puesto en lugar del contenido habitual.

CHICOS, ¿LE IMPORTARÍA A ALGUNO DE USTEDES DARME ALGO A CAMBIO DE UNA BOLSA DE MENDRUGOS?

A la hora de almorzar, hoy sucedió exactamente lo mismo: dos piezas de fruta y ni un solo snack de chocolate, ni una galleta de nata.

Como decía, dependo totalmente de la energía que obtengo de los dulces. Casi me caigo dormido durante la clase del Sr. Watson, en la sexta hora. Menos mal que me desperté de golpe cuando me di con la cabeza en el respaldo de la silla.

Cuando volví a casa, le dije a Mamá que no era justo que alguien se estuviera comiendo las galletas y los snacks y yo pagara el pato. Pero ella dijo que no pensaba volver a comprar al supermercado hasta el fin de semana y que hasta entonces iba a tener que aguantarme.

Papá tampoco me sirvió de ayuda. Cuando fui a él con mis quejas, tan sólo se sacó un castigo de la manga y dijo que no habría "ni batería ni videojuegos durante una semana" para quien fuera sorprendido robando los snacks de chocolate. Es evidente que piensa que somos Rodrick o yo.

Como ya he dicho, no soy YO. Por tanto, pensé que Papá podía estar en lo cierto respecto a Rodrick y aproveché cuando mi hermano fue al cuarto de baño después de cenar para bajar a su habitación a ver si encontraba envoltorios o migajas.

Mientras estaba husmeando en la habitación de Rodrick, le oí bajar las escaleras. Tuve que esconderme a toda prisa, porque por alguna razón Rodrick suele ponerse muy furioso cuando pilla a alguien en sus dominios, tal y como ocurrió ayer.

Antes de que Rodrick llegara abajo, me introduje en el armario de su mesa de estudio y cerré la puerta. Rodrick entró en la habitación, se tumbó en la cama y llamó a su amigo Ward.

Rodrick y Ward mantenían una conversación INTERMINABLE y empecé a pensar que iba a tener que pasar toda la noche allí encerrado.

Se enzarzaron en una animada discusión sobre si una persona podría vomitar o no mientras se encontraba haciendo el pino, y yo empecé a sentir ganas de vomitar. Por suerte, justo entonces se agotó la batería del móvil. Y cuando Rodrick se fue escaleras arriba para usar el teléfono fijo, aproveché para esfumarme de allí.

Si tuviera dinero, este asunto de los *snacks* de chocolate no tendría la menor importancia, ya que podría comprar comida todos los días en la máquina dispensadora del colegio.

Pero me temo que, por ahora, estoy en quiebra. Es porque invertí todo mi capital en objetos estúpidos que ni siquiera FUNCIONAN.

Hace más o menos un mes, vi unos anuncios en la contraportada de un cómic y encargué algunas de esas cosas que se supone que van a cambiar DEL TODO tu vida.

GAFAS CON
RAYOS X
Vea a través de
Paredes - Metales – Ropa

AERODESLIZADOR
Personal
DESLÍCESE POR TODA LA CIUDAD SOBRE UN COLCHÓN DE AIRE

FLOTE INGRÁVIDO A SEIS PIES DEL SUELO

IMPRIMA SU PROPIO
DINERO
con la
Impresora de billetes
Inserte un papel en blanco y obtenga un billete de 5 dólares

PROYECTE SU VOZ A
DISTANCIA
KIT DE VENTRILOQUÍA

Hace dos semanas empecé a recibir mis encargos por correo.

La Impresora de Billetes no era más que una máquina con un truco de magia, y para hacerla funcionar tenías que poner antes TU PROPIO dinero en un compartimento secreto. Mal asunto, porque tenía fe en que ese invento me iba a librar de buscar trabajo cuando fuera mayor.

Con las Gafas de Rayos-X todo se veía borroso y descolocado, también fue un fracaso.

El chisme Proyector de Voz tampoco funcionó EN ABSOLUTO, y eso que seguí el manual de instrucciones al pie de la letra.

Pero la compra en que yo había depositado más esperanzas era el Aerodeslizador Personal. Ya me veía regresando a casa desde el colegio en un abrir y cerrar de ojos, en cuanto mi encargo llegara por correo.

Resulta que, cuando hoy llegó el envío, no traía el aerodeslizador. Sólo había un esquema con las instrucciones para CONSTRUIR el aerodeslizador, y me quedé atascado en el paso 1.

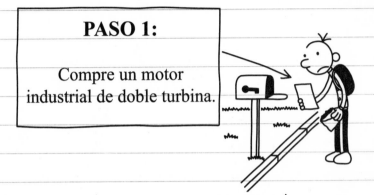

PASO 1:

Compre un motor industrial de doble turbina.

Me cuesta trabajo creer que quienes escribieron esos anuncios puedan engañar así a los chicos y quedarse tan tranquilos. Consideré la posibilidad de contratar a un abogado y querellarme con esa gente, pero los abogados cuestan dinero y, como ya he dicho antes, la Impresora de Billetes no era más que chatarra inútil.

Miércoles

Hoy, cuando he vuelto del colegio, Mamá me estaba esperando y no parecía muy contenta. Resulta que le han enviado mis notas del colegio y ha recibido el correo antes de que yo pudiera interceptarlo.

Mamá me enseñó la tarjeta con mis calificaciones y la cosa fue muy desagradable. Luego dijo que íbamos a esperar a que Papá volviera a casa, para ver qué pensaba del asunto.

Cuando estás en problemas, LO PEOR que puede ocurrir es que Mamá espere a que Papá vuelva a casa. Antes solía esconderme en el ropero, pero hace poco se me ocurrió otra forma mucho mejor de afrontar la situación. Ahora, lo que hago cuando las cosas se ponen feas, es decirle a la abuela que venga a cenar porque, con ella delante, Papá no se va a poner furioso conmigo.

Y durante la cena, tuve la precaución de sentarme justo al lado de la abuela.

Por suerte, Mamá no sacó a relucir el asunto de mis notas mientras cenábamos. Y cuando la abuela dijo que se marchaba porque tenía que ir al bingo, me pegué a ella como una lapa.

Escapar de Papá no era el único motivo para ir al bingo con la abuela. También iba porque necesitaba algún modo de conseguir dinero...

Supuse que pasar unas horas con la abuela y sus amigas del bingo era un precio que merecía la pena, a cambio de poder comprar golosinas a tope durante toda una semana, en la máquina expendedora de la cafetería del colegio.

La abuela y sus amigas son EXPERTAS en bingo y además se lo toman muy en serio. Para que les acompañe la suerte, tienen todo tipo de amuletos, mascotas, "Duendes del bingo" y cosas por el estilo.

Una de ellas es TAN rematadamente buena que memoriza todos los cartones y no necesita ir marcando los números.

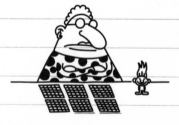

No sé por qué anoche la abuela y sus amigas no ganaban como de costumbre. Entonces fue cuando yo taché todos mis números y canté "¡BINGO!" en voz muy alta y el empleado vino a comprobar mi cartón.

Resulta que me había equivocado y había tachado erróneamente un par de números. El empleado anunció que mi premio no era correcto y todo el mundo en la sala se alegró de poder seguir jugando.

La abuela me recomendó no llamar la atención demasiado si volvía a cantar bingo, porque a los jugadores que frecuentan la sala no les hace gracia que gane un novato.

Debo admitir que en algún momento, hasta me sentí ALGO intimidado por los jugadores habituales.

Viernes
Está claro que hoy no ha sido el mejor día de mi vida. Para empezar, me han suspendido el examen de Ciencias. Deduzco que tal vez hubiera sido una buena idea quedarme a estudiar ayer, en lugar de pasarme cuatro horas en el bingo con la abuela.

Me entró el sueño durante la sexta clase, y esta vez me quedé totalmente FRITO. El Sr. Watson tuvo que darme un meneo para poder despertarme. Como castigo, tuve que sentarme en el fondo delantero del aula.

Mira tú por dónde, aquella fue la única manera de poder dormir a gusto.

Tan sólo hubiera deseado que alguien me despertara al marcharse el Sr. Watson, porque seguí durmiendo cuando empezó la siguiente clase.

Cuando abrí los ojos, me encontraba en mitad de la clase de la Sra. Lowry, que me impuso un arresto y el lunes voy a tener que quedarme castigado después de la última hora.

Esta tarde me encontraba más nervioso que un flan debido a la falta de azúcar, pero no tenía dinero para comprarme dulces o un refresco. Así que hice algo de lo que no me siento orgulloso.

Fui hasta casa de Rowley y desenterré la cápsula de tiempo que habíamos escondido en su patio. Pero lo hice únicamente porque me encontraba desesperado.

Regresé a mi casa con la caja, la abrí y saqué mis tres dólares. Entonces me fui al mercado y me compré un refresco grande, una bolsa de ositos-gominola y una barra de caramelo.

Creo que me siento un poco mal de que la cápsula de tiempo que Rowley y yo escondimos juntos no permaneciera enterrada unos cuantos cientos de años. Por otra parte, es bueno que haya sido yo el que la ha abierto, porque la verdad es que dentro pusimos un montón de cosas buenas.

Lunes

La verdad es que no tenía claro en qué iba a consistir mi castigo, pero cuando entré en aquella habitación mi primer pensamiento fue: "No pinto nada aquí, entre estos futuros delincuentes".

Me senté en la única silla que había libre, justo delante de un chico llamado León Ricket.

León no es precisamente el alumno más brillante del colegio. Estaba castigado por lo que hizo cuando una avispa se posó en la ventana de la clase.

Ahora ya sé que todo lo que haces cuando estás detenido es sentarte ahí y esperar a que acabe. No está permitido leer, ni hacer los deberes, ni NADA, lo que no deja de ser una norma del todo estúpida, considerando que la mayoría de los chicos podría aprovechar ese tiempo extra de estudio.

El Sr. Ray estaba encargado y nos vigilaba más o menos. Pero cada vez que el Sr. Ray apartaba la mirada de nosotros, León Ricket me daba un papirotazo en la oreja, o un cogotazo, o algo por el estilo. En una de ésas León se descuidó y el Sr. Ray lo pilló con el dedo junto a mi oído.

Le dijo que si lo sorprendía molestándome otra vez iba a verse en un problema SERIO.

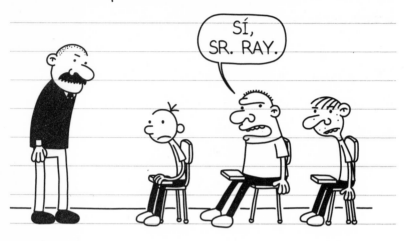

Yo sabía que León iba a seguir molestándome, así que decidí poner fin a su juego. Tan pronto como el Sr. Ray se dio la vuelta, di un palmetazo con las manos para simular que León me había pegado.

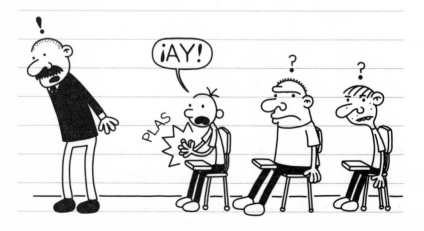

El Sr. Ray se giró y le dijo a León que se iba a tener que quedar otra media hora, y que MAÑANA estaba otra vez detenido.

De camino a casa, me preguntaba si había hecho bien. No soy un corredor demasiado rápido y media hora tampoco no es tanta ventaja.

Martes

Anoche me di cuenta de que todos mis problemas actuales empezaron cuando alguien de mi familia empezó a robar las galletas y los snacks de chocolate del almuerzo. Así que decidí atrapar al ladrón de una vez por todas.

Sabía que Mamá había ido a comprar a la tienda durante el fin de semana y por tanto había suministro de dulces en la despensa. Eso significaba también que muy probablemente el ladrón actuase de nuevo.

Después de la cena, me dirigí al cuarto de lavar y apagué la luz. Entonces me metí en un cesto de ropa vacío y esperé.

Una media hora más tarde, alguien entró en la habitación y encendió la luz, así que me escondí deba-jo de una toalla. Resulta que era Mamá.

Me quedé totalmente inmóvil mientras ella sacaba ropa de la secadora. No se dio cuenta de mi presencia cuando volcó toda la ropa en el cesto donde yo me encontraba.

Luego se marchó y yo seguí al acecho más tiempo. Estaba seriamente decidido a esperar todo el tiempo que hiciera falta.

Pero la ropa recién salida de la secadora estaba caliente y yo me empecé a sentir un poco aletargado. Antes de darme cuenta, me quedé dormido.

No sé cuántas horas estuve frito, pero SÍ SÉ que me despertó el ruido de papel celofán crujiendo.

Cuando escuché el sonido de alguien masticando, encendí mi linterna y atrapé al ladrón con las manos en la masa.

¡Era Papá! Vaya, debería haber sospechado que era él desde el principio. Cuando se trata de comer chucherías, es todo un ADICTO.

Empecé a decirle todo lo que pensaba, pero él me interrumpió. No estaba interesado en explicar por qué estaba robando los dulces y los snacks de chocolate de nuestros almuerzos. Sólo quería saber qué diablos estaba haciendo yo en mitad de la noche, debajo de un montón de ropa interior de Mamá.

Y en eso, oímos a Mamá que bajaba las escaleras.

Creo que tanto Papá como yo comprendimos que la situación no se presentaba bien para ninguno de los dos, así que cada uno agarró tantas galletas de nata como podíamos llevar en las manos y salimos huyendo.

Miércoles

Todavía me duraba la indignación de que fuera Papá el que robaba nuestros dulces del almuerzo, y había planeado tener unas palabras con él esta noche. Pero se fue a la cama a las 6:00, así que no tuve ocasión.

Papá se había acostado temprano porque estaba deprimido a causa de algo que había sucedido al llegar a casa después del trabajo. Estaba recogiendo el correo, cuando nuestros vecinos, los Snella, bajaban por la acera con su bebé. Se llama Seth y me parece que tiene sólo dos meses.

¡HOLA, FRANK!

Cada vez que los Snella tienen un niño, a los seis meses celebran una fiesta del "medio cumpleaños" e invitan a todos los vecinos.

El momento cumbre de las fiestas de medio cumpleaños de los Snella es cuando los mayores intentan por turno hacer reír al bebé. Los adultos hacen entonces todo tipo de cosas ridículas que les hacen parecer TOTALMENTE estúpidos.

He estado en todas las fiestas de medio cumpleaños de los Snella y hasta ahora ningún bebé se ha reído.

Todo el mundo sabe que la VERDADERA razón de que los Snella den estas fiestas es porque quieren ganar el Gran Premio de 10.000 dólares en "Las Familias Más Divertidas de América". Se trata de un concurso de televisión en el que ponen vídeos caseros de gente recibiendo un pelotazo de golf en la ingle y cosas así.

Los Snella esperan que algo divertido suceda en alguna de sus fiestas, de modo que puedan tenerlo grabado en vídeo. A lo largo de los años, se han hecho con una buena colección de imágenes. Durante la fiesta de medio cumpleaños de Sam Snella, el Sr. Bittner se rajó los pantalones dando saltos de rana. Y en la fiesta de Scott Snella, al andar hacia atrás, el Sr. Odom se cayó en la piscinita de los niños.

Los Snella presentaron esos vídeos al concurso, pero no ganaron nada. Así que me parece que van a seguir teniendo niños hasta que lo consigan.

Papá ODIA actuar en público, de modo que hará todo lo posible para no tener que hacer el tonto ante todo el vecindario. Hasta ahora, ha conseguido escabullirse astutamente de todas y cada una de las fiestas de medio cumpleaños.

En la cena, Mamá le dijo a Papá que este año TIENE que asistir en junio a la fiesta de medio cumpleaños de Seth Snella. Seguro que Papá sabe que esta vez le va a tocar.

Jueves
Todo el mundo en el colegio habla del Gran Baile de San Valentín, que se celebra la semana que viene.

Éste es el primer año que tenemos baile en el colegio, así que todo el mundo está muy nervioso. Algunos chicos de mi curso incluso están pidiendo a las chicas si quieren ser su pareja.

Rowley y yo por ahora no tenemos pareja, pero eso no va a impedir que nuestra llegada tenga mucho estilo.

Pensé que si Rowley y yo conseguíamos reunir algo de dinero los próximos días, podríamos alquilar una limusina para la noche del baile. Pero cuando llamé a la empresa de alquiler de limusinas, el empleado que me atendió me llamó "señora". De un soplo, se desvaneció su oportunidad de hacer negocio CONMIGO.

Como el baile es la semana próxima, me he dado cuenta de que voy a necesitar algo de ropa que ponerme.

Me encuentro en un aprieto, porque ya he usado la mayor parte de la ropa que me regalaron por Navidad y prácticamente no me queda nada que ponerme. Busqué entre mis prendas sucias, por si había algo que pudiera usar una segunda vez.

Separé todo mi vestuario en dos montones. Uno de cosas que podría volver a ponerme. Otra, con prendas que me enviarían directamente al despacho de la enfermera Powell para una lectura sobre higiene.

Encontré una camisa en el primer montón que no estaba mal, excepto por una mancha de gelatina en la manga izquierda. Así que durante el baile tendré que acordarme de mantener a Holly Hills a mi derecha todo el tiempo.

Día de San Valentín

Anoche estuve levantado hasta muy tarde, haciendo tarjetas de San Valentín para toda la gente de mi curso. Estoy seguro de que mi colegio es el único en todo el Estado que todavía obliga a sus alumnos a intercambiar tarjetas de felicitación por San Valentín.

El año pasado estaba deseando que llegara el intercambio de tarjetas. La víspera de San Valentín me pasé un montón de tiempo haciendo una tarjeta formidable para una chica que se llamaba Natasha y me gustaba mucho.

Amada Natasha,

Mi corazón arde por ti.

Tan intensamente, que sólo con el calor de las brasas podría hervir el agua de un millar de jacuzzis.

Tan intensamente, que todos los muñecos de nieve del mundo se derretirían en un instante.

Deja que el fuego de mi amor te envuelva en su calidez.

Tan sólo un beso tuyo podría sofocar las llamas que me consumen.

A ti te prometo mi amor, mi deseo, mi vida.

Greg

Le enseñé a Mamá la tarjeta, para que me corrigiera las faltas de ortografía, pero ella me dijo que lo que había escrito no era "apropiado para mi edad". Me dijo que quizá era mejor que le regalara a Natasha una caja de caramelos o algo así, pero no pensaba hacer caso de mi madre como consejera romántica.

En el colegio, todos fueron recorriendo la clase y depositando sus tarjetas de San Valentín en las cajas de los demás, pero yo le entregué la mía a Natasha personalmente.

Le dejé leerla y me quedé esperando para ver cómo reaccionaba CONMIGO.

Ella buscó en su caja y sacó una tarjeta barata comprada en la tienda que inicialmente era para su amiga Chantelle, que ese día no había ido al colegio porque estaba enferma.

Entonces Natasha tachó el nombre de su amiga y puso el mío en su lugar.

En cualquier caso, creo que se comprende por qué este año no me encontraba demasiado entusiasmado respecto al intercambio de tarjetas.

Por fin anoche tuve una gran idea. Sabía que tenía que hacer tarjetas para los de mi curso, pero en lugar de las cursilerías de siempre y cosas sin sentido, iba a decirle a todos EXACTAMENTE lo que opinaba de ellos.

La clave estaba en no firmar ninguna de las tarjetas.

Algunos de los chicos se quejaron del contenido de las tarjetas a la maestra, la Sra. Riser, y ella fue por toda la clase tratando de averiguar quién había sido el autor. Yo sabía que la Sra. Riser iba a pensar que quien no hubiera recibido una de esas tarjetas sería el culpable, pero había previsto eso y me había escrito también una tarjeta dirigida a MÍ MISMO.

Después del intercambio de tarjetas, llegó el Baile de San Valentín. Se suponía que iba a celebrarse POR LA NOCHE, pero parece que ningún padre se presentó como voluntario para hacernos compañía. Así que en lugar de eso, nos colocaron el baile en mitad de la jornada escolar.

A eso de la 1:00 los maestros empezaron a reunirnos a todos y a enviarnos al auditorium. El que no quisiera apoquinar los dos dólares de la entrada tenía que ir a estudio, a la clase del Sr. Ray.

Para la mayoría de nosotros era evidente que eso de "ir a estudio" era prácticamente lo mismo que permanecer bajo arresto.

Los demás desfilamos hacia el gimnasio y nos sentamos en las gradas. No sé por qué todos los chicos se sentaron en un lado de la pista y las chicas en el otro. Una vez que todos habíamos entrado, los maestros pusieron la música. Pero el encargado de elegir las canciones se había lucido, porque no tenía ni idea de lo que se escucha actualmente.

Durante el primer cuarto de hora o así, ninguno de nosotros movió un músculo. Entonces, el Sr. Phillips, el orientador profesional, y la enfermera Powell se dirigieron al centro de la pista y se pusieron a bailar.

Seguro que el Sr. Phillips y la enfermera Powell pensaron que si ELLOS empezaban a bailar todos nos animaríamos, bajaríamos a la cancha y nos uniríamos al baile. Pero consiguieron el efecto contrario y todo el mundo permaneció en su asiento.

Al final, la Sra. Mancy, la directora, agarró el micrófono y anunció que todos los ocupantes de las gradas estábamos OBLIGADOS a bajar a la pista y bailar, y que eso iba a subir un 20% la nota de Educación Física.

Llegados a este punto, otros dos chicos y yo intentamos escurrirnos para bajar al aula del Sr. Ray, pero nos lo impidieron varios maestros que bloqueaban las salidas.

Sin embargo, la Sra. Mancy no bromeaba respecto a las notas de Educación Física. La acompañaba el Sr. Underwood, el profesor de Educación Física, y llevaba la libreta de calificaciones.

Estoy a punto de suspender también en Educación Física y decidí que debía tomármelo en serio. Sin embargo, tampoco quería hacer el ridículo delante de los de mi curso. Así que me puse a hacer el movimiento más mínimo posible que técnicamente pudiera considerarse como "bailar".

Por desgracia, varios chicos que también andaban preocupados por su nota de Educación Física vieron lo que yo hacía y se pusieron a mi lado. Lo siguiente que recuerdo es verme rodeado por un grupo de cretinos que copiaban mis movimientos.

Quise alejarme de ellos lo más posible y miré a mi alrededor en busca de un lugar donde pudiera bailar tranquilo.

Entonces fue cuando divisé a Holly Hills en otra parte de la pista y recordé la principal razón por la que me había molestado en asistir al baile.

Holly bailaba en el centro del gimnasio con sus amigas, y yo comencé a hacer mi paso de baile desplazándome lentamente hacia ellas.

Todas las chicas formaban un grupo compacto y baila-
ban como profesionales, seguramente gracias a que
pasaban todo su tiempo libre viendo el canal de MTV.

Holly se encontraba justo en el centro del grupo.
Durante un rato, hice como que bailaba por fuera de
aquel círculo cerrado, mientras buscaba un hueco para
introducirme, pero no había manera.

Finalmente, Holly dejó de bailar y fue a buscar un
refresco. Supe que era mi gran oportunidad.

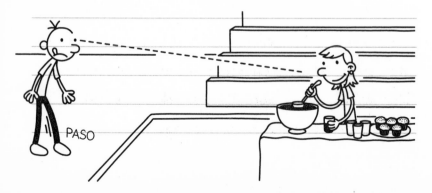

Y justo en el momento en que me dirigía hacia Holly para decirle algo divertido, aterrizó Fregley en escena como parachutado desde ninguna parte.

¡BOOGIE BOOGIE! BOOGIE!

Fregley llevaba la cara toda cubierta de crema azucarada de color rosa, seguramente se había puesto perdido con los pasteles que había en la mesa de los refrescos. En fin, todo lo que sé es que echó a perder por completo lo que hubiera sido un gran momento entre Holly y yo.

Pocos minutos más tarde se acabó el baile y yo perdí mi gran oportunidad de causarle a ella una buena impresión. Después del colegio regresé a casa solo, porque necesitaba un rato para estar a solas conmigo mismo.

Después de la cena, Mamá me dijo que en el buzón había una tarjeta para mí. Cuando le pregunté quién la enviaba, sólo me contestó que "alguien especial". Corrí al buzón y saqué la tarjeta y tengo que admitir que estaba muy nervioso. Estaba deseando que fuera de Holly, pero había al menos otras cuatro o cinco chicas en el colegio de las que tampoco me importaría recibir una tarjeta.

La tarjeta iba en un gran sobre de color rosa, con mi nombre escrito en letra cursiva. Lo abrí y dentro había una hoja de cartulina con un caramelo pegado. Lo enviaba ROWLEY.

A veces tengo la impresión de que no conozco a ese chico.

MARZO

<u>Sábado</u>

El otro día, Papá encontró en el sofá a Pringui, la
mantita de Manny, No creo que supiera lo que era
cuando la tiró al cubo de basura.

Desde entonces, Manny estuvo volviendo toda la casa
patas arriba en busca de su mantita y al final Papá tuvo
que decirle que, por equivocación, la había tirado. Bien,
pues Manny ayer se tomó la revancha, utilizando la
maqueta del campo de batalla de la guerra civil de Papá
como escenario para sus propios juegos.

Manny también ha descargado su ira sobre todos nosotros. Hoy estaba sentado en el sofá pensando en mis cosas, cuando apareció de pronto y me dijo:

Yo no sabía si "babón" era una especie de insulto gordo entre los niños pequeños o qué, pero no me gustaba nada como sonaba. Así que fui a preguntar a Mamá si ELLA sabía lo que significaba.

Por desgracia, Mamá estaba hablando por teléfono y, cuando se lía de palique con alguna de sus amigas, no hay manera de que te haga caso.

Al final conseguí que Mamá parara de hablar un momento, pero estaba enfadada porque la había interrumpido.
Le dije que Manny me había llamado "babón" y ella dijo:

¿Y QUÉ ES UN BABÓN?

Eso me dejó descolocado durante unos momentos,
porque era precisamente lo que yo trataba de preguntarle a ella. Y como yo no tenía una respuesta, ella
siguió hablando por teléfono.

Después de aquello, Manny se sintió con luz verde para
llamarme babón siempre que quería, y es lo que ha
estado haciendo todo el día.

¡LÍMPIAME
EL TRASERO,
BABÓN!

Tenía que haber pensado que decírselo a Mamá no me iba a llevar a ninguna parte. Cuando Rodrick y yo éramos pequeños, todo el tiempo nos estábamos acusando el uno al otro y volvíamos loca a Mamá. Entonces fue cuando ella se sacó de la manga la Tortuga Chismosa para solventar la situación.

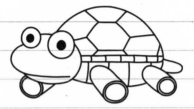

Mamá se inventó lo de la Tortuga Chismosa cuando era maestra de preescolar. La idea era que cuando Rodrick y yo tuviéramos un problema entre nosotros, en lugar de ir a Mamá, fuéramos a contárselo a la Tortuga Chismosa. Bien, pues aquella Tortuga Chismosa funcionó DE MARA-VILLA con Rodrick, pero no tanto conmigo.

Domingo de Resurrección

Hoy, cuando íbamos a la iglesia en el coche, sentí que me había sentado encima de algo asqueroso. Al bajar, me miré la parte de atrás de los pantalones y estaba TODA MANCHADA de chocolate.

Manny había traído con él en el coche su conejito de Pascua, y yo me había sentado encima de una oreja o algo así.

Mamá intentaba que toda la familia entrara de una vez, para que pudiéramos conseguir buenos asientos, pero le dije que DE NINGUNA MANERA iba a entrar con esa pinta.

Sabía que Holly Hills y su familia probablemente ya estaban dentro, y no me apetecía que ella pensara que me lo había hecho todo encima.

Mamá dijo que ni soñara con escabullirme de la iglesia el domingo de Resurrección, y nos pusimos a discutir. Entonces Rodrick intervino con SU solución.

Rodrick sabe que el domingo de Resurrección los servicios religiosos duran al menos dos horas, y buscaba cualquier pretexto para escurrirse. Y justo en ese momento pasaron a nuestro lado el jefe de Papá y su familia, camino del aparcamiento.

Mamá hizo que Rodrick se volviese a poner los pantalones, y a mí me dio su jersey rosa para que me lo
atara en la cintura.

No sé qué era peor, ir con los pantalones manchados de
chocolate o llevar el jersey rosa de Mamá como si fuera
una falda escocesa.

La iglesia estaba totalmente llena. Los únicos asientos
que quedaban vacíos estaban al frente, junto a tío
Joe y su familia, así que nos sentamos a su lado.

Miré a mi alrededor y pude distinguir a Holly Hills y
su familia tres filas más atrás. Estaba seguro de que
ella no podía ver lo que llevaba puesto de la cintura
para abajo, lo que no dejaba de ser un alivio.

Tan pronto como empezó la música, tío Joe nos cogió las manos a mí y a su mujer y se puso a cantar.

Traté de soltarme un par de veces, pero su presa parecía de acero. La canción duró sólo un minuto o así, pero a mí me pareció una hora.

Cuando terminó la canción, me volví hacia la gente que tenía detrás y señalando a tío Joe me llevé un dedo a la sien, para que todo el mundo supiera que yo no tenía nada que ver con la iniciativa de agarrarse de las manos.

Por alguna parte en el centro de la iglesia, empezaron a pasar una cesta para que la gente pudiera dar dinero para los necesitados.

Yo no tenía dinero, así que le dije susurrando a Mamá que si me podía dar un dólar. De este modo, cuando la cesta llegara hasta mí haría mi gran donación poniendo el dólar en la cesta y Holly podía ver lo espléndido que soy.

Pero cuando fui a poner el dólar en la cesta, me di cuenta de que Mamá no me había dado un billete de un dólar, sino uno de VEINTE. Quise sujetar la cesta para recuperarlo, pero ya era demasiado tarde.

En fin, ojalá que al menos ESA donación me haya valido algunos puntos en el Cielo.

He oído que cuando haces buenas acciones se supone que debes mantenerlo en privado, pero eso no tiene demasiado sentido para MÍ.

Si empiezo a ocultar mis buenas acciones, estoy seguro de que más tarde lo lamentaré.

Como dije antes, los servicios de Pascua son SÚPER largos. Uno de los himnos llevaba sonando ya como cinco minutos y empecé a buscar alguna manera de distraerme.

Cuando Rodrick está aburrido, se entretiene rascándose una cicatriz que tiene en la parte de atrás de su mano, de manera que nunca le termina de desaparecer. Pero a mí no me va ese rollo.

Manny sí que se lo ha montado bien en la iglesia. Papá y Mamá le dejan que se traiga todo tipo de cosas para mantenerlo entretenido. Pues a mí nunca me dejaban traerme nada a la iglesia cuando tenía su edad.

En cambio, Papá y Mamá siempre miman a Manny. Voy a poner un ejemplo de lo que estoy diciendo. La semana pasada, cuando Manny abrió la bolsa con su almuerzo en preescolar, su sándwich estaba cortado por la mitad y no a cuartos, como a él le gusta.

Entonces agarró una rabieta tremenda y los maestros tuvieron que llamar a Mamá. Ella dejó su trabajo y fue con el coche hasta la escuela de Manny para hacer al sándwich el corte que le faltaba.

Estaba pensando estas cosas en la iglesia, cuando de pronto se me ocurrió una idea. Me incliné sobre Manny y le susurré:

¡Ufff! Eso le hizo verdadero impacto.

Empezó a BERREAR y todo el mundo en la iglesia se volvía a mirar hacia nosotros. Incluso el predicador se calló para ver qué sucedía.

Mamá no consiguió aplacar a Manny, así que tuvimos que marcharnos. Sin embargo, en lugar de salir por la puerta lateral fuimos por uno de los pasillos centrales.

Traté de parecer totalmente impasible mientras pasábamos por delante de la familia Hills, pero en aquellas circunstancias no resultaba nada fácil.

La única persona más avergonzada que yo era Papá. Trató de taparse la cara con el boletín religioso, pero su jefe lo vio y le hizo una seña con el pulgar hacia arriba cuando salíamos.

Miércoles

Las cosas han estado algo así como tensas en casa desde el otro día. Para empezar, Mamá estaba enojadísima conmigo por haber llamado "babón" a Manny. Tuve que recordarle que a ella no le pareció mal cuando MANNY me lo llamó a mí. Entonces Mamá prohibió esa palabra a todo el mundo, y dijo que si pillaba a alguien diciéndola lo castigaría toda una semana. Claro que Rodrick no tardó en encontrar el modo de hacer trampa.

Ésta no es la primera vez que Mamá nos prohíbe decir determinadas palabras en casa. Hace algún tiempo nos impuso una "ley antipalabrotas", porque Manny empezaba a ampliar su vocabulario con nuevas palabras oídas aquí y allí.

Cada vez que alguien soltaba un taco delante de Manny, tenía que poner un dólar en su "Bote de las Palabrotas". Y así Manny se fue haciendo rico a costa mía y de Rodrick.

Entonces Mamá subió todavía más la apuesta y nos prohibió decir palabras como "estúpido" o "gilitonto" y cosas así.

Para no caer en la bancarrota, Rodrick y yo nos inventamos una serie de palabras en clave que significaban lo mismo que las palabras prohibidas, y así hemos estado funcionando desde entonces.

A veces se me olvida volver al lenguaje normal cuando voy al colegio y acabo dando la impresión de estar como una regadera. Hoy mismo, David Nester escupió un chicle que fue a parar a mi pelo. Le llamé de todo, pero no creo que se ofendiera demasiado.

Otra cosa que ha cambiado desde Pascua es que Papá ha estado más pendiente de Rodrick y de mí. Me parece que está harto de parecer un imbécil delante de su jefe.

A Rodrick lo ha matriculado en una clase para preparar el ACCESO a la universidad y a mí me ha hecho apuntarme en la Liga Recreativa de Fútbol.

Las pruebas para el fútbol fueron ayer por la tarde. Los entrenadores pusieron a todos los aspirantes en fila, para una "prueba de habilidad" que consistía en correr con el balón sorteando unos conos y cosas por el estilo.

Lo hice lo mejor que pude y quedé clasificado como un "Pre-Alfa-Minus", que supongo que significa algo así como "Pelotón de los Torpes".

Después de hacer las pruebas de habilidad nos pusieron en diferentes equipos. Esperaba que me tocara uno de esos entrenadores divertidos que no se toman demasiado a pecho lo de competir, como el Sr. Proctor o el Sr. Gibb, pero me cayó el peor de todos los posibles, el Sr. Litch.

El Sr. Litch es como uno de esos sargentos instructores que te gritan todo el tiempo. Antes fue el entrenador de Rodrick y ése es el motivo de que Rodrick ya no haga ningún tipo de deporte.

¡NECESITAS UN CORTE DE PELO!

En fin, mañana tenemos nuestro primer entrenamiento real. Como lo más seguro es que no me saquen a jugar, podré volver a casa para una sesión de videojuegos. Está a punto de salir Twisted Wizard 2, y me han dicho que es ALUCINANTE.

<u>Jueves</u>

Me pusieron en un equipo con un grupo de chicos que no conozco de nada. Lo primero que hizo el Sr. Litch fue darnos los uniformes y después nos dijo que pensáramos un nombre para el equipo.

Yo sugerí que nos llamásemos los "Twisted Wizards" y conseguir que la casa de videojuegos nos patrocinara.

Pero a nadie le gustó mi idea. Un chico dijo que podíamos llamarnos los "Red Sox", lo que me pareció una idea lamentable. En primer lugar, porque los Red Sox son un equipo de BÉISBOL y, en segundo lugar, porque nuestra camiseta de fútbol es AZUL.

Pero claro, a todo el mundo le tenía que gustar la idea y ese nombre fue el que salió por mayoría. Entonces el ayudante del entrenador, el Sr. Boone, dijo que le preocupaba que fueran a querellarse con nosotros si usábamos ese nombre.

Seguro que esa gente tiene otras cosas mejores que hacer que ponerles querellas a los equipos de fútbol de los colegios, pero ya he dicho que a nadie le interesaban MIS opiniones.

Por fin, el equipo votó cambiar el nombre a "Red SOCKS" y ahí quedó la cosa.

Cuando empezamos el entrenamiento, el Sr. Litch y el Sr. Boone nos hicieron correr varias vueltas al campo y hacer levantamientos de pierna y un montón de ejercicios más, que no tenían nada que ver con el fútbol. Entre carrera rápida y carrera rápida, me descolgué hacia el dispensador de agua junto a otros dos chicos Pre-Alfa-Minus. Siempre que nos hacíamos los remolones para volver al campo, el Sr. Litck nos gritaba:

¡MUEVAN EL TRASERO RÁPIDO HACIA AQUÍ!

Los otros chicos y yo pensamos que sería la mar de divertido si la siguiente vez que el Sr. Litch dijera eso corriéramos hacia él sacando los traseros hacia afuera.

Así que la siguiente vez que nos gritó lo de mover los traseros de ahí, yo corrí hacia él meneando exageradamente mi trasero. Pero los otros chicos me dejaron TOTALMENTE colgado de la brocha.

El Sr. Litch no apreció mi sentido del humor y me hizo correr tres vueltas más.

Cuando Papá me recogió después del entrenamiento le dije que, después de todo, quizá esto del fútbol no era tan buena idea y que debía permitirme dejarlo.

Eso enfureció a mi padre, que dijo:

¡NINGÚN HIJO MÍO ES UN RAJADO!

Lo cual no es cierto en absoluto. Yo soy un TREMEN-DO rajado y también Rodrick. Y no sé si Manny lleva ya tres o cuatro cursos en preescolar.

De todos modos, tengo la sensación de que si quiero perder el fútbol de vista voy a tener que enfocarlo desde otro ángulo.

Viernes

Desde que empecé con el fútbol, he ensuciado mi ropa el doble de rápido que antes. Hace tiempo que me quedé sin nada limpio que ponerme, así que he estado usando cosas del montón de ropa para lavar.

Pero me he dado cuenta de que reciclar ropa sucia también tiene sus riesgos.

Hoy pasaba por el pasillo cerca de unas chicas, cuando un par de calzoncillos sucios asomaron por una pernera de mi pantalón y cayeron al suelo. Me limité a seguir caminando como si nada, esperando que las chicas no pensaran que los calzoncillos eran míos.

Pero más tarde pagué muy cara aquella decisión.

Creo que debería apresurarme y aprender a lavar la ropa, porque se me están agotando las posibilidades. Mañana voy a tener que ponerme la camiseta de la primera boda de tío Gary y no me hace mucha ilusión precisamente.

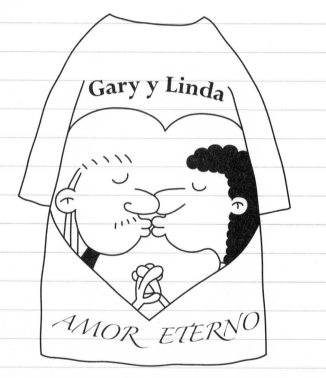

Iba un poco deprimido hoy al salir del colegio hacia casa, cuando de pronto ocurrió algo que cambió el panorama. Rowley me dijo que en casa de uno de sus amigos de karate tenía una fiesta de las de dormir fuera, y me preguntó si quería ir yo también.

Estaba a punto de decirle que "no" cuando Rowley dijo algo que me llamó la atención. El chico de la fiesta de pijamas vive en Pleasant Street, es decir, el mismo barrio donde vive Holly Hills.

Durante el almuerzo oí a un par de chicas decir que HOLLY también iba a tener en su casa otra fiesta de las de dormir fuera, así que ésta podría ser la ocasión de mi VIDA.

Esta tarde durante el entrenamiento de fútbol,
el Sr. Litch le dijo a cada uno de nosotros la posición en que
iba a jugar el domingo, en el primer partido de la temporada.

El Sr. Litch me dijo que yo iba a ser el "recuperador"
y eso me sonó la mar de bien. Así que cuando llegué a
casa se lo pasé por la cara a Rodrick.

Pensé que Rodrick se iba a quedar impresionado, pero en
lugar de eso se echó a reír. Me dijo que el recuperador no
es un puesto en el campo, sino que es el chico que se
encarga de ir a recuperar el balón cuando sale fuera.
Entonces me enseñó un reglamento con todos los puestos
de un equipo de fútbol y la verdad es que no aparecía eso
del recuperador.

Rodrick siempre me está tomando el pelo, de manera que voy a tener que esperar hasta el fin de semana para ver si esta vez ha dicho la verdad.

Domingo

Recuérdenme que nunca vaya otra vez a dormir fuera con Rowley.

Ayer por la tarde Mamá nos llevó a Rowley y a mí a casa de su amigo. La primera pista de dónde iba a pasar una larga noche fue que, al entrar en la casa, no vi ni un chico que tuviera más de seis años.

La segunda pista fue que todos llevaban puesto el quimono de karate.

La única razón por la que me había APUNTADO a esta fiesta era que quizá podríamos acechar e intentar colarnos en la fiesta de pijamas de Holly. Pero los amigos de Rowley estaban más interesados en ver "Barrio Sésamo" que en las chicas.

A aquellos chicos sólo les apetecía jugar a esos juegos de las fiestas de niños pequeños, como el ratoncito ciego y cosas así. Podía haberlo pasado chachi en la fiesta de Holly Hills y en lugar de eso tuve que estar toda la noche intentando que no me palparan un puñado de preescolares.

Los amigos de Rowley también jugaron a otras cosas, como "Enredos" y "Stop".

Cuando alguien sugirió que podíamos jugar a "¿Quién me ha lamido?", aproveche para excusarme y marcharme escaleras arriba.

Traté de llamar a Mamá para que viniera a recogerme, pero había salido con Papá. Supe que tenía que aguantar toda la noche en casa de aquel chico.

A eso de las 9:30, decidí irme a dormir y que de ese modo la noche pasara más deprisa. Pero los chicos subieron al dormitorio y se organizó una batalla campal con las almohadas. Permítanme decir que no es nada fácil dormir cuando un niño sudoroso te cae encima cada cinco minutos.

Finalmente subió la mamá del anfitrión y dijo que ya era hora de dormir todo el mundo.

Pero incluso con las luces apagadas, Rowley y sus amigos siguieron hablando y montando follón. Debieron pensar que me había dormido, porque en un momento dado varios de ellos se acercaron a mí con sigilo y trataron de hacerme la broma de poner-la-mano-en-un-bol-de-agua-tibia.

Aquello fue definitivo para MÍ. Bajé las escaleras para irme a dormir al sótano, a pesar de que estaba a oscuras y no podía encontrar el interruptor de la luz. Me había dejado arriba mi saco de dormir y eso sí que fue un error, porque el sótano estaba helado.

Sin embargo, NO quise regresar escaleras arriba a buscar mis cosas. Me hice un ovillo y traté de conservar tanto calor corporal como me fuese posible, para resistir hasta la mañana siguiente.

Creo que probablemente fue la noche más larga de mi vida.

Cuando salió el sol esta mañana, supe por qué hacía tanto frío en el sótano. Había estado durmiendo junto a la puerta de cristal deslizante, que alguien se había dejado abierta toda la noche.

Y eso sí que fue un fallo, porque si llego a saber que había una vía de escape, POR SUPUESTO que la habría utilizado.

Cuando llegué esta mañana a casa, me fui a la cama a dormir hasta que Papá me despertó y me dijo que era la hora de ir al partido de fútbol.

Resulta que Rodrick tenía razón respecto a lo del recuperador. Me pasé todo el partido sacando balones de las zarzas, cosa que no tiene ninguna gracia.

Nuestro equipo ganó el partido y después de eso se supone que teníamos que ir todos a celebrarlo. Papá no podía quedarse, así que le preguntó al Sr. Litch si luego me podía llevar a casa.

Bueno. Hubiera preferido que Papá me preguntara a MÍ primero qué me parecía la idea, porque me habría ido a casa con él.

Con todo, me sentía hambriento después de toda aquella actividad de recuperar balones de la maleza y me hice a la idea de ir con los del equipo.

Fuimos a un restaurante de comida rápida y pedí para mí veinte nuggets de pollo. Fui un momento al cuarto de baño y cuando regresé, toda mi comida había desaparecido. Pero entonces Erick Bickford volvió a poner mis nuggets sobre la mesa con sus manos sudorosas.

Si alguien quiere saber por qué no me gusta el equipo deportivo, ahora ya lo sabe.

Después de aquel almuerzo, Kenny Keith, Erick y yo volvimos en el coche del Sr. Litch. Kenny se sentó en la parte de atrás con Erick y yo me senté delante, al lado del conductor.

Tuvimos que esperar un montón de tiempo, porque el
Sr. Litch estaba sentado en el capó del coche, charlando con el Sr. Boone. Después de estar allí aburri-
dos un buen rato, Kenny se inclinó hacia delante
desde el asiento trasero y pegó un claxonazo de al
menos tres segundos.

Entonces Kenny se dejó caer rápidamente de nuevo hacia
el asiento de atrás, de manera que cuando el Sr. Litch se
dio la vuelta parecía que había sido yo quién había tocado la bocina del coche.

El Sr. Litch me dirigió una mirada desagradable y luego
se volvió y siguió hablando con su ayudante al menos
durante otra media hora.

De regreso a casa, el Sr. Litch paró unas cinco veces para hacer varios recados. Tampoco parecía tener prisa alguna por acabar.

¡Y chúpate ésta! Kenny y Erick se enojaron CONMIGO por hacerles llegar tan tarde a casa. Esto puede dar una pista del tipo de intelectuales con los me ha tocado bregar.

El Sr. Litch me dejó en casa el último. Al subir la cuesta, vi a los Snella en su jardín y parecía que intentaban grabar algunas escenas para enviarlas a "Las Familias Más Divertidas de América".

Me da la impresión de que no quieren esperar unos pocos meses hasta la fiesta de medio cumpleaños de Seth.

ABRIL

Jueves

Ayer fue primero de abril y así empezó el día para mí.

Durante el resto del año había que ARRASTRAR a Rodrick para sacarlo de la cama antes de las 8:00 A.M. Pero todos los días uno de abril, siempre madrugaba para poner sus gracias en práctica.

Es necesario que alguien le explique seriamente a Rodrick el concepto de lo que es una broma, porque todas sus "bromas" me tienen a mí como víctima.

El año pasado Rodrick apostó conmigo cincuenta centavos a que yo no era capaz de atarme los zapatos estando de pie. Y yo caí por completo en la trampa.

Entré en casa y le dije a Papá que Rodrick me había disparado en el trasero con la pistola de bolas de pintura. Papá no quiso meterse en medio de nuestra bronca, y tan sólo le dijo a Rodrick que tenía que pagarme cincuenta centavos, porque yo había ganado la apuesta.

Rodrick sacó de su bolsillo dos monedas de veinticinco centavos y las tiró al suelo. Está claro que yo no había aprendido la lección, porque me agaché a recogerlas.

Al menos, yo pongo algo de inteligencia en mis bromas. El año pasado le gasté una buenísima a Rowley. Estábamos en los servicios de un cine y le convencí de que un chico cualquiera que estaba en los urinarios era un atleta profesional.

Y Rowley fue a pedirle un autógrafo.

Y hoy un par de chicos y yo le hemos gastado una broma estupenda a Chirag Gupta.

Decidimos que sería muy gracioso si le hacíamos creer que se estaba quedando sordo, así que nos pusimos de acuerdo en hablar muy bajito siempre que él estuviera cerca.

Cuando Chirag se dio cuenta de lo que estábamos haciendo, fue directo al maestro para acabar con el juego antes de que la cosa fuese a más. No tenía ganas de que se repitiera la broma del "Chirag invisible" que le gastamos el año pasado.

Viernes

Esta tarde tenemos nuestro segundo partido de fútbol. Algunos adultos se prestaron voluntarios para ir a recuperar los balones, así que me tuve que pasar todo el partido sentado en el banquillo.

Hacía AUTÉNTICO frío y le pregunté a Papá si podía ir al coche a buscar mi chaqueta, pero no me dejó.

Papá dijo que debía estar preparado por si el entrenador decidía sacarme a jugar, y por tanto tenía que aguantarme.

Quise decirle a Papá que el único momento en que iba a pisar el campo iba a ser cuando el Sr. Litch me ordenara recoger durante el descanso las cáscaras de naranja que los otros chicos habían tirado. Pero me mantuve callado, mientras intentaba impedir que las espinilleras me helaran las piernas.

Cada vez que el entrenador llamaba a los jugadores para dar instrucciones, Papá me hacía levantarme del banquillo y unirme al resto del equipo. Al ver un partido por la tele, ¿nunca se han preguntado qué pasa por la cabeza de los que calientan el banquillo, cuando están ahí de pie con el corro de jugadores, mientras el entrenador les explica la estrategia?

Pues ahora lo puedo decir por mi propia experiencia.

Cuando el sol se ocultó, sentí frío DE VERDAD.
De hecho, hacía tanto frío que Mackey Creavey y
Manuel Gónzales fueron y se trajeron SACOS DE
DORMIR del coche de los Creavey.

Y Papá ni siquiera me dejaba ir a buscar mi
chaqueta.

Durante el siguiente tiempo muerto, todos hicimos un corro. Y cuando el entrenador vio a Mickey y a Manuel, les dio permiso para quedarse en el coche de los Creavey el resto del partido.

Y así Mackey y Manuel fueron a sentarse en el interior de un todoterreno calentito, mientras yo podía sentir el frío metal del banquillo a través de mis pantalones cortos. Me CONSTA que el coche de los Creavey tiene televisión, así que esos chicos se encontraban muy a gusto allí dentro.

<u>Lunes</u>

Tengo que ponerme DE UNA VEZ POR TODAS
a resolver lo de mi montón de ropa sucia. Llevo ya
tres días sin ropa interior y he tenido que usar un
traje de baño como sustituto.

Hoy teníamos Educación Física y al ir a ponerme la
ropa de gimnasia, he olvidado totalmente que llevaba
el bañador.

Y todavía podría haber sido mucho PEOR. Tengo unos
calzoncillos de Wonder Woman que no he llegado a sacar
de su envoltorio, y esta mañana he estado tentado de
ponérmelos tan sólo porque estaban limpios.

De veras, yo no pedí que me regalaran los calzoncillos de Wonder Woman. El verano pasado, algunos familiares le preguntaron a Mamá qué me haría ilusión por mi cumpleaños y ella les dijo que estaba totalmente enganchado a los cómics y los superhéroes.

Los calzoncillos fueron el regalo de tío Charlie.

Teníamos otro partido de fútbol después del colegio, pero últimamente está haciendo mejor tiempo, así que no me preocupaba pasar frío.

En el colegio, Mackey, Manuel y yo habíamos acordado llevar esta tarde algunos videojuegos, y así por primera vez lo pasamos BIEN en el fútbol.

Sin embargo, no duró mucho. A los veinte minutos de empezar el partido, el Sr. Litch nos llamó a los tres del banquillo para que saliéramos al campo.

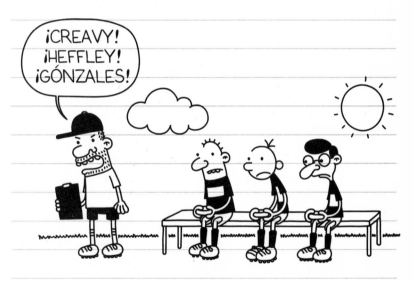

Por lo visto, algunos padres se habían quejado de que a sus chicos no los sacaban nunca a jugar y en la Liga Recreativa han impuesto como norma que TODOS tenemos que participar en el juego.

Bien. Pues ninguno de nosotros habíamos prestado la menor atención al desarrollo del juego y cuando salimos al campo no sabíamos qué hacer ni dónde ponernos.

Un par de chicos de nuestro equipo nos dijeron que los del otro equipo iban a sacar un tiro "libre directo" y se suponía que teníamos que permanecer codo con codo, formando una barrera para impedir que pasara el balón.

Pensé que los de mi equipo estaban de broma, pero resultó que era verdad. Manuel, Mackey y yo nos pusimos delante de nuestra portería. Entonces el árbitro hizo sonar el silbato y un chico del otro equipo corrió hacia el balón y le dio una patada hacia nosotros.

¡PIIIIIII!

La verdad es que no hicimos un gran papel como barrera y el balón entró en nuestra portería.

El Sr. Litch nos sacó del juego a los tres a la
primera oportunidad, y nos echó una bronca por no
aguantar de pie, bloqueando la trayectoria del balón.

Pero permítanme decirles que si tengo que elegir
entre que me echen una bronca o recibir un balonazo
en la cara, lo tengo clarísimo.

Jueves

Después del partido de la semana pasada, le pregunté al Sr. Litch si yo podía ser el portero suplente del equipo y me dijo que sí.

Fue una jugada genial por mi parte, por dos razones. En primer lugar, porque los porteros no tienen que correr cientos de vueltas al campo en los entrenamientos. Sólo hacen unos ejercicios especiales para los porteros, con el ayudante del entrenador.

Segundo, los porteros llevan un uniforme diferente al del resto del equipo y eso significa que el Sr. Litch no me va sacar al campo cuando haga falta hacer una barrera en los tiros directos.

Nuestro portero titular, Tucker Fox, es la estrella del equipo, así que sabía que era prácticamente imposible que me tocara salir a jugar. De alguna manera, estos últimos partidos han estado bien. Pero ayer por la tarde ocurrió algo. Tucker se lesionó una mano al tirarse para parar un balón y tuvo que salir del campo. Eso significaba que el entrenador iba a ponerme A MÍ.

¡Uf! Papá estaba REALMENTE nervioso. Al fin iba a salir a jugar de verdad. Se acercó hasta el fondo del campo para asesorarme desde la línea de banda. Sin embargo, parece que no llegué a necesitarlo. Nuestro equipo mantuvo el balón en su poder en el otro lado del campo hasta terminó el partido y yo no llegué a tocarlo UNA SOLA VEZ.

149

Me parece que sé lo que le preocupaba a Papá.

La verdad es que en la época en que jugaba a béisbol tenía ciertas dificultades para concentrarme en el juego. Ayer por la tarde Papá sólo quería asegurarse de que no me iba a dispersar de la misma manera que entonces, cuando me dedicaba a jugar con las flores que crecían en el campo.

Tengo que admitir que quizá fue una buena cosa que Papá estuviera ayer pendiente de mí.

En el extremo del campo en que yo me encontraba, había MILLONES de margaritas dispersas por la hierba y durante la segunda parte estaba empezando a ponerme inquieto.

Lunes

Pues ayer tuvimos otro partido y por suerte Papá no estuvo allí para verlo. Perdimos por primera vez en lo que va de temporada, 1-0. De alguna manera, en los últimos segundos de juego, los del otro equipo consiguieron que el balón entrara en mi portería y ganaron el partido. Eso echó por tierra nuestro récord de imbatibilidad.

Después del partido, todos los del equipo se encontraban sumidos en una nube de amargura, así que intenté levantarles la moral.

¡CHICOS, NO ES PARA TANTO! ¡DESPUÉS DE TODO, SÓLO ES UN JUEGO ESTÚPIDO!

Mis compañeros agradecieron mi actitud positiva lanzándome cáscaras de naranja.

De regreso a casa, no sabía cómo decirle a Papá lo sucedido en el fútbol.

Al principio, pareció un poco disgustado, pero luego se le fue pasando.

Sin embargo, esta noche cuando Papá regresó a casa del trabajo, parecía muy enojado. Dejó caer ruidosamente el periódico frente a mí, sobre la mesa de la cocina. Y aquí está la foto de la página de Deportes:

La imbatibilidad que voló de un soplo

Greg Heffley, el guardameta de los Red Socks, se toma un respiro mientras entra rodando en su portería el balón disparado desde cincuenta yardas por el centrocampista de los Demon Dawgs, James Byron. Este tanto da al traste con las aspiraciones de los Red Socks de terminar la temporada imbatidos.

Por lo visto, Papá supo lo del periódico porque se lo dijo su jefe en el trabajo.

Bueno, quizá no le conté a Papá TODOS los detalles del partido.

En mi defensa puedo decir que no me enteré realmente de lo que había sucedido hasta que lo leí yo mismo en el periódico.

Papá no me dirigió la palabra durante el resto de la noche. Si todavía está enojado conmigo, espero que se le pase pronto. Hoy han sacado por fin a la venta Twisted Wizard 2 y pensaba pedirle dinero para comprarlo.

<u>Viernes</u>

Esta noche, después de cenar, Papá nos llevó al cine a Rodrick y a mí. Sin embargo, no lo hizo porque estuviera tratando de ser agradable. Sólo tenía necesidad de salir de casa.

¿Recuerdan que mencioné que Mamá se había apuntado a unas clases de gimnasia hace unos meses? Pues lo dejó después de la primera sesión. Papá le hizo una foto vestida con su atuendo deportivo el primer día que fue al gimnasio, y esta tarde llegaron por correo todas las fotografías ya reveladas.

Como la tienda de fotografías envía un duplicado de cada una de las impresiones, Papá escribió algo sobre las dos fotos de Mamá y las pegó en la nevera.

154

Bien, Papá estaría encantado porque se le había ocurrido esa broma ingeniosa, pero me temo que a Mamá no le hizo ninguna gracia.

¡JE, JE!

En cualquier caso, sospecho que Papá ha preferido poner un poco de distancia entre él y Mamá esta noche.

Fuimos al nuevo cine que acaban de inaugurar en el centro comercial. Después de sacar las entradas, entramos y se las dimos al acomodador, que era un adolescente con el pelo rapado al estilo militar. No lo reconocí al principio, pero parece que Papá sí.

SUS ENTRADAS, POR FAVOR.

Leí el nombre del adolescente en su identificador, y no podía dar crédito a mis ojos. Era LENWOOD HEATH, el gamberro que vivía en nuestra calle. La última vez que le vi llevaba el pelo largo y prendía fuego al cubo de basura de alguien. Pero ahora ahí estaba, con un aspecto como si acabara de graduarse en las Fuerzas Aéreas o algo así.

Papá parecía MUY impresionado con la nueva imagen de Lenwood, y los dos entablaron conversación.

Lenwood dijo que asistía a la Academia Militar de Spag Union y que sólo estaba trabajando en el cine durante el periodo de vacaciones de primavera.
También dijo que está intentando sacar buenas notas en Spag Union, para poder ingresar en West Point.

Y de pronto, Papá trataba a Lenwood como si fuera su mejor amigo. Era demencial, especialmente si tenemos en cuenta toda la historia anterior entre ellos.

ANTES   DESPUÉS

En cualquier caso, Papá siguió charlando con Lenwood, así que Rodrick y yo cogimos nuestras palomitas de maíz y pasamos a la sala. Y hasta la mitad de la película no caí en la cuenta de lo que EN REALIDAD estaba sucediendo.

Si Papá veía que en la escuela militar podían convertir en un hombre a un delincuente juvenil como Lenwood Heath, no le quedaba mucho trecho para pensar que también podían hacer un hombre de un renacuajo como YO.

Rezo para que a Papá no se le pasen esas ideas por la cabeza. Me preocupa bastante que esta noche, después del cine, Papá pareciera encontrarse de mejor humor de lo que ha estado durante MUCHO tiempo.

Lunes

Es exactamente lo que me temía. Papá se ha pasado todo el fin de semana leyendo cosas sobre Spag Union y esta noche ha dicho que ha decidido apuntarme.

Esto es lo peor de todo: los "nuevos reclutas" tienen que incorporarse el día 7 de junio, cuando se supone que empiezo las VACACIONES de verano.

Papá trató de convencerme de que iba a ser estupendo para mí, cómo Spag Union iba a modelarme. Pero ir a un campamento militar NO es precisamente el plan que yo tengo para mis vacaciones escolares.

Le dije a Papá que no duraría ni un día en Spag Union. Para empezar, mezclan a chicos como yo con adolescentes, y eso no puede ser bueno.

Estoy seguro de que los chicos mayores la tomarían conmigo desde el primer día.

Pero lo más me preocupa es la situación en el cuarto de baño. Apuesto a que Spag Union es uno de esos sitios donde no tienen cabinas individuales para las duchas, y a mí eso no me va.

Necesito mi privacidad en el cuarto de baño. Ni siquiera uso los servicios del colegio excepto en caso de absoluta emergencia.

Algunas aulas tienen aseos, pero ni siquiera esos puedo utilizar, porque el menor ruido que hagas se escucha en toda la clase.

Una última posibilidad son los servicios de la cafetería, y ese sitio es una verdadera casa de locos. Hace algunas semanas, a alguien se le ocurrió empezar a lanzar papel higiénico mojado y ahora aquello es como una zona de guerra.

No soy capaz de concentrarme en ese tipo de entornos, así que no me queda más remedio que aguantarme las ganas hasta que regreso a casa del colegio.

Hace un par de días, ocurrió algo que cambió la situación. El conserje instaló en el cuarto de baño varios ambientadores.

Entonces fui corriendo el rumor de que los ambientadores eran cámaras de seguridad camufladas, para captar a cualquiera que tirase papel higiénico mojado.

Creo que elegí a la gente apropiada, porque desde entonces el cuarto de baño de la cafetería está tan apacible como la biblioteca.

Tal vez haya resuelto el problema del cuarto de baño en el colegio, pero no creo que el mismo truco fuera a colar en Spag Union. Y la verdad, dudo muy SERIA-MENTE de que pueda resistir todo el verano sin hacer mis necesidades.

Sabía que no iba a convencer a Papá para que cambiara de opinión, así que me dirigí a Mamá. Le dije que no quería ir a un sitio donde te hacen afeitarte la cabeza y se ponen a hacer flexiones a las cinco de la mañana todos los días. Supuse que estaría de acuerdo conmigo y haría entrar en razón a Papá.

Pero parece que no va a serme de mucha ayuda, después de todo.

¡ME PARECE QUE ESTARÍAS MUY GUAPO EN UNIFORME!

Miércoles

Supe que tenía que hacer algo rápidamente para convencer a Papá de que yo era un tipo recio y no necesitaba ir a la academia militar. Así que le dije que quería apuntarme a los Boy Scouts.

La idea pareció entusiasmar a Papá, lo cual es un alivio.

Aparte de buscar una manera de quitarme a Papá de encima, tengo otras dos razones para hacerme Boy Scout. Primero, que los Boy Scouts hacen sus reuniones los domingos, lo que significa que podré dejar el fútbol.

Y segundo, ya va siendo hora de que los demás chicos del colegio me vayan teniendo un poco de respeto.

En mi ciudad hay dos brigadas de los Boy Scouts: la Brigada 24, que se encuentra cerca de nuestro vecindario, y la Brigada 133, situada a unas cinco millas por la carretera. La Brigada 133 siempre está organizando barbacoas y fiestas de piscina y cosas así, pero la Brigada 24 dedica los fines de semana a trabajar en proyectos de servicios comunitarios. Así que, definitivamente, mi perfil se ajusta más a la Brigada 133.

Ahora la jugada reside en procurar que Papá no se entere de que existe la Brigada 24, porque SEGURO que me hace apuntarme a esa.

De hecho, anoche nos dirigíamos al centro comercial y
había gente de la Brigada 24 limpiando el parque. Por
suerte, pude distraer a Papá en el último momento.

Domingo

Hoy ha sido mi primera reunión con los Boy Scouts,
afortunadamente con la Brigada 133. Me llevé conmigo
a Rowley para que se apuntara también. Cuando
llegamos al pabellón, conocimos al Sr. Barrett, el
Scoutmaster, que nos hizo repetir la Promesa de
Lealtad y hacer una serie de cosas y nos aceptaron. El
Sr Barrett incluso nos dio los uniformes.

Rowley estaba encantado porque pensaba que su uniforme era muy chulo, pero yo estaba contento por
tener una muda limpia de camisa.

Nos pusimos los uniformes y nos unimos al resto de la brigada y empezamos a trabajar para ganarnos las insignias al mérito. Las insignias al mérito son esos parches que consigues por aprender a hacer todo tipo de cosas varoniles.

Yo y Rowley lo pasamos bien echando un vistazo al libro de insignias al mérito y decidiendo qué *misión* elegir.

Rowley quería apuntarse a Supervivencia en la Jungla o Buena Forma Física Personal, pero le convencí para que desistiera de la idea. Le dije que debíamos empezar con algo fácil y agradable, así que nos apuntamos a Talla de Madera.

Pero tallar era mucho más duro de lo que yo había pensado. Lleva una ETERNIDAD intentar dar a un bloque de madera forma de cualquier cosa, y a los cinco minutos Rowley se clavó una astilla.

Así que fuimos a ver al Sr. Barrett y le preguntamos si podíamos hacer algo que fuera menos PELIGROSO.

El Sr. Barrett dijo que si estábamos teniendo problemas con la madera, quizá podíamos intentarlo usando jabón en su lugar. Y entonces fue cuando supe que había tomado la decisión correcta al apuntarme en la Brigada 133.

Rowley y yo empezamos a tallar el jabón, pero entonces me di cuenta de una cosa formidable. Si humedeces la pastilla de jabón lo suficiente, puedes moldearlo a voluntad usando las manos. Así que dejamos a un lado nuestros cuchillos de tallar y nos dedicamos a darle forma al jabón por el procedimiento de estrujarlo.

Mi primera creación fue una oveja. Se la llevé al Sr. Barrett, y tachó una talla de mi lista.

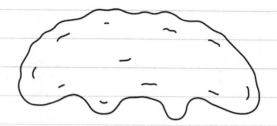

La verdad es que no sabía qué hacer para mi siguiente talla, de modo que puse mi oveja bocabajo y la volví a presentar diciendo que era el Titanic.

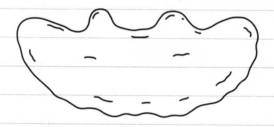

Podrán no creerlo, pero lo cierto es que el Sr. Barrett también aceptó esa talla como válida.

De este modo, Rowley y yo conseguimos nuestras insignias al mérito en Talla de Madera, que nos cosimos en los uniformes. Cuando volví a casa, Papá se quedó muy impresionado. Si llego a saber que bastaba con eso para hacerle feliz, me habría apuntado a los Boy Scouts hace seis meses.

MAYO

Domingo

El otro día el Sr. Barrett anunció que este fin de semana nuestra brigada de los Boy Scouts tendría una acampada de hijos y padres, de modo que le pregunté a Papá si podría venir conmigo. Yo estaba sorprendido de lo fácil que había sido impresionar a Papá con una mínima insignia, y me imaginé que TODO un fin de semana viéndome hacer cosas propias de hombres recios y varoniles le dejaría totalmente noqueado.

Pero resulta que ayer por la mañana desperté sintién-
dome enfermo de veras. Estaba hecho un asco. No
podía ir. Sin embargo, Papá tenía que ir porque se
había comprometido a conducir.

Me quedé en la cama casi todo el día. Sólo hubiese
preferido ponerme enfermo un día de clase y no en fin de
semana. El año pasado no falté al colegio ni un solo día,
y me prometí a mí mismo que eso no volvería a ocurrir.

La acampada de hijos y padres fue un DESASTRE.
El teléfono sonó anoche a las diez, y era Papá, que
llamaba desde Urgencias.

Habían puesto a Papá a dormir en una tienda con los her-
manos Woodley, Darren y Marcus, porque su padre no
había podido ir. Darren y Marcus estuvieron alborotando
por toda la tienda, a pesar de que Papá les decía que se
fueran a dormir. En un momento dado, Darren le tiró un
balón de fútbol a Marcus y le dio en el estómago.

Marcus se mojó los pantalones, y eso le pareció gra-
ciosísimo a Darren.

Entonces Marcus se puso como una FIERA. Mordió
a Darren y no soltaba su presa.

A Papá le costó un buen rato separarlos, y luego tuvo
que llevar a Darren a Urgencias.

Papá regresó esta mañana y no parecía muy contento conmigo por haberle dejado en la estacada.
Algo me dice que, después de este fin de semana, no
va a ser demasiado forofo de la Brigada 133.

Domingo
Hoy era el Día de la Madre, y no tenía regalo
para Mamá.

Iba a pedirle a Papá que me llevase a la tienda, de
modo que al menos pudiera comprarle a Mamá una tarjeta o alguna cosa, pero Papá todavía se estaba recu-
perando de la acampada de hijos y padres.
Y tampoco creo que tuviera ganas de hacerme favores.

Así que tuve que arreglarme con un regalo de
fabricación doméstica.

El año pasado le hice a Mamá un "talonario de tareas" por el Día de la Madre. En cada talón ponía
algo así como "Vale por una cortada de césped" o
"Vale por un lavado de cristales a las ventanas".

Cada Día del Padre, le regalo a Papá un talonario de
tareas y siempre resulta bien. Para mí es una manera
de cumplir con la obligación de hacer un regalo, sin
tener que gastar dinero. Y Papá nunca usa ninguno de
los talones.

En cambio Mamá hizo efectivos TODOS y cada uno de los talones que le había regalado. Por supuesto que este año no pienso cometer el mismo error.

Intenté pensar en algo original para regalarle hoy a Mamá, pero se me acabó el tiempo. Así que al final me limité a añadir mi firma a la tarjeta que le había hecho Manny.

<u>Lunes</u>

Creo que la mejor manera de hacer que Papá supere el desastre de la acampada de hijos y padres es recomponer la jugada. De manera que esta noche durante la cena le he preguntado si quería venirse a acampar, él y yo solos.

He estado estudiando el manual de los Boy Scouts y estoy deseando mostrarle todo lo que he aprendido.

No es que Papá saltara de alegría con mi ofrecimiento, pero a Mamá le pareció que era una GRAN idea. Dijo que fuéramos este fin de semana y que Rodrick también podría ir. Dijo también que esta experiencia contribuiría a crear "vínculos afectivos" entre los tres.

Yo no estaba tan entusiasmado con la idea y tampoco Rodrick.

De hecho, una de las razones por las que quería salir de casa este fin de semana es porque Rodrick y yo estamos en guerra.

Anoche Mamá estaba cortándole el pelo a Rodrick en la cocina. Cuando Mamá nos corta el pelo, suele ponernos una toalla alrededor del cuello para que el pelo no nos caiga sobre la ropa. Pero ayer, en lugar de una toalla, utilizó uno de sus antiguos vestidos de maternidad. Y en cuanto vi el aspecto de Rodrick supe que tenía que sacar partido de la situación.

Corrí escaleras arriba y me encerré en el cuarto de
baño, antes de que Rodrick pudiese atraparme y
quitarme la cámara. Y no salí hasta que estuve seguro
de que se había marchado.

Rodrick, sin embargo, se cobró su venganza. Anoche
soñé que estaba durmiendo sobre un hormiguero y fue
gracias a él.

Según lo veo, estamos iguales. Pero si hay algo que he
aprendido de Rodrick es que no deja así las cosas.
Por eso no me gusta la idea de dormir con él en la
misma tienda.

Sábado

Hoy salimos Papá, Rodrick y yo de acampada. Elegí
un lugar en el que se podían hacer muchas actividades
importantes.

De camino al campamento, el cielo se puso oscuro y empezó a llover.

No me preocupó, porque nuestra tienda era a prueba de agua y Mamá había puesto ponchos impermeables para todos. Pero cuando llegamos al lugar de la acampada, se encontraba sumergido un palmo bajo el agua.

Estábamos muy lejos de casa, así que Papá decidió buscar un sitio para pasar la noche.

Yo estaba bastante fastidiado, porque el objetivo de la expedición era impresionar a Papá con mis habilidades de acampada, y ahora íbamos a dormir en algún estúpido hotel.

Papá encontró un sitio y alquiló una habitación con dos camas y un sofá plegable. Estuvimos viendo la tele un rato y luego nos preparamos para irnos a dormir.

Papá bajó las escaleras hasta recepción para quejarse de que la calefacción estaba demasiado fuerte. Y me quedé a solas con Rodrick.

Fui al cuarto de baño para cepillarme los dientes y cuando salí Rodrick estaba mirando hacia fuera por la mirilla de la puerta.

Dijo que Holly Hills y su familia se encontraban afuera, en el vestíbulo, y que se iban a alojar en la habitación de en frente.

Tenía que comprobarlo por mí mismo. Así que le aparté a un lado y me puse a espiar por la mirilla.

El vestíbulo estaba totalmente desierto. Antes de que me diese cuenta del engaño, Rodrick me dio un fuerte empujón y caí en el exterior.

Entonces las cosas se pusieron feas de verdad. Rodrick cerró la puerta, dejándome fuera. Me había quedado tirado en el vestíbulo, vestido tan sólo con mi calzoncillo superajustado.

Aporreé la puerta, pero Rodrick no quiso abrirme.

Estaba armando mucho jaleo y me di cuenta de que la gente de las habitaciones vecinas iba a empezar a asomarse para ver qué pasaba. Así que corrí y me escondí detrás de un recodo del pasillo, para evitar pasar la vergüenza de que me vieran. Durante los siguientes quince minutos estuve rondando por los pasillos y escondiéndome cada vez que escuchaba voces.

Quise regresar a la habitación para pedirle a Rodrick que me dejara entrar, pero entonces me di cuenta de que ni siquiera sabía cuál era el número de nuestra habitación. Y todas las puertas me parecían iguales.

No tenía intención de bajar hasta recepción y que
me viera todo el mundo, así que la única posibilidad
era intentar encontrar a Papá.

Entonces recordé que Papá es un adicto a los dulces.
Sabía que era posible que estuviera donde las máquinas
expendedoras y me dirigí hacia allí.

Me escondí entre una máquina de refrescos y otra de
dulces y esperé. Tuve que esperar un buen rato, pero
al fin apareció Papá.

Pero al ver la cara de Papá, deseé haber tenido el
coraje de haber ido hasta la recepción.

<u>Domingo</u>

En fin, en vista del éxito de nuestra acampada, supongo que ya no hay manera de quitarle a Papá la idea de enviarme a Spag Union, así que no pienso molestarme en intentarlo.

Me he dado cuenta de que sólo faltan tres semanas para que me manden allí, de modo que es mi última oportunidad de intentar ligar con Holly Hills. Si tengo suerte, puede que pueda llevarme algún buen recuerdo a la academia militar y entonces el verano no se me haría tan cuesta arriba.

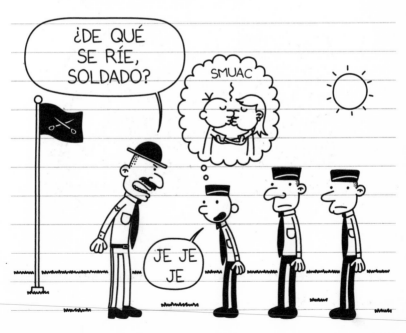

He estado reuniendo valor para mantener una conversación con Holly y he decidido que tiene que ser ahora o
nunca.

Cuando fuimos a la iglesia hoy, intenté que nos sen-
táramos al lado de la familia Hills. Pero al final termi-
namos dos filas por delante de ellos, lo cual es bastante
cerca. Y durante la parte en que todo el mundo se da la
mano, llevé a cabo mi jugada.

Lo de estrecharle la mano fue sólo el primer paso de
mi plan de dos pasos. La segunda parte vendría
esta noche. El siguiente paso era llamar a Holly por
teléfono y utilizar como excusa lo de darse la paz
para entablar una conversación.

HOLA, HOLLY, SOY GREG HEFFLEY. SEGURO QUE TE ACUERDAS DE MÍ POR LA FORMA ESPECIAL DE DECIRTE "QUE LA PAZ SEA CONTIGO".

(RISITA)

Por la noche, durante la cena, les dije a todos que no ocuparan el teléfono porque tenía que hacer una llamada muy importante. Pero supongo que Rodrick se debió imaginar que iba a llamar a una chica, porque agarró todos los auriculares y los escondió.

Eso significaba que sólo podía llamar desde el teléfono de pared de la cocina pero, claro, no había manera de hacerlo.

Le dije a Mamá que Rodrick se había llevado todos los teléfonos y ella le hizo devolver cada uno de ellos a su sitio.

Más tarde, aprovechando que Rodrick había bajado al sótano, me colé en el dormitorio de Papá y Mamá para hacer mi llamada. Dejé apagadas las luces para que Rodrick no pudiera localizarme, y me escondí debajo de una manta. Esperé unos veinte minutos para estar seguro de que no me había seguido.

Antes de que pudiera marcar el número de Holly, alguien entró en la habitación y encendió la luz. Estaba seguro de que era Rodrick.

Pero resulta que no. Era PAPÁ.

Decidí permanecer totalmente inmóvil y esperar a que Papá agarrara lo que había ido a buscar y se marchara.

Pero no se marchó. Se acostó en la cama y empezó a leer un LIBRO.

Debería haber descubierto mi presencia cuando Papá entró en la habitación, porque si ahora me incorporaba y salía hacia la puerta seguro que le daba un infarto. Comencé a arrastrarme muy despacio.

Apenas avanzaba nada. A ese paso de hormiga coja, iba a tardar media hora en alcanzar la salida de la habitación, pero todavía me quedaba tiempo para llamar a Holly.

Estaba ya rozando la puerta del dormitorio cuando el
teléfono que llevaba en la mano empezó a sonar y me
dio un susto tremendo.

Creo que de veras faltó MUY POCO para que a
Papá le diera un ataque al corazón. Cuando se repuso
del sobresalto, no pareció muy contento de verme.

Me hizo salir de su habitación y luego cerró de un
portazo.

Este episodio no ha mejorado mi posición ante Papá,
pero supongo que de todos modos ya es demasiado
tarde.

Martes

Han pasado ya dos días desde que le estreché la
mano a Holly y no quiero dejar pasar más tiempo
antes de dirigirme a ella de nuevo.

Por suerte, Papá y Rodrick no estaban en casa esta
tarde y se podía hablar por teléfono sin problemas.
Ensayé un millón de veces lo que le iba a decir y
finalmente reuní valor para hacer la llamada.

Marqué el número de Holly y escuché el sonido de la
llamada al otro lado. Pero justo entonces Mamá
descolgó el teléfono de abajo.

Mamá tiene la MALA costumbre de ponerse a marcar
un número sin comprobar antes si alguien está usando
el teléfono, y eso es lo hizo esta noche.

Traté de que lo dejara, pero no hubo manera.

El teléfono siguió sonando en casa de los Hill hasta que alguien lo cogió. Era la madre de Holly.

Mamá estaba confusa, ya que ella no había marcado ese número. Contuve la respiración y aguardé el desenlace.

Le llevó menos de un minuto a Mamá y a la señora Hills averiguar cada una de ellas quién estaba al otro lado de la línea. Y luego se pusieron a charlar como si nada extraño hubiera sucedido.

Se liaron en una larguísima conversación sobre el PTA y el Comité Fundador y cosas así. Yo no podía colgar, ya que entonces Mamá escucharía el chasquido y sabría que alguien más estaba escuchando.

En un momento dado, Mamá y la Sra. Hills empezaron a hablar sobre mí.

Entonces dejé el teléfono y me fui a dormir. Supongo que el destino no quiere que Holly y yo podamos hablar por teléfono, así que definitivamente me rindo.

Viernes

Hoy en el colegio escuché a Holly quedar con dos amigas para ir por la tarde a la pista de patinaje. Y de pronto se me encendió una bombilla en la cabeza.

Después de clase le pregunté a Mamá si esta tarde me podía llevar a la pista de patinaje y ella me dijo que sí, siempre que los padres de alguien me trajeran de regreso a casa. Así que le dije a Rowley que viniera conmigo.

Tan pronto como apareció por la puerta, supe que había cometido un error al llamarle.

Rowley iba todo repeinado y vestía como Joshie, su cantante favorito.

Y podía ser que incluso llevara puesto brillo de labios, aunque no estoy seguro. No podía dejar de preocuparme por la pinta que llevaba Rowley, porque yo tenía mis PROPIOS problemas. Un rato antes se me había perdido una de mis lentillas de contacto y eso me obligaba a llevar puestos los lentes, que tienen unos cristales de medio palmo de grosor y me dan un aspecto RIDÍCULO.

Si no llevo las lentillas o los lentes, estoy más ciego que un murciélago. Supongo que soy afortunado de no vivir en la Edad de Piedra, porque no sería capaz de cazar, ni de hacer nada útil. Los de mi tribu se desharían de mí en la primera ocasión que tuvieran.

Probablemente tendría que convertirme en un sabio consejero o algo así, para hacer creer a todo el mundo que merecía la pena tenerme con ellos.

Esta tarde, cuando nos dirigíamos a la pista de patinaje, le di a Rowley instrucciones sobre cómo debía comportarse si teníamos una conversación con Holly Hills. Conociéndole, podía meter la pata y comprometer seriamente mis posibilidades con Holly.

Debería haber esperado hasta que bajáramos del coche, porque Mamá escuchó nuestra conversación.

Cuando llegamos a la pista de patinaje, salí del coche antes de que Mamá dijese más cosas que yo no quería escuchar.

Rowley y yo pagamos las entradas y pasamos al interior. Alquilamos patines para los dos y cargamos con ellos hasta el área de recreo, donde observé el panorama.

Divisé a Holly en la cafetería con un grupo de amigas, así que todavía no era el momento de acercarme y ponerme a hablar con ella.

Más tarde, a eso de las 9:00, el DJ anunció "Patinaje en Parejas". Mucha gente se fue emparejando, mientras Holly estaba allí sola, en una mesa. Supe que aquella era la ocasión que había estado esperando.

Comencé a acercarme a ella, pero moverse en patines resultaba mucho más difícil de lo que me había imaginado. Tuve que apoyarme en la pared para mantenerme sobre los pies.

Estaba tardando una ETERNIDAD y me di cuenta de que la canción se iba a terminar para cuando consiguiera llegar hasta Holly. Así que me senté en el suelo y me fui arrastrando sobre el trasero para ganar tiempo.

Casi me atropellan un par de veces, pero al fin conseguí llegar hasta la cafetería.

Holly todavía estaba allí, sentada sola. Se me estaba
acabando el tiempo y tuve que atajar pasando por
encima de un charco de refresco para llegar hasta ella.

Mientras atravesaba la cafetería, intentaba pensar lo
que iba a decirle a Holly. Me di cuenta de que no tenía
un buen aspecto en ese momento y que, por tanto, iba
a tener que decirle algo verdaderamente dulce para com-
pensarlo. Pero antes de que llegara a abrir la boca,
Holly dijo cuatro palabras que lo cambiaron todo:

Empecé a decirle que yo me llamaba Greg Heffley, el
chico del chiste de la chocolatina que un perro había
tirado al suelo, pero justo entonces se acabó el Patinaje
en Parejas y aparecieron las amigas de Holly, que la
arrastraron a la pista.

Regresé al área de recreo y permanecí allí el resto de la tarde. Y es que, pueden creerlo, no me sentía con ánimo de ponerme a patinar.

Ya saben, debería haberme dado cuenta hace bastante de que no vale la pena perder el tiempo con Holly. Alguien que es capaz de CONFUNDIRME con FREGLEY no puede estar en sus cabales.

He TERMINADO oficialmente con las chicas. Debería preguntarle a Papá si es posible adelantar mi incorporación a Spag Union, porque aquí ya no me retiene nada.

Viernes

Hoy era el último día de colegio y todo el mundo estaba alegre excepto yo. Todos los DEMÁS están deseando pasárselo bien este verano, pero a mí todo lo que me espera es hacer flexiones y desfilar con los tambores.

Durante el almuerzo, todo el mundo pasó sus anuarios al resto para que los firmaran, y cuando me devolvieron el mío, esto es lo que estaba escrito en la última página.

No seas tonto
Levanta el ánimo

Firmado: El Tigre

Al principio, no podía imaginar quién podía ser el que firmaba como "El Tigre", pero luego deduje que sólo podía ser Rowley. Hace un par de días, se encontraba de pie delante de la taquilla de un chico mayor y el tipo, para que Rowley se quitara de en medio, le dijo:

Por eso pienso que Rowley le ha gustado lo de
"Tigre" y lo ha adoptado como una especie de apodo
o algo así. Supongo que no querrá que yo también
se lo diga.

Hojeé las páginas del anuario para ver quién más
había firmado y de pronto vi una que me produjo un
sobresalto. Estaba escrita de puño y letra por
Holly Hills. En primer lugar, ella había escrito mi
nombre, así que después del viernes ella ya sabía
quién yo era. Después, escribió las iniciales "SEC."
que como todo el mundo sabe, significan "Sigue En
Contacto". Pueden estar seguros de que pienso
seguir su recomendación.

Greg,
Todavía no te conozco muy bien,
pero me da la impresión de que eres
un tío estupendo.
S.E.C.
Holly

Le pasé a Rowley mi anuario, para que viera lo que
Holly me había escrito. Pero entonces él me enseñó lo
que Holly había escrito en SU anuario, y sentí algo
parecido a la envidia.

Querido Rowley,
¡Eres un encanto y muy divertido!
Espero que el año que viene nos
toque juntos en la misma clase.
¡Preciosón!

Besazos,
Holly

203

Un par de minutos después el anuario de Holly pasó
por mi lado y tuve ocasión de firmarlo. Esto es lo
que puse:

> Querida Holly,
> Eres una persona agradable y todo eso,
> pero sólo pienso en ti como una amiga,
>
> Firmado: El Tigre

A mi modo de ver, le hice a Rowley un ENORME
favor. No quiero verle con las orejas gachas por
culpa de Holly Hills, porque lo cierto es que las chicas
a veces pueden llegar a ser un poco crueles.

Sábado

Hoy era mi único día de vacaciones de verano y tenía
que ir a la fiesta de medio cumpleaños de Seth Snella.
Le pedí a Mamá que me dejara quedarme en casa para
que pudiera estar tranquilo, pero ella me dijo que
íbamos a asistir toda la familia.

Papá ni se molestó en discutir, porque sabía que él tampoco tenía escapatoria.

Así que a la 1:00 cruzamos la calle en dirección a casa de los Snella.

La verdad es que este año los Snella sí que lo han montado bien. Había un payaso inflando globos con formas de animales y una luna que botaba haciendo las delicias de los críos.

Incluso había música en vivo. Rodrick se sentía dolido, porque su grupo Celebros Retorcidos se había ofrecido para actuar pero los Snella los habían rechazado.

Todo el mundo comió el almuerzo y a las 3:00 empezó la parte principal de la fiesta.

Los señores Snella habían hecho que todos los adultos formaran una fila delante de Seth, y todos esperaban su turno para intentarle hacer reír. El Sr. Henrich fue el primero.

Me di cuenta de que Papá se encontraba al final de la fila y parecía estar muy nervioso. En cierto momento, me acerqué a esa parte para tomar un bizcocho y él me detuvo. Me dijo que si conseguía sacarle de aquella situación me debería una.

Yo pensé que resultaba irónico que Papá me estuviera pidiendo un favor, sobre todo cuando mañana me iba a enviar a la academia militar. Fue divertido ver cómo me rogaba.

Eso tampoco significaba que yo deseara ver a mi padre imitar a los babuinos delante de todo el vecindario. Estuve tentado de escabullirme y marcharme a casa para ahorrarme el espectáculo.

Entonces vi a Manny al otro lado de la terraza, curioseando entre los regalos de Seth.

Manny encontró el regalo de nuestra familia y lo abrió rasgando el papel que lo envolvía. Tan pronto como vi lo que era, supe que las cosas iban a complicarse.

Era una mantita azul de punto, exactamente igual a la que Manny había tenido cuando era un bebé. No resulta extraño que Manny pensara que había encontrado una Pringui nuevecita.

Me acerqué a Manny y le dije que iba a tener que dejar la manta, porque no era para él sino para Seth. Pero Manny se había aferrado a la nueva Pringui y no la soltaba.

Cuando se dio cuenta de que le iba a quitar la mantita, Manny se dio la vuelta y la tiró por encima de la barandilla.

La manta fue a parar a la rama de un árbol. Supe que tenía que recuperarla antes de que Mamá se diera cuenta, así que bajé de la terraza y empecé a trepar por el árbol.

Cuando estaba a punto de alcanzar la manta, mi pie resbaló y me quedé colgado. Intenté subir de nuevo, pero me faltaban fuerzas.

Normalmente hubiera podido hacerlo, pero lo único que había comido hoy era un refresco de uva y la corteza dulce de un trozo de pastel, así que estaba bajo de energías.

Grité para pedir ayuda, pero en realidad no deseaba
que la gente se fijara en mí, porque justo cuando
todos se asomaron para ver qué ocurría, mis pantalones se deslizaron hasta los tobillos.

Esto no habría sucedido si hubiera llevado puestos mis
propios pantalones, pero no llegué a lavarlos después de
que se pusieran perdidos de chocolate y por eso había
tomado prestados unos de RODRICK, que eran dos
tallas más grandes que la mía.

La situación ya era bastante humillante, pero
entonces me di cuenta de algo PEOR todavía.
Llevaba puestos los calzoncillos de Wonder Woman.

Llegó Papá y me ayudó a bajar del árbol, pero no antes de que el Sr. Snella grabara en vídeo toda la escena. Algo me dice que esta vez sí que dispone de buen material para el Gran Premio de "Las Familias Más Divertidas de América".

Después de aquello, Papá me llevó hasta casa y yo pensaba que estaba enojado conmigo. Pero resulta que mi accidente había sucedido justo cuando él se encontraba a punto de actuar delante de Seth Snella, así que se había librado por los pelos.

Y chúpate ésta: ¡Papá cree que lo FINGÍ todo para sacarle de apuros!

Claro que tampoco iba a sacarle de su error. Me preparé una gran bola de helado y me senté a ver la tele, tratando de pasar lo mejor posible el resto de mi único día de libertad.

Domingo

Cuando me desperté hoy eran ya las 11:15 pasadas.
No podía entender que todavía estuviera en la cama,
porque se suponía que Papá me iba a llevar a las
8:00 a Spag Union.

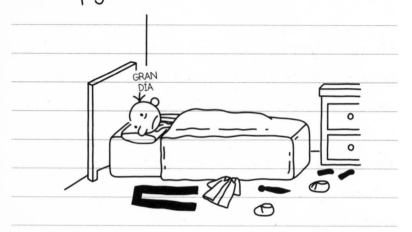

Bajé las escaleras y vi a Papá en la cocina, leyendo
tranquilamente el periódico mientras desayunaba. Ni
siquiera se había vestido.

Cuando entré, me dijo que podíamos "replantearnos" eso de la academia militar. Dijo que tal vez podría hacer flexiones y esas cosas de vez en cuando, y que eso me sentaría tan bien como pasar el verano en el campamento de Spag Union.

No podía creer lo que estaba oyendo. Creo que Papá se sentía en deuda conmigo por sacarle ayer del apuro y ésta era su forma de pagarlo.

Antes de que cambiase de idea, salí de casa y me fui a buscar a Rowley. Mientras iba subiendo la cuesta, me di cuenta de que ¡estaba de vacaciones !

PIO
PIO

Llamé a la puerta de la casa de Rowley y, cuando abrió, le dije que DESPUÉS de todo, ya no tenía que ir a Spag Union.

Rowley ni siquiera sabía de qué estaba hablando, lo que dice mucho de lo despistado que puede llegar a ser, en ocasiones.

En casa de Rowley estuvimos jugando con el Twisted Wizard 2 un buen rato y luego sus padres nos hicieron salir a tomar el aire. Entonces agarramos unos bombones helados y fuimos a sentarnos delante de la casa, en el bordillo de la acera.

No se van a creer lo que sucedió a continuación. Una chica estupendísima que nunca había visto antes se acercó a nosotros y se presentó.

Dijo que se llamaba Trista y que se acababa de mudar a la parte de abajo de esta misma calle.

Miré a Rowley y era evidente que estaba pensando lo mismo que yo. Elaboré mi plan en menos de dos segundos.

Pero luego se me ocurrió una idea MEJOR.

La familia de Rowley es socia de un club de campo y
pueden llevar dos invitados a la piscina.

Eso podría ser una ventaja muy importante.

Parece que por fin la suerte se pone a mi favor.
Como es sabido, ya iba siendo hora. No conozco a
nadie que se merezca una buena racha más que yo
porque, como dije al principio, soy una de las
mejores personas que conozco.

Y como sería una cursilada terminar con un "final feliz" y además se me está terminando el papel, me parece que hemos llegado al

RECONOCIMIENTOS

Gracias a mi esposa, Julie, ya que sin su amor y su apoyo estos libros no hubieran sido posibles. Gracias a mi familia — Mamá, Papá, Re, Scott y Pat— y a mi familia ampliada —los Kinney, los Cullinan, los Johnson, los Fitch, los Kennedy y los Burdett. ¡Todos han sido de gran ayuda y ha sido formidable compartir esta experiencia con ustedes!

Gracias, como siempre, a mi editor Charlie Kochman por apostar por esta serie; a Jason Wells, el mejor director de publicidad de todo el mercado, y a toda la gente estupenda de Abrams.

Gracias a mi jefe, Jess Brallier, y a todos mis compañeros de Familiy Education Network.

Gracias a Riley, Silvie, Carla, Nina, Brad, Elizabeth y a Keith, de Hollywoodland.

Gracias a Mel Odom por sus maravillosas críticas de los dos primeros libros.

Y gracias a Aaron Nicodemus por animarme para que volviera a coger mi pluma de ilustrador, cuando ya había tirado la toalla.

SOBRE EL AUTOR

Jeff Kinney es un autor #1 en ventas de *The New York Times* y ha ganado en cinco ocasiones el premio Nickelodeon Kid's Choice del Libro Favorito. Jeff está considerado una de las 100 personas más influyentes del mundo, según la revista *Time*. Es el creador de Poptropica, que es una de las cincuenta mejores páginas web según *Time*. Pasó su infancia en Washington D. C. y se trasladó a Nueva Inglaterra en 1995. Hoy, Jeff vive con su esposa y sus dos hijos en Massachusetts, donde tienen una librería, An Unlikely Story

THE WRITER'S RESOURCE GUIDE

EDITED BY
William Brohaugh

ASSISTANT EDITOR
JoAnne Moser Gibbons

Writer's Digest Books

CINCINNATI, OHIO

A Note of Appreciation

The editors wish to acknowledge the following Writer's Digest Books staff members for their assistance in the preparation of The Writer's Resource Guide: Connie Achabal, Judy Beraha, Barb Kuroff, Barb O'Brien, and Becky Rogers.

The Writer's Resource Guide. Copyright © 1979. Published by Writer's Digest Books, 9933 Alliance Rd., Cincinnati, Ohio 45242. Publisher/Editorial Director: Richard Rosenthal. Managing Editor: Douglas Sandhage. Printed and bound in the United States of America. All rights reserved. No part of this book may be reproduced in any manner whatsoever without written permission from the publisher, except by reviewers who may quote brief passages to be printed in a magazine or newspaper. Second Printing, 1979.

Library of Congress Cataloging in Publication Data

Brohaugh, William
  The Writer's Resource Guide
  Cincinnati, Ohio
  Writer's Digest Books
  480 pages
  7904   790112

Library of Congress Catalog Card No. 79-3935

International Standard Book Number 0-911654-68-2

PREFACE

Let me tell you about excitement.

In many ways, excitement is a realization of possibilities. It's the thrill you feel when you recognize something's potential. That's why we're excited about *The Writer's Resource Guide*.

The book you're holding is more than a list of places to get information; it's a compilation of *possibilities*. Paging through *The Writer's Resource Guide*, you'll find story ideas, research strategies, advice and inspiration from sources with fascinating stories to tell.

The Writer's Resource Guide isn't intended to be the last word on research. We think of the book more as the first word. The book directs you to almost 2,000 places to get facts, quotes, background information, etc.—and, in doing so, introduces you to the types of sources available to you. We provide leads to information. We provide possibilities.

We provide excitement.

CONTENTS

ON DOING RESEARCH

Using
The Writer's Resource Guide

The Writer's Resource Guide is much more than a compilation of places to find information; it's a warehouse of leads, ideas, contacts and sources. To effectively use this book—to explore that warehouse—you must use this book methodically and innovatively.

Begin by reading the introductory articles that follow. This material was written by people who have researched the field of research, people who have all but haunted libraries, museums and a variety of other places searching for info. In their articles, they advise you on practical research methods, and start you thinking about other ways to unearth that important fact.

Then move on to the resource listings themselves, cataloged in the Sources section. Sources are categorized according to type (as examples, museums, organizations, government agencies, hospitals and medical centers and historical societies). The table of contents outlines the wide variety of subjects and sources covered by this book.

Let's say you're doing an article on professional athletes in US recreational sports. The Organizations & Associations section carries a sports subcategory—a logical place to begin your research. In the sports subcategory is this listing, offered here as a sample:

> **Professional Golfers' Association of America (PGA)**, Box 12458, Lake Park FL 33403. (305)844-5000. News Director: James C. Warters.
> **Purpose:** "The Professional Golfers' Association of America is an association of 16,000 members and apprentices. The organization carries out various administrative functions for members, including education; operation of various activities, such as professional golf tournaments; a credit union; membership processing; and annual business and executive meetings." Information covers business, celebrities, economics, entertainment, history, how-to, industry, new products, recreation, sports and technical data.

Services: Offers aid in arranging interviews, annual reports, bibliographies, biographies, statistics, brochures/pamphlets, information searches,
placement on mailing list, newsletter, photos,
press kits and films. Publications include *PGA
Media Reference Guide* and *PGA Apprentice Program*.
How to Contact: Write or call. Charges $10/film,
plus shipping costs.

If you want to interview professional athletes or other people involved in the golf
profession, PGA will help arrange interviews; if you need background information on
golfers or golfing, the organization will supply you with statistics, bibliographies and
biographies; if you need photos, PGA will help you get them.

When consulting specific listings in this book, read them carefully. If you don't,
you might miss some important information that you must know to use the source
effectively.

A close reading helps in other ways. Each listing is designed to inform you of the
scope and depth of each source's information, as well as a few specifics about it. The
United States Golf Association (USGA), for example, maintains a golfing museum and
library, a useful bit of information you might have missed had you only skimmed the
USGA listing. All information in the listing is pertinent to your consultation, even
though the pertinence might not be immediately obvious. We allow each source to
outline its purpose, for instance, so you can understand what information is available,
what areas it covers, and what bias the people supplying the information might have.

In the Sports subcategory, you'll find other sources (for example, the USGA) able
to help you with your article on professionals in sports. You might be tempted to put
away this book once you've scoured that category. *Don't.* You've only begun exploring
The Writer's Resource Guide's potential. Check the Sports subcategory in the Industrial & Commercial Firms section, and you'll find professional baseball, soccer, football, hockey and basketball teams, as well as professional league offices.

How many people claim athletics as their sole source of income? Maybe the
Bureau of Labor Statistics or the Census Bureau (both in the Government Information
Sources section) can help you. Check the Libraries & Archives and the Museums
sections for sports-related information facilities.

Done? Not by any means. The Sports Information Resource Center, listed in the
Data Bases section, is a computer bibliographic base that can lead you to many
different sources. *The Writer's Resource Guide* also has a section devoted to university
athletic departments. Your article might concentrate on athletes who have made
professional careers of coaching. Know of any professional athletes who have come to
the US for money and stardom? Check with the embassy or tourism office of their home
country for information about those athletes, and about any others who may be
involved in US professional sports.

If you seek a particular source, check the index at the back of the book. A source
not listed has been left out for one of these reasons: It is uninterested in or unable to aid
writers and/or researchers; it hasn't responded to any of our solicitations; it has asked
to be omitted.

Used correctly, *The Writer's Resource Guide* can lead you to the right information
to help you complete your article, book, script, etc. Yet, the book can be useful even if
you don't have a specific project in mind. *The Writer's Resource Guide* can be used
innovatively as an idea-generator. Skim through the book; read it. Ideas will force
themselves on you. What writer could encounter sources like the World Association of
Detectives, the American Spice Trade Association or the National Ballroom & Entertainment Association without coming up with at least one potential story?

The sources listed here are eager to tell the press about their organizations and
their work. They have stories to tell. All *you* have to do is contact them in the way they
want to be contacted, and then listen.

Here are the Postal Service's two-letter state codes used in the addresses in this book.

STATE CODES

AK	Alaska	MT	Montana
AL	Alabama	NC	North Carolina
AR	Arkansas	ND	North Dakota
AZ	Arizona	NE	Nebraska
CA	California	NH	New Hampshire
CO	Colorado	NJ	New Jersey
CT	Connecticut	NM	New Mexico
DC	District of Columbia	NV	Nevada
DE	Delaware	NY	New York
FL	Florida	OH	Ohio
GA	Georgia	OK	Oklahoma
HI	Hawaii	OR	Oregon
IA	Iowa	PA	Pennsylvania
ID	Idaho	PR	Puerto Rico
IL	Illinois	RI	Rhode Island
IN	Indiana	SC	South Carolina
KS	Kansas	SD	South Dakota
KY	Kentucky	TN	Tennessee
LA	Louisiana	TX	Texas
MA	Massachusetts	UT	Utah
MD	Maryland	VA	Virginia
ME	Maine	VI	Virgin Islands
MI	Michigan	VT	Vermont
MN	Minnesota	WA	Washington
MO	Missouri	WI	Wisconsin
MS	Mississippi	WV	West Virginia
		WY	Wyoming

Research:
Search & Search Again

You can't let research intimidate you. But you can let it push you around.

Research should push you from source to source, from fact to fact, from idea to idea. It should push you to follow leads and verify information. But intimidate you? Friends don't intimidate you. Business partners shouldn't intimidate you. Research mustn't intimidate you, because, in loose terms, it's both friend and business partner.

That relationship is established because of the necessity of research to any writing. A writer's "memory—and his charm, and contacts, and rich writing style—are for naught if he is not, above all, a researcher," says Writer's Digest editor John Brady in his book, The Craft of Interviewing. Skillful writing is useless if it doesn't illuminate new information for the reader, or if it doesn't use up-to-date, accurate information to establish its credibility.

Readers demand information and accuracy. Harvard sociologist Daniel Bell says we're living in an "information society," and Andrew Molnar of the National Science Foundation claims that "information has become a national commodity and a national resource." If a writer doesn't meet the challenge of being accurate when addressing a society that lives in an atmosphere of information, the writing will fail to interest or prove useful to readers. "Successful ideas need inspiration and creativity," says Mary Ann Grass, research librarian with the Warner Research library, "but most important, they need accurate information."

Establishing credibility with readers is only one advantage to research. Another is establishing credibility with editors. A well-documented article is more salable because the editor can stand behind its accuracy. The more research the writer does, the less research an editor must do to verify facts, and the greater is the sales potential of the piece in question. Besides, proper research can tell you if other writers have preceded you; there's no point in writing an article if it's already been done. Or, if the article has been done, research will tell you if it was done correctly; if it wasn't, you can rectify the situation by writing an accurate piece.

Research also provides you with the elements that give depth and texture to writing: background, sidelights and details. These elements make research valuable to fiction writers, too—and not just to historical novelists. Granted, novelists and short story writers deal in that-which-is-not-necessarily fact, but research can provide information about settings, costume and dress, events and even characters that can give fiction the verisimilitude necessary to the reader suspending disbelief. Robert Ludlum, author of The Chancellor Manuscript, consults newspaper and magazine stories and personal memoirs when describing locations—that is, when he can't get to the location himself. "I like to get the point of view of someone who was actually on the scene," he says.

Clive Cussler couldn't visit his location, so he build a model of the Titanic while writing his bestseller, Raise the Titanic! The model helped establish mood not only in the writing, but in the writer.

Few rules can be applied to research. Do enough to enable you to write your *material intelligently* is perhaps the only useful rule; *Then do some more* is good advice.

The ways to do research are many, but can be boiled down, as Alden Todd has done in *Finding Facts Fast*, to four basic procedures: "Reading, interviewing the expert or source person, observing for ourselves, and reasoning from what we have learned." (*Finding Facts Fast* is an excellent guide to research strategies.) Each writer must decide just how these procedures are applied.

Yet, that decision isn't nearly as important as the realization that research is vital to good writing, and that research isn't—mustn't—be intimidating.

Getting Cozy
in Public (Libraries)

Giving advice on how to use the library is a little like telling Admiral Byrd how to explore the South Pole. Two recommendations apply: Go there and explore.

The library is useless if you don't investigate everything the library offers. Even small libraries are more than just orderly book warehouses. The natural gravitational center of a library seems to be the card catalog, because most library users are drawn toward it first. Certainly the card catalog and the books to which it leads you form the core of the library, but other contents of the library can be equally useful, if not more so.

Libraries house and catalog magazines, pamphlets, files of newspaper clippings, and microfilm and microfiche collections. What's more, collections don't stop at compilation of the printed word. Libraries maintain collections of photos and illustrations; they file and store phonograph and tape recordings; they loan films and filmstrips; they provide computer terminals for access to data bases.

Libraries also boast a research aid that's indispensible: the librarian. Librarians are more than willing to help a researcher on the trail of a fact. Facts and finding them are the librarian's business, so much so that librarians will go out of their way to approach you if they notice you wandering around the building, as if the puzzled look on your face is an affront to their professional integrity. Librarians are the guides that Admiral Byrd never had; they can transform a library from a seemingly vast and formidable landscape into a friendly, useful and even cozy place.

The first step in getting cozy with a library is to find the one that's right for your research. The basic library, of course, is the public library—the primary subject of this article. Myriad specialized libraries are scattered about the country, however, and writers/researchers should be aware of what these libraries can offer. The first place to look for specialized libraries is in the Libraries & Archives section of this book. Here you'll find a number of collections covering specialized topics. Other libraries, specialized and general, can be found in *American Library Directory* (R.R. Bowker Co.) and *Directory of Special Libraries and Information Centers* (Gale Research). Consulting your phone book will reveal local libraries, as will queries to librarians and people involved in the field you're researching.

Having found the proper library, you will be wise to acquaint yourself with it. Ask the librarian if a map of the library is available. Walk around the library and see how it's arranged. Explore the library (prior to or during your researching) well enough that you know what sections will provide you with useful information. Alden Todd, in his book, *Finding Facts Fast*, recommends that researchers *practice* researching. Practice will teach you about the most fruitful sources, as well as the obscure sources that you might not know exist unless you take the effort to explore the library and its holdings. Practice and exploration will also tell you about the most efficient ways to find information.

Let the kind of information you need control your research plan. Here's some guidelines:

Do you need detailed rundowns of a topic? Check the card catalog for books published on the topic. Card catalogs often carry instruction cards in each card tray; read these before looking something up. Also consult bibliographies of the books you find. Ask the reference librarian if specialized bibliographies on your topic have been published. Also inquire about collections of unpublished works—doctoral dissertations and the like. These often make useful sources.

Do you need short briefings about the subject? Consult encyclopedias, and don't stop with the *Britannica.* Many encyclopedias cover specialized topics. *The Encyclopedia of Military History* is one such encyclopedia. Check the reference room for these sources.

Do you need updates on current developments in a particular area of interest? Periodical indexes will direct you to articles published about your topic. The most famous of these indexes is the *Readers' Guide to Periodical Literature,* but don't stop with this standby. Specialized periodical indexes like *Applied Science & Technology Index* and *Biological & Agricultural Index* cover a greater range of magazines than does *Reader's Guide,* allowing you to explore a subject in more detail. Some publications, such as the *New York Times,* publish indexes which cover their publication only. *Facts on File* is a carefully indexed digest newsletter that can keep you up-to-date on news events. The English version of *Facts on File* is *Keesing's Contemporary Archives* (Longman Group, Ltd.), and the Canadian version is *Canadian News Facts.*

Do you need information about a specific person? Good sources include *Current Biography* (containing short biographies) and *Biographical Index.* Also available are a number of "who's who" type directories: *Who's Who in America, Who's Who in the USSR* and *Who's Who in Music* are examples. In the reference room you'll find biographical dictionaries broken down by fields of interest (e.g., education, writing, music, etc.).

These are only examples of available sources. Libraries house a multitude of specialized dictionaries, directories, anthologies, companions, quick histories, atlases, yearbooks and books of abstracts. Finding them depends only on knowing the library, on taking the time to look, or on being willing to ask a librarian for help. Information is also more easily accessible if you refuse to stop at consulting a couple of obvious sources. Search. Follow leads you've found in sources; go to books mentioned in bibliographies; interview people quoted in articles and books. These secondary sources found by following such leads can often prove more valuable than the primary sources.

Other help you can seek includes books written about libraries and research. Todd's *Finding Facts Fast* is a brief, well-written guide to research, especially in libraries. *Writer's Research Handbook* (Barnes & Noble), written by Keith M. Cottam and Robert W. Pelton, is an annotated list of useful sources and source guides ranging from subject encyclopedias to specialized dictionaries to government publications.

One last word about using the library: Your research doesn't stop there. The library is your primary source for background information, but your research must extend beyond those book stacks. Libraries provide facts, but never the final word. By the time you're able to find information in the library, it could already be out of date. Events that occurred between the time the information was printed and the time you walked into the library might change "facts" or shed new light on them. Respond to change by conducting interviews with people knowledgeable about your subject, or by consulting information provided by sources such as those listed later in this book. This way you get the most current information possible, as well as differing viewpoints (or concurring viewpoints, which would serve to strengthen the credibility of your information).

Bolstered by such a wide base of information, you can write the article or book that *someone else* will someday look up in the library.

"References on Request": The Home Library

By Leon Taylor

The folks who coin old, trusty maxims say that a writer needs only a ream, an IBM, and a flaming imagination to prosper. But then, the folks who write old, trusty maxims don't write nonfiction. That's a shame. For if they did, they would know that a journalist does not live by his keyboard alone: That he also needs a keyring to facts, situated within quick and easy reach. In short, he needs a collection of reference books, wide-ranging in subject but reasonable in cost, his home arsenal for researching articles.

Ergo, here are some suggestions for his shopping list. For painless shopping, we've listed paperback versions where they are available.

A good almanac should be the centerpiece for the reference bookshelf. However, no almanac is definitive, although I find *The World Almanac & Book of Facts* (Newspaper Enterprise Association, annual, $3.95) to be the most cooperative when I need a statistic pronto. I suggest that you buy at least two almanacs: *The World Almanac* and *The U.S. Fact Book* (Grosset & Dunlap, annual, $4.95), which is the statistical abstract of the country. *The Fact Book* is indispensable for public affairs reporting, although it is not as easy to manipulate as the *World Almanac*. *The Hammond Almanac* (Hammond Almanac, annual, $3.95) and the *Information Please Almanac* (Information Please, annual, $3.95) also have their merits, and they demonstrate why one almanac is not enough. *Information Please* has the strongest section on education, for instance—but *Hammond* has the strongest on states and countries.

The sharpest almanac I've seen is *The Almanac of American Politics* (E.P. Dutton & Co. $7.95) by Michael Barone, Grant Ujifusa and Douglas Matthews. It has the low-down on each congressional district and state—socially, economically, and above all, politically. It is as essential for a political writer as an inside source.

For those hard-to-reach facts, try *The Trivia Encyclopedia*, by Fred L. Worth (Brooke House, 1974, $3.95). It is the only book I know of that reveals the address of poor Mrs. O'Leary's barn (hint: the Chicago Fire Academy is now here).

You would do well to keep *The People's Almanac* (Doubleday, 1975, $8.95; volume II, Bantam 1978, $10.95) just beyond your comfortable grasp. Some writers have been known to dip into it, only never to be heard from again. When used in moderation, however, the *Almanac* is a dandy idea-starter, with pieces on everything from the Legend of Paper Plates to the Men from Interpol. Any writer whose sense of journalistic wonder is not rekindled by this book should opt for accounting. Another rejuvenator is *The Book of Lists* (Bantam, 1978, $2.50), also by David Wallechinsky and his slightly famous father, Irving Wallace, as well as Amy Wallace.

Former managing editor of Writer's Digest, Leon Taylor is now a reporter with the Sunday Courier and Press in Evansville, Indiana.

People-watchers will find *Webster's Biographical Dictionary* (G. & C. Merriam, 1976, $15) a quick and reliable guide to more than 40,000 famous people. And despite its title, *Issac Asimov's Biographical Encyclopedia of Science and Technology* (Equinox, 1972, $5.95) is intriguing as well as informative.

For what's in a name, try *The Merriam-Webster Pocket Dictionary of Proper Names* (Pocket Books, 1972), compiled by Geoffrey Payton. The book is eclectic and sometimes frustratingly incomplete—but a bargain at $2.50.

Little-known oddities can lend a touch of surprise to an article, like chocolate chips to a cookie. For flavoring, consult the *Kane Book of Famous First Facts and Records* (Ace, 1976, $1.95). One revelation is that the smallest violin is 5.5 inches long—proof that good strings come in small packages.

For an odd phrase rather than an odd fact, you would do well to haunt the used bookstores in search of *A Dictionary of American Proverbs and Proverbial Phrases 1820-1880* (Belknap Press of Harvard Univ., 1958). It contains a proverb for nearly every occasion—and where one is lacking, a wisecrack is supplied. One book quoted is *Col. Crockett's Exploits and Adventures in Texas*, a saga with sage advice for anyone who would freelance in word or in wilderness: "If a man is only determined to go ahead, the more kicks he receives in his breech, the faster he will get on his journey."

Tracking the right fact is one task, but tracking the right source—particularly one that inhabits the marble halls of government—is another, and a Herculean one at that. Two reference books, however, will shed some light. The *Congressional Directory* (U.S. Government Printing Office, 1977, $6.50, order stock number 052-070-03929-2; 1978 supplement, 052-070-04351-2) lists the offices and officers of government and some private organizations. It also includes a variety of other information—for instance, newsmen who can be admitted to congressional press galleries. (Woodward is listed; Bernstein is not.) And the *U.S. Government Manual* (USGPO, $6.50, stock number 022-003-00948-5) describes the purposes and programs of most government agencies, as well as listing key officials.

Government agencies are also covered by Rod Nordland's *Names and Numbers* (John Wiley & Sons, 1978), but Nordland doesn't stop there. This reference is the writer's phone book, and includes phone numbers of people, firms and organizations.

For further nurturing of your reference shelf, you might consult *Reference Books in Paperback '76* (Libraries Unlimited, Inc.), a cogent guide to the best and the cheapest—ironically, it is not available in paperback.

The weakness of reference books is that they cannot provide the local angle. That will come from your files of newspaper clippings.

All you need are scissors in hand, paste at hand—and two rules in mind: Date each story and make the file names as specific as possible. A file called "Elementary Schools" will only slow you down if you plan to specialize in educational reporting, but a file entitled "Elementary Schools—Mainstreaming" will prove much easier to handle.

Begin clipping the back page first: Therein lie those nuggets of stories that the dailies bypass in their rush to press. Often they are tailor-made for a magazine article or even a book. Thomas Thompson was intrigued by a Texas murder item one day, and decided to follow up. He followed it straight into a bestseller, *Blood and Money*.

Certainly a versatile reference shelf and efficient clip files will start you off right—if not immediately for a bestseller, then for better-selling articles.

Paying for Research

By Fred 'Bert Woodress

In a broad sense, research is a way of defying the rule: "You can't get something for nothing." By investing only time and imagination into a research project, you receive valuable, useful information. Times arise, however, when you don't have the time and imagination to devote to finding all the facts. During those times, you might find that paying someone else to help with the research is valuable.

Computers, for example, can trim research time. Experts predict that the computerized Magazine Index Data Base (a base accessible through computer terminals at libraries and other locations) may someday make the manual system of consulting *Readers' Guide to Periodicals* obsolete. "Writers don't understand computers, but they should," comments one information specialist. The difference between researching *Readers' Guide*, as you might do now, and conducting a computer research of the magazine index, lies in the time and money you invest in the search. Computers can accomplish a tremendous amount of searching in seconds, while a manual investigation for the information may take hours.

Consulting the Magazine Index Data Base costs $45 for each hour of computer time used during the search, plus a charge for the overhead of the organization doing the search. Your own time, on the other hand, is free—or is it? Time spent in research is time you don't spend on writing, but you can't forego research just to do more writing.

Another major difference between manual and computer searches lies in what information you're left with when the search is completed. *Readers' Guide*, for example, covers 190 publications, and its coverage dates back to 1890 (another index, *Pooles Index*, goes to 1802), while the new Magazine Index Data Base indexes 370 publications. As of the first of the year, the Magazine Index had access to references going back to Jan. 1, 1976, although the coverage will be extended backward. Besides, not everything is indexed on computer. *Books in Print*, for instance, is not. (More about the advantages and disadvantages of computer searches is discussed in the Data Bases section of this book.)

Once you've decided to consult a computer data base, where do you go? The listings in the Data Bases section provide a good start, but you might want to look for other sources. If you live in a college town, go to the university library. Other possible locations for a public computer terminal with access to data banks include medical centers, government installations and local industries. You can possibly gain access to a privately owned terminal if you agree to pay the charges.

Another good place to begin is your public library, which might have its own

---

Fred Woodress is a freelance writer who teaches a course in use of the university library at the University of Kentucky. His work has appeared in publications ranging from American Libraries *to the* National Enquirer.

terminal or a working arrangement with your state library, historical society or archives office. Those on rural routes can usually make computer search requests through a bookmobile.

Even if you do find one or more computer terminals in your town, shop around in nearby cities for lower prices or, possibly, free usage. "There's no logic to the way they charge for computer use," says one data librarian about data bases. "The charges don't always relate to the costs." Comparison shopping, therefore, is wise.

After locating a terminal, you must prepare a research strategy. In researching this article, I located a computer data base terminal and asked the librarian to search "research-techniques" into the Magazine Index Data Base. Instead of retrieving items about how writers research books and articles, the machine started producing facts about scientific research. Because this useless information cost more than $45 an hour, I abruptly ended the search. Timothy Sineath, dean of Kentucky's graduate library school, explains what was wrong with this strategy: "One thing data bases have taught us is that 'indexing languages' for manual searches are not very adequate for machine searches. The clue to a successful search is to be as precise as you can about what it is you're looking for."

Next time, I asked the librarian to key in "research-techniques, author, writer, journalist, poet, playwright, photographer." This narrowly-defined request brought better results.

When deciding whether to use a data base, remember that the computer supplies you with references to articles and other information *only*. You still must look up the complete articles after you find the citations.

Clipping Services

Another valuable research service is provided by clipping services, firms that watch newspapers, magazines, etc., and clip out articles relevant to your area of interest. Most writers operate their own informal clipping services to collect ideas from their own magazines and newspapers, but can't possibly cover all the publications a clipping service can cover. On a systematic basis, a state, regional or national clipping service can provide you with stacks of clippings related to your topics. Like computers, however, clipping services are expensive.

Persons using clipping services actually subscribe to the service, and must subscribe for a minimum time length. A charge is also made for each clipping supplied to the subscriber. Bill Shirk of the Luce Clipping Bureau, headquartered in Mesa, Arizona, explains how his firm operates: A client pays $86 a month as a subscription fee for a minimum of three months, plus 44¢ per clipping supplied. The 250 professional readers employed by Luce daily scan 1,900 daily newspapers, 8,200 weeklies, and 3,800 to 4,000 consumer trade publications. They search different topic headings for writers working on various projects as part of the basic charge, and keep an eye out for reviews of the author's latest book.

If you decide to use a clipping service, consider these ways of saving money: Two or three writers could split the reading fee, with one in the group sending the subscription order. Because clipping services also monitor wire service releases and syndicated material, avoid paying for duplication by limiting the service to reading one only. Finally, you can place a dollar limit on the total number of clippings supplied so you can avoid exceeding your budget.

The usefulness of clipping services is demonstrated by the fact that Ruth Annan, the former *Time* researcher who organized the 30-member research department at the *National Enquirer* several years ago, says the *Enquirer* has its own clipping service for checking for facts and article ideas. Another research aid used by some publishers that can also be used by writers is use of an independent researcher. That was the technique used by Alex Haley when researching *Roots*.

When, in 1960, Haley took his Coast Guard discharge and went to Greenwich Village to become a full-time writer, he teamed up with boyhood friend George Sims, who became his researcher. The ex-Coast Guard cook/writer and the former gold-stacker/porter/researcher shared good times and tough times, and, most important, shared *Roots*. Research paid off for Haley and Sims. Today, 19 years after teaming up with Haley, Sims is still at work, now a salaried member of Alex Haley's team at Kinte Corporation, Century City, California.

The advantages of using an independent researcher lie in the time it frees up for you to spend in writing or doing additional research, and in the skills of the independent researcher—skills you might not have. The disadvantages, obviously, are in the additional cost. Another, less obvious, disadvantage is that an independent researcher can't know exactly what you seek, and may not recognize an interesting find that's only *indirectly* related to your project. If you decide to use independent researchers, give them clear instructions about what you're seeking.

One place to look for research help is the Association of American Library Schools (471 Park Lane, State College, Pennsylvania 16801). Using the association's annual directory (available for $5.50), you can contact member schools seeking a graduate student or a moonlighting faculty member to help you. How much? Whatever the going hourly or per-project rate happens to be.

Writer's Guild West supplies a list of 56 research sources for scriptwriters; telephone numbers are provided, and the subject specializations of the researchers range from "adoptions" to "YMCA."

Yellow Pages directories from other cities (available at your local telephone company or library) provide additional sources. A glance at the Washington, D.C. Yellow Pages reveals a number of listings under "Library Research" and "Writers, Writing and Editing Services."

You could also contact a temporary-help service, but this is risky, and success depends on finding the right person for the assignment.

If money is no object, however, the best route might be to hire an information broker or research firm. "We get the toughest questions," says Alice Warner, co-owner of Warner-Eddison Associates, Inc. of Cambridge, Massachusetts. A few years ago, Warner and Betty Eddison saw a need for such a research outfit while in graduate library school. The company, now in new offices, has its own computer terminal and official memberships in the Harvard and Massachusetts Institute of Technology (MIT) libraries, and keeps an extensive file of published indices in the firm's growing library. Typical are questions like "What FDA regulations since April 1977 affect manufacturers of titanium dioxide?" and "What are the policies of the Big Seven nations on buffer stocks as a method of stabilizing commodity prices?", as well as requests like "Please prepare a complete package on Brazil." Warner-Eddison's most frequent clients include utilities, Fortune 500 companies, the US government, and Harvard and Boston Universities. Research firms like Warner-Eddison can be excellent in getting information on complex, obscure subjects, but, again, the cost is generally prohibitive. "I frankly wonder whether *Writer's Resource* readers want to pay our kind of money," says Warner. "But one can never tell."

"Travel Light This Weekend . . ."

Explore more inexpensive research methods before turning to research firms. For instance, one excellent investigative tool hangs on your wall: the telephone. Using the telephone doesn't seem to be a method of research that you pay for, but check your monthly bill and reconsider. The telephone cuts out your dependence on the postal service, it gets you right to the source in a hurry, and it saves your interviewees from having to write you letters. On a recent writing assignment that involved considerable fact-gathering in a short time, I made 47 long-distance calls to all parts of the mainland US and Hawaii for $138, or an average of $2.94 per call. The cost was worth it because I got the information I needed quickly.

Not all long-distance calls cost money, however. Industry, business and government provide toll-free "800" numbers that can be called with no cost to the caller, i.e., no cost to you. *Toll Free Digest* publishes an annual directory of toll-free numbers ($5 from Box 800, Claverack, New York 12513). *Toll Free Digest* maintains a toll-free number for book orders on charge cards: 800/447-4700.

To give this article a practical flavor, *The Writer's Resource Guide* provided me $50 with the instructions, "See what you can do with this in paid research." I first made an appointment with Trudi Bellardo, computer librarian at the University of Kentucky's M.I. Library in Lexington. There I wanted to conduct a search through the New York Times Information Bank, but the cost of $110 per hour—plus overhead—stopped me. Magazine Index Data Base with references to 370 popular publications (from *Aging* to *Yankee*) at $45 per hour seemed most appropriate. Bellardo, using the telephone, keyed in her library number and the secret password into Lockheed's DIALOG, the world's largest online (that is, tied directly to a computer memory) system, and started the machine.

The computer was sluggish, and took a long time—for a computer—to answer my questions. "It's 1:15 p.m. at Palo Alto, California" (where the data base is located), Bellardo explained. She indicated that Eastern time zone users were crowding it before quitting time, while users in other time zones were getting underway for the afternoon.

In a matter of seconds, however, the index reported that it had found 2,315 items cataloged under "research," 2,747 under "techniques," 178 under "writer," 32 under "research and technique," 371 under "author," 100 under "journalist," 15 under "playwright," 182 under "photographer" and 132 under "poet." When all of the references were combined with "techniques," the machine located 28 references. Bellardo had them printed off-line (independent of the main computer) to save time and money; the copies were mailed to me in care of the library several days later. She then asked the machine to tally charges, signed off, and added in the library's 30% overhead charge. I owed 9.60.

For the second search, we used Social Science Citation Index, a $70-an-hour-plus service. Thirty items printed off-line cost $8.60.

At this point I took some time out for some long-distance telephone interviews. My six calls cost $15.30, leaving $16.50 in the original $50 allotment.

I next decided to stretch my search by trying to find some free computer sources. I discovered that the National Aeronautics and Space Administration (NASA) maintained a State Technology Applications Center on the University of Kentucky-Lexington campus. A search of the Smithsonian Information Exchange through the NASA terminal produced a number of references, but the information contributed little to my project. Typical of the citations was a reference to a project sponsored by the Department of Health, Education and Welfare on "behavioral significance of the functional modifications produced in an identified neural circuit in the abdominal ganglion of the marine mollusk, Aplysis." Lesson: Be selective about the information bases you consult.

I then consulted the Educational Resources Information Center (ERIC), which retrieved 279 references under "journalist," 422 for "poet," 60 for "playwright" and 66 for "photographer." Three citations and abstracts printed off-line were interesting. One titled "Ethnic Live-In," for instance, told how to observe and seek information in ethnic enclaves within large cities and in the countryside. My cost, if this one hadn't been given me free, would have been $49.

As it was, I had spent only $33.50 of the original $50, and for that price, came to these conclusions:

First, the computer is best used when searching for information in the fields of science, technology and health—or when searching for the latest in any field—but it is still uneven in cultural areas. Use it carefully now. In a few years you might use it for everything.

Second, the next best thing to doing your own research is to have a skilled, paid research assistant, but we all can't be Alex Haley. Try to find a well-informed librarian, and wait your turn in line to consult this person.

Third, clipping services—your own or one you pay for—as well as long-distance calls, travel, photocopies and interlibrary loans are the necessities of "paid-for" research.

Fourth, do the best you can with your budget, taking advantage of everything free you can find, from computer time to "800" long-distance numbers.

No matter how expensive or extensive the research you pay for is, however, remember that your writing is what really counts in the final analysis. Before you pay for research, make certain that it will pay for itself in the time it frees you for writing, and in contributing to the quality of your writing.

Junk Mail Can Be Good for You

By Hartley E. Howe

Article ideas keep a freelance writer alive. No matter how good a reporter he is, how astute in organizing his material, how skilled in writing, the freelancer writer lacking ideas might as well become a freelance plumber. Even the staff writer soon finds that his own article ideas often earn a raise.

Successful article writers know this, of course; that's one reason they are successful. Clay Schoenfeld, who has conceived and sold several hundred articles to top markets, knows where to find ideas. Not long ago, Schoenfeld was leafing through a big pile of morning mail, when his eye was caught by an item in a Sierra Club fact sheet: "Grizzly Bear Management in the Wilderness." *Management? Wilderness? A contradiction? Hmmm.*

Schoenfeld recalls this incident with some satisfaction; the end result has been the sale of a dozen articles and a soon-to-be published book, all on the problems involved in running the wilderness areas Congress has established. This is, by no means, the first time Schoenfeld found a first-class article subject in his mail box. "It happens all the time," he says.

That's why he's happy to be on a variety of mailing lists. Like many other successful freelancers, Schoenfeld has found that the great flood of releases, press kits, fact sheets, "backgrounders," newsletters, in-house publications and speech texts— cranked out by a vast army of public relations people—is a great source of ideas.

Not everything you receive as a result of being on mailing lists will provide salable ideas, of course. About as many good ideas can be found in a square mile of press releases as fish can be found in a cubic mile of ocean. The smart writer is the one who knows the best places to cast his net, and has the patience to keep fishing. Hidden away among the product plugs, personnel changes, financial reports and pure junk, are enough fat, juicy ideas to keep the persistent writer/researcher well-fed for a lifetime.

Net Gains

Whose lists are the best ones to get on? If you have begun to specialize, you obviously want to hear about innovators in your fields of interest. If your interests are broad, then cast your net wide. In either case, plenty of places to try your luck are available.

Industry: Nearly every company of any size has a public relations operation with clusters of mailing lists to which it sends news of its activities. Concerns that deal with advanced technologies or have active research and development (R&D) divisions are particularly likely idea sources: manufacturers of such products as computers, energy equipment, automatized machines, drugs. (On the other hand, at least one good article lies in a company that has turned out the same product for generations.)

Hartley E. Howe teaches writing courses at the University of Wisconsin–Madison. He has worked as senior editor of Popular Science *and a contributing editor with* Atlantic Monthly.

Research centers and laboratories are in the idea business. Both commercial concerns and nonprofit institutes are constantly developing new products, techniques, tools and methods.

Universities, both public and private, are hives of people poking into things, exploring new concepts, finding better ways to reach goals and new goals to be reached. The University of Wisconsin alone spends more than $90 million a year on studying everything from weather satellites to self-fertilizing food plants. Harvard, Loyola, Berkeley and dozens of others can keep a writer at his typewriter for years, and they aren't shy about telling writers/researchers about what they're doing.

Government agencies like NASA, the National Academy of Sciences and the National Weather Service are among scores of federal agencies doing major research. What's more, don't forget United Nations agencies and foreign government information sources that deal with many of the same problems on a worldwide basis.

Business and trade associations and industry organizations are concerned with presenting their members' views on political and economic questions. Many are also investigating new technology, environmental problems, energy conservation, and other areas of special concern. The National Automobile Dealers Association and the Institute of Scrap Iron and Steel are among thousands of such organizations. Many circulate idea-rich reports of their activities.

Advocacy organizations, lobbying groups and special interest societies from Action for Children's Television to the Sierra Club and the League of Women Voters are in a constant battle to enlist public support. In exploring and expounding on everything from wilderness preservation to political prisoners, they spark ideas and provide valuable information.

Professional and scientific societies include such powerhouses as the American Medical Association and the American Association for the Advancement of Science, as well as the more specialized learned societies. Some sponsor research themselves; many report to their members and to the general public on significant new developments in their fields.

Museums, libraries, archives and historical societies chronicle and maintain valuable information sources, and often maintain mailing lists used to announce the installment of special collections or the hiring of a new expert.

A bewildering array of sources—and lists—to draw on obviously exists, and hundreds of sources in each of the above-mentioned categories are listed in *The Writer's Resource Guide*. A good place to start is with companies and organizations mentioned in news stories concerning companies and organizations mentioned in news stories about your fields of interest. Smaller organizations that don't often hit the papers turn up in the pages of trade publications and specialized magazines. One short cut to finding good sources is through public relations firms that specialize in certain areas. Many are listed in this book; more can be found in *O'Dwyer's Directory of Public Relations Firms*. This directory, available in most libraries, lists agencies and their clients under 12 headings ranging from Beauty and Fashion to Trave. You can write either to the leading PR firms in each category that interests you—which might enable you to get on several lists with one request—or to the individual clients.

Some journalists and researchers profess to scorn public relations people as paid advocates who have sold their independence. So far as the writer is concerned, this is short-sighted. In our immense and complex society, information specialists have become essential links between the writer and a host of sources. In controversial matters, public relations people will present their clients in as favorable light as possible, to be sure, but sheer self-interest—not to mention good professional standards—assures that the basic information will be reliable. In any case, no writer or researcher will be misled if he remembers the basic rule of good journalism and always checks controversial points with sources that have other points of view.

Professionalism & the Wombat

The PR person's need to show his clients that he's getting the word out makes getting on mailing lists pretty easy, but it's up to you to make a case for yourself. Here are some suggestions:

To start with, your request should be on some sort of professional letterhead. This is for psychological impact; it conveys the message that you are serious about writing. Of course, you make the same point directly in your letter: You are a freelance writer with a special interest in your respondent's field. Back this up, if you can, by mentioning where your writing has appeared. Name the publications if they're likely to impress the recipient. This can be done deftly with an offhand reference such as, "Perhaps you recall seeing my article on wombats in *Animal Times* last December." Be sure to mention your assocation with any of the widely recognized professional societies of writers, such as the Outdoor Writers Association or the National Association of Science Writers. (Actually, members of such organizations often find themselves on many mailing lists without even asking.)

Be specific about the kinds of information you want to receive. Mailing lists are usually broken down by categories and, as postage and production costs soar, companies are trying harder than ever to limit mailings to people who really want them. This is also important to you: If you are interested in information on new drugs, you don't want to be flooded with releases on company promotions or quarterly earnings.

If you find an organization's mailings useful, be sure to return the cards, sent to you every year, that ask whether you want to be kept on the list; otherwise your name will be dropped. Since the PR people who send you their releases survive by showing how successful they are in getting their client's name in print, they will appreciate tearsheets of published articles using their material. (Of course, if your piece was unkind to his client, the public relations person will probably just as soon not know about it.)

A minor problem: In writing to large, far-flung universities—and to some decentralized corporations, as well—figuring out just where to send your request might be difficult. The University of Wisconsin—Madison, for example, has some half-dozen schools, departments and centers that have their own mailing lists quite apart from those of the university's official news bureau. An old hand at touring academic labyrinths advises addressing your letter simply to "University Relations"; the request will be distributed to the appropriate university divisions.

Once you've sent off your requests, you can enlarge your mail box and wait for the flood to come rolling in. Don't, however, expect full-fledged stories ready to be written to be handed to you. Even the announcement of an interesting new product can rarely be sold as such; the same release has almost certainly been sent directly to your target market, and no editor will pay a freelancer for a simple rewrite. Most announcements of news events are also useless; they will be history long before a magazine could get a piece into print.

What you're seeking as you thumb through your mail is not stories, but *ideas and sources.* Clay Schoenfeld didn't write his articles on grizzly bears in the Yosemite, the subject of the item that caught his eye. Imagination, plus his wide knowledge of the conservation field, enabled him to see that the problems of *Ursus horrobilis* in one national park are representative of a host of problems affecting all kinds of wildlife in all kinds of wilderness environments.

This is typical. The creative spark that fires the writer's imagination is often only an incidental part of the original release. Not long ago Judi Kesselman and Franklynn Peterson, a team of successful and prolific freelance article writers, received a three-page release from a Midwestern university telling about attempts to construct a mathematical formula to describe a tornado. This seemed of little interest to the general reader, but buried in the release was a paragraph mentioning that the research required building a machine that created a miniature tornado in the laboratory.

A table-top tornado? A natural! So natural that the writers sold the article over the telephone, before it was even written, to *Popular Science.*

The flow of ideas and information never stops. Here are a couple of examples that came to hand as this piece was being written:

A release put out by the University of Wisconsin reports that a professor of biochemistry has synthesized a substance that treats a group of bone diseases, a discovery that could affect hundreds of thousands of people. The culmination of many years of research, the drug may lead also to effective treatment of several animal diseases, so there's an angle for farm magazines, as well.

That one is pretty obvious, but here's a fat press packet from a division of General Motors (via its PR firm) announcing the production of 100-million horsepower in diesel engines. A trade paper story, right? Another release enclosed, though reports that "the world's largest industrial laser process" is used to harden the cylinder liners of the company's engines. More of a real story, but still too technical and specialized for consumer publications.

Yet, wait a minute—*lasers*? That's at the limits of basic science. We've read about some advanced applications in eye surgery or fusion research, but now lasers are being applied on a massive scale in heavy industry. Maybe there's a story here after all, not just in engine liners alone, but in a round-up of how this laboratory device is finding a wide range of practical applications.

Where can you find more information on the subject?

Start turning pages.

Advertising for Information

By Robert Cassidy

Articles and books often require interviews with a special kind of person, and sometimes finding the right people to interview is difficult. That's the problem I ran into when I signed a contract to do a book about the man's side of divorce. To make the book interesting and unique, I needed to relate the experiences of real men. Without dozens of first-person accounts, the book would be just another rehash of previous books, and that wasn't good enough for me. I wanted my book to come alive with the stories of men facing divorce. But I lacked sources.

An avid reader of classified ads, I realized the solution: Advertise for sources, and let them find me. I took ads in the *New York Review of Books*, *New York* magazine and *The New Republic*. "DIVORCED MEN. Serious author seeks interviews with men hurt by divorce," read my ad. The cost at the time ranged from 60¢ to $1 a word, usually with a 15-word minimum (prices have since gone up, of course).

Responses came from all over the country. The response from a Pittsburgh man was typical: "I saw your ad and would be willing to relate experiences of my recent divorce. I'm quite certain mine was not the most exciting or tragic, but the details are yours for the asking." In all, I got some 25 responses to my ads. I was surprised by both their quality and the high degree of interest in my project. Many respondents gave me names of others to contact. A young St. Louis woman wrote me about how her father was being mistreated by the divorce courts. I wrote all the respondents, then followed up with a phone call or personal interview. I was able to use material from *every one of them* in my book.

Since then, I have used personal ads to gather information for other articles. For a piece I'm doing on writers who have published their own books, I've received a dozen excellent responses from an ad in *Writer's Digest*. When *Cosmopolitan* asked me to do a piece about women who are dating men with children by a previous marriage, the classifieds helped once more.

The Straight Dopes

It's not a perfect system, of course. Writer Donald Carroll took a 64-word, $200 ad in *New York* for "funny" hate mail, which he hoped to collect in a book. The result: "It was an expensive washout. Useless," he reflects. "One good letter—from an inmate—and the rest a collection of playground insults from the proud authors themselves. No kooks, just dopes. Literate people have better things to read than classified ads."

Yet, other writers have found classified ads useful. Bruce Mays, a young Chicago writer, had an idea for a book about the riots at the 1968 Democratic convention. "I thought it would be no trouble finding people who had been there, but I kept running into dead ends," he says. With three ad insertions in *The Reader* (a Chicago weekly),

Based in Chicago, Robert Cassidy is the author of What Every Man Should Know About Divorce. *His magazine credits include* Writer's Digest, *where this article originally appeared.*

however, he found more than 20 interviewees. "The people who called were obsessed by the riots," says Mays. "They'd invite me to their homes and give up an evening just to talk."

Jean Stein and George Plimpton also found classifieds useful. When researching a book on Robert Kennedy, Stein and Plimpton took ads in the newspapers of towns where Kennedy's funeral train had passed, asking people for first-person accounts. This material was used in *American Journey: The Times of Robert Kennedy*.

If you have a tough research problem, therefore, you can try to get one of the major newspapers or book reviews like the *New York Times Book Review* to carry your "author's query" ("For a biography of James Jones, send letters, memoirs, etc., to. . . ."); the *Times* and other publications are swamped with such requests, however, and there's no guarantee they'll ever run it, particularly since they favor more "literary" requests. I recommend use of the classifieds, however. You're sure to get your message across precisely as you want it, when you want it. All you need are a few dollars and the know-how to get the most bang for your advertising buck.

First, know where to place your ad. "If there's a lesson here, I think it's that one only advertises for very specialized material, in specialized magazines," says Donald Carroll. Pick the right market to reach the kind of person you want. Bill Novak, while working on a book about personal uses of marijuana, received a disappointing response from ads in magazines like *Psychology Today*, *The New Republic*, *Mother Jones* and *New York Review of Books*. Novak decided that an ad in *High Times* would have worked better for him.

Test the market. Don't blow your whole advertising budget in one publication. Try several, and see what kind of response you get. Then go with the winners. Look for bargains. Chicago has *The Reader* with its free classifieds. Does your area have a publication with free or inexpensive ads? If not, do any publications give special rates? (*The New Republic*, for example, will run an ad three times for the price of two insertions.)

Writing an effective ad is important, too. If you have only ten words, make them clear and strong. Don't skimp to save a few dollars, however. The more information you give potential respondents, the greater your chances of getting them to reply. By the same token, the easier you make getting in touch with you, the greater will be the response. Give your phone number. Agree to accept collect calls, if you can afford to do so. At least give your full address.

This also opens the way for crank calls and pests, of course. One man who responded to my divorce ads made a homosexual advance when I attempted to interview him. I've also encountered one or two heavy phone breathers over the years. I don't think that's such a bad record, though, considering the number of times I've used classifieds. If this concerns you (and women writers are more often the target of such abuse), however, take precautions. Use a "reply box number" instead of an address, or use only your first initial along with your real last name and a friend's address. That way your phone number can't be detected. If you give a phone number, use an answering service. If the call gets through and the caller doesn't seem right for your story, politely thank the person and say that you've already filled your quota of interviews for this particular project. Do the same for crank mail. As a writer, you must take a certain number of risks to get the story. From my own experience, though, I'd say that crank calls and letters are almost inconsequential.

Trust & Classified Information

Remember that people will be suspicious of you. They'll figure you're trying to sell them something—or worse. "They thought I might be a police spy, using the cover of being a journalist," says Bruce Mays, the writer interested in the Chicago riots. The only antidote for this paranoia is to be as professional and straightforward as possible with the people who respond to your ad. You must win their trust with the force of your personality. It's amazing what people will tell you once they get talking: the intimate details of their sex lives, their financial statuses, anything you want to know. It's all a matter of establishing *trust*. Besides, people like to talk about themselves; it's the subject they know best. Many people feel, quite rightly, that they are helping others by telling you their stories.

Once the ad is running, be ready to deal with the responses. Have your pen and paper by the phone in case people call. Better still, take notes on your typewriter, or record the conversation on tape. (It's not illegal if you get permission from the caller.) Don't discourage respondents by failing to be prompt, efficient, eager and interested. If they want a personal interview, meet them. These people are going out of their way to help you. Respond in kind.

Some respondents may press you for money. One woman called me twice asking if I paid a fee for granting an interview. "I'm out of work, and I'm looking for a little extra money," she told me. My policy is to not pay for interviews. I'll buy an interviewee lunch; that's almost a courtesy. But no cash. If you're paying for the information, the interviewee may feel compelled to make up "interesting" anecdotes. If you're doing research requiring people to take tests or devote an inordinate amount of time to the interview, however, you might offer a modest fee. In my bones, though, I feel it's wrong to pay for information.

Finally, quality, not quantity, counts. A few good interviews can make an article. One man told me, "The average man can't afford a divorce." That's the only quote I used from him, but it became a subhead to a chapter on money problems, and television and radio interviewers picked up on it when I did a promotional tour for the book. Nina Gaspich, a legal secretary and freelancer, ran an ad seeking people who had been backstage at rock concerts. Four people responded—not a great number, she says, "but the ones that I got were talkative. They gave me some absolutely fascinating information." Would she use personal ads again? "Definitely."

I got only two or three responses from my ad in the *New York Review of Books*, but one of them was from Mel Roth, a psychoanalyst in New York who runs counseling groups for divorced and separated men. Roth not only gave me a good interview, but he also reviewed chapters of my book and helped me rewrite certain crucial sections.

Remember, too, that one lead can open doors. Bruce Mays got a tip from one of his interviewees about how he could find the names and addresses of thousands of people involved in the 1968 Chicago demonstrations. That tip alone will save Mays hundreds of hours of research time.

There's no guarantee that using personal ads will solve your problems, of course, but the technique has proved useful to some writers; it may help you get out of that tough research problem. The next time you're stuck trying to find interviewees for an article, book or any other sort of research project, remember the maxim: It pays to advertise.

THE SOURCES

Aquariums, Arboretums, Planetariums & Zoos

Zoos, planetariums and arboretums are great places to spend a pleasant Sunday afternoon, but few writers realize that they're also fascinating sources of practical information on everything from plants to planets.

Housed here are more than just cute animals and pretty flowers; you'll also find people whose expertise comes from day-to-day dealings with flora, fauna, environment and stars. Information available from these sources can be much more valuable than textbook data.

For example, "When writing animal stories or articles, first go to a zoological park or aquarium to see the specimens," advises Thomas H. Livers, zoo superintendent with the Lafayette Zoological Park in Norfolk, Virginia. "Spend a couple of hours observing before the first word is placed on paper. The time spent will provide invaluable insight to behavior, and will give a clue to the accuracy of other literature sources. Many popular animal articles and books are riddled with inaccuracies."

Writers are welcome at the places listed below. As Colvin L. Randall of Longwood Gardens says, "We welcome freelance writers and will try to accommodate them, especially if their work will directly publicize Longwood." Better yet, more than just information can be had by consulting these sources. For instance, "We can provide some story ideas, assistance on photos and technical information," says Joseph B.C. White, director of the Dawes Arboretum.

Livers concurs. "Zoos offer more resources than most realize. Each staff member may be an expert in a particular species or animal group and can ease the writer's research problems by guiding him/her to good sources in literature, often unpublished, and to other experts."

Getting such help often entails a visit to the place in question, though many questions can be answered by mail. If you request information by mail, give the source as much time as possible to answer. "Plenty of lead time is absolutely essential," Randall says.

Names and addresses of other places like those listed here can be found in *Zoos and Aquariums in the Americas*, published by the American Association of Zoological Parks and Aquariums (Oglebay Park, Wheeling, West Virginia 26003).

Aquariums, Arboretums & Zoos

Arizona/Sonora Desert Museum, Rt. 9, Box 900, Tucson AZ 85704. (602)883-1380. Public Affairs Officer: Christopher Helms.

Purpose: Natural living museum of the Sonora Desert region. Information covers agriculture, business, celebrities, economics, food, health/medicine, history, how-to, industry, nature, recreation, science, sports, technical information, travel, geology, flora/ fauna, ecology and conservation.
Services: Offers aid in arranging interviews, annual reports, bibliographies, biographies, statistics, brochures/pamphlets, clipping services, information searches, placement on mailing list, photos and press kits. Publishes *Sonorensis* (quarterly).
How to Contact: Write.

The Birmingham Zoo, 2630 Cahaba Rd., Birmingham AL 35223. (204)879-0409. Zoo Director: Bob Truett.
Purpose: Public zoological park. Information covers nature and technical data.
Services: Offers assistance.
How to Contact: Write or call.

Chicago Zoological Park, Brookfield Zoo, Golf Rd., Brookfield IL 60513. (312)0263. Contact Public Relations Department.
Purpose: "The preservation of wildlife, education of the public and research of animals." Information covers agriculture, art, business, celebrities, economics, entertainment, food, health/medicine, history, how-to, industry, law, nature, new product information, politics, recreation, science, self-help, technical information, travel and horticulture.
Services: Offers aid in arranging interviews, annual reports, bibliographies, biographies, statistics, brochures/pamphlets, information searches, placement on mailing list, newsletter, photos and press kits. Publications include *Brookfield Bison* (bimonthly).
How to Contact: Write. Charges for photos "when used for profit."

Cincinnati Zoo, 3400 Vine St., Cincinnati OH 45220. (513)281-4703. Contact: Janet Ross.
Purpose: "Conservation, recreation and education. We have the best educational department in the country, and offer a two-year high school alternative program with the Cincinnati Public Schools. We have the world record for successful gorilla births in captivity and in an outdoor display, and we're the only zoo with a whole building devoted to insects." Information covers entertainment, food, health/medicine, history, how-to, nature, politics, recreation, science, self-help, technical data and travel.
Services: Offers aid in arranging interviews, bibliographies, biographies, statistics, brochures/pamphlets, information searches, placement on mailing list, newsletter, photos, press kits, and data on breeding endangered species. Publications include a zoo brochure, *Cincinnati Zoo News*, a fact sheet, *Purpose of Zoos and Aquariums*, and *Zoo and Aquarium Careers*.
How to Contact: Write or call.

The Dawes Arboretum, 7770 Jacksontown Rd. SE, Newark OH 43055. (614)323-2355. Director: Joseph B.C. White.
Purpose: "To encourage the planting of forest and ornamental trees and to demonstrate the value of the different varieties of trees for these purposes: to promote practical and scientific research in horticulture and agriculture, but particularly in the growth and culture of trees and shrubs able to support the climate of the state of Ohio; to give pleasure to the public and education to the youth; to increase the general knowledge of trees and shrubs; and to bring about an increase and improvement in their growth and culture." Information covers agriculture, history, nature, and environment education.
Services: Offers brochures/pamphlets and newsletter.
How to Contact: Write or call. "We can provide some story ideas, assistance on photos, and technical information."

Denver Zoo, City Park, Denver CO 80205. (303)575-2432. Director: Clayton Freiheit.
Purpose: "The Denver Zoo is dedicated to the preservation of wildlife through a variety of breeding and conservation plans." Information covers food, how-to, nature, recreation, science, technical information and animal management.
Services: Offers aid in arranging interviews, annual reports, statistics, brochures/pamphlets, information searches, placement on mailing list, newsletter and photos. Publications include *Zoo Review* (quarterly).
How to Contact: Write or call.

Lafayette Zoological Park, 3500 Granby St., Norfolk VA 23504. (804)441-2706. Zoo Superintendent: Thomas H. Livers.
Purpose: "To exhibit zoological and botanical specimens to the visiting public in an attempt to educate in an entertaining manner about animals, plants, conservation and wildlife preservation and to conduct animal breeding programs in an attempt to stem the tide of extinction." Information covers nature and technical data.
Services: Offers annual reports. "We also provide insights into zoological/zoo biology data, animal observations, exhibit design, zoological fundraising techniques, and animal/plant propagation programs."
How to Contact: Write, call or schedule an appointment. Zoo hours are 10 a.m to 5:00 p.m. (winter and daily) and 10 a.m to 6 p.m. (summer). Office hours are 8:30 a.m to 5 p.m. (Monday through Friday). "Please schedule appointments at least two weeks in advance. All information published must note the source, and credit must be clearly displayed."
Tips: "When writing animal stories or articles, first go to a zoological park or aquarium to see the specimens if possible, then spend a couple of hours observing before the first word is placed on paper. The time spent will provide invaluable insight to behavior, and will give a clue to the accuracy of other literature sources. Many popular animal articles and books are riddled with inaccuracies. Zoos offer more resources than most realize. Each staff member may be an expert in a particular species or animal group and can ease the writer's research problems by guiding him/her to good sources in literature, often unpublished, and to other experts."

Los Angeles State and County Arboretum, Plant Science Library, 301 N. Baldwin Ave., Arcadia CA 91006. (213)446-8251, ext. 32.
Purpose: "The arboretum is concerned with plants, particularly woody ones, that are suitable for growth in southern California. Many of our plants are from South Africa and Australia. The library collects books in support of these interests. Our holdings are both horticultural and botanical and include floras of many countries. The library is for reference only, but anyone may use our facilities." Information covers horticulture and botany.
Services: Offers routine library services: ready answers to reference questions in person or by phone, and assistance with finding information from our collection.
How to Contact: Write or call. "Anyone may use the library for reference. We work with closed stacks, but a user can have access to any material desired. If a person is interested in a topic that would take time to research, it would be better to call ahead so that we can start looking for relevant material."

Longwood Gardens, Kennett Square PA 19348. (215)388-6741. Publicity Coordinator: Colvin L. Randall.
Purpose: "Longwood Gardens is a 1,000-acre horticultural showplace attracting 700,000 visitors yearly. Open every day of the year, the gardens have nearly four acres of heated conservatories, 14,000 types of plants, lavish fountain displays and an open air theatre." Information covers entertainment, music, nature, recreation, travel, horticulture, landscape architecture and landscape architectural history.
Services: Offers aid in arranging interviews, brochures/pamphlets, placement on mailing list, publicity photos and press kits. Publications include a schedule of events, general informational brochure and *Balcony Gardening*, a booklet.

How to Contact: Write or call. "There is a $2 per day (plus admission) fee to use the library. We welcome freelance writers and will try to accommodate them, especially if their work will directly publicize Longwood. Plenty of lead time is absolutely essential."

Miami Seaquarium, 4400 Rickenbacker Causeway, Miami FL 33149. Public Relations: Zoe Todd.
Purpose: Marine tourist attraction.
Services: Offers b&w and color photos of the seaquarium and a variety of sea creatures. The Miami Seaquarium makes photographs available to all writers and editors free of charge, providing either the seaquarium is given a credit line ("Photo Courtesy Miami Seaquarium"), or the seaquarium is mentioned in the caption.
How to Contact: Write. Tearsheets of the published photo required. Return required for color only. Nonpayment situation subject to change.

Milwaukee City Zoological Park, 10001 W. Bluemound Rd., Milwaukee WI 53226. (414)771-3040. Director: Robert Bullerman.
Purpose: "To keep and breed animals, to exhibit vanishing species, and to provide an educational program." Information covers art, food, health/medicine, history, how-to, nature, recreation, science, technical information and horticulture.
Services: Offers aid in arranging interviews, annual reports, bibliographies, biographies, statistics, brochures/pamphlets, information searches, placement on mailing list and photos.
How to Contact: Write or call.

Missouri Botanical Garden, 2345 Tower Grove Ave., St. Louis MO 63110. (314)772-7600. Director, Publications: Barbara Pesch.
Purpose: "Nonprofit botanical garden. Activities include research in botany, education and displays (open to public year-round, plus special shows)." Information covers horticulture, botany and ecology.
Services: Offers biographies, statistics, brochures/pamphlets, newsletter and photos. Publications include *Botanical Garden Bulletin* (monthly), *Annals of the Missouri Botanical Garden*, a visitors' guide, a Japanese garden guide, education booklets, and a biography of Henry Shaw.
How to Contact: Write or call publications or public relations department. Open 9 a.m. to 6 p.m., May through October; 9 a.m. to 5 p.m., November through April. Charges for commercial photography inside garden; subscription rates for regular publications vary.

National Arboretum, 24th and R Sts. NE, Washington DC 20002. (202)399-5400. Curator of Education: Erik A. Neumann.
Purpose: "To provide research and education on woody landscape plants." Information covers horticulture.
Services: Offers aid in arranging interviews, annual reports, brochures/pamphlets, information searches, placement on mailing list and photos. Publications include general brochures on the National Arboretum, *National Bonsai Collection*, *Azaleas at the Arboretum*, *Camellias at the Arboretum*, *Hollies at the Arboretum* and *Fern Valley at the Arboretum*.
How to Contact: Write or call.

National Zoological Park, Smithsonian Institution, 3001 Connecticut Ave., Washington DC 20008. (202)381-7335.
Purpose: "To operate for the advancement of science, instruction and recreation. The official depository of animals donated by heads of state." Information covers history, nature, science, exotic animal science, medicine and zoo management.
Services: Offers aid in arranging interviews, annual reports, statistics, brochures/

pamphlets, information searches, placement on mailing list, newsletter, photos and press kits.
How to Contact: Write or call. Charges for photos "depending on use."

New York Zoological Society, Bronx NY 10462. (212)220-5197. Contact: Jeanette Genova.
Purpose: "Conservation of wildlife and breeding of endangered species. Supported by grants, contributions and private funds." Information covers health/medicine, nature, science and technical data.
Services: Offers aid in arranging interviews, brochures/pamphlets, statistics and photos. Publication available to members only.
How to Contact: Write or call. Charges for photos.

A photo of this Australian native doesn't have to come from Down Under; this shot by Ron Garrison is from the San Diego Zoo, the only zoo outside Australia that houses koalas. "We have thousands of negatives on file," says Carole Towne, director of public relations and marketing for the zoo. "Describe in detail what you want in order to speed and simplify our search through our files." The zoo charges $10 for b&w and $30 for color, for one-time use in a book or magazine.

Oklahoma City Zoo, 2101 NE 50th St., Oklahoma City OK 73111. (405)424-3344. Public Information Curator: Timothy O'Connor.
Purpose: "Education, recreation, conservation, research, and information on most aspects of zoological functions." Information covers entertainment, food, health/medicine, nature, recreation, science and travel.
Services: Offers statistics, brochures/pamphlets, information searches and photos.
How to Contact: Write or call. "Make research data requested as clear and concise as possible. Give dates needed. Send a form that can easily be filled out."

Clyde Peeling's Reptiland, Ltd., Box 66, Allenwood PA 17810. (717)538-1869. President: Clyde Peeling.
Purpose: "We are a specialized zoo for reptiles and feature live specimens from all over the world. Lecture/demonstrations provide visitors with information and an opportu-

nity to touch or even hold specimens." Information covers nature and travel.
Services: Offers aid in arranging interviews, brochures/pamphlets and press kits.
How to Contact: Write or call. "We will work with a professional writer or photographer and set up interviews or photo sessions at no charge as long as we receive credit. Please set up date with us in advance."

Riverbanks Zoological Park, 500 Wildlife Pkwy., Columbia SC 29210. (803)779-8717. Public Relations Manager: Linda Johnson.
Purpose: "The Riverbanks Zoological Park is a refuge for wildlife and a cultural and educational environment for the people who visit." Information covers food, health/medicine, law, nature, science and wildlife conservation.
Services: Offers aid in arranging interviews, statistics, brochures/pamphlets, information searches, placement on mailing list, newsletter and photos. Publications include *Riverbanks Society Newsletter* (quarterly).
How to Contact: Write or call. "Personal phone calls get faster attention." Offers photos on a limited basis.

St. Louis Zoo, Forest Park, St. Louis MO 63110. (314)781-0900. Community Relations Director: Janet Powell.
Purpose: A free zoo for family entertainment. Information covers agriculture, business, celebrities, economics, entertainment, food, health/medicine, history, how-to, law, nature, new product information, recreation, science and travel.
Services: Offers aid in arranging interviews, annual reports, biographies, brochures/pamphlets, information searches, placement on mailing list, newsletter and photos.
How to Contact: Write. Open daily, 9 a.m. to 5 p.m., except Christmas and New Year's Day.

San Diego Wild Animal Park, Rt. 1, Box 725-E, Escondido CA 92025. (714)747-8702. Contact: Public Relations Department.
Purpose: "A sprawling 1,800-acre sanctuary enabling animals to roam freely in settings similar to their native homelands. The park has gained worldwide recognition for its conservation efforts directed to the preservation of plants and animals." Information covers entertainment, health/medicine, nature, recreation, science and endangered species.
Services: Offers brochures/pamphlets. Publications include *San Diego Wild Animal Park*, *Wild World of Animals* and *Colorful World of Animals*.
How to Contact: Write or call. Charges $2/copy for *Wild World of Animals* and *Colorful World of Animals*.

San Diego Zoo, Box 551, San Diego CA 92112. (714)231-1515. Contact: Public Relations Department.
Purpose: "A zoo where animals are displayed year-round in outdoor settings that look like the animals' natural homes in the wild; a zoo with one of the world's best collections of rare animals; a zoo where tropical plants cover the 100-acre grounds. Purposes of the zoo include recreation, education, conservation and research in zoology, zoo medicine, zoo management and botany." Information covers entertainment, health/medicine, nature, recreation and science.
Services: Offers brochures/pamphlets and photos. Publications include *San Diego Zoo*, *Zoonooz* (monthly), *Colorful World of Animals* and *Wild World of Animals*.
How to Contact: Write or call. For publications, address request to Public Services Department. For photos, address request to San Diego Zoo Photo Lab. Charges $1/copy for *Zoonooz*, $8/one-year subscription; $2/copy for books. Charges varying rates for photos, depending on use; also charges handling fee. "A credit line must be given on all photos. Permission to use photos is not authorized until full payment has been made."

Sealand of Cape Cod, Inc., Rt. 6A, Brewster MA 02631. (617)385-9252. President: George R. King.
Purpose: Keeps marine mammals and marine fish. Information covers business, entertainment, recreation, science and technical data.
Services: Offers aid in arranging interviews and brochures/pamphlets.
How to Contact: Visit. Charges depend on time involved.

Washington Park Zoo, 4001 SW Canyon Rd., Portland OR 97221. (503)226-1561. Public Information Director: Jack McGowan.
Purpose: Information covers "operation of our zoo, animal collection, funding, and our history."
Services: Offers brochures/pamphlets. Publications include *Looking For Something Wild?*.
How to Contact: Write or call.

Wye Marsh Wildlife Center, Box 100, Midland, Ontario, Canada L4R 4K6. (705)526-7809. Assistant Biologist-in-Charge: Eva Giesecke.
Purpose: "Wye Marsh Wildlife Center is a nature interpretation facility operated by the Canadian Wildlife Service, Environment Canada. It is a place for public visitors to explore the natural environments of the Great Lakes Natural Region of Canada." Information covers nature.
Services: Offers brochures/pamphlets and photos. "Writers are welcome to participate in the program of naturalist-led nature walks, talks, canoe trips and wildlife demonstrations, and to interview the interpretation biologists at Wye Marsh Wildlife Center." Publications include *Wye Marsh Wildlife Center*, *Hinterland Who's Who* (about wildlife), *Wye Marsh Bird Checklist*, and many handout fact sheets and identification booklets of plants and insects.
How to Contact: "Write or call to arrange a date for a visit or for more information. We suggest suitable attire for the outdoors if the writer plans a visit on-site."

Planetariums

Casey Observatory, University of Wisconsin—Eau Claire, Eau Claire WI 54701. (715)836-5731. Contact: Robert C. Elliott.
Purpose: "An astronomical data service." Information covers astronomy and science.
Services: Offers information searches and photos. "We can use extensive data files to help you solve astronomical problems. For example: What stars and planets were visible or will be visible at a specific time and place. We have an extensive collection of astronomical photographs.
How to Contact: Write or call. Charges $10-25/hour, "depending on the job. Estimates will be given."

Goldendale Observatory, Box 555, Goldendale WA 98620. (509)773-3141. Director: William F. Yantis.
Purpose: "We are here to educate the public and show them celestial objects and describe their formation and their meaning in astronomy." Information covers science.
Services: Offers newsletter.
How to Contact: Write or call.

Griffith Observatory, 2800 E. Observatory Rd., Los Angeles CA 90041. (213)664-1181. Director: Dr. E.C. Krupp.
Purpose: "Our purpose is the communication of astronomy and related sciences to the general public." Information covers science.
Services: Offers consultation. "We will answer inquiries of a reasonable magnitude." Publications include a monthly magazine.

How to Contact: Write or call. "Consulting may be done free, depending on the nature of project and the demand on our resources."

Hayden Planetarium, 81st St. and Central Park W., New York NY 10024. (212)873-1300, ext. 478. Librarian: Sandra Kitt.
Purpose: "We are a department of astronomy, connected with a natural history museum. We are a public department which offers a major planetarium, with topical sky shows to the public. We have floors of exhibits, two multimedia theaters, classrooms, a research library and a gift shop. Our library (and the department) specializes in astronomy, astrophysics, meteorology and space technology. Our resource library is considered the best available to the general public in this field." Information covers history, how-to, new product information, science and technical data. "We also have NASA technical information and mission reports."
Services: Offers bibliographies, information searches, and photos for research only.
How to Contact: Write or call. The planetarium is opened daily except Thanksgiving and Christman. The library is open by appointment Monday through Friday, 1 to 5 p.m. Charges for photocopies. Research must be done in-house.

Lick Observatory, University of California, Santa Cruz CA 95064. Contact: Administrative Office.
Purpose: Observatory.
Services: Offers b&w 2¼x2¼, 8x10 and 14x17 photos. Catalogs are free on written request. Information concerning color materials is contained in the catalog.
How to Contact: "Users of astronomical photographs should make their selections from the standard list in the current catalog of astronomical photographs available as slides or prints from negatives obtained at Lick Observatory, since it is not possible to supply views of other objects or special sizes. Purchasers are reminded that permission for use of Lick Observatory photographs for reproduction or commercial purposes must be obtained in writing in advance from the director of the observatory.

Morrison Planetarium, California Academy of Sciences, Golden Gate Park, San Francisco CA 94118. (415)221-5100, ext. 269. Director: Dr. Lee W. Simon.
Purpose: "Morrison Planetarium is part of the California Academy of Sciences, located in San Francisco's Golden Gate Park near the Japanese Tea Garden and the DeYoung Museum. Morrison Planetarium's unique Sky Theater consists of a 65-foot hemispherical dome which arcs above a comfortably appointed seating area. In the center stands the Academy Projector, designed and constructed at the California Academy of Sciences. This projector can depict the appearance of the sky as seen from the Earth, at any time—past, present or future. On the dome overhead can be seen the sun and moon, the five planets visible to the unaided eye, star clusters, nebulae and almost 4,000 stars. Special effects projectors and a new panorama system can take the viewer on a space voyage to Mars and Jupiter, enable one to land on the surface of an alien planet or vividly display such events as exploding stars, whirling galaxies and black holes." Information covers science and astronomy.
Services: Offers programs on astronomy.
How to Contact: Write or call.

Trailside Nature and Science Center and Planetarium, Coles Ave. and New Providence Rd., Mountainside NJ 07092. (201)232-5930. Director: Donald W. Mayer.
Purpose: "Our specialty is astronomy and science." Information covers nature and science.
Services: Offers information searches.
How to Contact: Write or call.

Clipping Services

Good writers are good readers; they read in order to stay current with developments in their field of interest.

Covering all publications that might publish something related to your field, however, is usually impossible. When you believe wide coverage of current publications is important, therefore, clipping services can serve as your eyes on hundreds of publications. For a subscription fee, these services monitor newspapers, magazines and other publications, and clip out articles covering the topic in which the subscriber is interested. One clipping service, for example, monitors 4,000 business, trade, farm and consumer magazines—and the top daily newspapers—in the US and Canada.

The clipped articles are then delivered to you, along with the name of the publication in which the article appeared and the date of publication.

Using a clipping service is a good way to cast a research net for current material published on a specific subject, but it's also an expensive way. Clipping services charge a monthly subscription fee in the range of $40-70, plus a per-clipping fee in the range of 25-40¢ an item. Another smaller monthly fee is added if you want the service to check for additional subjects.

For a more detailed discussion of the benefits and disadvantages of consulting clipping services, see "Paying for Research" in the introductory material of this book.

Allen's Press Clipping Bureau, 657 Mission St., San Francisco CA 94105. Owners: John McCombs, Phillip McCombs.
Purpose: "We've been in business for 90 years. We supply information from local (California), national and international newspapers." Information covers agriculture, art, business, celebrities, economics, entertainment, food, health/medicine, history, how-to, industry, law, music, nature, new products, politics, recreation, science, self-help, sports, technical data and travel.
How to Contact: Write or call. Charges vary.

ATP Clipping Bureau, Inc., 5 Beekman St., New York NY 10038. (212)349-1177. General Manager: Helen Surrey.
Purpose: Trade press and newspaper bureau for media research services.
How to Contact: Write. Charges for services; "rates and details on request."

Bacon's, 14 E. Jackson Blvd., Chicago IL 60604. (312)922-8419. President: Robert H. Bacon Jr.
Purpose: "To keep pace with today's information explosion, more and more businesses are using Bacon's services both here and abroad. With over 45 years experience in reading, evaluating and analyzing magazines and newspapers, Bacon's provides you with a highly trained staff that gives you the specific information required."
How to Contact: Write or call. Charges $60/month plus 33¢/clipping for clipping service (3 months minimum), and $95 plus $1.95 shipping for publicity checker.

Bureau Internationale de Press, 68 E. 7th St., New York NY 10003. (212)533-7420. Director: J.P. Knapp.

Purpose: Worldwide press clipping service.
How to Contact: Write to inquire about rates.

Burelle Press Clipping Bureau, 75 E. Northfield, Livingston NJ 07039. (201)992-6600.
Contact: Arthur Wynne Jr.
Purpose: "Burelle covers all national newspapers and consumer trade magazines on any subject." Information covers agriculture, art, business, celebrities, economics, entertainment, food, health/medicine, history, how-to, industry, law, music, nature, new products, politics, recreation, science, self-help, sports, technical data and travel.
Services: Offers clipping services.
How to Contact: Write or call. Charges for services.

Congressional Record Clippings, Suite 402, 1868 Columbia Rd. NW, Washington DC 20009 (202)332-2000. Chief Reader: Ruth Prince.
Purpose: Monitors Senate, House of Representatives and daily *Congressional Record* appendix.
How to Contact: Write or call.

Empire State Press Clipping Service, 455 Central Ave., Scarsdale NY 10583. (914)723-2792. Contact: Sales Dept.
Purpose: "Clipping bureau covering the state of New York." Information covers specific companies, general information on all areas.
How to Contact: Write or call. Charges monthly reading fee and a per- clipping fee.

Home Economics Reading Service, Inc., 1341 G St. NW, Washington DC 20005. (202)347-4763. President: Alice Brueck.
Purpose: "We can make available information from 1,350 daily metropolitan newspapers on women's interests and publicity." Information covers food, home furnishing and household equipment.
How to Contact: Write or call. Charges a monthly rate plus a per-clipping fee.

International Press Clipping Bureau, Inc., 5 Beekman St., New York NY 10038. (212)267-5450. President: Irving Paley.
Purpose: "We cover virtually every daily and weekly newspaper. We have domestic and foreign coverage." Information covers agriculture, art, business, celebrities, economics, entertainment, food, health/medicine, history, how-to, industry, law, music, nature, new products, politics, recreation, science, self-help, sports, technical data and travel.
How to Contact: Write or call. Charges for services.

International Press Clipping Bureau, Inc., 1868 Columbia Rd. NW, Washington DC 20009. (202)332-2000. President: Irving Paley.
Purpose: "Clipping service." Provides coverage of domestic and foreign publications. Information covers agriculture, art, business, celebrities, economics, entertainment, food, health/medicine, history, how-to, industry, law, music, nature, new products, politics, recreation, science, self-help, sports, technical data and travel.
How to Contact: Write or call. Charges for services.

Latin American Press Clipping Service, Division of Burelle Press Clipping Service, 75 E. Northfield Ave., Livingston NJ 07039. (201)992-6600. (212)227-5579 (New York). Contact: Arthur Wynne Jr.
Purpose: "We cover 350 leading newspapers and magazines from Latin American countries." Information covers agriculture, art, business, clebrities, economics, entertainment, food, health/medicine, history, how-to, industry, law, music, nature, new products, politics, recreation, science, self-help, sports, technical data and travel.
How to Contact: Write or call. Charges for services.

Luce Press Clippings, Inc., 420 Lexington Ave., New York NY 10017. (800)528-8226.
Purpose: Clipping bureau offering national coverage. Information covers "all subjects, specific companies, institutions, etc."
How to Contact: Write or call. Charges reading charge plus a per- clipping.

New England Newsclip Agency, Inc., Division of Burelle's Press Clipping Service, 5 Auburn St., Framingham MA 01701. (617)879-4460. Contact: Arthur Wynne Jr.
Purpose: "New England Newsclip Agency covers only those newspapers and magazines which cover the New England area." Information covers agriculture, art, business, celebrities, economics, entertainment, food, health/medicine, history, how-to, industry, law, music, nature, new products, politics, recreation, science, self-help, sports, technical data and travel.
How to Contact: Write or call. Charges for services.

New Jersey Clipping Service, Division of Burelle's Press Clipping Service, 99 E. Northfield Ave., Livingston NJ 07039. (201)994-3333. Contact: Arthur Wynne Jr.
Purpose: "New Jersey Clipping Service covers all New Jersey newspapers and magazines." Information covers agriculture, art, business, celebrities, economics, entertainment, food, health/medicine, history, how-to, industry, law, music, nature, new products, politics, recreation, science, self-help, sports, technical data and travel.
How to Contact: Write or call. Charges for services.

New York State Clipping Service, Division of Burelle's Press Clipping Service, 75 E. Northfield Ave., Livingston NJ 07039. (212)233-1373. Contact: Arthur Wynne Jr.
Purpose: "New York State Clipping Service covers only those newspapers and magazines which cover the state of New York." Information covers agriculture, art, business, celebrities, economics, entertainment, food, health/medicine, history, how-to, industry, law, music, nature, new products, politics, recreation, science, self-help, sports, technical data and travel.
How to Contact: Write or call. Charges for services.

Newsvertising, Suite 603, 1868 Columbia Rd. NW, Washington DC 20009. (202)332-2000. General Manager: Prescott Dennett.
Purpose: Clipping service.
Services: Offers "all media monitoring, clipping and retrieval services—news, editorial, TV-radio commentary, legislative, diplomatic researching on any subject."
How to Contact: Write or call.

Pacific Clippings, Box 11789, Santa Ana CA 92711. (714)542-7201.
Purpose: "Covers Orange County newspapers and magazines, including *Los Angeles Times, Los Angeles Examiner* and the *Long Beach Press Telegram.*"
How to Contact: Write or call.

Packaged Facts, 274 Madison Ave., New York NY 10016. (212)532-5533. President: David Wise.
Purpose: "Packaged Facts is a research company with files of clippings on literally thousands of topics. We will research historical background; we have access to any material desired." Information covers agriculture, art, business, celebrities, economics, entertainment, food, health/medicine, history, how-to, industry, law, music, nature, new products, politics, recreation, science, self-help, sports, technical data and travel.
How to Contact: Write or call. Charges for services; write for free estimate.

Press Intelligence, Inc., 734 15th St. NW, Washington DC 20005. (202)783-5810. Owner: Ese Crash.
Purpose: "To provide information from most of the nation's newspapers." Information covers agriculture, art, business, celebrities, economics, entertainment, food, health/

medicine, history, how-to, industry, law, music, nature, new products, politics, recreation, science, self-help, sports, technical data and travel.
How to Contact: Write or call. Charges for services; write for specific information.

Pressclips, Inc., 47 Lawrence St., New Hyde Park NY 11040. (516)437-1047. Contact: N. H. Halberstadt.
Purpose: "We tailor our service to the client's requirements. Our coverage is local, regional or national." Information covers "everything, specific and general."
How to Contact: Write or call. Charges monthly reading fee and a per-clipping fee. Annual contract also available.

Review on File, Walton NY 13856. Contact: D. Brant.
Purpose: "Book review clippings from newspapers and magazines from 1929-1970. Our service covers fiction, nonfiction and technical works."
How to Contact: Write or call. Clippings indexed according to author. Charges a per-clipping fee.

Colleges & Universities

General Information Offices

Colleges and universities are structured around the discovery, interpretation and dissemination of information. Though teaching is one of these institutions' most important purposes, finding new information and making it useful are also important. Colleges and universities are, therefore, logical—and valuable—places to seek information.

What's more, colleges and universities are willing to share discoveries with writers. Says Kenneth Service, Carnegie-Mellon University's director of PR: "Anyone writing material for publication is encouraged to call," because, he says, getting information to writers "justifies our existence. The PR office exists to provide information about university faculty, programs and research projects."

University and college news bureaus and public relations departments, then, are prepared and willing to work with writers. The news bureau of the University of Pennsylvania, for instance, spends about half of its time responding to reporters' queries, estimates Ronald D. Hurt, assistant director of communications services. Hurt has faith in the worth of the information he can provide to writers and the information to which he can direct writers: "When all else fails, call the Penn News Bureau." He continues, tongue in cheek, "When the Penn News Bureau fails, make up stuff!"

University information specialists seem less concerned with the specificity of the requests they receive than are information people in other fields. "The form in which we are most used to working with writers is the simple inquiry: a phone call asking, 'do you have anyone working on solar energy, or disarmament policies, or computer speech-understanding systems?'," says Service. "If we have people conducting research in the appropriate area, we're happy to point you to them, set up interviews, shoot photos, or provide background information. We do not have a comprehensive listing of research underway; the best bet is simply a phone call." Many, though certainly not all, college and university people are willing to entertain generalized inquiries. Yet, a spokesperson for one university notes that writers should explore textbooks and other sources to learn the basics of the particular subject before making inquiries.

Writers, however, won't always get information simply by asking, even if the university in question has access to the needed information. "Because research projects are in various stages, all details cannot always be provided," explains Annette Henderson, assistant director of communications and public affairs of the Polytechnic Institute of New York. Some information can be released only with permission by university authorities, as is the case at Troy State University in Alabama. "This," says Don Griffis of the university, "is simply a formality and should not interfere with or constrict a responsible journalist/writer."

Writers also can't expect immediate answers to inquiries, especially complex ones. "If writers have special needs for individual interviews or detailed information, allow as much time as possible" for a response, says Donna Chitwood of Gallaudet College's public relations office. The first office you contact often can't answer your specific question, so it will route the information request to a department or individual that can. (A brief discussion of such academic pathways is included in "Junk Mail Can Be Good for You.") Allow éxtra time for this extra routing; it's important because it ensures that your question is answered by the person most qualified to respond, or by the one with the time to give you an adequate answer.

Answers aren't the only product of universities that's useful to writers; ideas are also available. "The writer needing data for an article, or contemplating one on a specific or general topic, might discuss this with the public relations department," says George W. Belk III, director of public relations at Thomas Jefferson University. "Information and story leads are numerous and constantly developing." Ron Hurt of the University of Pennsylvania concurs: "We typically provide people and/or information on specific topics for reporters. We also have, at any given point, dozens of ideas for stories, using Penn research or personalities." Colleges and universities listed here are those that expressed to us their interest in working with writers.

When asked what kind of information is available from the Penn News Bureau, Hurt could have been speaking for any number of colleges and universities when he replied, "Almost any topic; give us a try!" If you'll excuse the expression, give it the old college try.

American University, Office of University Relations, Massachusetts and Nebraska Aves. NW, Washington DC 20016. (202)686-2100. Assistant Director of University Relations: Jody Goulden.
Purpose: "Assessment of prior experiential learning. Earn college credit for learning outside of classroom—for students in real world experiences. Earn up to 30 credit hours. We are also an institution for advanced studies in justice."
Services: Offers aid in arranging interviews, annual reports, biographies, brochures/ pamphlets, information searches, placement on mailing list, newsletter and some photos. Publications available.
How to Contact: Write or call.

Carnegie-Mellon University, Public Relations Department, Schenley Park, Pittsburgh PA 15213. (412)578-2900. Director of Public Relations: Kenneth Service.
Purpose: "Carnegie-Mellon is a private university with approximately 5,000 students. Though there is a comprehensive range of programs, the university is particularly strong (ranked within the top 10 nationally) in graduate business education, computer science, engineering (electrical, mechanical, civil, chemical, and metallurgy and materials science), molecular biology, drama, art, design, cognitive psychology and public management. The PR office will provide information about faculty, programs and research projects." Information covers art, business, economics, entertainment, history, industry, music, science and technical data.
Services: Offers aid in arranging interviews, annual reports, bibliographies, brochures/pamphlets, placement on mailing list and photos. Publications include "dozens of brochures; most are about specific educational programs."
How to Contact: Write or call. "The form in which we are most used to working with writers is the simple inquiry: a phone call asking, 'Do you have anyone working on solar energy, or disarmament policies, or computer speech understanding systems, etc.' If we have people conducting research in the appropriate area, we're happy to point you to them, set up interviews, shoot photos, or provide background information. We do not have a comprehensive listing of research underway; the best bet is a simple phone call."

John Carroll University, University Heights OH 44118. (216)491-4321. Director, Public Affairs: Paul Kantz.
Purpose: "John Carroll University enrolls 3,800 students in 40 degree programs in the arts and sciences, business, and teacher education. It offers degrees at both the bachelor's and master's levels." Information covers business, economics, history, industry, politics, science, sports and earthquake analysis.
Services: Offers aid in arranging interviews, annual reports, biographies, statistics,

brochures/pamphlets, placement on mailing list and photos.
How to Contact: Write or call.

The Catholic University of America, 620 Michigan Ave., Washington DC 20064.
(202)635-5000. Director of Public Relations: Suzanne Nelson.
Purpose: "We are the most eminent school of religious studies and a pontifically
chartered faculty in three departments: theology, canon law and philosophy. Some
unique aspects of the university include the following: an outstanding drama department (in the last few years, nine of their productions have been done on Broadway and
three graduates have been Pulitzer Prize winners); music (in the last three years
graduates have won or have been first runners-up in the national audition of the
Metropolitan Opera); scientists here recently discovered neutrinos and a glass that can
contain radioactive material; the anthropology department is using NASA equipment
to find ancient civilizations in South America; and the Boy's Town Center on campus
is studying youth development."
Services: Offers biographies and brochures/pamphlets.
How to Contact: Call.

De Paul University, 25 E. Jackson Blvd., Chicago IL 60604. (312)321-7600 (admissions
office), (312)321-7656 (public relations office). Contact: Admissions or Public Relations Office.
Purpose: Educational institution. Information covers art, business, economics, history, law, music and science.
Services: Offers aid in arranging interviews, annual reports and newsletter.
How to Contact: Write or call.

Drew University, Madison NJ 07940. (201)377-3000. Director, Public Information:
Lois F. Bell.
Purpose: "At Drew, founded in 1866 as a theological seminary, there are three
divisions—a college of liberal arts, a graduate school and a theological school. Enrollment is over 2,000. Further information upon request." Information covers art, economics, entertainment (at Drew), history, music, politics, science, sports (Drew sports)
and liberal arts studies.
Services: Offers biographies, brochures/pamphlets, placement on mailing list, newsletter and promotional material. Publications available.
How to Contact: Write or call. Sometimes charges for services.

Duquesne University, 800 Forbes Ave., Room 405, Administration Bldg., Pittsburgh
PA 15219. (412)434-6050. Director of Communications: Mary R. Kukovich.
Purpose: "Duquesne is a private urban university (one of only six urban Catholic
universities in the US). It has 7,000 students enrolled in its eight schools: pharmacy,
law, education, music, business, liberal arts and sciences, nursing and education."
Information covers business, economics, health/medicine, history, law, music, science, sports, education (especially in the area of reading deficiencies, the handicapped
and the retarded), literature, psychology and religion.
Services: Offers aid in arranging interviews, annual reports, biographies, statistics,
brochures/pamphlets, clipping services, placement on mailing list, photos and press
kits. Publications include "standard catalogs, student recruitment items and special
pieces on a wide range of topics."
How to Contact: Write or call.

Eastern Kentucky University, Office of Public Information, Richmond KY 40475.
(606)622-2301. Director: John Winnecke.
Purpose: "General news service for the university programs." Information covers
agriculture, art, business, celebrities, economics, entertainment, food, health/
medicine, history, how-to, music, nature, recreation, science, self-help, sports and
technical data.

Services: Offers aid in arranging interviews, biographies, statistics, brochures/ pamphlets, placement on mailing list, newsletter and photos. Publications include pamphlets and brochures on most academic programs, sports, and general university information.
How to Contact: Write or call.

Fairleigh Dickinson University, Montross and W. Passaic Aves., Rutherford NJ 07070. (201)933-5000. Public Information Officer: Carol Wintemberg.
Purpose: "The university serves 20,000 students on 3 main north Jersey campuses: Rutherford, Florham-Madison and Teaneck-Hackensack, and on overseas campuses at Wroxton, England and St. Croix, Virgin Islands. Contact can be made with faculty members possessing unusual expertise in these subjects: accounting, biology, business administration, communications, dentistry (and specializations), desalination, engineering (including construction engineering), futures forecasting, planning and assessment, gerontology, health professions, hotel and restaurant management, human development, humanities, marine biology, mothering, nutrition, research, oceanography, pharmaceutical/chemical marketing, recreation and leisure services, social sciences and women's studies." Information covers art, business, economics, entertainment, food, health/medicine, history, industry, music, politics, recreation, science, sports and technical data.
Services: Offers aid in arranging interviews, statistics, brochures/pamphlets, placement on mailing list and newsletter.
How to Contact: Write or call.

Ferris State College, Big Rapids MI 49307. (616)796-9971, ext 503. Director of College Relations: Donald F. Scannell.
Purpose: "Ferris is a pioneer and national leader in career and vocational education with more than 100 different programs, ranging from certificates through doctor of optometry degrees."
Services: Offers aid in arranging interviews, brochures/pamphlets and photos. Publications include *This Is Ferris State College* and brochures about individual programs.
How to Contact: Write or call.

Simon Fraser University, Burnaby, British Columbia, Canada V5A 1S6. (604)291-3210. Director, University News Service: Dennis Roberts.
Purpose: "The office of university news service serves as an information/publicity office for Simon Fraser University. The university has faculties of arts, science, education and inter-disciplinary studies." Information covers business, economics, health/medicine, history, nature, politics, recreation, science, sports, archeology, computers and sociology.
Services: Offers aid in arranging interviews, biographies, brochures/pamphlets, placement on mailing list, newsletter and photos. Publications include general information pamphlets and *Comment* magazine, "about the people of our university and their special interests."
How to Contact: Write. "We would greatly appreciate seeing articles or the 'end result' of interviews, etc. Such feedback is essential if we are to improve or modify our service."

Gallaudet College, 7th St. and Florida Ave. NE, Washington DC 20002. (202)447-0741. Senior Writer, Public Relations: Donna Chitwood.
Purpose: "Gallaudet serves deaf individuals internationally in a great variety of ways. For example, educationally the college offers demonstration programs on the elementary and secondary school levels, a liberal arts college, a graduate school, and a network of continuing education programs. The library houses one of the largest collections of materials on deafness. The National Center for Law and the Deaf and the International Center on Deafness are located at Gallaudet, and research related to

deafness is being conducted at the college." Information covers the following areas as related to deafness: art, economics, health/medicine, history, how-to, law, politics, science, self-help, sports, technical data and communication (sign language).
Services: Offers aid in arranging interviews, annual reports, statistics, brochures/pamphlets, photos and "individual assistance as requested." Publications include *Gallaudet College, The Look of a Sound, Deafness Briefs, Gallaudet Today* (quarterly magazine) and related materials.
How to Contact: Write or call office of alumni and public relations. "If writers have special needs for individual interviews, detailed information, etc., allow as much time as possible. We have a small office working extensively with radio, television, film, newspaper, magazine and other media personnel."

Georgetown University, Office of Public Relations, 37th and O Sts. NW, Washington DC 20057. (202)625-0100. Director of Public Relations: Brent Breedin. Director of News Bureau: David Fulghum.
Purpose: The university's special features include the oldest and largest school of foreign service in the country; the Joseph and Rose Kennedy Institute of Ethics; the Lombardy Cancer Research Center; research in oral surgery and weight reducation; and work in international diplomacy, cryo-biology, animal behavior and environmental biology.
Services: Offers aid in arranging interviews, biographies, brochures/pamphlets, placement on mailing list and newsletter. Publications include *Press Contacts*, a directory of persons to call for more information.
How to Contact: Write or call.

Georgia Institute of Technology, 225 N. Ave. NW, Atlanta GA 30332. (404)894-2452. News Bureau: Charles Harmon.
Purpose: "Includes four colleges (architecture, industrial management, engineering, science and liberal studies). We are also heavily involved in solar energy research and alternate energy research."
Services: Offers aid in arranging interviews, bibliographies, biographies, brochures/pamphlets, information searches, placement on mailing list, statistics and news releases.
How to Contact: Write.

Hampshire College, West St., Amherst MA 01002. (413)549-4600. Public Relations Director: Peter Gluckler.
Purpose: "Hampshire College was planned beginning in 1958 by a committee representing Amherst, Mount Holyoke and Smith Colleges and the University of Massachusetts. The college was founded in 1965 when Amherst College alumnus Harold F. Johnson pledged $6 million. The college opened in 1970. Its mission was to find new ways in which to organize knowledge and new ways in which to teach it. Hampshire is a nontraditional, experimenting college eager to export the results of its findings." Information covers agriculture, art, economics, history, law, music, nature, politics, recreation, science, self-help, sports, some technical data, educational theory and philosophy and TV.
Services: Offers aid in arranging interviews, annual reports, biographies, brochures/pamphlets, information searches, placement on mailing list and photos.
How to Contact: Write or call.

Harvard University, 1000 Holyoke Center, Cambridge MA 02138. (617)495-1585. Contact: Harvard University News Office.
Purpose: "Higher education: graduate; undergraduate; professional; doctoral programs; research; social, physical and biological sciences; and the arts. We have a center for international affairs and European studies. The John F. Kennedy School of Government is at Harvard." Information covers agriculture, art, business, celebrities, economics, entertainment, food, health/medicine, history, how-to, industry, law, music, na-

ture, politics, recreation, science, self-help, sports and technical data.

Services: Offers aid in arranging interviews, annual reports, bibliographies, biographies, statistics, brochures/pamphlets, information searches, placement on mailing list, newsletter and photos. Publishes a weekly newspaper, *Harvard University Gazette.*

How to Contact: Write or call. Charges $5/year for newspaper.

Sam Houston State University, Huntsville TX 77341. (713)295-6211. Director, Information Services: Frank Krystyniak.

Purpose: "Education and service in all fields. We are especially strong in criminal justice, education, agriculture, business and music. We have a great deal of expertise and recent research underway and completed in the Criminal Justice Center on all aspects of the criminal justice system." Information covers agriculture, art, business, economics, food, history, how-to, industry, music, nature, politics, recreation, science, self-help, sports and technical data.

Services: Offers aid in arranging interviews, statistics, brochures/pamphlets, information searches, placement on mailing list and photos. Publications include *Texas Crime Poll* (semiannual).

How to Contact: Call.

Indiana University, Bloomington IN 474045. (812)337-3911. Press Secretary: Susan Hays.

Purpose: "Indiana University is one of the oldest universities west of the Allegheny Mountains." Information covers art, business, celebrities, economics, entertainment, food, health/medicine, history, how-to, industry, law, music, nature, new products, politics, recreation, science, self-help, sports, technical data and travel.

Services: Offers aid in arranging interviews, annual reports, bibliographies, biographies, statistics, brochures/pamphlets, clipping services, placement on mailing list, newsletter, photos, press kits, TV film or video clips, and radio spots.

How to Contact: Write or call.

Iowa State Center, Iowa State University, Ames IA 50011. (515)294-3347. Public Relations Coordinator: Wayne P. Davis.

Purpose: "Performing arts complex and conference center for Iowa State University. The center consists of four buildings: a 2,749-seat auditorium, a 14,800-seat arena, a 450-seat little theater, a conference center with meeting and banquet rooms, a 450-seat auditorium, and the Brunnier Art Gallery. Our information supports utilization of the complex." Information covers art, celebrities, entertainment, music and sports.

Services: Offers aid in arranging interviews, statistics, brochures/pamphlets, placement on mailing list and photos. Publications include *The Iowa State Center* and *Front and Center* (monthly newsletter).

How to Contact: Write or call. "Since service to writers is not our primary responsibility, we need as much lead time as possible in gathering material."

Thomas Jefferson University, 1020 Walnut St., Philadelphia PA 19107. (215)928-6300. Director, Public Relations: Geroge W. Belk III.

Purpose: "Thomas Jefferson University consists of Jefferson Medical College, Thomas Jefferson University Hospital, The College of Allied Health Sciences, and the College of Graduate Studies. Its mission is health care, medical education and clinical and basic research. Founded in 1824, it is the largest private medical/teaching institution in the US, and has graduated more practicing physicians than any other school in the country." Information covers health/medicine and science.

Services: Offers aid in arranging interviews, annual reports, newsletter and photos. Publications include annual reports, newsletters, brochures/pamphlets and reprints of scientific papers.

How to Contact: Call. For brochures/pamphlets, contact Vincent Walsh, director, department of publications. "Specify the type of data needed and the general purpose for which it is to be used. Writers/photographers desiring to interview physicians, administrators or researchers should arrange this through the PR department. Interviews and photographs of patients in the hospital are allowed only with patient permission, which must be obtained through the PR department."

Tips: "The writer needing data for an article, or contemplating one on specific or general topics, might discuss this with public relations department. Story leads and information are numerous and constantly developing."

Juilliard School, Lincoln Center, New York NY 10023. (212)799-5000. Contact: Public Relations Department.
Purpose: A private, professional school of dance, music and drama. Has students from 36 foreign countries.
Services: Offers brochures/pamphlets. Publications include school catalog.
How to Contact: Write or call.

Kansas State University, Anderson Hall 111, Manhattan KS 66502. (913)532-6415. Director of Information: Robert Bruce.
Purpose: "This Department of Information manages media relations for Kansas State University, a major multifaceted land grant university with programs in agriculture, engineering, arts and sciences, business administration, grain science, home economics and graduate studies." Information covers agriculture, art, business, economics, history, industry, music, nature, politics, recreation, science, sports and education.
Services: Offers aid in arranging interviews, biographies, statistics, brochures/pamphlets, placement on mailing list, newsletter and photos. Publications include *KSU Bulletin.*
How to Contact: Write or call.

Sarah Lawrence College, Public Relations Office, Bronxville NY 10708. (914)337-0700, ext. 219. Director of Public Relations: Jane Klang or William Klein.
Purpose: "One of our most important programs is the conference system—in each course the student gets involved in an independent study project and meets with the instructor biweekly. Also each student has her own advisor." Information covers art, history, music, nature, politics, science, self-help, technical data, theater, dance and writing.
Services: Offers aid in arranging interviews, annual reports, biographies, brochures/pamphlets, information searches, placement on mailing list, statistics, quarterly newsletter and photos.
How to Contact: Write or call.

Loyola College of Maryland, 4501 N. Charles St., Balitimore MD 21210. (301)323-1010, ext. 280. Contact: Public Relations Director.
Purpose: Higher education. Information covers art, business, economics, entertainment, health/medicine, history, how-to, industry, music, nature, politics, recreation, science, self-help, sports, technical data and travel.
Services: Offers aid in arranging interviews, biographies, statistics, brochures/pamphlets, information searches, placement on mailing list, newsletter, photos and press kits. "We offer monthly editions of *Story Possibilities*, feature and interview suggestions researched by us on a wide range of academic, faculty, and human interest topics developed at/by Loyola College."
How to Contact: "We request that writers call the PR office directly for best assistance, background information, etc."

Medical College of Ohio, C.S. 10008, Toledo OH 43699. (419)381-4267. Director of Information: Jim Richard.
Purpose: Medical college. Information covers health/medicine and science.
Services: Offers aid in arranging interviews, brochures/pamphlets and newsletter.
How to Contact: Write or call.

New Mexico State University, Las Cruces NM 88003. (505)646-0111. Director of Information Services: Eddie Groth.
Purpose: Institution of higher learning. Information covers agriculture, history, recreation, science, sports and technical data.
Services: Offers aid in arranging interviews, biographies, brochures/pamphlets and press kits.
How to Contact: Write Director of Information Services, Box 3K, New Mexico State University; or call (505)646-3221.

New York State College of Agriculture and Life Science, Cornell University, 170 Van Rensselaer Hall, Cornell University, Ithaca NY 14853. (607)256-3290. News Editor: Kay Barnes.
Purpose: "We are land-grant colleges of New York State, with research information on agriculture and human ecology disseminated through cooperative extension." Information covers agriculture, economics, food, health/medicine, how-to, nature and biological science.
Services: Offers aid in arranging interviews, brochures/pamphlets and placement on mailing list. Publications include "many bulletins—request the *Know How Catalog* for topics such as home care, nutrition, energy, gardening, farming, consumer buying and child care."
How to Contact: Write or call. "Request *Know How Catalog* from Mailing Room, 7 Research Park, Cornell University, Ithaca NY 14853."

North Texas State University, NT Station, Denton TX 76203. (817)788-2521. Sports News Director: Fred Graham. Director of News and Information: Keith Shelton.
Purpose: "We are a university offering higher education." Information covers art, business, celebrities, economics, entertainment, food, health/medicine, history, industry, music, recreation, science and sports.
Services: Offers aid in arranging interviews, statistics, brochures/pamphlets, information searches, newsletters and photos.
How to Contact: Write or call.

Northern Illinois University, Office of Information, Lowden Hall, DeKalb IL 60115. (815)753-1681. Director, Office of Information: Don Peterson.
Purpose: "The Northern Illinois University (NIU) Office of Information writes and distributes news and feature stories and photographs about the university, ongoing research, and various academic events and activities. The office also arranges interviews, conducts news conferences, and issues an annual directory of faculty and staff specialists. We have two geologists and several students who are active in Antarctic research. Northern Illinois Regional History Center also is located here—a good source for anyone interested in the history of this area." Information covers art, business, economics, food, history, music, nature, science and sports.
Services: Offers aid in arranging interviews, annual reports, brochures/pamphlets, placement on mailing list, statistics and photos. Publications available.
How to Contact: Write or call. "We would appreciate appropriate recognition for the university in any article that might result from interviews or research. If a writer quotes one of our professors or staff members, a phone call to check quotes or other attribution would be a good idea."

Northwestern University, Department of University Relations, 1810 Hinman, Evanston IL 60201. (312)492-5000. Director, University Relations: Jack O'Dowd.
Purpose: "Northwestern University (NU) is a major private university of controlled enrollment that puts a dual emphasis on research and teaching. All members of the faculty are engaged in both research and teaching. NU is one of the ten top private universities in the nation." Information covers art, business, celebrities, economics, entertainment, health/medicine, history, how-to, industry, law, music, nature, new products, politics, recreation, science, self-help, sports and technical data.

Services: Offers aid in arranging interviews, annual reports, bibliographies, statistics, brochures/pamphlets, information searches, placement on mailing list, newsletter, photos and press kits. Publications include experts list and monthly magazine, *Northwestern University Memo.*
How to Contact: Write or call. "Fee charged only for involved research."

Northwestern University, Dearborn Observatory, Evanston IL 60201. Professor of Astronomy: W. Buscombe.
Purpose: Steller astrophysics. Information covers science.
Services: Offers star catalogs. Publications include MK spectral classifications for 1974 and 1977.
How to Contact: Write. "I regret that time does not permit lengthy telephone conversations. The basic principles of this work are available in most of the elementary textbooks of astronomy."

Ohio State University, 102 Administration Bldg., Columbus OH 43210. (614)422-2711. Office of Communication Services: Bill Merriman.
Purpose: "We are a state university with an enrollment of 55,900 students. We have the largest center for professional and graduate programs in the state." Information covers agriculture, art, business, economics, entertainment, food/nutrition, health/medicine, history, how-to, industry, law, music, nature, politics, recreation, science, self-help, sports and technical data.
Services: Offers aid in arranging interviews, annual reports, bibliographies, biographies, brochures/pamphlets, information searches, placement on mailing list, statistics, newsletter, photos and press kits. Publications include information sources booklet.
How to Contact: Write or call.

Oregon State University, Marine Science Center, Marine Science Dr., Newport OR 97365. (503)867-3011. Contact: Don Giles.
Purpose: "The Marine Science Center is an extension of Oregon State University, and is involved in scientific research, an educational program for university students and an educational program for the public. We have a museum area which includes an aquarium displaying Pacific Northwest marine animals and exhibits explaining the coastal and marine environments. The university offers courses (primarily at upper division levels) in marine science, and there are a number of researchers concerned with various research projects, including fisheries, environmental studies and oceanography." Information covers argiculture, recreation, science, self-help and technical data.
Services: Offers brochures/pamphlets and placement on mailing list. Publications available.
How to Contact: Write or call.

Pennsylvania State University, 201 Old Main, University Park PA 16802. (814)865-7517. Contact: Public Information Office.
Purpose: "We are a state university with 11 colleges (agriculture, arts and architecture, business administration, earth and mineral sciences, education, engineering, health/ physical education and recreation, human development, liberal arts, science, medicine and graduate school for each area)."
Services: Offers aid in arranging interviews, annual reports, biographies, brochures/ pamphlets, information searches, placement on mailing list, statistics and photos on request. "Our library is also available."
How to Contact: Write or call. "Give us enough time—several weeks especially for photos."

Polytechnic Institute of New York, 333 Jay St., Brooklyn NY 11201. (212)643-8035, 643-8036. Assistant Director of Communications and Public Affairs: Annette Henderson.

Purpose: "Polytechnic is the largest technological university in New York State. Information that would be of most interest to writers covers research primarily in engineering; also in chemistry, life sciences, management, history of science, psychology, physics, mathematics and computer science. Some specific research areas include solar and wind energy; effects of microwaves on living systems; continuing education for engineers; emergency water supplied from groundwater; hydroelectric power; and energy advantages of public transportation." Information covers health/medicine, history, industry, science, sports and technical data.
Services: Offers aid in arranging interviews, biographies, brochures/pamphlets, placement on mailing list and photos. "Various departments at Polytechnic publish brochures and pamphlets that detail research projects."
How to Contact: Write or call. "Because research projects are at various stages, all details cannot always be provided. It is best to check first with the communications/public affairs office. Most of our research is conducted at our main campus in Brooklyn and at our Long Island campus (Route 110, Farmingdale, Long Island NY 11735). We also have a graduate center in Westchester (456 North St., White Plains NY 10605)."

Purdue University, West Lafayette IN 47907. (317)749-2062. Contact: Public Information.
Purpose: "One of the leading scientific, technological and engineering schools in the country." Also has outstanding schools of management, consumer and family sciences, pharmacy, and veterinary medicine.
Services: Offers information searches.
How to Contact: Call.

Saint Louis University, 221 N. Grand, St. Louis MO 63108. (314)658-2540. Director, Public Relations: Michael A. Blatz.
Purpose: "The university, one of 28 Jesuit colleges and universities in the country, recongnizes and accepts three main responsibilities: teaching, research and community service. The component schools and colleges are the following: College of Arts and Sciences, Graduate School, School of Business and Administration, Parks College (aeronautical technology), School of Nursing and Allied Health Professions, School of Medicine, School of Law, School of Social Service, College of Philosophy and Letters and Metropolitan College." Information covers art, economics, health/medicine, history, industry, law, music, nature, politics, recreation, science, self-help, sports, technical data and travel.
Services: Offers aid in arranging interviews, biographies, statistics, brochures/pamphlets, placement on mailing list, photos and press kits.
How to Contact: Write or call.

San Diego State University, San Diego CA 92182. (714)286-5204. Contact: University News Service.
Purpose: "Four-year university granting degrees in 72 areas of study to more than 30,000 students." Information covers agriculture, art, business, celebrities, economics, entertainment, food, health/medicine, history, how-to, industry, law, music, nature, new products, politics, recreation, science, self-help, sports and technical data.
Services: Offers aid in arranging interviews. Has a "limited quantity of SDSU Experts List, a compilation of resource persons available on campus to writers. Individuals are listed by subject areas."
How to Contact: Write or call. "We may institute a charge for the experts list if we are forced into a second printing by demand."

State University of New York at Albany, News Bureau AD237, 1400 Washington Ave., Albany NY 12222. (518)457-4901. Manager, News Bureau: Mr. Lynn C. Newland.
Purpose: "Generally, the purpose of my office is to publicize the university, its activities and its faculty. Specifically, the university offers resources in three fields: criminal justice, Meso-American studies and atmospheric science research. All three

schools boast internationally known scholars."
Services: Offers aid in arranging interviews and information searches.
How to Contact: Write or call. Outline the type of information or interview desired. "Queries for interviews should be initiated well in advance of the writer's deadline."

Troy State University, University Relations, Wallace Hall, Troy AL 36081. (205)566-5814. Coordinator of University Relations: Don Griffis.
Purpose: "We're Alabama's third largest multi-campus university. Information and possible feature ideas range from the activities of our faculty members here in Troy to the operations of our European campuses. Our faculty has the highest percentage of Phi Beta Kappa members in the state, and more Rhodes scholars are connected with Troy State than any other institution of higher education in the state. In addition, each individual school is involved in some type of project or research. For example, the TSU biology department is currently working with the Department of Agriculture in waste disposal." Information covers art, business, celebrities economics, entertainment, health/medicine, history, industry, music, politics, science, self-help, sports and technical data.
Services: Offers aid in arranging interviews, annual reports, bibliographies, biographies, statistics, brochures/pamphlets, information searches, placement on mailing list, newsletter, photos and press kits. Also has audio tapes and videotapes from university-run television and radio station, and print materials from Troy State University Press. Publications include *Troy Statement*, quarterly review of activities; *The Trop*, student newspaper; *The Illiad*, weekly faculty bulletin; *Student Handbook*; *Radio Program Guide*; and general information pamphlets on each area of academic study.
How to Contact: Write or call. "Everything must be cleared through the offices of university relations and the special assistant to the president. This is simply a formality, and should not interfere or constrict a responsible journalist/writer."

Union College, College Grounds, Schenectady NY 12308. (518)370-6172. Assistant to the President: Jack L. Makanville.
Purpose: "Education—traditional and continuing; strong pre-medical, pre-law and engineering programs. Many faculty members are capable of commenting on current events in their specialties; some are nationally recognized authorities." Information covers economics, health/medicine, history, industry, music, nature, politics and science.
Services: Offers aid in arranging interviews, annual reports and placement on mailing list.
How to Contact: Write or call.

United States Military Academy, West Point NY 10996. (914)938-4011. Contact: Public Affairs Office.
Purpose: "Military academy with 4,200 students."
Services: Offers biographies, brochures/pamphlets and informational papers.
How to Contact: Write.

United States Sports Academy, University of South Alabama, Mobile AL 36688. (205)460-7000. Director of Public Relations: Eric Williams.
Purpose: "The United States Sports Academy is dedicated to upgrading sport and sport education through graduate education, research and service. We have, or know the best source, for information on almost all phases of sport and sport-related information. We also offer a sport facilities consulting service. We are active both nationally and internationally. We have several sport and sport-related contracts with foreign nations, especially in the Middle East." Information covers law and science as they relate to sports.
Services: Offers newsletter and information on sport medicine, graduate sport education, and sources of best information on all aspects of sport and sport-related activities.

How to Contact: Write or call. "We would prefer to work with known publications and writers with experience in the sports and sport-related field."
Tips: "Get plenty of views on controversial subjects, pro and con; don't go only to the well known sources on a topic. Don't take all information at face value; separate facts and statistics from opinion; and keep all promises made; you might have to use a source many times."

University of California—Berkeley, Public Information, 101 Sproul Hall, Berkeley CA 94720. (415)642-3734.
Purpose: "University of California—Berkeley is a major university." Information covers agriculture, art, business, celebrities, economics, entertainment, food, health/medicine, history, how-to, industry, law, music, nature, new products, politics, recreation, science, self-help, sports, technical data and travel.
Services: Offers placement on mailing list. Publications available.
How to Contact: Write the University Relations Office, Attention: Editor, University of California, Systemwide Administration, Berkeley CA 94720. "Please be very specific in your request."

University of California—Los Angeles (UCLA), 405 Hilgard Ave., Los Angeles CA 90024. (213)825-2585. Director, Public Information: Chandler Harris.
Purpose: "University of California (UCLA) is a major university with faculty members who are authorities in many fields." Information covers art, business, economics, health/medicine, history, law, music, nature, politics, science and technical data.
Services: Offers assistance. "We will assist writers who have definite assignments by attempting to secure comments or quotations from authorities, or by putting such writers in touch with authorities able to answer their questions."
How to Contact: Write or call; a letter is preferred. "We may not be able to help in every instance, because faculty members are reluctant to comment on subjects on which they have not personally conducted research or have firsthand knowledge; a match with a writer's area of interest and faculty expertise is not automatic."

University of California—San Diego, Public Information Office, Q-036, LaJolla CA 92093. (714)452-3120. National News Coordinator: Paul Lowenberg. Director of Public Information, UCSD: Paul West (714)452-3120. Public Information Representative, UCSD: Chuck Colgan (714)452-3120. Director of Public Information, School of Medicine, UCSD: Winifred Cox (714)452-3714. Director of Public Information, University Hospital, UCSD: Pat JaCoby (714)294-6163. Director of Public Information, Scripps Institution of Oceanography, UCSD: Dale Walker (714)452-3624.
Purpose: "Undergraduate and graduate education in liberal arts, humanities and sciences, including medical school and university (community) hospital; Scripps Institution of Oceanography (graduate programs and research); and research and development on myriad of subjects for private and government funded agencies. Some $83 million in federal R&D annually." Information covers art, economics, health/medicine, history, music, nature, politics, recreation, science, and most everything from educational trends to radio-astronomy.
Services: Offers aid in arranging interviews, annual reports, biographies, statistics information, brochures/pamphlets, information searches, placement on mailing list, photos and press kits. Publications include *ReSources,* "a media tip sheet of story leads primarily in the science and/or research field. Topics run from educational trends to quasars."
How to Contact: Call. "We ask writers to contact the proper individual rather than contacting the university personnel."

University of Detroit, 4001 W. McNichols, Detroit MI 48214. (313)927-1256. News Bureau Manager: Connie Ruohomaki.
Purpose: "Founded over 100 years ago, the University of Detroit has three campuses in the city of Detroit. Its eight schools and colleges include: law, dentistry, business and

administration, architecture, engineering and science, education and human services, psychology and liberal arts. The school's research programs have developed a computerized folklore archive, a polymer institute, an accounting aid service, a psycho-diagnostic center, an urban law clinic, adult and pediatric dental clinics, an international management instutute, a center for counselor education, a small business institute for public use, and a library for the visually handicapped." Information covers art, business, economics, entertainment, health/medicine, history, industry, law, new products, politics, science, self-help, sports, technical data and travel.

Services: Offers aid in arranging interviews, annual reports, bibliographies, biographies, brochures/pamphlets, information searches, placement on mailing list, photos and press kits; "reference resources pertaining to the research specialty of faculty members."

How to Contact: Write or call. "We prefer a written request with reasonable lead time to arrange interviews or gather information."

University of Iowa Health Center Information & Communication, 283 Medical Laboratories, Iowa City IA 52242. (319)353-7302. Assistant Director: Ken Koopman.

Purpose: "This office serves as information and communication liaison between the University of Iowa colleges of dentistry, nursing, pharmacy and other related health center units." Information covers health/medicine and science.

Services: Offers aid in arranging interviews, newsletter and photos. "We offer help in providing sources for stories writers are working on or are researching and we will arrange interviews. We also can provide private office space with a typewriter and phone in a central location for writers working on campus; writing research facilities, including MEDLINE computerized services of the National Library of Medicine for literature searches; professional photographic assistance; and audio taping of sources' answers to writers' questions." Publications include *Leads*, "capsule story ideas based on research and innovations in health care developed at the University of Iowa, which is mailed bimonthly to leading health science writers and editors."

How to Contact: Write or call.

Tips: "Writers should have prior experience in writing health science articles. We suggest that writers give sources an opportunity to review stories before publication if at all possible. Our years of experience indicate that our sources do not wish to rewrite but do appreciate a review for accuracy."

University of Maine, Orono ME 04469. (207)581-7336. Director, Public Information: Leonard N. Harlow.

Purpose: "Public Information and Central Services promotes, publicizes and informs the public about the three missions of a land-grant university—teaching, research and public service. This department is also responsible for all the printing of university publications and the handling of all university-connected mail." Information covers agriculture, art, business, economics, food, history, how-to, music, science, sports and technical data.

Services: Offers aid in arranging interviews, biographies, statistics, brochures/pamphlets, placement on mailing list, newsletter and photos. Publications include undergraduate and graduate catalogs, *Welcome to the University of Maine*, *Sports Digest*, *UMO News*, and annual report.

How to Contact: Write or call. "The only restrictions are those dictated by federal guidelines on confidentiality of some student and faculty records."

University of Michigan, 6008 Administration Bldg., Ann Arbor MI 48109. (313)764-7260. Information Services: Joel Berger.

Purpose: "We are a university and will soon house the President Ford Library to be built on our campus. This library will contain all Ford papers, congressional through the presidency. We also have the Michigan Historical Collections Library, with strong collections of materials of the Dutch, Germans, Poles and Finns; a pre-Civil War library; and general libraries."

Services: Offers aid in arranging interviews, annual reports, bibliographies, biographies, statistics, brochures/pamphlets, information searches, placement on mailing list, newsletter and photos. "We also have a pocket facts card for the university. (Start with this for basic facts.)
How to Contact: Write or call.

University of North Carolina at Chapel Hill, Chapel Hill NC 27514. (919)933-2091. Contact: News Bureau.
Purpose: Oldest graduate program among state universities in US; outstanding medical school, dental research center, child development center, pharmacy school and nursing school.
Services: Offers aid in arranging interviews, biographies, statistics, brochures/pamphlets, information searches, placement on mailing list and photos. Publications include general information booklet, brochures on university programs, weekly calendar and research center newsletters.
How to Contact: Write or call. "Give as much lead time as possible."

University of Notre Dame, Notre Dame IN 46556. (219)283-7367. Information Services: J. Kane.
Purpose: "We are a Catholic university." Information covers earth science, art, business, health/medicine, history, law, music, politics, science, self-help and technical data.
Services: Offers aid in arranging interviews, annual reports, bibliographies, biographies, statistics, brochures/pamphlets, information searches and placement on mailing list. Publications available.
How to Contact: Write or call. "We also have offices in New York, Chicago and Los Angeles."

University of Pennsylvania, News Bureau, 525 Franklin Bldg., Philadelphia PA 19104. (215)243-8721. Assistant Director of Cummunications Services: Ron Hurt.
Purpose: "A member of the Ivy League, Penn is a university with an international reputation for academic and research excellence. A community of nearly 30,000 students, faculty and staff can offer information and expert opinion on nearly any topic. Penn's professional schools and research activities provide particularly rich ground for writers." Information covers agriculture, art, business, economics, health/medicine, history, industry, law, music, nature, politics, recreation, science and technical data. "Almost any topic; give us a try!"
Services: Offers aid in arranging interviews, biographies, statistics, placement on mailing list and photos. "We typically provide people and/or information on specific topics for reporters. We also have, at any give point, dozens of ideas for stories using Penn research or pesonalities. We are able to respond quickly to requests for quotes/reactions from experts. The only brochures we provide are those describing courses, programs and the university."
How to Contact: Write, call or visit. "When all else fails, call the Penn News Bureau!"

University of Rochester, Rochester NY 14627. (716)275-4124. Contact: Director of Public Relations.
Purpose: Independent, coed, nonsectarian university with about 8,400 students. Information covers business, economics, health/medicine, history and science.
Services: Offers aid in arranging interviews, biographies and placement on mailing list.
How to Contact: Call. May be charge for mailing list or some photos. "Calls or queries should refer to writing projects actually contracted for by publications or other form of media rather than to purely speculative projects; material can be provided only in our specific areas of expertise with the permission of the relevant individuals involved."

University of Toledo, 2801 W. Bancroft St., Toledo OH 43606. (419)537-2675. Contact: Public Information Office.
Purpose: "To disseminate information about the university generally and specific programs in each college, as well as research activities carried on in the colleges." Information covers art, business, celebrities, economics, entertainment, history, law, music, nature, recreation, science, self-help and sports.
Services: Offers brochures/pamphlets, placement on mailing list and newsletter.
How to Contact: Write.

University of Tennessee Space Institute (UTSI), Tullahoma TN 37388. (615)455-0631.
Purpose: "Graduate educational institution offering degrees in aerospace sciences, with a heavy emphasis on research. The University of Tennessee Space Institute (UTSI) is a leader in research activities, particularly the MHD process, the production of electricity directly from burning coal. MHD will lead to the production of about 50/ of the possible energy in coal, versus the present 35 percent. Other research activities include high speed aerodynamics, low speed aerodynamics, modeling, remote sensing, weather phenomena, composite materials, jet propulsion, lasers, gas diagnostics, flight mechanics, aviation systems and mathematics computations. We would cooperate with writers in these fields."
Services: Offers aid in arranging interviews and placement on mailing list.
How to Contact: Write or call.

University of Texas—El Paso, News Service, El Paso TX 79968. (915)747-5526. Assistant Director: Nancy Hamilton.
Purpose: "We are a state university, part of the University of Texas system (15,752 students registered in the colleges of business administration, education, engineering, liberal arts, nursing, science and graduate school)." Information covers business, economics, history, science and information related to activities of the university, including research programs.
Services: Offers aid in arranging interviews and statistics information. "Our library has special collections on military history, borderlands studies, history of Mexico and Southwest US, microfilmed documents of northern Mexico, and others of value to researchers."
How to Contact: "Contact the University News Service. Our usual procedure is to put the writer in contact with the information source on campus."

West Virginia University, 102 Communications Bldg., Morgantown WV 26506. (304)293-6366. Director, University Relations: Harry Ernst.
Purpose: "Comprehensive and land-grant university devoted to teaching, research, and off-campus service programs." Information covers agriculture, art, business, economics, health/medicine, history, law, music, nature, recreation, science, sports and technical data.
Services: Offers aid in arranging interviews, bibliographies, biographies, brochures/pamphlets, placement on mailing list, statistics, photos and press kits. Publications available.
How to Contact: Write or call.

Yale University, New Haven CT 06520. (203)436-3440. Contact: Office of Communications and Information.
Purpose: "Established in 1701. We are a high-quality educational university."
Services: Offers brochures/pamphlets. A library and archives are also available.
How to Contact: Write or visit.

Sports Information Offices

"We are happy to provide information. Just ask."

This statement by Rosa Gatti of the Brown University Athletic Department, though it may not hold true for every sports information office, reflects the willingness of many college and university sports information people to work with writers and the press.

The degree of eagerness to accommodate writers, of course, varies from university to university, and from sport to sport. The sports information department of Pennsylvania State University, fore example, basking in the limelight drawn to it by its highly ranked football team, tells us that it regularly turns away writers. The coverage given their football team by the *New York Times* and other large daily newspapers is sufficient for them. On the other hand, other Penn State sports—like coed riflery—receive less coverage than does football.

Smaller universities that lack the exposure given to larger schools are often the most eager to work with writers. With a smaller university, however, "help is limited," says Frank Morgan, sports information director of Ohio University at Athens. "Thus, many of us—most of us—are one-man operations, and there may be times when the forwarding of requested information must wait on a 'priority' basis."

Ways to give your information request "priority," whether you're approaching a large or small institution, include simple courtesy and professionalism. "Enclosing a self-addressed and stamped envelope gets prompt attention," says Morgan, who adds that offering to accept a collect call from the information office in order to get the information also helps. Professionalism is demonstrated with such courtesy, but a stronger display of your professional status might also be needed. When writing, use stationery with a professional-looking letterhead, and try to have a firm assignment in hand when you approach the school. "Writers and photographers on assignment get preference," says John Zane, sports information director for the University of Maryland. "Freelance (work), and writing and shooting on speculation will be judged on merit (i.e., the professionalism you demonstrate)." Terry Ross of California State University—Long Beach charges for photos and some brochures "if the person requesting is not, in our judgment, a legitimate writer or media person."

Also, be aware of busy seasons in college sports. Seasons for fall sports like football overlap with seasons for winter sports like basketball and hockey. Frank Morgan calls the overlapping fall-winter sports seasons his "busiest times. Ditto for winter to spring" when, for example, hockey and basketball seasons run concurrently with the baseball and track seasons for a time.

Listed below are sports information offices for individual universities. Organizations related to collegiate sports can be found in the Sports category of the Organizations & Associations section. The following list is somewhat selective, based on responses from information offices that have indicated willingness to work with writers. Information on other sources of college and university sports information can be found in *The National Directory of College Athletics*, published in two editions (one for men's sports, another for women's) by Ray Franks Publishing Ranch, Box 7068, Amarillo, Texas 79109).

Alabama A&M University, Sports Information Office, Normal AL 35762. (205)859-7404. Sports Information Director: Wallace Dooley.
Purpose: To provide sports information.
Services: Offers statistics, brochures/pamphlets, placement on mailing list, newsletter and photos.
How to Contact: Write or call.

Boston University, Case Athletic Center, 285 Babcock St., Boston MA 02215. (617)352-2000, 353-2873. Contact: Sports Information Department.

Purpose: Intercollegiate athletics; 27 varsity sports.
Services: Offers aid in arranging interviews, biographies, statistics, brochures/pamphlets, clipping services, placement on mailing list, newsletter, photos and press kits. Publications include media guides on football, hockey and basketball.
How to Contact: Write. Charges $4/subscription to newsletter.

Brown University, Athletic Department, Box 1932, Providence RI 02912. (401)863-2211. Sports Information Department: Rosa Gatti.
Purpose: "To publicize athletic programs." Information covers sports.
Services: Offers aid in arranging interviews, brochures/pamphlets, biographies, placement on mailing list, statistics, newsletter, photos, and press kits. Publications available.
How to Contact: Write or call. "We charge if we do not feel the outlet will utilize the information."

California State University—Long Beach, Sports Information Bureau, 1250 Bellflower Blvd., Long Beach CA 90840. (213)498-4667. Sports Information Director: Terry Ross.
Purpose: "To gather and disseminate information on men's and women's intercollegiate sports at California State University—Long Beach. This includes media relations, hosting of athletic events and acting as an aid to the media who cover these events and our teams. We help in the promotion of intercollegiate athletics." Information covers sports.
Services: Offers aid in arranging interviews, biographies, statistics, brochures/pamphlets, information searches, placement on mailing list, newsletter, photos and press kits. Publications include media guides that contain records, rosters and biographical material on coaches and athletes.
How to Contact: Write or call. "Writers should be accredited media or freelance writers. We do charge for some brochures and photos if the person requesting is not, in our judgment, a legitimate writer or media person."

California State University—Northridge, Sports Information, 18111 Nordhoff St., Northridge CA 91330. (213)885-3243. Sports Information Director: Barry Zepel.
Purpose: "Publicity, public relations and promotion of California State University—Northridge sports teams. Records and statistics are also maintained."
Services: Offers aid in arranging interviews, statistics, brochures/pamphlets, placement on mailing list, newsletter, photos and press kits.
How to Contact: Write or call.

Duke University, Box BM, Durham NC 27706. (919)684-2633. Sports Information Director: Tom Mickle.
Purpose: Information covers entertainment, history, recreation and sports.
Services: Offers aid in arranging interviews, bibliographies, biographies, statistics, brochures/pamphlets, information searches, placement on mailing list, newsletter, photos and press kits.
How to Contact: Write or call.

Florida Technological University, Orlando FL 32816. (305)275-2256. Sports Information Director: Neil LaBar.
Purpose: "To give individuals a chance to compete in athletics. Our activities are concerned with providing information to the news media about our intercollegiate sports program." Information covers intercollegiate sports.
Services: Offers statistics, brochures/pamphlets, photos and press kits. Publications include press releases and press guides.
How to Contact: Write or call.
Tips: "We're not interested in writers that want information to be used for gambling purposes."

Georgetown University, McDonough Arena, Washington DC 20057. (202)625-4182. Sports Information Director: John Blake.
Purpose: "The sports information office provides any and all information concerning athletics at Georgetown University." Information covers celebrities, history, recreation and sports.
Services: Offers annual reports, statistics, brochures/pamphlets, placement on mailing list, newsletter, photos and press kits.
How to Contact: Write or call.

Georgia Institute of Technology, 190 3rd St., Atlanta GA 30332. (404)894-5445. Sports Information Director: Jim Schultz.
Purpose: "Our athletes compete in football, basketball, track, cross country, golf, swimming and wrestling; mens' and womens' basketball and volleyball. Starting in July, 1979, Georgia Tech will be in the Atlantic Coast Conference." Information covers sports.
Services: Offers aid in arranging interviews, bibliographies, biographies, statistics, brochures/pamphlets, information searches, placement on mailing list, newsletter, photos and press kits.
How to Contact: Write or call.

Indiana University at Bloomington, Department of Intercollegiate Athletics, Assembly Hall, Bloomington IN 47405. (812)337-4770. Women's Sports Information: Ann Bastianelli.
Purpose: "Women's sports (field hockey, volleyball, golf, tennis, track, cross county, gymnastics, softball, swimming and basketball). Member of the Big 10 Conference." Information covers sports.
Services: Offers aid in arranging interviews, annual reports, bibliographies, biographies, statistics, brochures/pamphlets, information searches, placement on mailing list, weekly newsletter, photos and press kits.
How to Contact: Write or call. "Give us as much time as possible—at least one week—to get the information needed."

Indiana University at Bloomington, Department of Intercollegiate Athletics, Assembly Hall, Bloomington IN 47405. (812)337-2421. Sports Information Director: Tom Miller.
Purpose: "Men's sports (football, basketball, soccer, swimming, track and field, cross country, golf, tennis, gymnastics, wrestling). Member of the Big 10 Conference." Information covers sports.
Services: Offers aid in arranging interviews, annual reports, bibliographies, biographies, statistics, brochures/pamphlets, information searches, placement on mailing list, newsletter, photos and press kits.
How to Contact: Write or call.

Louisiana State University, Drawer V, Baton Rouge LA 70893. (504)388-3202, 388-8226. Sports Information Office: Paul Mannasseh.
Purpose: "Men's and women's sports. Member of the Southeastern Conference." Information covers sports.
Services: Offers aid in arranging interviews, brochures/pamphlets, information searches, placement on mailing list and photos. Publications available.
How to Contact: Write. Charges for material distributed to the general public. Information free to sports writers.

Marquette University, Milwaukee WI 53222. (414)224-7700, 224-7447. Sports Information Director: Greg Sparaglia.
Purpose: Men's sports at Marquette include golf, cross country, soccer, basketball, wrestling, tennis, and track and field. Women's sports include volleyball, basketball,

tennis, cross country, and track and field. The women's athletic program is part of the Wisconsin Women's Intercollegiate Athletic Conference. The men's program is independent.

Services: Offers aid in arranging interviews, annual reports, biographies, statistics, brochures/pamphlets, information searches, placement on mailing list, newsletter, photos and press kits. Publications include a guide for each sport.

How to Contact: Write or call. Call (414)224-6980 for taped pre- and post-game interviews. May charge writers without credentials for basketball guide. "If your request is not for basketball, then make your request before or after basketball season; this is a one-man staff."

Marshall University, Box 1360, Huntington WV 27515. (304)696-3190. Sports Information Director: John Evenson.

Purpose: "Marshall University athletics includes 16 sports (10 for men, 6 for women). Marshall is a member of the NCAA's Division 1-A, along with major colleges and universities across the country. The sports information office deals with any type of information involving the school's athletic teams. Marshall's office of university relations handles informational needs and inquiries about the university in general." Information covers sports.

Services: Offers aid in arranging interviews, biographies, statistics, brochures/ pamphlets, clipping services, information searches, placement on mailing list, newsletter, photos, press kits, video and audio clips, chroma-keyed TV slides and features. Publications include *Marshall's Football Media Guide*, available August 1 each year, and *Marshall's Basketball Media Guide*, available November 1 each year.

How to Contact: Write or call.

This photo by Norm Schindler demonstrates the form of a collegiate javelin champion, says Michael Sondheimer, public relations director of UCLA's department of women's athletics. "This is typical of our photos in all 11 of our women's sports. We also have mug shots of most of our athletes." Photos are usually provided free to writers, though a charge might be made for a rush print. Like most people who supply photos to writers, Sondheimer asks for time to fill requests. "Call a couple of weeks in advance of needing the picture so we can get it printed and sent in time," he says.

North Texas State University, NT Station, Denton TX 76203. (817)788-2521. Sports News Director: Fred Graham.
Purpose: Information covers sports.
Services: Offers aid in arranging interviews, statistics, brochures/pamphlets, information searches, placement on mailing list and photos.
How to Contact: Write or call.

Northwestern University, 1501 Central St., Evanston IL 60201. (312)492-7503. Director of Sports Information: Jim Vruggink.
Purpose: Men's sports include football, basketball, baseball, tennis, wrestling, swimming, cross country, fencing and golf. Member of the Big 10 Athletic Conference. Women's sports include swimming, field hockey, volleyball, indoor and outdoor track, tennis, softball, basketball and cross country.
Services: Offers aid in arranging interviews, annual reports, bibliographies, biographies, statistics, brochures/pamphlets, clipping services, information searches, placement on mailing list, newsletter, photos and press kits. Publications include media guides.
How to Contact: Write or call. Preference given to queries written on business letterhead. May charge for some material, especially if writer is not accredited. Allow at least one month lead time for queries

Ohio State University, Sports Information Office, 410 W. Woodruff, Department of Athletics, 237 St. John Arena, Columbus OH (614)422-6861. Sports Information Director: Marvin Homan.
Purpose: Information covers sports.
Services: Offers aid in arranging interviews, biographies, brochures/pamphlets, statistics, information searches, placement on mailing list, newsletter and photos.
How to Contact: Write or call.

Ohio University, Sports Information Office, 103 Convocation Center, Richland Ave., Athens OH 45701. (614)594-5031. Sports Information Director: Frank Morgan.
Purpose: "Beyond the purpose of educating young men and women, I specifically handle all athletic publicity (weekly releases, brochures, photos, radio tapes and TV slides) for the Ohio University athletic department." Information covers sports.
Services: Offers aid in arranging interviews, biographies, statistics, brochures/pamphlets, information searches, placement on mailing list, newsletter, photos and press kits. Publications include brochures on football, basketball, baseball, wrestling, golf, tennis, track and swimming.
How to Contact: "Write or call with specific request. Give us ample time to fill the request. The end of fall (when fall and winter sports overlap) is my busiest time; ditto for winter to spring. Enclosing a self-addressed, stamped envelope gets prompt attention, as will a phone call (if it's a deadline matter) and an offer to accept a collect call from us with the requested information."

Oklahoma State University, Sports Information Office, Room 202, Gallagher Hall, Stillwater OK 74074. (405)624-5749. Assistant Sports Information Director: Tim Allen.
Purpose: "To aid media coverage of Oklahoma State University intercollegiate athletics." Information covers sports.
Services: Offers aid in arranging interviews, statistics, brochures/pamphlets, newsletter and photos. "Brochures covering all intercollegiate sports at Oklahoma State University are available to media."
How to Contact: Write on company letterhead. "There is a charge for telecopier and computer (VDT) transmission of data. Research is done by request but student workers are expected to be paid for work done for a profitmaking project (i.e., books)."

Oregon State University, Athletic Department, 103 Gill Coliseum, Corvallis OR 97331. (503)754-2611, 754-3720. Public Relations and Promotions Director: Hal Cowan.
Purpose: Intercollegiate athletics. Information covers entertainment and sports.
Services: Offers aid in arranging interviews, annual reports, biographies, statistics, brochures/pamphlets, newsletter, photos and press kits. Publications include press books on all sports for both men and women.
How.to Contact: Write or call. "All interviews must be cleared through the sports information office."

Pennsylvania State University, 206 Recreation Bldg., University Park PA 16802. (814)865-1757. Contact: Sports Information.
Purpose: "Independent varsity sports program. Sports for women include basketball, bowling, cross country, fencing, field hockey, golf, gymnastics, lacrosse, softball, swimming, volleyball, tennis, indoor track, and outdoor track. Men's sports include baseball, basketball, bowling, cross country, fencing, football, golf, gymnastics, lacrosse, soccer, swimming, tennis, indoor track, outdoor track, volleyball and wrestling." Information covers sports.
Services: Offers aid in arranging interviews, statistics, information searches, placement on mailing list, newsletter, photos and guides on each sport.
How to Contact: Write or call. "You must have credentials to qualify for our mailing list. To arrange interviews, contact John Morris."

Purdue University, Sports Information Office, Mackey Arena, Purdue University, West Lafayette IN 47907. (317)494-8561. Sports Information Director: Tom Shupe.
Purpose: "We have varsity and nonvarsity sports and coed sports." Information covers sports.
Services: Offers aid in arranging interviews, brochures/pamphlets, information searches, placement on mailing list, statistics, newsletter, photos and press kits. Publications include media guides.
How to Contact: Write or call.

Saint Louis University, Sports Information Department, 3672 W. Pine, St. Louis MO 63108. (314)658-3180, 658-3187. Sports Information Director: Dick O'Connor.
Purpose: "We handle the publicity for Saint Louis University's intercollegiate athletic teams. We cover team records and rosters and supply photos for sports reporters, opponents, fans and anyone else who's interested in the teams." Men's sports include basketball, soccer, hockey, cross country, track and field, baseball, tennis, golf and swimming. Women's sports include field hockey, volleyball, basketball, swimming, tennis, softball, track and field, and cross country. Information covers sports.
Services: Offers aid in arranging interviews, biographies, statistics, brochures/pamphlets, placement on mailing list, photos, press releases, feature stories and general information. Publications include press guides on Saint Louis University's intercollegiate varsity teams.
How to Contact: Write or call.

San Diego State University, San Diego CA 92182. (714)286-5547. Sports Information Director: Bruce Herman.
Purpose: "Publicity of all goings-on of the athletic department. We handle all media requests and compile press guides, game programs and other printed material, such as weekly press release updates of athletic events." Information covers sports.
Services: Offers aid in arranging interviews, annual reports, biographies, statistics, brochures/pamphlets, information searches, placement on mailing list, newsletter, photos and press kits. Publications include media guides on all sports conducted at San Diego State University.
How to Contact: "We handle a high-volume workload, so please make all requests well in advance, in writing."

San Francisco State University, Athletic Department, 1600 Holloway Ave., San Francisco CA 94132. (415)469-1579. Sports Information Director: Dirk W. Smith.
Purpose: "Publicity, promotion and press releases concerning San Francisco State University sports. Publicity covers all varsity squads and information is available on past years. Press passes for all games are also secured through this office." Information covers sports.
Services: Offers aid in arranging interviews, bibliographies, biographies, statistics, brochures/pamphlets and placement on mailing list. "Press and media guides are available."
How to Contact: Write or call.

Southwest Texas State University, Towers Center, San Marcos TX 78666. (512)245-2263. Sports Information Director: Gordon McCullough.
Purpose: "Sports Information office for the university's intercollegiate athletic programs."
Services: Offers aid in arranging interviews, statistics, brochures/pamphlets, placement on mailing list ("where merited") and photos.
How to Contact: Write or call.

Stanford University, Department of Athletics Publicity Office, c/o Department of Athletics, Stanford CA 94305. (415)497-4418. Director of Sports Publicity Promotion: Gary Cavalli.
Purpose: "Information service and publicity for Stanford University's 22 varsity intercollegiate sports, ranging from football to field hockey."
Services: Offers aid in arranging interviews, biographies, statistics, brochures/pamphlets, placement on mailing list and photos. Publications include press brochures on all 22 sports, including football, basketball, baseball, tennis and swimming.
How to Contact: Write or call. "Only sports writers and broadcasters need apply for the press materials sent weekly."

State University at Buffalo, Sports Information Office, 136 Crofts Bldg., Amherst NY 14260. (716)636-2626. Director: Larry G. Steele.
Purpose: "To disseminate information on intercollegiate athletic teams through the publication of news releases, schedules and brochures."
Services: Offers aid in arranging interviews, annual reports, biographies, statistics, brochures/pamphlets, placement on mailing list, photos and press kits. Publications include Men's Intercollegiate All-Sports and Women's Intercollegiate All-Sports brochures, schedules and roster information. Also publishes schedules, brochures, rosters, records, biographies and information on these varsity sports: football, soccer, baseball, basketball and wrestling.
How to Contact: Write or call. "Writers may receive one copy of the material, with exceptions."

State University of New York at Albany, News Bureau, AD 263, 1400 Washington Ave., Albany NY 12222. (518)457-4901. Sports Information Director: Gary Swatling.
Purpose: "To provide written and broadcast media information on university personnel, including staff, faculty and students. My emphasis is sports information concerning Albany State's intercollegiate teams, individual coaches and participants."
Services: Offers aid in arranging interviews, statistics, brochures/pamphlets, placement on mailing list, newsletter and photos. "Some individual sports pamphlets are available; however, most brochures are of a more general level, such as a winter sports press guide."
How to Contact: "Contact the office by mail or phone Monday through Friday, 8:30 a.m. to 5 p.m. We can provide more information at lower cost and with fastest results if the initial contact is by phone."

Syracuse University, Women's Athletic Department, 820 Comstock Ave., Syracuse NY 13210. (315)423-2508. Sports Information Director: Barbara Jacobs.
Purpose: "The women's athletic department supports a program of intercollegiate competition in tennis, field hockey, volleyball, basketball, swimming/diving and crew." Information covers entertainment and sports.
Services: Offers aid in arranging interviews, statistics, brochures/pamphlets, placement on mailing list, photos and press kits. Publications include an annual program brochure and individual press guides for each sport.
How to Contact: Write or call. "Making an appointment in advance would be helpful. We can arrange personal appointments with coaches and/or top players."

Texas A&M University, Sports Information Office, College Station TX 77843. (713)845-5725. Sports Information Director: Spec Gammon.
Purpose: "To supply information on Texas A&M intercollegiate athletics to news media."
Services: Offers aid in arranging interviews, statistics, brochures/pamphlets, placement on mailing list, newsletter, photos and press kits. Publications include press guides on football, basketball, baseball, golf, tennis, track and swimming.
How to Contact: Write or call. "To nonmedia, we charge for guides and offer paid subscriptions to our weekly press releases."

University of Colorado at Boulder, Field House Annex #53, Boulder CO 80309. (303)472-1818, 472-2313. Sports Information Director: Hal Bateman.
Purpose: Sports include football, basketball (men's and women's), ice hockey, cross country (men's and women's), gymnastics (men's and women's), indoor track (men's and women's), pistol (men's and women's), riflery (men's and women's), baseball, golf (men's and women's), lacrosse, tennis (men's and women's), outdoor track (men's and women's), volleyball (women only) and wrestling.
Services: Offers aid in arranging interviews, annual reports, bibliographies, biographies, statistics, brochures/pamphlets, placement on mailing list and photos.
How to Contact: Write or call. Allow adequate lead time for information searches.

University of Alabama, Department of Athletics, Box K, University AL 35486. (205)348-6084. Sports Information Director: Kirk McNair.
Purpose: "Information on all coaches and athletes in intercollegiate competition. We also issue press credentials for coverage of athletic events at the University of Alabama."
Services: Offers aid in arranging interviews, biographies, statistics, brochures/pamphlets, placement on mailing list and photos. "Brochures are available on all men's intercollegiate athletics—football, basketball, swimming, wrestling, track and field, baseball, golf and tennis. In the event of our participation in a football bowl, we publish a special brochure. Women's sports brochures are also available."
How to Contact: Write.
Tips: "Credentials are normally issued only to sports reporters on daily newspapers or national publications. Others wishing credentials should specify the reason."

University of Arkansas, Sports Information Office, N. End Zone Bldg., Fayetteville AR 72701. (501)575-2751. Sports Information Director: Butch Henry.
Purpose: "To serve as media and public contact for all intercollegiate activities of men's athletics."
Services: Offers aid in arranging interviews, annual reports, biographies, statistics, brochures/pamphlets, clipping services, information searches, placement on mailing list, newsletter, photos, press kits, and films.
How to Contact: Write or call.

University of California at Berkeley, Women's Athletics, 100 Heosst Gym, Berkeley CA 94720. (415)642-2098. Sports Information Director: Chris Dawson.

Purpose: "Women's basketball, cross country, field hockey, gymnastics, softball, swimming and diving, tennis, track and field, volleyball, badminton (coed) and fencing (coed). We are members of the Northern California Athletic Conference, Western Association for Intercollegiate Women and Association for Intercollegiate Athletics for Women." Information covers sports.
Services: Offers aid in arranging interviews, annual reports, biographies, brochures/pamphlets, information searches, placement on mailing list, statistics, newsletter and photos (limited). "We also have feature stories on some athletes."
How to Contact: Write or call. "Make requests one or two weeks before material is needed."

University of California at Berkeley, Men's Athletics, 61 Harmon Gym, Berkeley CA 94720. (415)642-5363. Public Relations Director: John McCasey.
Purpose: "Men's football, baseball, basketball, gymnastics, golf, swimming, tennis, track and field, wrestling, water polo, rugby, soccer and volleyball. Member of the Pacific 10 Conference." Information covers men's sports.
Services: Offers aid in arranging interviews, annual reports, biographies, brochures/pamphlets, information searches, placement on mailing list, statistics, newsletter and photos.
How to Contact: Write or call. "For credentials to an event, put in your request at least one week in advance."

University of California at Los Angeles, Athletic News Bureau, 405 Hilgard Ave., West Los Angeles CA 90024. (213)825-3732. Manager: Dick Kelley.
Purpose: "We are part of the NCAA and the Pacific-10 Athletic Conference. We have 18 intercollegiate sports." Information covers sports.
Services: Offers aid in arranging interviews, bibliographies, biographies, brochures/pamphlets, information searches, statistics, newsletter and photos.
How to Contact: Write or call. "It is best to write and have your letter on file."

University of California at Los Angeles, Women's Athletics, 405 Hilgard Ave., Los Angeles CA 90024. (213)825-9541. Public Relations/Promotions Director: Michael Sondheimer.
Purpose: "We have 11 intercollegiate sports for women athletes, who compete around the country. Several athletes are on scholarships and most have won many honors before entering UCLA. We have had the top all-around women's athletic program in the country for 1976-1977 and 1977-1978. Basketball is the big sport in women's athletics, and UCLA is the defending national champion. We are trying to encourage as many people as possible to see our events." Information covers business, entertainment, recreation and sports.
Services: Offers aid in arranging interviews, biographies, statistics, brochures/pamphlets, placement on mailing list, newsletter, photos and press kits. Publications include "a 36-page departmental brochure with information on all 11 sports and other data on UCLA women's athletics; press guides in basketball, volleyball and other sports; schedule cards in most sports; and informational releases and press data."
How to Contact: Write or call. "Each case will be reviewed individually to determine needs."

University of Colorado at Boulder, Field House Annex #53, Boulder CO 80309. (303)492-6128. Contact: Sports Information Director.
Purpose: The men's athletic program is part of the Big 8 Athletic Conference and includes football, basketball, baseball, tennis, golf, wrestling, gymnastics, swimming, cross country and skiing. Women's sports include swimming, gymnastics, skiing, tennis, track, cross country and basketball.
Services: Offers aid in arranging interviews, bibliographies, biographies, statistics, brochures/pamphlets, information searches, placement on mailing list, newsletter and photos. Publications include press guides on men's football and basketball and

women's basketball. Information sheets available on all players.
How to Contact: Write. Credentials needed to cover games; request permission on media letterhead.

University of Connecticut, U-78, Storrs CT 06268. (203)486-3531. Sports Information Director: Joseph J. Soltys.
Purpose: "Sports information related to college sports."
Services: Offers aid in arranging interviews, statistics, brochures/pamphlets, placement on mailing list, photos and press kits. Publications include brochures on football, basketball, baseball, hockey and track.
How to Contact: "Send request by mail on stationery of recognized media."

University of Florida, Box 14485, Gainesville FL 32604. (904)392-3261, 392-0641. Sports Information Director: Norm Carlson.
Purpose: Men's sports include football, basketball, track, baseball, tennis, golf, wrestling, swimming and cross country; men's program is part of the Southeastern Athletic Conference. Women's sports include basketball, track, cross country, softball, gymnastics, volleyball, swimming and tennis.
Services: Offers aid in arranging interviews, bibliographies, biographies, statistics, brochures/pamphlets, information searches, placement on mailing list, newsletter and photos. Publications include media guides to individual sports, *Gator Tales* (periodical) and general information material.
How to Contact: Write or call.

University of Kentucky, Memorial Coliseum, Lexington KY 40506. (606)257-3838. Sports Information Director: Russell Rice.
Purpose: Men's sports program, part of the Southeastern Athletic Conference, includes basketball, football, track, baseball, cross country, water polo, swimming, golf, track and field, and riflery. Women's sports include basketball, gymnastics, volleyball, track and cross country.
Services: Offers aid in arranging interviews, biographies, statistics, brochures/pamphlets, information searches, placement on mailing list, newsletter and photos. Publications include yearbooks on men's football and basketball and women's basketball, and media guides.
How to Contact: Write. May charge writers without credentials.

University of Louisville, Sports Information Office, Belknap Campus, Louisville KY 40208. (502)588-6581. Sports Information Director: Joe Yates.
Purpose: "To promote intercollegiate athletics at the University of Louisville."
Services: Offers aid in arranging interviews, biographies, statistics, brochures/pamphlets, information searches, placement on mailing list, newsletter, photos and press kits. "We supply all statistical information and brochures on all men's and women's sports at the University of Louisville."
How to Contact: Write on company letterhead or call. "Please notify our office of your needs in advance, as last-minute requests cannot always be fulfilled."

University of Maryland, Athletic Department, Box 295, College Park MD 20740. (301)454-2123. Sports Information Director: John W. "Jack" Zane.
Purpose: "Information service for University of Maryland intercollegiate athletics, associated with the Atlantic Coast Conference and NCAA."
Services: Offers aid in arranging interviews, biographies, statistics, brochures/pamphlets and photos. Publications include brochures on 23 teams for men's and women's sports.
How to Contact: Write or call.
Tips: "Writers and photographers on assignment get preference. Freelance writing or shooting on speculation will be judged on merit."

University of Michigan, 1000 S. State St., Ann Arbor MI 48109. (313)663-2411. Contact: Sports Information Director.
Purpose: Men's football program, part of the Big 10 Athletic Conference, includes football, basketball, baseball, track (indoor and outdoor), cross-country, wrestling, swimming, diving, tennis, golf, gymnastics and ice hockey. Women's sports include field hockey, volleyball, tennis, golf, basketball, softball, swimming and diving, synchronized swimming, gymnastics and track.
Services: Offers aid in arranging interviews, bibliographies, biographies, statistics, brochures/pamphlets, information searches and photos. Publications include press guides for all sports.
How to Contact: Write or call.

University of Missouri—Columbia, 321 Hearnes Bldg., Columbia MO 65205. (314)882-6501. Sports Information Supervisor: Dru Ann Hancock.
Purpose: "To handle publicity and promotion for eight women's intercollegiate sports, including media guides, statistics, photos and newspaper coverage."
Services: Offers aid in arranging interviews, statistics, brochures/pamphlets, newsletter, photos and press kits.
How to Contact: Write or call.

University of Nebraska, 116 S. Stadium, Lincoln NE 68588. (402)472-2263. Sports Information Director: Mr. Bryant. Assistant Director: Bill Bennett.
Purpose: Men's program is part of the Big 8 Athletic Conference. Men's sports include football, basketball, swimming, wrestling, gymnastics, baseball, tennis, golf, cross country and indoor and outdoor track. Women's sports include volleyball, basketball, gymnastics, swimming, softball, golf, track, cross country and tennis.
Services: Offers aid in arranging interviews, annual reports, bibliographies, biographies, statistics, brochures/pamphlets, information searches, placement on mailing list, newsletter, photos and press kits.
How to Contact: Write or call. Credentials required.

University of New Hampshire, Women's Sports Information, 223 Field House, Durham NH 03824. (603)862-1822. Sports Information Director: Laurel A. Milos.
Purpose: "We operate one of the finest women's athletic programs in the Northeast, with regionally and nationally prominent teams in 12 sports. In addition to standard promotion of our teams and athletes, our staff periodically releases photo-essays and general interest articles on women in sports." Information covers recreation, sports and women.
Services: Offers aid in arranging interviews, statistics, brochures/pamphlets, placement on mailing list, newsletter and photos.
How to Contact: Write or call.

University of New Mexico, Sports Information, Women's Athletics, Carlisle Gym, Albuquerque NM 87131. (505)277-2338. Director: Susan Craig.
Purpose: "We are responsible for promotion and publicity of all nine women's sports sponsored and funded by the University of New Mexico."
Services: Offers aid in arranging interviews, annual reports, statistics, brochures/pamphlets and photos. Publications include a program brochure on all women's sports and sports brochures on each sport individually.
How to Contact: Write.

University of North Carolina at Chapel Hill, Sports Information Office, Box 2126, Chapel Hill NC 27514. (919)933-2123, 933-1376. Sports Information Director: Rick Brewer. Assistant: Karen Croake.
Purpose: Men's program and some women's sports are part of the Atlantic Coast Athletic Conference. Men's sports include football, basketball, baseball, tennis, golf,

wrestling, gymnastics, swimming, cross country, soccer, fencing and lacrosse. Women's sports include basketball, tennis, swimming, field hockey, golf, cross country, indoor track, gymnastics, basketball, fencing, softball, outdoor track and volleyball.

Services: Offers aid in arranging interviews, annual reports, bibliographies, biographies, statistics, brochures/pamphlets, information searches, placement on mailing list and photos. Football and basketball telecopier service available. Publications include media guides for individual sports.

How to Contact: Write or call. Write for credentials to cover sporting events. Charges for telecopier services.

University of Notre Dame, Notre Dame IN 46556. (219)283-7516. Sports Information Director: Roger O. Valdiserri.

Purpose: Sports include football, basketball, track, baseball, tennis, golf, wrestling, swimming, cross country, ice hockey, fencing, lacrosse and soccer.

Services: Offers aid in arranging interviews, annual reports, biographies, statistics, brochures/pamphlets, information searches, placement on mailing list, photos and press kits. Publications include media guides on individual sports.

How to Contact: Write or call. Press credential requests should be in writing.

University of Oklahoma, 900 ASP, Room 500, Norman OK 73019. (405)325-3751. Contact: Sports Information Director (men's sports). Women's Sports Information.

Purpose: Men's athletic program is part of the Big 8 Athletic Conference. Men's sports include football, basketball, baseball, wrestling, tennis, golf, track, cross country and swimming. Women's sports include volleyball, golf, tennis, basketball, swimming, indoor and outdoor track, cross country and softball.

Services: Offers aid in arranging interviews, annual reports, bibliographies, biographies, statistics, brochures/pamphlets, clipping services, information searches, placement on mailing list, newsletter and photos. Publications include 124-page preseason football booklet, bowl game brochure, spring football prospectus, basketball brochure and publications for other sports.

How to Contact: Write. Allow adequate lead time during football season.

University of Oregon, Sports Information, McArthur Court, Eugene OR 97403. (503)686-5494. Sports Information Director: George Beres. Assistant Sports Information Director, Women's Athletics: Janet Heinonen.

Purpose: "To publicize and disseminate information about the University of Oregon athletic teams."

Services: Offers aid in arranging interviews, biographies, statistics, brochures/pamphlets, placement on mailing list, newsletter and photos. Publications include brochures on all varsity sports.

How to Contact: Write or call. Charges for archival photos.

University of Pittsburgh, Box 7436, Pittsburgh PA 15213. (412)624-4588. Contact: Sports Information Office.

Purpose: Men's sports include football, basketball, baseball, cross country, golf, gymnastics, soccer, swimming, tennis, track and field, water polo and wrestling. Women's sports include basketball, cross country, field hockey, track and field, volleyball, gymnastics, swimming and tennis.

Services: Offers information searches and press kits. Publications include brochures for individual sports.

How to Contact: Write or call. For interviews, contact individual coaches. Charges for most materials.

University of Southern California (USC), University Park, Los Angeles CA 90007. Men's Sports: (213)741-2224. Sports Information Director: Jim Perry. Women's Sports: (213)741-7693, 741-7770. Women's Sports Information Director: Becky Kummerfeld.

Purpose: Men's athletic program is part of the Pacific 10 Conference. Men's sports include football, baseball, track, crew, gymnastics, sailing, basketball, tennis, golf and cross country. Women's sports include volleyball, basketball, swimming, gymnastics, track and field, cross country, tennis and golf.
Services: Offers aid in arranging interviews, annual reports, bibliographies, biographies, statistics, brochures/pamphlets, information searches, placement on mailing list, photos and press kits. Publications include media guides for individual sports and men's sports yearbook.
How to Contact: Write or call. Men's sports information office prefers first contact in writing.

University of Southwestern Louisiana, Sports Information, Box 44050, University of Southwestern Louisiana, Lafayette LA 70504. (318)264-6331. Director of Sports Information: George Foster.
Purpose: "To disseminate information and neutralize hostile opinion on the University of Southwestern Louisiana (USL) athletic department." Information covers sports.
Services: Offers aid in arranging interviews, biographies, statistics, brochures/pamphlets, placement on mailing list, newsletter, photos and press kits. Publications include brochures and programs in 7 Division I sports.
How to Contact: "Make request on company letterhead." Charges "only for publications for persons or organizations that are not deemed professional."

University of Tennessee at Chattanooga, 5th and Lansing Sts., Chattanooga TN 37402. (615)755-4148. Sports Information Director: Jim Bell. Assistant Sports Information Director: Gary Wanat.
Purpose: Men's program is part of the Southern Athletic Conference. Sports include football, basketball, wrestling, golf, tennis, track, cross country, baseball and riflery. Women's sports include volleyball, basketball and tennis.
Services: Offers aid in arranging interviews, biographies, statistics, brochures/pamphlets, information searches, placement on mailing list, newsletter, photos and press kits. Publications include yearbooks and media guides in individual sports.
How to Contact: Write or call.

University of Texas at Arlington, Athletic Department, Arlington TX 76019. (817)273-2261. Sports Information Director: Jim Patterson.
Purpose: "To provide sports information for the university." Information covers sports.
Services: Offers aid in arranging interviews, statistics, brochures/pamphlets, placement on mailing list, photos, and press kits. Publications available.
How to Contact: Write or call.

The University of Toledo, 2801 W. Bancroft, Toledo OH 43606. (419)537-2675. Sports Information Director: Max E. Gerber.
Purpose: Education and sports.
Services: Offers aid in arranging interviews, biographies, brochures/pamphlets, placement on mailing list and newsletter.
How to Contact: Write or call. Charges "persons not on a newspaper or with a radio or TV station. Service restricted to press-radio-TV only on a non-fee basis. Photos, brochures, etc. supplied to others only on a cost basis."

University of Virginia, Sports Information, Box 3785, University Hall, Charlottesville VA 22901. (804)924-3011. Sports Information Director: Todd Turner.
Purpose: "To promote and publicize all 20 intercollegiate sports at the University of Virginia."
Services: Offers aid in arranging interviews, statistics, brochures/pamphlets, information searches and photos. Publications include brochures and pamphlets.

How to Contact: Write or call. Charge "depends upon cost of services provided—usually no charge."

Wright State University, Dayton OH 45435. (513)873-2771. Sports Information Director: David Stahl. Assistant Sports Information Director: Steve Kelly.
Purpose: "To promote and publicize the athletic programs at Wright State University under the department of intercollegiate athletics."
Services: Offers aid in arranging interviews, annual reports, biographies, statistics, brochures/pamphlets, placement on mailing list and photos. "We print brochures for all 13 varsity sports, plus a basketball program for 17 home games."
How to Contact: Write or call.

Data Bases

"New computer data bases enable you to find out quickly what's been written about just about anything." So claims FIND/SVP, an information and research service.

A representative of System Development Corporation Search Service talks about data bases in the same way: "Tremendous time savings can result from beginning the research of any topic via online bibliographic searching. Studies indicate that not only can references be identified in less than half the time, but also that more information can be located."

You'd expect these firms to talk enthusiastically about data bases; they're commercial enterprises that make a business of conducting computer searches. Independent viewers, however, also have praise for computer data banks. "Extensive research in many contemporary fields of interest can be simplified by using the frowing number of computer banks located across the country," says writer John Rothrock. "Computers can now supply researchers with information at moderate cost that an individual could not possibly locate by other means without taking a year or more to do it."

Computer data banks are generally bibliographic in nature; that is, the banks will supply you with a list of articles, books, abstracts, etc. that pertain to the subject you're researching. You must track down the actual materials yourself, but, as Rothrock points out, the time spent in discovering the existence of the materials in the first place is greatly reduced. Some data banks can supply abstracts (brief descriptions) of the materials to which they refer you, though most simply supply the references.

Consulting a data bank is more complex than using a vending machine; you don't drop in a coin and expect a list of references to drop into your lap. A data bank is also more expensive than a vending machine. The cost for a computer search varies widely from the searches that are free of charge to those that cost $50 or more for each hour of computer time used in the search. See "Paying for Research" for a more detailed rundown of the craft of consulting data banks, and of potential costs of doing a computer search.

A computer search for information yields more than a computer printout filled with leads; it also yields peace of mind. By consulting a data base, "a researcher can be more confident that he or she has not overlooked any important citations," says Roger W. Christian in listing the advantages of data bases in his book, *The Electronic Library*.

Data bases, of course, have their disadvantages—cost and accessibility, among them—so the writer/researcher must weigh the disadvantages against the advantages when determining the efficiency and worth of consulting a data base.

Some of the firms listed here are separate data bases; others can tie into a number of individual bases. (FIND/SVP has access to more than 115 bases.) A unique system is that of the Educational Resources Information Center (ERIC), operated by the National Institute of Education of the Department of Health, Education and Welfare. A service to educators in the US, ERIC is a system of clearinghouses—16 in all—which collate massive amounts of educational documents, journal annotations and other materials on many specialized educational topics. Decentralized by virtue of their locations and the unique specialties which each handles, the ERIC clearinghouses are bound by a centralized computer facility, which enables ERIC facilities to handle the reproduction and distribution of material throughout the world. For information about the material available at any of the ERIC clearinghouses, consult the ERIC entries included in this category.

The *Electronic Library* (Knowledge Industry Publications) contains information about additional bases, as does *Information Sources* (membership directory of the Information Industry Association, 4720 Montgomery Lane, Suite 904, Bethesda, Maryland 20014). The *Electronic Library* also covers specific uses of data bases.

Capital Systems Group, Inc. (CSG), 6110 Executive Blvd., Rockville MD 20852. (301)881-9400. President: William A. Creuger.
Purpose: "A technically oriented information services firm, CSG can serve writers in the following ways: library research and information gathering, automated literature searching, and finding and delivering desired documents." Information covers agriculture, business, food, health/medicine, science and technical data.
Services: Offers bibliographies, statistics, information searches and document delivery. Publications include a description of CSG's information research services, and a fee schedule.
How to Contact: "Call or write for a preliminary consultation, for which there is no charge."

Central Abstracting & Indexing Service, American Petroleum Institute, 275 Madison Ave., New York NY 10016. (212)685-6254. Assistant Manager: Irving Zarember.
Purpose: "Our department monitors technical journals and business news publications of importance to the petroleum industry to call attention to pertinent new developments, and to create an archival index to the information in these publications." Information covers technical data and news related to petroleum and energy.
Services: Offers information searches.
How to Contact: Write Clara Martinex, American Petroleum Institute. Charges $150/information search.

Congressional Information Service, Inc. (CIS), 7101 Wisconsin Ave., Suite 900, Washington DC 20014. (301)654-1500. Publicity Director: Richard K. Johnson.
Purpose: "Congressional Information Service is the leading commercial indexer, abstracter and micropublisher of government publications. Our indexes to federal statistical publications and Congressional publications are available in most major libraries. In addition, many libraries subscribe to our microfiche reproductions of publications identified in the indexes. The microfiche are also available individually 'on demand' from CIS." Information covers agriculture, business, economics, health/medicine, history, industry, law, politics and science.
Services: Offers bibliographies and microfiche reproductions of Congressional publications and Federal statistical publications. Publications include *DocKit* (instructions for ordering individual microfiche from CIS); *CIS Catalog* (a complete listing of our indexes and abstracts, outline data bases, microforms, and special publications and services), *Periodicals and Sources: A List of Federal Statistical Periodicals and Their Issuing Sources*; *CIS/Index User Handbook* (instructions on how to research Congressional publications) and *ASI User Handbook* (instructions on how to research federal statistical publications).
How to Contact: "Visit a major academic or public library which subscribes. Our customers are libraries and information centers. Individual researchers pay only when they choose to order microfiche reproductions of publications identified in our indexes. They also have the option of obtaining the original printed version from the government, or of using the documents collection of their library. CIS *does not* provide custom research services."

Data Courier, Inc., 620 S. 5th St., Louisville KY 40202. (502)582-4111.
Purpose: "To produce abstracting and indexing services for science, technology and business/management, available as printed journals, on-line access and magnetic tape leasing." Information covers business, health/medicine, science and technical data.
Services: Offers "information services by calendar-year subscription; magnetic tape leasing of data bases." Publications include catalog of services.
How to Contact: Write or call, and request a catalog.

Engineering Index, Inc., 345 E. 47th St., New York NY 10017. (212)644-7881. Communications Coordinator: Nancy F. Hardy.
Purpose: "Engineering Index, Inc., is a nonprofit organization recognized as the leading international publisher of multidisciplinary engineering bibliographic information." Information covers agricultural engineering, food technology and technical data.
Services: Offers bibliographies, brochures/pamphlets and newsletter.
How to Contact: Write or call.

ERIC Clearinghouse on Adult, Career and Vocational Education (CE), Ohio State University, 1960 Kenny Rd., Columbus OH 43210. (614)486-3655. Director: Dr. Peterson. Senior Research Specialist: Wes Budke.
Purpose: "ERIC (Educational Resources Information Center) is a national information system that obtains and makes available hard-to-find information in all areas of education." One of 16 such facilities in the US, this clearinghouse serves these areas: "adult and continuing education, career education and vocational and technical education. Within these areas, professional staff review periodicals and documents on exemplary programs, research and development efforts, instruction, personnel preparation, and related educational activities."
Services: Offers bibliographies and information searches. Publications include research reports, position papers, speeches, evaluation studies, curriculum materials and conference proceedings.
How to Contact: Write or call. Will respond to individual inquiries by mail or telephone and will refer researcher to additional information sources. Charges $25/computer search of the data base, plus searching time and printing of abstracts off-line.

ERIC Clearinghouse on Counseling and Personnel Services (CaPS), 2108 School of Education, University of Michigan, Ann Arbor MI 48109. (313)764-9492. Senior Information Specialist: Helen Mamarchev.
Purpose: "ERIC (Educational Resources Information Center) is a national information system which obtains and makes available hard-to-find, often unpublished information in all areas of education." Information covers the preparation, practice and supervision of counselors at all educational levels and in all settings.
Services: Offers aid in arranging interviews, bibliographies, statistics, brochures/pamphlets, information searches, placement on mailing list and newsletter. Publications include the counselor renewal series, the new vistas in counseling series, monographs and publications list.
How to Contact: Write, call or visit.

ERIC Clearinghouse on Early Childhood Education (ECE), 805 W. Pennsylvania Ave., Urbana IL 61801. (217)333-1386.
Purpose: "ERIC (Educational Resources Information Center) is a national information system which obtains and makes available hard-to-find, often unpublished information in all areas of education." Collects documents relating to all aspects of the development and education of children to 12 years of age, excluding special elementary school curriculum areas. Information covers prenatal and infant development and care; preschool and day care programs; and related community services at the local, state and federal levels.

Services: Offers bibliographies, statistics, brochures/pamphlets, information searches, newsletter, resource lists, microfiche abstracts, indexes and library (no lending). Publications include a day care legal handbook, a bibliography on fathering, research reviews and the *ERIC/ECE Newsletter*.
How to Contact: "Requests must be very specific. Call or write ahead as far as possible and indicate specific hours between 8 a.m. to 5 p.m. weekdays when you can come in." Charges for information searches; $3/year for newsletter subscription.

ERIC Clearinghouse on Educational Management (EA), University of Oregon, Eugene OR 97403. (503)686-5043. Director: Dr. Philip Piele.
Purpose: "ERIC (Educational Resources Information Center) is a national information system which obtains and makes available hard-to-find, often unpublished information in all areas of education." This clearinghouse monitors, acquires and processes information on educational management.
Services: Offers aid in arranging interviews, annual reports, bibliographies, statistics, brochures/pamphlets, information searches, placement on mailing list, newsletter, and reproduction on microfiche or paper of most reports. Publications include thesaurus, *Best of ERIC* (monthly), *School Management Digest, Resources iln Education* (monthly), and *Current Index to Journals in Education*.
How to Contact: Write, call or visit. "Be specific in your request." Charges for information search.

ERIC Clearinghouse on Handicapped and Gifted Children (EC), CEC Information Center, Council for Exceptional Children, 1920 Association Dr., Reston VA 22091. (703)620-3660. Assistant Director: Joyce Aegerter.
Purpose: "ERIC (Educational Resources Information Center) is a national information system which makes available hard-to-find, often unpublished information in all areas of education." Processes information and conducts computer searches "on the education of children and youth deemed exceptional."
Services: Offers bibliographies, brochures/pamphlets and information searches. Will refer researchers to other ERIC clearinghouses or agencies if needed. Library and microfiche collection are available for use. Publications include information packets and a fact sheet of little-known information.
How to Contact: Write, call or visit. Charges for information searches and microfiche copies according to a sliding scale.

ERIC Clearinghouse on Higher Education (HE), George Washington University, 1 DuPont Circle, Washington DC 20036. (202)296-2597.
Purpose: "ERIC (Educational Resources Information Center) is a national information system which obtains and makes available hard-to-find, often unpublished information in all areas of education." Information source on all aspects of higher education: students; all facets of colleges and universities; faculty; graduate and professional education; and the governance, management and development of higher educational institutions.
Services: Offers information searches.
How to Contact: Write, call or visit.

ERIC Clearinghouse on Information Resources (IR), Syracuse University School of Education, 150 Marshall St., Syracuse NY 13210. (315)423-3640. Librarian: Marilyn Laubacher.   •
Purpose: "ERIC (Educational Resources Information Center) is a national information system which obtains and makes available hard-to-find, often unpublished information in all areas of education." Collects and disseminates information on library science and educational technology. Information covers libraries, learning centers, instructional design, development and evaluation systems, analysis, instructional media, the delivery of information and instruction through the media.
Services: Offers aid in arranging interviews, bibliographies, statistics, brochures/

pamphlets, information searches, placement on mailing list and newsletter. Will answer reference questions. Publications include *ERIC/IR Update* (newsletter) and *Current Index to Journals in Education*.
How to Contact: Write, call or visit.

ERIC Clearinghouse on Junior Colleges (JC), University of California—Los Angeles, Room 96, Powell Library, 405 Hilgard Ave., Los Angeles CA 90024. (213)825-3931. Director: Arthur M. Cohen.
Purpose: "ERIC (Educational Resources Information Center) is a national information system which obtains and makes available hard-to-find, often unpublished information in all areas of education." Conducts computer searches on "the development, administration and evaluation of public and private community and junior colleges."
Services: Offers annotated bibliographies, information searches, placement on mailing list and newsletter. Will refer researchers to other ERIC clearinghouses or agencies if needed. Publications include information packets, state of the art papers, and a publications list.
How to Contact: Write, call or visit. Charges for more than one copy of printed materials; $20 for up to 50 citations in computer search. "Writer may use materials on premises free of charge."

ERIC Clearinghouse on Languages and Linguistics (FL), Center for Applied Linguistics, 1611 N. Kent St., 10th Floor, Arlington VA 22209. (703)528-4312. User Services Assistant: Linda Turner.
Purpose: "ERIC (Educational Resources Information Center) is a national information system which obtains and makes available hard-to-find, often unpublished information in all areas of education." Conducts computer searches on languages and language sciences.
Services: Offers bibliographies. Will refer researchers to other ERIC clearinghouses or agencies if needed. Publications include information packets.
How to Contact: Write, call or visit. Charges for information searches. "Writer may use materials on premises free of charge."

ERIC Clearinghouse on Reading and Communication Skills (CS), 111 Kenyon Rd., Urbana IL 61801. (217)328-3870.
Purpose: "ERIC (Educational Resources Inforamtion Center) is a national information system which obtains and makes available hard-to-find, often unpublished information in all areas of education." Collects and disseminates information in these areas: reading instruction and appreciation; written English for natives and non-natives, research, teacher training and instruction in writing; journalism education; production, interpretation and analysis of print and broadcast journalism; speaking and listing communications skills; and mass media communications skills.
Services: Offers bibliographies, statistics, brochures/pamphlets, information searches and newsletter. Publications include print abstracts and indexes to journals and publications.
How to Contact: Write or call. Open Monday through Friday, 8 a.m. to 4:30 p.m. Charges for computer searches or books. Writers should indicate their specific areas of interest, and information will be compiled and sent.

ERIC Clearinghouse on Rural Education and Small Schools (RC), New Mexico State University, Box 3AP, Las Cruces NM 88003. (505)646-2623.
Purpose: "ERIC (Educational Resources Information Center) is a national information system which obtains and makes available hard-to-find, often unpublished information in all areas of education." Has information on all aspects of education pertaining to rural areas, small schools, migrants, Mexican Americans, American Indians and outdoor education.
Services: Offers aid in arranging interviews, annual reports, bibliographies, statistics,

brochures/pamphlets, information searches, placement on mailing list and newsletter. Publications include publications list and ERIC brochure.

How to Contact: Write or call with questions on a specific topic. Charges for information searches; fee based on percentage of computer time used.

ERIC Clearinghouse on Science, Mathematics and Environmental Education (SE), 1200 Chambers Rd., 3rd Floor, Columbus OH 43212. (614)422-6717. Director: Robert W. Howe.

Purpose: "ERIC (Educational Resources Information Center) is a national information system which obtains and makes available hard-to-find, often unpublished information in all areas of education." Conducts searches on "all levels of science, mathematics and environmental education."

Services: Offers information searches. Publications include information packers, publications list and list of free services.

How to Contact: Write or call. "Charges for searches vary, as do the charges for printed materials provided. We will not provide services without a written request."

ERIC Clearinghouse on Social Studies/Social Science Education (SO), Education and Demonstration Center, Social Science Education Consortium, 855 Broadway, Boulder CO 80302. (303)492-8434. Executive Director: Dr. Irving Morrissett.

Purpose: "ERIC (Educational Resources Information Center) is a national information system which obtains and makes available hard-to-find, often unpublished information in all areas of education." Conducts computer searches on "All levels of social studies and social science education."

Services: Offers bibliographies, information searches, placement on mailing list, newsletter and access to microfiche collection. Will refer researchers to other ERIC clearinghouses or agencies if needed. Publications include publications list and information packets.

How to Contact: Write, call or visit. Charges $20/computer search for up to 50 citations. "Writer may use materials on premises free of charge."

ERIC Clearinghouse on Teacher Education (SP), American Association of Colleges for Teacher Education, 1 DuPont Circle NW, Suite 616, Washington DC 20036. (202)293-7280. Director: Karl Massanari.

Purpose: "ERIC (Educational Resources Information Center) conducts computer searches of material on school personnel at all levels, from preschool through university education; health and physical education; and recreation.

Services: Offers bibliographies, information searches, placement on mailing list and newsletter.

How to Contact: Write, call or visit. Charges vary for information searches.

ERIC Clearinghouse on Tests, Measurement and Evaluation (TM), Educational Testing Service, Princeton NJ 08541. (609)921-9000, ext. 2181. Users Services Representative: Barbara Hunt.

Purpose: "ERIC (Educational Resources Information Center) is a national information system which obtains and makes available hard-to-find, often unpublished information in all areas of education." Collects and disseminates materials on testing and measurement devices, programs, procedures and techniques. "ERIC offers background and quotable sources to education writers."

Services: Offers brochures/pamphlets, information searches and placement on mailing list. Will provide sources for statistical information. Publications include publications list.

How to Contact: Write, call or visit by appointment. Open Monday through Friday, 8:30 a.m. to 4:45 p.m. Charges $18.50 initial fee for computerized search; 10¢/citation.

ERIC Clearinghouse on Urban Education (UD), Box 40, Teachers College, Columbia

University, New York NY 10027. (212)678-3437. User Services Specialist: Alberta Stevenson.

Purpose: "ERIC (Educational Resources Information Center) is a national information system which obtains and makes available hard-to-find, often unpublished information in all areas of education." Collects and disseminates information and research on urban young people, from third grade through college entrance. Information covers Puerto Rican, black, Asian/American and other minority groups in urban and suburban schools. (Native Americans and Mexicans are not included.) Conducts computer research and will refer to other ERIC clearinghouses or agencies if needed.

Services: Offers bibliographies, brochures/pamphlets, information searches, placement on mailing list and newsletter. Publications include information packets, information bulletin and publications from the urban diversity series and doctoral research series. (The latter publications are available for a fee from the Institute of Urban and Minority Education, Columbia University).

How to Contact: Write, call or visit. Charges reprint fee for microfiche information and for information searches.

FIND/SVP, 500 5th Ave., New York NY 10036. (212)354-2424. Contact: Business Development Manager.

Purpose: "FIND/SVP is a total information resource offering a wide variety of research services. Small and large projects are undertaken. Searching of computer bibliographic data bases is a specialty." Information covers agriculture, art, business, celebrities, economics, entertainment, food, health/medicine, history, how-to, industry, law, music, nature, new products, politics, recreation, science, self-help, sports, technical data and travel.

Services: Offers bibliographies, biographies, statistics, brochures/pamphlets and information searches. Publications include: *Computer Bank Book: Executive Guide to Computer Data Banks*, *Findex: The Directory of Market Research Reports, Studies & Surveys*; *Findout: The Newsletter for People Who Use Information*; and a brochure describing the services of FIND/SVP.

How to Contact: Call. "Information searches generally cost between $25-50/hour. Computer data base searches start at $50, plus computer on-line costs."

The Foundation Center, 888 7th Ave., New York NY 10019. (212)975-1120. Director, Library Services: Carol M. Kurzig.

Purpose: "The Foundation Center is a national service organization which collects, analyzes and disseminates factual information about philanthropic foundations and their grants. It publishes a variety of reference publications which deal with foundations and their grants. It produces three computer data bases dealing with these topics. It also provides free library reference service to foundations, grant seekers and other interested publics in over 70 collections nationwide. It operates libraries in New York, Washington, Cleveland and San Francisco which offer special services to library users."

Services: Offers annual reports, bibliographies, biographies, statistics, brochures/pamphlets, information searches and placement on mailing list. Publications include *Foundation Directory*, grants index, directory of grants to individuals, *Foundation Center Source Book Profiles*, *International Philanthropy*, national data book, printouts, *About Foundations*, *How to Find the Facts You Need to Get a Grant*, and several brochures on grant proposals.

How to Contact: Call, write or visit. Offers special service program for $200/year; includes telephone reference, copying and computer searches.

Health Planning and Administration, 8600 Rockville Pike, Bethesda MD 20014. (301)496-6308. Chief, Office of Inquiries and Publications Management: Robert Maynard.

Purpose: Data base developed by the National Library of Medicine and the American Hospital Association, containing citations on health care management, manpower,

organization and administration, planning, standards, facilities, economics and financing. Information covers health planning and administration.
Services: Offers information searches.
How to Contact: Call American Hospital Association library information—(312)280-6263—for the nearest access center (about 900 centers—medical schools, hospitals, medical libraries, etc.—are available). "Cost of a search varies from center to center."

Institute for Monetary Research, Inc., 1200 15th St. NW, Washington DC 20005. (202)223-9050. Secretary/Treasurer: F.J. Broderick.
Purpose: Researches monetary questions. Information covers business, economics, industry and politics.
Services: Offers information searches.
How to Contact: Write or call. Charges for searches.

International Food Information Service, Lane End House, Shinfield, Reading RG2 9BB, England. 0734-883895. Joint Managing Director: E.J. Mann.
Purpose: "To provide a world information service in food science and technology. We have a data base of 18,000 items (abstracts) from world literature. Data base information is available as a monthly journal (*Food Science and Technology Abstracts*) and on magnetic tape."
Services: Offers bibliographies, information searches and newsletter. Publications include information kit describing service.
How to Contact: Write. Charges $10 minimum/inquiry; 20¢/photocopy.

MEDLINE Data Base, 8600 Rockville Pike, Bethesda MD 20014. (301)496-6308. Chief, Office of Inquiries and Publications Management: Robert Maynard.
Purpose: Data base containing 500,000 references to recently published articles in health science. MEDLINE is accessible at about 900 medical schools, hospitals and government agencies.
Services: Offers information searches. Publications include an informational brochure.
How to Contact: "Write or call for exact MEDLINE locations. The cost of a search varies from center to center."

National Automated Accounting Research System (NAARS), American Institute of Certified Public Accountants, 1211 Avenue of the Americas, New York NY 10036. (212)575-6393. Information Retrieval Department: Hortense Goodman.
Purpose: "Provides computer-assisted research of the published annual reports to shareholders of over 4,000 companies." Information covers business and industry.
Services: Offers information searches.
How to Contact: Write. Charges $200/hour, $50 minimum, for information search.

National Technical Information Service, 5285 Port Royal Rd., Springfield VA 22161. (703)557-4600.
Purpose: "The National Technical Information Service (NTIS) is an information service organization. It promotes the general welfare by channeling information about technological innovations and other specialized information to business, industry, government, and the public. Its products and services are intended to increase the efficiency and effectiveness of the US research and development enterprise, to support US foreign policy goals by assisting the social and economic development of other nations, and to increase the availability of foreign technical information in the US. NTIS undertakes and develops products and programs having the potential for self-support and which are appropriate for government, instead of private enterprise. NTIS information covers science, technology, social sciences, administration, urban planning, health, law, business, and dozens of other categories.
Services: Offers help in location of useful reports through published searches and on-line computer search service; lease of the NTIS bibliographic data file (on magnetic

tape); and current summaries of new research reports in 26 abstract newsletters—each devoted to a different subject (usually published weekly); Selected Research in Micro-fiche (SRIM) automatically sends subscribers full texts of new research reports in their selected field of interest."
How to Contact: Write or call.

Smithsonian Science Information Exchange (SSIE), Room 300, 1730 M St. NW, Washington DC 20036. (202)381-4211. Marketing Manager: Janet D. Goldstein.
Purpose: "SSIE collects, indexes, stores, and disseminates prepublication information about current research projects in every field of science. Because information about projects is collected when work begins or is continued for another year, the resulting data provides a unique source of information about scientific research from the time it begins until the time results are disseminated at meetings and in professional litera-ture. Single-page notices of research projects include supporting and performing organization names and addresses, investigator name(s) and department(s), project title, period for the description, and a 200-word technical summary prepared by the investigator outlining the work to be performed during the specified period." Informa-tion covers agriculture, economics, food, health/medicine, nature, politics, recreation, science and technical data.
Services: Offers brochures/pamphlets, information searches and newsletter. "On-line search services supplement off-line search services provided by SSIE staff. On-line searches may be conducted on the SDC or Lockheed systems." Publications include *SSIE Science Newsletter* and brochures describing search services available in agricul-tural science, medical and biological science, chemistry and chemical engineering, earth sciences, energy and environmental sciences, engineering and materials, physics, mathematics, electronics, behavioral science and social science.
How to Contact: Write or call. Charges vary according to services required. "Search results from the SSIE data base are copyrighted, and may not be reproduced in any form without prior permission. The Smithsonian Science Information Exchange will become part of the National Technical Information Service, Department of Commerce, during 1979. It will become a federal agency at that time."

Southern California Answering Network (SCAN), 630 W. 5th St., Los Angeles CA 90071. (213)626-7461. Director: Evelyn Greenwald.
Purpose: "SCAN is a federally funded reference referral service for libraries in south-ern California. SCAN is designed to make the information resources of the Los Angeles Central Library available to residents of the area through their nearest community library." Information covers agriculture, art, business, celebrities, economics, enter-tainment, food, health/medicine, history, how-to, industry, law, music, nature, new products, politics, recreation, science, self-help, sports, technical data and travel.
Services: Offers bibliographies and information searches. "SCAN provides a means of access to the wealth of collections in the Los Angeles Central Library, and it provides the services of specialist reference librarians. The SCAN headquarters has no book collection. The reference specialists use the collections in all the Central Library subject departments."
How to Contact: "Contact the reference librarian in a local or community library. "Since SCAN is a referral service for libraries, individual patrons have access to the service only through their local library."

Sport Information Resource Center (SIRC), Coaching Association of Canada (CAC), 333 River Rd. Vanier, Ottawa, Ontario, Canada K1L 8B9. (613)746-5693. Executive Director: Lyle Makosky.
Purpose: The Coaching Association of Canada is a national nonprofit organization. Its major aims are to increase coaching effectiveness in all sports and to encourage the development of coaching by providing programs and services to coaches at all levels. SIRC is a unique sport library and documentation center, and its services are accessible to all CAC members as well as the sports community at large." Information covers

health/medicine, how-to, recreation, science, sports and technical data.
Services: Offers annual reports, brochures/pamphlets and information searches. Publications include pamphlets on the CAC and SIRC in English and French.
How to Contact: Write or call. Charges for computerized information searches. "Our library doesn't lend books."

System Development Corp. Search Service, 2500 Colorado Ave., Santa Monica CA 90406. (213)829-7511, (800)421-7229. In California: (800)352-6689. Contact: Action Desk.
Purpose: "Our major product consists of more than 50 data bases that provide on-line access to scientific, technical, business and social science information. Our information retrieval program, ORBIT, provides rapid retrieval of this information, which points the user to fuller source documents found in journal articles, books, government reports, etc." Information covers agriculture, art, business, economics, food, health/medicine, history, industry, law, music, nature, new products, politics, recreation, science, sports and technical data.
Services: Offers bibliographies, statistics, brochures/pamphlets, information searches and newsletter. Publications include "manuals and other documentation concerning the data bases available for on-line searching."
How to Contact: "Write or call, and a user password will be assigned that will allow on-line access to all data bases. The user pays only for what is used, similar to a utility. Charges include connect time charges and off-line printing, which averages about $12 per search, including about 100 bibliographic citations, often with descriptive abstracts."
Tips: "You will need access to a teletypewriter terminal; these can be rented. Services can be obtained through major university and college libraries. Some major public libraries are also performing searches for the general public."

Foreign Information Sources

Governments establish embassies, consulates and tourism offices in foreign countries to promote better relations—diplomatic and otherwise—between nations. An *embassy* is the office of an ambassador, who is primarily concerned with diplomatic relations. The services of the Embassy of Bolivia, for instance, include "press and cultural services, economic and commercial affairs, consulate offices (visas and requirements for entry to Bolivia) and military offices," according to Nina Tamayo B., an attache. A *consulate* is the office of a consul, who concerns himself with promoting trade with the foreign government, with protecting the rights of his country's citizens or subjects, etc. Says an official from the Consulate of Ecuador in California: "Basically, our duties are to promote the good relations between Ecuador and the place where we perform our duties, and to look after the well-being of the Ecuadorian citizens who live in this area." A *tourism office* promotes the particular country as a possible vacation spot. For example, "We are funded by the Australian government to promote travel and tourism to Australia among the North American travel industry and consumers," notes Peter Harding, regional director of the Australian Tourist Commission.

Representatives of foreign countries are generally open to information requests, but remembering a few courtesies will make dealing with them easier. Information officials in embassies, consulates and tourism offices, for example, generally prefer written queries. The details of a verbal request can be forgotten if some time must be spent in gathering the needed information. Besides, language will present a barrier in some cases, and having the request in writing is preferable to having it garbled in a quick translation over the phone.

Allow a long time for a reply to any request. Information available from these offices is usually of a general nature, and the embassy or consulate sometimes must forward the request to its home country for an answer. Embassies and consulates will try to supply current information, but with countries in constant flux and/or upheaval, up-to-date information might be unavailable.

Foreign information sources in this section are listed alphabetically according to country name. The Embassy of South Africa, therefore, is listed before the Consulate General of Spain. While each country that maintains diplomatic relations with the US maintains only one embassy in the US, most maintain a number of consulates scattered across the country. Most major cities house at least a few foreign consulates, and these can be located by checking your Yellow Pages under a heading like "Consulates and Other Foreign Government Representatives." A source of consulate and embassy addresses and telephone numbers is the *National Directory of Addresses and Telephone Numbers* (Bantam), though the information is out-of-date in many cases. *Congressional Quarterly* publishes a useful sourcebook called *Washington Information Directory*, which lists not only the addresses and phone numbers of foreign embassies in Washington DC, but also the phone number of the Department of State offices assigned to monitor political, cultural and economic trends and developments in particular countries. The Department of State Office of Media Services, (202)632-1394, can help you locate the individual office you seek.

Another US government source that can supply information about foreign countries is the Government Printing Office (N. Capitol and H Sts. NW, Washington, D.C. 20401).

Statistics Sources (Gale Research Co.) is a helpful sourcebook that can direct you to specific sources of statistical data about foreign countries.

Foreign Embassies, Consulates & Tourism Offices

Embassy of the Argentine Republic, 1600 New Hampshire Ave. NW. Washington DC 20009. (202)387-0705. Contact: Cultural Office.
Purpose: "To disseminate information on the Argentine Republic." Information covers agriculture, art, business, industry, recreation and travel.
Services: Offers brochures/pamphlets and photos. "We will lend slides."
How to Contact: Write or call.

Australian Information Service, 636 5th Ave., New York NY 10020. (212)245-4000. Press Assistant: Paula J. O'Connor.
Purpose: "To inform the North American public of Australian news, human interest stories and all developments." Information covers agriculture, art, business, celebrities, economics, entertainment, food, health/medcine, history, industry, law, music, nature, new products, politics, recreation, science, self-help, sports, technical data and travel.
Services: Offers a wide selection of b&w photos, a few color transparencies. Offers reproduction rights.
How to Contact: Write or call.

Australian Tourist Commission, 1270 Avenue of the Americas, #2908, New York NY 10020. (212)489-7550. Regional Director: Peter Harding.
Purpose: "We are funded by the Australian government to promote travel and tourism to Australia among the North American travel industry and consumers. Information covers all states and territories in Australia." Information covers recreation, travel, visitor attractions and facilities.
Services: Offers aid in arranging interviews, statistics, brochures/pamphlets, placement on mailing list, newsletter, photos and press kits. Publications include *Australia—Your Travel Planner*, listing Australia's visitor attractions and facilities, transportation, entertainment and bargain travel plans together with wide range of practical information for travelers.
How to Contact: Write or call.

Austrian Press and Information Service, 31 E. 69th St., New York NY 10021.
Services: Offers general information and b&w photos of Austria.
How to Contact: Write. Charges no fees, but credit line and return of pictures are required.

Embassy of Belgium, 3330 Garfield St. NW, Washington DC 20008. (202)333-6900. Contact: Cultural Section.
Purpose: "To disseminate information on Belgium." Information covers agriculture, art, business, economics, history, industry, music and general information.
Services: Offers brochures/pamphlets, statistics and photos (available by mail).
How to Contact: Write or call. "We also have a library for research, but no information is sent by mail. Writers can also contact Belgium National Tourist Office, 745 5th Ave., New York NY 10022."

Embassy of Bolivia, 3014 Massachusetts Ave. NW, Washington DC 20008.

(202)483-4410. Attache: Miss Nina Tamayo B.

Purpose: "We provide diplomatic representation of Bolivia in the United States, including press and cultural services, economic and commercial affairs, consular duties (visas and requirements for entry to Bolivia) and military affairs. We also have a small library of Bolivian books covering the history, economy, literature, mining, international relations, geography and anthropology in Bolivia." Information covers art, economics, history, law, politics and travel.

Services: Offers bibliographies, statistics, brochures/pamphlets and information searches. Publications include *Bolivia*, a handbook of information issued by the cultural department of the Bolivian embassy in London; *Image of Bolivia*, a booklet published and issued by the Organization of American States; and *Tourism in Bolivia*, tourist information sheets.

How to Contact: Write or call. "If a writer needs immediate information on any specific research, it is best to request a bibliography instead of requesting the research to be done by us. In general, we have a limited amount of material already published and classified to be distributed to the public."

Embassy of Brazil, 3006 Massachusetts Ave. NW, Washington DC 20008. (202)793-0212. Contact: Information Office.

Purpose: "To disseminate information on Brazil." Information covers business, travel and general information.

Services: Offers brochures/pamphlets and information searches.

How to Contact: Call.

Tourism, Government of the Province of British Columbia, 1117 Wharf St., Victoria, British Columbia, Canada V8W 2Z2. (604)387-5498. Public Information Officer: Ben J. Pires.

Purpose: "To promote travel to British Columbia." Information covers entertainment, nature, recreation and travel.

Services: Offers annual reports, brochures/pamphlets, newsletter, photos and press kits. Publications include travel features on British Columbia, *Beautiful British Columbia* (quarterly magazine) and *Discover British Columbia* (mini travel stories for newspapers).

How to Contact: Write.

Canadian Consulate General, 1251 Avenue of the Americas, New York NY 10020. Contact: Photo Librarian.

Purpose: To supply information about Canada to Connecticut, New Jersey and New York State only.

Services: Offers 8x10 b&w glossy prints of Canadian scenes and the people of Canada on a loan basis.

How to Contact: Write. Credit line required. Return of pictures requested.

Canadian Embassy, Public Affairs Division, 1771 N St. NW, Washington DC 20036. (201)785-1400. Contact: Library.

Purpose: "The Public Affairs Division includes the press office and the library. The library is open to the public Monday through Friday, 1:30 p.m. to 5 p.m.; telephone reference service is available from 8:30 a.m. to 5 p.m. Our collection covers the entire range of Canadian issues with emphasis on current events." Information covers agriculture, art, business, celebrities, economics, entertainment, food, health/medicine, history, industry, law, music, nature, politics, recreation, science and sports.

Services: Offers aid in arranging interviews "on a selective basis," annual reports of Canadian government agencies, bibliographies, biographies, statistics, brochures/pamphlets, information searches, placement on mailing list, and "referral to other sources of Canadian information." Publications include *Canada Handbook*, a summary of recent social, cultural and economic development published by Statistics

Canada; *Canada Today/D'Aujourd'hui*, an embassy magazine (back issues available); *Canada Photosheet*, a poster with photos and brief text material covering contemporary Canada; press releases; and reference papers on selected topics.
How to Contact: Write, call or visit. "Preference is given to professional journalists and scholars."

Consulate of the Republic of Chile, 739 Hoomalimali St., Pearl City HI 96782. (808)456-9650. Consul: Fernando A. Marenco.
Purpose: Consulate of the Republic of Chile in the state of Hawaii. Information covers agriculture, art, business, celebrities, economics, entertainment, food, health/medicine, history, how-to, industry, law, music, nature, new products, politics, recreation, science, self-help, sports, technical data and travel.
How to Contact: Write or call.

Chinese Consulate General, 222 N. Dearborn St., Chicago IL 60601. (312)263-4669. Contact: Information Section.
Purpose: "To disseminate information on China." Information covers agriculture, art, economics, entertainment, food, history, industry, music, nature, recreation and travel. General and cultural information also available.
Services: Offers aid in arranging interviews, brochures/pamphlets, information searches, statistics, newsletter and photos.
How to Contact: Write or call.

Chinese Information Service, 159 Lexington Ave., New York NY 10016. (212)725-4950. Director: I-Cheng Loh.
Purpose: "To disseminate information on China." Information covers art, history and music.
Services: Offers brochures/pamphlets.
How to Contact: Write or call.

Embassy of Denmark, 3200 Whitehaven St. NW, Washington DC 20008. (202)234-4300. Contact: Cultural Affairs or Information Officer.
Purpose: "To disseminate information about Denmark." Information covers agriculture, art, business, celebrities, economics, entertainment, food, health/medicine, history, industry, music, nature, recreation, science, sports and travel.
Services: Offers aid in arranging interviews and information searches. Publications, publications list and films available.
How to Contact: Write or call.

Embassy of the Dominican Republic, 1715 22nd St. NW, Washington DC 20008. (212)332-6280.
Services: Offers fact sheet on Dominican Republic and *Investor's Guide*.
How to Contact: Write or call.

Consulate of Ecuador, 870 Market St., #858, San Francisco CA 94116. (415)391-4148.
Purpose: "Basically, our duties are to promote good relations between Ecuador and the places where we perform our duties, and to promote the well-being of Ecuadorian citizens living in an area." Information covers business, economics, entertainment, food, history, law and travel.
Services: Offers "general economic and investment information about Ecuador" and brochures/pamphlets. Publications include *Image of Ecuador* ("general information about different cities and a brief review of history and arts"); *This Is Ecuador* ("general information about Ecuador, such as transportation, places to visit, hotels, clothing, weather, etc."); *Monumental Cities: Quito* ("general information about Quito, the political capital of Ecuador"); *Invest in Ecuador*; and *Ecuador in Figures*.
How to Contact: Write, call or visit. "All the information and brochures are free; we charge for some services."

Consulate General of Ecuador, 25 SE 2nd Ave., Suite 1130, Miami FL 33131. (305)371-8366. Consul General: Col. Jaime A. Mino.
Purpose: "Promotion of the country of Ecuador, including the areas of economics (imports and exports), culture, Ecuadorian laws in general, visa applications and tourism." Information covers art, business, economics, history, industry, law, music, nature, new product information, recreation, self-help, science, sports, technical data and travel.
Services: Offers aid in arranging interviews, annual reports, brochures/pamphlets and photos. Publications include coverage of economics and tourism in Ecuador.
How to Contact: Write.

Embassy of the Arab Republic of Egypt, 2300 Decatur Plaza NW, Washington DC 20008. (202)234-0980. Press and Information Officer: Ms. Esmet Wahab.
Purpose: "To disseminate information on the Arab Republic of Egypt." Information covers business, history, industry, culture, education and religion.
Services: Offers aid in arranging interviews, brochures/pamphlets, information searches and photos (slides and films).
How to Contact: Write or call.

Consulate General of El Salvador, 403 W. 8th St., Suite 404, Los Angeles CA 90014. (213)622-2984. Consul General: Julio Cesar Bermudez.
Purpose: Information covers agriculture, business, economics and travel.
Services: Offers statistics, brochures/pamphlets and information searches.
How to Contact: Write or call.

Consulate General of El Salvador, 870 Market St., Room 721, San Francisco CA 94102. (415)781-7924.
Purpose: "To provide information about commercial investments in El Salvador as well as tourist information."
Services: Offers brochures/pamphlets.
How to Contact: Write or call.

Embassy of Finland, 1900 24th St. NW, Washington DC 20008. (202)462-0556. Contact: Press Section.
Purpose: Information covers agriculture, art, business, celebrities, economics, entertainment, food, health/medicine, history, industry, law, music, nature, politics, recreation, science, sports and travel.
Services: Offers statistics. Publications include *Suomi-Finland*, which answers most commonly asked questions on Finland and its relations with the US.
How to Contact: "Information on Finland will be sent upon request and questions will be answered over the phone, but we will not accept collect calls."

Finland National Tourist Office, 75 Rockefeller Plaza, New York NY 10019. (212)582-2802. Public Relations: Pat Patricof. Assistant Director: Nino de Prado.
Purpose: "To promote tourism from North America to Finland through the travel trade, travel trade press and consumer news media. To distribute informative tourist literature, conduct seminars and workshops for the travel trade. To participate in trade shows and the like. To invite press/travel agents on familiarization trips to Finland. To distribute visual sound material and otherwise engage in all facets of travel promotion. We also supply the general public with informational material and aid them in their travel plans when requested." Information covers art, entertainment, food, history, music, nature, sports and travel.
Services: Offers statistics, brochures/pamphlets, newsletter, photos and press kits.
How to Contact: Write or call. Also contact Scandinavian National Tourist Offices, 3600 Wilshire Blvd., Los Angeles, California 90010.

Embassy of France, 972 5th Ave., New York NY 10021. (212)570-4400. Contact: Library of French Cultural Services.
Purpose: "To disseminate information of France." Information covers art, economics, history, music, politics and literature.
Services: Offers information searches.
How to Contact: Write or call. Much of the information is in French.

Embassy of the Federal Republic of Germany, 4645 Reservoir Rd. NW, Washington DC 20007. (202)331-3000. Contact: Attache (Press Affairs).
Purpose: "The Embassy furnishes information about the Federal Republic of Germany. Specific information can be obtained from the German Information Center, 410 Park Ave., New York NY 10022. (212)888-9840." Information covers agriculture, art, business, celebrities, economics, food, history, industry, law, music, politics, science, sports and travel.
Services: Offers aid in arranging interviews, bibliographies, biographies, brochures/pamphlets, placement on mailing list, statistics, newsletter, photos and press kits. Publications available.
How to Contact: Write.

Embassy of the German Democratic Republic, 1717 Massachusetts Ave. NW, Washington DC 20036. (202)232-3134. Press Department: Frank Teutschbein.
Purpose: "To disseminate information on the German Democratic Republic." Information covers economics, travel, and general and cultural information.
Services: Offers information searches and photos.
How to Contact: Write or call. Please be specific about subject or area of interest.

Embassy of Greece, 2211 Massachusetts Ave. NW, Washington DC 20008. (202)332-2727. Contact: Press and Information Office.
Purpose: "To dissminate information on Greece." Information covers art, history, music, travel, general and cultural information. Information available from archives in person or by mail. Publications available.
How to Contact: Write or call. Be specific on subject or area of interest.

Hungarian Embassy, 3910 Shoemaker St., Washington DC 20003. (202)362-6730. Press Attaché: Mr. Fazekas.
Purpose: Information covers agriculture, economics, health/medicine, history, law, politics, science and travel.
Services: Offers statistics, brochures/pamphlets and placement on mailing list.
How to Contact: Write.

Consulate General of Iceland, 370 Lexington Ave., Suite 370, New York NY 10017. (212)686-4100.
Purpose: "To provide commercial and general information about Iceland." Information covers agriculture, art, business, celebrities, economics, entertainment, food, health/medicine, history, how-to, industry, law, music, nature, new product information, politics, recreation, science, self-help, sports, technical data and travel.
Services: Offers aid in arranging interviews, annual reports, statistics, brochures/pamphlets and photos. Publications cover "general information and special subjects."

Icelandic National Tourist Office, 75 Rockefeller Plaza, New York NY 10019. (212)582-2802. Director: Stefan J. Richter.
Purpose: "To promote Iceland as a tourist destination; to give tourist information on Iceland to prospective visitors; to supply travel agencies with tourist material; to supply the travel trade press and the general news media with travel oriented information on Iceland, mostly in the form of releases." Information covers nature and travel.
Services: Offers brochures/pamphlets, placement on mailing list, photos and press kits. Publications include *Iceland, Country and People, Some Facts on Iceland*,

Iceland Awaits You, Practical Tourist Information, and *Reykjavik, The Smokeless Capital.*
How to Contact: Write or call.

Embassy of the Republic of Indonesia, 2020 Massachusetts Ave. NW, Washington DC 20036. Contact: Information Division.
Purpose: "To provide information on Indonesia." Information covers general and cultural data.
Services: Offers information searches.
How to Contact: Write.

Embassy of Iraq, 1801 P St. NW, Washington DC 20036. (202)483-7500. Contact: Information Office.
Purpose: "To provide information on Iraq." Information covers business, economics, history, politics and travel.
Services: Offers information searches.
How to Contact: Write or call.

Irish Tourist Board, 590 5th Ave., New York NY 10036. (212)246-7400.
Purpose: "To provide information on Ireland." Information covers art, entertainment, food, history, music, nature, recreation, sports and travel.
Services: Offers brochures/pamphlets.
How to Contact: Write or call.

Consulate General of Israel, 800 2nd Ave., New York NY 10017. (212)697-5500. Information Officer: Ralene Levy.
Purpose: "To disseminate information on the various aspects of Israel's life and development and background material on the Middle East situation through printed materials, films, speaking engagements, and radio programs from Israel." Information covers agriculture, economics, health/medicine, history, politics, recreation, science, sports and general descriptive material on Israel.
Services: Offers aid in arranging interviews, biographies, brochures/pamphlets, placement on mailing list, photos, speakers, and films. Publications available.
How to Contact: Write or call. Charges for large quantities of materials; charges $7.50 for film rentals.

Italian Cultural Institute, 686 Park Ave., New York NY 10020. (212)879-4242.
Purpose: "Foreign government agency." Information covers art, history, music and cultural information.
Services: Offers information searches and photos. Library facilities available for research and loan of books.
How to Contact: Write.

Italian Government Travel Office, 630 5th Ave., New York NY 10021. (212)245-4822.
Purpose: "Foreign government travel office." Information covers art, entertainment, food, history, music, nature, recreation, sports, travel and museums.
Services: Offers brochures/pamphlets, photos (to borrow) and maps. Publications available.
How to Contact: Write or call.

Embassy of Jamaica, 1666 Connecticut Ave. NW, Washington DC 20009. (202)387-1010. Contact: Information Office.
Purpose: "To provide information on Jamaica." Information covers economics and politics.
Services: Offers aid in arranging interviews and information searches. Requests for information will be forwarded to Jamaica if information not available in Washington.
How to Contact: Write or call.

Embassy of Japan, 2520 Massachusetts Ave. NW, Washington DC 20008. (202)234-2266. Contact: Information Department.
Purpose: "To provide information on Japan." Information covers agriculture, art, history, music, nature and travel.
Services: Offers information searches. Material available is of general nature, but requests for specific information will be referred to proper sources.
How to Contact: Write or call.

Kenya Consulate General/Tourist Office, 60 E. 56th St., New York NY 10022. (212)486-1300. Consul General: Mr. Mohamed Ali.
Purpose: "Ours is a Kenyan government body dealing with consulate matters. Our activities also cover promotional activities for Kenya tourism within South and North America. We provide visas to visitors to Kenya and tourism information to travel agents, airlines and to the general public." Information covers history and travel.
Services: Offers aid in arranging interviews. Publications include *People of Kenya*, *Wildlife of Kenya*, *Culture of Kenya*, and *Tourism in Kenya*.
How to Contact: Write or call. "Depending on the topic of research, it would be advisable to go to Kenya to obtain firsthand information."

Consulate General of the Republic of Korea, 3500 Clay St., San Francisco CA 94118. (415)921-2251. Assistant to Information Director: Elizabeth Eshleman.
Purpose: "To promote an understanding of Korea and its culture by the American people, for the mutual benefit of both Korea and the US, through an exchange of personnel, trade and culture." Information covers art, economics, history, industry, music, politics and travel.
Services: Offers brochures/pamphlets, newsletter, photos and press kits. Publications include *Facts About Korea* (descriptive booklet) and *Korean Newsletter* (bimonthly newsletter).
How to Contact: Write.

Embassy of Lebanon, 2560 28th St. NW, Washington DC 20008. (202)462-8600. Legal and Cultural Affairs: Mrs. Mickeline Samara. Contact: Director of Commercial & Economics Affairs.
Purpose: "To provide information on Lebanon." Information covers business, economics, history, music and travel.
Services: Offers bibliographies and information searches.
How to Contact: Write or call.

Luxembourg National Tourist Office, 1 Dag Hammarskjold Plaza, New York NY 10017. (212)751-9650. Director: Anne Bastian.
Purpose: "We provide information on all aspects of tourism to Luxembourg." Information covers business, economics, entertainment, food, history, industry, sports and travel.
Services: Offers aid in arranging interviews, statistics, brochures/pamphlets, photos (b&w glossies and color slides), and press kits.
How to Contact: Write or call.

Embassy of Malaysia, 2401 Massachusetts Ave. NW, Washington DC 20008. (202)234-7600. First Secretary (Information): G. N. Nair.
Purpose: "To represent Malaysia in the United States, to promote Malaysia's political and economic interests, and to engage in normal diplomatic pursuits. The embassy provides general information on Malaysia and its policies. Specialized information is provided by separate trade, investment, tourism, rubber industry and tin industry offices." Information covers economics, industry, politics, travel and Malaysian foreign affairs.
Services: Offers aid in arranging interviews, statistics, brochures/pamphlets, placement on mailing list, and newsletter. Publications include *Malaysian Digest*, a semi-

monthly review of Malaysian affairs; *Foreign Affairs Malaysia*, a quarterly anthology of foreign policy speeches; *Malaysian Panorama*, a quarterly cultural magazine; *Malaysia in Brief*, a booklet of general information on Malaysia; and travel, investment and other brochures. "We have no restrictions on writers using our services, but acknowledgment or credit would be appreciated."
How to Contact: "Write to the embassy."

Consulate of the Republic of Malta, 249 E. 35th St., New York NY 10016. (212)725-2345. Information Officer: Mr. S. Giusti.
Purpose: "Consular and information on Malta tourism, trade and industrial promotion." Information covers tourisum, trade and industrial promotion in Malta.
Services: Offers brochures/pamphlets.
How to Contact: Write or call.

Consulate of Mexico, 700 Brazos St., Austin TX 78701. (512)478-2866. Consul General: Lic. Manuel Elizaldi
Purpose: "We collaborate with this city and other counties in our jurisdiction in any matter regarding Mexico." Information covers agriculture, business, celebrities, history, how-to, industry, law, recreation and travel.
Services: Offers aid in arranging interviews, brochures/pamphlets and placement on mailing list. Publications include tourism pamphlets of various recreational areas in Mexico, maps, etc.
How to Contact: "Write describing needs and giving us a detailed description of purpose for information needed. Our office is open Monday through Friday, 9 a.m. to 2 p.m. and on Saturday, 9 a.m. to 12 p.m."

Royal Netherlands Embassy, 4200 Linnean Ave. NW, Washington DC 20008. (202)244-5300. Contact: Counselor for Press and Cultural Affairs.
Purpose: "To furnish residents of the United States with information about the Netherlands."
Services: Offers aid in arranging interviews, brochures/pamphlets and placement on mailing list. Publications available. (Some may be under copyright restrictions.)
How to Contact: Write or call.

New Zealand Embassy, 19 Observatory Circle NW, Washington DC 20008. (202)265-1721. Information Officer: Mr. Rau Kirikiri.
Purpose: "The Information Office, Embassy of New Zealand, provides general information about New Zealand. We will provide addresses of organizations in New Zealand from which specific information may be obtained if information is not available at the embassy." Information covers all aspects of New Zealand, including agriculture, art, business, economics, food, health/medicine, history, industry, law, music, nature, politics, sports and travel.
Services: Offers government annual reports, limited biographies, statistics, brochures/pamphlets, placement on mailing list, regular informational newsletter, and a limited number of photos of a general nature about New Zealand. Publications include a variety of tourist pamphlets and booklets on New Zealand.
How to Contact: Write. Credit line and return of pictures are requested.

Nigerian Embassy, 2201 M St. NW, Washington DC 20037. (202)223-9300. First Secretary (Information): Chibueze Eke.
Purpose: "We represent the Federal Republic of Nigeria in all manifestations of government functions. However, contact is through his excellency, the Nigerian ambassador to the United States." Information covers agriculture, business, celebrities, economics, entertainment, food, health/medicine, history, industry, law, music, nature, politics, sports and travel.
Services: Offers aid in arranging interviews, annual reports, bibliographies, bio-

graphies, brochures/pamphlets, information searches, placement on mailing list and statistics.

How to Contact: Write or call. All material must be used in the way mutually agreed to between the embassy and the receiver.

Embassy of Norway, 2720 3rd St., Washington DC 20008. (202)333-6000. Contact: Information Service.

Purpose: Information covers agriculture, art, business, economics, food, health/medicine, history, industry, law, music, nature, politics, recreation, science, sports and travel.

Services: Offers brochures/pamphlets and information searches. Publications include booklet of general information and resource guide.

How to Contact: Write or call. Also contact: The Norwegian Information Service, 825 3rd Ave., New York NY 10022, (212)421-7333; Norwegian National Tourist Office, 75 Rockefeller Plaza, New York NY 10092, (212)582-2802 and the Norway Export Council, 800 3rd Ave., New York NY 10022, (212)421-9210.

The ballroom of the Royal Castle in Warsaw is shown in this photograph taken before German soldiers destroyed the painted ceiling in 1939. Photos to illustrate articles about Poland—past and present—are available free of charge from the Embassy of the Polish People's Republic, as they are from many embassies.

Panama Canal Information Office, Box M, Balboa Heights, Canal Zone. 52-3165. Assistant Information Officer: V.G. Canel.

Purpose: "The Panama Canal Company operates and maintains the Panama Canal. We furnish information on the history, operation and maintenance of the waterway." Information covers history.

Services: Offers aid in arranging interviews, annual reports, bibliographies, bio-

graphies (limited), brochures/pamphlets, information searches (limited), statistics, photos (limited) and press kits. "We publish a semiannual magazine, *Panama Canal Review*, which features a wide variety of articles on living and working in the Canal Zone. Also, a weekly house organ, *Panama Canal Spillway*, which deals more directly with employees and operations."
How to Contact: Write. "Our staff is limited and we are unable to provide extensive researching for replies to written queries. However, on-the-spot writers are accorded every privilege, through appointments made through this office, for assistance in gathering material."

Consulate General of the Philippines, Press Office, 2433 Pali Hwy., Honolulu HI 96817. (808)595-7263. Information Attaché: José T. Panganiban Jr.
Purpose: "To provide information about the Philippines, primarily by distributing a daily summary of the news, newsletters, brochures and pamphlets to newspapers and radio-TV stations in the state of Hawaii. We also answer queries." Information covers politics, travel and news.
Services: Offers brochures/pamphlets and placement on mailing list. "We issue a limited number of news summaries/newsletters daily, Monday through Friday."
How to Contact: Write or call.

Consulate General of the Philippines, 2975 Wilshire Blvd., Suite 450, Los Angeles CA 90010. (213)387-5321. Information Representative: Luis V. Ople.
Purpose: "To provide general information and news about the Philippines." Information covers economics, history and politics.
Services: Offers brochures/pamphlets, placement on mailing list, newsletter and press kits. Publications include *The Republic*, "a fortnightly journal on Philippine events"; *Archipelago*, "international magazine of the Philippines"; and *FID Backgrounders*, "briefing on important events."
How to Contact: "Write a formal letter addressed to Information Representative. Business hours: Monday through Friday, 9 a.m. to 4 p.m." Requires publication credits.

Embassy of the Polish People's Republic, 2640 16th St. NW, Washington DC 20009. (202)243-3800. Information Officer: Margaret Romaniuk.
Purpose: "To promote better relations between Poland and the US." Information covers agriculture, art, economics, food, politics, recreation, science and travel.
Services: Offers biographies, statistics, brochures/pamphlets, placement on mailing list and photos. Publications include "standard informational material."
How to Contact: Write or call.

Embassy of Portugal, 1875 Connecticut Ave. NW, Washington DC 20008. (202)265-1643.
Purpose: Information covers economics and politics.
Services: Offers brochures/pamphlets and information searches.
How to Contact: Write. "Requests for information should be written, not telephoned. For travel information, call the Portugal Travel Agency, (212)243-8799."

Puerto Rico Tourism Co., 1290 Avenue of the Americas, New York NY 10019. (212)541-6630, ext. 21. Public Relations Coordinator: Marianne M. Roig.
Purpose: "To promote tourism to Puerto Rico—directed to travel agents, corporate and incentive groups and the public." Information covers entertainment, food, history, music, nature, recreation, sports and travel.
Services: Offers aid in arranging interviews, statistics, brochures/pamphlets, newsletter and press kits.
How to Contact: Write or call.

The Embassy of the Republic of Rwanda, 1714 New Hampshire Ave. NW, Washington DC 20009. (202)232-2882.
Services: Offers "information."
How to Contact: Write or call.

Embassy of South Africa, 3051 Massachusetts Ave. NW, Washington DC 20008. (202)232-4400. Contact: Information Counselor.
Purpose: Information covers agriculture, art, business, economics, health/medicine, history, industry, law, music, nature and politics.
Services: Offers statistics, information searches and photos. Publications include *All the Facts About South Africa; Backgrounders*, a six-page periodical brochure on specific subjects; and printed excerpts from the *Official Yearbook*.
How to Contact: Write or call the following offices: West Coast Director, Information Service, 1801 Century Park E., Suite 1818, Los Angeles 90067, (213)553-5741; Consul Information, South African Consul General, 444 N. Michigan Ave., Chicago 60611, (312)838-9200; Deputy Consul General, Information, South African Consulate General, 425 Park Ave., New York City 10022, (212)838-1700; or the Information Counselor at the Washington DC address.

Consulate General of Spain, 333 World Trade Bldg., Houston TX 77002. (713)223-1694.
Purpose: "We provide any information regarding Spain."
Services: Offers brochures/pamphlets. Publications include tourist brochures.
How to Contact: Write or call. Charges $1 to cover postage.

Embassy of Sweden, 600 New Hampshire Ave., Suite 1200, Washington DC 20037. (202)965-4100. Contact: Information Department.
Purpose: Information covers agriculture, art, business, economics, history, industry, music, nature, politics, recreation, sports, travel, education, social insurance and taxes.
Services: Offers brochures/pamphlets and information searches. "Requests may be forwarded to Stockholm when necessary." Publications include fact sheets and pamphlets on specific subjects.
How to Contact: Write or call.

Swedish Information Service, 825 3rd Ave., New York NY 10022. (212)751-5900. Information Officer: Ami Sandstedt.
Purpose: To disseminate information on Sweden.
Services: Offers photos of Swedish subjects except tourism. B&w, some color.
How to Contact: Write or call. Photos must be returned after use.

Embassy of Switzerland, 2900 Cathedral Ave. NW, Washington DC 20008.
Services: Offers information on Switzerland. Publications include *Swiss in American Life* and several tourism booklets.
How to Contact: Write to the embassy or to the nearest consulate general: 307 N. Michigan Ave., Chicago 60601; 3440 Wilshire Blvd, Suite 817, Los Angeles 90010; 1106 International Trade Mart, New Orleans 70130; 444 Madison Ave., New York City 10022; or The Russ Bldg., 235 Montgomery St., Suite 1035, San Francisco 94104. For travel information, contact the Swiss National Tourist Office, 608 5th Ave., New York City 10022, (212)757-5944.

Swiss National Tourist Office, 608 5th Ave., New York NY 10020. Public Relations Director: Walter Bruderer.
Purpose: Promotion of tourism in Switzerland.
Services: Offers photos.
How to Contact: Write. Credit line and return of pictures required.

Embassy of Thailand, 2300 Kalorama Rd. NW, Washington DC 20008. (202)667-1446.
Contact: Public Relations Office.
Purpose: Information covers business, economics, history and politics.
Services: Offers brochures/pamphlets.
How to Contact: Write or call.

Embassy of the Republic of Turkey, 1606 23rd St. NW, Washington DC 20008.
(202)667-6400, 667-7581, or 667-1024. Contact: Information Department.
Purpose: "Representation, bilateral relations with the US, and information on Turkey." Information covers agriculture, art, business, economics, entertainment, food, history, industry, law, music, nature, politics, recreation and travel.
Services: Offers statistics, brochures/pamphlets, information searches and tourist and travel photos. Publications include fact sheets on a variety of subjects. Cancelled stamps and flags are also available.
How to Contact: Write or call.

Embassy of the Republic of Uganda, 5909 16th St. NW, Washington DC 20011.
(202)726-7100. Contact: Information Department.
Purpose: Information covers business, economics, history, music, politics, travel and culture.
Services: Offers brochures/pamphlets and information searches.
How to Contact: "Written requests preferred."

Embassy of the Union of Soviet Socialist Republics, 1125 16th St. NW, Washington DC 20036. (202)232-3756. Contact: Information Office.
Purpose: Information covers business, industry and politics.
Services: Offers brochures/pamphlets and information searches. Publications include *One Hundred Questions and Answers about the U.S.S.R.* and pamphlets on industry, construction, etc.
How to Contact: Write. Suggests that writers also consult *Soviet Life* magazine.

Consulate General of Venezuela, 7 E. 51st St., New York NY 10022. (212)826-1660
Contact: Public Relations Department for general information and the Visas Department for information on visas.
Purpose: "This is a consulate general and the main purpose of this office is to deal with the corresponding consular affairs." Information covers specific data on the country of Venezuela and cultural and economic facts.
Services: Offers brochures/pamphlets.
How to Contact: Write.

Consulate General of Venezuela, 20 N. Wacker Dr., Chicago IL 60606. (312)236-9655.
Consul General: F. Ganteaume Pantin.
Purpose: Provides "Venezuelan visas, information, cultural affairs information, passports, tourist information, Venezuelan notary public, etc." Information covers agriculture, art, business, celebrities, economics, food, health/medicine, history, industry, law, music, politics, science and travel.
Services: Offers brochures/pamphlets.
How to Contact: Write or call.

Venezuelan Government Tourist and Information Center, 450 Park Ave., New York NY 10022. (212)355-1101. Assistant Director: Berta Zurumay.
Purpose: "To inform people about Venezuela." Information covers art, food, history, music, recreation and travel.
Services: Offers brochures/pamphlets, information searches and photos. Publications include *Caracas Guide, Adventurous Things To Do in Venezuela* and *Venezuela A to Z.*
How to Contact: Write or call.

West Indies Department of Tourism, Ministry of Home Affairs and Tourism, St. Vincent, West Indies. Contact: Director of Tourism.
Purpose: "To promote tourism to St. Vincent." Information covers entertainment, food, nature, recreation, sports and travel.
Services: Offers statistics, brochures/pamphlets, newsletters, and photos. Publications include map, brochures and travel guides of St.Vincent.
How to Contact: Write.

Embassy of the S.F.R. of Yugoslavia, 2410 California St. NW, Washington DC 20008. (202)462-6566. Counselor: Dusko Trifunovic.
Purpose: "We represent our country." Information covers agriculture, art, business, economics, entertainment, history, law, music, nature, new product information, politics, science, sport and technical data.
Services: Offers aid in arranging interviews, annual reports, bibliographies, biographies, statistics, brochures/pamphlets, information searches, placement on mailing list, newsletter, photos and press kits. Publications include brochures and pamphlets on "facts about Yugoslavia, Yugoslav survey, Yugoslav news, Yugoslav information bulletin, Socialist thought and practice and many others."
How to Contact: Write.

International & United Nations Organizations

External Publications-Department of Public Information, United Nations, 1 United Nations Plaza, Room 530, New York NY 10017. (212)754-8262. Executive Publications Office: Mr. Aung.
Purpose: "We put out daily press releases on all activities of the UN." Information covers economics, science, technical data, housing, and population development.
Services: Offers annual reports, brochures/pamphlets, information searches, statistics, and newsletter and press kits (which are not mailed).
How to Contact: Write or call.

Food and Agriculture Organization of the United Nations, Liaison Office for North America, 1776 F St. NW, Washington DC 20437. (202)634-6215. Regional Information Advisor: Keith Smith.
Purpose: "The Food and Agriculture Organization (FAO) of the UN works to raise levels of nutrition and standards of living of rural people. It also attempts to improve the efficiency of production and distribution of all food and agricultural products. The FAO is headquartered in Rome, Italy, and has a membership of 144 nations. FAO personnel were working in 118 countries and territories at the beginning of 1978. These field project activitie involved 1,800 specialists in various aspects of agriculture, forestry and fisheries projects. FAO also serves as a forum for world exchange of various agricultural questions and gathers global statistics. In addition, it sponsors major events such as the World Conference in Agrarian Reform and Rural Development (WCARRD)." Information covers agriculture.
Services: Offers aid in arranging interviews, bibliographies, statistics, brochures/pamphlets, placement on mailing list, newsletter and photos. "Basic brochures on the work of FAO are available—e.g., *The FAO, What it Is, What it Does, How it Works*; *Seeds of Progress*; summary sheets on various aspects of FAO's work in forestries, fisheries and agriculture; and the FAO catalog, *Books in Print*.
How to Contact: "Contact the information section of the FAO Liaison Office for North America. No fees are charged for any material furnished by this office. If it's necessary to request either black and white prints or color slides from FAO headquarters, however, a charge of $5/item, plus a $25 flat research fee, is made."

International Civil Aviation Organization (ICAO), 1000 Sherbrooke St. W., Montreal, Quebec, Canada H3A 2R2. (514)285-8219. Contact: Public Information Office.

Purpose: "To foster the development of international air transport by establishing international standards and procedures, and to promote safety, uniformity and efficiency in air navigation throughout the world. This organization provides the machinery for the achievement of international cooperation in the air."
Services: Offers brochures/pamphlets. Publications include *Facts about ICAO*.
How to Contact: Write or call.

Organization of American States, Great Secretariat, Washington DC 20006. (202)381-8700. Librarian: Carl L. Headen.
Purpose: "Photo records. We have 45,000 photos in our collection."
Services: Offers photos, agriculture, antiquities, art, cities and towns, education, historical, industry, minerals, native activities, natural history, political, portraits, public welfare, recreation, topography and transportation.
How to Contact: Write or call. Offers editorial, advertising, reproduction and all rights. Charges $2 service charge and $2.50 print fee. Free catalog on request.

Organization of American States, Photographic Records, Graphic Services Unit, 19th St. and Constitution Ave. NW, Washington DC 20006. (202)381-8700. Contact: C.L. Headen.
Purpose: Organizations of nations in the Western Hemisphere. Information covers agriculture, antiquities, art, cities and towns, education, history,industry, minerals, native activities, natural history, politics, portraits, public welfare, recreation, topography, transportation, Latin America, Barbados, Jamaica, Trinidad and Tobago.
Services: Offers 35,000 b&w photos. Collection is in the public domain.
How to Contact: Charges $2/print. Credit line required. Return of pictures not required.

Standards Council of Canada, 350 Sparks St., Suite 1203, Ottawa, Canada K1R 7S8. (613)238-3222. Manager, Communications: Jacques Robitaille.
Purpose: "The Standards Council of Canada (SCC) was established in 1970 by act of Parliament 'to foster and promote voluntary standardization' in fields relating to the construction, manufacture, production, quality, performance and safety of buildings, structures, manufactured articles and products and other goods. The SCC carries out its task through the National Standards System (NSS), a federation of accredited independent organizations concerned with standards-writing, certification and testing coordinated by the SCC." Information covers standards and the National Standards System of Canada.
Services: Offers annual reports and brochures/pamphlets. Publications include various brochures and pamplets pertaining to voluntary standardization in Canada.
How to Contact: Write or call.

United Nations, UN Plaza and 42nd St., New York NY 10017. Distribution Officer: Marvin Weill.
Purpose: Represents the work of the UN in economic and social development and human rights throughout the world.
Services: Offers more than 140,000 selected negatives, b&w and color, on the work of the UN and its specialized agencies throughout the world. Also provides meeting coverage.
How to Contact: Material may not be used for advertising purposes and must be used in a UN context. Credit must be given to UN. Charges print fee of $1/b&w photo; service fee of $6/color transparency; and $25/each color photo published. Unused transparencies must be returned, in usable condition, within 30 days.

United Nations Center Against Apartheid, United Nations Plaza, New York NY 10017. (212)754-535. Chief, Unit for Publicity Against Apartheid: Mr. Abdennour Abrous.
Purpose: "To administer the UN Trust Fund for South Africa, the UN Educational and Training Programme for Southern Africa and the UN Trust Fund for Publicity Against Apartheid. To service the General Assembly's Special Committee against Apartheid,

the Advisory Committee on the United Nations Educational and Training Programme for Southern Africa and the Committee of Trustees of the United Nations Trust Fund for South Africa." Information covers economics, health/medicine, history, law, politics, sports and all aspects relating to apartheid in South Africa.
Services: Offers aid in arranging interviews, statistics, brochures/pamphlets, placement on mailing list, newsletter and photos. Publications include pamphlets, posters and *Notes and Documents* (weekly).
How to Contact: Write.

United Nations Development Program, 1 United Nations Plaza, New York NY 10017. (212)754-4690. Director, Special Services: John L. von Arnold.
Purpose: "We provide assistance to the development projects of developing countries, at their request, in the form of experts' services, equipment, consultations and fellowships. Projects assisted are in all economic and social areas (agriculture, industry, education, health, planning, transportation, communication, etc.)." Information covers agriculture, health/medicine and industry.
Services: Offers annual reports and brochures/pamphlets. Publications include basic information brochures on activities, background briefs on development issues, descriptions of technical cooperation among developing countries and fact sheets on various sectors of activity.
How to Contact: Write or call. "We can provide information only on development activities with which the UN Development Programme is concerned. We do not have basic information on individual countries."

United Nations Economic Commission for Europe, Palais des Nations, CH-1211, Geneva 10, Switzerland. (022)34-60-11. Contact: Information Officer.
Purpose: "All UN member countries in Europe and the US and Canada (34 countries) are members of the Economic Commission for Europe (ECE), which provides a permanent means of intergovernmental consultation and action on a wide variety of economic, scientific and technological subjects. Priorities are in the fields of promoting trade (particularly East-West trade), scientific and technological exchange, protection of the environment, and long-term projections and programming." Information covers agriculture, economics, industry, technical data, inland transport, timber, trade and technology.
Services: Offers aid in arranging interviews, statistics and placement on mailing list. Publications include *ECE: A Key to Economic Cooperation*.
How to Contact: Write. "Most ECE documents (as distinct from publications) are for restricted circulation only. An enquiry to the Information Officer will determine whether a particular item may be made available."

United Nations Office of Assistant Secretary General. (see United Nations Office of Press and Publications Division listing).

United Nations Office of Non-Governmental Organizations, (see United Nations Office of Press and Publications Division listing).

United Nations Office of Press and Publications Division, Room 378, United Nations, New York NY 10017. (212)754-7160. Contact: Director of Press and Publications:
Purpose: "We release information to the press on all organizations and committees through news briefings and give out information for publication."
Services: Offers aid in arranging interviews, annual reports, bibliographies, biographies, brochures/pamphlets, information searches, statistics, placement on mailing list and newsletter. Publications available.
How to Contact: Write.

United Nations Public Information Office of the Center for Economics and Social Information, United Nations Plaza, Room 1061, New York NY 10017. (212)754-6864.

Director of Agency: Leon Magairac.
Purpose: "Dissemination of information on the activities of UN, especially to developing and developed countries. Our services are aimed more at developing nations. We
also help different offices with information programs." Information covers agriculture, business, economics and technical data.
Services: Offers aid in arranging interviews, annual reports, brochures/pamphlets,
information searches, placement on mailing list, newsletter and press kits. Publications available.
How to Contact: Write or call.

World Bank, International Development Association, 1818 H St. NW, Washington DC
20433. (202)477-2403. Contact: Publications Office.
Purpose: "The World Bank provides financial and technical help for the development
of poor countries. It is now lending about $7,000 million a year to help raise the
standard of living in developing countries. The bank has also committed itself to
helping member countries with their more intractable development problems. Thanks
to increased contributions in recent years by the wealthier members of the bank's
affiliate, the International Development Association (IDA), more assistance has gone
to the very poor countries that are most in need. The World Bank and International
Development Association are two legally and financially distinct entities. The two
constitute, however, a closely integrated unit and are administered by the same staff."
Information covers agriculture, economics, education, population and public health,
trade, regional integration, environment, industry, transportation and many other
subjects relating to development aid and economics.
Services: Offers annual reports, statistics, brochures/pamphlets and placement on
mailing list. Publications include *World Bank Catalog of Publications*, which lists
available materials; *World Bank*, a descriptive brochure; *IDA: International Development Association*, a descriptive booklet; and various others.
How to Contact: Write. The World Bank distributes free publications as listed in the
publications catalog; orders for publications for sale must be placed with the publisher
or distributor of the work as listed in the catalog. Some World Bank publications may
be available in bookstores.

World Citizen Assembly, 312 Sutter St., Room 608, San Francisco CA 94108.
(415)421-0836. Secretary General: Douglas Mattern.
Purpose: "To organize people and organizations into an effective global movement for
controlled disarmament and world peace, and to build a representative UN able to
settle disputes between nations through the framework of world law. We hold a large
World Citizen Assemblies every two years, which are attended by people and organi-
zatons from many countries." Information covers politics.
Services: Offers statistics, brochures/pamphlets and newsletter.
How to Contact: Write or call.

Government Information Sources

Despite highly publicized wars between government officials and the press, writers and the government are *not* natural enemies. In many ways, they are actually allies able to help one another. Writers help the government by communicating a variety of information to the public; the government helps writers by locating specific information to which the government has access.

The amount of information available from government sources makes superlatives like "vast" seem lame. Thousands of documents, reports, press releases and other publications useful to writers/researchers are issued by departments, bureaus, offices, boards, commissions and so on, and these only preview the available information that isn't distributed in the form of public documents. The information available is as immense as the government itself.

That fact may cause you to fall back on another adjective describing government and its information: "formidable." If you remember a few suggestions, however, you'll find that the word can be temporarily dropped from your vocabulary.

The immensity of the available information requires writers/researchers to be specific in their requests. "Know *exactly* what you are looking for," advises Vincent J. Tuscher, an emergency information officer with the Defense Civil Preparedness Agency. Precision when requesting information pays off in precise information. A "tell me everything you know about..." kind of request often results in no information at all, or in information of such a generalized nature as to be useless. A general information request also presents problems timewise. Some materials are "of such a constantly changing nature that extensive compilation time could render that information useless," says Ronald L. Henderson, a public information officer with the US Dept. of Energy. Henderson's recommendations about requesting information from the energy department can be applied to almost every government agency or office: "Focus carefully upon your subject matter, since the field of energy information and data is fantastically broad and incredibly complex. Determine exactly what time span you want to cover in your work and allow us extra time for a response since we may encounter difficulty in researching your request. Familiarize yourself with the existing energy legislation and the organization of the Department of Energy so you will know to what division to direct your request."

Other government information officials agree with various points of Henderson's recommendations, particularly those related to allowing the sources as much time as possible to respond, and with knowing what department to approach with your request. That latter consideration isn't as important as the former because, in many cases, you won't have any conception of whom to approach first; the extra time for which you must allow comes in routing your request to the appropriate authority.

"Some of that routing time can be avoided by consulting government offices in your area," says Tacy Cook, public information officer of the US Treasury Bureau of Alcohol, Tobacco and Firearms. "Talk to local offices of government agencies first to narrow down the agency and its record group that may have the information you need. Then come to or contact the headquarters office with the name of a specific individual or the name of a specific file that you seek." Specific contact people are often, but not always, listed in the listings that follow; where no person is listed, anyone in the office may be able to help you. In fact, just getting to the right office is enough in most cases. "Personnel changes are as unpredictable as the Washington weather," write the editors of *Washington Information Directory 1978-79*. "When someone retires or is transferred, his office and telephone do not go with him." The *Washington Information Directory* editors also recommend contacting your local Congressman to get yourself pointed in the right direction.

When consulting government sources, remember that they provide *information*, not *research*. "Organize your inquiries and try not to place the whole burden of *finding* information from the information source," says Frances B. King, public information officer with the New England River Basins Commission. "We can suggest the directions a researcher can take, but cannot carry out research projects *for* him by ourselves."

Not all government sources will gladly hand out everything you request, of course. As Ronald Henderson points out, "Certain information is classified and cannot be released due to national security considerations." Other information may be embarrassing to government officials, so you'll occasionally encounter reluctance in releasing it. In cases like this, the Freedom of Information Act can be a valuable tool. The Freedom of Information Office of the Department of State (listed below) can provide procedural information about using the act. *Government Manual*, published by the Office of the Federal Register, National Archives and Records Service, also discusses the Freedom of Information Act, as well as other federal regulations that affect writers.

If you're unsure about which government office to approach with a question, write the Federal Information Center (601 E. 12th St., Kansas City, Missouri 64106). Information officers at the center will refer you to the appropriate authority.

Other sources of information about government information sources include *Washington Information Directory* (published by *Congressional Quarterly*, 1414 22nd St. NW, Washington, D.C. 20037); *Washington Information Workbook* and *A Researcher's Guide to Washington* (both published by Washington Researchers, 910 17th St. NW, Washington, D.C. 20006); and *Government Manual*. The Government Printing Office (Washington, D.C. 20402) publishes monthly catalogs like *Selected U.S. Government Publications*, which are useful in keeping track of the myriad books and reports published by the government.

Approached properly, government offices can be helpful and informative. As Frances King comments, "Since a good part of our business is to *provide* information to the public, we gear our work accordingly and welcome inquiries."

Action, Office of Communications, 806 Connecticut Ave. NW, Room P-303, Washington DC 20525. (202)254-7526. Director: Marylou Batt.
Purpose: "Action, the federal agency for volunteer services, administers the Peace Corps, VISTA, Retired Senior Volunteer Program, Foster Grandparent Program and various demonstration programs. The Office of Communications responds to media inquiries, issues press releases and feature articles, publishes various publications for volunteers and staff, produces brochures and flyers, and conducts print and broadcast advertising campaigns for recruitment of volunteers." Information covers agency news and activities of volunteers.
Services: Offers aid in arranging interviews, annual reports, biographies, brochures/ pamphlets, photos and press kits. Publications include general recruitment and information brochures for each program.
How to Contact: Write or call.

Action, 515 Congress, #1414, Austin TX 78701. (512)397-5925. Area Manager: Catherine Weir.
Purpose: "Action is the umbrella federal agency for volunteer programs." Information

covers agriculture, economics, health/medicine, development how-to and self-help. **Services:** Offers annual reports, bibliographies, biographies, statistics, brochures/ pamphlets, regular informational newsletter, photos and press kits. Publications include "numerous pamphlets on the Peace Corps and Vista, describing the programs, requirements, how to apply, and benefits."
How to Contact: Write or call.

Administrative Conference of the United States, 2120 L St. NW, Suite 500, Washington DC 20037. Contact: Office of Chairman.
Purpose: To identify the causes of inefficiency, delay and unfairness in administrative proceedings affecting private rights and to recommend improvements to the president, the agencies, the Congress and courts.
Services: Offers volumes I, II and III of the *Recommendations and Reports of the Administrative Conference of the U.S.*, published in July, 1971, June, 1973, and June, 1975, respectively, which contain the official texts of the recommendations adopted by the assembly (available from Superintendent of Documents, Government Printing Office, Washington DC).
How to Contact: Write.

Agricultural Marketing Service, Department of Agriculture, Washington DC 20250. Contact: Director, Information Division.
Purpose: Responsible for market news, standardization and grading of cotton and tobacco, marketing agreements and orders, packer and stockyard regulations, and specified regulatory programs. Provides various marketing services for nearly all agricultural commodities.
Services: Offers publications, photos, a catalog of available publications, and other assistance.

Agricultural Stabilization and Conservation Service, Department of Agriculture, Box 2415, Information Division, Washington DC 20013. (202)447-5237. Contact: Director.
Purpose: "A service agency dedicated to providing the best possible administration of farm programs." Information covers agriculture.
Services: Offers statistics and brochures/pamphlets. Publications include material on many agricultural topics, particularly those related to farm programs.
How to Contact: Write or call.

Air Force Accounting and Finance Center, Denver CO 80231. (301)320-7741. Director of Information: Lt. Col. Guy E. Brown.
Purpose: "We account for all Air Force money; pay all Air Force active duty, reserve, guard and retired personnel; design all financial management systems for worldwide accounting and finance network; and handle all the accounts, bill and collections for all Department of Defense foreign military sales." Information covers business, technical data and financial management.
Services: Offers aid in arranging interviews, biographies, statistics, information searches, photos and press kits.
How to Contact: Write. Charges for costs incurred in search (copies, etc.).
Tips: "Special areas of current interest to writers are electronic funds transfer (three-fourths of the USAF is paid this way) and the extensive computer remote network for pay data for individual members."

Air Force Central Still Photo Depository, 1221 S. Fern St., Arlington VA 22202.
Services: Offers approximately 300,000 photos with a corresponding visual print file for research use. "The collection consists of b&w and color still photos, negatives and transparencies depicting the history and progress of the Air Force. This coverage includes equipment, aircraft, personnel, missiles, officer portraits, unit insignia, etc."
How to Contact: Charges 75¢-$6.50/ b&w, $1-17.50/ color.

Air Force Service Information and News Center, Magazine and Book Division, HNB, Kelly Air Force Base TX 78241. (512)925-6781. Contact: Chief of Magazine and Book Division.
Purpose: "Established writers seeking information for use in articles concernng any aspect of the Air Force should contact the Magazine and Book Division. This division also provides a referral service for those authors engaged in historical research on the Air Force."
Services: Offers assistance.
How to Contact: Write. Field offices: 663 5th Ave., Room 340, New York NY 10022, (212)753-5609; 219 Dearborn Ave., Room 246-D, Chicago IL 60604, (312)353-8300; and 11000 Wilshire Blvd., Los Angeles CA 90024, (213)824-7517.

Alaska Outer Continental Shelf Office, Bureau of Land Management, Department of the Interior, Box 1159, Anchorage AK 99510. (907)276-2955. Public Information Officer: Consuelo (Connie) Wassink. Assistant Manager: Robert J. Brock.
Purpose: "This office, plus three others (New Orleans; New York and Pacific, located in Los Angeles), are field offices implementing the marine minerals management program of the BLM, under the Submerged Lands Act and OCS Lands Act, both of 1953, plus the 1978 amendments to the OCS Lands Act. This includes day-to-day operations of the minerals leasing (oil and natural gas) programs and granting of marine pipeline rights-of-way associated with offshore oil-gas exploration and, if successful, production outside the limits of the territorial seas; also involves all aspects of data collection pertinent to production of site-specific environmental impact statements." Information covers business, economics, law, science, technical data and "public participation in federal government decision making (in this case, two-year leasing process with specific steps of public involvement)."
Services: Offers aid in arranging interviews, bibliographies, statistics, brochures/pamphlets, placement on mailing list, photos and press kits (at specific occasions). "For a specific request for background information, we can supply certain clips from the public information office morgue directly related to sale proposal. A literature survey is conducted by a socioeconomic study contractor on all aspects of activities in Alaska; if supplies are exhausted, accession numbers for the documents are made available at low cost by National Technical Information Services." Publications available.
How to Contact: Write. "Send an inquiry detailing something of the writer's interest so that appropriate background information can be supplied together with the latest news releases. We cannot supply proprietary information that the petroleum furnishes to the Geological Survey nor details on the nominations the industry makes during a Bureau of Land Management call for nominations and comments, the initial step in the 2-year leasing process that examines an area for potential sale of leases by the federal government."

Alcohol, Drug Abuse and Mental Health Administration, National Clearinghouse for Alcohol, National Clearinghouse for Drug Abuse, National Clearinghouse for Mental Health, 5600 Fishers Lane, Rockville MD 20857. (301)443-3783. Contact: Director of the Office of Communications and Public Affairs.
Purpose: "To provide research, service and training in the areas of alcohol, drugs and mental health." Information covers economics, food, health/medicine, history, how-to, industry, law, music (as therapy), recreation (as therapy), science, self-help and technical data.
Services: Offers aid in arranging interviews, bibliographies, biographies, statistics, brochures/pamphlets, information searches, placement on mailing list, newsletter, photos and press kits. "Three publication lists are available—one each for alcohol, drug abuse and mental health."
How to Contact: Write or call the National Clearinghouse for Alcohol, the National Clearinghouse for Drug Abuse or the National Clearinghouse for Mental Health at the

above address and phone number. Charges only for Freedom of Information request or for some publications that are available only from the superintendent of documents.

American Battle Monuments Commission, 4C014 Forrestal Bldg., 1000 Independence Ave. SW, Washington DC 20314. Director of Operations: Col. William E. Ryan Jr.
Purpose: "The principal functions are to commemorate the services of the American forces where they have served since April 6, 1917; to design, construct, operate and maintain permanent American military burial grounds."
Services: Offers "reference information concerning the cemeteries, photographs, individual cemetery booklets, and a general information pamphlet which briefly lists and describes the cemeteries under our care. The commission publishes an information newsletter and periodically updates it as required. A copy of the newsletter may be obtained by writing to the commission."
How to Contact: Write.

Appalachian Regional Commission, 1666 Connecticut Ave. NW, Washington DC 20235. (202)673-7835. Editor: Elise Kendrick.
Purpose: "We are a Federal and state partnership governed and funded by the Federal government and 13 Appalachian states. We are the largest regional economical development program in United States history. The commission, created in 1965, includes all of West Virginia and parts of Alabama, Georgia, Maryland, Mississippi, New York, North Carolina, Ohio, Pennsylvania, South Carolina, Tennessee and Virginia." Information covers arts and crafts, business, personalities, economics, entertainment, health/medicine, history, industry, music, recreation and any information pertaining to development of the area.
Services: Offers aid in arranging interviews, annual reports, bibliographies, brochures/pamphlets, placement on mailing list, statistics, newsletter and press kits. Publications available.
How to Contact: Write or call. "We have a limited staff and must prioritize in answering requests. We also have a library and reading room available."

Army Corps of Engineers, Lower Mississippi Valley Division, Box 80, Vicksburg MS 39180. (601)636-1311, ext. 5757. Chief, Public Affairs Office: Herbert A. Kassner.
Purpose: "This agency provides for flood protection and improvement to navigation on the lower Mississippi River from Cape Girardeau, Missouri, to the Gulf of Mexico. We distribute brochures and pamphlets on request throughout our division, covering 149,000 square miles in parts of eight states, plus the public at large."
Services: Offers brochures/pamphlets. Publications include *Mississippi River Navigation* ("fully illustrated, reviews the history of the river, early navigation and flood control works, as well as present day commerce") and *Flood Control—Lower Mississippi River Valley* ("history and description of the flood protection project").

Army Corps of Engineers, Omaha District, 215 N. 17th St., Omaha NE 68102. (402)221-3917. Public Affairs Officer: Betty M. White.
Purpose: "The district has extensive military engineering, construction and real estate responsibilities for the Army and Air Force in 12 states. We are also actively engaged in planning and building projects for flood control, navigation and water conservation—and during emergencies, we assist local authorites. We also manage recreation at a number of lakes and operate and maintain dams." Information covers history, nature, recreation and science.
Services: Offers aid in arranging interviews, statistics, brochures/pamphlets, placement on mailing list, and photos. "We also have recreation brochures for each lake we operate and historical highlights of the Corps of Engineers."

How to Contact: Write or call. "Generally we would not charge unless there was an excessive amount of duplicating involved which is most unlikly.

Army Hometown News Center, 607 Hardesty, Kansas City MO 64124. (816)374-6231. Executive Officer: Maj. Robert Bernard.
Purpose: "To provide news stories, feature stories and feature TV releases on soldiers to appropriate local media or special interest publications." Information covers recreation and sports.
Services: Offers aid in arranging interviews and photos. "We constantly identify, write or rewrite and distribute stories on service members. When requested, we have some capability to develop information on specific service members."
How to Contact: Call or write. "We can provide output on soldiers from any area specified; however, we cannot provide output solely on the basis of race, religion or national origin."
Tips: "Call us to discuss any concept. In many instances, we are not the best source, but we can normally refer the writer to an appropriate POC."

Army Public Affairs Office (New York Branch), 663 5th Ave., New York NY 10022. (212)688-7572. Branch Chief: Colonel John C. Grant.
Purpose: "We provide an accessible contact point for New York based media on military matters and facilitate a better understanding of the Army. Capabilities include: providing photographs and slides to illustrate magazine or newspaper articles or books; providing stock footage for motion pictures and TV programming; assistance in research of Army related topics; checking ads and commercials for military accuracy; review of magazine articles, movie scripts, TV scripts and other copy; providing releases, articles and story ideas for publications; and providing contacts within the Army for interviews or technical information." Information covers health/medicine, history, new product information and military affairs.
Services: Offers aid in arranging interviews, biographies, statistics, information searches, photos and press kits. Publications include a wide range of internal military pamphlets/brochures.
How to Contact: Write, call or visit. "There is a minimal charge for film loan or extensive research."

Army Reserves, 120th US Army Reserve Command, Lee Rd., Ft. Jackson SC 29207. (803)751-7579. Public Information Officer: Michael W. Quinn.
Purpose: "The command and control of all US Army Reserve units in both North and South Carolina which are not attached to a division. This includes approximately 6,000 reservists in 83 units in 36 cities and towns." Information covers Army Reserves military information and activities.
Services: Offers aid in arranging interviews, biographies, statistics, brochures/ pamphlets, clipping services, information searches, newsletter, photos and press kits. Publications include *The Role of Reserve Components in Today's Army*, *Pay and Benefits* and *Misconception About the Army Reserve*.
How to Contact: Write or call.

Bureau of Economic Analysis, Department of Commerce, Washington DC 20230. Contact: Public Information Officer.
Services: Offers basic economic measures of the national economy (such as gross national product), current analysis of the economic situation and business outlook, and general economic research on the functioning of the economy.
How to Contact: Write.

Bureau of Economics and Business Affairs, Department of State, 2201 C St. NW,

Washington DC 20520. Special Assistant for Legislative and Public Affairs: Walter Lockwood.
Purpose: "To formulate and implement policy on international economic affairs in relation to domestic economic affairs." Information covers agriculture, business, economics, food, industry, energy, transportation, international finances and international trade.
Services: Offers aid in arranging interviews and brochures/pamphlets.
How to Contact: Write or call.

Bureau of Engraving and Printing, 14th and C Sts. SW, Washington DC 20228. Information Specialist: Betty L. Russell.
Purpose: "The Bureau of Engraving and Printing manufactures US paper currency, postage stamps and approximately 800 miscellaneous security products."
Services: Offers statistics, brochures/pamphlets and information searches. Publications include *Production of Government Securities*.
How to Contact: Write. Charges $5/hour if research exceeds one hour, and 10¢/photocopy.

Bureau of Labor Statistics, 1515 Broadway, New York NY 10036. (212)399-5405. Chief, Branch of Information and Advisory Services: Martin Karlin.
Purpose: Statistics gathering agency of the Department of Labor. "We disseminate information on and advise the public on the use of our statistics. We have information on consumer and producer prices, employment and unemployment productivity, occupational outlook, wages and industrial relations." Information covers business, economics, food, health/medicine and technical data.
Services: Offers bibliographies, statistics, brochures/pamphlets, placement on mailing list, and newsletter. Brochures/pamphlets include *Handbook of Labor Statistics, Monthly Labor Review, Occupational Outlook Quarterly, Occupational Outlook Handbook, Occupational Outlook for College Graduates, BLS Handbook of Methods, BLS Catalog of Publications, BLS Major Programs* and *Employment and Earnings*.
How to Contact: Write, call or visit. Charges 10¢/photocopy. Government Printing Office publications are for sale.

Bureau of Land Management, Office of Public Affairs, Department of the Interior, Washington DC 20240.
Services: Offers information and photos on the management of 473 million acres of national resource lands (public domain) mostly in 10 western states and Alaska; on forest, range, water, wildlife and recreation resources; on resource uses, including camping, hunting, fishing, hiking, rock hunting and off-road vehicle use; and on primitive, historic, natural and scenic areas.
How to Contact: Write or call.

Bureau of Mines, Department of the Interior, 2401 E St. NW, Washington DC 20241. (202)634-1004. Chief, Office of Mineral Information: R.O. Swenarton.
Purpose: "A research and statistics agency. We conduct scientific and engineering research in metallurgy and mining, compile and analyze statistical information on nonfuel mineral supply and demand, and investigate mineral potential of federal lands proposed for preservation as parks, refuges and other special purposes. Because of a series of US government reorganizations, several important functions historically associated with the Bureau of Mines have been transferred out of the bureau and reassigned to newly established federal agencies. Mine safety regulations and inspections are now the responsibility of the Labor Department's new Mine Safety and Health Administration, although mine safety and health research are still responsibilities of the Bureau of Mines. All Bureau of Mines programs directly concerned with energy (fuel statistics, technology of oil, coal and natural gas production and use) have been transferred to the Department of Energy." Information covers industry, science and

technical data on mining, metallurgy, mineral commodities, mine safety and health, and recycling metals."

Services: Offers aid in arranging interviews, annual reports, statistics, brochures/ pamphlets, placement on mailing list, informational motion pictures on mineral subjects, and free subscriptions to a monthly list of new Bureau of Mines technical publications. Publications include "popular-style descriptive booklets on the bureau and its programs"; *Mineral Commodity Summaries*, (free, on request, from Bureau of Mines); and other material available through the Government Printing Office, including *Dictionary of Mining, Mineral and Related Terms* and *Mineral Facts and Problems.*

How to Contact: Write or call. "Many reports are distributed by the bureau without charge, and many university and other federal depository libraries keep a complete file of Bureau of Mines publications. Other bureau reports are issued on a sales basis by the Government Printing Office. Reprints and papers or microfiche copies of unpublished 'open file reports' are sold by the commerce department's National Technical Information Service, Springfield VA 22161.

Bureau of Reclamation, Department of the Interior, Public Affairs Service Center, Denver Federal Center, Bldg. 67, Denver CO 80225. (303)234-6260. Acting Chief, Public Affairs Service Center: Kathy Wood Loveless.

Purpose: "The Bureau of Reclamation is the primary water resource development agency of the federal government operating in the 17 western states. We construct dams and other water conveyances. Our reservoirs are used for numerous kinds of recreation, such as boating, fishing, water skiing, camping and sightseeing. We are conducting research in new sources of energy, such as solar, wind and geothermal. Two of our new programs, environmental education and public involvement, are aimed at providing the public with more information regarding the environment and with receiving more input from the public regarding our activities and decisions." Information covers agriculture, nature, recreation and water resources.

Services: Offers aid in arranging interviews, annual reports, biographies, statistics, brochures/pamphlets, limited information searches, placement on mailing list, newsletter, photos and press kits.

How to Contact: Write or call.

Census Bureau, Department of Commerce, Washington DC 20233. (301)763-2400, 763-7024. Contact: Data User Services Division. Assistant Division Chief for Statistical Reports: William Lerner.

Purpose: "The Bureau of the Census is a general-purpose statistical agency whose primary function is to collect, process, compile and disseminate statistical data for the use of the general public and other government agencies. The Census Bureau occupies a unique place in the federal statistical system—it publishes more statistics than other federal statistical agencies do, covers a wider range of subjects, and serves a greater variety of needs. Through censuses and surveys, the Census Bureau collects data on population, housing, state and local governments, agriculture, construction, business, manufacturers, mineral industries, foreign trade, transportation, and other subjects. Resulting statistics are available in printed reports, microform, and computer tape. Depending on the type of statistics, they are reported for city blocks, census tracts, ZIP code areas, cities, counties, and various other geographic areas. The bureau also offers such related products and services as population estimates and projections, guides, maps, press releases, a monthly newsletter, statistical compendia, reports on survey methodology, and training programs." Information covers agriculture, business, economics and industry.

Services: Offers statistics, brochures/pamphlets and newsletter. "A variety of pamphlets describing the statistical products and services of the Census Bureau are available."

How to Contact: "Write or call the Data User Services Division and indicate the types of statistical information needed. Relevant pamphlets and order forms will be sent. For press releases and other news media services, write or call the public information office(301)763-7273. Statistical reports, reference publications, and statistical data on computer tape are sold by the Census Bureau or, in some cases, the Government Printing Office. Introductory materials, such as the pamphlets, and assistance in dertermining what relevant data are available are generally provided free of charge. The Census Bureau has user services specialists in its regional offices in the following cities: Atlanta, Boston, Charlotte, Chicago, Dallas, Denver, Detroit, Kansas City, Kansas, Los Angeles, New York, Philadelphia and Seattle. These specialists can assist users in locating data and obtaining publications. They also conduct training programs on census products and services."

Census Bureau, 1700 Westlake Ave. N., Seattle WA 98109. (206)442-7080. Data User Services Officer: Lyle Larson.
Purpose:"The Census Bureau collects a myriad of information of a demographic and economic nature. Each of the 12 regional offices of the Census Bureau has a data users service to assist users in locating census statistics, either in person or by telephone. Information covers business and technical data.
Services: Offers bibliographies, statistics, and brochures/pamphlets. "Through data delivery services, Bureau products are made available in a variety of formats: printed reports, machine-readable data files and computer programs, maps and geographic products, microfiche and microfilm, and printouts prepared from data files. For a complete description of these products and how to obtain them, see the *Bureau of the Census Catalog*, which is available on subscription through the Government Printing Office. Other reference publications include such works as *Data Users News*(monthly), *Pocket Data Book, USA* (biennial), *Historical Statistics of the United States, Colonial Times to 1970,* and *Congressional District Data Book.* "The Census Bureau also condusts an educational program consisting of semiars, workshops, and training courses to inform users of the products available and to provide guidance in their use. The bureau maintains data files from which special tabulations covering specific geographic or subject matter areas can be prepared. These tabulations are supplied only on request and at user cost, and all materials are subject to review to make certain no individual information is disclosed. Bureau reports can be found in many libraries across the country, icnluding more than 1,000 libraries designated as federal depositories. Additionally, the publications are available for use in the 43 Department of Commerce district offices located in major cities. Trade specialists are available in these offices to provide marketing assistance and technical information to businesses.
How to Contact: Write or telephone the Data User Services Division at the above address.

Center for Disease Control, 1600 Clifton Rd. NE, Atlanta GA 30333. Director, Office of Information: Donald A. Berreth.
Purpose: "The Center for Disease Control (CDC) is one of six agencies of the U.S. Public Health Service. It is responsible for surveillance and control of communicable and vector-borne diseases, occupational safety and health, family planning, birth defects, lead-based paint poisoning, urban rat control, and health education. Programs include epidemic and/disease outbreaks, foreign travel (health recommendations and requirements), international activities, training of foreign health workers, etc."
Services: Offers reference and background materials and photographs on communicable diseases and other subjects. Publications include the *Morbidity and Mortality Weekly Report* and *Surveillance Reports.* Mailing lists are maintained and anyone may request these publications."
How to Contact: Write.

Coast Guard, Boating Information Branch, Washington DC 20590. (202)426-9716. Branch Chief: F.J. Lynch, Lt., U.S. Coast Guard.
Purpose: "To keep the public informed of safety procedures involved in recreational

boating. This is done through pamphlets, posters, news releases, feature articles, and radio and television public service announcements." Information covers boating safety.

Services: Offers statistics and brochures/pamphlets. Publications include *Visual Distress Signals, Boating Statistics, Emergency Repairs Afloat, Federal Requirements for Recreational Boats, Hypothermia and Cold Water Survival, First Aid for the Boatman* and *Passport to Pleasure Cruising.*

How to Contact: Call or write.

Coast Guard, Headquarters, 400 7th St. SW, Room 8315, Washington DC 20590. Contact: Chief, Public Affairs Division.

Services: Offers 100,000 photos of "vessels, light stations, other shore stations, rescues, Alaskan Patrols, Arctic, Antarctic, boating safety, and various others illustrating the multi-roles of the Coast Guard. Mostly 8x10 b&w glossies are available; some 35mm color transparency slides."

How to Contact: "Generally no fee when photos are to be used for publication. There is a fee of $1.25 for each 8x10 b&w glossy print for mere personal use. Color is not available for personal use. If for publication, the Coast Guard credit line must be used. The number of photos selected must be kept within reason. Photos not used are requested to be returned."

Coast Guard News and Photo Center, Bldg. 108, Room 1, Governors Island NY 10004. (212)668-7189. Center Supervisor: Bob Jones.

Purpose: Information office with material on search and rescue; marine safety patrols; aids to navigation; bridge construction; oil pollution, clean-up and control; lighthouses; fisherie patrols; ice-breaking; etc.

Services: Offers 2,000 b&w photos and 1,000 color slides. Material is in the public domain.

How to Contact: No charge to publications, "small charge for personal collections."

Coast Guard News and Photo Center, Third Coast Guard District, New York NY 10004. (212)264-4996. Contact: Photographic Officer.

Purpose: Government agency. Information covers the U.S. Coast Guard, search and rescue, marine safety, aids to navigation, recreational boating, oil pollution abatement, lighthouses, etc.

Services: Offers photos on a loan basis. "The collection is in the public domain."

How to Contact: Write or call. Generally makes no charge to qualified sources for publication. Makes modest charges for personal collections, etc. Credit line required. Fees: Prints made to order, $1.25/b&w; $3-50/color. Photocopies, $3.15/b&w; $6-25/color.

Commandant of Marine Corps, Washington DC 20380. (202)694-4309. Information Chief: Bob Jordon, Captain, USMC.

Purpose: "To inform Marine Corps family of important matters and to inform public of Marine Corps matters." Information covers history and sports.

Services: Offers aid in arranging interviews, annual reports, bibliographies, biographies, statistics, brochures/pamphlets, clipping services, and photos.

How to Contact: Write or call.

Commission on Civil Rights, 1121 Vermont Ave. NW, Washington DC 20425. (202)254-6697. Director of Public Affairs: Joan Larson Kelly.

Purpose: "The commission is an independent, bipartisan, fact-finding agency established by Congress. It appraises laws and policies concerned with the civil rights of minorities and women and makes recommendations to the President and Congress."

Services: "We can provide writers with copies of press releases on studies we have done on civil rights."

How to Contact: Write or call. "Studies are available at no charge by writing the publications division of the commission."

Committee for the Preservation of the White House, 1100 Ohio Dr. SW, Washington DC 20242. (202)426-6725. Executive Secretary: Elmer S. Atkins.
Purpose: "To recommend and approve decorating and furnishing projects at the White House and to preserve its museum character." Information covers art and history.
Services: Offers annual reports and brochures/pamphlets. Publications include "reports on accomplishments of each administration."
How to Contact: Write or call.

Congressional Record Index, Room 507B, Senate Courts, 120 C St. NE, Washington DC 20510. (202)224-1385. Chief Indexer: Jack W. Parsons.
Purpose: "We publish a biweekly and annual index to the *Congressional Record*. Information covers every subject in the *Congressional Record*.
Services: Offers biweekly and annual *Indexes to the Congressional Record* sent to all subscribers of the *Record* on request, sent to all depository libraries, and can be purchased from the Government Printing Office.
How to Contact: "There is no charge for the *Index* if you are a subscriber to the *Congressional Record*; if purchased from Superintendent of Documents, Government Printing Office, Washington DC, the *Index* is 25¢/biweekly and $25/annually."
Tips: "*Index* is by members, listing, subjects, and history of bills (by legislative numbers). Any one using our *Indexes* and having a problem should write us and we would be happy to help them."

Consumer Product Safety Commission, Press Office, 1111 18th St. NW, Washington DC 20207. (202)634-7780. Contact: Public Information Specialist.
Purpose: "We are an independent federal regulatory agency responsible for reducing inquires from consumer products used in homes, schools and recreational areas." Information covers agriculture, art, business, economics, health/medicine, how-to, industry, law, new products, recreation, science, self-help, sports, technical data and consumer complaints.
Services: Offers aid in arranging interviews, annual reports, bibliographies, biographies, statistics, brochures/pamphlets, information searches, placement on mailing list, newsletter, photos, press kits and toll-free numbers for consumer complaints. Publications include *CPSC Memo*, a monthly newsletter.
How to Contact: Write or call. Toll-free number for consumer complaints is (800)638-2668 or 492-2937 (for Maryland residents) and (800)638-8833 (for Alaska, Hawaii, Porta Rico and the Virgin Island residents). "Give us time for extensive research."
Tips: "Consumer Product Safety Commission (CPSC) has 13 area offices in major cities that can serve Action Line Reporters with answers to product safety questions." Write for a list of offices. "We can't recommend one particular brand of product over other brands, or compare the quality of one particular brand with others."

Copyright Office, Office of Information and Publications, Library of Congress, Washington DC 20559.
Purpose: Registers claims to copyright.
Services: Offers copyright searches, free circulars on copyright subjects, and other related services.
How to Contact: Write.

Customs Service, Room 6316, 1301 Constitution Ave. NW, Washington DC 20229. (202)566-5288. Contact: Director of Public Information.
Purpose: "The US Customs Service is the principal border enforcement agency of the US. It enforces the Tariff Act of 1930 as well as some 400 other provisions of law for 40 other federal agencies concerned with international trade. The service collects duties

and other revenues; regulates the movement of commerce and people between the US and other nations; and detects and investigates contraband smuggling and other actitivites, including arms trafficking, unreported movement and other law violations." Information covers agriculture, art, business, economics, food, health/medicine, history, how-to, industry, law, nature (endangered species), new products, technical data and travel.

Services: Offers aid in arranging interviews, annual reports, bibliographies, biographies, statistics, brochures/pamphlets, clipping services, placement on mailing list, photos and press kits. Publications include publications list.

How to Contact: Write or call. "We have a limited staff but will do our best to answer requests; give us as much lead time as possible. We've worked successfully in the past with a number of article and book authors."

Defense Civil Preparedness Agency, The Pentagon, Washington DC 20301. (202)695-9441. Assistant Director for Information Services: Vincent A. Otto.

Purpose: "To work with federal, state and local government; national organizations; business and industry; and the general public to inform of the dangers of peacetime disasters, and of possible attack on the United States; and how to prepare to mitigate or withstand and recover from disasters or attack." Information covers disaster and attack preparedness.

Services: Offers "a wide range of information concerning disaster and attack preparedness, including publications and audiovisual materials. However, most Defense Civil Preparedness Agency (DCPA) publications are designed for use by key persons in civil preparedness work; or key persons in government, business and industry; or national organizations who may be concerned with defense preparedness." Publications include *In Time of Emergency: A Citizen's Handbook on Nuclear Attack, Natural Disasters; Introduction to Civil Preparedness* and *DCPA Motion Picture Catalog.*

How to Contact: "Contact local or state civil defense agencies or the Washington DC office."

Defense Civil Preparedness Agency, Region One, Federal Regional Center, Maynard MA 01754. (617)897-9381. Emergency Information Officer: Vincent J. Tuscher.

Purpose: "To provide funding and guidance to state and local civil defense organizations on nuclear, natural and man-made disasters." Information covers how-to, self-help and technical data.

Services: Offers statistics and brochures/pamphlets. Publications include *In Time of Emergency.*

How to Contact: "Write a letter and know *exactly* what you are looking for. Be thoroughly certain the information is not available from state or local units."

Defense Civil Preparedness Agency, Region Six, Denver Federal Center, Denver CO 80225. (303)234-2582. Contact: Public Information Officer.

Purpose: "We are one of eight regional offices of Defense Civil Preparedness Agency (DCPA) and are responsible for helping state and local governments build an effective civil preparedness program. The agency provides matching funds, technical expertise, training programs and grants to improve the preparedness of state and local communities. At one time the agency was mandated by Congress to provide assistance for only nuclear attack preparedness, but now the agency is involved in natural disaster preparedness as well as man-caused emergencies such as chemical spills." Information covers how-to and technical data.

Services: Offers brochures/pamphlets. "We can provide technical information dealing with construction of home fallout shelters, as well as safeguards against natural disasters. Civil Defense courses are also available for home study. A wide variety of personal, family, community and industry preparedness publications are available to acquaint the public with the hazards of various types of disasters and ways they can prepare themselves. The *In Time of Emergency* book is available to help families protect themselves against nuclear and natural disasters. *Your Chance To Live* is a

public school course covering essentially the same information."
How to Contact: "Call or write. However, we would recommend that the writer query the local or state level emergency preparedness agency prior to contacting us. We try to encourage more local and community involvement in civil preparedness and feel that it would be more beneficial for the writer to contact them first. We will be glad to provide whatever information they cannot provide."

Defense Logistics Agency, Cameron Station, Alexandria VA 22314. Special Assistant for Public Affairs: Chester C. Spurgeon.
Purpose: Responsible for supply support to the military services, administration of defense contracts and various other logistics services.
Services: Offers information on Defense Logistics Agency areas of activity. Publications include *Introduction to the Defense Logistics Agency*.
How to Contact: Write.

Defense Mapping Agency, Bldg. 56, US Naval Observatory, Washington DC 20305. (202)254-4140. Contact: Public Affairs Officer.
Purpose: "To provide support to the Secretary of Defense, the military departments, the Joint Chiefs of Staff, and other Department of Defense components as appropriate, on matters concerning mapping, charting and geodesy. By law, the Defense Mapping Agency (DMA) also provides nautical charts and marine navigation data for the use of all vessels of the US and navigators in general." Information covers "mapping, charting and geodesy (MC&G)."
Services: Offers aid in arranging interviews, brochures/pamphlets, world maps, aeronautical and ocean charts outside the continental US, notices to mariners, and flight information publications. Publications include a kit with flyers about each of the 5 DMA components and the *DMA Fact Sheet*.
How to Contact: For general inquiries, write or call. "For product inquiries contact DMA Office of Distribution Services, Brookmont MD 20315, (202)227-2496. A price list is available. Aeronautical charts are available from the National Ocean Survey, Rockville MD 20852, (301)436-6990. Nautical charts can be purchased from authorized sales agents in major ports in the US and in more than 80 foreign countries. Maps and charts for public sale are sold at a nominal fee stated in the price list. Sales agents may add handling charges. DMA's products don't cover maps or charts for the continental US, which are the responsibility of other government agencies. Except for limited products given in the price list, maps and charts prepared by DMA are for military use."
Tips: "DMA products are for current use. For historical materials, research should turn to the National Archives or the Library of Congress. For current MC&G information for other than military purposes, try the National Cartographic Information Center, Reston VA 22092, (703)860-6045. For general research and development information, use the National Technical Information Service, 5285 Port Royal Rd., Springfield VA 22161, (703)557-4600."

Department of Agriculture, Independence Ave. between 12th and 14th Sts. SW, Washington DC 20250. (202)447-5247. Contact: Director of Governmental and Public Affairs.
Purpose: Directed by law to acquire and diffuse useful information on agricultural subjects in the most general and comprehensive sense. Performs functions relating to research, education, conservation, marketing, regulatory work, nutrition, food programs and rural development.
How to Contact: Write or Call.

Department of Agriculture, Photography Division, Office of Governmental and Public Affairs, Washington DC 20250. Contact: Chief, Photography Division.
Services: Offers 500,000 or more photos; some very technical, others general. No charge to publications, "small charge for personal collection."

How to Contact: Write or call. Charges $3.30/8x10, 35¢/duplicate 35mm color. Credit line requested. "Slide sets and filmstrips ($14.50 and up) available on Department programs."

Department of Commerce, 14th St. & Constitution Ave. NW, Washington DC 20230. (202)377-4901. Chief of News Room: Anne M. Wiesner.
Purpose: "Department established by Congress to foster, promote and develop the foreign and domestic commercial, manufacturing and shipping industry of the United States." Information covers agriculture, business, economics, food, health/medicine, industry, nature, recreation, science, sports (equipment), technical data, travel and population and census.
Services: Offers aid in arranging interviews, annual reports, bibliographies, biographies, statistics, brochures/pamphlets, placement on mailing list, photos and press kits. Publications available.
How to Contact: Write. Charges for some publications. "We do no research but can put you in touch with the proper official. We also have a 4-page subject directory which lists the agency, the official, address and phone number that would cover a particular topic."

Department of Defense, Office Assistant Secretary, Room 2E-772, The Pentagon, Washington DC 20301. Contact: Betty Sprigg.
Purpose: "We provide the national news media with coverage (press releases, speech texts, film, photos) on the activities of the Defense Department." Information covers business, economics, history, industry, law, nature, new products, science, travel and civilian and military leaders of the department.
Services: Offers aid in arranging interviews, annual reports, bibliographies, biographies, statistics, brochures/pamphlets, photos and press kits.
How to Contact: Write. "Be as specific as possible. Due to limited staff, priorities must be made and requests will be answered as time permits."

Department of Defense, Room 2E773, Acquisitions Branch, AV Division, The Pentagon, Washington DC 20301. Contact: Office of the Assistant Secretary of Defense for Public Affairs.
Services: Offers assistance in gathering information about the Department of Defense and its components.
How to Contact: Write.

Department of Energy, Washington DC 20585. (202)566-9820. Contact: Office of Public Affairs.

Department of Energy, Region Four, 1655 Peachtree St. NE, Atlanta GA 30309. (404)881-2062. Public Information Officer: Ronald L. Henderson.
Purpose: "To develop and implement national energy policy and regulate activities within the national energy sectors. We have information on all aspects of energy resources, supplies, production, research and development, regulation, statistics and projections. We also have literature and audiovisual materials, a speakers bureau, and information mailings. We *do not* have information that would normally be found in various state agencies pertaining to within-state energy activities." Information covers business, economics, health/medicine, history, how-to, industry, law, nature, politics, science, self-help and technical data.
Services: Offers aid in arranging interviews, bibliographies, biographies, statistics, brochures/pamphlets, clipping services, information searches, placement on mailing list, newsletter, photos and press kits. "This office can tailor responses to meet our needs within reason and with sufficient time allowance to permit outside compilation of information and resource materials. We will be able to inform inquirers if their requests fall outside our capabilities." Publications include *Monthly Energy Review*, *Solar Energy R&D Report*, and "numerous statistical summaries dealing with petro-

leum supply/price and electrical energy supply/price."
How to Contact: Write or call. "Focus carefully on your subject matter, since the field of energy information and data is fantastically broad and incredibly complex. Determine exactly what time span you want to cover in your work, and allow us extra time for a response. Familiarize yourself with the existing energy legislation and the organization of the Department of Energy so you will know to what division to direct your inquiry. Depending on the extent of the request, reference may be made to the Freedom of Information Act, which provides response times and fees for professional time spent in information compilation. Ordinarily, requests for readily available data or records are not chargeable but, if extensive professional time is required or computer runs must be made, then charges might be assessed." For a complete list of department publications, write Technical Information Center, Box 62, Oak Ridge TN 37830.
Tips: "Certain information is classified and can't be released due to national security considerations. Other material are of such a constantly changing nature that extensive compilation time could render that information useless. The Privacy Act may be invoked for certain classes of information, but such invocation is determined on a case-by-case basis."

Department of Health, Education and Welfare, 26 Federal Plaza, New York NY 10007. (212)264-5285, 264-5286. Special Assistant to the Assistant Secretary for Public Affairs: Robert B. O'Connell.
Purpose: Information covers business, economics, food, health/medicine, how-to, industry, law, science, self-help, sports, technical data, travel, education, civil rights and smoking.
Services: Offers aid in arranging interviews, bibliographies, biographies, statistics, brochures/pamphlets, information searches, placement on mailing list, photos and press kits. "I will suggest topics to authors and alert writers to news stories in their field of interest." Publications include publications list.
How to Contact: Write or call. Wants "only serious inquiries."

Department of Housing and Urban Development, Office of Fair Housing and Equal Opportunity, 451 7th St. SW, Room 5204, Washington DC 20410. (202)755-5735. Equal Opportunity Specialist: Marian Humbles.
Purpose: "The office of Fair Housing and Equal Opportunity in the Department of Housing and Urban Developemnt is charged with assuring fair housing for all citizens throughout the United States and ensuring that HUD-assisted programs are administered without discrimination based on race, sex, color or national origin."Information covers fair housing and equal opportunity in HUD programs.
Services: Offers annual reports, bibliographies and brochures/pamphlets. Publications available.
How to Contact: Write or call.

Department of Justice, Office of Public Information, 10th St. and Constitution Ave. NW, Room 5114, Washington DC 20530. (202)739-2007. Deputy Director, Public Information: Robert J. Havel.
Purpose: "As the largest law firm in the nation, the Department of Justice serves as counsel for its citizens. It represents them in enforcing the law in the public interest. Through its thousands of lawyers, investigators, and agents, the department plays the key role in protection against criminals and subversion, in ensuring healthy competition of business in our free enterprise system, in safeguarding the consumer, and in enforcing drug, immigration and naturalization laws. The department also plays a significant role in protecting citizens through its efforts for effective law enforcement, crime prevention, crime detention, and prosecution and rehabilitation of offenders."
How to Contact: Write or call.

Department of Labor, 3rd and Constitution Ave. NW, Washington DC 20210. (202)523-7316. Contact: Office of Information, Publications and Reports.

Department of Labor, Region V, Information Office, 230 S. Dearborn, Room 772, Chicago IL 60604. (312)353-6977.
Purpose: "This office is responsible for the Labor Department's public information program in six Midwestern states. The office provides general information about labor law and issues, prepares and disseminates public information on the department, distributes publications, and issues department news releases." Information covers labor law and data related to employees.
Services: Offers aid in arranging interviews, statistics and information searches. "Probably the greatest assistance we offer writers is help in finding specific research materials. This is particularrly true in the cases of employment studies, minority work force studies, and other materials related directly to work in the US."
How to Contact: Call or write. Doesn't usually charge; "some publications are priced, but in most cases we try to find complimentary copies."

Department of Labor, Southwest Region, Office of Information, 555 Griffin Square Bldg., Room 220, Dallas TX 75202. (214)767-4776. Regional Information Director: Les Gaddie.
Purpose: "This is one of ten regional offices operated by the Labor Department in various parts of the country. We provide information about US labor department policies, programs and activities in general, with emphasis on such matters in the states of Arkansas, Louisiana, New Mexico, Oklahoma and Texas. In general, the department enforces laws that protect the safety and health of workers, helps them find jobs, sponsors training, helps strengthen free collective bargaining, guides unemployment insurance system, tracks changes in employment and prices, ensures their pension rights, sets wage rates and equal employment goals in general contract work, etc." Information covers agriculture, business, economics, health/medicine, industry and wage earners.
Services: Offers aid in arranging interviews, annual reports, biographies, statistics, brochures/pamphlets and placement on mailing list. "Our publications cover a broad and constantly expanding range relating to composition, character and size of the nation's work force; employment problems; benefits and protection available to workers."
How to Contact: "Telephone or mail contact. There is a small charge for a few of our many documents."

Department of State, 2201 C. St. NW, Washington DC 20520. Press Office: (202)632-2492. Freedom of Information Office: (202)632-0772. Office of Historian: (202)632-8888. Contact: Press Officer.
Purpose: "To inform the press on daily activities of the Department of State. The Freedom of Information Office can provide access to classified documents under the Freedom of Information Act. The Office of Historian declassifies and publishes documents of United States foreign policy of the past 20 years." Information covers business, celebrities (within the department), economics, history, how-to, international law, politics and science (limited).
Services: Offers aid in arranging interviews, annual reports, bibliographies, biographies, statistics, brochures/pamphlets, information searches, placement on mailing list, photos (of department heads), daily press briefings and document searches under Freedom of Information Act. Publications available.
How to Contact: Write or call. Charges for some documents and 10¢/page copied material from Freedom of Information Office.
Tips: "Journalists must apply for press status and press pass. Response from the Freedom of Information Office usually averages 6 weeks. The Office of Historian arranges occasional briefs on research procedures which would benefit in-depth scholarly research."

Department of the Air Force, Magazine and Book Branch, SAF/OIPM, The Pentagon, Room 4C914, Washington DC 20330. (202)697-4065.

Services: Offers information on the Air Force and a referral service to those authors engaged in historical research on the Air Force. The Air Force also has the following field offices: 663 5th Ave., New York City,(212)753-5609; 219 S. Dearborn Ave., Room 246-D, Chicago, (312)353-8300; and 11000 Wilshire Blvd., Room 10114, Los Angeles, (213)824-7517.

Department of the Army, The Pentagon, Washington DC 20310. (202)695-5608. Contact: Office, Chief of Public Affairs.

Department of the Interior, Interior Bldg., Washington DC 20240. Contact: Director of Public Affairs.
Purpose: The nation's principal conservation agency, with responsibilities for energy, water, fish, wildlife, mineral, land, park, and recreational resources, and Indian and territorial affairs.
How to Contact: Requests for information should be directed to the office most concerned with specific subjects of interest. See listings for individual bureaus and agencies to locate the best source for information.

Department of the Treasury, 15th St. and Pennsylvania Ave., NW, Washington DC 20220. (202)566-2041. Contact: Public Information Director.
Purpose: "To raise revenues for the United States government." Information covers business, economice and technical data.
Services: Offers annual reports, biographies, placement on mailing list and news releases.
How to Contact: Write or call.

Department of Transportation, 400 7th St. SW, Washington DC 20590. Contact: Office of Public Affairs, S-80.
Services: Offers "a limited supply of photos and reference material, but we can usually put the writer in touch with the right people in the department."
How to Contact: Write.

86th Information Office, APO NY 09009, Ramstein AB, Germany 09009. Chief, Internal Information: Andrew C. Henderson.
Purpose: "We support all information function for this base." Information covers military.
Services: Offers aid in arranging interviews, annual reports, biographies, statistics, brochures/pamphlets, information searches, photos and press kits. Publications include *Air Force History and Aerospace Vehicles* and *Contemporary Issues and Policy*.
How to Contact: Write. Charges for reproduction.

Environmental Protection Agency, Washington DC 20460. Contact: Public Information Center (PM215).
Services: Offers pamphlets/brochures. Publications include popular booklets and leaflets on water and air pollution, solid waste management, radiation and pesticides control and noise abatement and control. 16mm color films on pollution control and photos of pollution problems are available by contacting the Communications Division of Office of Public Affairs.
How to Contact: Write.

Equal Employment Opportunity Commission, Office of Public Affairs, 2401 E St. NW, Washington DC 20506. (202)634-6930. Contact: Public Information Specialist.
Purpose: "To enforce Title 7 of the 1964 Civil Rights Act, which prohibits employment discrimination in the federal and private sector on the basis of race, color, sex, religion and national origin. As of July 1, 1979, the commission will also enforce the Age Discrimination Act and the Equal Pay Act." Information covers business, economics, how-to, industry, law, self-help and technical data.

Services: Offers aid in arranging interviews, annual reports, bibliographies, biographies, brochures/pamphlets, placement on mailing list, newsletter, photos and speakers' bureau. Publications includes publications list.
How to Contact: Write or call. "No information is given on individual companies or complainants."

Farm Credit Administration, 490 L'Enfant Plaza SW, Washington DC 20578. (202)755-2170. Contact: Public Affairs Division.
Purpose: Responsible for the supervision and coordination of activities of the farm credit system, which consists of federal land banks and federal land bank associations, federal intermediate credit banks and production credit associations, and banks for cooperatives. Information covers agricultural credit and finance.
Services: Offers annual reports, brochures/pamphlets and placement on mailing list. Publications include *Farm Credit Facts* (a summary of operations of Farm Credit Bands and Associations); *Investor's Guide to Farm Credit Securities* (answers to frequently asked questions about Farm Credit Bonds); *Banks for Cooperatives: How They Operate* (an explanation of lending operations); *The Cooperative Farm Credit System (an explanation of the functions and organization of the system); Federal Land Banks: How They Operate* (a description of lending operations of the banks); *Production Credit Associations: How They Operate.*
How to Contact: Write or call.

Federal Aviation Administration, Public Inquiry Center, APA-430, Dept. of Transportation, 800 Independence Ave. SW, Washington DC 20591. (202)426-8058.
Purpose: "We provide the public with publication and inquiry service, a documents copying service, and a document inspection facility. We provide basic informational publications and other nontechnical directives, plans, studies and reports. We refer requests for all statistical, forecast or planning publications to the originating offices." Information covers "career information regarding aviation."
Services: Offers statistics, brochures/pamphlets and placement on mailing list. Publications include *Federal Aviation Administration*, a brochure explaining the workings of the agency, and *Guide to FAA Publications*, listings and descriptions of agency publications.
How to Contact: Write or call. "Writers should contact the new division, APA-300, for assistance on aviation matters currently in the news. Orders and handbooks of a technical nature are quoted on an individual basis by APA-420, Document Inspection Section." Write for a list of regional headquarters offices; "public affairs offices in each region can assist writers wanting help in their local area."

Federal Bureau of Investigation, 9th St. and Pennsylvania Ave. NW, Washington DC 20535. (202)324-3000. Contact: Public Affairs Office.
Purpose: "The Federal Bureau of Investigation (FBI) investigates violation of certain federal statutes, collects evidence in cases which the United States is or may be interested party, and performs other duties specified by law or presidential directive." Information is pertinent to FBI duties.
Services: Offers aid in arranging interviews. Will furnish annual reports, brochures/ pamphlets, statistics, and some news clippings. Publications available.
How to Contact: Write. "We serve legitimate authors and members of the media. We can provide information regarding cases which have been fully adjudicated. Freedom of Information document requests processed through separate channels."

Federal Communications Commission, 1919 M St. NW, Washington DC 20554. Public Information Officer: Samuel M. Sharkey Jr.
Purpose: Regulation of all forms of telecommunications, broadcasting, cable, common carrier (telephone, telegraph, satellite), CB, safety or special radio.
Services: All material, except for certain special information (trade secrets, etc.), is

available for public inspection. Does not do research for writers. Detailed material is available in Federal Communications Commission (FCC) public reference rooms.
How to Contact: Write.

Federal Disaster Assistance Administration, 1111 18th St. NW, Washington DC 20410. (202)634-6666. Information Director: Bob Blair.
Purpose: "The Federal Disaster Assistance Administration (FDAA) coordinates all federal and volunteer agencies in providing natural disaster assistance following presidential disaster declarations."
Services: Offers aid in arranging interviews, annual reports, bibliographies, biographies, statistics, brochures/pamphlets, information searches, placement on mailing list, photos and press kits. Also offers phone information on disaster assistance. Publications include press kit of background information.
How to Contact: Call.
Tips: "Remember each disaster is different. One can't be compared to another or to the so called 'average.' "

Federal Energy Regulatory Commission, 825 N. Capitol St. NE, Washington DC 20426. Acting Director of Public Information: Joyce R. Morrison.
Purpose: Regulation of interstate aspects of natural gas and electric power industries, and licensing of nonfederal hydroelectric power projects.
Services: Offers lists of publications and special reports, and general information on regulatory activities. Media representatives may also receive, upon request, a complimentary copy of nonsubscription items on the publications list.
How to Contact: Write.

Federal Information Center, 601 E. 12th St., Kansas City MO 64106. (816)374-2466.
Purpose: "The Federal Information Center is primarily a small office that is equipped to answer specific questions about government agencies and will direct the caller to the particular agency which could best answer his questions. It is a referral service for the federal government." Information covers agriculture, economics, health/medicine, industry, law, nature, politics, science, technical data, travel and federal government agencies.
Services: Offers information searches and referral services.
How to Contact: Write or call. "This particular office will not be able to answer specific questions on the topics covered in each government office. It is very useful in referring people to the office that can provide the information they need."

Federal Judicial Center, Dolly Madison House, 1520 H St. NW, Washington DC 20005. Contact: Mrs. Sue Welsh, Information Service.
Purpose: To further the development and adoption of improved judicial administration in the US courts.
Services: Offers books, articles, periodicals, reference services and a few bibliographies. Publications include *The Third Branch*, free monthly newsletter of the federal courts.
How to Contact: Write or visit. The information service is open to the public for research purposes; written requests within the realm of jurisdiction will be answered, with first priority given to federal judicial personnel.

Federal Labor Relations Authority, 1900 E St., NW, Washington DC 20424.
Purpose: "Established by the Civil Service Reform Act of 1978, Federal Labor Relations Authority (FLRA) oversees creation of bargaining units, supervises elections and deals with labor-management issues in federal agencies. Within FLRA, a general counsel investigates alleged unfair labor practices and prosecutes them before the FLRA. Also within FLRA and acting as a separate body, the Federal Service Impasses Panel will resolve negotiation impasses." Information covers law and federal labor-management relations information.

Services: Offers a wide range of information services not yet established. Address initial inquiry to Office of Personnel Management, Office of Public Affairs.
How to Contact: Write.

Federal Law Enforcement Training Center, Department of the Treasury, Glynco GA 31520. (912)267-2447. Public Affairs Officer: William M. Allen Jr.
Purpose: "The Federal Law Enforcement Training Center is a bureau of the Department of the Treasury which serves as an interagency training center for federal police officers and investigators. The center provides basic training for new officers and investigators from more than 30 federal law enforcement organizations. In addition, the center provides administrative and logistical support for the organizations to conduct advanced and specialized training required to meet their individual needs." Information covers federal law enforcement.
Services: Offers annual reports, brochures/pamphlets, photos, and press kits. "The public information office will be happy to provide all available assistance to writers."
How to Contact: Write.

Federal Mediation and Conciliation Service, 2100 K St. NW, Washington DC 20427. Assistant Director of Information: John Rogers.
Purpose: The settlement and prevention of labor-management disputes. Collective bargaining is the general subject of programs.
Services: Offers brochures and annual reports.
How to Contact: Write.

Federal Trade Commission, Public Reference Branch, 6th St. and Pennsylvania Ave. NW, Washington DC 20580. (202)523-3600.
Purpose: The commission is a law enforcement agency whose mission is to protect the public (consumers and businessmen) against abuses caused by unfair competition and unfair and deceptive business practices; to guide and counsel businessmen, consumers, and federal, state, and local officials.
Services: Offers reprints, copies of speeches, or other documents pertinent to his subject. Publications include *News Summary*, a weekly roundup of news stories emanating from the commission.
How to Contact: Write or call. "Be specific in your requests."

15th Air Base Wing, Office of Information, Hickam Air Force Base, HI 96853. (808)449-2490.
Purpose: "To provide information on Air Force activities and personnel in Hawaii." Information covers economics, enterainment, food, health/medicine, history, recreation and sports.
Services: Offers aid in arranging interviews, biographies, statistics, placement on mailing list, and photos.
How to Contact: Write or call.

Fish and Wildlife Service, Room 3240, Interior Bldg., Washington DC 20240. (202)343-5634. Contact: Office of Public Affairs.

Fish and Wildlife Service, Southwestern Region, Box 1306, Albuquerque NM 87103. (505)766-3940. Public Affairs Officer: Tom Smylie.
Purpose: "The US Fish & Wildlife Service (FWS) is the principal agency through which the federal government carries out its responsibilities for conserving the nation's wild birds, mammals and fish for the enjoyment of all people. In the southwestern states of Texas, Oklahoma, New Mexico and Arizona, the FWS operates 29 national wildlife refuges, 9 national fish hatcheries and several research stations. The FWS also administers programs in animal damage control, habitat preservation, endangered species, interpretation and recreation, law enforcement, youth conservation corps and young adult conservation corps." Information covers nature, wildlife

oriented recreation, biological and ecological science, and biological data.
Services: Offers aid in arranging interviews, annual reports, statistics, brochures/
pamphlets, information searches, placement on mailing list, photos and press kits.
Publications include *Fish, Wildlife and People; The US Fish and Wildlife Service;
Ducks at a Distance; The Way of the Whooping Crane; The Unique Ecosystem Pro-
gram; The US Fish and Who?;* and *Directory of National Wildlife Refuges and Hatche-
ries in the Southwest.*
How to Contact: Write or call.

Food and Drug Administration, 5600 Fishers Lane, Rockville MD 20857. Chief, Press
Relations: Wayne Pines.
Purpose: "To protect consumers in the areas of food (except meat and poultry);
medicines, cosmetics, medical devices, biologicals and electronic equipment emitting
radiation."
Services: Offers press releases, placement on mailing list and brochures on many
subjects. Publications include *FDA Consumer* magazine, available by subscription
through the Government Printing Office.
How to Contact: Write.

Food and Nutrition Service, Child Care and Summer Programs Division, 201 14th St.
SW, Washington DC 20019. (202)447-8211. Acting Director: Jordan Benderly.
Purpose: "The Food and Nutrition Service is concerned with ensuring the nutritional
well-being of the children in this country. The child care food program offers a
year-round reimbursement plan for food service in establishments which offer licensed day care for preschoolers. The summer food program is the summer replacement for those high school aged and younger students who participate in the national
school lunch program during the academic year." Information covers food, how-to
and technical data.
Services: Offers brochures/pamphlets and regulations. Publications available.
How to Contact: Write. "Only licensed day care facilities are eligible for participation
in the child care food program. Those interested in sponsoring the summer feeding
program must be an approved site or a summer camp. Camps may be residential or
nonresidential as long as they serve four meals a day. Mentally and/or physically
handicapped persons regardless of age who participate in public school programs are
eligible for these programs."

Forest Service, Department of Agriculture, Box 2417, Washington DC 20013.
(202)447-4211. Press Officer: Diane O'Connor.
Purpose: "The Forest Service is dedicated to the principles of multiple-use management of the nation's forest resources for sustained yields of water, forage, wildlife,
wood and recreation. Through management of the national forests and national
grasslands and cooperation with states and private forest owners and forestry research,
it strives, as directed by Congress, to provide increasingly greater service to a growing
nation."
Services: Offers reference services, reference information, photos and news releases.
How to Contact: Write.

General Services Administration, 18th and F Sts. NW, Washington DC 20405.
(202)566-1231. Contact: Office of Information.
Purpose: The General Services Administration (GSA) establishes policy and provides
for a system for the management of federal property and records, including construction and operation of buildings, procurement and distribution of supplies, utilization
and disposal of property, transportation, traffic and communications management,
stockpiling of strategic materials and management of government-wide Automated
Data Processing resources program.
How to Contact: Write or call.

Geological Survey, Department of the Interior, Information Office, National Center, Reston VA 22092. (703)860-7444. Information Officer: Frank H. Forrester.
Purpose: "Major federal earth science research agency. Through field and lab studies and investigations, obtains fundamental data and makes assessments of the nation's mineral, energy, and water resources. Programs include resource estimates, mapping, studies of surface and ground water, supervision of leases on federal lands, studies of geologic hazards (earthquakes, volcanoes, landslides, subsidence and glaciers)."
Services: Offers "news media services: press releases, backgrounders, news photos, arranges interviews, etc." Publications include a variety of nontechnical leaflets, and writers may request press release mailings.
How to Contact: Write or call. "We would be pleased to receive inquiries from any writer on general earth science subjects, including natural resources and environmental monitoring."

Geological Survey, Public Inquiries Office, 169 Federal Bldg., 1961 Stout St., Denver CO 80294. (303)837-4160. Inquiries Specialist: Alice M. Coleman.
Purpose: "To make available to the general public both published and unpublished material gathered and prepared by US Geologic Survey (USGS) personnel. We have a complete USGS reference (nonlending) library, plus state agency information at our office for research, specializing particularly in the Rocky Mountain region." Information covers nature, new products, recreation, science, technical data and energy (oil, gas, coal, uranium, water, minerals and thermal energy).
Services: Offers bibliographies, statistics, brochures/pamphlets, information searches, and placement on mailing list. Also offers professional papers, bulletins, water supply papers, miscellaneous geologic publications, and topographic and geologic maps—all individually priced; and research journals and earthquake bulletins—individually priced or available by subscription. Publications include nontechnical pamphlets and technical circulars on the earth sciences: geology, water, energy, land use, etc.; topographic map indices, thematic map indices, USGS publication lists and USGS water lists—all for every state. "The pamphlet series also includes teachers' aids and layman articles on rock collecting, volcanoes, earthquakes, caves, national parks, the moon, Mercury, Mars and space, minerals, prospecting, etc."
How to Contact: "A concise, detailed description of information needed will aid us in researching and selecting the information to fill the inquiry." Request information by mail, stating your subject, the type of information needed, and the geographic area of interest (including state, county and site). "Print your name and mailing address clearly. Handwriting is frequently misinterpreted." Charges fees for maps and books. "We will provide data concerning availability, cost, and instructions for ordering." No charge for research service or brochures/pamphlets.

Government Printing Office, N. Capitol and H Sts. NW, Washington DC 20401. Special Assistant to the Public Printer: David H. Brown.
Purpose: Printing and binding services for the Congress, Judicial and Executive branches of the federal government; distribution of 25,000 titles of federal documents to the public. Programs include printing production and innovations and a mail order sales program.
Services: Offers "reference materials or information on an individual request basis. Writers may obtain federal reference publications on a broad range of subjects—available through mail order or in 25 bookstores throughout the country."
How to Contact: Write. Charges for some publications.

Health Resources Administration, Department of Health, Education and Welfare, 3700 East-West Hwy., Hyattsville MD 20782. (3012)436-6716. Acting Director, National Health Planning Information Center: Frank Morrone.
Purpose: "To facilitate the exchange of information concerning health services, health resources, and health planning and resources development practice and methodology." Information covers health/medicine.

Services: Offers statistics, brochures/pamphlets and information searches. Publications include *Catalog of Publications*.
How to Contact: Write or call.

Indian Arts And Crafts Board, US Department of the Interior, Washington DC 20240. (202)343-2773.
Purpose: "The board encourages and promotes the development of traditional and innovative native American arts and crafts—the creative work of American Indian, Eskimo and Aleut people—and related cultural concerns. The agency's general subject of expertise is contemporary native American arts." Information covers art, business and law.
Services: Offers bibliographies, brochures/pamphlets and "referral to other appropriate sources of information about native American arts." Publications include *Source Directory of Native American Arts and Crafts Businesses*, *Bibliography on Native American Arts and Crafts* and *Fact Sheet: General Information About the Activities of the Indiana Arts and Crafts Abroad*. "A publications list is available. Only single copies of publications are provided."
How to Contact: "Request by letter or phone. The board exists primarily to serve native American artists, craftsmen and organizations. Staff time devoted to others, including writers, is secondary and only provided as time permits. The more specific a writer can be about the information needed, the more effectively we can respond."

Institute of Museum Services, 200 Independence Ave. SW, 326H, Washington DC 20202. (202)472-3325. Assistant Director for Public Affairs: Sam Eskenazi.
Purpose: "The Institute of Museum Services (IMS) was created by Congress in 1976 to assist the nation's museums in maintaining and improving their services to the public. IMS does this with grants to museums for operating expenses, project support and workshops and by serving as a museum information clearinghouse. IMS supports all types of museums including art, natural history, science and tecnology, planetariums, aquariums, zoos, botanical gardens, historic house and buildings, etc." Information covers museums of all types.
Services: Offers aid in arranging interviews, statistics, brochures/pamphlets, information searches, placement on mailing list, press kits, museum library and slide library.
How to Contact: Write or call.

Interagency Committee on Handicapped Employees, Civil Service Commission, 1900 E St. NW, Washington DC 204l5. (202)632-4437. Program Manager: Judy Gilliom.
Purpose: "To provide a focus for federal and other employment of handicapped individuals and to review in cooperation wth the Civil Service Commission the adequacy of hiring, placement and advancement practices with respect to handicapped individuals in the federal service." Information covers employment of handicapped individuals.
Services: Offers aid in arranging interviews, annual reports, statistics, brochures/pamphlets and placement on mailing list. Publications include "government publications concerning employment of handicapped individuals, and annual reports and statistics on the employment of handicapped individuals."
How to Contact: "The Interagency Committee addresses policy and program issues concerning nondiscrimination and affirmative action. Persons interested in how the federal government implements section 501 of the Rehabilitation Act of 1973 should get in touch with the Interagency Committee."

Internal Revenue Service (IRS), 1111 Constitutional Ave. NW, Washington DC 20224. (202)566-4021. Spokesman for IRS: Larry Battorf.
Purpose: "To administer federal tax laws of the United States." Information covers all types of information bearing on income received and deductions claimed.
Services: Offers aid in arranging interviews, annual reports, statistics, brochures/

pamphlets, placement on mailing list and press kits. Publications available.
How to Contact: Write or call. "We do not divulge individual tax information."

International Trade Commission, 701 E St. NW, Washington DC 20436.
(202)523-0161.
Purpose: "We are a government agency." Information covers trade/imports.
Services: Offers aid in arranging interviews, annual reports, biographies, brochures/
pamphlets, information searches, placement on mailing list, newsletter and press kits.
Publications include an annual report and investigation reports that are issued period-
ically.
How to Contact: Write or call.

Interstate Commerce Commission, 12th and Constitution Ave., Washington DC
20423. (202)275-7301. Contact: Public Information Office.
Purpose: The Interstate Commerce Commission (ICC) has regulatory responsibility for
interstate surface transportation by railroads, trucks, buses, barges, coastal shipping,
oil pipe lines, express companies, freight forwarders and transportation brokers.
Jurisdiction includes rates, mergers, operating rights and issuance of securities.
How to Contact: Write for free list of publications.

Marine Corps, Historical and Museums Division, Headquarters, United States Marine
Corps, Washington DC 20380. (202)433-3840. Contact: Director of Marine Corps History and Museums.
Purpose: "The Division oversees the Marine Corps Historical Program which includes
Marine Corps museums. Its offices are located in the Marine Corps Historical Center in
the Washington Navy Yard (9th & M. St., SE) The Historical Center is a comprehensive
archival and museum facility which houses artifact collections of personal papers, oral
history interviesw, still photographs, military music, art, reference files, writing and
publications offices, and administrative offices. All collections and activities are
oriented toward Marine Corps history and amphibious operations." Information covers art, history, music and technical data.
Services: Offers bibliographies, brochures/pamphlets, information searches, statistics,
newsletter, photos and personal papers and oral histories interviews of United States
Marines. Publications available.
How to Contact: Write. Charges for copying of documents, photos, and motion picture
films, which are currently 5¢/page for documents, $1.25 for each 8x10 b&w still photo
prints and 7¢/foot for motion pictures. There is frequently an additional charge for
clerical time. "Basically, there are few restrictions exception those on access to
classified documents (the majority of holdings are not classified) and those placed on
personal papers and oral history holdings by donors (which are not extensive)."

Merit Systems Protection Board, Office of Public Affairs, Washington DC 20419.
Purpose: "Also established by Civil Service Reform Act of 1978, MSPB is an independent Federal agency to safeguard both the merit system of public employment and
individual Federal employees against abuses and unfair personnel actions. The Board
will hear and decide employee appeals and order corrective and disciplinary actions
against an employee or agency when appropriate. It also reports annually to Congress
on how the merit system is functioning. Within MSPB will be an independent Special
Counsel empowered to investigate charges of prohibited personnel practices and
bring disciplinary charges before MSPB against those who violate merit system law."
Information covers law (federal personnel law and regulation policy).
Services: Offers aid in arranging interviews, annual reports, biographies, brochures/
pamphlets, information searches, statistics, placement on mailing list, photos and
press kits. Publications available.
How to Contact: Write or call. "No restrictions on general information. Privacy Act,
however, restricts information that legally can be provided regarding cases or investigations in process."

Missouri River Basin Commission, Suite 403, 10050 Regency Circle, Omaha NE 68114. Information Officer: William C. Ramige.
Purpose: To coordinate and conduct water resources planning in the ten states of the Missouri River Basin. Information covers water resources planning.
Services: Offers annual reports, brochures/pamphlets, placement on mailing list, newsletter, and periodic reports of planning and coordination activities. Brochures/ pamphlets include administrative, planning-coordination and natural water assessment documents.
How to Contact: Write the Information Officer. For brochures/pamphlets, request a copy of the publication list. Sometimes charges a fee of 5¢/page for publications that are out of print.

National Academy of Sciences, National Academy of Engineering, National Research Council, Institute of Medicine, 2101 Constitution Ave. NW, Washington DC 20418. (202)389-6511. Director of Media Relations: Barbara Jorgenson.
Purpose: A private organization which acts as an official, but independent adviser to the federal government in matters of science and technology.
Services: For writers on assignment, the academies often can be helpful by identifying authorities in various scientific disciplines and sometimes by providing state-of-the-art reports on broad scientific and environmental subjects prepared by their committees.
How to Contact: Write.

National Aeronautics and Space Administration, 400 Maryland Ave. SW, Washington DC 20546. (202)755-8370. Contact: Public Information Branch.
Purpose: "Civilian space program." Information covers agriculture, art, health/ medicine, history, science, technical data and travel.
Services: Offers aid in arranging interviews, annual reports, biographies, statistics, brochures/pamphlets, placement on mailing list, photos and press kits. Publications available.
How to Contact: Write or call. "Be specific in your request."

National Archives and Records Service, Pennsylvania Ave. at 8th St. NW, Washington DC 20408. (202)523-3054. Contact: William H. Leary.
Purpose: The National Archives is the repository for valuable, official records of the US government. All treaties, laws, proclamations, executive orders and bills are retained. It is also authorized to accept some private papers which deal with government transactions. Administering all presidential libraries from Herbert Hoover to Lyndon Johnson and 15 federal records centers across the nation, the National Archives was created to serve the government, scholars, writers and students. Also, pictorial records (primarily b&w) from some 140 federal agencies illustrating all aspects of American history from the colonial period to the recent past, and many aspects of life in other parts of the world. Included are several large collections such as the Mathew Brady Civil War photographs, the picture file of the Paris branch of the *New York Times* (1923-1950), and the Heinrich Hoffmann files illustrating activities of the Nazi party in Germany (1923-45)."
Services: Offers sound recordings, films, some artifacts, and five million photos (available for purchase). "Most are in the public domain and may be freely reproduced."
How to Contact: Write.

National Bureau of Standards, Department of Commerce, Washington DC 20234. (301)921-3181. Chief, Media Liaison, Public Information Division: Madeleine Jacobs.
Purpose: "The National Bureau of Standards (NBS) is the nation's central laboratory for measurement and advanced physical science research. It develops and maintains the US system of physical, chemical and materials measurement, with the aid of five centers devoted to absolute physical quantities, radiation research, thermodynamics

and molecular science, analytical geometry and materials science. The bureau provides services to industry and government, helps facilitate technological innovation, and operates seven centers dealing with applied mathematics, electronics and electrical engineering, mechanical engineering, and process technology, building technology, fire research, and consumer product technology. NBS is organized into three major units: National Measurement Laboratory, National Engineering Laboratory, and the Institute for Computer Sciences and Technology." Information covers health/ medicine (related to physical and measurement standards), how-to, industry, new product information, science and technical data.

Services: Offers aid in arranging interviews, annual reports, bibliographies, biographies, brochures/pamphlets, information searches, placement on press mailing list, photos and press kits. Publications include *Dimensions/NBS* (magazine published ten times a year), general and technical press releases, special publications, technical notes, safety codes, handbooks, monographs and research reports. *NBS List of Publications* describes the bureau's publication program, including periodicals, nonperiodicals, NBS interagency reports, publications catalogs and many other items. "NBS scientists and engineers are happy to grant personal interviews. The courtesy of reviewing the writer's article for technical accuracy prior to publication is requested. We request credit to NBS when reprinting *Dimensions/NBS* articles and similar items."

National Center for Health Services Research, OASH, PHS, Department of Health, Education, and Welfare, 3700 East-West Hwy., Hyattsville MD 20782. (301)436-8970. Chief, Publications and Information Branch: Daniel W. Taylor.
Purpose: "The National Center for Health Services Research (NCHSR) is the primary federal agency responsible for research to improve the delivery and quality of health services in the United States. Through grants and contracts, it supports research in the accessibility, acceptability, planning, organization, distribution, utilization, and quality of systems for the delivery of health care."
Services: Offers brochures/pamphlets and placement on mailing list.
How to Contact: Write or call. List of publications available on request.

National Credit Union Administration, 2025 M St. NW, Washington DC 20456. Administrator: Lawrence Connell.
Purpose: "The National Credit Union Administration (NCUA) is a federal regulatory agency responsible for chartering, supervising, examining and insuring some 13,000 federal credit unions and for providing federal share insurance to qualifying state credit unions requesting it."
Services: "Reference services are not available, although a specific request may be honored if the information is at hand. Publications include *Annual Report of the Administration, Your Insured Funds, NCUA Research Report, Administrator's Letter* and *NCUA Quarterly.*"
How to Contact: Write.

National Endowment for the Arts, 2401 E St. NW, Washington DC 20506. (202)634-6033. Contact: Assistant to the Chairman for the Press.
Purpose: "Independent agency of the federal government set up in 1965 to encourage and assist national cultural progress." Information covers art, entertainment and music.
Services: Offers aid in arranging interviews.
How to Contact: Write or call the General Program and Publications Office, (202)634-6369, for additional information and brochures/pamphlets on National Endowment for the Arts.

National Fire Prevention and Control Administration, Department of Commerce, Washington DC 20230. Director of Information Services: Peg Maloy.
Purpose: "To reduce human and property losses from fire in the US by half, within a

A National Bureau of Standards (NBS) specialist works with a two-kilogram mass standard on a precision balance; an "antique" standard made in the 1850s stands in the foreground. This photo, taken by Mark Helfer, is in the public domain and is offered free to the press and media. "The photo typifies one aspect of NBS work," says public information specialist Stan Lichtenstein. "Other available photos illustrate many other NBS activities on the frontiers of science and technology." Lichtenstein adds, "We will work closely with the writer to provide appropriate and appealing pictures. If laboratory or experimental procedures will be photographed, give us enough notice to set something up before your deadline."

generation. Programs include fire prevention and control through the National Academy for Fire Prevention and Control, The National Fire Safety and Research Office, and the National Fire Data Center and the Public Education Office."

Services: Publishes a monthly newsletter, *Fireword*; bulletins; news releases; public education materials; brochures; reports (such as *Arson: America's Malignant Crime*); annual reports; and annual conference proceedings.

How to Contact: Write.

National Flood Insurance Program, National Insurance Administration, 451 7th St. SW, Washington DC 20410. (800)424-8892. Special Assistant: Sarah Mason. Secretary: Deborah Cowan.

Purpose: "To provide low-cost, federally subsidized flood insurance to consumers, to alert communities and individuals to the hazard they face from flooding, and to reduce the exposure of new construction to flood loss." Information covers economics, history, law, nature, new products, self-help and technical data. "Our information includes the history and background of flood insurance, as well as specific design guidance to builders to effect safer flood plain and coastal building."

Services: Offers statistics, brochures/pamphlets, reports of flood hazard exposure for individual areas, articles and speeches about the program. Publications include manuals on flood plain management and safe building techniques in hazardous areas, *Questions and Answers: The National Flood Insurance Program, Elevated Residential Structures*, and the Community Assistance Series.

How to Contact: Write or call. Contact Joe Sredl at (202)426-1891 about the Community Assistance Series.

National Highway Traffic Safety Administration, 400 7th St. SW, Washington DC 20590. (202)426-9550. Chief of Public Affairs: Bobby A. Boaz.

Purpose: "We are a regulatory agency charged by Congress with reducing the number of fatalities and injuries on US highways occurring because of motor vehicle accidents." Information covers motor vehicle and traffic safety.

Services: Offers aid in arranging interviews, annual reports, statistics, brochures/pamphlets, placement on mailing list and press kits. Publications available.

How to Contact: Write.

National Institute of Health, Division of Research Resources, Bethesda MD 20014. (301)496-5545. Assistant Information Officer: Jerry Gordon.

Purpose: "The Division of Research Resources identifies and strives to meet the research resource needs and opportunities of the National Institute of Health. The division conceives, develops and assures the availability of resources that are essential to the conduct of human health research. The division administers and manages six major programs that serve as the backbone for important health research at universities, hospitals and research institutes throughout the US. These programs are primate research centers (apes and monkeys), general clinical research centers (human patients), biotechnology resource centers (biomedical research computers, mass spectrometry, million-volt electron microscopes, nuclear magnetic resonance spectrometry, etc.), animal resources (laboratory animals other than apes and monkeys), and minority biomedical support (biomedical research activities at predominantly black, Indian and Spanish-speaking colleges)." Information covers health/medicine and science.

Services: Offers aid in arranging interviews, statistics, brochures/pamphlets and photos. Publications include *Division of Research Resources: Meeting the Research Resource Needs of the Biomedical Sciences*.

How to Contact: Write or call.

National Institute of Neurological and Communicative Disorders and Stroke (NINCDS), National Institutes of Health, Bethesda MD 20014. (301)496-5751. Chief, Office of Scientific and Health Reports: Sylvia Shaffer. Public Information Specialist: Lynn Shields.

Purpose: "We conduct and support research in neurological and communicative disorders and stroke. Information covers all areas within these general categories: research progress, current research activity, and health information literature for laymen." Information covers health/medicine, science and technical data.
Services: Offers aid in arranging interviews, annual reports, bibliographies, statistics and brochures/pamphlets. Publications include material for physicians, scientists and other professional health workers, and for the general public.
How to Contact: For publications, write to Publications Department, Room 8A-06, NINCDS, National Institutes of Health, Bethesda MD 20014. For work on specific features for magazines, contact Lynn Shields for discussion of what help can be offered.
Tips: "For features, we suggest working closely with Ms. Shields to determine appropriate slant, to discuss recent research on the disorder, and to obtain relevant quotes from the scientists."

National Library Service for the Blind and Physically Handicapped, Library of Congress, 1291 Taylor St. NW, Washington DC 20542. (202)882-5500. Head, Publication Service: Martha N. Robinson.
Purpose: "We provide braille and talking books and magazines to blind and physically handicapped individuals." Information covers agriculture, art, business, celebrities, economics, entertainment, food, health/medicine, history, how-to, industry, law, music, nature, politics, recreation, science, self-help, sports, technical data and travel. "We also have the same range of books/magazines as in any public library."
Services: Offers bibliographies, brochures/pamphlets and newsletters. Publications include *Reading Is for Everyone, Books That Talk?, Volunteers in Library Services*, talking books for physically handicapped readers, and many others.
How to Contact: Write.

National Marine Fisheries Service, National Oceanic and Atmospheric Administration, Department of Commerce, Washington DC 20235. Contact: Public Affairs Office.
Purpose: Biological and technical research administration and enforcement of the Marine Mammal Protection Act, the Endangered Species Act and the Fishery Conservation and Management Act, statistical facts on commercial fisheries and marine game fish, and economic studies.
How to Contact: Write.

National Oceanic and Atmospheric Administration, 11400 Rockville Pike, Rockville MD 20852. (30l)443-8243. Director, Public Affairs: Stanley B. Eames.
Purpose: "Major civilian agency in the provision of scientific services and research in oceanography and marine and atmospheric sciences. Components include the National Weather Service, National Ocean Survey, National Marine Fisheries Service, National Environmental Satellite Service, Environmental Data and Information Service, Office of Coastal and Ocean Management, Office of Sea Grant, and the National Oceanic and Atmospheric Administration (NOAA) Corps. Information covers food, nature, science and technical data.
Services: Offers aid in arranging interviews, biographies, statistics, brochures/ pamphlets, placement on mailing list, and photos. "Brochures are available on all forms of severe weather (tornados, hurricanes, etc.), commercial fisheries, scientific research in the ocean and atmospheric sciences." .
How to Contact: "Write or call for a NOAA brochure describing the agency's range of activities. If face-to-face interviews are needed, arrangements can be made."

National Park Service, Division of Public Inquiries, Room 1013, Interior Bldg., Washington DC 20240.
Services: Offers publications about the national park system. Publications include "minifolders" on individual parks, an index of the national park system, and *Map Guide to the National Parks*.
How to Contact: Write.

National Park Service, Office of Communications, Room 3043, Interior Bldg., Washington DC 20240. (202)343-7394. Chief, Media Information: Tom Wilson.
Services: Offers information on more than 290 areas of the national park system which the service administers. Information available includes park acreage and attendance statistics, and data on camping, swimming, boating, mountain climbing, hiking, fishing, winter activities, wildlife research and management, history, archeology, nature walks and scenic features.
How to Contact: Write.

National Park Service, Photo Library, Room 8060, Interior Bldg., Washington DC 20240.
Services: Offers photos of many National Park Service areas and recreational activities.
How to Contact: Write.

National Park Service, Public Affairs Office, 1895 Phoenix Blvd., Atlanta GA 30349. (404)996-2520, ext. 240. Assistant to Regional Director of Public Affairs: Jim Howard. Writer/Editor: Paul Winegar.
Purpose: "The National Park Service (NPS) is responsible for managing areas in the national park system so that they can remain in their original state as much as possible. Our office is responsible for disseminating information on those NPS areas in the southeast region (Kentucky, Tennessee, Mississippi, Alabama, North Carolina, South Carolina, Florida, Puerto Rico and the Virgin Islands)." Information covers history, nature, recreation, travel and the environment.
Services: Offers aid in arranging interviews, annual reports, bibliographies, brochures/pamphlets, placement on mailing list, photos and press kits. Publications include conservation yearbooks and visitors' interpretive guides to each area in the Southeast under NPS administration.
How to Contact: Write or call. "Be specific about what material is to be used for. We do not prepare term papers for students, but we are happy to provide materials for research."

National Park Service, St. Croix NSR, Box 708, St. Croix Falls WI 54024. (715)483-3280. Public Information Officer: Albert L. Seidenkranz.
Purpose: "A conservation organization set up to protect natural and historical areas throughout the United States." Information covers nature and local history.
Services: Offers answers concerning history and natural history of our area which is a 252-mile-long national scenic riverway.
How to Contact: Write or call.

National Park Service, White House Liaison, 1100 Ohio Dr. SW, Washington DC 20242. (202)426-6622. Executive Assistant: Jim McDaniel.
Purpose: "We manage the White House and grounds as a national historic site. We have information on history, landscaping, visitor services, architecture, environmental concerns, etc." Information covers agriculture/horticulture, art, history, nature, recreation and technical data.
Services: Offers aid in arranging interviews, statistics, brochures/pamphlets, information searches and photos. "Staff historian, curator, and architect are available for consultation. Brochures/pamphlets include *The White House, The White House Gardens and Grounds,* and a brochure for children about the White House. Also available are color photographs of the White House and several books about the White House.
How to Contact: Write. Charges for some publications.

National Science Foundation, 1800 G St. NW, Washington DC 20550. (202)632-5728. Contact: Public Information Officer.
Purpose: "To promote the progress of science through the support of research and education in the sciences. Major emphasis is on basic research." Information covers economics, food, nature, science and technical data.

Services: Offers aid in arranging interviews, annual reports, bibliographies, statistics, brochures/pamphlets, placement on mailing list, newsletter and press kits. Publication available.
How to Contact: Write or call. "Be specific; the exact topic should be specified and the topic must be limited to the area of the National Science Foundation."

National Transportation Safety Board, 800 Independence Ave. SW, Washington DC 20594.
Purpose: Responsible for the investigation and cause determination of transportation accidents and the initiation of corrective measures. "Work is about 80x in the field of aviation; balance is in selected cases involving highways, railroad, pipeline and marine accidents."
Services: Offers accident reports and special studies involving transportation safety.
How to Contact: Case history details of all cases available for review are in the public inquiry section of the safety board.

National Weather Service, National Oceanic and Atmospheric Administration, Department of Commerce, 8060 13th St., Silver Spring MD 20910. Contact: Public Affairs Officer.
Purpose: Reports the weather of the US and its possessions; provides weather forecasts to the general public; and issues warnings against tornadoes, hurricanes, floods, and other weather hazards.
Services: Offers specialized information which supports the needs of agricultural, aeronautical, maritime, space, and military operations. Some 300 weather service offices in cities across the land maintain close contact with the general public to ensure prompt and useful dissemination of weather information.
How to Contact: Write. Agency publications may be purchased from Superintendent of Documents, Government Printing Office, Washington DC 20402.

Navy Department, Office of Information, Attention: Media Service, The Pentagon, Washington DC 20350. (202)695-0911. Contact: Head, Media Service Branch.
Purpose: "To provide Navy department information." Information covers anything pertaining to the Navy.
Services: Offers aid in arranging interviews, annual reports, bibliographies, biographies, statistics, brochures/pamphlets, information searches, photos and press kits. Publications available.
How to Contact: Write. "We cannot provide classified information or information that would violate the National Privacy Act."

New England River Basins Commission, 53 State St., Boston MA 02109. (617)222-6244. Public Information Officer: Frances B. King.
Purpose: "New England River Basins Commission (NERBC) coordinates the water and related land resource management plans of New England agencies—state and federal. It is composed of representatives of the six New England states, New York, nine federal agencies and six New England interstate agencies. It produces in-depth studies of water and related land source problems and recommended solutions for the region, and serves as a forum for state/federal/local discussions of these issues. Information produced by the commission is usually in the form of staff papers, reports (some single, some multi-volume), newsletters, press releases, workshops and seminars, and speaking engagements. The commission meets four times per year, receives funding from the New England states and the federal government annually, and frequently serves as a clearinghouse for other publications about water and related land source topics." Information covers nature, technical data and water and related land resource material.
Services: Offers aid in arranging interviews, annual reports, statistics, brochures/pamphlets, information searches, and regular informational newsletters. "We can provide copies of our annual reports (which cover our water and related land research

work in synopses), copies of our regional report series (covering in-depth articles on topics related to our work, as well as news of related issues in the New England region), and a range of natural resources reports we've produced covering a multitude of subjects. We try to make our staff as available as is reasonable to those who need information from us. Our extensive library is open for public use and is staffed by a part-time librarian; for writers doing natural resource research, it is an excellent source of information."
How to Contact: Write or call.

Nuclear Regulatory Commission, Washington DC 20555. (202)492-7715. Contact: Office of Public Affairs.

Occupational Safety and Health Review Commission, 1825 K St. NW, Washington DC 20006. (202)634-7943. Director of Information: Linda Dodd.
Purpose: An independent agency of the executive branch of the government. Functions as a court by adjudicating contested cases under the Occupational Safety and Health Act (OSHA) of 1970. Operates under the mandates of the Freedom of Information Act.
Services: Files are open to anyone who wishes to inspect them. Publications include press releases, *Rules of Procedure* and *Guide to the Procedures of OSHRC.*
How to Contact: Write.

Office of Consumer Affairs, Consumer Information Division, 621 Reporters Bldg., Washington DC 20201. (202)755-8830.
Purpose: "We can furnish general information on consumer affairs, especially related to federal activity (or we can refer researchers to more appropriate sources of help)."
Services: Offers aid in arranging interviews and brochures/pamphlets. Publications include *Consumers' Shopping List of Inflation-Fighting Ideas* and *Consumers' Resource Guide.*
How to Contact: Write or call.

Office of Air Force History, HQ USAF, Bldg. 5681, Bolling Air Force Base, Washington DC 20332. (202)767-5088. Historian: William Heimdahl.
Purpose: "The Office of Air Force History formulates policy for, directs and administers the Air Force historical program. Our historians prepare objective, comprehensive and accurate historical accounts of USAF activities in peace and war. Provides historical reference sevices to the Air staff, other public and private agencies, and individuals. Our historical records cover military aeronautics from its early beginnings to the mid 1970s. Unclassified records are available to any individual or organization who visits our office for the purpose of conducting research. Records are not loaned; must be used here." Information covers history.
Services: Offers bibliographies, biographies, brochures/pamphlets, information searches and statistics. "We will make available all unclassified materials, including microfilm, to any researcher who wishes to utilize our facilities. Our microfilm holdings include most Air Force unit histories for World War II, pre-World War II and post-World War II. A brochure describing the Albert F. Simpson Historical Research Center of the United States Air Force is available. The center maintains the official Air Force historical document collection. A few pamphlets pertaining to Air Force history and aircraft and answering pertinent questions are available. Although these are published by the Office of the Secretary of the Air Force, Office of Information, we have a small quantity available for distribution."
How to Contact: "Because of a very limited staff, only minor research requests can be taken care of by mail. Researchers and writers should make arrangements to perform their research in our facilities. Our office hours are Monday through Friday, 7:45 a.m. to 4:15 p.m."

Office of Education and Public Affairs, 400 Maryland Ave. SW, Washington DC

20202. (202)245-8564. Chief, Information Service Branch: Jeanne S. Park.
Purpose: "To administer federal education legislation." Information covers anything pertaining to education.
Services: Offers aid in arranging interviews, annual reports, bibliographies, biographies, placement on mailing list, photos, and press releases.
How to Contact: Write or call.

Office of Human Development Services, Public Affairs, Department of Health, Education and Welfare, Room 329D, 200 Independence Ave. SW, Washington DC 20201. (202)472-7257. Director, Office of Public Affairs: Ann Gropp.
Purpose: "The Office of Human Development Services administers programs for the elderly; native Americans; low-income families; the mentally and physically handicapped; and children, youth, and families." Information covers human services programs.
Services: Offers aid in arranging interviews, annual reports, brochures/pamphlets, placement on mailing list and newsletter.
How to Contact: Write or call. "Writers are expected to credit the appropriate publication."

Office of Management and Budget, Old Executive Office Bldg., Washington DC 20503. (202)395-4854. Contact: Information Office.

Office of Personnel Management, 1900 E St. NW, Washington DC 20415. (202)632-5491. Contact: Office of Public Affairs.
Purpose: "The Office of Personnel Management (OPM) was established by the Civil Service Reform Act of 1978 (Public Law 95-454, signed October 13, 1978) to help the President carry out his responsibilities for management of the federal work force. The new agency takes over many of the responsibilities of the former Civil Service Commission. These include central examining and employment operations, and training, investigation, personnel program evaluation, executive development and training. OPM also administers the retirement and insurance programs for federal employees and exercises management leadership in labor relations and affirmative action." Information covers federal and personnel law, regulation, and management.
Services: Offers aid in arranging interviews, annual reports, bibliographies, biographies, statistics, brochures/pamphlets, information searches, placement on mailing list, photos and press kits. Publications available.
How to Contact: Write or call. "Restrictions on information are very few. The agency complies with the Freedom of Information act and the Privacy Act. Most of the agency's information is public information. Any restrictions would be discussed in relation to a particular inquiry."

Office of Territorial Affairs, C St. between 18th and 19th Sts. NW, Washington DC 20240. Contact: Director of Territorial Affairs.

Office of Veterans' Reemployment Rights, Room N5414, New Dept. of Labor Bldg., 200 Constitution Ave. NW, Washington DC 20216. (202)523-8611. Director: Joseph R. Beever.
Purpose: "To assist veterans, reservists and National Guard members in exercising their statutory rights to unemployment and other benefits from the employers they left to enter military training or service. We investigate and mediate claims under the reemployment rights law for reemployment, as well as for promotions, seniority, pay raises, pension credits, and other advantages that would have gone to the claimant but for his military service. Where we do not succeed, we refer the case to the Department of Justice for litigation." Information covers law and labor-management relations. "Our material relates to a very narrow part of the broad field of labor law."
Services: Offers brochures/pamphlets. Publications include *Veterans' Reemployment*

Rights Handbook, Field Letter 24 (containing the text of the reemployment statute), *Facts* (about reemployment rights for veterans), *17 Key Answers* (for reservists and National Guard members), and *Alabama Power v. Davis* (a Supreme Court decision on pension credits for military service time).
How to Contact: Write or call. Write for a list of area offices.

Patent and Trademark Office, Department of Commerce, Washington DC 20231. Contact: Public Information Officer.
Purpose: Administers the patent and trademark laws, examines applications, and grants patents when applicants are entitled to them under the law.
Services: Offers patent information, maintains search files of US and foreign patents and a patent search room for public use, and supplies copies of patents and official records to the public. Performs similar functions relating to trademarks.
How to Contact: Write or visit.

Peace Corps, 515 Congress, #1414, Austin TX 78701. (512)397-5925. Area Manager: Catherine Weir.
Purpose: "The Peace Corps oversees social and economic development." Information covers agriculture, economics, health/medicine and development how-to.
Services: Offers annual reports, bibliographies, biographies, statistics, brochures/pamphlets, regular informational newsletter, photos and press kits. Publications include "pamphlets on the Peace Corps, describing programs, requirements, how to apply and benefits."
How to Contact: Write or call.

Postal Rate Commission, 2000 L St. NW, Suite 500, Washington DC 20268. (202)254-5614. Director of Information: Ned Callan.
Purpose: "The Postal Rate Commission is a public forum for consideration of domestic postal rate fee, service and classification changes proposed by the Postal Service." Information covers postal rates and mail classifications.
Services: Offers aid in arranging interviews, biographies, statistics and placement on mailing list.
How to Contact: Write or call. Charges for substantial copying.

Postal Service, 475 L'Enfant Plaza, Room 10945, Washington DC 20260. (202)245-4168. New Information Officer: Robert A. Becker.
Purpose: "The US Postal Service (USPS) throughout the country (encompassing some 40,000 post offices) is charged with delivering mail to its customers at a reasonable rate. The public and employee communications department is charged with providing information about all facets of the Postal Service to all external media and internal offices and departments through agency publications." Information covers "how USPS functions, and current and new ways to deliver messages, both printed and electronic."
Services: Offers aid in arranging interviews, annual reports, biographies, statistics, brochures/pamphlets, information searches, placement on mailing list, photos and press kits. Publications include *Annual Report of the Postmaster General* and "miscellaneous brochures/pamphlets on various services of USPS, e.g., *Presort, Express Mail, Parcel Post, Consumer's Guide to Postal Services & Products, Mailers Guide, Philately* and *Mail Fraud Laws.*"
How to Contact: Write or call. "Placement on press release lists is limited to accredited members of the press."

President's Council on Physical Fitness and Sports, 400 6th St. SW, Washington DC 20201. (202)755-7478. Director of Information: V.L. Nicholson.
Purpose: "The council promotes national fitness and health in every segment of the population, including schools, business and industry. It provides assistance to groups seeking to formulate health and fitness programs." Information covers business,

celebrities, entertainment, health/medicine, industry, recreation and sports.
Services: Offers aid in arranging interviews with professional staff, annual reports, bibliographies, biographies, statistics, brochures/pamphlets and "limited publications."
How to Contact: Write or call. "Request information about the subject area you're interested in and we'll advise you if we have a publication, or where publications may be obtained if we don't."

Saint Lawrence Seaway Development Corp., Box 520, Massena NY 13662. (315)764-0881. Public Information Officer: Madelyn Pruski.
Purpose: "The Seaway Corporation is a government-owned enterprise responsible for the construction, development, operation and maintenance of that part of the Saint Lawrence Seaway within the territorial limits of the US. The corporation is part of the Department of Transportation and is self-sustaining, being financed by income received from tolls and other charges assessed for the use of its facilities." Information covers history, industry, technical data, shipping, cargoes, tolls, lock maintenance, marine services, pleasure craft and tourism sites.
Services: Offers aid in arranging interviews, annual reports, biographies, statistics, brochures/pamphlets, placement on mailing list, photos and press kits. Publications include a publications list.
How to Contact: Write or call.
Tips: "Writers are encouraged to visit the public information office to examine extensive reference works that cannot be checked out. In-depth research must be conducted by the writer, since our staff is very small."

Savings Bonds Division, Department of the Treasury, Washington DC 20226. Director of Public Affairs: Carolyn M. Johnston.
Purpose: "To sell US savings bonds. The office of public information provides information on savings bonds—their sales, redemption, relationship to the treasury's debt management, purposes and qualities of the bonds. We also provide information on changes in the bond program, the division's personnel and so on." Information covers economics and US savings bonds.
Services: Offers aid in arranging interviews, statistics, brochures/pamphlets, photos and press kits. Publications include several different brochures describing Series E and H US savings bonds, a booklet on legal aspects of savings bonds, a booklet for bond tellers on cashing and selling bonds, various booklets for bond canvassers in companies and organizations, a history of the bond program, monthly sales releases on bond sales, other news releases as necessary, and questions and answers on specific bond questions.
How to Contact: Write or call.

Secret Service, 1800 G St. NW, Washington DC 20223. (202)634-5708. Contact: Office of Public Affairs.

Securities and Exchange Commission, 500 N. Capitol St., Washington DC 20549. Contact: Office of Public Information.
Purpose: "To administer the securities laws, which have two basic objectives: to provide investors with financial material and other information on securities and to prohibit fraud in the sale of securities."
Services: Offers biographies of commissioners.
How to Contact: Write for publications list.

Senate, Senate Office Bldg., Washington DC 20510.

Small Business Administration, 450 Golden Gate, San Francisco CA 94102. (415)556-0860. Assistant Regional Director for Public Affairs and Communications: Jo Ann Semones.

Purpose: "The Small Business Administration's (SBA) mandate is to aid, counsel and protect the interests of small business through programs of financial management and procurement assistance." Information covers business.

Services: Offers aid in arranging interviews, annual reports, bibliographies, biographies, statistics, brochures/pamphlets, information searches, placement on mailing list, newsletter, photos and press kits. Publications include management and small marketers aids, and small business management information.

How to Contact: "Contact any SBA district office." Write for a copy of the SBA publications list, and a list of SBA field offices.

Social Security Administration, Office of Information, 6401 Security Blvd., Baltimore MD 21235. (301)592-1200. Press Officer: Michael Naver.

Purpose: Administers the federal retirement, survivors and disability insurance programs; health insurance for the aged and certain severely disabled people (Medicare); and a program of supplemental security income for the aged, blind and disabled.

Services: Offers biographies, statistics, historical information, brochures/pamphlets, news releases, photos and "other information materials."

How to Contact: Write. "The Social Security Administration (SSA) can't provide information about any individual social security record or beneficiary. Under the law, all social security records are confidential.

Soil Conservation Service, Information Division, Department of Agriculture, Box 2890, Washington DC 20013. (202)447-4543. Director, Information Division: Hubert Kelley.

Purpose: To help landowners and operators to use their land and water in the best possible manner. Assists local groups with flood, drought, excessive sedimentation or other water problems. Information covers soil, water, plant and wildlife conservation; flood prevention; better use of water by individuals and communities; and improvement of rural communities through better use of natural resources, and preservation of prime farmland. In addition to material of interest to the agricultural and outdoor media, also has work in urban and educational fields that offer article possibilities.

Services: Offers "background materials on all phases of our work," aid in arranging interviews, and photos. "We publish a variety of general and technical publications on practically all aspects of our programs and on soil and water conservation."

How to Contact: Write. Single copies of publications are available from the publications Unit.

Soil Conservation Service, Department of Agriculture, Box 2890, Washington DC 20013. (202)447-5063. Chief, Education and Publications Branch: Walter E. Jeske.

Purpose: "To conduct a national program of conservation of soil, water, and related natural resources. With local offices in nearly every county of the United States, Soil Conservation Service (SCS) provides technical help and information on protection and management of natural resources, with special emphases on control of erosion and sedimentation on private and public lands. The professional staff includes agronomists, biologists, soil scientists, soil conservationists, hydrologists, range conservationists and engineers." Information covers agriculture, nature, science, technical data, conservation of natural resources, and environmental education information.

Services: Offers aid in arranging interviews, brochures/pamphlets, statistics and photos. "We also produce published soil surveys, generally on a county basis, that provide detailed information and maps on the kinds of soil in the area covered, as well as on conservation management of that soil." Other publications available.

How to Contact: Write or call. "Writers will obtain more complete information faster if they are specific in defining their needs and interests—information on soil erosion and control, water pollution by sediment, conservation plant materials, land use, conservation planning, materials for environmental education, and the like."

Southeastern Power Administration, Department of Energy, Samuel Elbert Bldg.,

Elberton GA 30635. (404)283-3261. Chief, Division of Administrative Management: Mary George Bond.
Purpose: Responsible for transmission and disposition of electrical energy generated at reservoir projects under the control of the Corps of Engineers in the southeastern US, and for water resources development.
Services: Offers answers to inquiries.
How to Contact: Write or call.

Supreme Court, 1 1st St. NE, Washington DC 20543. (202)252-3211. Director of Public Information: Barrett McGurn.
Services: Offers annual reports, biographies, statistics, brochures/pamphlets and placement on mailing list.
How to Contact: Write or call.

Tennessee Valley Authority, 400 Commerce Ave., Knoxville TN 37902. (615)632-3257. Director of Information: John Van Mol.
Purpose: "The Tennessee Valley Authority (TVA) is an independent federal agency created by Congress in 1933 to develop the resources of the Tennessee Valley region. This comprehensive effort involves a broad range of activities that includes flood control, navigation development, electric power production, environmental protection control, navigation development, energy research, agricultural and forestry development, fish and wildlife, land use planning, area and community development, outdoor recreation and related fields." Information covers agriculture, economics, health/medicine, history, how-to, law, nature, recreation and technical data.
Services: Offers aid in arranging interviews, annual reports, bibliographies, biographies, statistics, brochures/pamphlets, placement on mailing list and photos. Publications include maps and navigation charts, and various publications covering power, flood control, history, navigation, energy conservation, recreation and visitors, projects and a fertilizer program.
How to Contact: Write to Map Information and Records Unit (101 Haney Bldg., Chattanooga TN 37401) or Engineering Records Section (102-A Union Bldg., Knoxville TN 37902) for maps, charts or drawings; write to the main TVA address for other services.

Veterans Administration, 810 Vermont Ave. NW, Washington DC 20420. Director, News and Media Liaison Division: Stratton Appleman.
Purpose: Administers laws authorizing benefits principally for former members and certain dependents of former members of the armed forces. Major Veterans Administration (VA) programs include medical care and research, education and training, compensation, pension, loan guaranty, death benefits, rehabilitation and insurance.
Services: Offers specialized pamphlets describing individual VA benefits.
How to Contact: Write. Information is available at 58 VA regional offices and 172 hospitals.

Vista, 515 Congress, #1414, Austin TX 78701. (512)397-5925. Area Manager: Catherine Weir.
Purpose: "Vista is a volunteer program committed to community empowerment of low-income communities in the US." Information covers agriculture, economics, health/medicine, development how-to and self-help.
Services: Offers annual reports, bibliographies, biographies, statistics, brochures/pamphlets, newsletter, photos and press kits. Publications include "numerous pamphlets describing Vista programs, requirements, how to apply, and benefits."
How to Contact: Call or write.

Women's Bureau, Department of Labor, 911 Walnut St., Room 2511, Kansas City MO 64106. (816)374-6108. Regional Administrator: Euphesenia Foster.
Purpose: "To foster and promote women in the work force." Information covers

women in the labor force.
Services: Offers statistics, brochures/pamphlets, publications and technical assistance to organizations.
How to Contact: Write for publications list.

Historical Societies, Sites & Monuments

Historical Societies

Historical societies are America's cultural catch-alls. Generally relaxed and oriented toward people, they offer a wide variety of information and are often fun. Historical societies can find "beauty" in suspenders and false teeth if they have a story to tell.

What's more, these stories make fascinating material for salable articles. My story, "Augustus vs. Terrible Mountain," which I sold to *Vermont Life*, resulted from my dealings with one historical society. It was a story I didn't expect to write, and wouldn't have without the help of the society.

When consulting information provided by historical societies, remember these tips:

Because of the nature of the material stored, historical societies are often concerned with security. For your own protection, report immediately any damage you find when going through materials.

Historical societies will often supply photographs, but will often prohibit you from taking photographs on your own. Strobe flash, for instance, ages original works many times faster than daylight, and curators of historical societies are concerned with potential damage from flash units and excessive handling.

Historical societies often receive bequests in bulk (for instance, "The Papers of . . .), and, being understaffed, just don't have time to index or catalog properly. This means that either the material won't be available to the public or, if it is, you might gently and patiently search "raw" material. Discovering unpublished letters or journals on your subject can be exciting, but it may take five cartons of blind leads to find them. If you write, asking for uncataloged material, the answer will almost certainly be: "Unavailable."

Another curious indexing habit of some institutions is the use of "curatorial files"—rather like newspaper morgues—which are kept in "staff-only" areas. These files may also have old, hand-written file cards, which may contain notes not transcribed onto modern open files. Sometimes dedicated volunteers may have made a listing of, say, 19th-century band boxes used to store hats. Usually, however, you will never know of these "secret" files until you have established some rapport with the person involved by demonstrating that you've exhausted the obvious channels.

Once you're inside the door, listen. Say enough to establish your credentials, and then let the curator talk because, like writers, curators love attention and usually love to be helpful. This is especially crucial in smaller historical societies, because their indexing systems are often under the curators' hats. The curator who's been with a historical society for a long time and who knows where everything is may be your only clue to discovering material related to your project.

Newport Historical Society was invaluable when one of its employees suggested my piece on whaling manuscripts might be helped by the journal of a whaler's wife that was filed under her family papers, not whaling. Ultimately, we found a cross-reference that would have led to the journal, but that very day the employee hauled out Lucy P. Smith's journal written aboard her husband's command, the *Nautilus*. From that journal I sought out information from other seagoing wives who faced childbirth, storms and, above all, isolation. From Mrs. Bolhouse's suggestion resulted the tale of 100,000 bittersweet miles, logged by Victorian ladies amidst the roughest crews afloat.

Not all material in historical societies is necessarily "historical." The State Historical Society of Wisconsin, for example, carries copies of all weeklies published in the state. The Dearborn Historical Society in Michigan carries local newspapers, as do several other societies. Able to concentrate their funds for publications more narrowly than most libraries, historical societies can be the source for specialized contemporary material that's otherwise difficult to locate. Larger state historical societies, like those in Texas and Michigan, are likely to carry such material as well as being repositories for noncurrent state documents. Naturally, state houses themselves are, in effect, historical societies.

The starting point for information about this Mulligan's stew of the American experience is found in the following listings, which are broken down according to the states in which the historical societies are located. More information is available from the American Association for State and Local History (1400 8th Ave. S., Nashville 37203), which publishes a biennial directory titled *Directory of Historical Societies and Agencies in the United States and Canada*. Equally helpful, if not more so, is the American Historical Association (400 A St. SE, Washington, D.C. 20003). Additional information can be found in the *Encyclopedia of Associations* (Gale Research Co.), which lists historical groups concerned with everything from pilgrims to the Polish underground in World War II. (*The above introduction was written by William B. Stevens Jr., a freelance writer who has sold many articles based on what he calls "antics in the archives."*)

Alabama

Alabama Department of Archives and History, 624 Washington Ave., Montgomery AL 36130. (205)832-6510. Contact: Director.
Purpose: "The preservation, care and custody of the official archives collection of the materials of Alabama, from earliest times; the publication of state historical materials; and the diffusion and encouragement of research. Contains unique private manuscript records of Confederate materials, plantation records, diaries, biographic files, geological surveys and Southeastern map collection." Information covers agriculture, art, business, celebrities, economics, entertainment, food, health/medicine, history, how-to, industry, music, nature, politics, recreation, self-help, sports, technical data and travel.
Services: Offers aid in arranging interviews, annual reports, bibliographies, biographies, brochures/pamphlets, information searches and photos. Publications include *Alabama Historical Quarterly*.
How to Contact: Write or visit. Open Monday through Friday, 8 a.m. to 5 p.m., except on state holidays. Charges for photocopies.

Alabama Historical Commission, 725 Monroe St., Montgomery AL 36130. (205)832-6621. Contact: Executive Director.
Purpose: "To preserve and assist in preserving sites and structures of significance to Alabama history and to provide information on historical sites statewide." Information covers history, primarily historic preservation of houses.
Services: Offers aid in arranging interviews, bibliographies, statistics, brochures/pamphlets, information searches, placement on mailing list, newsletter, photos and press kits. Willing to provide writers with help on historical settings for novels.

Publications include *Preservation Report* (bimonthly).
How to Contact: Write or visit. Open Monday through Friday, 8 a.m. to 5 p.m., except on state holidays. Charges for photocopies.

Henry County Historical Society, Box 222, Abbeville AL 36310. (204)585-3901. President: William W. Nordan.
Purpose: "To discover and collect any materials which may help establish or illustrate the history of Henry County, Alabama: its exploration, settlement, development and varied activities; its progress in population, wealth, education, arts, science, agriculture and manufacturers. We shall collect printed materials such as histories, genealogies, biographies, descriptions, directories, newspapers, pamphlets, circulars and handbills to illustrate life, conditions, events and activities of our past and present." Information covers agriculture, art, business, celebrities, economics, entertainment, history, industry, music, nature, politics, recreation, science, sports, technical data and travel.
Services: Offers aid in arranging interviews and newsletter.
How to Contact: Write or call. Charges "nominal basic rates on time required for services."

Historic Chattahoochee Commission, Box 33, Eufaula AL 36027. (205)687-9755/6631. Executive Director: Douglas Clare Purcell.
Purpose: "The purpose of the Commission is to promote tourism and historic preservation throughout the Chattahoochee Valley of Alabama and Georgia. Our geographic area includes those 18 Alabama and Georgia counties which border the Chattahoochee River from Lanett, Alabama to the Florida state line. This number includes Dale County, Alabama and Randolph County, Georgia—two counties which do not touch the Chattahoochee River." Information covers history, recreation and travel.
Services: Offers statistics, brochures/pamphlets, newsletters and press kits.
How to Contact: Write or call.

Russell County Historical Commission, Lakeside Dr., Seale AL 36875. (205)855-4595. Vice President: Mrs. George Williams.
Purpose: "Research, restoration and preservation in Russell County, Alabama and other areas." Information covers celebrities and history.
Services: Offers clipping services and information searches.
How to Contact: Write or call.

Alaska

Alaska State Museum (see listing in Museums section).

Tanana—Yukon Historical Society, Box 1794, Fairbanks AK 99701. Vice President: Renée Blahuta.
Purpose: To foster the preservation and study of the history of interior Alaska (Fairbanks and the Tanana and Yukon River drainages). Information covers history.
Services: Offers aid in arranging interviews.
How to Contact: Write.
Tips: "One of the greatest resources anywhere for the study of Alaska history is the Elmer Rasmuson Library with its archives and special polar collection. It presently contains over 80,000 historical photographs and 30,000 volumes on Alaska and the Arctic. It is located on the University of Alaska campus in Fairbanks."

Valdez Historical Society, Inc., "Archives Alives," Keystone Mall, Box 6, Valdez AK 99686. (907)835-4367. Director: Dorothy I. Clifton.
Purpose: "To provide correct Valdez information on history and what is going on today." Information covers Valdez for the most part, "but we have much more informa-

tion. We seem to have the largest collection of religious publications in Alaska. Many denominations represented."
Services: Offers brochures/pamphlets. "We have several hundred different Alaskan brochures to choose from."
How to Contact: Write or call. "We would just love to have you come and stay awhile and research our material. We can help, but time is limited. Several blocks away is the recording district for the Valdez area, and all books are here in Valdez back to at least 1890. There is no charge for personal services—just for copies. Someone can visit and work long hours in our archives if he gives us a little notice."

Arizona

Sharlot Hall Historical Society, 415 W. Gurley, Prescott AZ 86301. (602)445-3122. Director: Dr. Kenneth Kimsey.
Purpose: "To preserve and disseminate historical information and photos of Arizona and Southwest history. Also to preserve the authenticity of the pioneer spirit through the preservation of historical buildings." Information covers history.
Services: Offers photos. Brochures available.
How to Contact: Write or call Sue Chamberlain, achivist. Charges 15¢/photocopy; plus photo reproduction—rates depend on size. "Please notify us in advance of the subject interest, so we can be checking our files before your arrival. This will save time on all sides. All reproduction of material in this museum is subject to the copyright law."

Arkansas

Arkansas Historical Association, University of Arkansas, History Department, Fayetteville AK 72701. (501)575-3001. Secretary/Treasurer: Walter L. Brown.
Purpose: "To publish Arkansas history and to promote interest in Arkansas." Information covers agriculture, art, business, economics, health/medicine, history and law.
Services: Offers quarterly journal.
How to Contact: Write or call. Charges for subscription to publications.

Benton County Historical Society, Box 355, Siloam Springs AR 72761. (501)524-3217. Secretary Editor: J. Roger Huff.
Purpose: "Devoted to preserving the history (architectural, oral, etc.) of Benton County." Information covers agriculture, art and history.
Services: Offers aid in arranging interviews, biographies, brochures/pamphlets, information searches, and photos. Publications available.
How to Contact: Write or call. Charges for extensive research, photocopies and photo reproduction.

Civil War Round Table Associates, Box 7388, Little Rock AR 72217. (501)225-3996. National Chairman: Jerry Russell.
Purpose: "Dedicated to a continuing interest in the history of the American Civil War and to the protection and preservation of Civil War historic sites." Information covers history and current status of Civil War sites.
Services: Offers newsletters and reports on developmental pressures facing Civil War historic sites.
How to Contact: Write or call. Charges $10/year for newsletter.

Washington County Historical Society, 118 E. Dickson St., Fayetteville AR 72701. (501)521-2970. Secretary: Kathy Lively.
Purpose: "To preserve the past for future generations. We work with genealogical research. We have census records (1850 and 1860), marriage records (1845-1890),

cemetery records and a few specific family histories available." Information covers history.
Services: Offers brochures/pamphlets. Publications include material dealing with family histories, cemetery records, marriages, churches and early settlements of Washington County, Arkansas.
How to Contact: "Write for list of publications. Ask for information required. When requesting information on a family who lived in Washington County, send specific names and dates. Please send SASE." Charges for publications and for postage. Charges 10¢/photocopy.

California

California Historical Society, 2090 Jackson St., San Francisco CA 94109. (415)567-1848. Contact: Library Staff.
Purpose: "The collection, preservation and dissemination of information about the history of California. Library collections include 40,000 books, 5,000 manuscripts, 200,000 historic photographs and art collections. We are a publisher, with a quarterly magazine and regular publishing program. We also provide lectures, tours and other public service activities and programs." Information covers history.
Services: Offers biographies, newsletter and photos. Publications include magazine for members.
How to Contact: Write or visit. "All resources of the library are available on a noncirculating basis. As a privately funded nonprofit organization, we have limited staff time available for research, so a personal visit is preferable. (Researcher will be assisted by our reference librarians.) It is advisable to call before making visit to check what materials are broadly available. The library is open Wednesday through Saturday, 10 a.m. to 4 p.m. (excluding Saturday). Art collections are open by appointment." Charges for photos and photocopies; "fee schedule depends on use of material, time spent and kind of material supplied." Magazine available with membership only.

Fort Crook Historical Society, Box 432, Fall River Mills CA 96028. Curator: Lillian Kent.
Purpose: "To collect and house information and artifacts of the area, including including biographies, history, pictures, and information on families and homes." Information covers agriculture, art, business, health/medicine, history, how-to, industry, law, music, nature, politics and recreation.
Services: Offers aid in arranging interviews, annual reports, bibliographies, biographies, statistics, brochures/pamphlets, clipping services, information searches and photos. "We have many artifacts from local ancestry, also from Indians of the valley and surrounding places."
How to Contact: Write or call.

Lake Tahoe Historical Society, Box 404, South Lake Tahoe CA 95731. (916)544-6249. Publications Chairwoman: Del Laine.
Purpose: "Dedicated to the collection, preservation and distribution of historical information and devoted to the study of the developments of the Lake Tahoe Basin." Information covers history.
Services: Offers aid in arranging interviews, brochures/pamphlets, placement on mailing list, newsletters and photos. Publications include *Legends of Tahoe* and *Lake Valley's Pass*.
How to Contact: Write or call. Charges $5, plus charge for photos.

Napa County Historical Society, 1219 1st St., Napa CA 94558. (707)224-1739. Executive Director: Jess Doud.
Purpose: "To study the history of the state of California, and, in particular, the history of Napa County; to collect and preserve native artifacts, pioneer relics and all other evidences of the life and activities of the early inhabitants of California, with emphasis

on Napa County; to educate the public about the treasures of our pioneer heritage by the collection and dissemination of information of historical value and interest; to engage in educational and social activities and services of every kind and nature." Information covers agriculture, business, history, industry, politics and recreation.
Services: Offers brochures/pamphlets, information searches, newsletter and photos. Publications include monographs published on an irregular basis under a *Gleanings* heading. "A new program of *Sketches* from our archives will include unedited copies of stories of Napa County pioneers. Twenty-eight manuscripts are planned, and they will be published on a bimonthly schedule at about $3.50 each, plus tax."
How to Contact: Write. "We operate wholly with volunteers and, therefore, are limited in the volume and the effort required to respond. SASE must accompany each request for information. All copy work is at the rate of 25¢/page (minimum $1), plus postage. Photo work is $5/negative, plus the cost of the print and postage. Rates are subject to change without notice. No material may be removed from our archives or library except by a certified staff volunteer."

Held Poage Memorial Home and Research Library, 603 W. Perkins St., Ukiah CA 95482. (707)462-6969. Librarian: Mrs. Robert J. (Lila) Lee.
Purpose: Historical society and library; preserves history of Mendocino County, the Pomo Indians, the US, Civil War, school books, secondary Old West, early novels and local authors. Information covers history.
Services: Offers brochures/pamphlets, clipping services and information searches. Publications include the writings of Dr. John Whiz Hudson, Helen McCowen Carpenter and Edith Van Allen Murphy.
How to Contact: Visit. Open Tuesday and Saturday, 2 to 4 p.m., or by appointment in the evening. "Books and materials must be used in the library."

San Antonio Valley Historical Association, Box 157, Lockwood CA 93932. Contact: President.
Purpose: "To maintain and promote preservation of various archeological and historical elements concerning south Monterey County." Information covers agriculture and history.
Services: Offers brochures/pamphlets, newsletter and photos. "We have oral tapes, a few books and pamphlets in the public library at King City. In homes there are various source materials that pertain to prehistory and to the present; interview at home."
How to Contact: Write.

San Diego Corral, Westerners, Box 7174, San Diego CA 92107. (714)222-4491. Round-up Foreman: Horace Dodd.
Purpose: "Research and publication of history of the Far West." Information covers history.
Services: Offers newsletters. "We offer no other services other than publications."
How to Contact: Write for list of publications.

Santa Clara County Historical Heritage Commission, 70 W. Hedding, 6th Floor, East Wing, San Jose CA 95110. Staff to the Commission: Arthur L. Ogilvie.
Purpose: Information covers heritage resources preservation.
Services: Offers brochures/pamphlets. Publications include the *Heritage Resources Inventory*.
How to Contact: Write or call. Charges for 1979 edition of Heritage Resources Inventory and 50¢/photocopy.

Colorado

Partisan Prohibition Historical Society, Box 2635, Denver CO 80201. (303)572-0646. President: Roger C. Storms.
Purpose: "To honor the partisan campaigns for prohibition, to provide a source of

information sympathetic to the prohibition movement, and to encourage the study of the temperance movement and its impact on the broader historical movements of America." Information covers history and politics.
Services: Offers aid in arranging interviews, bibliographies, biographies, information searches, statistics and newsletter.
How to Contact: Write or call. "We are primarily a middleman type of service referring, the inquirer to other eources of information. We have limited sources and staff at our Denver office. Our archival service is located in Ann Arbor, Michigan, and is far more extensive."

State Historical Society of Colorado, 1300 Broadway, Denver CO 80203. (303)839-2305. Curator of Documentary Research: Maxine Benson.
Purpose: "To collect, preserve and present Colorado history." Information covers agriculture, art, business, celebrities, entertainment, food, history, industry, law, music, politics and recreation.
Services: Offers bibliographies, biographies, information searches, newsletter and photos.
How to Contact: Write or call. Charges for photocopies, extensive information searches and photos used for publication. "Restrictions vary but are minimal; credit must be given."

Connecticut

Connecticut Historical Society, 1 Elizabeth St., Hartford CT 06105. (203)236-5621. Library Director: Christopher Bickford.
Purpose: Research library and records museum of Connecticut. Information covers agriculture, art, business, celebrities, economics, entertainment, food, health/ medicine, history, how-to, industry, law, music, nature, politics, recreation, science, sports and travel.
Services: Offers photos and complete library services.
How to Contact: Visit.

Harwinton Historical Society, Inc., Box 84, Harwinton CT 06791. President: Bonnie F. Kochiss.
Purpose: "We are a small, local, nonprofit historical society, organized to preserve local history." Information covers agriculture and history.
Services: Offers statistics, newsletter and photos.
How to Contact: Write.

Litchfield Historical Society, Ingraham Memorial Library, Box 385, Litchfield CT 06759. (203)567-5862. Director: Lockett Ford Ballard Jr.
Purpose: "The Litchfield Historical Society (LHS) is a local history museum and research library with manuscript holdings covering the local area from 1750-1900, genealogical materials, special collections of the first law schools, Pierce Academy, local industries, institutions, etc. We also have newspaper holdings and research materials pertaining to Litchfield. Photographs and other visual materials are available in-house." Information covers art, economics and history.
Services: Offers general research services.
How to Contact: Write or visit. Charges 15¢/photocopy and $1 service charge/request for photocopies (up to 100 copies). "There are no loans or interlibrary loan service. All books and manuscripts are to be used in-house."

Rocky Hill Historical Society, Inc., Box 185, Rocky Hill CT 06067. President: Peter J. Revill.
Purpose: "To collect and preserve historical material of Rocky Hill and, to some extent, the region." Information covers local history.

Services: Offers research facilities. "Our small 1,000-volume library is available to researchers on request."
How to Contact: Write. "Staff (volunteer) is not always available to assist and host visitors for extended periods."

Stamford Historical Society, 713 Bedford St., Stamford CT 06901. (203)323-1975. Director: Elizabeth Gershman.
Purpose: "To promote Stamford history and educate area residents of their geographic heritage." Information covers history.
Services: Offers newsletter. Publications and price list is available.
How to Contact: Write or call. "If research is involved on our part, a donation is requested."

Stowe-Day Foundations, 77 Forest St., Hartford CT 06105. (203)522-9258. Director: Joseph S. Van Why.
Purpose: "To maintain the restored Harriet Beecher Stowe House and the Stowe-Day Library which is a research collection of 19th Century Americana." Information covers art and history.
Services: Offers bibliographies, photos and an annual teacher's workshop.
How to Contact: Call for an appointment. Library hours are Monday through Friday, 9 a.m. to 5 p.m. "Like many institutions which make available original manuscript material and have a limited staff, we suggest that the researcher have a basic knowledge of the subject of interest before calling on us."

The Wethersfield Historical Society, Inc., 150 Main St., Wethersfield CT 06109. (203)529-4757. Director: C. Douglass Alves Jr.
Purpose: "We are a local historical society with collections dealing with Wethersfield in particular and the surrounding area in general. We provide exhibits, house museums, lectures, and house tours. We maintain holdings of genealogical information on Wethersfield families." Information covers history and local genealogy.
Services: Offers brochures/pamphlets and information searches. Brochures include general information on the nine historic sites in Wethersfield open to the public.
How to Contact: Write or call. Charges 15¢/photocopy. Photographs can be reproduced on a per-job basis. Send 2 loose first-class stamps to cover return postage.

Delaware

The Historical Society of Delaware, 505 Market Street Mall, Wilmington DE 19801. (302)655-7161. Contact: Library.
Purpose: "Historical society of Delaware with material covering 1700 to present." Information covers agriculture, art, business, food, health/medicine, history, industry, music and nature.
Services: Offers brochures/pamphlets and information searches. "We also have a museum, an educational program, and a library open to the public with an extensive collection of manuscripts on the history of Delaware."
How to Contact: Write. Charges for research based on time and copy.

District of Columbia

Columbia Historical Society, 1307 New Hampshire Ave. NW, Washington DC 20036. (202)785-2068. Executive Director/Librarian: Perry Fisher.
Purpose: To chronicle "Washington DC history from approximately 1783 to present." Information covers agriculture, art, business, economics, food, health/medicine, history, industry, law, music, nature and politics.
Services: Offers brochures/pamphlets, information searches (on limited basis), statistics and photos. "Our library is open to the public and contains pamphlets, books,

scrapbooks, manuscripts, maps, and an extensive collection of prints and photographs."
How to Contact: Write. Charges for services.

United States Capitol Historical Society, 200 Maryland Ave. NE, Washington DC 20515. (202)543-8919. Historian: William M. Maury.
Purpose: To promote the history of the Capitol building and Congress.
Services: Offers aid in arranging interviews, bibliographies and newsletter. Publications include a calendar and *Capitol Journal*; also has informational recording.
How to Contact: Write.

Florida

Broward County Historical Commission, 201 SE 6th St., Room 800, Courthouse, Fort Lauderdale FL 33301. (305)765-5872. Director: Elizabeth S. Bolge.
Purpose: "The Broward County Historical Commission (BCHC) is a government agency devoted to the protection and promotion of local history and heritage. We maintain, for both inhouse and public use, an archives and library, a resource collection on historical and museum administration, technical information on preservation, and a photograph collection. The BCHC regularly publishes research in its semiannual magazine, *Broward Legacy*." Information covers history and archeology.
Services: Offers bibliographies, brochures/pamphlets, information searches and newsletter. "Upon request, the county historian can conduct a limited degree of research on special projects. We also act as a clearinghouse for references to collections held by other groups and agencies." Publications available.
How to Contact: Write or call. Charges for publications.

Florida Historical Society, University of South Florida Library, Special Collections, Tampa FL 33620. (813)974-2731.
Purpose: "The study, preservation and conservation of Florida history. The society is an important repository of primary sources." Information covers agriculture, art, business, celebrities, economics, entertainment, food, health/medicine, history, how-to, industry, law, music, nature, politics, recreation, science, sports, technical data, travel and anthropology.
Services: Offers aid in arranging interviews, annual reports, bibliographies, biographies, statistics, brochures/pamphlets, information searches and newsletter. Also has a few photos and a noncirculating library. Publications include *Florida Historical Quarterly* and *Florida History Newsletter*.
How to Contact: Write, call or visit. Written requests preferred. Open Monday through Thursday, 8 a.m. to 9 p.m.; Friday, 8 a.m. to 5 p.m. Time varies between academic quarters. Will allow photocopying of some materials.

Fort Lauderdale Historical Society, Inc., 219 SW 2nd Ave., Box 14043, Fort Lauderdale FL 33302. (305)463-4431. Executive Director: Marjorie D. Patterson.
Purpose: "To collect and disseminate information concerning the city of Fort Lauderdale and its residents." Information covers history.
Services: Offers copies of materials (photographs) if reimbursed.
How to Contact: Write or call.

Historical Society of Okaloosa and Walton Counties, Inc., Historical Society Museum, 115 Westview Ave., Box 488, Valparaiso FL 32580. (904)678-2615. Director: Mrs. James N. LaRoche.
Purpose: "The historical society and the museum it sponsors collects, records and preserves documentary and photographic data and material objects which help to establish and illustrate the history of Okaloosa and Walton Counties and the panhandle of northwest Florida. Of particular interest is the cultural, educational and industrial development of the area including farming, fishing, turpentine and lumber

industries, and pioneer life until 1940 and the beginning of Eglin Air Force Base."
Information covers agriculture, business, history and genealogy.
Services: Offers brochures/pamphlets, information searches and newsletters.
How to Contact: Write or call.

Historical Society of Palm Beach County, 1 Whitehall Way, Box 1492, Palm Beach FL
33480. (305)655-1492. Librarian: Maxine W. Banash.
Purpose: "To discover, collect and preserve all materials (especially originals) pertaining to the history of Palm Beach County; to disseminate knowledge to our members
and to the public; and to promote historical research." Information covers agriculture,
art, celebrities, history and music.
Services: Offers some photos and assistance. "We see researchers by appointment only
on Tuesday and Thursday, noon to 4 p.m. We are a small library with very little help;
however, we have a wealth of information. Unfortunately, we do not have a research
program available."
How to Contact: Write or call.

Georgia

Georgia Department of Archives and History (see listing in Libraries & Archives
section).

Northwest Georgia Historical and Genealogical Society, Inc., Box 2484. Rome GA
30161. (404)291-6697. President: Roy E. Bottoms.
Purpose: "Our society is a nonprofit organization that is made up of some 300
members in 30 states. Our purpose is to preserve history and research in genealogy of
the area (northwest Georgia). Our society meets eight times per year in our local library
auditorium." Information covers history and genealogical research.
Services: Offers a quarterly publication.
How to Contact: Write or call. "Our quarterly is free to use at the society. To become a
member costs $10/year. Members automatically receive four copies of our quarterly or,
if they choose, they can purchase single copies at $2.50 each. I personally do genealogical research in this area, mostly in   Floyd County, Georgia. My fee for this service is
$5/hour. Our genealogical library contains over 5,000 volumes of valuable information. Write to my personal address: Roy Bottoms, Box 60003, Rome GA 30161."

Hawaii

Hawaii Foundation for History and the Humanities, 1151 Punchbowl St., Room 233,
Honolulu HI 96813. (808)548-2070. Executive Director: David Yamamoto.
Purpose: Historic preservation and promotion of Hawaii's cultural heritage. Information covers agriculture, business, food, health/medicine, history, how-to, nature and
the humanities.
Services: Offers aid in arranging interviews, annual reports, bibliographies, biographies, statistics, brochures/pamphlets, information searches, placement on mailing
list and newsletter. Publications include *Hawaii Heritage News* (quarterly).
How to Contact: Write.

Idaho

Idaho State Historical Society, 610 N. Julia Davis Dr., Boise ID 83706. (208)384-2120.
Purpose: Contains state archives; historical and genealogical libraries; papers of
former governors, senators, congressmen, etc.; and other material pertaining to Idaho
and the Pacific Northwest. Information covers agriculture, art, business, celebrities,
economics, entertainment, food, health/medicine, history, how-to, industry, law, music, nature, politics, recreation, science, self-help, sports, technical data and archeology.
Services: Offers aid in arranging interviews, annual reports, statistics, brochures/

pamphlets, 600,000 photos available for reproduction, and newspaper and manuscript files.
How to Contact: Write or visit. Materials must be used in the library, located at 3rd and State Sts., Boise.

Latah County Historical Society, 110 S. Adams, Moscow ID 83843. (208)882-1004. Director: Keith Petersen.
Purpose: "Our research collection consists of manuscripts, archives, oral histories, photographs, clippings, books, pamphlets and ephemera dealing with Latah County and northern Idaho history. The collections are organized much as the collections at a large historical society, and much the same policy governs their use. We welcome all serious researchers and attempt to be as helpful as possible." Information covers history.
Services: Offers the *Oral History Guide*, which details some of the subjects covered in the 300 interviews the society did with Latah County old-timers between 1971 and 1978. Most of these oral histories have been transcribed and, with a few exceptions, are available to researchers either in typewritten or tape form. A guide to genealogical and historical resources available in Latah County will be published in 1979, until then, access to the collections is gained through the card catalogs in the library.
How to Contact: Write or call. Charges for copying or photo duplication; also $6/hour for research done by the staff (the first hour is free). Some of the manuscript collections and oral histories are restricted, but most are open to all serious researchers. Credit must be given to the Latah County Historical Society for any materials used in a publication.

Lemhi County Historical Society, Box 645, Salmon ID 83467. Contact: Museum Director.
Purpose: "We are a society sponsoring the local museum." Information covers display cases of local history and an Oriental Room.
How to Contact: "We operate on a limited basis and do not have the finances for dealing with all the mail. The museum is open to the public from April to October."

Illinois

Chicago Historical Society, Clark St. at North Ave., Chicago IL 60614. (312)642-4600. Contact: Larry A. Viskochil.
Services: Offers 450,000 photos on Chicago history. "The collection is in the public domain. We exercise proprietary rights and sell or rent photographic copies of items in the collection."
How to Contact: Write or call. Print fee: $10 (b&w); $40 (color transparency). "In certain instances—e.g., for advertising use, we charge $75." Charges 15¢ each, plus 50¢ service charge, for photocopies.
Tips: "Unless copies are available in our 'ready' file, photo orders take 4-8 weeks for completion."

Hancock County Historical Society, Box 68, Carthage IL 62321. Corresponding Secretary: Robert M. Cochran, Warsaw IL 62379.
Purpose: "To acquire and preserve knowledge and material of historic significance to Hancock County. We will soon have a genealogical card index listing families or heads of families who have lived in Hancock County and every source of related information appearing in our reference library." Information covers history (family data).
Services: Offers biographies, newsletter and photos. "We are currently working on the publication of *Historic Sites and Structures of Hancock County, Illinois*. This book will contain about 1,000 old photos and related information and should be available in midwinter at $20 per copy."
How to Contact: Write. Charges only if copying is required or if lengthy research is involved. Some of the material is copyrighted.

The Historical Society of Arlington Heights, 500 N. Vail Ave., Arlington Heights IL 60004. (312)255-1225. Executive Director: Virgil K. Horath.
Purpose: "For all those who treasure history of the pioneer beginnings of Arlington Heights, the society is dedicated to the preservation of the historical imprint of all the persons who have made this area their home." Information covers history.
Services: Offers biographies, brochures/pamphlets, information searches and photos.
How to Contact: Write or call.

Illinois State Historical Library (see listing in Libraries & Archives section).

Indiana

Brown County Historical Society, Box 668, Nashville IN 47448. (812)988-6089. President: Hazel S. Davis.
Purpose: "To collect and preserve history, records and artifacts pertaining to Brown County."
Services: Offers genealogical and archival information on Brown County. Publications include *Cemeteries of Brown County* and *Goodspeed's History of Brown County*.
How to Contact: Write and enclose SASE.
Tips: "Archival materials are now in the process of being organized and filed, and are not always easily available. But a sincere attempt will be made to be helpful."

Fulton County Historical Society, Inc., 7th and Pontiac, Rochester IN 46975. (219)223-4436. President: Shirley Willard.
Purpose: "To preserve Fulton County and northern Indiana history by preserving old records, newspapers and artifacts and by publishing books and quarterly magazines of historically documented stories and photos. We have much information on local schools, businesses, the Cole Brothers Circus from 1935 to 1940, genealogy, railroads and farm equipment." Information covers agriculture, business, celebrities and history.
Services: Offers bibliographies, biographies and brochures/pamphlets. Publications include reprints of *1883 Fulton County Atlas* ($12); *1910 Home Folks* ($10), tales told by pioneer settlers of Fulton County; and *1941 Wagoner Genealogy* ($12.50). All these will be mailed for an additional $1 mailing charge. Also offers a *Fulton County Historical Society Quarterly* and brochures on the museum, the Trail of Courage Rendezvous and the Round Barn Festival.
How to Contact: Write. "We charge for postage, photocopying and labor."

Historic Fort Wayne, Inc., 107 S. Clinton, Fort Wayne IN 46802. (219)424-3476. Managing Director: Brian Leigh Dunnigan.
Purpose: "Museum and living history program primarily concerned with the history of northeast Indiana to 1819. The living history program focuses primarily on life on the military frontier in 1816." Information covers history.
Services: Offers brochures/pamphlets.
How to Contact: Write or call. Request list of publications. "Most publications are for sale. Information on our museum programs is generally free of charge."

Indiana Historical Society, 315 W. Ohio St., Indianapolis IN 46202. (317)633-5277. Head Librarian: Thomas Rumer.
Purpose: "The collection and preservation of all materials calculated to shed light on the natural, civil and political history of Indiana; the publication and circulation of historical documents; and the promotion of useful knowledge." Information covers agriculture, art, business, celebrities, economics, entertainment, food, health/medicine, history, how-to, industry, law, music, nature, politics, recreation, science, sports and military education.
Services: Offers annual reports, bibliographies, biographies, brochures/pamphlets, information searches, placement on mailing list, newsletter and photos. "No geneal-

ogy." Publications include *Indiana Historical Society Newsletter* (monthly).
How to Contact: Write or call ahead of visit. Open Monday through Friday, 8:15 a.m. to 5 p.m.; Saturday, 8:15 a.m to noon, except in summer.

Michigan City Historical Society, Inc., Old Lighthouse Museum, Box 512, Michigan City IN 46360. (219)872-6133. Curator: Mrs. William H. Harris.
Purpose: "The assimilation and dissemination of historical data relating to Michigan City, the Lakefront, and the Lighthouse at Michigan City and the Lighthouse service. We also have a historical newsletter *Old Lighthouse Museum News* and have a museum with historical displays and guided tours." Information covers business, history, industry, music and genealogy.
Services: Offers brochures/pamphlets and information searches. Publications available.
How to Contact: Write. Charges for publications, photocopies (10¢/page plus postage) and genealogy searches ($3/hour plus 10¢/photocopy). Appointments with curator or her delegate are requested as most of the help is volunteer.

Washington County Historical Society, 307 E. Market, Salem IN 47167. (812)883-6495. President: Ruby Williams.
Purpose: "To collect, preserve and share local history and family genealogy. A museum in connection with the historical society houses relics. In addition to much material on our county history, we also have information on our neighboring counties in Indiana, Kentucky and North Carolina. Our church records include Baptist, Presbyterian and Quaker records. We have many stories of Morgan's Raid during the Civil War, underground railroad stations and Knights of the Golden Circle. We have several area folk stories. Many scrapbooks of newspaper clippings are indexed by subject as well as by the person's name. We have a file of a newspaper printed in Salem, covering 1885 to 1937." Information covers history.
Services: Offers bibliographies, biographies, and information searches.
How to Contact: Write or visit. Museum open Tuesday through Sunday. "Even though we are not officially open until 1 p.m., out-of-towners are admitted for research at 9 a.m. Plan to spend plenty of time with us. Any of our material is available for use in the library, not for rental." Charges 15¢/page for photocopies. "We usually suggest a donation for maintenance of our facilities for research done by our staff."

Wayne County Historical Society/Museum, 1150 N. A St., Richmond IN 47374. (317)962-5756. Director: Stephen R. Williams.
Purpose: "To preserve and promote local history; we have other interests in industry, communications and international cultures." Information covers historical aspects of agriculture, art, business, health/medicine, industry and music.
Services: Offers brochures/pamphlets, information searches and photos. Publications include a museum brochure, a society newsletter, and various publications on local history.
How to Contact: Write or call. Make an appointment in advance.

Iowa

Calhoun County Historical Society, 8th St., Rockwell City IA 50579. (712)297-8307. President: Judy Webb.
Purpose: "To preserve historical material and artifacts of this rural community and to assist genealogist in research." Information covers agriculture and history.
Services: Offers brochures/pamphlets and information searches. Publications available.
How to Contact: Write or call. There is no charge unless some extra expense is involved, such as copying, then the inquirer is expected to reimburse the society.

Grundy County Historical Society, 1009 H. Ave., Grundy Center IA 50638. (319)824-6451. Agent: Jean Evans.

Purpose: "To search out and record history of the area in Grundy County, Iowa." Information covers history.
Services: Offers aid in arranging interviews, brochures/pamphlets, and information searches.
How to Contact: Write or call.

Iowa Division of Historical Museums and Archives (see listing in Libraries & Archives section).

Tama County Historical Society, State and Broadway, Box 64, Toledo IA 52342. Executive Secretary: Marie K. Vileta, 310 W. 7th St., Tama IA 52339. (515)484-3028.
Purpose: "To preserve Tama County history and artifacts. We have a museum in the two-story former county jail (built in 1869); information and artifacts concerning Mesquakie Indians and early settlers of Tama County; information on Tama County history of 1879, 1883 and 1910; Tama County plates and atlases of 1875, 1892, 1916 and 1926; Tama County newspapers on microfilm as far back as 1868; 200 rolls of microfilm (two viewers) concerning newspapers, genealogies and censuses (Tama County) of 1860, 1870 and 1880; scrapbooks of county obituaries; old county school records; etc. This historical society also houses a genealogical library and is the site for meetings of the county genealogical society. Information covers history.
Services: Offers information searches. "We have information on burials in Tama County cemeteries (over 60); we have access to some county records of births, deaths, marriages and probate previous to 1914. (Unfortunately, not all were recorded.)
How to Contact: Write or call. Charges for photos of "primitives" or artifacts and copies of printed materials (20¢/sheet). "Please be explicit in requests. We help with genealogical searches for ancestors in Tama County, but must have a few clues. We ask that a contribution be made to the Tama County Historical Society."

Kansas

Kansas State Historical Society, 10th and Jackson St., Topeka KS 66617. (913)296-3165. Curator of Photographs: Nancy Sherbert.
Purpose: "Our purpose is to preserve and promote Kansas history. We have a large collection of Kansas newspapers and extensive collections of manuscripts, maps and photographs. We are the official state archives, and our library specializes in Kansas, Western and Indian history and genealogy." Information covers agriculture, art, business, celebrities, economics, entertainment, food, health/medicine, history, industry, music, nature, politics, recreation, science, sports and travel.
Services: Offers 85,000 b&w photos and 1,000 color photos of Indians, the American West, railroads, military, Kansas and Kansans.
How to Contact: "A limited amount of information can be obtained by correspondence. The research departments are open to the public from 8 to 5, Monday through Friday." Charges fee for photocopies and photographs. For photos, offers reproduction rights, advertising rights, first rights and second rights. Collection is in the public domain. B&w glossy or matte finish fee: $1 (4x5); $1.50 (5x7); $2.75 (8x10); $5 (11x14); $8.50 (16x20). Minimum order: $1. Color transparencies will be made in special cases—where such work is feasible—for $7. Mounting charge: 75¢/square foot Charges $1.50 if a new negative is required. Credit line required.

Osage County Historical Society, Rt. 2, Osage City KS 66523. (913)528-4778. President: Noble E. Hunsicker.
Purpose: "We receive by notation, to store and display, any historical souvenirs, artifacts and personal effects of any known historical figure or area, and any general historical information for future generations." Information covers history and self-help.
Services: Offers aid in arranging interviews, bibliographies, brochures/pamphlets, information searches and placement on mailing list. "We will try to answer any

questions pertaining to family or general history of the area."
How to Contact: Write or call. "Please give us as much information as possible to begin our answers. Also give your name and address for return mail."

Kentucky

The Filson Club, Inc., 118 W. Breckinridge St., Louisville KY 40203. (502)582-3727. Librarian: Martin F. Schmidt. Secretary: James R. Bentley.
Purpose: "The Filson Club collects historical material, especially that pertaining to Kentucky. We also have an extensive holding of genealogical data. We collect books, pamphlets, newspapers, pictures, maps, manuscripts and ephemera as well as museum objects dealing with Kentucky." Information covers history.
Services: Offers brochures/pamphlets.
How to Contact: "We prefer that researchers visit us and use the collections. We can answer limited questions through correspondence or by telephone, but cannot give extensive time to reference. We charge for photocopies (25¢/page). We prefer to have a stamped return envelope for letters; contributions are welcome. We are a reference collection and our holdings do not circulate nor do we participate in interlibrary loans."

Kentucky Covered Bridge Association, Box 151, Fort Thomas KY 41075. (606)441-7000. Executive Director: Mr. L.K. Patton.
Purpose: "Gathering and dissemination of covered bridge information and history, of bridges past and present, of Kentucky in particular, and the US in general." Information covers history, technical data and travel.
Services: Offers statistics, brochures/pamphlets, newsletters, photos and press kits. Publications available.
How to Contact: Write. Charges for photocopies and photograph duplication.

Kentucky Historical Society, 300 W. Broadway, Box H, Frankfort KY 40601. (502)564-3016. Director: William R. Buster.
Purpose: "To preserve and promote the history of Kentucky. We have two history mobiles that go to fairs, schools and celebrations." Information covers art, celebrities, economics, entertainment, food, history, how-to, industry, law, music, politics, recreation, genealogy and the military.
Services: Offers aid in arranging interviews, brochures/pamphlets, information searches, newsletter and photos. Publications available.
How to Contact: Write or visit. "We have a small staff but will be able to assist in the library. If you need to work with photos or manuscripts give us time to get it ready." Charges for photocopies and some publications.

Rowan County Historical Society, Rt. 6, Box 498, Morehead KY 40351. (606)784-9145. President: Lloyd Dean.
Purpose: "We collect historical information of Morehead and Rowan County. We collect information past and present." Information covers agriculture, art, celebrities, history, music and politics.
Services: Offers bibliographies, biographies, brochures/pamphlets, clipping services and information searches.
How to Contact: Write. "We will pass on information we have available or supply information as to where it can be found."

Louisiana

Louisiana Historical Association, Box 44211, Baton Rouge LA 70804. (504)342-5440. Secretary/Treasurer: Donald J. Lemieux. Assistant Secretary-Treasurer: Rose Angelle.
Purpose: "To promote Louisiana history for educational purposes, and to preserve

Louisiana's rich heritage. An annual meeting is held in the spring." Information covers history.
Services: Offers newsletter (a historical quarterly on Louisiana history).
How to Contact: Write or call. Charges for membership and back issues of the quarterly.

Maine

Bethel Historical Society, Inc., 15 Broad St., Bethel ME 04217. (207)824-2908. Director: Stanley Russell Howe.
Purpose: "To preserve and interpret the local past. The society's resources include an archives (containing manuscripts, diaries, letters and maps); a library (containing technical and regional history), and a museum (effectively portraying life in mid-19th century America and focusing on Dr. Moses Mason and his wife Agnes)." Information covers agriculture, art, business, celebrities, economics, entertainment, food, health/ medicine, history, industry, music, politics, recreation, sports and travel.
Services: Offers bibliographies, biographies, brochures/pamphlets, information searches, newsletter and photos. Publications include *Moses Mason House Museum*, *Dr. Moses Mason and His House*, *The Family Farm*, *Bethel's Broad Street*, *Molly Ockett*, *Made in Bethel* and *Special Edition*.
How to Contact: Write or call. "The society is willing to provide any information that can be retrieved from its collections at no cost to the writer." Charges 25¢/photocopy, 50¢-$1/each for publications, and cost of processing for photos. "Copies of our photos may be used with permission."

Maine State Museum (see listing in Museums section).

Pejepscot Historical Society, 11 Lincoln St., Brunswick ME 04011. (207)729-4622. President: Irving Stetson.
Purpose: "We are basically a local history museum concerned with Brunswick, Topsham and Harpswell, Maine. Archival material contains genealogical material from the 17th to 20th centuries, with emphasis on the 18th century." Information covers history, industry and genealogy.
Services: Offers brochures.
How to Contact: Write. Charges for publications.

Pemaquid Historical Association, c/o Harrington Meeting House, Pemaquid ME 04558. Vice President: Mrs. Stuart Condon.
Purpose: "To encourage and promote interest in the historical background of the Bristol, Maine, area. We maintain Harrington Meeting House (1772), a national historic site, and staff a museum of old Bristol in the Meeting House." Information covers history of Bristol area.
Services: Offers brochures/pamphlets. "Museum contains old photos, maps, books, memorabilia and artifacts of the area. Bristol was incorporated as a town in 1765." Publications include *Eighteenth Century Meeting Houses* and *The Pemaquid River*.
How to Contact: Write. Enclose SASE. Be specific about inquiries.

The Society for the Preservation of Old Mills, Box 435, Wiscasset ME 04578.
Purpose: To preserve the history of old mills.
Services: Offers newsletters.
How to Contact: Write. "We are not a writers service bureau, our newsletters are for our members. Dues are $6/year."

Maryland

The Historical Society of Frederick County, Inc., 24 E. Church St., Frederick MD 21701. (301)662-1188. Contact: President or Curator.

Purpose: "The object of our society shall be to promote the study of the history and antiquities of this county and the collection and conservation of the records thereof, as well as all ancient articles of personal property; and to acquire, maintain, restore and preserve monuments structures and areas deemed to be of historic importance to Frederick County, Maryland." Information covers history.
Services: Offers research information. Publications available.
How to Contact: Write or visit. "Contributions to our tax-exempt operation are welcomed."

Maryland Historical Society, 21 State Circle, Annapolis MD 21401. (301)269-2438. Contact: Librarian.
Purpose: "To provide information on the architecture and history of structures in Maryland, 1634 to present; and on prehistoric archaelogy."Information covers history, architecture, and archaelogy.
Services: Offers information searches (limited) and a library for research (with permission). Publications available.
How to Contact: Write or call. Charges for services depending on time and subject.

Steamship Historical Society of America, University of Baltimore Library, 1420 Maryland Ave., Baltimore MD 21201. (301)727-6350, ext. 455. Reference Librarian: James Foster.
Services: Offers 15,000 b&w photos of steamships (oceans, coastal, inland, etc.). "Photos arranged by vessel name, not by type of ship or geographical area of service."
How to Contact: Offers one-time rights for commercial use. Charges $5/hour service charge for inquiries involving lengthy research, $6/copy negative.

Massachusetts

American Jewish Historical Society, 2 Thornton Rd., Waltham MA 02154. Librarian: Dr. Nathan M. Karanoff.
Purpose: "To collect, preserve, exhibit and disseminate information related to the history of Jews in America." Information covers history.
Services: Offers bibliographies, brochures/pamphlets, photos and books. Publications include publications list.
How to Contact: Write detailed request. "Restrictions on usage of collections must be adhered to and proper credit must be given."

Amherst Historical Society, Inc., Box 739, Amherst MA 01002. (413)253-7204. Treasurer: Sheila M. Rainford.
Purpose: "To promote activities of historic and civic interest in and about Amherst, Massachusetts. This includes operation of the Strong House as a museum of local history." Information covers history.
Services: Offers assistance. Publications include *Amherst: A Guide to Its Architecture*, by Paul Norton; and *Essays on Amherst's History*, edited by Theodore Green.
How to Contact: "Local history is a broad category. Send your request in writing, and we will try to forward it to the proper source. We are an all-volunteer society and cannot do lengthy research for you. Please plan far ahead. If you just 'turn up' in Amherst one day, there may be no one available to help you. Sending your request and schedule in writing—early—is the best system. Questionnaires are more likely to be returned if they are brief, if enough time is allowed, and if a return envelope is enclosed. If I get a questionnaire ten pages long on June 10 and it is due by June 11, I simply don't respond."

The Bostonian Society, Old State House, 206 Washington St., Boston MA 02109. (617)523-7033. Librarian: Mary Leen.
Services: Offers 10,000 b&w photos of people, places (e.g., buildings, streets), and

events related to Boston. Most material pertains to the 19th century, with some about the 20th century.
How to Contact: Write or call. Charges $5-50 for one-time editorial or advertising use; $5-15 print fee.

Dighton Historical Society, Inc., 1217 Williams St., Dighton MA 02715. Acting President: E. Varley.
Purpose: "We cover mostly Dighton area information, including account books, letters, deeds, etc. We also have material things, all donated from Dighton families: clothing, pictures and furniture."
Services: Offers genealogy records. Publications available.
How to Contact: Write. Charges for genealogy searches. Material cannot be removed from the historical house.

Massachusetts Historical Commission, 294 Washington St., Boston MA 02108. (617)727-8470. Public Information Officer: Kim Davis.
Purpose: "The historic preservation and protection of historic sites." Information covers agriculture, art, business, economics, history, how-to, industry, technical data, travel and archeology.
Services: Offers aid in arranging interviews, annual reports, bibliographies, statistics, brochures/pamphlets, placement on mailing list, newsletter, photos and press kits. Publications include *Massachusetts Historical Commission Newsletter* (bimonthly).
How to Contact: Write. Open Monday through Friday, 9 a.m. to 5 p.m. Some files are classified by law.

Northampton Historical Society, 58 Bridge St., Northampton MA 01060. (413)584-6011. Executive Director: Ruth E. Wilbur.
Purpose: "Collecting, preserving and exhibiting artifacts of the history of man in Northampton and the Connecticut Valley." Maintains three historic house museums and an 1840 barn, creates exhibits, sponsors lectures and programs, and conducts tours. Information covers agriculture, art, business, celebrities, economics, entertainment, food, health/medicine, history, industry, law, music, politics and recreation.
Services: Offers brochures/pamphlets, information searches and photos. Publications include pamphlets on houses, and books and charts on the Parsons and Bliss families.
How to Contact: Write or call. Write for rate schedule. Appointment necessary to use collection for research. "Use the Forbes Library (46 West St., Northampton) first before coming to the society. They are apt to have more information than we do."

Norton Historical Society, Box 1776, Norton MA 02766. President: Curtis Dahl.
Purpose: "Maintaining an old school house museum and holding meetings relevant to Norton and American history. Those interested in Norton genealogy should refer to the Mormon Church's genealogical records in Salt Lake City rather than to this society. Norton records have been microfilmed by the Mormons and are available through them. We have no paid staff and cannot do research, though we can answer general questions that can be answered from general knowledge. This is not a research institution." Information covers history.
Services: Offers brochures/pamphlets.
How to Contact: Write. Charges for publications.

Pilgrim Society, Pilgrim Hall, 75 Court St., Plymouth MA 02360. (617)746-1620. Curator of Books and Manuscripts: Jeanne M. Mills. Director: Lawrence Pizer.
Purpose: "The Pilgrim Society was founded in 1820 to study and interpret Pilgrim history, to preserve Pilgrim artifacts and to promote a continuing awareness of the Pilgrims' contributions to the founding of our nation. We maintain a museum, library and manuscript collection relating to the Pilgrim experience and to the founding and continuing development of Plymouth town and colony." Information covers agriculture, art, business, economics, history, industry, music and politics.

Services: Offers brochures/pamphlets, information searches and "assistance with historical research within the Pilgrim experience—scholarly and, to a lesser extent, genealogical." Publications include *The Pilgrim Society (1820-1970), A Guide to Manuscripts of the Pilgrim Society, The Pilgrim Story* and *Sparrow Hawk*.

How to Contact: Write. "If coming in person, arrange beforehand with curator, as office is open only on part-time basis." Charges $1/photocopy; varying rates for published material. "Most requests for genealogical information would have greater success with other organizations, such as the Massachusetts Historical Genealogical Society in Boston."

The Plymouth Antiquarian Society, 27 North St., Plymouth MA 02360. (617)746-9697 (summer); (617)747-0346 (winter). Curator: Carla A. Crawley.

Purpose: "We are a society of 500 members who own and maintain three historic homes open to the public. We are trying to preserve history by maintaining these homes and the local history involved around them. The earliest dates 1677, 1749 and 1809. Each contains beautiful furnishings appropriate to its specific period and collections of many porcelains, costumes, quilts and coverlets." Information covers art and history.

Services: Offers brochures/pamphlets. "We maintain our collections for insight into the past and especially for research. All of our things are available for use as documentation and as research material." Publications available.

How to Contact: Write or call.

Sandy Bay Historical Society, 40 King St., Rockport MA 01966. Curator: Dr. William D. Hoyt.

Purpose: "To collect and process information and materials related to the history of Rockport, Gloucester and the Cape Ann area; and to make these available to researchers and through exhibits." Information covers art, business, economics, industry, politics and recreation.

Services: Offers response to queries.

How to Contact: Write or call. "This is a small society with no regular staff. We try to respond to inquiries for information, and we gladly arrange for visitors to see the exhibits and collections when there is advance notice. The only request is that persons using our collections do give credit when work is published." Charges for photocopies.

Society for the Preservation of Colonial Culture, 235 Old Westford Rd., Chelmsford MA 01824. Curator: Vincent J.R. Kehoe.

Purpose: To preserve information on British military history in the American colonies, 1770-1783. Information covers history.

Services: Offers statistics, information searches and consultation services. Publications include *The Military Guide: British Infantry of 1775*.

How to Contact: Write, explaining needs. Charges $10/hour for research; $100/day for technical services.

Titanic Historical Society, Inc., Box 53, Indian Orchard (Springfield) MA 01151. Cofounder/General Secretary: Edward S. Kamuda.

Purpose: "To perpetuate the history of the *Titanic* and her sister ships by the establishment of an archives and a quarterly newsletter for distribution to members." Information covers history.

Services: Offers newsletter.

How to Contact: Write.

Michigan

Michigan History Division, 208 N. Capitol, Lansing MI 48918. (517)373-3703.

Purpose: "We are a governmental history organization with a museum, brochures and

informational pieces, archives, stored primary resources, publications, a bimonthly magazine, how-to manuals and information leaflets." Information covers history, how-to and politics.
Services: Offers brochures/pamphlets.
How to Contact: Write or call. Make appointment in advance to use archives.

Michilimackinac Historical Society, Box 451, St. Ignace MI 49781. President: Robert Sposito.
Purpose: "To preserve the history of the straits area with emphasis placed on Marquette and photo history plus archaeological. We also provide archaeological research of the area." Information covers history.
Services: Offers aid in arranging interviews, brochures/pamphlets, information searches, photos and family history.
How to Contact: Write. Charges for copies of photos or negatives. "We would like credit as an information source. Our museum has office space available for use by writers and researchers."

Newaygo County Historical Society, Box 482, White Cloud MI 49349. (616)689-6966. President: Martha Evans.
Purpose: "To preserve and disseminate the history of Newaygo County. We maintain two museums and a historical collection in the E. Jack Sharpe Public Library at White Cloud. Collection is strong in genealogical, lumbering and railroading material." Information covers history and genealogy.
Services: Offers aid in arranging interviews and information searches. A limited amount of historical or genealogical research can be arranged for a small fee. Publications available.
How to Contact: Write or call. "A search of our indexes will be done for $3/ surname. More detailed search, including courthouse research, is done for $5/hour."

Minnesota

Brown County Historical Society, 27 N. Broadway, New Ulm MN 56073. (507)354-2016. Director: Paul Klammer.
Purpose: "Our purpose is the preservation and dissemination of the history of our county. We maintain a museum and publish a magazine, newsletter and occasionally a book or pamphlet. We also maintain a small library/archives containing primary and secondary sources on the history of Brown County and the pioneer families who settled here." Information covers history.
Services: Offers information searches.
How to Contact: "Write (please include SASE) or visit our library/archives. We charge $4/hour for research done by our staff for nonresidents of Brown County. The first hour of research is free. It is best to make an appointment in advance to do research in our library."

Crow Wing County Historical Society, Box 722, Brainerd MN 56401. (218)829-2695; 829-3268. Curator: Catherine M. Ebert.
Purpose: "To collect, preserve and catalog material and artifacts pertaining to the history of this area. Some of our collection is on display to the public." Information covers agriculture, art, business, celebrities, economics, entertainment, health/ medicine, history, industry, law, politics, recreation and sports.
Services: Offers aid in arranging interviews, biographies and photos.
How to Contact: "Our archives are open to the public, and time may be arranged by contacting the curator. We are not adequately staffed to do research for the public. Our materials must be used under supervision in the museum."

Grant County Historical Society, Elbow Lake MN 56531. (218)685-4864. President: George M. Shervey.

Purpose: "To collect and preserve biographies, historical events and artifacts." Information covers history.
Services: Offers aid in arranging interviews and biographies.
How to Contact: Write or call.

Immigration History Society, 690 Cedar St., St. Paul MN 55101. Editor: Carlton Qualey.
Purpose: To provide bibliographical and informational service. Information covers history.
Services: Offers newsletter.
How to Contact: Write.

LeSueur County Historical Society and Museum, Box 557, Elysian MN 56028. (507)362-8350 or 267-4620. Director: James E. Hruska.
Purpose: "Our purpose is to collect and preserve local and county history and artifacts showing how our ancestors lived; and to preserve all county, church and cemetery and business records for genealogy purposes." Information covers agriculture, art, business, health/medicine, history and politics.
Services: Offers biographies and information searches. Publications include "brochure telling of our county society's holdings."
How to Contact: Write. Charges $2 minimum; also charges for costs of photocopying, postage, use of telephone and mileage needed for researching service. "The library is open from May 1 to October 1. The records and materials can be used only on the museum site. Please send SASE for your inquiries, or you may not receive an answer."
Tips: "We are developing our genealogy interpretive center to contain all of Le Sueur County's newspapers before 1900 on microfilm. We hope to have eventually a complete record of the cemeteries and of all church vital statistics in the county."

Minnesota Historical Society, Audio-Visual Library, 690 Cedar, St. Paul MN 55101. (612)296-2489. Contact: Bonnie Wilson.
Purpose: To preserve Minnesota history.
Services: Offers photos. 150,000 photos available for purchase; reproduction rights offered for some. Provides information on Minnesota persons, places and activities. Emphasis on Indians, agriculture, mining, lumbering, recreation, transportation and family life.
How to Contact: Charges $10 for reproduction service; $3 for prints; 10¢ for photocopies and $2.50 for copy negative. Credit line required.

Northfield Historical Society, Box 372, Northfield MN 55057. Co-Directors: Liz Holum, Cindy Robinson.
Purpose: "We are a chapter of the Rice County Historical Society. Our headquarters are at the site of the defeat of Jesse James. Northfield is the actual site of the last attempt of the James-Younger gang to rob a bank. Every September we celebrate the defeat of Jessie James. This usually occurs the first of the second weekend of September. The society also preserves the history of the town of Northfield." Information covers history.
Services: Offers annual reports and newsletter. "We offer a booklet of the *Northfield Bank Raid*, a paperback book of the history of Northfield, a paperback book in the history of Rice County, and picture postcards (e.g., of the eight men involved in the bankraid, etc.)"
How to Contact: Write.

Todd County Historical Society, Inc., 215 1st Ave. S., Long Prairie MN 56347. (612)732-6181; 732-2231. Curator: Morrie A. Olson.
Purpose: "To display the history and artifacts of Todd City and the state." Information covers agriculture, art, business, celebrities, entertainment, history and self-help.

Services: Offers aid in arranging interviews, biographies, information searches and photos.
How to Contact: Write or call. No fee charges but will except donations.

Wright County Historical Society, 101 Lake Blvd. NW, Buffalo MN 55313. (612)682-3900, ext. 191. Historian: Mrs. Marion Jameson.
Purpose: "To gather and disseminate the history of our county. We have a small historical museum with an office that is open daily 8 to 4:30 (Monday to Friday) and 2 to 5 on Sundays. We have a large collection of photographs, genealogical material, county histories, cemetery surveys and maps. We have restored log buildings; a restored frame school; work with the schools in teaching local history; and publish a curriculum. We are restoring an old grist mill and have an art fair to raise funds. We also have special projects such as marking homesteads, historic sites, and territorial roads with signs. "Information covers agriculture and history.
Services: Offers brochures/pamphlets, information searches, newsletters and photos. Publications available.
How to Contact: Write or call. Charge for reproduction; fees depend on work required. The library may be used during business hours only; "we do not lend out materials or books."

Mississippi

Bolivar County Historical Society, 104 S. Leflore Ave., Cleveland MS 38732. (601)843-2774. Director, County Library: Mrs. LePoint C. Smith.
Purpose: "To promote interest in the history of Bolivar County, Mississippi." Activities include the restoration of an antebellum home, maintenance of a museum, and collection of data and artifacts. Information covers history.
Services: Offers "voluntary membership assistance on queries relating to Bolivar County history." Publications include *Bolivar County Historical Journal*, annual.
How to Contact: Write. Enclose SASE. Services rendered are voluntary; any expense involved should be paid by those requesting service. No extensive research is possible. Only valid queries relating to Bolivar County history should be made."

Cottonlandia Foundation, Inc., Box 1635, Greenwood MS 38930. (601)453-0925, 455-1416. Executive Director: Peggy H. McCormick.
Purpose: "To preserve the heritage of the geographical region." Information covers history and travel. "We also have information on the archeology of northern Mississippi and the southeastern US."
Services: Offers aid in arranging interviews, brochures/pamphlets, photos and press kits. "We also offer tours of museums, conferences on related subjects and exhibits of contemporary crafts and arts." Publications include *Going Our Way* (information on travel in northwest Mississippi).
How to Contact: Write or call.

Mississippi Department of Archives & History, Box 571, (100 S. State St.,) Jackson MS 39205. (601)354-6218, 354-6219. Contact: Jo Ann Bomar.
Purpose: "To collect, preserve and make available information on Mississippi. We also run a museum and have historical preservation programs." Information covers history.
Services: Offers bibliographies, biographies, brochures/pamphlets, information searches, newsletter and photos. Photos include: Civil War prints from *Harper's Weekly* and Frank Leslie's *Weekly* (some hand-colored); prominent Mississippians; and historic spots and other Mississippi scenes (e.g., historic buildings, antebellum mansions, the Mississippi River and steamboats.)
How to Contact: "We prefer the writer to come in to get information. We do little by phone or mail except to tell the writer what type of information we have. The

department cannot do research but will help the writer do his own research." Charges $8 for magazines; $3.50 for positive photostat; and $3/8x10 glossy print. Credit line required.

Missouri

Andrew County Historical Society and Museum, Clasbey Community Bldg., Savannah MO 64485. (816)324-9207. Director: Roy E. Coy.
Purpose: "We are a historical society and museum specializing in genealogical research." Information covers agriculture, art, celebrities and history.
Services: Offers bibliographies, biographies, statistics, and brochures/pamphlets. Publications include *Diggin History* (sent quarterly to all members).
How to Contact: Write. "Membership in our society is $3/year for 12 genealogical publications. We also have marriage records from 1841-1856 ($4); 1850 federal census ($6); *Andrew County School Report of 1911* ($6.50); Andrew County cemetery inscriptions ($5); *Women of Andrew County* ($5); Andrew County births ($1.50); *Bible Records of Andrew County*, Vol. 1, ($2); and 1890 federal census ($4). You must let us know at least two weeks in advance if you wish to use our library and do research here. There is no charge for this service."

DeKalb Co. Historical Society, c/o Martha Spiers, Rt. 2, Box 90, Maysville MO 64469. (816)449-5377. Secretary: Martha Spiers.
Purpose: "We are attempting to uncover and preserve DeKalb County history. This includes present and past history, business, churches, schools, rivers, trails, railroads and persons." Information covers history (DeKalb County only).
Services: Offers biographies, information searches, newsletters and photos. Publications available.
How to Contact: Write or call. Charges $1 for search and photocopies, $3 minimum/ hour for other research; $5 to nonmembers using newspapers, publications or microfilm.

Graham Historical Society, Inc., Box 72, Graham MO 64455. (816)939-2275. Files Secretary: Letha Marie Mowry.
Purpose: "We are organized for preservation in Hughes Township. We began by restoring a calaboose, then followed the publication of the known burial listings for the township. We then compiled a two-volume set of histories (*On the Banks of the Elk Horn*) and a cookbook (*Iron Kettle Cookbook*). We own and maintain a museum, 'Simpson's College,' which was named to the National Register of Historic Sites on January 31, 1978." Information covers history and genealogy.
Services: Offers information searches. "For a fee we will search our files of more than 50,000 cards on any given surname. SASE must accompany any request for information. We will send our fees by return mail." Publications available.
How to Contact: Write. "We charge $1 plus SASE (business size please) for each surname requested."

Missouri Historical Society, Jefferson Memorial Bldg., Lindell & Debaliviere, St. Louis MO 63112. (314)361-1424. Contact: Library or Judith Ciampoli, Pictorial History Department.
Purpose: "We are a privately supported organization dedicated to the collection and preservation of objects and information relating to the history of St. Louis, the state of Missouri and the Louisiana Purchase Territory." Information covers history.
Services: Offers information searches and photos. Collection contains 100,000 photos on Missouri and western life, the World's Fair, early St. Louis, early aviation, the Lindbergh Collection and the Steamboat Collection.
How to Contact: Write or call the photos or library department. The library department is open Tuesday-Saturday, 9:30-4:45; "strongly advised to write or call for an appoint-

ment." Charges $5/hour "for lengthy searches," $10/8x10 b&w glossy print; $40/4x5 color transparency; and varying rates for reproduction rights.

Vernon County Historical Society, Bushwhacker Museum, 231 N. Main St., Nevada MO 64772. President: Patrick T. Brophy.
Purpose: "To preserve and study local and regional (western Missouri border) history and display artifacts of same." Information covers history.
Services: Offers assistance. "We will attempt to supply information on the history of the area, notably: Osage Indians, explorers, the border troubles of 1854-1865, Civil War, Bushwhackers, outlaws, etc. Some printed material is available." Publications include a brief area history, a newspaper supplement on area history, and xeroxed summaries of several subjects.
How to Contact: Write. "In most cases we must charge a nominal fee—usually no more than $5 for the whole request."

Montana

Montana Historical Society, 225 N. Roberts, Helena MT 59601. (406)449-2694. Contact: Reference Librarian.
Purpose: "For the preservation of Montana History." Information covers history.
Services: Offers annual reports, bibliographies, biographies, brochures/pamphlets, information searches and photos. Publications available.
How to Contact: Write or call with informational needs. "We'll see what we can do, or come in. We have microfilm of all Montana newspapers."

Nebraska

American Historical Society of Germans from Russia, 631 D St., Lincoln NE 68502. (402)477-4524. Executive Director: Ruth M. Amen.
Purpose: "We are an international, nonprofit educational organization, actively engaged in researching the history of all Germans from Russia. The society publishes historical and genealogical materials which are distributed throughout the year to its members." Information covers folk art, ethnic food, history, folk music and genealogical studies.
Services: Offers biographies and information searches (for members only). Publications available.
How to Contact: Write or call. Charges for extensive research, depending on time involved.

Cherry County Historical Society, Hwy. 20 and Main St., Valentine NE 69201. Curator: Dora Cronin.
Purpose: "We are a historical organization maintained by the county for the preservation of the heritage of our county since its beginning. This is a large county but sparsely settled. We have microfilm and a good reader of all the newspapers that have been printed in this county." Information covers history, recreation and travel.
Services: Offers annual reports, bibliographies, biographies, brochures/pamphlets, clipping services, information searches and photos.
How to Contact: Write. Operates April 15 to October 15. "We do not loan our material, but it can be used on the premises. We are a small museum, but we had 1,300 visitors last season. At least half were asking for help or information on either family trees or just the history of some early settlers."

Cozad Historical Society, 503 Lake Ave., Gothenburg NE 69138. President: Keith Buss.
Purpose: "To preserve the history of the Cozad, Nebraska, area. Mostly Western frontier historical information is provided." Information covers agriculture and history.
Services: Offers information searches and photos.
How to Contact: Write. Charges for reproduction of photos.

Nebraska State Historical Society, Ft. Robinson Museum Branch, Box 304, Crawford NE 69339. (308)665-2852. Curator: Vance Nelson.
Purpose: "To collect and preserve items related to the history of Nebraska, and here especially items pertaining to Ft. Robinson. To disseminate historical information through our exhibits and library programs." Information covers agriculture, history and Western Americana.
Services: Offers research facilities. "The library is open to the public for on-premise use only."
How to Contact: Visit. Open April 1 to November 15, 8 a.m. to 5 p.m. Monday through Friday and 1 p.m. to 5 p.m. Sunday; by appointment during winter months.

Nebraska State Historical Society, 1500 R St., Lincoln NE 68503. (402)432-2793. Editor: Marvin F. Kivett.
Purpose: "To collect materials of Nebraska history and archeology." Information covers history.
Services: Offers research facilities and photos. Photographs available of historical subjects pertaining to Nebraska and the trans-Missouri West, agriculture, steamboats and Indians. Publications include *Nebraska History* (quarterly).
How to Contact: Write, call or visit. Charges $2.50/b&w 8x10 glossy print. Credit line required.

North Platte Valley Historical Association, Inc., Box 495, 11th & J Sts., Gering NE 69341. (308)436-5411. Director: C.H. Scott.
Purpose: "We are a historical association making available to the people the history of the North Platte Valley, beginning with the Indians, then the trappers and so forth to the present day. Besides the museum, we also have a log cabin and sod house which adjoin the main museum building." Information covers history and travel.
Services: Offers brochures/pamphlets.
How to Contact: Write or call. Enclose SASE.

Nevada

Nevada Historical Society, 1650 N. Virginia St., Reno NV 89503. (702)784-6397.
Purpose: "We are the historical agency for the state of Nevada." Information covers history.
Services: Offers aid in arranging interviews, brochures/pamphlets, information searches and photos (over 100,000 in files). Publications available.
How to Contact: Write or call. Charges for photos.

New Hampshire

Atkinson Historical Society, Academy Ave., Atkinson NH 03811. Curator: Eleanor M. Zaremba.
Purpose: "To provide information on the town of Atkinson." Information covers history.
How to Contact: Write.

Effingham Historical Society, Rt. 153 CTR, Effingham NH, Box 33, South Effingham NH 03882. President: Paul D. Potter.
Purpose: "To preserve the history of the area, both in preservation and in recording of facts." Information covers history.
Services: Offers "small resource center, dealing mostly with the history of the town and the surrounding area."
How to Contact: Write. "Don't expect information quickly; we have no full-time staff, so requests have to be taken as time is found free."

Hudson Historical Society, Inc., 18 Ledge Rd., Hudson NH 03051. (603)882-9522. Clerk: Arlene MacIntyre.

Purpose: "To preserve local artifacts and maintain the Alvirne Hills House as a historical and cultural center. We have a small genealogical library and local histories." Information covers history and craft classes.

Services: Offers museum house, 1890s period; has excellent samples of early American and Victorian furnishings. Publications include *History of Hudson, New Hampshire: Town in Transition 1913-1977* and an updated edition.

How to Contact: Write or call Arlene MacIntyre or Mr. and Mrs. Louis Pecce, at the Alvirne Hills House, Derry Rd., Hudson NH, (603)882-7474. "Donations to help defray expenses of maintaining the society's home are welcome; we also welcome return postage for answering inquiries. No article or books may be taken on loan from the house."

Littleton Area Historical Society, 4 Merrill St., Littleton NH 03561. (603)444-6586. President: Frances Heald.

Purpose: "To collect and record historical data of the town of Littleton, and to preserve local memorabilia and to stimulate interest in local history." Information covers art, celebrities and history.

Services: Offers annual reports, newsletters and photos.

How to Contact: Write or call. No fees, but welcomes contributions.

New Hampshire Historical Society, 30 Park St., Concord NH 03301. (603)225-3381. Assistant Librarian: Bill Copeley.

Purpose: "To collect and preserve New Hampshire history." Information covers agriculture, art, business, celebrities, economics, entertainment, food, health/medicine, history, industry, law, music, nature, politics, recreation, science, self-help, travel, archeology and geneology.

Services: Offers aid in arranging interviews, annual reports, bibliographies, biographies, statistics, brochures/pamphlets, information searches, placement on mailing list, newsletter and photos. Publications available.

How to Contact: Write, call or visit.

Nottingham Historical Society, c/o Julia Case, Rt. 156, Nottingham NH 03290. President: Julia Case.

Purpose: "To furnish information so far as possible on local families and their affiliations since the establishment of the town of Nottingham, New Hampshire." Information covers history.

Services: Offers information searches.

How to Contact: Write. No fees, but donations are welcomed.

New Jersey

New Jersey Historical Society, 230 Broadway, Newark NJ 07104. (201)483-3939. Librarian: Dr. Robert C. Morris. Curator: Howard W. Wiseman.

Purpose: "To collect and preserve all materials pertaining to the history of the state of New Jersey." Information covers history.

Services: Offers information searches, newsletter and photos.

How to Contact: Write. "We are open Monday through Saturday 12 noon to 4:15 p.m. Be as specific as possible in your request, as our library is a specialized one in detail on New Jersey history." Photos filed by name of town, not by subject. Charges $1.25/selection fee for photos, $10/photo for one-time use; about $15/print fee; $5/copy negative. Credit line required.

Thomas Warne Historical Museum and Library, Rt. 516, Old Bridge Township NJ 08857. (201)566-0348. Curator: Alvia D. Martin.

Purpose: "History of South Amboy Township, Madison Township, Old Bridge Township in Middlesex County of the western area of Monmouth County, New Jersey. This include genealogy, craftsmen, agriculture, business, folk art, folklore, colonial homes

and living, diaries, receipts and shipping. Vertical file contains miscellaneous information on areas of local interest and the state of New Jersey. Displays of Indian artifacts, pottery (stoneware), clothing, tools, textiles, baskets, school-related items, maps and photographs." Information covers agriculture, history, music and genealogy.
Services: Offers aid in arranging interviews and information searches.
How to Contact: Write or call Alvia Martin, Rt. 1, Box 150, Matawan NJ 07747. "Call ahead for appointment."Charges 20¢/photocopy, $2/hour for research material. Material may not be taken out of the building. Open for public research on Wednesday 9:30 a.m.-12 p.m. and on the first Sunday of each month, 1-4 p.m.; otherwise by appointment. "Write or call ahead with an outline of information needed."

New Mexico

Historical Society of New Mexico, Box 5819, Sante Fe NM 87502. Executive Director: E.C. Kubicek.
Purpose: "To collect and preserve artifacts and documents with particular reference to the southwestern states in the last 100 years." Information covers history.
Services: Offers brochures/pamphlets and newsletter. Publications available.
How to Contact: Write.

New York

American Italian Historical Association, 209 Flagg Place, Staten Island NY 10304.
Purpose: "The association promotes American-Italian studies nationally, publishes a quarterly national newsletter, publishes the proceedings of the annual conference, presents the Leonard Covello Award annually for best written essay in American-Italian studies, sponsors joint conferences and programs, etc."
Services: Offers brochures/pamphlets and newsletter.
How to Contact: Write.

Aurora Historical Society, Inc., 5 S. Grove St., East Aurora NY 14052. Town Historian: Virginia Vidler.
Purpose: "To document and preserve town history and to make it available to the public in three small museums, including President Millard Fillmore House (a national landmark) and Elbert Hubbard's Roycroft Campus." Information covers history.
Services: Offers brochures/pamphlets and photos.
How to Contact: Write. "We charge only if there is a lot of copying to be done or if file photos have to be sent out for copying. We request a courtesy credit line on photos. Writer must pay print cost but no publication use fee."

Buffalo and Erie County Historical Society, 25 Nottingham Ct., Buffalo NY 14216. (716)873-9644. Curator of Iconography: C.E. Helfter. Head Librarian: H. Sass. Manuscripts Curator: Arthur Deimers.
Purpose: "The society procures and disseminates information relating to western New York history. This is done through an education and exhibits program and numerous publications, as well as an active involvement in community affairs that relate to the society's goal." Information covers art, entertainment, history and industry.
Services: Offers information searches and photos. Publications include publications list. Offer photos "which emphasize 19th and 20th century materials of the Niagara frontier."
How to Contact: Write or call. "Our materials must be used at the society. Restrictions may depend upon the collection being used."Charges 14¢/photocopy, $5/8x10 b&w photo, $1/2x2 Ektachrome slide ($5, minimum order). "Inquire about other sizes and types of reproductions. The society charges for the publication of its materials. Explanation upon request." Credit line required.

Chemung County Historical Society, 304 William St., Elmira NY 14901. (607)737-2900. Director: Constance Barone.
Purpose: "Historical society with archives of 50,000 items (photos, manuscripts, genealogy, cemetery records, obituaries, newspapers, diaries) and a library of 3,500 volumes. Material covers Chemung County; Elmira, New York; Mark Twain; Civil War prison camp; Elmira College; Chemung Canal; regional Indians (Lamoka culture and Iroquois); railroads; etc." Information covers agriculture, art, business, celebrities, economics, entertainment, history, industry, law, music, politics, recreation, sports and travel.
Services: Offers brochures/pamphlets, information searches, newsletter and photos. Publications include *Chemung County Historical Journal* (quarterly publication since 1955; index and reprints available), *Chemung County—Its History*, *Chemung County 1876-1976* and *The Rambles* (driving tour information).
How to Contact: Write, call or visit. "Visting hours are Monday through Friday, 9 a.m. to 5 p.m." Charges 75¢/copy for *Journal*, $2/copy for *Chemung County—Its History*, $20/copy for *Chemung County 1876-1976*, and 15¢/page for photocopies. "The society requests acknowledgment when using materials from collections in publications."

Civil War Round Table of New York, Inc., 289 New Hyde Park Rd., Garden City NY 11530. (516)437-2821. Secretary/Treasurer: Arnold Gates.
Purpose: "This organization is a gathering of people deeply interested in all aspects of the Civil War period in American history. Meetings are held about 8 times a year, battlefield tours are conducted; a newsletter and an occasional yearbook are issued." Information covers history.
Services: Offers information on certain aspects of the Civil War story.
How to Contact: Write or call. "Members will probably respond to a few questions without charge. Any extensive research material would require a charge. The amount could be arranged between a writer and the individual member."

Cortland County Historical Society, Inc., 25 Homer Ave., Cortland NY 13045. (607)765-6071. Executive Secretary: Anita H. Wright.
Purpose: "This society is dedicated to the restoration and strengthening of a sense of tradition and continuity in Cortland County. The museum collection covers 1783 to the present, with displays of military artifacts; it includes a typical home of the 1850s through 1900. Library resources include genealogical and historical research, manuscripts, microfilms, books and newspapers (1700 through present)." Information covers history.
Services: Offers information searches and newsletters.
How to Contact: Write, including SASE for information searches. Must join society to receive newsletter and bulletin. "We charge 20¢/photocopy and $5/search of our holdings."

Greene County Historical Society, Vedder Library, R.D., Coxsackie NY 12051. (518)731-6822. Librarian: Raymond Beecher.
Purpose: "The library, opened by appointment and on Tuesday during the summer months, contains a wealth of printed and manuscript material related to Greene County, the Catskill Mountains and the mid-Hudson River section." Information covers history.
Services: Offers quarterly historical journal by purchase or subscription.
How to Contact: Call for appointment. No charge unless information requires extensive time. "If a user can take out a $5 membership in the society, it helps. We cannot photostat complete holdings in certain categories. Some historical material also is being saved for journal articles. A few family manuscript holdings are restrictive in nature."

Horseheads Historical Society & Museum, Grand Central Ave. and Broad St., Horseheads NY 14845. (607)739-3938. President: Leah Cramer.

Purpose: "The purpose of the museum and society is the preservation and research of artifacts and historical buildings and sites, and the presentation of exhibitions, displays, programs, demonstrations and instruction. We have many 'Zim' original cartoons and advertising art posters. 'Zim' (Eugene Zimmerman, 1862-1935) was a Horseheads resident, the internationally known cartoonist for *Puck* and *Judge* magazines." Information covers history.
Services: Offers brochures/pamphlets and newsletter; also, museum and historical tours, exhibits and monthly programs. Publications include books and pamphlets on Eugene Zimmerman and local genealogical information.
How to Contact: Write, call or visit.

Huntington Historical Society, Box 506, 2 High St., Huntington NY 11743. (516)427-7045, 427-3981. Administrative Assistant: Mitzi Caputo.
Purpose: "To stimulate community interest in the preservation of Huntington's heritage." Information covers history.
Services: Offers photos and help with genealogical and historical research.
How to Contact: "While we will answer a limited number of inquiries by mail, we would prefer to have the researcher visit us. Appointments should be made by phone or letter. There are fees for services; please inquire."

Long Island Historical Society, 128 Pierrepont St., Brooklyn NY 11201. (212)624-0890. Director: Russell Bastedo. Librarian: Anne Gordon.
Purpose: "Founded in 1863, the Long Island Historical Society has concentrated on collecting written materials about Brooklyn and communities on Long Island since its inception. Grants for the conservation, preservation and microfilming of newspapers, voter registration records, printed pamphlets and other such materials are currently being sought. In addition, extensive holdings of fine arts and decorative arts are currently in storage, but will come out if funding can be found." Information covers many aspects of Brooklyn/Long Island.
Services: Offers photos, genealogical facilities, work space and trained staff for help in searches. "Restrictions depend on materials being sought. We ask that the society be given credit in articles or books prepared with our help." Collection includes 6,000 b&w photos dating from 1870 to present of Brooklyn, Queens and Long Island streets, houses, factories, landscapes, transportation and marine topics.
How to Contact: Write or call. Charges $1/day for nonmembers; charges for photocopies. Offers reproduction rights. Charges $10 for one-time editorial or advertising use; $2 service charge; $12.50 print fee. "All negatives retained by the society. Credit line required."

Montgomery County Department of History and Archives, Old Court House, Fonda NY 12068. (518)853-3431. Historian: Anita Smith.
Purpose: "To preserve the heritage of our county and to complete genealogical searches." Information covers agriculture, celebrities, history, law, politics, technical data, travel and genealogical material (3rd largest collection in New York State).
Services: Offers annual reports, brochures/pamphlets, information searches and statistics. "We are willing to assist in any way we can. We have records for other counties as well as Montgomery, except for Columbia, Pennsylvania, Schoharie, Albany and Schenectady." Publications available.
How to Contact: Write. Charges $5/search of indexed records, 15¢/photocopy and $3/day department charges for out-of-state residents. Charges $3/catalog of genealogical material.

New York Genealogical and Biographical Society, 122 E. 58th St., New York NY 10022. (212)755-8532. Executive Secretary: Carolyn G. Stifel.
Purpose: "To discover, procure, preserve and perpetuate whatever may relate to genealogy and biography and local history, primarily for educational purposes." Information covers history, genealogy and biography.

Services: Offers research facilities of the society's library which is open to the public for use on the premises. No materials circulate; no interlibrary loan. "Because of limited staff we are unable to do research in response to mail inquiries." Publications available.

How to Contact: Write the library, stating the question specifically. Enclose SASE. "We cannot render general research services. Our library staff, to the extent possible, will help direct persons working in the library to proper source materials. Persons must do their own genealogical research, or the society can provide names of professional researchers in genealogy with whom writer would make own arrangements."

Blue and yellow pike, bass, sturgeon and muskelunge were caught from this wharf on the Niagara river, photographed in 1898. This is a typical photo in the collection of the Buffalo and Erie County Historical Society, which houses many regional historical photos. "The Niagara River is a dominant force in the history of this area," says Clyde Eller Helfter, curator of iconography. The society charges $5 for 8x10 b&w prints, and $20 for each photo used in a commercial publication. This photo, which has been used in a newspaper and in two society publications, could illustrate features on costume, the environment and ichthyology, as well as history, says Helfter.

New York Historical Society, Print Room, 170 Central Park W., New York NY 10021. (212)873-3400. Curator of Prints: Wendy Shadwell.

Purpose: "A historical society, founded in 1804 and still privately funded. It specializes in New York state and city history. We have much general material on the early years of the American colonies and the United States. Materials include maps, broadsides, postcards, prints, photos, architectural drawings, books, manuscripts and a special collection of business and advertising art, silver, furniture, portraits, paperweights, etc." Information covers art, business and history.

Services: Offers annual reports, newsletter and photos. Publications include annual reports, a quarterly periodical, seasonal newsletters, occasional observers, and *Portrait Catalogue*.

How to Contact: Write or call. "Advance appointment is required to use special research collections. Call in advance." Charges for services. "There is an admission charge for nonmembers to use research facilities, a research fee for out-of-towners who undertake research, fees for photocopies and photos, and reproduction fees for material used in films, books or periodicals. A credit line is required."

Tips: "Do general book research first and know specifically what you are looking for, instead of requesting permission to browse through valuable and fragile original material."

Niagara Falls Historical Society, Inc., c/o Public Library, 1425 Main St., Niagara Falls NY 14305. (716)278-8229. President: Donald E. Loker.
Purpose: "Niagara Falls items—newspapers, indexes, books, pamphlets and photographs." Information covers history.
Services: Offers biographies, brochures/pamphlets, information searches and photos. "Nothing circulates: photocopying available. (photos may be taken here.)" Publications available.
How to Contact: Write or call. "We can arrange a time to visit or answer some requests by phone." Charges for photocopies and photo reproduction.

Orange County Community of Museums and Galleries, Box 527, Goshen NY 10924. (914)294-5657. Secretary of the Board: Malcolm A. Booth.
Purpose: "This agency is concerned with promoting visitation to museums and similar agencies in Orange County, New York; providing professional information to these museums; and maintaining a local history reference collection dealing with Orange County." Information covers agriculture, art, economics, history, how-to, law, nature, politics, recreation and travel.
Services: Offers aid in arranging interviews, bibliographies, statistics and brochures/pamphlets. Publications include *Orange County: Inviting, Historic*, and *Where to Stay, Where to Dine in Loveable Orange County*.

Rome Historical Society, 113 W. Court St., Rome NY 13440. (315)336-5870. Executive Director: Joseph G. Vincent.
Purpose: "To maintain research facilities and historical artifacts as applied to central New York, especially in the Rome-Utica area." Offers cultural displays and records history. Information covers art, entertainment, history and genealogy.
Services: Offers statistics and information searches. Publication available.
How to Contact: Write or call. Charges for services.

Schoharie County Historical Society, Old Stone Fort, N. Main St., Schoharie NY 12157. (518)295-7192. Director: William H. Seeger.
Purpose: "We are a local history museum and research library." Information covers agriculture, art, history, nature and politics.
Services: Offers local history and research. Publications include *Schoharie County Historical Review*.
How to Contact: Visit; material available on premises only.

Somers Historical Society, Box 336, Somers NY 19589. (914)277-4977. Acting Curator: Florence S. Oliver.
Purpose: "To provide information on local history (early circus posters, pamphlets, ledgers, correspondence, etc.)" Information covers history and information on early circuses.
Services: Offers fact sheets.
How to Contact: Write or call.

Staten Island Historical Society, 302 Center St., Staten Island NY 10306.

(212)351-1611. Contact: Raymond Fingado.

Purpose: To preserve the history of Staten Island.

Services: Offers 10,000 photos, "mostly Staten Island scenes, houses, landscapes. However, we own the famed Alice Austen Collection—excellent shots of New York City street scenes circa 1895 to 1910, waterfront scenes of old sailing ships, Quarantine Station, famous old steamships, immigrants and life of the society set on Staten Island." Primarily b&w prints.

How to Contact: Offers "usually one-time publication rights for each picture." Fees are "flexible, but generally average $30/plate—sometimes, but rarely, lower and sometimes higher. Negotiated according to the nature of the project."

US Catholic Historic Society, St. Joseph's Seminary, Dunwoodie, Yonkers NY 10704. (914)968-6200, ext. 51. Executive Secretary: James J. Mahoney.

Purpose: "To provide for the publication of documents, books and papers relating to the history of the Catholic Church and the development of Catholic culture in America." Information covers history.

Services: Offers bibliographies, biographies, information searches and newsletter.

How to Contact: Write. "Request to be placed on our mailing list or give particulars of specific problem or question."

Wayne County Historical Society, 21 Butternut St., Lyon NY 14489. (315)946-4943. Curator Director: Gary Walrath.

Purpose: "To collect, preserve and exhibit records, writings of historical items and artifacts, and to preserve and disseminate information in the fields of history and genealogical information connected with Wayne County. At present, the society owns over 10,000 articles of historical interest, many of which are on display in the museum." Information covers history.

Services: Offers newsletters and archival library for on-site research.

How to Contact: Write. Charges 15¢/photocopy for genealogical research work."For best service, on-site research is advised."

Yates County Genealogical & Historical Society, Inc., 200 Main St., Penn Yan NY 14527. (315)536-7318. Director: Virginia H. Gibbs.

Purpose: "Dedicated to preserve, procure, and disseminate information (and artifacts) relating to the history of western New York in general and Yates County in particular." Information covers agriculture, business, celebrities, economics, history, industry, politics, science and genealogical information.

Services: Offers aid in arranging interviews, statistics (on genealogy), and information searches.

How to Contact: Write or call.

North Carolina

North Carolina Division of Archives and History, 109 E. Jones St., Raleigh NC 27611. (919)733-3952. Contact: History Branch.

Purpose: To preserve historical information and artifacts of North Carolina.

Services: Offers photos.

How to Contact: Write or call.

North Carolina Folklore Society, Department of English, Appalachian State University, Boone NC 28608. (704)262-3098. Secretary/Treasurer: Thomas McGowan.

Purpose: "To promote the collecting and study of North Carolina folklore by publishing a scholarly journal, *North Carolina Folklore Journal*, and an occasional newsletter; by sponsoring programs and symposia; and by serving as a clearinghouse for information. Information covers folk art and the history and music of folklore and folklife.

Services: Offers newsletters.

How to Contact: Write.

North Dakota

State Historical Society of North Dakota, Research and Reference Division, State Capitol Grounds, Bismarck ND 58505. (701)224-2668, Library. (701)224-2663, Archives. Librarian: Duane E. Crawford. Archivist: Frank Vyzralek.
Purpose: "The library is a major source for genealogical, historical, governmental and newspaper information through censuses, plat books, state newspapers, state documents, and the newspaper indexes and indexes to publications of the State Historical Society of North Dakota, and catalogs which give access to the materials. Microfilm newspapers are sent to libraries on request." Information covers history.
Services: Offers bibliographies, biographies, information searches, newsletter (*Plains Talk*), photos and photocopies of specific items. "The staff will do searches on request. The historians, archeologist, architectural historian, librarian and archivist will consult, if necessary." Publications include genealogical resources and services, census search application forms, index to the journals of the North Dakota Historical Society, *North Dakota History* and *Journal of the Northern Plains.*
How to Contact: Write, call or visit. "We charge $1/census search. We often get $1 for searches for obituaries. We have been charging 10¢/photocopy and 25¢/microfilm print. Be specific and make our job easier by telling us what information you already have on the subject so we can focus in on the data more easily."
Tips: "Abide by copyright law. Illustrate with a good photograph or art reproduction, and send us a manuscript when you are finished."

Ohio

Anderson Township Historical Society, Inc., Box 30174, Cincinnati OH 45230. (513)231-2114 or 231-6453. Coordinator: Marjorie A. Frame.
Purpose: "To collect and preserve the local history of our township, and to restore and exhibit our 1796 log house." Information covers history.
Services: Offers brochures/pamphlets. "We also provide genealogical help for families stemming from Anderson Township. Guided tours of the area and of our historic holdings are also available."
How to Contact: Write. Charges no fees, but donations are accepted.

Berlin History Project, Inc., Box 164, Berlin Heights OH 44814. Director: Dr. William F. Vartorella.
Purpose: "Primarily, we are a group of professionals dedicated to the historic preservation of Victorian communitarian sites (e.g., utopian experiments) and to allied research efforts. Our network of historians can provide information relative to Victorian perfectionism, socialism, free loveism, and a plethora of other reform doctrinal experiments. We are especially interested in the literary contributions of Victorian female writers and editors." Information covers health/medicine, history, politics and reform editorial ventures.
Services: Offers aid in arranging interviews (with appropriate scholars) and information searches.
How to Contact: Write. "While we do not charge any fees for services, we do require acknowledgment in published works as well as a copy of the published article/book."
Tips: "Writers/researchers should provide a brief *vita* describing their qualifications and interests, as well as a brief statement indicating how the materials will be used and in what context. It is always helpful if we know precisely what the researcher needs in terms of sources or expert aid in order to match the writer with the appropriate professional."

Cincinnati Historical Society, Eden Park, Cincinnati OH 45202. Picture Librarian: Edward Malloy.
Services: Offers more than 350,000 b&w and color prints and slides of Cincinnati and Cincinnati-related material, and general pictures on subjects such as World War I,

urban decay and Ohio River transportation.
How to Contact: Write. Charges fee for commercial use.

Cleveland Landmarks Commission, Room 28, City Hall, Cleveland OH 44114. Director: John D. Cimperman.
Purpose: "The inventory and designation of sites and structures of historic significance." Information covers art and history.
Services: Offers annual reports, bibliographies, information searches and newsletter.
How to Contact: Write.

Ohio Historical Society, I-71 and 17th Ave., Columbus OH 43211. (614)466-1500. Special Events Coordinator: Sharon Antle.
Purpose: "The society contains state archives, research library for genealogy, and natural history mall. It's a major repository of primary research." Information covers agriculture, business, celebrities, economics, entertainment, health/medicine, history, how-to, industry, law, music, nature, politics, science, self-help, sports, technical data and travel.
Services: Offers aid in arranging interviews, annual reports, biographies, statistics, brochures/pamphlets, information searches, placement on mailing list, newsletter, photos and press kits. Publications include *Society Page* (monthly).
How to Contact: Write, call or visit. Requires credit line on photos.

Portage County Historical Society, Inc., 6549-51 N. Chestnut, Ravenna OH 44266. (216)296-3523. Secretary: Ruth A. Engelhardt.
Purpose: "To preserve the history of Portage County and America through display of items, documents, art, facts, etc.; to educate the general public through monthly programs on topics related to history, visits, tours of individuals and groups, on a reservation basis." Information covers agriculture, art, business, history, industry and genealogy (county records).
Services: Offers biographies and statistics. "We also have facilities for genealogical reserach of Portage County residents, past and present."
How to Contact: Write or call. Charges for genealogical research (cost based upon time needed). All resources must be used within confines of museum. No loans.

Rogues' Hollow Historical Society, 17459 Galehouse Rd., Doylestown OH 44230. (216)658-4561. Director: Russell Frey.
Purpose: "Actively researching early history of area on the western edge of Barberton, Ohio." Information covers history.
Services: Offers biographies and newsletter. "We also have historical research on pioneer woolen mill, two grist mills, and 170 coal mines which supplied coal and coke to pioneer steel mills of northeast Ohio." Publications include *History of Rogues' Hollow*.
How to Contact: Write or call.

Sandusky County Historical Society, 1337 Hayes Ave., Fremont OH 43420.
Purpose: "A county historical society with programs and projects in the local history field. The society has a historical crafts division called the Crafts Guild and a genealogy division called the Kin-Hunters. Questions on county and area history and genealogy are referred to us for answer by libraries, Chambers of Commerce, postmasters, etc." Information covers history.
Services: Offers brochures/pamphlets.
How to Contact: Write. "No mail is answered unless it's accompanied by a#10SASE. We expect the inquirer to pay in advance the costs of photo duplication. Inquiries should be specific. We will not do extended historical research or extensive photocopying. Our resources are housed at the local library, which will not do research."

Tuscarawas County Historical Society, 435 W. High Ave., Box 462, New Philadelphia

OH 44663. (216)364-6448. Director: Paul A. Goudy.
Purpose: "The society serves as an educational and a cultural institution to the Tuscarawas Valley. We have programs in education, historic preservation, tourist development and museum preservation. Holdings include manuscripts, photographs, newspapers, county records, private business papers and antique artifacts." Information covers agriculture, art, business, history, law, music and politics.
Services: Offers aid in arranging interviews, bibliographies, biographies, brochures/pamphlets, information searches, placement on mailing list and photos. Publications include brochures on the annual heritage tour program, pamphlets on cultural and historic institutions and museums, and several historical publications.
How to Contact: Write. "We charge only for some services, and rates are available on request. In general, no restrictions apply. Contact should be made well in advance of deadlines. All queries should include a legal-size SASE."

Oklahoma

Cherokee National Historical Society, Inc., Box 515, TSA-LA-GI, Tahlequah OK 74464. (918)456-6007. Executive Vice President: M.A. Hagerstrand.
Purpose: "Preservation of the Cherokee heritage and culture; education of members of the tribe in their own history; education of the general public about Cherokee history and culture. We own and operate TSA-LA-GI, which includes the Cherokee National Museum; the Cherokee National Archives and Library (currently in the process of accumulating material); the Theatre at TSA-LA-GI which presents each summer the historical drama 'Trail of Tears'; the Ancient Museum Village at TSA-LA-GI (living museum circa 1650-1700 AD). Our collection of several hundred original newspapers dating back to 1762 and containing articles about the Cherokees is a fruitful source of interesting historical material. Our collection is particularly strong covering the late 18th and 19th centuries through the Civil War. Our archival collection includes, among others, the personal papers of W.W. Keeler, the former chief of the Cherokees for 26 years, amounting to approximately 35 linear feet." Information covers art and history.
Services: Offers aid in arranging interviews, bibliographies, biographies, brochures/pamphlets, placement on mailing list, photos and press kits. Also available are promotional material concerning TSA-LA-GI and limited genealogical service relating to Cherokee families. Publications include brochures/pamphlets on TSA-LA-GI (the Cherokee Cultural Center); short history of TSA-LA-GI and the Cherokee National Historical Society, the Cherokee tribe (incorporated in a souvenir program covering the Trail of Tears, an outdoor symphonic drama presented in the outdoor theater at TSA-LA-GI); and bibliography of books and pamphlets about the Cherokees.
How to Contact: Write or call. Research material may not be removed from the archives and library.

Oklahoma Historical Society, Historical Bldg., Oklahoma City OK 73105. (405)521-2491. Executive Director: Jack Wettengel.
Purpose: To promote the study of history in Oklahoma. Contains unique Indian archives. Information covers history.
Services: Offers aid in arranging interviews, brochures/pamphlets and photos. Publications include *Chronicles of Oklahoma* (quarterly).
How to Contact: Write or visit. Open Monday through Friday, 8 a.m. to 9 p.m.; Saturday, 8 a.m. to 6 p.m.

Oregon

Oregon Historical Society, 1230 SW Park Ave., Portland OR 97205. (503)222-1741. Photograph Librarian: Janice Worden.
Purpose: "To collect, preserve, exhibit and publish material of a historical character,

especially that related to the history of Oregon and of the US." Information covers history.

Services: Offers biographies, statistics, brochures/pamphlets, information searches, placement on mailing list, and over one million b&w photos (a few color photos); 300,000 are cataloged. Offers one-time rights. "All subjects in geographical range: Pacific Northwest (Oregon, Washington, Idaho, British Columbia), Alaska, North Pacific. Most are b&w prints and negatives; also color transparencies and negatives, engravings, lantern slides (color and b&w), etc." Publications include *A List of Western Imprints* and *Oregon Historical Society Quarterly*.

How to Contact: "Send written requests re information required. Cost for research can be figured on an hourly rate basis or contracted on a project basis. The Library charges $10/hour which includes hiring the research associate, assisting and supervising the researcher, providing desk and/or office space, a typewriter, supplies, etc. Virtually all material is available for publication; credit line required." Fees vary according to use. When ordering photos, "please allow up to four weeks from the date of order to completion." Charges $5-25 for editorial or advertising use; $2 minimum/print.

Southern Oregon Historical Society, Box 480, 206 N. 5th St., Jacksonville OR 97530. (503)899-1847. Librarian: Richard H. Engemen.
Purpose: "We are a historical society library and museum concerned with the history of southern Oregon and northern California. The library includes materials on local history, historic preservation (renovation, repair, reuse of historic buildings), and the care of museum artifacts."
Services: Offers brochures/pamphlets, information searches and photos.
How to Contact: Write or call. Charges 10¢/photocopy and 25¢/sheet for microfilm/fiche. Initial library search is free; charges $10/hour for additional library research over ½ hours. Price list on photographs is available on request; charges $3.50/8x10 print minimum; $5/photo for commerical use; $20/photo for advertising use.

Pennsylvania

American Motley Association, Valley Forge Office Colony, Valley Forge Pennsylvania 19481. (215)783-0857. Publisher: Thomas Motley-Freeman.
Purpose: To promote knowledge of and conduct research in Motley family heritage and ancestry. Information covers history and genealogy.
Services: Offers bibliographies, biographies, brochures/pamphlets, information searches, newsletter and photos. Publications include *Motley Ancestral Gleanings* (quarterly).
How to Contact: Write or call. Charges negotiable.

Pennsylvania Historical and Museum Commission, William Penn Memorial Museum and Archives Bldg., Harrisburg PA 17120. (717)787-2891. Chief Administrative Officer: William J. Wewer.
Purpose: "Preservation, promotion and dissemination of Pennsylvania history." Information covers agriculture, art, celebrities, economics, entertainment, food, health/medicine, history, how-to, industry, law, music, nature, politics, recreation, science, sports, technical information, travel, religion and maps.
Services: Offers statistics, brochures/pamphlets, information searches, photos and press kits. Publications include *Pennsylvania Heritage* (quarterly).
How to Contact: Write. Charges for copies.

Warren County Historical Society, 210 4th Ave., Box 427, Warren PA 16365. (814)723-1795. Executive Director: Chase Putnam.
Purpose: "Historical society and repository for artifactual and recorded history of Warren County from its founding to the present. Our services include programs, field trips, a museum, archives, genealogy services and a library." Information covers agriculture, art, business, celebrities, entertainment, health/medicine, history, indus-

try, law, music, politics, recreation and sports.
Services: Offers bibliographies, brochures/pamphlets and information searches. Publications include *History of Warren County, Under Three Flags, Chief Cornplanter* and a publications list.
How to Contact: Write, call or visit. Charges for genealogical research: $5 for initial research, $3.50/hour thereafter.

Rhode Island

Preservation Society of Newport County, 118 Mill St., Newport RI 02840. (401)847-1000. Public Relations Director: Mrs. Leonard J. Panaggio.
Purpose: "The Preservation Society of Newport County is a nonprofit educational organization dedicated to the preservation and restoration of Newport County's outstanding architectural heritage. It has eight properties open to the public: The Breakers, The Elms, Marble House, Chateau-sur-Mer, Rosecliff, Kingscote, Hunter House and Green Animals." Information covers art, history and museum houses.
Services: Offers annual reports, statistics, brochures/pamphlets, photos and press kits. Publications include *Newport Mansions*, a brochure about the properties open to the public.
How to Contact: Call or write. No charge is made for services if the information is to be used for editorial copy.

The Rhode Island Historical Society, 52 Power St., Providence RI 02906. (401)331-8575. Librarian: Nancy F. Chudacoff.
Purpose: "Four major programs of activity include library, education, museum and publication. Our aims include the collection, conservation and interpretation of Rhode Island artifacts through the maintenance of activities in the John Brown House Museum, the library and the Museum of Rhode Island History at Aldrich House." Information covers history.
Services: Offers a research facility. Publications include *Rhode Island History* (quarterly).
How to Contact: Write. Rhode Island History is available on microfilm from University Microfilm, 300 Zeeb Rd., Ann Arbor MI 48106. Charges 25¢/photocopy, $25 plus cost for graphics reproduction. "If visiting the library from out of town, please call ahead (401)331-0448 and make a firm appointment with appropriate staff member. Due to staffing restrictions, we are unable to engage in general research problems. We can advise on the availability of material in the collection, and make a limited number of copies."

South Carolina

Cherokee Historic and Preservation Society, Inc., Box 998, Gaffney SC 29340. President: A. Jack Blanton.
Purpose: "Finding, identifying, recording and preserving historical information, sites and artifacts in and near Cherokee County, South Carolina. Special emphasis on American Revolutionary period." Information covers history.
Services: Offers aid in arranging interviews and photos.
How to Contact: Write.

Laurens County Historical Society, 500 Cedar, Clinton NC. President: Sara Cronic.
Purpose: "To preserve the history of Laurens County, South Carolina." Information covers history.
Services: Offers information on Laurens County.
How to Contact: Write or call.

South Carolina Historical Society, 100 Meeting St., Fireproof Bldg., Charleston SC 29401. (803)723-3225. Research Consultant: Sallie Doscher.

Purpose: "Our purpose is to collect and make accessible materials relating to South Carolina history. We maintain a research library, publish the *South Carolina Historical Magazine* and sponsor tours and programs for our members." Information covers agriculture, art, business, celebrities, economics, entertainment, food, health/ medicine, history, law, music, politics, science and travel.

Services: Offers bibliographies, biographies and information searches. "The staff collects, cares for, and makes information available to researchers who visit the society. The staff cannot undertake research projects, but qualified freelance researchers can be recommended. We will be publishing a summary guide to our collections in 1979. A brief description of manuscript collections of the South Carolina Historical Society can be found in the *South Carolina Historical Magazine*, July, 1977."

How to Contact: Call. "Nonmembers are charged a $5/day research fee. Membership, which includes subscription to the *South Carolina Historical Magazine* and research privileges, is $15/year. Researchers may not quote or publish documents in the society's possession without permission in writing from the society. A look at John Hammond Moore's *Research Materials in South Carolina* will show how our holdings relate to other collections in the state. We tell genealogists that we are a place of last resort. They should first survey the public records in the South Carolina Department of Archives and History and in county court houses."

South Dakota

East River Genealogical Forum, 17 5th St. SW, Huron SD 57350. (605)883-4117. Moderator/President: Dorothy A. Sargent Wolsey.

Purpose: "To uncover and preserve items of historical and genealogical interest; to maintain such morgue files as will help the genealogist; to increase and make available to the public as much genealogical and historical material and how-to as our funds will allow. We cooperate with the local newspapers and the local libraries to make these materials available to the general public. We own and maintain the Pioneer Memorial Collection at the Huron Public Library, and place many materials on microfilm for use in the local library only." Information covers celebrities, history, how-to, self-help, geography and autobiographies.

Services: Offers aid in arranging interviews, bibliographies, biographies, clipping services, information searches, and photos. "We do actual detailed research on individual family names or individuals in South Dakota (past and present) for genealogical and historical purposes only (not legal)."

How to Contact: Write. Specific requests only-not general information on broad subjects. Enclose SASE.

South Dakota State Historical Society, Historical Resource Center, Memorial Bldg., Pierre SD 57501. (605)773-3615 or 224-3615. Director: Dayton W. Canaday. Library Technician: Bonnie Gardner.

Purpose: "To collect, preserve and publish material for the study of history. The resource center includes a historical library, photographs, South Dakota census records, South Dakota newspapers on microfilm, South Dakota state documents, manuscript material and maps." Information covers history.

Services: Offers information searches and 30,000 b&w photos. "The photograph collection is made up of early towns, forts, American natives, Black Hills, Badlands, farming, ranching, mining, recreation, sod houses, transportation, biographies, etc." Publications include *Dakota Highlights*, *Verendrye Plate*, *A Short History of South Dakota* and *Leaders of the Sioux Nation*.

How to Contact: "Request specific data by mail with 15¢ return postage. When planning a visit to the library, give advance notice." Offers one-time rights. Charges 10¢/photocopy, $7/roll for microfilm, $2/5x7 b&w photo and $4/8x10 b&w photo. Material restricted to one-time photos rights in publications and general copyright regulations. Charges $2/5x7 print, $4/8x10 print.

Tripp County Historical Society, E. Highway 18, Winner SD 57580. Secretary: Eldora Mathis.
Purpose: "We are a society to preserve the early-day items and history of Tripp County." Information covers history.
Services: Offers brochures/pamphlets. "We have brochures on the different early-day towns in Tripp County."
How to Contact: Write.

On an 1874 expedition through the Black Hills, Gen. George Custer (center), scout Bloody Knife (left) and two uinidentified men (rear) killed a grizzly bear. They posed with their kill for this photograph, now part of South Dakota State Historical Society's collection. An 8x10 b&w glossy copy of this shot costs $4, and a 5x7 costs $2, says director Dayton W. Canaday. The cost goes up if the photo is published or put to commercial use.

Tennessee

Tennessee Historical Society, 403 7th Ave. N., Nashville TN 37219. (615)741-2660. Editor: Robert McBride.
Purpose: "To record the history of Tennessee. We also will help writers get their information through society personnel or by referring them to the state library and archives." Information covers history.
Services: Offers aid in arranging interviews, brochures/pamphlets and photos. Publications include a magazine.
How to Contact: Write or call. Charges $10/year for magazine.

Texas

Chaparral Genealogy Society, Box 606, Tomball TX 77375. President: Flossie Bueckner.
Purpose: "To establish a nonprofit organization devoted to the collection and dissemination of factual genealogical data and to raising the standards of genealogical research." Information covers history and how-to.

Services: Offers bibliographies. Publications available.
How to Contact: Write. "Our society does not charge, but our time is limited. However, some of our members are professional genealogists and they do some research for people."

Cooke County Heritage Society, Inc., Box 150, Gainesville TX 76240. (817)668-8900. President: Mary McCain. Vice President: Margaret P. Hays.
Purpose: "To promote the public interest of Cooke County and its immediate environs through development of interest in the preservation of historical resources in Cooke County." Information covers history.
Services: Offers brochures/pamphlets and photos. "Our collection is aimed at the history of Cooke County, Texas. Archival material consists of essays and other material about early Cooke County. We also have a collection of photographs from the area, including many of the Gainesville Community Circus. Publications include *Early Days in Cooke County, 1848-1873* ($3.75); *First 100 Years in Cooke County* ($14.20); *Texas: Cooke County–Its People, Production and Resources* ($1.25); and *History of Cooke County, A Pictorial Essay* ($3.25). Pamphlets about the Gainesville Community Circus, old Gainesville city directories and various newspaper clippings about early Gainesville are also available.
How to Contact: Write or call. "Archival material may be examined by visiting the Morton Museum of Cooke County. Materials must be used on the premises."

Dallas Historical Society, Box 26038, Dallas TX 75226. (214)421-5136. Director: John W. Crain.
Purpose: "To acquire, preserve, exhibit and publish historical materials relating to the southwestern United States, more particularly northern Texas and Dallas." Information covers history.
Services: Offers newsletter and press kits.
How to Contact: "Become a member of the society or write the director for information. Contact the hisorical society in advance by letter and obtain permission; there is a permission fee for research and reproduction."

East Texas Historical Association, Box 6223, Stephen F. Austin State University, Nacogdoches TX 75962. (713)569-2407. Editor: Archie P. McDonald.
Purpose: "To promote study and writing in Texas history, we publish a journal and hold meetings (September and February) where papers are read." Information covers history.
How to Contact: Write or call.

Society for American Indian Studies & Research, Box 443, Hurst TX 76053. (817)281-3784. Director: William L. Turnbull.
Purpose: "A nonprofit consortium of individuals and institutions with no bond holders, mortgagees or other security holders, created to promote the discovery, collection, preservation and publication of materials in anthropology, history and literature, as they relate to Indians in North and Middle America." Information covers anthropology, history and literary criticism.
Services: Offers publications, including *American Indian Quarterly: A Journal of Anthropology, History, and Literature*, which contains in-depth research and review articles, book reviews, a bibliography of recent articles published in other journals, and news and notes.
How to Contact: "Become a dues-paying member of the society."

Society of Southwest Archivists, 3501 Quail Lane, Arlington TX 76016. Treasurer: C. George Younkin.
Purpose: "Professional association for archivists, librarians and historians interested in the techniques of preservation of records in the states of Louisiana, Arkansas,

Oklahoma, Texas and New Mexico." Information covers how-to.
Services: Offers newsletter and membership list.
How to Contact: Write individual members.

Texas State Historical Association, SRH 306, University Station, Austin TX 78712.
(512)474-3092.
Purpose: "To preserve and stimulate interest in Texas history." Information covers
history.
Services: Offers bibliographies, brochures/pamphlets and newsletter.
How to Contact: Write. Maintains no library or archives. "For research, go to the Texas
State Library, Box 1291, Capitol Station, Austin 78711."

Utah

Genealogical Society of Utah, 50 E. North Temple St., Salt Lake City UT 84150.
(801)531-2331.
Purpose: "Affiliated with the Church of Jesus Christ of Latter-Day Saints. Largest
genealogical library in the world open to the public." Information covers genealogy.
Services: Offers information searches and pedigree survey. Publications available.
How to Contact: Write or call. Charges depend on services. "Requests for specific
search on surname should be in writing. Include any pertinent information related to
search."

Utah State Historical Society, 307 W. 2nd St., Salt Lake City UT 84101. (801)533-5755.
Purpose: "To collect, preserve and publish history and prehistory." Information
covers agriculture, art, business, celebrities, economics, entertainment, food, history,
industry, law, music, nature, politics, recreation, science, self-help, sports, technical
information, travel, religion (emphasis on the Mormons), architecture, Indians, drama
and theater.
Services: Offers aid in arranging interviews, annual reports, bibliographies, biographies, statistics, brochures/pamphlets, information searches, placement on mailing
list, newsletter and b&w historic photos. Publications include bimonthly newsletter;
quarterly magazine; and an annual juvenile publication.
How to Contact: "Write, first, for appointment, and be specific." Charges for publications. Photos are made to order; allow 10 days to 2 weeks for delivery. Photos are not
sent on approval; they may not be returned once they are made. Charges $1.50
minimum/print; fees subject to change. Credit line required.

Vermont

Black River Historical Society, Box 16, Ludlow VT 05149. (802)228-5050. Director:
Milton G. Moore Sr.
Purpose: "To foster the history of the Black River Valley area in Windsor-Rutland
County." Information covers agriculture, celebrities and history.
Services: Offers brochures/pamphlets and information searches.
How to Contact: Write.

Springfield Art & Historical Society, 9 Elm St., Springfield VT 05156. (802)885-2415.
Director: Mrs. Fred R. Herrick.
Purpose: "A center for the arts, both visual and performing. Preserving historical items
pertaining to Springfield Vermont." Information covers art, history and music.
How to Contact: Write or call.

Vermont Historical Society, 109 State St., Montpelier VT 05602. Librarian: Laura
Abbott.
Purpose: A research library carrying information on **genealogy and** Vermont and New
England history, as well as maps, photos and broadsides. Information covers agricul-

ture, business, history and politics.

Services: Offers bibliographies and help with on-site research on Vermont topics.
How to Contact: Write ("always enclose SASE for a reply") or visit (hours are 8 a.m. to 4:30 p.m., Monday through Friday). Charges 15¢/page for photocopy. "Photographic copies are available through a local photographer only. Researchers should be aware that use of some material may constitute a violation of copyright unless permission is secured."

Woodstock Historical Society, 26 Elm St., Woodstock VT 05091. (802)457-1822. Director: Mrs. Raymond F. Leonard.
Purpose: "A local historical society located in a restored dwelling built in 1807. There are museum tours for vacationing visitors, plus services for local members of the historical society: summer lectures, research library and social events. There are research facilities for scholars and interested visitors. The society's research library has holdings in Woodstock history, Woodstock imprints, some manuscripts and genealogical materials, and local newspapers. The large photographic archive contains 19th century glass plate and celluloid negatives, prints, Daguerrotypes and tintypes of Woodstock scenes and subjects." Information covers art and history.
Services: Offers brochures/pamphlets, information searches and photos. Publications include *Jacob Collamer: Woodstock's U.S. Senator, My Grandmothers and Other Tales of Old Woodstock, The Vermont Heritage of George Perkins Marsh*, and *The Dana House Collection*.
How to Contact: Write or call. "Be as specific as possible in composing questions for research by the Society staff. Research requests which are too time-consuming for the staff to handle are generally referred to paid local researchers. Genealogical search requests are often referred in this way." Charges for reproduction of antique photo views from the society's photo archives. Charges $4/b&w print if negative is available, $5/b&w print when new negative must be prepared. "Photos must include credit line to the historical society when used for publication. No photo duplication or publication without permission. No negatives released from the collection."

Virginia

The Aaron Burr Association, Tremont, Inca Rd., Linden VA 22642. (703)636-6095. President General: Dr. Samuel Engle Burr Jr.
Purpose: "To do historical research and to publish the findings, with special regard to the life and career of Col. Aaron Burr." Information covers history and politics.
Services: Offers brochures/pamphlets and newsletter. Publications include *The Chronicle of the Aaron Burr Association* (quarterly) and *The Influence of His Wife and His Daughter on the Life and Career of Colonel Aaron Burr*.
How to Contact: Write. "Our library materials are available only by appointment."

Hampton Center for the Arts and Humanities, 22 Wine St., Hampton VA 23669. (804)723-1776. Manager: Jeanne Zeidler.
Purpose: "To provide a research center and programs in the arts and humanities for the community. Information provided on Hampton history and archeology, local artists and craftspeople, and local performing arts." Information covers art, entertainment, history, music and recreation.
Services: Offers aid in arranging interviews and photos.
How to Contact: Write or call.

Hampton Heritage Foundation, Inc., Box 536, Hampton VA 23669. (804)723-1776, 723-9940. President: Mrs. Sandidge Evans.
Purpose: "Historic preservation of sites and structures and the cultural heritage of Hampton." Information covers history, how-to and nature.
Services: Offers brochures/pamphlets. Publications include information on historic landmark house and survey of Hampton buildings and sites.

How to Contact: Write or call.
Tips: "We're volunteer only, hence restricted as to time/manpower to do work for others. We are, however, willing to assist and make data available."

Jamestown-Yorktown Foundation, Box JF, Williamsburg VA 23185. (804)229-1607. Director: Parke Rouse Jr.
Purpose: "This is an agency of the government of Virginia to operate Jamestown Festival Park and Yorktown Victory Center, both historical centers of important sites and events of early America. We research, write and distribute literature about Jamestown-Yorktown and the history, people and issues relative to them." Information covers agriculture, art, economics, food, history, recreation and travel.
Services: Offers aid in arranging interviews, brochures/pamphlets, information searches, photos and press kits. Publications include *Jamestown Festival Park*, *Yorktown Victory Center* and *John Rolfe and Tobacco*.
How to Contact: Write or call. "Give credit for any photos."

Richmond Bicentennial Commission, 900 E. Broad St., Room 404, Richmond VA 23234. (804)649-1775. Director: Dr. Lynn L. Sims.
Purpose: "To celebrate the Revolutionary Era for the city and also to act as city historian."
Services: Offers brochures/pamphlets, placement on mailing list, and newsletter. "We have two free films 'Richmond and the American Revolution' and 'Liberty or Death—Reenactment of Patrick Henry's Speech.' Also sponsor the summer production of the Patrick Henry re-enactment show at its original site (St. John's Church, Church Hill)." Publications available.
How to Contact: Write or call.

Spotsylvania Historical Association, Inc., Box 64, Spotsylvania VA 22553. (703)582-5672. President: F.L.N. Waller.
Purpose: "To preserve the sites and monuments of historic value in Spotsylvania County and vicinity and to encourage owners in their preservation and restoration; to promote research and publish findings regarding local history, arts, crafts and culture; to preserve and display artifacts of historic value; and to establish a research library." Information covers art, entertainment, history, music, nature and travel.
Services: Offers bibliographies, biographies, statistics, brochures/pamphlets, information searches and photos. Publications include *Early History of Spotsylvania County* ($9), *Patriots 1776 of Spotsylvania County* ($1.25), *Freedom of Worship–A Religious History of Spotsylvania County, 1776-1976* ($1.25), *Spotsylvania County (1710-1976)* (75¢), a historical map of the county (75¢) and a brochure on Spotsylvania County.
How to Contact: Write or visit. Charges 50¢ admission fee; 25¢/photocopy and $2/hour for research work. "Books and manuscripts are to be used on premises. The Association requests credit annotations."
Tips: "The court house, with records dating from 1717, is across the street. We can assist you with these records also."

Washington

Eatonville Historical Society, Rt. 2, Box 444, Eatonville WA 98328. Contact: Donald B. Baublits.
Purpose: "To research and print history and to accumulate and preserve artifacts." Information covers history.
How to Contact: Write.

Washington State Historical Society, 315 N. Stadium Way, Tacoma WA 98403. (206)593-2830. Director: Bruce LeRoy.
Purpose: "To preserve artifacts, books, maps, pictures, manuscripts, etc. for research, education and public information on the history of the Pacific Northwest." Informa-

tion covers agriculture, artists, business, celebrities, economics, entertainment, food, health/medicine, history, industry, law, music, nature, politics, recreation, sports, Indians and genealogy.

Services: Offers aid in arranging interviews, annual reports, bibliographies, biographies, brochures/pamphlets, information searches, placement on mailing list, newsletter and photos. Publications include numerous books and publications.

How to Contact: "Write to the society and be specific." Charges reproduction fees. "Arranging an appointment may save time. The staff of the museum will also help with research."

West Virginia

Chesapeake & Ohio Historical Society, Inc., Box 417, Alderson WV 24910. President: Thomas W. Dixon Jr.

Purpose: "To gather information on the Chesapeake & Ohio (C&O) Railway and its predecessors, and to disseminate this information and data through publications, displays, etc. We collect negatives and printed matter as well for reproduction and distribution, including engineering drawings and material associated with production of scale models." Information covers history and technical data.

Services: Offers newsletters and photos. "We publish a fully illustrated monthly magazine, which provides current news, history and modelling information on the C&O Railway and its predecessors. We also publish special pamphlets and other material. We offer over 1,500 different prints from our negative files of photos dating from the 1890s through the 1970s."

How to Contact: Write. Charges for photos and photocopies. "We answer informational questions without charge unless special research is required."

Grant County Historical Society, Inc., Box 665, Petersburg WV 26847. (304)257-1444. President: Harold D. Garber.

Purpose: "For the recovery, conservation and dissemination of information pertaining to the history of the Potomac Valley of West Virginia—Grant County, in particular." Information covers art and history.

Services: Offers information searches.

How to Contact: Write. "Allow plenty of time for replies."

Mingo County Historical Society, Box 245, Kermit WV 25674. Contact: Zona Hoke, Amanda Meade Thompson.

Purpose: "To provide regional history. We are a small organization interested in our area history. We'll be glad to pass along any information we may have, but we do not publish to distribute." Information covers history.

Services: Offers information whenever possible. Publications available.

How to Contact: Write or call Amanda Meade Thompson, 210 Palmetto St., New Smyrna Beach FL 32069, (904)428-5688.

General Adam Stephen Memorial Association, Box 862, Martinsburg WV 25401.

Purpose: "To collect information regarding Maj. Gen. Adam Stephen (Revolutionary general, founder of Martinsburg, statesman in Virginia House of Burgesses)." Information covers history.

Services: Offers bibliographies. Publications include brochures on General Stephen.

How to Contact: Write or visit. Open June through September, Saturday and Sunday, 2 p.m. to 5 p.m.

West Virginia Archives and History Division (see listing in Libraries and Archives section).

Wisconsin

Brown Deer Historical Society, 8248 N. 38th St., Milwaukee WI 53209. (414)354-9060.

Contact: Mrs. D. Grehn.
Purpose: "We have restored an 1888 schoolhouse and run classes in the spring and fall for the 4th grade. We do have historical information on the Brown Deer area." Information covers history.
How to Contact: Write.

LaCrosse County Historical Society, Box 1272, LaCrosse WI 54601. (608)784-9080. Curator: David L. Henke.
Purpose: "We are located on the historic banks of the Mississippi River. Our society and its three museums attempt to preserve local significant heritage of LaCrosse County and the river." Information covers art, business, celebrities, economics, food, health/medicine, history, industry, law, music, politics, recreation, science and sports.
Services: Offers brochures/pamphlets and newsletters. Publications available.
How to Contact: Write. "We do request a copy of the final work in which our information was used."

Manitowoc County Historical Society, 1115 N. 18th St., Manitowoc WI 54220. (414)684-3144. Secretary: Edward Ehlert.
Purpose: "For research, preservation and publication of local history." Information covers agriculture, business, entertainment, history, law and politics.
Services: Offers annual reports, brochures/pamphlets, placement on mailing list, and newsletter. Publications available.
How to Contact: Write or call. For services relating to genealogy, write to Mrs. William Larsen, 936 N. 12th St., Manitowoc WI 54220.

Marathon County Historical Society, 403 McIndoe, Wausau WI 54401. (715)848-6143. Librarian: Ester Wunsch.
Purpose: "The historical society is dedicated to the preservation, advancement and dissemination of the knowledge and history of Marathon County. We cover the early logging days of the county in photos and related materials. Logging artifacts are on display." Information covers history.
Services: Offers photos.
How to Contact: Write or call (between 9 a.m. and 1 p.m. if seeking library information). Charges $1 service fee for photostats of documents, plus 10¢/photostat and $6.50/photo. "Books are not loaned; they must be used at the museum."

Mayville Historical Society, Inc., Box 82, 11 N. German St., Mayville WI 53050. (414)387-5530, 387-4295. President: James Schinderle. Secretary/Treasurer/Supervisor: Evaline F. Boelk.
Purpose: "We catalog material: history of the Mayville area, family folders, business records (of out-of-business firms), manuscripts, records, artifacts of the area, and law material (an old collection of books)." Information covers business, economics, history, industry and law.
Services: Offers statistics, Mayville news articles, and photos. "We also help with information on families and business data—as much as we have."
How to Contact: Write or call. "We do not have regular heat in our building, so we do not know how long we will be here for the winter. If the heat is adequate, we will continue working."

Milwaukee County Historical Society, 910 N. 3rd St., Milwaukee WI 53203. (414)273-8288. Curator, Research Collections: Robert G. Carroon.
Purpose: "The historical society, through a wide range of programs, seeks to encourage research into facets of Milwaukee history. A local history museum and an archives/research center are two major parts of this effort." Information covers business, entertainment and history.
Services: Offers bibliographies, biographies, brochures/pamphlets, newsletter and photos. "Library and archives collections deal with major persons and events in

Milwaukee history." Publications include *Milwaukee History*, a quarterly magazine.
How to Contact: Write, call or visit. Charges $3/8x10 photo, $1.75/5x7 photo, 15¢/first
photocopy, and 10¢/additional photocopy.
Tips: "We do not undertake detailed searches for writers, but will answer brief
questions and assist researchers when they appear in person."

Monroe County Local History Room, Court House Annex North, Rt. 2, Sparta WI
54656. (608)269-3175. Acting County Historian: Kathleen Calhoon.
Purpose: "We have artifacts and papers on history of Monroe County. All county
census and newspapers through 1900 are on microfilm." Information covers history.
Services: Offers aid in arranging interviews, biographies, brochures/pamphlets, information searches and photos.
How to Contact: Write and enclose large SASE, or call. Charges 25¢/microfilm printout, and "current price" for photos, plus postage. Cannot publish any collection in its
entirety.

Outagamie County Historical Society, Inc., 320 N. Durkee St., Appleton WI 54911.
(414)733-8445. President: Carolyn Kellogg.
Purpose: To promote interest and educate young people in local history, to establish a
museum in Outagamie County, and to preserve landmarks. Activities include monthly
meetings, changing exhibits and special programs. Projects include tours of nearby
areas (guide provided) and oral histories. The reference library contains old newspapers and books. "We also have a file that lists about 150 Wisconsin authors; information on Outagamie County pioneers and businesses; a 1907 Felgemacher tracker organ
in good playable condition; and the Irving Schwerke Collection, which contains
antique furniture and art objects collected in Europe." Information covers history.
Services: Offers brochures/pamphlets, information searches and newsletter. "We also
offer programs to clubs, organizations and schools. Our building, 'Temple Zion,' is on
the National Register of Historic Places. Houdini and Edna Ferber were members of the
original congregation. The history workshop (Temple Zion) is open Monday through
Friday, 9 a.m. to 5 p.m."
How to Contact: Write or call. "Since we are nonprofit, we will be happy to accept
donations. For extensive information, it is best for the writer to come to our building if
possible, because we have a limited staff."

State Historical Society of Wisconsin, 816 State St., Madison WI 53706. (608)262-
3266. Public Information Director: George C. Cutlip.
Purpose: "To research, publish and disseminate historical material on Wisconsin, the
Midwest and the nation." Information covers agriculture, business, entertainment,
health/medicine, history, how-to, industry, politics, technical information, archeology and genealogy.
Services: Offers aid in arranging interviews, annual reports, bibliographies, biographies, statistics, brochures/pamphlets, information searches, placement on mailing
list and photos. Distributes 4 publications/year to members and the state at large.
How to Contact: Write. Make appointment to reserve office space. Extensive search
arranged by contract on fee basis.

West Salem Historical Society, Inc., 357 W. Garland St., West Salem WI 54669.
(608)786-1399. Curator: Errol Kindschy.
Purpose: "To preserve local history and the restored Hamlin Garland Homestead. We
have purchased a local octagon home. Most information is on Garland." Information
covers history.
Services: Offers aid in arranging interviews, bibliographies, biographies, brochures/
pamphlets, information searches and newsletters.
How to Contact: Write or call. Charges for items ordered.

Wyoming

Sublette County Historical Society, Inc., Box 666, Pinedale WY 82941. (307)367-4367 (office), 367-4737 (home). President: Alice E. Harrower. Secretary: Donna Dittman.
Purpose: "Organized in 1936 to put on a pageant to commemorate the 100th anniversary of the first passage of women through Wyoming and their stay at the Rendezvous near Daniel. The women were Narcissa Whitman and Eliza Spaulding, both missionary wives. The Rendezvous was reenacted sporadically at first, but has been moved to permanent quarters near Pinedale and is acted out every second Sunday of July, drawing large crowds from all over the country—even Europe. The society has marked the Oregon trails and emigrant graves, wherever found; has put up historical signs telling of the events that happened here years ago; and is building the Museum of the Mountain Men." Information covers history.
Services: Offers brochures/pamphlets, statistics and newsletter. Publications available.
How to Contact: Write. "Since the museum is not ready for use, the material we have pertaining to biographies of early settlers, or older reports, have not been organized yet. It will be a while before our proposed library will be functioning."

Wyoming State Archives & Historical Department, Barrett Bldg., Cheyenne WY 82002. (307)777-7518. Director: Vincent P. Foley.
Purpose: "Historical research. We have a depository for public archives." Information covers agriculture, art, business, celebrities, economics, entertainment, food, history, industry, law, music, nature, recreation, travel and geology.
Services: Offers aid in arranging interviews, annual reports, biographies, statistics, brochures/pamphlets, information searches, placement on mailing list and photos. Publications include *Annals of Wyoming*.
How to Contact: "Write ahead with specifics and for an appointment at the archives." Charges reproduction costs. Research vaults are restricted.

Canada

Archelaus Smith Branch of Cape Sable Historical Society, Centerville, c/o McGray Post Office, Shelburne County, Nova Scotia, Canada B0W 2G0. President: Alfred Newell.
Purpose: "Operation of a small museum that illustrates the history of Cape Sable Island."
Services: Offers assistance. "We endeavor to research, as far as our information will permit, questions." Publications include *The Wreckwood Chair*, an account of several shipwrecks.
How to Contact: Write.

Aurora and District Historical Society, Inc., Box 356, Aurora, Ontario, Canada I4G 3H4. (416)727-8991. Curator: W. John McIntyre.
Purpose: "To promote the study, practice and knowledge of any phase of historical and archeological research regarding the town of Aurora and its vicinity. To operate for the display and preservation of historical materials, documents, pictures and artifacts, a museum and an archival repository." Information covers art and history.
Services: Offers brochures/pamphlets, information searches, newsletter and photos. Publications include *Aurora: Its Early Beginnings* ($3.50) and *Hillary House ("The Manor")* ($2.50).
How to Contact: Write. Charges for publications and photos. Allow six weeks for replies.

La Société Historique Acadienne, C.P. 2363, Station A, Moncton, New Brunswick, Canada E1C 8J3. (506)388-3045. President: Maurice A. Leger.
Purpose: "The purpose is to organize all of those interested in Acadian history. Our

first objective is appropriation, discovery, collection and the publication of all of those who have contributed to the teaching and the love of Acadian history." Information covers history.
Services: Offers publications, including *Les Cahiers*, quarterly. Vol. 9, Nos. 2 and 3 contain an index of the last 15 years.
How to Contact: Write.

La Société Historique de Québec, Inc., Séminaire de Québec, C.P. 460, H.V., Québec, Canada G1R 4R7. Treasurer: Micheline Fortin.
Purpose: "Research and publication of local history." Information covers celebrities and history.
Services: Offers brochures/pamphlets. Publications include *Cahiers d'Histoire* and *L'invasion du Canada 1775-1776*.
How to Contact: Write or call.
Tips: "The secretary and the treasurer are French-speaking persons. We do not answer genealogical queries."

Manitoulin Historical Society, Western Chapter, Manitoulin Island, Gore Bay, Ontario, Canada P0P 1H0. (705)282-2595. Chairman: G.F. Porter.
Purpose: "To collect everything from old tapes to rattlesnakes and those in between." Information covers agriculture, art, business, celebrities, economics, history, how-to, industry, law, music, nature, new products, politics and technical data.
Services: Offers aid in arranging interviews.
How to Contact: Write (summer only).

Missisquo Historical Society, Box 186, Stanbridge East, Québec, Canada J0J 2H0. (514)248-3153. President/Archivist: Mrs. R.S. McIntosh.
Purpose: "We are dedicated to keeping alive the history of the pioneer settlers of Missisquo, and we have a good collection of original documents, manuscripts, diaries, journals, biographies, reference books, and many artifacts." Information covers agriculture, business, celebrities, entertainment, food, history, industry, law, music, nature and politics. Also researches genealogy and antiques.
Services: Offers aid in arranging interviews, annual reports, bibliographies, biographies, brochures/pamphlets, information searches, and newsletter. Publications available.
How to Contact: Write. Research at the museum library is free to members of the Society. Nonmembers charged $5/hour, $50 payable in advance. Research well in advance, as museum is closed October 15 to May 27, but research facilities are open by appointment only.

New Brunswick Historical Society, Loyalist House, 120 Union St., Saint John, New Brunswick, Canada E2L 1A3. (506)652-3590. Executive Director: Willard F. Merritt.
Purpose: "New Brunswick Historical Society was founded in 1874 for the purpose of promoting historical and scientific research and to collect, preserve and publish all historical and other facts and data relating to the history of the province." Information covers celebrities, entertainment, history and science.
Services: Offers aid in arranging interviews, annual reports, brochures/pamphlets and newsletters. Publications include *Collections of New Brunswick Historical Society* ($5), *Loyalist of New Brunswick* ($7), *Dr. Hannay History of New Brunswick* Vol. 2 ($25), *Champlain of St. John River* (1.50), and a newsletter published 8 times/year.
How to Contact: Write. "We do not have a staff to do extensive research. Check the archives department at New Brunswick Museum or Provincial Achives Federation, New Brunswick, Box 6000, for genealogical information. We do not have any here."

The Ontario Historical Society, 1466 Bathurst St., Toronto, Ontario, Canada M5R 3J3. (416)536-1353. Executive Assistant: U. Ernest Buchner.
Purpose: "The society operates to increase the public's awareness of and appreciation

for Ontario's heritage and to act as a central office for the numerous local historical societies and heritage groups throughout the province." Information covers history.
Services: Offers brochures/pamphlets, newsletter and referral service for questions on Ontario's history.
How to Contact: Write. Membership is $10/year. Other services are available at cost.

Porcupine Camp Historical Society, Box 115, Porcupine, Ontario, Canada P0N 1C0. (705)235-5682. President: John W. Campsall.
Purpose: "To research, collect and preserve historical material, pictures, and old-timers' pictures, and making such material available to researchers." Information covers history.
Services: Offers photos.
How to Contact: Write or call.

United Empire Loyalists' Association of Canada, 23 Prince Arthur Ave., Toronto, Ontario, Canada M5R 1B2. (416)923-7921. Chairman and Editor: Mr. E. J. Chard.
Purpose: "Our association is confined to the history of the Loyalists who left the American Colonies during and after the American Revolution and came to settle in Canada; and the genealogy of the descendants of those Loyalists." Information covers history and genealogy.
Services: Offers aid in arranging interviews, bibliographies, brochures/pamphlets and information searches. Publications include *The Loyalist Gazette* (a semiannual journal).
How to Contact: Write. Charges for research; journal costs $3.50/year.

Wallaceburg & District Historical Society, 171 Margaret Ave., Wallaceburg, Ontario, Canada N8A 2A3. (519)627-3296. President: Alan Mann.
Purpose: "Preservation of local history, collection of artifacts, documents, papers, etc." Information covers local history.
Services: Offers information searches and photos. Publications include a resource booklet outlining materials pertaining to history of Wallaceburg, including audiovisual presentations, resource personnel, taped interviews, reference materials, etc.
How to Contact: Write or call. Charges for searches and materials on microfiche. "We are strictly a volunteer organization, but are willing to offer our assistance as much as possible."

Yarmouth County Historical Society, 22 Collins St., Yarmouth, Nova Scotia, Canada B5A 3C8. (902)742-5539. Curator: Eric Ruff. Librarian: Helen Hall.
Purpose: Chronicles "Yarmouth's history and shipping, and Yarmouth genealogies." Information covers history and shipping.
Services: Offers photos and limited information searches. Publications include newspapers, manuscripts, documents, logs, etc. "which can be used on our premises."
How to Contact: Write. Charges for photocopying, photo reproduction and searches. "Rates vary, but are minimal. We insist on a credit line for photos, information, etc. from our sources."

Historic Sites and Monuments

Because historic sites and monuments are usually tourist attractions eager to get their names before the public, they are willing to aid writers/researchers with information. More than just willing, however, they are also *able* to help, and can offer a wide range of services.

The Stonewall Jackson House, for example, is much more than a place where the curators can say, "Stonewall Jackson slept here—a lot." It's "an educational center offering tours of the general's home, exhibits relating to Jackson and ante-bellum life in the Valley of Virginia, and a library and research referral center where researchers may be assisted in locating materials and sources about Jackson, his associates, and the Lexington-Rockbridge area." So says Dr. Katharine L. Brown, associate director for research of the house.

Historic sites comprise a variety of locations, structures, etc. Included in the following listings are homes, palaces, monuments, and even a battleship. These places primarily offer printed material, but sometimes can also provide photos, press kits, bibliographies, etc. What's more, information specialists employed by the sites are willing to answer specific questions. "Curators will be happy to help on answering any questions someone might have," notes Nora Ward, museum curator of the Spanish Governor's Palace in San Antonio. A visit to the site, if one is possible, is often helpful in determining the sorts of information available, though most sites will answer inquiries made by mail or phone.

Because these sites concentrate on the facets of only one subject (or only a few subjects), supplement the information obtained with research in historical societies, libraries, museums, etc. You might even begin your research in one of these places, and consult the historical site afterward. Writers "should always first check with their state archives and the US war department; then come to us," recommends G.B. Edge, historic site manager of the Mansfield State Commemorative Area, a Civil War period museum and battlefield. Historic sites are often (though not always) best used as a source of material that adds depth to material obtained from other sources.

A short list of additional names and addresses can be found in *Stock Photo and Assignment Sourcebook* (R.R. Bowker Co.); check your local library for this book.

Susan B. Anthony Memorial, Inc., 17 Madison St., Rochester NY 14608. (716)381-6202. President: Roberta LaChiusa.
Purpose: "Care and maintanence of the Susan B. Anthony home and site." Information covers history.
Services: Offers information searches. Publications available.
How to Contact: Write. "Admission to house is 50¢. Visiting hours for the public are Wednesday through Saturday, 11 a.m. to 4 p.m., except Christmas. Group tours are by appointment. No pictures are to be taken inside the house."

Big Bend National Park, National Park Service, Big Bend National Park TX 79834. (915)477-2251. Chief Park Naturalist: Frank Deckert.
Purpose: "To protect and provide for the enjoyment of an outstanding example of Chihuahuan Desert in the United States." Information covers history, nature, recreation, travel and Big Bend National Park.
Services: Offers statistics and brochures/pamphlets. Publications include general information folders, *El Paisano* (newspaper), and miscellaneous mimeographed sheets and brochures.
How to Contact: Write the park superintendent. "For writers/researchers who want more in-depth information about the park, a list of sales publications is available from Big Bend National History Association, Box 86, Big Bend National Park TX 79834. A writer/researcher should consider a trip to the park if he intends to write an article of any length or depth in order to get a feeling for this country that can be obtained only through personal experience with the park."

Charles Towne Landing—1670, 1500 Old Town Rd., Charleston SC 29407. (803)556-4450. Public Relations/Special Events: Deirdra Wintner.
Purpose: "Charles Towne Landing is a nature and history preserve commemorating the site of the first permanent English settlement in South Carolina in 1670. We are an educational and possibly recreational theme park, and we offer the visitor a rich variety of activities that interprets the state's early history and educates visitors about the area's natural history." Information covers agriculture, art, economics, entertainment, food, history, nature, recreation, science and travel.
Services: Offers aid in arranging interviews, bibliographies, statistics, brochures/pamphlets, placement on mailing list, newsletter, photos and press kits. Publications

include a general brochure, a group visit brochure, *Charles Towne Landing* (souvenir book), *Pictorial History of Charles Towne* and *The Carolinas and Adventure*.
How to Contact: Write, call or visit. "Nothing can substitute for a visit to the landing, as the park is unusual, and not like other state parks or theme parks. Writers are asked to acknowledge sources."

Columbia State Historic Park, Box 151, Columbia CA 95310. (209)532-4301. Area Manager: Neil E. Power.
Purpose: "A state historic park. Our main period of interest is a typical Gold Rush town of the period from 1850 to 1870." Information covers history.
Services: Offers brochures/pamphlets. Publications include *Columbia State Historic Park*.
How to Contact: Write. "We cannot do research in response to mail inquiries. Some local material is available to resident inquiries. Do not send lengthy questionnaires to be filled in."

Edison Winter Home, 2350 McGregor Blvd., Fort Myers FL 33901. (813)334-3614. Curator: Robert Halgrim.
Purpose: "The Edison Winter Home and Botanical Gardens are historical, scientific and educational. There are two historical homes, 14 acres of botanical gardens, a chemical laboratory and a museum housing all of Edison's inventions. Open 7 days/week." Information covers agriculture, history, and science.
Services: Offers brochures/pamphlets.
How to Contact: Write or call.

Fort George National Historic Park, Box 787, Niagara-on-the-Lake, Ontario, Canada L0S 1J0. (416)468-2741. Superintendent: Walter Haldorson.
Purpose: "We are a historic park emphasizing the War of 1812." Information covers history.
Services: Offers brochures/pamphlets. Publications include *Fort George, British Soldiery in Canada* and *Battle of Queenston Heights Battlefield Walking Tour*.
How to Contact: Write or call.

Fort Nashborough, Metro Board of Parks and Recreation, Metro Postal Service, Centennial Park Office, Nashville TN 37201. (615)255-8192. Museum Director: Wesley Paine. Museum Guide: Naomi Levia.
Purpose: "The fort is a small replica of the original beginning point of the city, run by the Metro Board of Parks and Recreation. We have a living history program consisting of guides in period dress demonstrating many activities of daily life for the original settlers. Our time period is 1780 to 1784 and is specifically geared to frontier life in that time frame. Textiles are a major thrust of our program." Information covers agriculture, food, history, how-to (spinning and natural dyeing, primarily) and music (limited).
Services: Offers brochures/pamphlets and answers questions. "If someone needs specific information with regard to the settlement of middle Tennessee and will drop us a line, we will do our best to find the answer."
How to Contact: Write or call.

Great Sand Dunes National Monument, Box 60, Alamosa CO 81101. (303)378-2312. Contact: Superintendent.
Purpose: "To maintain the natural features of the highest sand dunes in the United States, while providing access to the public for recreational and aesthetic purposes."
Services: Offers brochures/pamphlets. Publications include monument brochure, trail guide, and various publications on sale through the cooperating association.
How to Contact: Write (requesting specific information), call or visit.

President Benjamin Harrison Home, 1230 N. Delaware St., Indianapolis IN 46202.

(317)631-1898. Director: Dorothy Sallee.

Purpose: "Home of the 23rd president of the US. Contains original furnishings and mementos of the Harrison family. Also contains speeches, programs and books for research of the period 1889-1893 (the Harrison presidential term)." Information covers celebrities, history, law and politics.

Services: Offers bibliographies, biographies, brochures/pamphlets, placement on mailing list and press kits. Publications include pamphlets of speeches of politicians of the period, *Harrison Heritage*, *President Benjamin Harrison and Our Country's Flag* and "The City of Indianapolis" (*Harper's Weekly* reprint, August, 1888).

How to Contact: "Call the office or write. Writers must use our materials on the premises and by appointment. Pamphlets and booklets published by the Harrison Home about the family and the home are available through the gift shop or the office." Charges for items obtained through gift shop.

The Rutherford B. Hayes Library and Museum, 1337 Hayes Ave., Fremont OH 43420. (419)332-2081. Director: Watt P. Marchman. Manuscripts Librarian: Thomas A. Smith. Books Librarian: Linda C. Hauck.

Purpose: "A registered national historical landmark." It contains the 19th president's personal library of 10,000 volumes, as well as his correspondence, papers, diaries, scrapbooks, photographs, and memorabilia. There is also a research library of 19th century America with 100,000 books and over a million manuscripts. Information covers history.

Services: Offers brochures/pamphlets. Publications include *Hayes Historical Journal* (semiannual $5/year) and *The Rutherford B. Hayes State Memorial* (brochure $1).

How to Contact: Write or call. The reference library (Ohio Room) is open freely to the public for research and study, between regular hours (9:00 a.m. to 5:00 p.m. weekdays; Saturday until noon; closed Saturday afternoon, Sundays and holidays).

Historic Bath, State Historic Site, Box 124, Bath NC 27808. (919)923-3971. Site Manager: Mrs. John A. Tankard.

Purpose: "We offer an orientation film and a guided tour of historic homes. This covers from 1705 when the town was incorporated." Information covers history.

Services: Offers brochures/pamphlets.

How to Contact: Write or call. Charges $1/admission.

Historic Cherry Hill, 523½ S. Pearl St., Albany NY 12202. (518)434-4791. Director: Cornelia H. Frisbee.

Purpose: "To preserve the history of the house and family that occupied Cherry Hill from 1787 to 1903 by means of the objects left by the family, including documents, letters and diaries. We are interested in helping individuals who want to do research." Information covers art, history and how-to.

Services: Offers "documents that are part of the manuscripts and documents collection at the New York State Library. These are partially cataloged. There is a great deal of social history information available in the document collection."

How to Contact: Write or call. Charges $5/b&w 8x10 print, plus a $20 publication fee. "Materials need to be credited if used in a publication."

Hovenweep National Monument, Box 401, McElmo Route, Cortez CO 81321. (303)529-4461.

Purpose: "Hovenweep National Monument is an agency of the National Park Service, Department of the Interior, that was established to preserve and protect several ruin groups of the Anasazi Culture." Information covers recreation and archeology.

Services: Offers statistics and brochures/pamphlets. Publications include *Hovenweep Mini-Folder* and *Hovenweep Guide to the Outlying Ruins*.

How to Contact: Write.

Independence National Historic Park, 313 Walnut St., Philadelphia PA 19106.

(215)597-9986. Procurement Agent: Mr. T.H. Spence.
Purpose: "A national historic park." Information covers history.
Services: Offers brochures/pamphlets.
How to Contact: Write.

The Stonewall Jackson House, 8 E. Washington St., Lexington VA 24450.
(703)463-2552. Associate Director, Research: Dr. Katharine L. Brown.
Purpose: "The Stonewall Jackson House is an educational center offering tours of the General's home, exhibits relating to Jackson and ante-bellum life in the Valley of Virginia, and a library and research referral center where researchers may be assisted in locating materials and sources about Jackson, his associates, and the Lexington-Rockbridge area." Information covers history.
Services: Offers brochures/pamphlets. "We cannot conduct research for a writer, nor do we have manuscripts, but we can refer a writer to the proper places to get material that relates to General Thomas J. Jackson, his associates and Lexington. We have a library available to the researcher who visits us." Publications include a general information brochure about the Stonewall Jackson House; more detailed publications are anticipated in the future, which would be of more assistance to writers.
How to Contact: Write, giving details of the type of information needed. Charges by the page for photocopies and for mailing and handling costs. Writers may need permission to quote or to copy some material.

John Jay Homestead New York State Historic Site, Box AH, Katonah NY 10536.
(914)232-5651. Contact: Jane Begos.
Purpose: "Historic site: home and farm of John Jay (first chief justice of the US and second governor of New York) and his descendants." Information covers history.
Services: Offers biographies and historical information on the Jay family.
How to Contact: Write or call.

Katmai National Monument, US National Park Service, Box 7, King Salmon AK 99613. (907)246-3305.
Purpose: "To protect the scenic beauties and wildlife within the boundary of Katmai National Monument and provide for the enjoyment of the visiting public. Information of interest would be on the Valley of 10,000 Smokes, plus specifics on the wildlife and ecosystems of Katmai." Information covers history, nature, recreation and travel.
Services: Offers brochures/pamphlets and assistance in research for events connected with Katmai National Monument. Publications include a park brochure and general information.
How to Contact: Write. "The staff at the present time is small. Most of our assistance is in providing information about previous research in the Katmai area."

Vachel Lindsay Association, 1529 Noble Ave., Springfield IL 62704. (217)787-0619.
Curator: Dr. Dennis Camp.
Purpose: "To provide information on the heritage of poet/artist Vachel Lindsay. (The home includes manuscripts and artwork.) Information covers art, history and literature.
Services: Offers brochures/pamphlets. "We have daily guided tours in the summer and tours by appointment in fall, winter and spring."
How to Contact: Write. "We charge $1 for an open-ended tour of the home. Any work by writers will have to be done during the middle part of the day."

Mansfield State Commemorative Area, Mansfield LA 71052. (318)872-1474. Historic Site Manager: G.B. Edge.
Purpose: "We have a fine Civil War period museum and commemorative area for historians and students." Information covers history.
Services: Offers help with Civil War ancestry tracing and Civil War history. Publications include *Mansfield* (a pamphlet about the history of the Battle of Mansfield).

How to Contact: Write. "We have a fine library that is open to the public. Our books cannot be taken out of our building; researchers take notes or tape material with their personal tape equipment. We do not have a copy service, our research is answered by letter."

Navajo National Monument, Tonalea AZ 86044. (602)672-2366. Chief Ranger: Norman Ritchie.
Purpose: "To preserve and interpret three prehistoric Indian ruins of the Kayenta Anasazi culture, circa late A.D. 1200s." Information covers history, science and archeology.
Services: Offers brochures/pamphlets. Publications include brochure on monument.
How to Contact: Write, call or visit.

North Cascades National Park Service Complex, 800 State St., Sedroo Woolley WA 98284. (206)855-1331. Management Assistant: Alan D. Eliason.
Purpose: "The national park and two national recreation areas provide a wide range of recreational opportunity: backcountry hiking and camping, climbing, boating, fishing, etc." Information covers nature.
Services: Offers brochures/pamphlets. Publications include park brochure and a variety of mimeographed handouts.
How to Contact: Write.

James Knox Polk Ancestral Home, W. 7th St., Columbia TN 38401. (615)388-2354. President: Frances H. Rainey.
Purpose: "To maintain and open to visitors the home of President Polk. We have almost all of Polk's personal effects, such as furniture, clothes and account books.'We can answer questions about Polk and supply photos of these relics." Information covers history.
Services: Offers brochures/pamphlets and photos.
How to Contact: Write or call.

Ringling Residence, 5401 Bayshore Rd., Sarasota FL 33580. Chief, Information Department: Robert L. Ardren.
Purpose: "The Ringling Residence is fashioned after the Doge's Venetian Gothic palazzo. It is part of the Ringling complex (Ringling Museum of Art, Ringling Museum of the Circus and the Asolo Theater) which is the foremost cultural center in the Southeast." Information covers art and John Ringling.
Services: Offers aid in arranging interviews, annual reports, brochures/pamphlets, placement on mailing list, newsletter, photos and press kits. Publications include *Souvenir Book,* describing the Ringling complex; *Fifty Masterpieces in the Ringling Museum of Art;* and *Ringling Museum of the Circus.*
How to Contact: Write, call or visit.
Tips: "The board of trustees has ruled that the Ringling Museums may not participate in commerical advertising with the exception of the advertising we purchase."

Saint Gaudens National Historic Site, Rt. 2, Windsor VT 05089. (603)675-2055. Superintendent: John H. Dryfhout.
Purpose: "To commemorate the life of Augustus Saint Gaudens. Information is also available on Cornish Colony artists to a limited degree." Information covers art and history.
Services: Offers brochures/pamphlets, information searches, photos and on-site access to research materials.
How to Contact: Write or call.

St. Marie Among the Hurons, Government of Ontario, Box 160, Midland, Ontario, Canada. (705)526-7838. Manager: Bill Byrick.
Purpose: "To provide a living history experience for visitors to the site. Information

covers the 17th century history of Nouoelle, France, specifically missionary (Jesuit) activity in Huronia." Information covers agriculture, art, health/medicine and nature as they relate to the 17th-century mission.
Services: Offers brochures/pamphlets and information on request.
How to Contact: Write or call.

Spanish Governor's Palace, 105 Plaza DeArmas, San Antonio TX 78205. (512)224-0601. Museum Curator: Nora Ward.
Purpose: "The Spanish Governor's Palace in a restored aristocratic Spanish colonial home with period furnishings and handmade doors. Keystone has Hapsburg Coat of Arms, dated 1749. This is the original building on the original site." Information covers history.
Services: Offers brochures/pamphlets. "Brochures are available, and they explain the history of the place and its furnishings."
How to Contact: Send SASE. "Other than brochures, the museum curators will be happy to help answer any questions you might have."

Statue of Liberty National Monument, Liberty Island, New York NY 10004. (212)964-3451. Librarian: Harvey Dixon.
Purpose: "The Statue of Liberty National Monument includes Ellis Island and the American Museum of Immigration, as well as the Statue of Liberty. Our purpose is to interpret and protect the monument for people who visit and/or inquire. We have records of the monument and Ellis or referrals to them, museum records, historic photographs, oral history collections, slides, books on ethnic history, and material supplied by the National Park Service." Information covers history.
Services: Offers annual reports, brochures/pamphlets, information searches, and photos. Also has duplicate tapes and/or their transcripts of "immigrants, former Ellis Island workers, and relevant persons/materials. Searches are done to a certain, reasonable extent. The writer does the rest."
How to Contact: Write or call. Charges for photographs ($3.25/8x10 b&w glossy prints); tapes ($2-3/tape); and photocopies (25¢/first page, 5/each additional page. "Start your project early and do not expect the unreasonable. Bear in mind that certain historic photographs in our collection cannot be reproduced due to copyright restrictions."

William Trent House, 15 Market St., Trenton NJ 08611. (609)989-3027. Curator: Ellen L. Sablosky.
Purpose: "The William Trent House is a historic house museum owned by the City of Trenton. The house was built in 1719 by William Trent, chief justice, and is furnished according to a 1726 inventory." Information covers art and history.
Services: Offers brochures/pamphlets.
How to Contact: "Send SASE to our address. The Trent House is a resource for those writers interested in early American architecture and English and American decorative arts."

Tryon Palace Restoration Complex, Box 1007, 610 Pollock St., New Bern NC 28560. Administrator: Donald R. Taylor.
Purpose: "To show the life of the late 18th and early 19th centuries through restorations, and to depict the history of North Carolina which occurred here. Operated by the state of North Caroline and the Tryon Palace Commission." Information covers history.
Services: Offers photos and press kits. "We have a number of 18th century volumes which can be used with special advance permission." Publications include *History of Tryon Palace Commission* ($6.), *History of Stanly Family and Stanly House* ($1.25), *A Tryon Treasury* ($4.), *Garden Booklet* ($2.75), and free brochures.
How to Contact: Write or call. "We charge for reproducing photographs. If a writer or photographer wishes to take his own pictures throughout our complex, he should

make advance arrangements for a Monday when we are closed to the public. No photography or wandering around are allowed on regular conducted tours."

USS North Carolina Battleship Memorial, Box 417, Wilmington NC 28402. (919)762-1829. Superintendent: Cpt. F.S. Conlon, USN. Promotion Director: Lt.Col. Amo F. Judd, USMC.
Purpose: "A World War II battleship preserved in her active duty days, serving now as a memorial to the 10,000 North Carolinians who lost their lives in WWII. Nine decks and levels are open to vistors." Information covers history and travel.
Services: Offers brochures/pamphlets.
How to Contact: Write or call. "Certain financial information is not released by the Battleship Memorial; it is available through other sources." Charges for admission.

Victoria Mansion, Morse-Libby House, 109 Danforth St., Portland ME 04101. (207)772-4841. Historian: Roger D. Calderwood.
Purpose: "The purpose of this society shall include literary, scientific, musical, educational and social undertakings. To emphasize the quickening and ennobling influence of art, music, literature and other educational and social forces, and to provide a center at Victoria Mansion for the development of such activities. The society maintains a nonsectarian and nonpolitical spirit, and gives recognition to Maine women who have made noteworthy contributions to society." Information covers art, history, and music.
Services: Offers brochures/pamphlets and photos.
How to Contact: Write or call.

Booker T. Washington National Mounment, Rt. 1, Box 195, Hardy VA 24101. (703)721-2094. Park Ranger/Historian: William T. Wilcox.
Purpose: "The monument is the birthplace site of Booker T. Washington, the famous black educator and founder of Tuskegee Institute. It serves to help interpret Booker's childhood as a slave on a mid-l9th century tobacco farm." Information covers agriculture, history, nature and black culture.
Services: Offers brochures/pamphlets, placement on mailing list and a library open for on-site resource/reference use. Publications include a brochure of Booker T. Washington Park.
How to Contact: Write or call.

Hospitals & Medical Centers

"There's a story behind every door in a major hospital. Human drama, prevention, life-or-death, people caring. A hospital sees it all, round the clock. Behind the headlines and behind the white uniforms a multitude of stories wait."

This statement, quite promising to any writer in search of a lead, comes from Jo Ann Valenti, community public relations representative at Tampa General Hospital. But Valenti qualifies her observation with this directive: "Go to medical professionals for medical information. Only the attending physician, emergency room personnel, or other hospital spokesmen can give you accurate, factual information, and we are more than happy to work with the media and their representatives."

So, whether covering the latest medical discovery, writing a human interest piece on a hospital employee or patient, or compiling a financial study on hospitals, the writer's challenge is to acquire the needed information about the hospital scene, and to deal with it effectively. Here are some suggestions.

A well-written letter on your professional letterhead may well be your ticket to the back door of the emergency room, if that is your goal. A letter is almost always preferred as your initial contact with the hospital public relations department. Besides being a more gracious interruption than a phone call, a written approach enables you to clearly detail your interests in what is sometimes a highly technical field. Let the PR director know why you want the information and how it will be used. In your letter, carefully outline your questions and request an appointment if necessary. Above all, allow plenty of time for a response.

"Give us a day or two to find the information you need," requests Michael L. Firlik, director of public relations/communications at Blodgett Memorial Medical Center. Firlik also advises writers to know what they want: "Have a handle on what your topic is, what the thrust of the piece you are writing is all about." Your description of your angle on a given medical subject may help the hospital communications specialist to determine how he can best help you.

Writers pursuing material on medical research or other highly technical hospital-related topics should be sufficiently fluent in medical terminology and the functioning of the modern hospital. Alfred D. Bruce, Director of Public Affairs at the Psychiatric Institute, stresses that, "in the medical and mental health fields, writers should have a working knowledge of terms and specialties before they begin in-depth research." Lee Chmelik of the Alaska Treatment Center concurs, adding, "Don't try to become an authority in the field—just make sure you speak directly with established authorities."

Such specialized knowledge not only assures you of an understanding of medical jargon; it also assures the medical professionals whom you contact of their efficient use of the time spent with you. Too, you can then truly present yourself to them as a professional, well-informed writer.

A few reminders about handling the information you gather from hospital authorities:

• Patient information of all kinds—case histories, photos, interviews—is confidential. You must obtain release consent forms signed by the patient or his guardian before publication. The hospital public relations director usually has such forms, and may be willing to handle them for you.

• Sending a draft of your piece to the public relations director prior to publication is a good idea. "Not for editorial purposes or critique," says Chmelik, but to check for technical accuracy.

• Credit the hospital, when appropriate, in your published work.

• Always send a copy of the published piece to the public relations director who assisted in the information gathering, even if it seems negative about the hospital in any way. It's a professional courtesy that helps to demonstrate that both of you are doing your jobs.

The hospitals and medical centers in the list that follows are representative of the medical facilities throughout the country that are willing to work with writers in the development of material. Some will work only with writers who have firm assignments; others are happy to handle almost all requests for information. Their preferences, when known, are included in the entries.

An extensive list of hospitals and medical centers is contained in the American Hospital Association's *Guide to the Health Care Field*, available at most public libraries. *The National Directory of Addresses and Telephone Numbers* (Bantam Books) provides a by-state list of government, voluntary and private hospitals with over 300 beds.

Alaska Treatment Center, 3710 E. 20th Ave., Anchorage AK 99504. (907)272-0586. Director, Public Relations: Lee Chmelik.
Purpose: "We are a private, nonprofit rehabilitation agency for crippled children and adults." Information covers health/medicine.
Services: Offers brochures/pamphlets. Publications ·include the Alaska Treatment Center (ATC) general brochure and the Sensory Impairment Center brochure.
How to Contact: Write. "We would need to see the final draft of an article before it is submitted to the publisher, not for editorial purposes or critique but to make sure any technical material is correct."

Augustana Hospital & Health Care Center, 411 Dickens, Chicago IL 60614. (312)975-5000. Assistant Director, Public Relations: Michael Kulczycki.
Purpose: "Augustana is a 330-bed community general hospital, a nonprofit institution. A medium-sized community hospital in an urban market, Augustana is involved with two unique programs: a seniors' health program; a consumer health education program for the elderly; and FHHEA, a consortium effort dealing with homebound medical care for the elderly." Information covers health/medicine.
Services: Offers aid in arranging interviews, statistics, placement on mailing list, newsletter and photos.
How to Contact: Write or call.

Blodgett Memorial Medical Center, 1840 Wealthy St. SE, Grand Rapids MI 49506. (616)774-7622. Director of Public Relations/Communications: Michael L. Firlik.
Purpose: "We are a comprehensive medical treatment facility composed of a nonprofit, fully accredited hospital of 410 beds, including an ambulatory care center, a professional building, and a school of nursing. We are a regional medical center serving patients from around the state." Information covers health/medicine.
Services: Offers aid in arranging interviews, annual reports, statistics and brochures/pamphlets.
How to Contact: Write or call. "Know what you want. Have a handle on what your topic is, what the thrust of the piece you are writing is all about. Give us a day or two to find the information you need. Check with public relations first."

Children's Hospital and Health Center, 8001 Frost St., San Diego CA 92123. (714)292-3101. Public Affairs Director: Larry Anderson.
Purpose: "Medical facility doing research in neurophysiology (computer-assisted

brainwave analysis); the world's prototype gait (walking) analysis lab; and top pediatric specialists in psychiatry, neurology, cardiology, orthopedics and rehabilitation."
Information covers health, science, self-help and sports medicine.
Services: Offers aid in arranging interviews, annual reports, statistics, brochures/pamphlets, Information searches, placement on mailing list, newsletter, photos and press kits.
How to Contact: Write or call. "We prefer to respond to specific queries."

Cedars Sinai Hospital, 8700 Beverly Blvd., Los Angeles CA 90048. (213)855-3674. Assistant Director of Public Relations: Tess Griffin.
Purpose: "Largest hospital in Los Angeles, with 1,120 beds. Completely supported by the community and support groups." Information covers health/medicine.
Services: Offers articles on Cedars Sinai or any aspect of it. "Requests should be made to the public relations department. The department will then present the idea to the public relations committee, which must grant approval for the piece. Only then will the department cooperate with the writer."
How to Contact: Write.

Children's Hospital Medical Center, Elland and Bethesda Ave., Cincinnati OH 45229. (513)559-4421. Director of Public Relations: Marian Knight.
Purpose: "To provide health care for newborns through adolescents. Children's Hospital Medical Center (CHMC) is one of the largest and most sophisticated pediatric centers in the United States. It definitely has the most sophisticated electronic equipment in the country for pediatric health care. Within the pediatric area, Children's Hospital specializes in kidney and heart disease, internal organs, cancer and congenital problems, mental retardation, kidney transplants and open heart surgery, correcting newborn defects, dental problems, and diagnosis and treatment of physical and mental handicaps. It is one of the few juvenile arthritis centers in the United States. Doctors here carry on genetic investigation and counseling. CHMC specializes in total intravenous feeding." Information covers health/medicine.
Services: Offers aid in arranging interviews, bibliographies, biographies, brochures/pamphlets, newsletter and photos.
How to Contact: Write or call. Charges for photocopies. "We will steer writers to research information and will tailormake information for writers, if necessary."

Cleveland Clinic Foundation, 9500 Euclid Ave., Cleveland OH 44106.
Purpose: "The Cleveland Clinic Foundation is a group practice of more than 300 physicians and scientists who provide specialty medical and surgical care to patients. It is considered by federal officials as a national health resource, renowned for optimal patient care, research, and education."
Services: Offers aid in arranging interviews and placement on mailing list.
How to Contact: Write. "All members of the media, who might want specific information about any phase of the Cleveland Clinic Foundation, should contact the public relations department. Interviews can be arranged with professional staff members and others in administration of the facility. If established writers wish press releases issued by the foundation, they can send a written request to be added to the mailing list."

Columbus-Cuneo-Cabrini Medical Center, 2520 N. Lake View Ave., Chicago IL 60614. (312)883-6798. Public Relations Director: James D. Monahan. Contact: Ellen Greenberg.
Purpose: "The Columbus-Cuneo-Cabrini Medical Center (3Cs) is the nation's largest Catholic medical center. It includes three unified hospitals in Chicago, owned and operated by the Missionary Sisters of the Sacred Heart. In addition to caring for in-patients (over 31,000 a year), the 3Cs sponsors many ambulatory and reachout programs. It has established 14 private physicians in the medically scarce neighborhoods of the Near West Side. It was founded by St. Frances Xavier Cabrini, the first American citizen-saint, in 1905. The 3Cs sponsors one of the most successful em-

ployee fundraising programs in the nation. Funds go to improve patient care via purchase of color TVs that will carry educational and entertainment programs." Information covers health/medicine and religious objectives of the Missionary Sisters of the Sacred Heart.

Services: Offers aid in arranging interviews, annual reports, biographies, statistics, brochures/pamphlets, information searches, placement on mailing list, photos and press kits. Publications include *3Cs Quarterly*; an internal, bimonthly newspaper; an annual report; a booklet on the life of Mother Cabrini; other special purpose publications pertaining to various care programs; and fundraising publications.

How to Contact: "A written request is preferred. Limited staff and the fact that the Medical Center is nonprofit makes it difficult to fulfill every request a writer might have, but every effort will be made to cooperate."

Tips: "Have as specific an objective in mind as possible when trying to secure information. If material is used in an article, send copies to the provider in all cases."

Eastern Women's Center, 14 E. 60th St., New York NY 10022. (212)832-0033. Director, Public Relations: Ilene Cooper.

Purpose: "To provide medical services to women, including family planning, pregnancy testing, counseling, abortion and gynecology." Information covers health/medicine.

Services: Offers statistics, brochures/pamphlets, information searches and newsletter. Publications include *Abortion, Every Woman's Right* and *Rape Resources Guide—New York Metro Area*.

How to Contact: Call.

Fairfax Hospital Association, 3300 Gallows Rd., Falls Church VA 22204. (703)698-3481. Director, Public Affairs: Peggy Pond.

Purpose: "Fairfax Hospital Association is a nonprofit, citizen-run organization that operates Commonwealth Doctors Hospital, the Fairfax Hospital (including ACCESS) and the Mt. Vernon Hospital. ACCESS is an unbedded emergency service and ambulatory service center located in Reston, which operates as part of the emergency department of Fairfax Hospital." Information covers health/medicine and science.

Services: Offers annual reports, brochures/pamphlets and placement on mailing list.

How to Contact: Write or call.

Fairview Community Hospitals, 2312 S. 6th St., Minneapolis MN 55454. (612)371-6612. Public Relations Director: Deborah Swanson.

Purpose: "A nonprofit hospital association, working together to share services, to purchase supplies at quantity discount, and to provide quality health care at lowest possible cost through good hospital management systems." Information covers health/medicine.

Services: Offers aid in arranging interviews, annual reports, bibliographies, biographies, statistics, brochures/pamphlets, newsletter, photos and press kits. Publications include annual report, reprints and information on services.

How to Contact: Write or call. "Contact our office with concrete suggestions about publishing opportunities. Midwestern residence of writer would be helpful. Published material must be appropriately credited."

Henry Ford Hospital, 2799 W. Grand Blvd., Detroit MI 48202. (313)876-2882. Public Relations Director: Patricia R. McCarthy.

Purpose: "A full service hospital with emphasis on patient care, medical education and research. We offer 39 specialties with more than 300 staff physicians, 300 physicians-in-training and 1,000 nurses. We have a major affiliation with the University of Michigan for training of medical students and affiliations with institutions including the University of Minnesota and Wayne State Unversity (Detroit) for allied health education programs. We have more than 200 research projects in more than 30 laboratories. Information covers food, health/medicine, history, how-to, industry, new product information, science, self-help, sports, technical information, medical education, health trends, psychology, social services, urban health, care and community education and revitalization. Publications include an annual report, a quarterly magazine and numerous health care informational brochures.

How to Contact: Write or call. "Patient privacy is always protected. Only if the patient, or legal guardian, signs a written waiver would we release a name or any other specific information on an individual."

Grossmont District Hospital, Box 158, La Mesa CA 92041. (714)465-0711, ext. 370 Director of Information Services: Ruth E. Messing.

Purpose: "General acute care nonprofit district hospital serving east San Diego (city and county). One of the three largest hospitals in San Diego County. Activities include physical rehabilitation, mental rehabilitation, maternity—delivery, intensive care, special community health services, pediatrics, emergency room with paramedic radio base station, laminar air flow operating room, laboratory and radiology (including body scanner)." Information covers health/medicine.

Services: Offers aid in arranging interviews, brochures/pamphlets, placement on mailing list and newsletter. Publications cover most hospital activities and services.

How to Contact: Write or call. "Writers contacting us must be working on assignment, not on speculation."

Harbor-UCLA Medical Center, 1124 W. Carson St., Torrance CA 90502. (213)533-3611. Communications Director: Carol Schmidt.

Purpose: "Harbor-UCLA Medical Center excels in patient care, medical education and medical research, especially in these areas: women's health care, perinatology, endocrinology and metabolism, genetics, fetal physiology, skeletal dysplasia, polypeptide research, development of radioimmunoassay tests, obesity, rheumatism, multiple sclerosis, lupus and immunology." Information covers health/medicine.

Services: Offers aid in arranging interviews, annual reports, statistics, brochures/pamphlets, information searches, placement on mailing list, newsletter and photos. Publications include an "annual report summarizing the 430 or so research projects underway here each year."

How to Contact: Write or call. "Still films shot for a commercial enterprise by an outside photographer cost $75/day; filming that is not for nonprofit educational uses costs $200/day for shooting on the campus/hospital."

Tips: "We will be particularly helpful to any writer whose work may help to convey the message that there are excellent medical research projects underway at Harbor-UCLA Medical Center."

Health Central, Inc., Suite 601, 2810 57th Ave. N., Minneapolis MN 55430. (612)566-6600. Vice President, Public Relations: James F. Moffet.

Purpose: "To promote the viability of the voluntary community hospital as the basis of the American health care system, and to assist in the maintenance of the highest standards of care and service through resource and service sharing as well as cost-effective management and operation. The Health Central system owns or manages 10 hospitals, some with attached nursing care facilities, in Minnesota and South Dakota. Through a broad share services program, it is involved with more than 100 community health facilities, representing more than 9,500 acute and nursing care beds in seven Upper Midwestern states." Information covers business (health management), economics, health/medicine, how-to, new products, politics, recreation, science, self-help and technical data.

Services: Offers aid in arranging interviews, annual reports, bibliographies, biographies, statistics, brochures/pamphlets, information searches, placement on mailing list, newsletter, photos and press kits. Publications include *Health Central TODAY* (quarterly) and *Updater* (monthly newsletter).

How to Contact: Write or call.

Jackson Memorial Hospital, 1611 NW 12th Ave., Miami FL 33136. (305)325-7304. Coordinator, Medical Center Communications: Betty Baderman.
Purpose: "To provide health care, Jackson Memorial is primarily a teaching hospital for the University of Miami school of medicine." Information covers health/medicine and medical research.
Services: Offers aid in arranging interviews, annual reports, statistics, and photos.
How to Contact: Write or call. "Most patient information is confidential unless we receive a release consent form. If the writer wishes to interview patients, it is best to let us make arrangements before writer comes to the hospital."

Jewish Hospital, 3200 Burnet Ave., Cincinnati OH 45229. (513)872-3322. Director of Public Relations: Judith Bogard.
Purpose: "Jewish Hospital is a nonprofit, nonsectarian hospital and the oldest Jewish hospital in the United States. It provides patient care and research and education and community health." Information covers food, nutrition, history, how-to, science, self-help and technical information.
Services: Offers aid in arranging interviews, annual reports, bibliographies, biographies, statistics, brochures/pamphlets, information searches, newsletter and photos.
How to Contact: Write or call. "Health/medical writers should contact Medline, a data base that can do a complete bibliographic search in seconds. Most hospitals belong to Medline and a hospital librarian can put the writer in touch with its services."

Lexington County Hospital/Lexington County Health Education Foundation, 2720 Sunset Blvd., West Columbia SC 29169. (803)791-2771. Coordinator for Public Relations: Ned B. Barnett.
Purpose: "The foundation underwrites innovations in health education, especially community-oriented programs. Lexington County Hospital is currently engaged in a community-oriented hospital-based health education program that the American Hospital Association has singled out as a model program for hospitals in the 1980s." Information covers health/medicine and self-help.
Services: Offers aid in arranging interviews, annual reports, bibliographies, brochures/pamphlets, placement on mailing list, statistics and photos. Also offers assistance in publicity efforts directed at informing public about specific health and health education programs.
How to Contact: Write or call. Charges, depending on the nature of the services.

Methodist Hospital of Indiana, 1604 N. Capitol Ave., Indianapolis IN 46202. (317)924-8517. Public Relations Director: Fred B. Price.
Purpose: "Methodist is the largest hospital in Indiana with 1,150 beds, 750 medical staff personnel, an annual budget of $110 million, and 39,000 admissions last year. We have a special care nursery for high risk infants, and operate a separate children's pavilion for 100 patients. Members of our staff perform open heart surgery and kidney transplants. We have one of the country's dialysis centers, a very active research department, and one of the most active and busiest emergency rooms. Methodist has over 25 contracts with other hospitals for shared services; it boasts the state's largest family practice program, 130 interns and residents in 15 different specialities; and 1,800 outpatient visits daily to 35 services." Information covers health/medicine and science.
Services: Offers aid in arranging interviews, annual reports, biographies, brochures/pamphlets, statistics, newsletter and photos.
How to Contact: Write or call.

Minneapolis Children's Health Center, 2525 Chicago Ave., Minneapolis MN 55404. (612)874-6192. Public Relations Coordinator: Suzi Hagen. Director of PR and Development: Margaret Sand.
Purpose: "Comprehensive inpatient and outpatient health care for children, from birth

through teen years. Built in 1973, Minneapolis Children's Health Center (MCHC) is unique because of its human ecology program, which places primary concern on caring for the total needs of children." Information covers health/medicine.

Services: Offers aid in arranging interviews and "background information, photos and interviews on general and specialized pediatric services, including nutrition, human ecology, mental health, reconstructive surgery, neonatal intensive care, cardiac surgery, cancer in children, pediatric dentistry and hypnosis as adjutant therapy." Publications include *Children's Magazine* and an annual report.

How to Contact: "We prefer a letter explaining the information needed and why, with lead time given for response. Generally, we want to know how information will be used."

Psychiatric Institute, 4460 MacArthur Blvd. NW, Washington DC 20007. (202)467-4538. Director, Public Affairs: Alfred D. Bruce.

Purpose: "The Psychiatric Institute is the only private comprehensive mental health center in Washington, D.C. that offers inpatient, outpatient and day treatment services to children, adolescents, adults and the aging in the metropolitan Washington area. In addition, the institute provides specialized services, including separate centers for the treatment of alcoholics and drug abusers, and it has a school of special education for youngsters in treatment at the institute. Information and referral services are provided. The institute trains mental health students from many disciplines, in addition to offering extensive conferences and workshops for area mental health professionals." Information covers health/medicine.

Services: Offers aid in arranging interviews, brochures/pamphlets and placement on mailing list. Publications include information folder of services offered at the institute.

How to Contact: Call.

Tips: "In the medical/mental health fields, writers should have a working knowledge of terms and specialties before they begin in-depth research."

Walter Reed Army Medical Center, 6825 16th St. NW, Washington DC 20012. (202)576-2177. Public Affairs Officer: Brian Sullivan.

Purpose: "To provide medical care for active duty military personnel and their families, families of deceased service members and others designated by the Secretary of the Army. We offer care in all phases of medicine. Walter Reed is a teaching center, providing internship and residencies in nearly all specialized medical practive. Medical research units include the Army Institute of Research, the Armed Forces Institute of Pathology and the Army Institute of Dental Research. We are currently the newest hospital in the Army." Information covers health/medicine, science and technical data.

Services: Offers aid in arranging interviews, information searches, placement on mailing list, statistics, photos and press kits.

How to Contact: Write. "No medical information on, photos of, or interviews with specific patients without that patient's consent. No identifiable photos of patients or interviews without their consent."

St. Paul Children's Hospital, 311 Pleasant Ave., St. Paul MN 55104. (612)227-6521. Public Relations Director: George Ryan.

Purpose: "We are a hospital for adolescents and children. We have information on pediatric medicine, pediatric social services, dietary subjects, pharmacy, safety, hospital shared services, etc." Information covers health/medicine.

Services: Offers aid in arranging interviews, placement on mailing list and newsletters. Publications include *Day Care Surgery* (information for day care surgery patients), *Hospital Education, Social Services, Clinic Information, Children's Hospital . . . How to Serve* (general information), and *Story of Children's Hospital* (history).

How to Contact: Write or call.

St. Paul Hospital, 5909 Harry Hines Blvd., Dallas TX 75235. (214)689-2496. Vice

President: John W. Roppolo.
Purpose: "A 600-bed general hospital operated by the Daughters of Charity, who also operate a charity clinic. Dallas's oldest private hospital, St. Paul performed the city's first open heart operation, and opened the first intensive care unit, the first coronary care unit and first school of nursing. The hospital has emphasized family-centered maternity services (fathers in the delivery rooms, rooming-in for new mothers, sibling visiting, birthing room, high risk pregnancy unit). We have a cancer treatment center."
Services: Offers aid in arranging interviews, statistics, brochures/pamphlets and photos (historical photos of hospital available).
How to Contact: Write or call. "Please give us a little time on your request; sometimes we don't have information immediately available. Please credit the hospital in your research."

Scripps Memorial Hospitals, Box 28, La Jolla CA 92037. (714)453-3400. Community Relations Director: Greg McQuerter.
Purpose: "To handle Scripps Memorial Hospital community relations, act as news brokers to the popular press and raise funds for hospital operations." Information covers health/medicine.
Services: Offers aid in arranging interviews, annual reports, brochures/pamphlets, placement on mailing list and newsletter.
How to Contact: Write or call.

Shriners Burns Institute, 202 Goodman St., Cincinnati OH 45219. (513)751-3900. Public Relations: Sue Anthony.
Purpose: "We are supported by Shriners of North America. We are a burns hospital (one of three in the US) specializing in pediatrics (burns only—limit age up to 16). We provide treatment, research and teaching. Our staff currently is conducting research in skin grafting and new burn dressings. We stress total patient treatment—rehabilitation emotionally as well as physically. The institute does have an out-patient clinic and follow-up care." Information covers health/medicine and technical data.
Services: Offers aid in arranging interviews, bibliographies, biographies, information searches and access to reprint file (most material is highly technical). "If writing on burns, we could assist in checking for medical accuracy."
How to Contact: Write or call. "Case studies by request only."

Edward W. Sparrow Hospital, 1215 E. Michigan Ave., Lansing MI 48912. (517)487-6111. Communications Director: Ann J. Heglin.
Purpose: "Sparrow Hospital is a 500-bed, privately owned, general medical/surgical/teaching hospital. It specializes in cancer treatment, the care of critically ill newborns, burnpatients and rehabilitation; it serves as a perinatal center for central Michigan." Information covers health/medicine.
Services: Offers aid in arranging interviews, annual reports, brochures/pamphlets, information searches, placement on mailing list, statistics, newsletter and photos.
How to Contact: Write or call.

Tampa General Hospital, Community Relations Dept., Administration Bldg., Davis Islands FL 33606. (813)251-7671. Community Relations Representative: Jo Ann Myer Valenti.
Purpose: "Tampa General Hospital is a 600-bed hospital serving the west coast and central region of Florida. We have specialized medical service areas, such as a burns unit, cardiac center (with four open heart surgical suites and three catheterization labs), neonatal intensive care unit, kidney transplant and dialysis unit, and numerous specialized clinic facilities for outpatient as well as inpatient services. We offer many educational and informational programs to the community as well as medical care." Information covers health/medicine.
Services: Offers annual reports, statistics, brochures/pamphlets, information searches,

placement on mailing list, newsletter, photos and press kits. Publications include *Critical Care for Your Heart*, an informational brochure on the hospital, pamphlets and flyers pertaining to medical services and health care, and *Hospitopics* (bimonthly). **How to Contact:** Write or call.
Tips: "Please go to medical professionals for medical information. Only the attending physician, emergency room personnel or other hospital spokesmen can give you accurate, factual information, and we are more than happy to work with media and their representatives. There's a story behind every door in a major hospital. Human drama, prevention, life-or-death situations, people caring. A hospital sees it all, around the clock. Behind the headlines and behind the white uniforms a multitude of stories wait."

University Hospital, 1405 E. Ann St., Ann Arbor MI 48109. (313)764-2220. Assistant Director, Public Relations: Joseph Owsley.
Purpose: "Teaching, research and patient care." The hospital specializes in research, preventive heart attack care, pediatric surgery, orthopedic surgery, cancer research and treatment and prenatal care. Information covers medical economics, food, health/medicine, new medical products, science, self-help and technical data.
Services: Offers aid in arranging interviews, annual reports, biographies, statistics, brochures/pamphlets, placement on mailing list ("for writers with credentials only"), and photos.
How to Contact: Write or call. "Writers should be able to produce credentials or demonstrate they have bonafide assignments."

University of Cincinnati Medical Center, Eden and Bethesda Aves., Cincinnati OH 45229. (513)872-5676. Contact: Public Information Officer.
Purpose: "The University of Cincinnati Medical Center operates six different units; College of Medicine, College of Nursing and Health, College of Pharmacy, Cincinnati General Hospital, Holmes Hospital and Medical Center Libraries. It is billed as a teaching institution that also delivers health care for the greater Cincinnati area. The medical center is especially known for the following: the major burn and trauma center for Ohio, Kentucky and Indiana; a major training center for family medicine physicians (operates a family practice center); the operation of a 24-hour psychiatric emergency center; the training program for emergency physicians; the Sports Medicine Institute for the rehabilitation of athletes; and its leadership in southwestern Ohio in pre-hospital emergency care. The medical center has the largest and most sophisticated newborn intensive care unit in the United States." Information covers health/medicine.
Services: Offers aid in arranging interviews, annual reports, bibliographies, biographies, brochures/pamphlets, information searches, placement on mailing list, newsletter and photos.
How to Contact: Write or call.

University of Kansas Medical Center, 39th and Rainbow Blvd., Kansas City KS 66103. (913)588-5240. Director, University Relations: Susan Shipley.
Purpose: "To improve the quality of health care by educating health care professionals; to provide direct health care services; and to conduct research in the basic sciences and clinical investigations into the causes and treatment of diseases." Information covers health/medicine.
Services: Offers aid in arranging interviews, biographies and placement on mailing list.
How to Contact: Write or call.

Vanderbilt University Medical Center, 21st Ave. S. at Garland, CCC-3312, Nashville TN 37232. (615)322-4747. Director, Public Affairs: Dr. Beverly Flykes.
Purpose: "We provide tertiary health care to persons in middle Tennessee and in some specialties to the entire Southeast. We have special research and treatment programs

in cancer, hypertension, lung disease, heart disease, diabetes, infertility, neuromuscular disease, pharmacology, toxicology and other medical specialties and subspecialties. We also have a comprehensive children's hospital with major specialties." Information covers health/medicine.

Services: Offers aid in arranging interviews, annual reports, brochures/pamphlets, placement on mailing list, newsletter, photos and press kits.

How to Contact: Write or call.

Industrial & Commercial Firms

"Always call public relations people first," Noreen Jenney, president of Noreen Jenney Communicates advises writers. "They'll do half your work for you."

Some public relations people associated with industrial and commercial firms might call Jenney's "half-the-work" estimate a bit extravagant; yet, the public relations departments of companies large and small are eager to supply information to you. You are their link to the public—to consumers. "If you're writing about (the PR person's client)," Jenney says, "you're doing *them* the favor."

Industrial and commercial firms can be valuable sources of information, facts, story leads, interviews and statistics. Inventions, discoveries, new procedures, interesting people, economic milieus—all are parts of the business world, and all have their effects on the world in general. (See "Junk Mail Can Be Good for You" for a more detailed discussion of information available to writers, and how it can be used.)

What's more, the public relations person has a concept of what you as a writer will want—and what readers will find interesting—because most PR people are trained communicators, and many have journalism backgrounds. "We are experienced in working with all levels of public and trade media, and emphasize meeting editorial and technical requirements and providing up-to-date, accurate, fact-laden material that the media and their target publics will find useful," says John Ross, public relations representative of R.J. Reynolds Industries. Though Ross's statement borders on being PR for PR, if gives you an idea of the value of consulting public relations departments of companies.

Still, the PR person's job is to present his employers in the best possible light, and to give the employers images of untainted, untarnished American superheroes. Be wary, therefore, of using *only* information supplied from public relations sources. PR information can make good background material, or provide a good supplement to information you get from other sources, but is rarely useful by itself. "Never be content with only one source of information," says Thomas Keating, western director of public relations with the John Hancock Mutual Life Insurance Company. "Where possible, make at least three contacts with different sources."

Besides, knowing something about your topic *before* approaching a company has advantages. "We are happy to assist writers and students, *if* they do their homework first," says W.A. Nail, director of public relations with Zenith Radio Corporation. Though eager to help, companies won't do all the writer's work for him. "We welcome inquiries and the opportunity to explain our businesses," says a representative of Ford Motor Company's diversified products division, but "we are *not* a research agency, and can offer only what we have in stock or what is available by interview."

Demonstrating your preparation is a way of demonstrating your professionalism to these people, and a show of professionalism is important. Other ways of exhibiting professionalism include typing inquiries on letterhead stationery and mentioning the magazine/publishing house you're working with—if you're on assignment. "In making inquiries, it would be helpful if writers provided their telephone numbers, the use for which the information is being sought (e.g., an article in such-and-such publication), and a *reasonable* time to respond," says the Ford representative in discussing a view of a professional writer.

Be courteous when requesting information, and follow up by giving the company you've consulted copies of the published work. Attribute the information to the company as you would to any other source, but don't go out of your way to give the company a plug. "We do like credit," says Nail, "but we don't insist on it."

Listed below are the companies that have indicated to *The Writer's Resource Guide* that they're willing to supply information and other assistance to writers. This list, besides providing specific sources, will also give you an indication of what help other companies can provide. Names and address of more industrial and commercial firms can be found in *National Directory of Addresses and Telephone Numbers* (Bantam Books), and in *Public Relations Register*. Published by the Public Relations Society of America (845 3rd Ave., New York City 10022), *Public Relations Register* carries lists that are broken down by individual members' names, by company names, and by geographic location. *Public Relations Register* costs nonmembers $45, so check your local library for a copy.

Many companies maintain toll-free numbers you can use. To find out if a particular company has such a number, call 800/555-1212 (which is, itself, toll-free), and give the operator the name of the company in which you're interested. You'll be given the toll-free number, if one is available.

Aeronautics & Aerospace

The Boeing Co., Box 3707, Seattle WA 98124. (206)655-6123. Corporate Public Relations Director: Peter Bush.
Purpose: "Commercial air transports, missiles and space programs." Information covers business, economics, industry, new products, science, technical data and travel.
Services: Offers aid in arranging interviews, annual reports, bibliographies, biographies, statistics, brochures/pamphlets, information searches, placement on mailing list, photos and press kits.
How to Contact: Write. Charges for some photos.

General Electric Co., Aerospace Group, Box 8555, Philadelphia PA 19101. (215)962-2832. Manager, Aerospace Business Communications: J.C. Hoffman.
Purpose: "Research, development, manufacturing and testing activities for aircraft control and instrumentation systems; sonar, airborne and ground-based radar, ballistic missile and space reentry systems; earth observatory and communication satellites; manned space programs; simulation systems; advanced energy systems and related technology." Information covers new products, science and technical data.
Services: Offers aid in arranging interviews, biographies, statistics, brochures/pamphlets, placement on mailing list, photos and press kits. Publications include pamphlets, brochures, folders and product information in general.
How to Contact: Write or call.

Grumman Corp., 1111 Stewart Ave., Bethpage NY 11714. (516)575-7521. Assistant Manager, NY Press Relations: Peter Costiglio.
Purpose: "Grumman Corp. is a diversified aserospace company—primarily a manufacturer of military aircraft—that also makes solar and wind energy systems, fire trucks, ambulances, buses, truck bodies, canoes, boats, yachts, storage and transportation systems for perishable products." Information covers industry.
Services: Offers aid in arranging interviews, annual reports, biographies, brochures/pamphlets, placement on mailing list, photos and press kits. Publications include brochures on products and activities.
How to Contact: Write or call. "We prefer that requests be written, specific and reasonable."

Lockheed Corp., 2555 N. Hollywood Way, Burbank CA 91503. (213)847-6515.Public Relations Director: G. Mulhern.
Purpose: "Products, electronics, shipbuilding, missiles, space and services division." Information covers business, health/medicine, history, industry, new product information and science."
Services: Offers aid in arranging interviews, annual reports, bibliographies, biographies, statistics, brochures/pamphlets, information searches, placement on mailing list, newsletter, and press kits.
How to Contact: Write or call. "Make an appointment to get into our plant.

Amusements

African Safari Park, Box 7129, Naples FL 33941. (813)262-5409. President/ General Manager: Col. Larry Tetzlaff.
Purpose: Commercial zoological park. Information covers agriculture, entertainment, food, nature, recreation and travel.
Services: Offers aid in arranging interviews, biographies, brochures/pamphlets, photos and press kits.
How to Contact: Write. Charges for photos and books.
Tips: "There are scores of human interest stories here, and lots of history."

The Alligator Farm, Drawer E, St. Augustine FL 32084. (904)824-3337. Director of Shows: Ross Allen.
Purpose: Commercial attraction. Information covers entertainment, nature and science.
Services: Offers brochures/pamphlets on reptile information.
How to Contact: Write or call.

Assiniboia Downs Racetrack, 3975 Portage Ave., Winnipeg, Manitoba, Canada R3K 1W5. (204)885-3330. Director of Public Relations: John Matheson.
Purpose: "Thoroughbred horse racing, May through October." Information covers entertainment and sports.
Services: Offers statistics, brochures/pamphlets and placement on mailing list. Publications include 1979 Assiniboia Downs brochure and *They're Off!*, a guide to horse racing.
How to Contact: Write or call.

The Buckeye State Society Circus, Box 74, Barnesville PA 18214. (717)467-2316; toll-free (800)824-7888, ext. A263. Manager/Owner: Col. Jerry Lipko.
Purpose: "A circus playing schools and colleges as a fundraiser, supported by circus stars as well as trained animals; also a program lecturing on chimps and having them perform." Information covers entertainment.
Services: Offers brochures/pamphlets, photos and press kits.
How to Contact: Write or call. "I have owned and trained chimps for over 29 years; I've owned 19 in my life and am considered an authority."

Busch Bird Sanctuary, 16000 Roscoe Blvd., Van Nuys CA 91406. (213)997-1171. Contact: Patricia McCauley.
Purpose: Bird sanctuary and free tourist attraction. Information covers agriculture, health/medicine (for birds), how-to, nature, recreation, sports, technical data and travel; also migration, training and endangered birds.
Services: Offers aid in arranging interviews, bibliographies, biographies, statistics, brochures/pamphlets, information searches, placement on mailing list, photos and press kits.
How to Contact: Write or call Patricia McCauley, 835 Hopkins Way, Suite 505, Redondo Beach CA 90277. (213)376-6978.

Busch Gardens, 3000 Busch Blvd., Tampa FL 33618. (813)977-6606. Publicity Manager: Glinda Gilmore.
Purpose: Theme park. Information covers art, entertainment, health/medicine (of animals), history, nature, recreation, science, technical data, travel, horticulture, botany and zoology.
Services: Offers aid in arranging interviews, annual reports, bibliographies, biographies, statistics, brochures/pamphlets, information searches, placement on mailing list, photos and press kits.
How to Contact: Write or call. Allow one to two weeks for a response. "Get a press kit first and peruse it before writing."

Cedar Point, Inc., Box 759, Sandusky OH 44870. (419)626-0830. Public Relations Coordinator: Don Ingle. Public Relations Representative: Lynn Williams.
Purpose: "We are the nation's second largest amusement/theme park in terms of size and development. We have the most rides of any park (56) and the most coasters (6). We can provide information on amusement parks, coasters, the coastermania phenomenon, carrousels and their history, ride safety, fast foods, etc., plus information about the Grand National Offshore Powerboat Race." Information covers business, entertainment, food, history, crafts, how-to, new products, recreation, sports and travel.
Services: Offers aid in arranging interviews, annual reports, biographies, statistics, brochures/pamphlets, placement on mailing list, photos, press kits and tours of the park. Publications include *Cedar Point*, a color information brochure; *Cedar Point Marina*; *Frontier Trail*, brochure about Cedar Point crafts area; *Coaster Enthusiast's Guide to Cedar Point*; and summer employment opportunities information.
How to Contact: "Write or call the public relations department. Requests for information during our operating season (May to September) should allow a generous response time (two to three weeks)."

Churchill Downs, Inc., Box 8427, Louisville KY 40208. (502)636-3541, 637-8120. Publicity Director: William Rudy.
Purpose: "Best known as the home of the Kentucky Derby, Churchill Downs conducts two thoroughbred race meetings per year—one in the spring and one in the fall for a total of approximately 80 days. In existence since 1875, the track keeps historical and statistical information related to racing, specifically the Kentucky Derby." Information covers business, celebrities, racing and technical data.
Services: Offers aid in arranging interviews, annual reports, bibliographies, biographies, statistics, placement on mailing list, newsletter, photos and press kits (Derby press kits go only to accredited press). Publications include a Kentucky Derby press guide, Kentucky Derby Museum brochure, a King of Sports informational racing brochure, Kentucky Derby ticket information and a Churchill Downs Group Program brochure.
How to Contact: Write or call. "Members of accredited news media desiring press credentials must write on letterhead at least three weeks prior to the opening of the racing season. Prices for photography publication depend on use. Other photographs are $6.25 per 8x10 b&w print; $15 per 8x10 color photo; other sizes are available on request. Permission to use must be granted on photos for publication or commercial use."

Country Music Hall of Fame, Country Music Foundation, 2 Music Square E., Nashville TN 37202. Director of Library: Danny Hatcher.
Purpose: To preserve the history of country music. We have a fully functioning museum and research facility with 65,000-70,000 recorded items." Information covers history, music and new products; also information on new artists.
Services: Offers aid in arranging interviews ("possibly"), clipping services, information searches, placement on mailing list, photos and press kits. Includes vertical file system with biographical sketches of country music artists. "We can provide basically any information—records, videotapes, clips and films." Publications include *Journal*

of Country Music; Bill Munroe: An Illustrated Discography; My Husband, Jimmy Rogers; Truth Is Stranger than Publicity; and reprints of a 1921 Gibson Company catalog and a report of an 1890 Edison Phonograph Dealers convention proceedings.
How to Contact: Write or call. "The stack area is closed; write or call in advance for specific needs." Charges for photos.

Delaware Park, Box 6008, Stanton DE 19804. (302)994-2521. Public Relations Director: Bob Kelley.
Purpose: "The presentation of parimutuel throroughbred racing during the summer months." Information covers business, entertainment, recreation and sports.
Services: Offers aid in arranging interviews, brochures/pamphlets, placement on mailing list and photos. Publications include a press guide and press releases.
How to Contact: Write or call. "Prints requested during the off-season may require a production charge."

Walt Disney World, Box 40, Lake Buena Vista FL 32830. (305)824-2222, 824-4531. Manager of Publicity: Charles Ridgeway.
Purpose: "Most popular vacation destination in America." Information covers celebrities, entertainment, history, music, nature, recreation, sports and technical data.
Services: Offers aid in arranging interviews, annual reports, bibliographies, biographies, statistics, brochures/pamphlets, information searches and press kits. "Press kits are made to suit the writer's needs." Publications include *The Story of Steam Locomotives in the Magic Kingdom, Biography of Walt Disney,* and special press kits for special events.
How to Contact: Write or call. No charge to "the author or working pressperson." Requires an editor's OK on a story to give help to a writer. Written requests preferred. "We like to work with people, especially if they are writing from a new angle on our large and many-faceted operation. We must have control of Disney material."

Disneyland, 1313 Harbor Blvd., Anaheim CA 92801. (714)533-4456. Publicity Spokesperson: Frank Whiteley.
Purpose: "Amusement park." Information covers recreation.
Services: Offers press kits. Publications include a guide book.
How to Contact: Write or call. "We deal only with working journalists with credentials. A freelancer needs a letter from editor or managing editor."

Evangeline Downs, US Hwy. 167 N., Box 3508, Lafayette LA 70502. (318)896-6185. General Manager: Norman F. Faulk. Public Relations Director: Bob Henderson.
Purpose: "Thoroughbred horse racing season opens first week of April and extends until Labor Day (approximately 23 consecutive weeks, and total racing dates number about 90). 1979 race season: April 5 through September 3." Information covers entertainment, food and sports.
Services: Offers aid in arranging interviews, brochures/pamphlets, placement on mailing list, statistics and photos.
How to Contact: Write. "The 'welcome mat' is extended each and every day to one and all—fans and writers. Make arrangements in advance, if possible."

Florida Cypress Gardens, Box 1, Cypress Gardens FL 33880. (813)324-2111. Publicity Manager: Pete Johnson.
Purpose: "This is a family tourism total destination attraction." Information covers business, celebrities, entertainment, food, how-to, nature, new products, recreation, sports, technical data and travel.
Services: Offers aid in arranging interviews, annual reports, brochures/pamphlets, information searches, placement on mailing list, photos and press kits. Publications include *Ski Like a Pro.* Photos include pictures of flowers, plants, scenics, boating, water skiing, fishing, camping and "pretty girls."

How to Contact: Write. "All Cypress Garden photos must carry a credit line." Charges if photo used without credit line. Return of pictures required.

Geauga Lake, Funtime, Inc., 1060 Aurora Rd., Aurora OH 44202. (216)562-7131. Public Relations Director: Harry H. Peck.
Purpose: "We are a profitmaking organization whose operations entail attracting and entertaining in our park, approximately one million guests per year. We distribute travel, entertainment, historical, business and general interest information." Information covers business, entertainment, new products, recreation and travel.
Services: Offers aid in arranging interviews, annual reports, biographies, brochures/pamphlets, photos and press kits. Publications include *Geauga Lake Sales* brochure.
How to Contact: Write or call. "Any writer who would like to visit our facility may do so free of charge by giving us 24 hours notice."

Hersheypark & Arena, HERCO, Inc., Hershey PA 17033. (717)534-3977. Publicity and Press Relations Manager: Cynthia A. Roof.
Purpose: "Hersheypark & Arena seats 7,300 reserved and up to 11,000 festival seating. Home of the Hershey Bears hockey team, in the American Hockey League, Heritage is an important factor in Hershey—Milton S. Hershey brought his candy factory to the cornfields of Derry Church in 1907. Many attractions were originated for—and are still used by—employees of Hershey (now two separate corporations—HERCO, Inc. and Hershey Foods Corporation). Hersheypark has existed for 73 years, seven of those years as a theme park." Information covers entertainment, recreation and travel.
Services: Offers brochures/pamphlets, placement on mailing list, newsletter, photos and press kits. Publications include brochures (front gate handouts, special entertainment and coming attractions) and *Hershey Book*, describing all attractions in Hershey, Pennsylvania.
How to Contact: Write or call.

Kings Dominion, Box 166, Doswell VA 23047. (804)876-3371. Manager of Public Relations: Jack Yager.
Purpose: "Kings Dominion is a large family entertainment center with rides, shows, shops and restaurants, surrounded by beautiful landscaping. We also have live animals and the cartoon characters of Hanna Barbera." Information covers entertainment, nature (animals), recreation and travel.
Services: Offers aid in arranging interviews, photos and press kits.
How to Contact: Write.

King's Island, Box 400, Kings Mills OH 45034. (513)241-5600, ext. 461. Public Relations Director: Ruth Voss.
Purpose: Family entertainment center. Special features are the College Football Hall of Fame, 18-hole Jack Nicklaus Golf Center, Wild Animal Safari, and a major amusement park. Information covers nature and sports.
Services: Offers aid in arranging interviews, annual reports, statistics, information searches, placement on mailing list, photos (color transparencies) and press kits. Publications include *Rollercoaster* newsletter.
How to Contact: Write, call or visit. "Start with a press kit. Call a few days in advance for help."

Knott's Berry Farm, 8039 Beach Blvd., Buena Park CA 92801. (714)533-4456. Publicity Manager: Jane Kolb.
Purpose: Amusement park. Features an operating stage coach, an Old West ghost town, the largest miniature collection in the world, demonstrations of panning for gold, and a narrow-gauge railroad.
Services: Offers press kits. Publications include general farm brochures.
How to Contact: Write or call. "Start in the publicity department and state an area of specific interest." Must have credentials to use services.

Editors constantly ask for people pictures to accompany stories, and public relations sources can often provide such pictures. In this photo, the people are topping a 76-foot-tall loop of a roller coaster at Marriott's Great America theme park in Santa Clara, California. Paul Becker took the photo, available free (as are many photos supplied by PR sources) from Marriott's Great America.

Liberty Bell Park Racetrack, Knights & Woodhaven Rds., Philadelphia PA 19154. (215)637-7100. Publicity Director: Dave Terrell.
Purpose: "We have harness racing 200 days yearly and are always glad to answer any

questions that we can on harness horse racing here or elsewhere. Writers and/or press are admitted free with a prior call." Information covers sports.
Services: Offers placement on mailing list and newsletter.
How to Contact: Write or call.

Lookout Mountain Caverns, Inc., Rt. 4, Scenic Hwy., Chattanooga TN 37409. (615)821-2544. Administrative Secretary: Susan Davenport.
Purpose: Tourist attraction with natural rock formation and observation tower. Information covers history, nature, recreation, science, technical data and travel.
Services: Offers aid in arranging interviews, statistics, brochures/pamphlets, information searches, placement on mailing list, newsletter, photos and press kits. Publications include *Southern Highlands Attractions*.
How to Contact: Write or call.

Marine Land of Florida, Rt. 1, St. Augustine FL 32084. (904)829-5607. Contact: Charlene List.
Purpose: "The world's original marineland with the largest tropical fish display and 2 oceanariums." Information covers nature and science.
Services: Offers aid in arranging interviews, annual reports, biographies, brochures/pamphlets, information searches, placement on mailing list, photos and press kits.
How to Contact: Write or call. Charges depend on use. Direct queries on operations to Cecil Walker and on specific scientific information to Robert L. Jenkins, curator. A marine research lab of the University of Florida is maintained on Marine Land property and may be used for information.

Marriott's Great America, Box 1776, Santa Clara CA 95052. (408)988-1776. Public Affairs Manager: John Poimiroo.
Purpose: "We are a theme park featuring travel, family recreation, stage shows and amusements." Information covers celebrities, entertainment, history, music, recreation and travel.
Services: Offers aid in arranging interviews, annual reports, statistics, brochures/pamphlets, placement on mailing list, newsletters, photos and press kits.
How to Contact: Write and specify purpose for which information is needed.

The Meadows Racetrack, Box 499, Meadow Lands PA 15347. (412)225-9300. Public Relations/Publicity Director: Thomas J. Rooney.
Purpose: "The Meadows races 200 nights a year, February through November. We are the site of the $130,000 Adios Pace and $50,000 Currier & Ives trot, two of our sport's most prestigious races." Information covers sports.
Services: Offers statistics, brochures/pamphlets, placement on mailing list, newsletter, photos and press kits. Publications include *Fact Book* (annual), a monthly newspaper and a weekly news sheet.
How to Contact: Write. "Supplemental material can be obtained from the US Trotting Association in Columbus, Ohio (614)224-2291.

Opryland USA, Box 2138, Nashville TN 37214. (615)889-6600. Public Relations Director: Charlotte Davidson. Operator: Ray Camady.
Purpose: "Amusement park—rides, games, musical entertainment, Grand Ole Opry radio show every Friday and Saturday night, 600-room hotel and television productions center." Information covers celebrities, entertainment, history, music, recreation, technical information, travel and their own television and radio programs. Recent productions include TV specials featuring John Ritter, Ann-Margaret, Dolly Parton and Carol Burnett.
Services: Offers aid in arranging interviews, biographies, statistics, brochures/pamphlets, placement on press mailing list, newsletter, photos and press kits.
How to Contact: Write or call.

Ringling Bros. and Barnum & Bailey Circus, 1015 18th St. NW, Washington DC 20036. (202)833-2700. Public Relations Director: Jerry Digney.
Purpose: "World's largest and oldest (109 years old) circus. Popularly known as the Greatest Show on Earth." Information covers celebrities, entertainment, history and sports.
Services: Offers aid in arranging interviews, bibliographies, biographies, statistics, brochures/pamphlets, clipping services, placement on mailing list, photos and press kits.
How to Contact: Write or call.

Rockingham Park, Rt. 28, Salem NH 03079. (603)898-2311. Director of Publicity: Bruce A. Stearns.
Purpose: "Built in 1906, Rockingham Park is a horse-racing track which has conducted thoroughbred and harness racing over that period, and some auto racing thrown in for good measure during the 1920's." Information covers entertainment, history and sports.
Services: Offers aid in arranging interviews, statistics, brochures/pamphlets, information searches and press kits. Publications include yearly press guides.
How to Contact: Write or call.

Rockome Association of Commerce, Rt. 2, Arcola IL 61910. (217)268-4226. Public Relations Director: Leesa Willis.
Purpose: "Rockome Gardens is a 10-acre theme park, located in the heart of Illinois Amish country. Famous for its beautifully ornate rockwork and flower gardens, Rockome also offers a realistic look at frontier life in 19th- century Illinois. Surrounded by Amish farms and businesses, Rockome offers information on and some products of the Amish." Information covers agriculture, art, entertainment, food, history, nature, recreation and travel.
Services: Offers brochures/pamphlets, placement on mailing list, photos and press kits. "We have pamphlets and brochures concerning all of our activities and special events, including railsplitting days (spring); antique auto show; quilt show; German, bluegrass, old time fiddlers' and country western music festivals; children's days; broom corn festivities in Arcola (fall); and horse farming days (fall). We also have several stories available with background information on the gardens and the Amish. Press releases and kits are available."
How to Contact: Write or phone.
Tips: "No photography restrictions exist in the gardens or throughout the countryside. However, because of their religious convictions, the Amish prefer not to be photographed. Though they do not particularly mind being photographed at work, they do desire their facial features to be excluded from the picture. Most will find the Amish a very friendly sect, quite willing to discuss their way of life. Rather than having a battery of questions prepared, one will perhaps learn more by exhibiting a friendly conversational tone in interviews. This particular style will be more effective in our rural agricultural region."

Sea World of San Diego, 1720 S. Shores Rd., San Diego CA 92109. (714)222-6363. Public Relations Manager: Jackie O'Connor.
Purpose: An entertainment, education and research complex. Information covers nature and science.
Services: Offers aid in arranging interviews, placement on mailing list, photos and press kits. Publications include Sea World flyer.
How to Contact: Written request preferred. Allow as much lead time as possible.

Six Flags, Inc., 530 W. 6th St., Suite 800, Los Angles CA 90014. (213)680-2375. Director/Corporate Public Relations: Richard Tyler.
Purpose: "Six Flags owns/operates the following theme amusement parks: Six Flags Over Georgia (Atlanta), Six Flags Over Texas (Dallas/Fort Worth), Six Flags Over

Mid-America (St. Louis), Astroworld (Houston), and Six Flags Great Adventure (New Jersey). Six Flags also operates the Movieland Wax Museum (Southern California) and the Stars Hall of Fame (Orlando, Florida)." Information covers business, celebrities, entertainment, food, recreation and travel.
Services: Offers aid in arranging interviews, annual reports, biographies, statistics, brochures/pamphlets, photos, press kits and historical information on theme parks, amusement park rides and attractions.
How to Contact: Write or call.

Six Flags Over Georgia, Box 43187, Atlanta GA 30336. (404)948-9290. Contact: Debbie Lord.
Purpose: Theme park of Georgia history. Information covers entertainment, history, nature, recreation, science, landscape and architecture.
Services: Offers aid in arranging interviews, statistics, information searches, placement on mailing list and press kits. Publications include employee newsletters and a travel planner.
How to Contact: Call to arrange interviews. Contact one week in advance for complimentary ticket. Park open March to Thanksgiving, daily mid-May to Labor Day.

Six Flags Over Mid-America, Box 666, Eureka MO 63025. (314)938-5300. Public Relations Manager: Bob Kochan.
Purpose: "Six Flags Over Mid-America is a 200-acre theme park. It consists of six theme areas, representing the different flags that have flown over the Midwest. It contains more than 80 different rides, shows and attractions. The park is open from spring through fall." Information covers business, celebrities, entertainment, history, music, nature, recreation and travel.
Services: Offers aid in arranging interviews, brochures/pamphlets, placement on mailing list, photos and press kits (information on the park's operation, prices, attractions; feature stories on the theme park industry as it relates to Six Flags; and photos of the park).
How to Contact: Write or call. "We do not reveal information concerning marketing or research techniques, or operational procedures for the day-to-day running of particular facets of the park."

Six Flags Over Texas, Box 191, Arlington TX 76010. (817)461-1200. Public Relations Manager: Bruce Neal.
Purpose: Historical theme park. Information covers entertainment, history and recreation.
Services: Offers aid in arranging interviews, statistics, brochures/pamphlets, information searches, placement on mailing list, photos and press kits.
How to Contact: Write or call.

Sugarloaf/USA, Sugarloaf Mountain, Carrabassett Valley ME 04947. (207)237-2000. Director of Publicity: Chip Carey.
Purpose: "We specialize in ski vacations, ski instructions, and vacation real estate." Information covers business, economics, entertainment, food, how-to, recreation, self-help, sports and travel.
Services: Offers aid in arranging interviews, annual reports, brochures/pamphlets, clipping services, placement on mailing list, newsletters, photos and press kits. Publications include lodging guides, area brochures, and material about special deals and offers.
How to Contact: Write or call.

The Arts

Dance

American Ballet Theatre, 888 7th Ave., New York NY 10019. Press Director: Charles France.
Purpose: Ballet company. Information covers art (dance).
Services: Offers aid in arranging interviews, brochures/pamphlets, biographies, information searches and photos. Publications include a souvenir book.
How to Contact: Write. Charges for photos.

Boston Ballet Co., Inc., 19 Clarendon St., Boston MA 02116. (617)338-8034. Marketing Director: Mr. Murray.
Purpose: "We are a professional performing ballet and official ballet school. We are rated among the top ballet companies and schools of ballet professionals." Information covers art, business, celebrities, entertainment, how-to, music, recreation and ballet.
Services: Offers aid in arranging interviews, annual reports, biographies, brochures/pamphlets, statistics, clipping services, information searches, placement on mailing list, newsletter, photos and press kits.
How to Contact: Write.

Cincinnati Ballet Co., 1216 Central Pkwy., Cincinnati OH 45210. (513)621-5219. Marketing Assistant: Kim Wilson.
Purpose: "The Cincinnati Ballet Company, the only professional dance organization in the area, provides its patrons with an eclectic repertoire that reveals the range of talents within the company and illustrates the versatility of the act of dance itself." Information covers entertainment, repertoire, biographical and historical information.
Services: Offers aid in arranging interviews, biographies, statistics, brochures/pamphlets, placement on mailing list, newsletter, photos and press kits.
How to Contact: Write or call. "Due to the company's demanding work hours, all interviews should be arranged in advance."

Dance Theatre of Harlem, Inc., 466 W. 152nd St., New York NY 10031. (212)690-2800. Contact: Public Relations Director.
Purpose: "Dance Theatre of Harlem is a classical-based company. Arthur Mitchell, the founder, left the New York City Ballet Company to start the new group. The group has established a school to train their own dancers and has percussion and choral ensembles." Information covers art (dance) and music.
Services: Offers aid in arranging interviews, biographies, brochures/pamphlets, information searches, placement on mailing list, newsletter, photos and press kits. Publications include history of school and press material.
How to Contact: Write or call. Prefers written requests. Charges for copies of photos or photocopies of large quantities of material.

Dayton Ballet Co., 140 N. Main St., Dayton OH 45402. (513)222-3661. General Manager: Diane Dean.
Purpose: "To promote, foster and increase dance and theater arts knowledge and appreciation for the public by maintaining a Dayton-based company of professional quality to present performances, as well as lecture-demonstrations, in Dayton and the US." Information covers art, entertainment, recreation and dance.
Services: Offers biographies, statistics, brochures/pamphlets, placement on mailing list, newsletter, photos and press kits.
How to Contact: Write or call.

Cliff Keuter Dance Co., 330 Broome St., New York NY 10002. (212)966-5260. Director: Cliff Keuter.

Purpose: Information covers art and entertainment.
How to Contact: Write or call.

Martha Graham Dance Company, 316 E. 63rd St., New York NY 10021. Archivist: Bonnie Kleinberg.
Purpose: "Performing and organizing and training a performing group." Information covers art (dance) and music.
Services: Offers aid in arranging interviews, biographies, brochures/pamphlets, information searches, newsletter and photos. Publications include souvenir books and reviews.
How to Contact: Write or call. Charges for publications.

Jose Greco Foundation for Hispanic Dance, Inc., 866 United Nations Plaza, New York NY 10017. Artistic Director: Jose Greco.
Purpose: "To develop interest in hispanic dance in the US and the world through performances, workshops and clinics." Information covers art (dance), entertainment and music.
Services: Offers aid in arranging interviews, biographies, brochures/pamphlets, information searches, placement on mailing list, photos and press kits. Publications available.
How to Contact: Write or call. Prefers written requests, but will answer questions briefly by phone.

Houston Ballet, 615 Louisiana Ave., Houston TX 77002. (713)225-0275. Publicity Director: Rollin Bachman.
Purpose: "Houston Ballet Foundation (1954), which first performed in 1968, has 30 dancers and performs 36 weeks each year. It gives 45 performances in Houston." Information covers art (dance).
Services: Offers aid in arranging interviews, biographies, brochures/pamphlets, information searches, photos and press kits.
How to Contact: Write or call. Prefers written requests with time to gather the information, but will answer quick questions on the phone.

Joffrey Ballet, 130 W. 56th St., New York NY 10019. (212)265-7300. Press Assistant: Ken Marini.
Purpose: "We are the third largest ballet company in the country." Information covers art (dance), celebrities and music.
Services: Offers aid in arranging interviews, biographies, brochures/pamphlets, information searches, placement on mailing list, photos and press kits.
How to Contact: Write or call. Charges for copy of photos.

Lar Lubovitch Dance Company, 463 West St., New York NY 10014. (212)989-4953. Administrator: Jane Yockel.
Purpose: "Modern dance company." Information covers art (dance), celebrities, entertainment and music.
Services: Offers aid in arranging interviews, biographies, information searches, placement on mailing list, photos and press kits.
How to Contact: Write or call.

Los Angeles Ballet, 1320 S. Figuerelo St., Los Angeles CA 90015. (213)748-9975. Press and Public Relations Director: Dorathi Bock Peirre.
Purpose: "To support and make a fine ballet company, first all professional ballet company Los Angeles has had.
Services: Offers aid in arranging interviews, biographies, brochures/pamphlets, information searches, placement on mailing list, photos and press kits.
How to Contact: Write or call.

Multigravitational Aero Dance Group, c/o N.S.C., 414 W. 51st St., New York NY 10019. (212)265-1340.
Purpose: "A touring dance company that performs 'aerial structures.' " Information covers art.
Services: Offers aid in arranging interviews, biographies, brochures/pamphlets, information searches, placement on mailing list, photos and press kits.
How to Contact: Write or call.

Murray Louis Dance Company, 33 E. 18th St., New York NY 10003. (212)777-1120. General Manager: Anthony P. Micocci.
Purpose: "Established in 1953, the company has eight dancers doing modern dance. Music is varied (classic, jazz and popular)." Information covers art and music.
Services: Offers aid in arranging interviews, biographies, information searches, photos and press kits.
How to Contact: Write or call.

New York City Ballet, New York State Theatre, Lincoln Center, New York NY 10023. (212)877-4700. Public Relations Director: Leslie Bailey.
Purpose: "To have American dancers dancing American ballet. Our school was started in 1934 to train dancers." Information covers art (dance) and music.
Services: Offers biographies, brochures/pamphlets, clipping services, information searches, placement on mailing list, photos and press kits.
How to Contact: Write or call. Prefer written request for lengthy or involved information.

Nikolais Dance Theatre, 33 E. 18th St., New York NY 10003. (212)777-1120. Manager: William Bourne.
Purpose: "Established in 1948. The Nikolais Dance Theatre has 10 dancers." Information covers art (dance) and music.
Services: Offers aid in arranging interviews, biographies, information searches, photos and press kits.
How to Contact: Write or call.

Oakland Ballet Company, 2704 McArthur Blvd., Oakland CA 94602. (415)530-0447. Director of Public Relations: Doris Ober.
Purpose: "To bring art of ballet to the community." Information covers art (dance).
Services: Offers aid in arranging interviews, biographies, brochures/pamphlets, clipping services, information searches, placement on mailing list, newsletter, photos and press kits.
How to Contact: Write or call.

San Diego Ballet Company, 526 Market St., San Diego CA 92101. (714)239-4141. Public Relations Director: Carmen Rodriguez.
Purpose: "A professional dance company that employs 18 dancers year-round and includes at least two regular full-scale productions every season. This year those productions were The Nutcracker and Carmina Burana. We also do Swan Lake. In addition to the company, we have the SDB Association, which is a volunteer association that supports the company." Information covers art, entertainment and recreation.
Services: Offers brochures/pamphlets, newsletter, photos and press kits. Publications include season brochures, biographies and ballet history.
How to Contact: Write. "We need at least 2-3 weeks notice. We charge for photographs."

Music

Boston Symphony Orchestra, Inc., 301 Massachusetts Ave., Symphony Hall, Boston MA 02115. (617)266-1492. Director of Promotion: Peter Gelb.
Purpose: "The Boston Symphony Orchestra plays classical music September through April and May through July. The Boston Pops plays May through mid-July. Tanglewood is the summer home of the Boston Symphony Orchestra during July and August." Information covers art, celebrities, entertainment, history and music.
Services: Offers aid in arranging interviews, annual reports, bibliographies, biographies, statistics, brochures/pamphlets, clipping services, information searches, placement on mailing list, newsletter, photos and press kits.
How to Contact: Write.

Cincinnati Symphony Orchestra (CSO), 1241 Elm St., Cincinnati OH 45210. (513)621-1919. Director of Public Relations: Kenneth R. Miller.
Purpose: "The Cincinnati Symphony Orchestra (CSO), fifth oldest orchestra in the US, presents some 300 concerts annually—many at its historic, 100-year-old home, Music Hall." Information covers music.
Services: Offers aid in arranging interviews, statistics, brochures/pamphlets, placement on mailing list, photos and press kits.
How to Contact: Write or call.

Columbus Symphony Orchestra, 101 E. Town St., Columbus OH 43229. (614)224-5281. Director of Public Relations: Robert J. Moon.
Purpose: "We are an entertainment medium with programming ranging from symphonies to pops to opera. We also perform for student audiences in high schools and junior highs." Information covers music.
Services: Offers aid in arranging interviews, biographies, brochures/pamphlets, placement on mailing list and photos. Publications include programs, ticket brochures and fliers.
How to Contact: Write.

Kalamazoo Symphony Society, Inc., 426 S. Park St., Kalamazoo MI 49007. (616)349-7759. Publicity/Publications: Susan Magnuson.
Purpose: "To provide a cultural ambience to the community through music in addition to community service through summer park concerts. Our information covers many aspects of music."
Services: Offers brochures/pamphlets and newsletter. "We also provide an annual maintenance fund drive brochure and a season brochure."
How to Contact: Write.

Los Angeles Philharmonic Association, 135 N. Grand Ave., Los Angeles CA 90012. Director of Publicity and Promotion: Norma L. Flynn.
Purpose: "The Los Angeles Philharmonic Association is a symphony orchestra for Californian tours of symphonic music."
Services: Offers aid in arranging interviews, statistics, brochures/pamphlets and a press book.
How to Contact: Write. "We ask, that you get permission to do an article first and send copies when finished."

National Symphony Orchestra, John F. Kennedy Center for the Performing Arts, Washington DC 20566. Contact: Director of Public Relations.
Purpose: Established 48 years ago. Information covers celebrities and music.
Services: Offers aid in arranging interviews, bibliographies, biographies, brochures/pamphlets, clipping services and photos.
How to Contact: Write. Researchers "must be on assignment and must have an editor send information in writing."

New Orleans Philharmonic Symphony Orchestra, Suite 903, 203 Carondelet St., New Orleans LA 70130. (504)524-0404. Director, Public Relations and Advertising: Bette Moore.
Purpose: "Subscription series with guest artists and conductors, children's and young people's concert series, concerts tours through several states, convention and sports concerts, blanket concerts in stadiums, etc." Information covers entertainment, music and recreation.
Services: Offers aid in arranging interviews, biographies, brochures/pamphlets, placement on mailing list, newsletter, photos and press kits. Publications include programs for all concerts with annotated and copyrighted program notes by Arrand Parsons of the Chicago Symphony, fliers and posters.
How to Contact: Write or call. "If we are able to service the inquiry, we will be happy to do so."

New York Philharmonic Orchestra, Avery Fisher Hall, 65th St. and Broadway, New York NY 10023. (212)580-8700. Public Relations: Jack Murphy, Mary DeCamp.
Purpose: Concerts. Information covers celebrities, music and conductors.
Services: Offers aid in arranging interviews, annual reports, biographies, statistics, placement on mailing list, photos and press kits. Publications include promotional and fundraising material.
How to Contact: Write. Explain the intended use of the material requested.

Oklahoma Symphony Orchestra, 512 Civic Center Music Hall, Oklahoma City OK 73102. (405)232-4292. Contact: Public Relations Department.
Purpose: "To provide symphonic music to the city and state, educational programs for children and small-town concerts. Information covers art, celebrities, entertainment and music.
Services: Offers aid in arranging interviews, biographies, brochures/pamphlets, placement on mailing list, newsletter, photos and press kits.
How to Contact: Write or call.

Philadelphia Orchestra, 1420 Locust St., Philadelphia PA 19102. (215)893-1900. Director of Public Relations: Louis Hood.
Purpose: "To bring fine music to the public and to educate and maintain an orchestra in excellence." Information covers celebrities and music.
Services: Offers aid in arranging interviews, annual reports, biographies, statistics, brochures/pamphlets, placement on mailing list, newsletter, photos and press kits.
How to Contact: Write or call.

Rochester Philharmonic Orchestra, 20 Grove Place, Rochester NY 14605. (716)454-2620. Contact: Public Relations Director.
Purpose: "To provide the greater Rochester area with live symphonic music and other top-flight entertainment on a continuing basis." Information covers art, entertainment and music.
Services: Offers aid in arranging interviews, annual reports, biographies, brochures/pamphlets, placement on mailing list, newsletter, photos and press kits.
How to Contact: Write or call.

Savannah Symphony Society, Box 9505, Savannah GA 31412. (912)236-9536. General Manager: Ms. Sheridan Stricker.
Purpose: "The purpose of our organization is to bring music to our entire community, which we endeavor to do by having a subscription series of concerts (eight this year), eight free concerts in various locations, over 160 services to the school system (ensembles, lectures and full symphony), a youth orchestra, scholarships for young musicians, concerts for senior citizens and chamber music concerts." Information covers art, business, celebrities, entertainment and music.

Services: Offers brochures/pamphlets. Publications include subscription series brochure and maintenance fund pamphlet.
How to Contact: Write or call.

The Wheeling Symphony Society, Inc., 51 16th St., Room 102, Wheeling WV 26003. (304)232-6191. Contact: Public Relations Director.
Purpose: "To provide cultural activities for the upper Ohio valley. We sponsor a resident string quartet, children's concerts, a summer music series, winter subscription concerts and tour concerts. We are active in a school string program and present a contemporary arts festival. Brochures areavailable on most of these. Brochures contain schedules, prices, etc." Information covers entertainment and music.
Services: Offers brochures/pamphlets. Publications include a 50th anniversary commemorative booklet.
How to Contact: Write or call.

Opera

Charlotte Opera Association, 110 E. 7th St., Charlotte NC 28202. (704)332-7177. Director of Promotions: Paula Almond.
Purpose: "The Charlotte Opera Association (COA) produces and promotes opera. We have three basic programs: performance in Charlotte, opera-in-schools and a statewide tour. We have the capability of building sets, selling current sets, and co-production. Information covers our season, our history, our current programs, technical data, art, entertainment, music and technical data."
Services: Offers annual reports, brochures/pamphlets, placement on mailing list, newsletter, photos and performance schedules.
How to Contact: Write or call. "We ask for reimbursement for costs only."

Lyric Opera of Chicago, 20 N. Wacker Dr., Chicago IL 60606. (312)346-6111. Publicity Director: Danny Newan.
Purpose: Information covers art (opera), celebrities and music.
Services: Offers biographies, statistics, brochures/pamphlets, placement on mailing list, newsletter, photos and press kits.
How to Contact: Written request preferred. May charge for some photos.

Metropolitan Opera Association, Lincoln Center, New York NY 10023. Director of Press and Public Relations: David Reuben.
Purpose: "Opera company."
Services: Offers aid in arranging interviews, annual reports, bibliographies, biographies, information searches, placement on mailing list, photos and press kits.
How to Contact: Write or call. "The writer should have his editor write that he is on assignment for a specific topic, giving us time to set up the necessary arrangements. This is the only way we handle freelance writers."

Minnesota Opera Company, 850 Grand Ave., St. Paul MN 55105. (612)221-0122. Public Relations Director: Liz Beatty.
Purpose: "The Minnesota Opera Company is a fulltime, professional opera company dedicated to the production and performance of high quality music/theater entertainment. Special emphasis is placed on the performance of contemporary American operas, many of which are commissioned by the company and performed as world premieres. All operas are sung in English with equal attention given to the theatrical and musical elements. The company offers a nine month training program for singers and tours throughout the Midwest." Information covers music and theater.
Services: Offers aid in arranging interviews, biographies, statistics, brochures/pamphlets, placement on mailing list, photos and program magazines from past productions. Publications include season brochures from any of the company's recent seasons and fundraising brochure.

How to Contact: Write, call or visit. There may be a small charge for production photographs (color or b&w).

Nevada Opera Guild, Box 3256, Reno NV 89505. (702)786-4046. Artistic Director: Ted Puffer.
Purpose: "Production of professional opera with a nationally known company and cast. The Nevada Opera Guild is a member of Opera America." Information covers art, entertainment, music and recreation.
Services: Offers brochures/pamphlets.
How to Contact: Write or call.

New York Grand Opera, 270 W. 89th St., New York NY 10024. Director: Vincent LaSelva.
Purpose: "We perform in New York and perform only known works. We've performed in Central Park free for the last 6 summers." Information covers art (operas performed), history of New York opera and music.
Services: Offers aid in arranging interviews, biographies, brochures/pamphlets, statistics, information searches (only newspapers) and photos.
How to Contact: Write. "We will judge each request on its own merit."

Opera Company of Philadelphia, 1518 Walnut St., Suite 310, Philadelphia PA 19102. Director of Public Relations: Jane Nemeth.
Purpose: "Opera Company performing all year."
Services: Offers aid in arranging interviews, biographies, brochures/pamphlets, clipping services, placement on mailing list, and photos.
How to Contact: Write or call. Charges for copy of photos or specific services. Writer should contact early for specific information, but will answer brief questions on the phone.

San Francisco Opera Association, War Memorial Opera House, San Francisco CA 94102. (415)861-4008. Director of Public Relations: Herbert Sholder.
Purpose: Information covers art (opera), celebrities (singers) and music.
Services: Offers aid in arranging interviews, annual reports, biographies, statistics, brochures/pamphlets, placement on mailing list and photos. Publications include pamphlets about opera companies and the opera season.
How to Contact: Write or call. "Photo fee depends on who is asking for it and what it is to be used for." Written requests preferred.

The Santa Fe Opera, Box 2408, Santa Fe NM 87501. (505)982-3851. Public Relations Director: Saba McWilliams.
Purpose: "The Santa Fe Opera is a major opera company in the US. We have pioneered in both encouraging American young artists and premiering new works." Information covers art, celebrities, entertainment, history, music, nature, new products, self-help and technical data.
Services: Offers aid in arranging interviews, bibliographies, biographies, statistics, brochures/pamphlets, clipping services, information searches, placement on mailing list, photos and press kits.
How to Contact: Write. "During our season (June 30 through Aug. 25) conditions are too chaotic to be of great assistance in research."

The Washington Opera, Kennedy Center, Washington DC 20007. (202)223-4757. Director of Development and Public Relations: John R. Wilson.
Purpose: "To produce good opera. Through our guild, we issue *The Washington Opera Magazine.*"
How to Contact: Write or call.

Automobile

American Motors Corp., 27777 Franklin Rd., Southfield MI 48034. Press Relation Manager: Mr. Pichurski.
Purpose: "We manufacture passenger cars and jeep vehicles." Information covers business, economics, history, industry, new products, recreation and technical data.
Services: Offers aid in arranging interviews, annual reports, biographies, brochures/ pamphlets, information searches, placement on mailing list, photos and press kits.
How to Contact: Write.

Chrysler Corp., Box 1919, Detroit MI 48288. (313)956-5741. Contact: News Relations.
Purpose: "We develop, produce and market passenger cars, trucks, boats, outboards and military products, and are the largest Chrysler job-training program under government contract." Information covers business, how-to, industry, new products, recreation, science, self-help, technical data and travel.
Services: Offers aid in arranging interviews, annual reports, biographies, brochures/ pamphlets, information searches, placement on mailing list, statistics, photos and press kits.
How to Contact: Write. "We will try to answer anything related to Chrysler Corporation."

Ford Motor Co., The American Road, Dearborn MI 48121. (313)322-9600. Manager, Corporate News Department: J.W. Harris.
Purpose: "Financial reporting, executive changes, speeches, corporate (not product) legal matters, energy management, and personnel and labor issues." Information covers business (automotive only).
Services: Offers aid in arranging interviews, annual reports, biographies, brochures/ pamphlets, statistics and photos. Publications available.
How to Contact: Write or call. "We are not a research agency and can offer only what we have in stock or is available by interview. Photos are limited to our files, but we will occasionally fill special requests. We welcome the opportunity to explain our businesses. Give us your telephone numbers, the use for which the information is being sought and a reasonable time to respond. Also, we do not have time or staff to write term papers."

General Motors, 3044 W. Grand Blvd., Detroit MI 48202. (313)556-2027. Director of News Relations: Clifford D. Merriott.
Purpose: "We are engaged in the manufacture, assembly and distribution of various motor-driven products. Automotive products include passenger cars, trucks, coaches, major automotive components and parts and accessories. Nonautomotive products include diesel engines and locomotives and off-highway earthmoving equipment."
Services: Offers aid in arranging interviews, annual reports, biographies, statistics, brochures/pamphlets, placement on mailing list, photos and press kits.
How to Contact: Write or call.

Volkswagen, 818 Sylvan Ave., Englewood Cliffs NJ 07632. (201)894-6310. Director of Public Relations: Baron K. Bates.
Purpose: "Importation and sale of Volkswagen, Porsche and Audi vehicles; and parts and accessories."
Services: Offers aid in arranging interviews, annual reports, biographies, statistics, brochures/pamphlets, photos and press kits. Publications available.
How to Contact: Write or call. "We do not have information in-depth on research and development, which is located in Germany."

Broadcasting

American Broadcasting Co., Inc. (ABC), 1330 Avenue of the Americas, New York NY 10019.

Bonneville International Corp./WRFM Radio, 485 Madison Ave., New York NY 10022. (212)752-3322. Special Assistant to the President: Mark Bench.
Purpose: "Covers Latin American involvement in radio and television, representing US broadcasters to the Inter-American Association of Broadcasters; consultants to UNESCO on communications policies, etc." Information covers entertainment, music and communications.
Services: Offers statistics. Publications include *Doctrine for Public Broadcasting in the Americas, Statement of Ethics for Broadcasters throughout the Americas* and *Bases for Legislation throughout the Americas.*
How to Contact: Write.

Columbia Broadcasting System (CBS) Radio, 51 W. 52nd St., New York NY 10019. (212)975-4321. Manager, Radio Press Information: Robert A. Fuller.
Purpose: "Columbia Broadcasting System Radio is a network radio station." Information covers news, sports and dramatic productions.
Services: Offers aid in arranging interviews, statistics, placement on mailing list and press kits.
How to Contact: Write or call.

Columbia Broadcasting System (CBS) Television, 51 W. 52nd St., New York NY 10019.

Home Box Office, Inc., Time & Life Bldg., Rockefeller Center, New York NY 10020. (212)841-4461. Public Relations Director: Robbin Ahrold.
Purpose: "We are the nation's largest pay television network, serving over 700 cable affiliates in 50 states with approximately two million American homes subscribing to the service. Home Box Office provides a fully-formatted package of unedited, uncut theatrical movies, sports and specials, most of the latter produced exclusively for Home Box Office. We provide advertising, marketing, technical and administrative support to affiliated systems. The Home Box Office is primarily delivered via satellite." Information covers celebrities, entertainment, new products and technical data.
Services: Offers aid in arranging interviews, bibliographies, statistics, brochures/pamphlets, photos and press kits.
How to Contact: Write or call.

KGU Radio, 605 Kapiolani Blvd., Honolulu HI 96813. (808)536-3626. Promotion Director: Margot D. Samuels.
Purpose: Radio station. Information covers business, celebrities, entertainment, politics and sports.
Services: Offers aid in arranging interviews, newsletter and radio interviews and features.
How to Contact: Call or write.

Metromedia, Inc., 1 Harmon Plaza, Secaucus NJ 07094. (201)348-3244. Public Relations Director: Tom Reed.
Purpose: "Metromedia is the nation's largest group television and radio broadcaster and out-of-home advertising company." Affiliated touring groups include the Ice Capades, Inc. and the Harlem Globetrotters, Inc. Information covers business, celebrities, entertainment, recreation, sports, advertising and broadcasting.
Services: Offers annual reports, statistics, placement on mailing list, photos and press releases.
How to Contact: Write or call.

National Broadcasting Co. (NBC), 30 Rockefeller Plaza, New York NY 10020.

Public Broadcasting Service, 475 L'Enfant Plaza SW, Washington DC 20004.

Radio Free Europe/Radio Liberty, Inc. (RFE/RL), 1201 Connecticut Ave. NW, Washington DC 20036. (202)457-6915. Vice President and Secretary of the Corporation: Nathan Kingsley.
Purpose: "Radio Free Europe/Radio Liberty, Inc. (RFE/RL) is a nonprofit, private corporation, funded by congressional appropriations, broadcasting news and information in 22 languages to Eastern Europe and the Soviet Union." Information covers East European and Soviet affairs.
Services: Offers research subscription program. Publications include research reports.
How to Contact: Write.

RKO Radio, 6255 Sunset Blvd., Los Angeles CA 90028. (213)462-6255. Vice President: Harvey Mednick.
Purpose: "We own and operate 12 radio stations in six different formats in nine key cities in the US. We also own a tape duplication service and provide special programming for stations around the world. We represent, through our sales firm, 17 additional stations." Information covers entertainment, industry and technical data.
Services: Offers material on "contemporary radio philosophy, state of the broadcast industry, and developments within the art."
How to Contact: Write or call. "In rare cases, a consulting fee might be charged; it all depends mainly on the situation and the usage of the information."

Westinghouse Broadcasting Co., Inc., 90 Park Ave., New York NY 10016.

Builders & Building Manufacturers

American Standard Homes Corp., 700 Commerce Ct., Box 4908, Martinsville VA 24112. (703)638-3991. Public Relations Director: Sam B. Weddle.
Purpose: "We manufacture preassembled homes and spaces in six areas: small two-bedroom homes; econo-line two- and three-bedroom homes; two-, three- and four-bedroom homes; vacation and second homes; commercial line-office, restaurants, motels, clinics, etc.; and multifamily housing, duplexes, condominiums, townhouses and apartments. A seventh area of our production would be in our ease at working with 'specials'—in other words, our availability to work, design and manufacture some home outside of our standard line."
Services: Offers brochures/pamphlets and newsletter.
How to Contact: "Write, call or arrange for an office visit and tour of our manufacturing plant."

Cardinal Industries, 2040 S. Hamilton, Columbus OH 43227. (614)861-3211. Director of Public Relations: Jeff Thompson.
Purpose: "The nation's largest manufacturer of multifamily dwellings and motels in the United States. The firm also constructs and mamages all aspects regarding the construction of their apartment or motel projects." Information covers business, economics, industry, new products, technical data and manufactured housing.
Services: Offers aid in arranging interviews, annual reports, brochures/pamphlets, placement on mailing list, statistics, newsletter, photos and press kits.
How to Contact: Write or call.

Champion Home Builders Co., 5573 North St., Dryden MI 48428. (313)796-2211. Director of Public Relations: Gerald T. Kennedy.
Purpose: "Manufacturer and wholesaler of mobile homes, sectional homes, motor homes, pick-up campers and van conversions. We have 48 plants coast-to-coast."

Information covers industry and new products.
Services: Offers aid in arranging interviews, annual reports, brochures/pamphlets, placement on mailing list, statistics, photos and press kits.
How to Contact: Write or call.

US Home Corp., 1 Countryside Office Park, Clearwater FL 33519. (813)736-7111. Contact: Investor Relations Department.
Purpose: "US Home Corporation is an on-site manufacturer of homes." Information covers business and industry.
Services: Offers annual reports, bibliographies, biographies, statistics, brochures/pamphlets, placement on mailing list, newsletter, photos and press kits.
How to Contact: Write.

Chemicals

Allied Chemical Corp., Box 225 R, Morristown NJ 07960. Contact: Corporation Information Services.
Purpose: Manufacturer of chemicals, energy, fibers and fabricated products. Information covers chemicals, corporation headquarters operations and highly technical and scientific papers.
Services: Offers annual reports and corporate brochure.
How to Contact: Write.

American Cyanamid Co., Berdan Ave., Wayne NJ 07470. (201)831-1234. Director of Press Relations and Public Affairs: Jean Monaghan.
Purpose: "Manufacturer of chemicals. We produce speciality chemical pharmaceuticals and consumer products—personal care products, household cleaners and formica laminates." Information covers agriculture, business, economics, health/medicine, industry, new products, science, self-help and technical data.
Services: Offers aid in arranging interviews, annual reports, bibliographies, biographies, statistics, brochures/pamphlets, information searches, placement on mailing list and press kits.
How to Contact: Write.

CIBA-GEIGY Corp., 444 Saw Mill River Rd., Ardsley NY 10502. (914)478-3131. Senior Communications Specialist: Charles T. Keene.
Purpose: "We are a diversified chemical company engaged principally in the discovery, development, manufacture and marketing of a wide variety of special-purpose chemicals and chemical products throughout the United States." Information covers business, industry, new products and technical data.
Services: Offers aid in arranging interviews, annual reports, biographies, brochures/pamphlets, statistics, photos, and press kits. Publications available.
How to Contact: Write or call.

The Dow Chemical Co., 2030 Dow Center, Midland MI 48640. (517)636-0527. Communications Director: Mr. McKeller.
Purpose: Manufacturer of chemicals, plastics and agricultural products. Information covers agriculture, food, health/medicine, industry, new products, science and technical data.
Services: Offers aid in arranging interviews, annual reports, statistics, brochures/pamphlets, information searches, placement on mailing list, newsletter, photos and press kits. Publications include an extensive library of product literature.
How to Contact: Write.

Dynapol, c/o Simon/Public Relations, 11661 San Vicente, Los Angeles CA 90049. (213)820-2606. Executive Vice President: Joe Radoff.

Purpose: "A company researching new types of food additives that are not absorbed by the human body. Products, which involve the bonding of a large polymer to a small molecule, must be approved by the Food and Drug Administration." Information covers agriculture, business, food, health/medicine, new products and science.
Services: Offers aid in arranging interviews, brochures/pamphlets, placement on mailing list and photos.
How to Contact: Write or call.

W.R. Grace & Co., 1114 Avenue of the Americas, New York NY 10036. (212)764-6022. Manager, Press Elations: Fred Bona. Press Relations Representative: Mark Baxter.
Purpose: "An international chemical company with related natural resource activities and consumer services." Information covers agriculture, business, economics, industry, science, sports, technical data, chemicals and natural resources.
Services: Offers aid in arranging interviews, annual reports, biographies, brochures/pamphlets, placement on mailing list, photos and press kits.
How to Contact: Write.

M&T Chemicals, Inc., Woodbridge Ave., Rahway NJ 07065. (201)499-0200. Director, Advertising and Public Relations: John Porpora.
Purpose: "M&T Chemicals is a specialty chemical corporation. We are the world's leading producer of plating chemicals and processes. In addition we supply coatings and inks for packaging and industrial applications. We are basic in organotin chemicals as well as plastics, adhesives and chemicals for the aircraft and electronics industries." Information covers business, industry, science, technical data and chemicals.
Services: Offers aid in arranging interviews, annual reports, bibliographies, brochures/pamphlets, placement on mailing list and photos. "We offer information on any of our products and their application/use, case histories, ad reprints, slide presentations and etc. Most of our literature is technical and pertinent to industrial users only."
How to Contact: "All contact should be made through the director of advertising either by phone or mail. Any information written about our company or products must be reviewed by M&T for general content and technical accuracy prior to publication. It would be most helpful if the writer has developed an outline or theme for his article."
Tips: "We strongly recommend personal interviews and visits with our personnel whenever possible. M&T has fully cooperated in the development of stories and technical articles whenever we can offer information or expertise in the many markets we serve."

Monsanto Co., 1114 Avenue of the Americas, New York NY 10036. Eastern Public Relations Director: Philip P. Fried.
Purpose: "The 43rd largest company in the US and the third largest chemical company." Information covers agriculture, business, economics, food, health/medicine, industry, new products, science and technical data.
Services: Offers aid in arranging interviews, annual reports, bibliographies, biographies, statistics, brochures/pamphlets, placement on mailing list, newsletter, photos and press kits. Publications include *Chemical Facts of Life*, *Chemical Facts of Life Bulletin* and *Monsanto Public Affairs Bulletin*.
How to Contact: Write.

MortonNorwich, 110 N. Wacker Dr., Chicago IL 60606. (312)621-5419. Director of Communications: Carson B. Trenor. Communications Coordinator: Patricia St. Clair.
Purpose: "MortonNorwich is a Chicago-based company manufacturing and selling salt, pharmaceutical, household, and specialty chemical products throughout the world." Information covers health/medicine.
Services: Offers annual reports, biographies and placement on mailing list.
How to Contact: Write or call.

Diversified Products

American Can Co., American Lane, Greenwich CT 06830. (203)552-2000. Public Relations Department: Bryan Martin.
Purpose: "Diversified packaging from frigid containers to flexible plastics. Consumer products—dixie cups, paper towels, tissues, records and tapes. Resource recovery—alum and steel recycling and chemicals from wood pulping process." Information covers business, economics, entertainment, how-to, industry, music, new products, self-help and technical data.
Services: Offers aid in arranging interviews, annual reports, bibliographies, biographies, statistics, brochures/pamphlets, information searches, placement on mailing list, newsletter, photos and press kits.
How to Contact: Write.

Armco Steel Corp., General Office, Middletown OH 45043. (513)425-5646. Media Relations: Robert W. Hawk.
Purpose: "We are a highly diversified steel company." Information covers agriculture, business, health/medicine, history, industry, new products and environment.
Services: Offers annual reports, biographies, brochures/pamphlets, photos and press kits.
How to Contact: Write. "Please give plenty of lead time for request."

DuPont, E. L. De Nemours and Co., 1007 Market St., Wilmington DE 19898. (302)774-1000. National and Financial Press Representative: Clint Archer.
Purpose: "We are a manufacturer of chemicals and allied products. We also do research and development in all areas." Information covers agriculture, graphic art, business, food, health/medicine/pharmaceticals, how-to, industry, science, sports (raw material supplied to sporting goods industry), technical data and instruments.
Services: Offers aid in arranging interviews, annual reports, bibliographies, brochures/pamphlets, statistics, information searches, placement on mailing list and photos. Publications available.
How to Contact: Write. Charges for photocopies and reproduction. "Research should be done at Wilmington, but if research is mailed, there is a fee."

Esmark Inc., 55 E. Monroe St., Chicago IL 60603. Director of Public Relations: A. Michael Finn.
Purpose: "Esmark is a holding company with major interests in foods, chemicals and industrial products, energy, personal products and automotive products. It owns Swift & Company; Estec, Inc.; Bickers Energy Corporation; International Playtex, Inc.; STP Corporation; and Pemcor, Inc." Information covers food, new products, technical data and anything related to any of the companies.
Services: Offers aid in arranging interviews, annual reports, biographies, photos and press kits.
How to Contact: Write or call.

Ex-Cell-O Corp., Troy MI 48084. (313)649-1000. Manager, Press Relations: C. E. Westberg.
Purpose: "We manufacture machinery and products in the metalworking, packaging, aerospace and agricultural markets. We are the suppliers of components to the automotive industries and we also manufacture some ordnance products." Information covers agriculture, business, industry, new products and technical data.
Services: Offers aid in arranging interviews, annual reports, biographies, brochures/pamphlets, placement on mailing list, newsletter, photos and press kits. Publications include annual reports, biographies of personnel, directory of products and services, capabilities brochures, specific product literature and press releases on most products and lines.

How to Contact: Write or call with specific requests. "We will respond freely to requests for information on products and services, etc. We do not have staff capabilities to respond to elaborate requests for information on research papers, doctoral theses, etc."

Ford Motor Co., Diversified Products Operations, Public Relations Office, World Headquarters Bldg., Dearborn MI 48121. (313)323-4308. Public Relations Service Manager: Michael W.R. Davis. Technical Information Specialist: James A. Allen. Director: Richard W. Judy.

Purpose: "Diversified Products Operation is the nonautomotive part of the Ford Motor Company. Its worldwide operations include steel; castings; plastics; paint; vinyl; automotive, architectural and mirror glass; automotive radiators and air conditioning components; electrical and electronic components; farm and industrial tractors and equipment; and aerospace and communications equipment (weather and communications satellites, command and control systems, and missile defense systems)." Information covers history, industry, new products and technical data.

Services: Offers aid in arranging interviews, annual reports, brochures/pamphlets, photos and press kits. Publications include a general descriptive brochure and brochures on glass, steel, casting, plastics and automotive electronics. "Photos are limited generally to what we have in our files, but we are willing to shoot if the opportunity warrants. We welcome inquiries and the opportunity to explain our business."

How to Contact: Write or call. "It would be helpful if writers provided their telephone numbers, the use for which the information is being sought (i.e., article in such-and-such publication), and a reasonable time to respond. We do not have time or staff to write term papers!"

GAF Corp., 140 W. 51st St., New York NY 10017. (212)582-7600. Manager of Public Relations: R.G. Button.

Purpose: "GAF is nation's leading producer of asphalt roofing; it also produces flooring, siding, insulation, chemicals, specialty black & white films for such uses as x-ray and graphic arts, office reprographic equipment and papers." Information covers new products and technical data.

Services: Offers aid in arranging interviews, annual reports, brochures/pamphlets, photos and press kits. Public Relations materials available are mostly press releases and related fact sheets about company and its products. 35mm transparancies available from Pictorial Products Division. These are from GAF's Pana-Vue collection and involve fees for commercial uses.

How to Contact: Write. "Allow plenty of time, indicate your deadline, and ask specific questions."

Tips: "Know something about the company before writing. Get general industry information from industry associations and government agencies. Public relations departments are not equipped to perform research for nonmedia researchers, such as college students, etc."

The Group, Inc., 633 3rd Ave., New York NY 10017. (212)551-7000. Contact: Corporate Communications.

Purpose: "We have five operations: Continental Can (rigid and composite containers); Continental Forest Industry (all packaging of paper and craft products); Continental Financial Services (insurance—life, title and casualty); Continental Plastics (all variety of containers); and Continental Diversified Operations (meat casings, vacuum closures and automotive parts)." Information covers business, economics, food, health/medicine, industry, nature, new produtcs, science and technical data.

Services: Offers aid in arranging interviews, annual reports, biographies, brochures/pamphlets, statistics, placement on mailing list, information searches, newsletter and photos. Publications available.

How to Contact: Write. "We try to respond to all inquiries."

Gulf and Western, 1 Gulf and Western Plaza, New York NY 10023. (212)333-2816, 333-2817. Assistant Vice President, Corporate Communications: William A. Blodgett.
Purpose: "Gulf and Western operates in the following areas: manufacturing; natural resources; automotive replacement parts; leisure-time products; consumer and agricultural products; financial services; apparel products; and paper and building products."
Services: Offers annual reports, biographies, statistics, brochures/pamphlets, information searches, photos and press kits.
How to Contact: Write or call. "Information services are offered to writers on assignment."

International Telephone and Telegraph, 320 Park Ave., New York NY 10022. Public Information: David Varner.
Purpose: "We have five areas of business: telecommunications and electronics, consumber products and services, insurance and finance, engineered products and natural resources." Information covers business, economics, new products and technical data.
Services: Offers annual reports, brochures/pamphlets, statistics, photos and press kits.
How to Contact: Write or call. "We prefer written requests."

Litton Industries, 360 N. Crescent Dr., Beverly Hills CA 90210. (213)273-7860; (800)421-0768 (toll free). Director, Advertising and Public Relations: C.V. Meconis.
Purpose: "Litton Industries is engaged in approximately 80 different kinds of businesses: electronics, geophysical exploration, medical and dental products, machine tools, inertial navigation, military command and control systems, specialty paper, microwave ovens, educational publishing and shipbuilding."
Services: Offers annual reports, bibliographies, biographies, statistics, brochures/pamphlets, clipping services, information searches, placement on mailing list and photos. Publications include reprints and directories.
How to Contact: Write or call C.V. Meconis or one of the following persons: Bob Knapp, Suite 8206, 490 L'Enfant Plaza, Washington DC 20024, (202)554-2570; Ray Noble, 201 E. 42nd St., New York NY 10017, (212)661-1111; or Bob Sohngen, 111 E. Wacker, Chicago IL 60601, (312)664-4558. "We have been especially useful to writers polling a number of companies on some peg or symposium line, since our experience is so wide-ranging."

Mobil Corp., 150 E. 42nd St., New York NY 10017. (212)883-4408. Press Relations Coordinator: John Flint.
Purpose: "We are one of the four largest companies in the United States with gross assets of over $34 billion net income in 1977. Mobil Corporation (formed July 1, 1976) owns Mobil Oil Corp. (including worldwide energy interests and growth oriented chemical interests), Montgomery Ward (one of the largest retailers) and Container Corp. of America (the leading United States manufacture of paperboard packaging)." Information covers business, new products and technical data on Mobil Oil only.
Services: Offers aid in arranging interviews (Mobil Oil only), annual reports (all companies), brochures/pamphlets (Mobil Oil only), statistics (all companies) and press kits.
How to Contact: Write.

The Procter and Gamble Co., 301 E. 6th St., Cincinnati OH 45201. (513)562-1100. Public Relations Director: P.S. Bacon.
Purpose: "Procter and Gamble is the leading manufacturer of household and industrial cleaning products, food, health and beauty aids and paper products." Information covers business, food, health/medicine, how-to and new products.
Services: Offers aid in arranging interviews, annual reports, brochures/pamphlets, photos and press kits.
How to Contact: Write or call. "A written request is preferable."

R.J. Reynolds Industries, Inc., RJR World Headquarters, Winston-Salem NC 27102. (919)748-2861. Public Relations Representative: John Ross.
Purpose: "R.J. Reynolds Industries (RJR) is a diversified, multinational firm involved in tobacco, foods and beverages, energy, shipping, packaging, flavoring and fragrances, and conducting business in more than 140 nations. Sales and revenues were $6.36 billion in 1977 or 41st on the *Fortune* 500 list. The firm has some 37,000 employees worldwide. RJR corporate public relations offers annual and quarterly financial reports covering the whole corporation, as well as capabilities booklets covering each subsidiary. Also available is information on unique corporate programs in health and dental care, pastoral counseling, alcoholism, art, minority affairs, rodeo and auto racing." Information covers art, business, economics, food, health/medicine, how-to, industry, new products, science, self-help and sports.
Services: Offers aid in arranging interviews, annual reports, biographies, brochures/pamphlets, placement on mailing list, photos and press kits. Publications include an annual report, a quarterly report, "capabilities booklets" on all subsidiaries; facts about smoking and health, *RJR Corporate Social Responsibility Report* (minority affairs, art, educational and community support work, etc.), booklets on prepaid employee health care and dental care centers, RJR Foods recipe and party booklets, and booklets on company building programs.
How to Contact: Write or call. "Due to the technical nature of the subjects, we prefer review opportunities regarding pieces on health and dental care programs, pastoral counseling, alcoholism programs and building programs."
Tips: "We are experienced in working with all levels of public and trade media and emphasize meeting editorial and technical requirements and providing up-to-date, accurate, fact-laden material that the media and their target publics will find useful."

Rockwell International Corp., 600 Grant St., Pittsburgh PA. 15219. (412)565-7177. Contact: Communications Department.
Purpose: "Rockwell International Corporation is a major international corporation applying advanced technology to a wide range of products." Information covers business, economics, health/medicine, history, how-to, industry, new products, science, technical data, electronics and automotive power tools.
Services: Offers aid in arranging interviews, annual reports, bibliographies, biographies, statistics, brochures/pamphlets, information searches, placement on mailing list, photos and press kits.
How to Contact: Write or call.

The Signal Companies, 9665 Wilshire Blvd., Beverly Hills CA 90212. (213)278-7400. Vice President, Public Relations: John W. Bold.
Purpose: "The Signal Companies, Inc., is a conglomerate operating in several industries with strong, strategic positions in the transportation, aerospace and energy service industries. Major units include Mack Trucks, Inc.; UPO Inc.; the Garrett Corporation. Sales for 1978 are $3.5 billion."
Services: Offers aid in arranging interviews, annual reports, biographies, statistics, brochures/pamphlets, information searches, placement on mailing list, newsletter, photos and press kits.
How to Contact: Write or call.

Sperry Rand Corp., 1290 Avenue of the Americas, New York NY 10019. (212)956-2027. Manager Corporate News Services: Terry Souers.
Purpose: "We are a worldwide industrial enterprise with over $4 billion in revenues and major interests in computer systems, farm and industry equipment, fluid power components, and aircraft and marine guidance and control systems." Information covers business, economics, industry and technical data.
Services: Offers aid in arranging interviews, annual reports, brochures/pamphlets, placement on mailing list, statistics, photos and press kits.
How to Contact: Write or call. "We prefer written requests."

Tenneco, Inc., Box 2511, Houston TX 77001. (713)757-3430. Director of Public Relations: George O. Jackson.
Purpose: "We are the corporate public relations office for Tenneco, Inc., a diversified company with major business interests in oil, natural gas pipelines, construction and farm equipment, automotive components, chemicals, shipbuilding, packaging and agriculture/land management."
Services: Offers aid in arranging interviews, annual reports, biographies, statistics, brochures/pamphlets, placement on mailing list and photos.
How to Contact: Write or call.

3M Co., Public Relations Service Center, 3M Center 224-4SW St., Paul MN 55101. (612)733-9504. Public Relations Supervisor, Information Resources: Ms. D.E. Follmer.
Purpose: Has information on "some 50 major product lines in 17 basic technologies; also selected information on such 'social' issues as energy conservation, pollution control, the role of multinational corporations, etc." Information covers agriculture, art, business, economics, health/medicine, how-to, industry, recreation, science and technical data.
Services: Offers aid in arranging interviews, annual reports, biographies, brochures/pamphlets, placement on mailing list, newsletter, photos, press kits, speech reprints and positon papers. Publications available.
How to Contact: Write or call. "Some 3M publications involve a nominal charge."
Tips: "Questions should be reasonably specific. Staff limitations require that initial response will usually be with existing 3M materials. The PR information center does not offer individual research or reference services. Indicate intended use of material and specific media, if possible."

TRW, Inc., 23555 Euclid Ave., Cleveland OH 44117. (216)383-2332. Director, Public Relations: M. J. Jablonski.
Purpose: "Cleveland-headquartered TRW is a major industrial supplier of high-technology products and services for the electronics and space systems, car and truck, and industrial and energy markets."
Services: Offers aid in arranging interviews, annual reports, biographies, brochures/pamphlets, statistics, information searches, placement on mailing list, photos and press kits.
How to Contact: Write or call.

Trans World Corp., 605 3rd Ave., New York NY 10016. (212)557-6107. Vice President, Communications: Jerry Cosley.
Purpose: "Trans-World Corporation subsidiaries include Trans World Airlines, Canteen Corporation and Hilton International." Information covers business, economics. food and travel.
Services: Offers annual reports, statistics, brochures/pamphlets, placement on mailing list and press kits.
How to Contact: Write for a list of regional offices, then write the appropriate office.

Union Camp Corp., 1600 Valley Rd., Wayne NJ 07470. (201)628-9000. Assistant Director of Public Relations: Thomas C. Hunter.
Purpose: "Union Camp's major national resource base is 1.7 million acres of woodlands in the Southeast. Its activities—concentrated in the eastern third of the United States but extending to Colorado and Texas with sales activity on the West Coast—include paper manufacture, bagging, school supplies and stationery, printing papers, building products, chemicals, minerals exploration and mining, development of residential communities, and the retailing of building products and home improvement materials." Information covers business, industry, new product information, environmental protection and woodlands management.
Services: Offers aid in arranging interviews, annual reports, biographies, brochures/pamphlets, placement on mailing list, newsletter, photos and press kits.

How to Contact: Write or call. Prefers to work with writers on assignment.

Whittaker Corp., 10880 Wilshire Blvd., Los Angeles CA 90024. Corporate Communications Director: Robert W. Murray.
Purpose: "Whittaker is a publicly held corporation with business activities in the metals, technology, marine, life sciences and chemicals fields. The company is listed on the New York Stock Exchange." Information covers company information only.
Services: Offers annual reports and placement on mailing list. Publications include annual and interim reports.
How to Contact: Write.

Electronics & Data Processing

Basic Four Corp., c/o Simon Public Relations, Inc., 11661 San Vicente Blvd., #903, Los Angeles CA 90049. (213)820-2606. Vice President: Marlane McGarry.
Purpose: "A Management Assistance, Inc. (MAI) company, Basic Four Corp. manufactures and sells small business computers and communications systems around the world." Information covers business, economics, new products and technical data.
Services: Offers aid in arranging interviews, brochures/pamphlets, information searches, placement on mailing list, photos, press kits and "case history articles on how the systems are used."
How to Contact: Write or call.

Bunker Ramo Corp., Information Systems Division, 35 Nutmeg Dr., Trumbull CT 06609. (203)377-4141. Director of Public Relations: Walter Clark.
Purpose: "Bunker Ramo Information Systems Division is the pioneer supplier of on-line data processing and communications systems. The division designs, builds, sells, and services on-line terminal systems to banks, insurance companies, and other financially oriented users; operates a nationwide system to supply stock brokers with market quotations and other investment information; and specializes in terminals and communications control for on-line, real-time applications. It does not supply mainframe computers." Information covers business and industry.
Services: Offers aid in arranging interviews, annual reports, biographies, brochures/pamphlets, placement on mailing list, newsletters, photos and press kits.Publications include brochures/pamphlets for on-line systems for commercial banking, thrift banking, insurance operations and the financial community (stock, bond, and commodity exchanges; over-the-counter markets; options; order processing; instant news retrieval; ticker displays).
How to Contact: Write or call.

Calma, c/o Simon Public Relations, Inc., 11661 San Vicente, Suite 903, Los Angeles CA 90049. (213)820-2606. Senior Account Executive: Steven Ludwig.
Purpose: "We manufacture and market computer systems for designing electronic circuits, mechanical parts and architectural/engineering/construction schematics, plus mapping." Information covers computer-aided design and mapping products, technology and case studies.
Services: Offers aid in arranging interviews, brochures/pamphlets, placement on mailing list, photos and press kits.
How to Contact: Write or call.

Centronics Data Computer Corp., 1 Wall St., Hudson NH 03051. (603)883-0111. Public Relations Specialist: Sterling Hager.
Purpose: "Founded less than 10 years ago, Centronics has become the leading independent producer of computer printout products, serving a variety of worldwide markets. We desgn, manufacture and market high-quality impact dot matrix printers, teleprinters, line printers and nonimpact printers. Since our first printer was shipped

in March, 1971, more than 125,000 have been installed throughout the world." Information covers printers.

Services: Offers aid in arranging interviews, annual reports, statistics, brochures/pamphlets and photos. Publications include annual and quarterly reports, *The Evolution of Printers into the Office Environment*, *Trends in the Computer Printer Industry*, ad and article reprints, product brochures, and specification sheets.

How to Contact: Write or call. "Ask to speak with public relations/marketing group."

Computer Micrographics, Inc., c/o Simon Public Relations, Inc., 11661 San Vicente, Suite 903, Los Angeles CA 90049. (213)820-2606. Account Executive: Frank L. Pollare.

Purpose: "Computer Micrographics (CMI) is a nationwide network of micrographics service centers providing diverse services to business and industry in trying to alleviate the growing amount of paper-based information. Data, both computer-generated and paper-based, is converted to various types of microfilm." Information covers business.

Services: Offers aid in arranging interviews, brochures/pamphlets, placement on mailing list, newsletter, photos, press kits and case histories on customers' use of CMI.

How to Contact: Write or call.

Eaton Corp., 100 Erieview Plaza, Cleveland OH 44114. (216)523-5270. Contact: Director of Communications.

Purpose: "Manufacturer and supplier of major industrial companies of automobile and truck components, materials handling vehicles and systems, industrial power transmission systems components, major suppliers of electrical and electronic systems and subsystems appliance controls." Information covers agriculture, business, economics, history, industry, new products, science and technical data.

Services: Offers aid in arranging interviews, annual reports, bibliographies, biographies, statistics, brochures/pamphlets, information searches, statistics, placement on mailing list, newsletter, photos and press kits.

How to Contact: Write.

Honeywell, 200 Smith St., Waltham MA 02154. (617)890-8400, ext. 3248. Public Relations Specialist: Thomas A. Eifler.

Purpose: "We manufacture and sell computers—minis, small, medium and large. The PR department disseminates information about these activities." Information covers business, industry, new products and technical data.

Services: Offers aid in arranging interviews, annual reports, biographies, statistics, brochures/pamphlets, photos and press kits. "Dozens of brochures on Honeywell products/services are available."

How to Contact: "Send a formal request in writing. Be as clear as possible when explaining why the information is needed and/or how it will be used."

Integrated Software Systems Corp. (ISSCO), c/o Simon Public Relations, Inc., 11661 San Vicente, Suite 903, Los Angeles CA 91307. (213)820-2606. Senior Account Executive: Steven Ludwig.

Purpose: "Integrated Software Systems Corp. (ISSCO) markets computer software for using computers to create charts, graphs and line illustrations of data." Information covers technical data for computer use in chartmaking.

Services: Offers aid in arranging interviews, brochures/pamphlets, placement on mailing list, photos and press kits.

How to Contact: Write or call.

International Business Machines (IBM), Old Orchard Rd., Armonk NY 10504. (914)765-1900. Contact: Information Department.

Purpose: "International Business Machine's (IBM) main activity is information processing." Information covers business, new products,science and technical data.
Services: Offers aid in arranging interviews, annual reports, biographies, brochures/pamphlets, photos and press kits. Publications include *IBM Yesterday and Today*, a profile and history of the company.
How to Contact: Write or call.

Lear Siegler Data Products, c/o Simon Public Relations, Inc., 11661 San Vicente, Los Angeles CA 90049. (213)820-2606. Executive Vice President: Joe Radoff.
Purpose: "The data products division of Lear Siegler is a pioneer and leader in the design, manufacture and marketing of Dumb terminals and computer printers." Information covers business, economics, new products, science and technical data.
Services: Offers aid in arranging interviews, brochures/pamphlets, placement on mailing list, photos and press kits.
How to Contact: Call.

Magnavox Consumer Electronics Co., 1700 Magnavox Way, Fort Wayne IN 46804. (219)432-6511. Public Relations Director: Robert V. Jones.
Purpose: "The manufacture and marketing of consumer electronics products—color and b&w TVs, console and component stereo systems, video cassette recorders, videodisc players, video games, portable radios, and tape cassette players." Information covers entertainment and new products.
Services: Offers aid in arranging interviews, brochures/pamphlets and press kits. Publications include product brochures, product information on technological advances, and information about the consumer electronics industry.

NCR Corp., Main and K Sts., Dayton OH 45409. (513)449-2150. Director of Public Relations: C.V. Truax.
Purpose: "To provide information about the company and its products, including computers, terminals, communication systems and other areas such as electronic funds transfer."
Services: Offers annual reports, brochures/pamphlets, placement on mailing list, photos and press kits.
How to Contact: Write or call.

Prime Computer, Inc., 40 Walnut St., Wellesley Hills MA 02181. (617)237-6990. Public Relations: Andre P. Beaupre.
Purpose: "Prime Computer manufactures very powerful 'super-minicomputers' that are medium- and large-scale computer systems for computational time-sharing and interactive data processing. Public relations is responsible for building awareness, understanding and acceptance of Prime Computer and its products." Information covers business, economics, industry, new products and technical data.
Services: Offers aid in arranging interviews, annual reports, statistics, brochures/pamphlets, placement on mailing list, newsletter, photos and press kits. Publications include product bulletins describing Prime's hardware and software offerings; annual reports; article reprints; and "an introductory brochure providing insight into company history, marketing philosophies and financial success. Application profiles describe in detail how several customers use our computers."
How to Contact: Write.

ROLM Telecommunications, c/o Simon Public Relations, Inc., 11661 San Vicente Blvd., #903, Los Angeles CA 90049. (213)820-2606. Vice President: Marlane McGarry.
Purpose: We manufacture and sell computerized switching systems to replace 'old-fashioned' switchboards." Information covers business, new products and technical data.

Services: Offers aid in arranging interviews, brochures/pamphlets, placement on mailing list, photos, press kits, and articles on how the systems are used.
How to Contact: Write or call.

Terminal Data Corp., c/o Simon Public Relations, Inc., 11661 San Vicente, Los Angeles CA 90049. (213)820-2606. Executive Vice President: Joe Radoff.
Purpose: "We are the leader in high-speed systems for microfilming thousands of pages of data per hour. Systems are used by the nation's largest companies, banks and government bureaus." Information covers business, industry, new products, science and technical data.
Services: Offers aid in arranging interviews, annual reports, brochures/pamphlets, placement on mailing list, photos and press kits.
How to Contact: Call.

Tracor, Inc., 6500 Tracor Lane, Austin TX 78721. (512)926-2800. Corporate Director of Public Relations: Judith Newby.
Purpose: "Tracor is an international technological products and services company performing research and development, engineering, manufacturing, and worldwide marketing through three operating groups—sciences and systems, instruments, and components. Tracor is a leading manufacturer of scientific and electronic instuments, advanced systems, and small electronic components; and conducts research programs in such important fields as sonar and environmental health." Information covers industry, new products, science and technical data.
Services: Offers aid in arranging interviews, annual reports, biographies, statistics, brochures/pamphlets, placement on mailing list, photos and press kits.
How to Contact: Write or call.

TRW Datacom, International, c/o Simon Public Relations, Inc., 11661 San Vicente, Los Angeles CA 90049. (213)820-2606. Executive Vice President: Joseph Radoff.
Purpose: "We are a subsidiary of TRW, Inc., and a leading company in the international sales of data processing and communications equipment in 51 countries around the world." Information covers business, economics, new products and technical data. "We also have case histories on the application of US computer products in foreign countries."
How to Contact: Call.

United Computing Systems, c/o Simon Public Relations, Inc., 11661 San Vicente, Suite 903, Los Angeles CA 90049. (213)820-2606. Senior Account Executive: Steven Ludwig.
Purpose: "We are a diversified computing services vendor which provides remote-batch and time-share data processing services, and also markets computer systems for certain specialized and general business applications." Information covers computer services products, technical dataand case studies.
Services: Offers aid in arranging interviews, brochures/pamphlets, placement on mailing list, newsletter, photos and press kits.
How to Contact: Call.

Xerox Corp., High Ridge Park, Stamford CT 06904. Public Relations Manager: James R. Lamb Jr.
Purpose: "To develop, make and market xerographic copies and duplicators, facsimile transceivers, electrostatic printers, processor memory discs/drives, high-speed terminals, electronic typing systems and electronic printing systems." Information covers business, economics, entertainment, industry, new products, science, technical data and educational materials.
Services: Offers aid in arranging interviews, annual reports, bibliographies, biographies, statistics, brochures/pamphlets, information searches, placement on mailing

list, photos and press kits.
How to Contact: Write or call.

Zenith Radio Corp., 1000 Milwaukee Ave., Glenview IL 60025. (312)391-8181.Director, Public Relations: W.A. Nail.
Purpose: "Zenith is the leading TV company in the US and a leader in audio and video—in research and development, engineering, and marketing. The company has been a pioneer in the industry for 60 years. Our information services cover these fields, as well as pay TV, international trade, public affairs, history of the industry, and collectors' information, business, celebrities, economics, history, how-to, new products, recreation, science and technical data."
Services: Offers aid in arranging interviews, annual reports, statistics, brochures/pamphlets, clipping services, information searches, placement on press mailing list, photos and press kits. Publications include "fact sheets on industry history and brochures on audio components and video cassette recorders."
How to Contact: "Writers may contact us by mail or phone, but please do your homework before phoning. Coverage of *Readers' Guide* and other library information on a subject is essential before narrowing to a source such as Zenith. We do like credit, but we don't insist on it."

Energy

Ashland Oil, Inc., 1401 Winchester Ave., Ashland KY 41101. Manager of Public Relations: **Dan Lacy.**
Purpose: "Ashland Oil, Inc. is the 42nd largest corporation in the United States. Major operating divisions include Ashland Petroleum Company (with seven refineries), which transports crude oil and refined products and markets petroleum products. Valvoline Oil Company markets broad lines of automotive lubricants, chemicals and filters. Ashland Chemical Company manufactures and distributes a variety of specialty chemicals including foundry products; industrial chemicals and solvents; carbon black; resins; plastics; and petrochemicals. Through wholly owned and affiliated companies, Ashland Oil has become the fifth largest coal producer in the United States with mines in southwestern Illinois, Wyoming, Alabama and Appalachia."
Services: Offers aid in arranging interviews, annual reports, biographies, statistics, brochures/pamphlets, placement on mailing list, newsletter, photos, press conferences and background information to news editors/directors.
How to Contact: Write or call.

Atlantic Richfield, 515 S. Flower St., Los Angeles CA 90051. Manager of News Services: Raymond E. Parr. Manager of Media Relations: Anthony P. Hatch.
Services: Offers aid in arranging interviews, annual reports, biographies, statistics, brochures/pamphlets, information searches, placement on mailing list, photos and press kits.
How to Contact: Write.

Chevron U.S.A., Inc., 555 Market St., San Francisco CA 94105. (415)894-4358, 894-0776. Contact: Dale Basye, Jerry Martin.
Purpose: "We provide material on all oil industry data and issues." Information covers business, economics, industry, new products, science and technical data.
Services: Offers aid in arranging interviews, annual reports, biographies and statistics.
How to Contact: Write or call. "Our services are limited to bonafide representatives of the news media or professional freelance writers."

Commonwealth Edison Co., 1 First National Plaza, Chicago IL 60609. Supervisor of News Information: John F. Hogan.
Purpose: "One of the largest electric utility companies. Provides 2.8 million customers with electric power in northern fifth of Illinois." Information covers business, econom-

ics, technical data and information related to the electric industry.
Services: Offers aid in arranging interviews, annual reports, brochures/pamphlets, placement on mailing list and statistics.
How to Contact: Write or call. "Writers must be bonafide members of the news media."

Consolidated Edison Co. of New York, Inc., 4 Irving Place, New York NY 10003. Director, Public Information: Bernard P. Stengren.
Purpose: Information covers electricity, gas, steam generation and distribution facilities.
Services: Offers photos.
How to Contact: Write.

Entex, Inc., Box 2628, Houston TX 77001. (713)659-5111. Manager, PR and Publicity: Benny Hill.
Purpose: "We engage in natural gas distribution, oil and gas exploration and production, contract drilling and savings and loan affairs." Information covers business.
Services: Offers aid in arranging interviews, annual reports, biographies, statistics, brochures/pamphlets and photos. "We are willing to provide background information on the natural gas business and oil and gas business (drilling, exploration, etc.)." Publications include material on energy conservation and efficiency of gas appliances.
How to Contact: Write or call.

General Atomic Co., Box 81608, San Diego CA 92138. (714)455-2100. Director, Public Relations and Advertising: Earl D. Zimmerman.
Purpose: "Research and development and manufacturing of nuclear energy systems for power production, nuclear research reactors, solar energy conversion systems, and fusion power research." Information covers science and technical data.
Services: Offers aid in arranging interviews, brochures/pamphlets, placement on mailing list, photos and press kits.
How to Contact: Write or call.

Getty Oil Co., Southern Division, Box 1404, Houston TX 77001. (713)658-9361. Public Affairs Manager: Michelle Beale.
Purpose: "Involved in exploration and production of oil and natural gas offshore (US) and in the southeastern US." Information covers business and petroleum.
Services: Offers aid in arranging interviews, annual reports, biographies, statistics, photos and press kits.
How to Contact: Write or call.

Gulf Oil Corp., Gulf Bldg., Pittsburgh PA 14230. (412)391-2400.

Marathon Oil Co., 539 S. Main St., Findlay OH 45840. (419)422-2121, ext. 3577. Contact: Manager, Press and Publications.
Purpose: "A fully integrated domestic oil company with significant international operations." Products include crude oil, natural gas and a full range of petroleum products. Information covers business, economics, how-to, industry, new product information, politics, science and technical information.
Services: Offers aid in arranging interviews, annual reports, biographies, statistics, brochures/pamphlets, information searches, placement on mailing list, photos and press kits.
How to Contact: Write. "Inquiries should be limited to Marathon or petroleum."

Middle South Services, Inc., Box 61000, New Orleans LA 70161. (504)529-5262. Cummunications Director: James J. Wallace. Communications Associate: A. R. Lentini.
Purpose: "To provide technical/professional services to the companies of the Middle South utilities system." Information covers finances and energy.

Services: Offers aid in arranging interviews and annual reports.
How to Contact: Write.

Missouri Public Service Co., 10700 E. 50th Hwy., Kansas City MO 64138. (816)353-5811. Manager, Public Information and Advertising: John Gilbert.
Purpose: "We provide gas, electric and water service in 28 counties in Western Missouri." Information covers utility information.
Services: Offers aid in arranging interviews, annual reports, statistics, and brochures/pamphlets. Publications include brochures on energy conservation and company operations.
How to Contact: Write or call.

Occidental Petroleum, 10889 Wilshire Blvd., Los Angeles CA 90024. (213)879-1700. Director of Public Relations: Carl W. Blumay. Assistant: Bruce McWilliams.
Services: Offers aid in arranging interviews, annual reports, bibliographies, biographies, statistics, brochures/pamphlets, information searches, photos, press kits and progress reports.
How to Contact: Write or call.

Peabody Coal Co., 301 N. Memorial Dr., St. Louis MO 63102. (314)342-3593. Director of Public Relations: Mr. Whitney.
Purpose: "Peabody Coal Company is in the coal mining industry exclusively." Information covers agriculture, business, economics, how-to, industry, law, nature, recreation and technical data.
Services: Offers aid in arranging interviews, bibliographies, biographies, statistics, brochures/pamphlets, information searches, placement on mailing list, newsletter and photos.
How to Contact: Write or call.

Public Service Co. of New Hampshire, Box 330, Manchester NH 03105. (603)669-4000. Editor: K.C. Disch.
Purpose: Electric utility company. Information covers business, economics, health/medicine and politics.
Services: Offers annual reports, statistics, brochures/pamphlets and newsletter.
How to Contact: Write or call.

Shell Oil Co., Box 2463, Houston TX 77001. (713)241-4544. Media Relations Representative: Lynn Johnson.
Purpose: "Shell Oil is a petrochemical company." Information covers "business and energy areas affecting the company and the energy industry."
Services: Offers aid in arranging interviews, annual reports, brochures/pamphlets and placement on mailing list.
How to Contact: Write or call. "Shell publishes a variety of position papers on energy issues."

Standard Oil Co. of California, 225 Bush, San Francisco CA 94104. (415)894-7700.

Sun Dance Oil Co., 1776 Lincoln St., Suite 510, Denver CO 80203. (303)861-4694.
Purpose: "Strictly exploration. We sell oil and gas at well head to crude oil purchaser or pipeline company." Information covers industry (oil and gas), law, technical data and travel.
Services: Offers annual reports, information searches and placement on mailing list.
How to Contact: Write or call.

Financial

American Express Co., 125 Broad St., New York NY 10004. (212)480-3603. Director, News Services: Jess Gregory.
Purpose: "Our information covers charge cards, travelers cheques and travel."
Services: Offers annual reports and brochures/pamphlets. Publications include *Credit Handbook for Women* (an overview of credit rights), *Consumer on the Go* (tips for travelers), *Report on Travelers Cheque Counterfeiting* (1978 speech by the vice president of corporate security), and *New Air Charters . . . What's the Consumer Being Told?* (1977 study).
How to Contact: Write. Single copies of *Credit Handbook for Women* are free; quantities are 50¢/copy.

Bank of Montreal, 129 St. James St., Montreal, Quebec, Canada H2Y 1L6. (514)877-2154. Director, Public Relations: Stanley N. Conder.
Purpose: "Bank of Montreal is a $30 billion asset bank offering a complete range of banking and related financial services with 1,260 offices in Canada and offices in every major financial center in the world." Information covers banking.
Services: Offers aid in arranging interviews, annual reports, biographies and photos. "We offer complete assistance in providing nonconfidential background information, on running stories covering banking and related subjects, and with feature articles (including statements and interviews)."
How to Contact: Write or call. "In the absence of the director of public relations, ask for one of his support managers."

The Chase Manhattan Bank, 1 Chase Manhattan Plaza, New York NY 10015. (212)552-2222. Vice President, Public Relations: Fraser P. Seitel.
Purpose: "The Chase Manhattan Bank is a commercial bank, headquartered in New York City, with branches throughout New York State and the world. The public relations division can handle any questions dealing with the bank's business; its subsidiaries, affiliates and associate banks; and, through the archives, inquiries about the bank's history and development." Information covers banking business, economics and the history of the bank and its antecedents.
Services: Offers aid in arranging interviews, annual reports, biographies, statistics, brochures/pamphlets, limited information searches, placement on mailing list and photos. Publications include the speeches of the chairman, president and others; historical pamphlets on the bank; miscellaneous publications on energy, finance and business; annual and quarterly reports.
How to Contact: "Inquiries made by mail are more desirable than telephone inquiries."

Chicago Board of Trade, LaSalle at Jackson, Chicago IL 60604. (312)435-3620. Director of Public Relations: Edward M. Lee.
Purpose: A commodity futures exchange. "The Chicago Board of Trade (CBT) is an open auction market of 1,502 members and associated members who buy and sell commodity futures contracts for customers or for themselves. Listed contracts cover the following areas: agriculture and food (grains and poultry), metals (precious), forest products and financial instruments (interest rate related contracts). Founded in 1848, the CBT is the world's oldest and largest commodity futures exchange." Information covers agriculture, business, economics, food, technical data and finance.
Services: Offers aid in arranging interviews, annual reports, bibliographies, biographies, statistics, brochures/pamphlets, information searches, placement on mailing list, newsletter, photos and press kits. Publications include "pamphlets and brochures covering commodity futures trading in general; specific futures in wheat, corn, oats, soybeans, soybean oil, soybean meal, iced broiler chickens, plywood, gold, silver, US Treasury bonds, commercial papers, and government National Mortgage Association mortgage-backed certificates."

How to Contact: Write or call.

Tips: "While the CBT PR department can offer much information on futures trading, it can also put writers/researchers in touch with market experts knowledgeable on subjects such as food prices; farm commodity prices; crop production forecasts; transportation of commodities; impact of inflation on food, metals, forest products and credit; efects of government regulation; exports and imports; and free markets vs. government-controlled markets."

S.N. Conder, director of public relations for the Bank of Montreal, envisions this photo of the bank's main office building in Toronto used to illustrate a general article about banking. The building is "the tallest bank building in the world, and the eighth tallest office building, according to the Guinness Book of World Records," says Conder. "There is no charge for photographs accompanying articles or features in which the Bank of Montreal is mentioned."

Deak-Perera, 29 Broadway, New York NY 10006. (212)480-0280. Vice President/ Marketing: R.L. Deak.

Purpose: ."We are foreign exchange specialists, precious metals specialists and a bank." Information covers business and economics.

Services: Offers brochures/pamphlets, placement on mailing list and newsletter.

How to Contact: Write or call.

Federal Reserve Bank of New York, 33 Liberty St., New York NY 10038. Chief: John Reich.

Purpose: "The Federal Reserve Bank of New York is part of the US central bank. It regulates monetary policy and bank holding companies, and acts as fiscal agent for the US Government."

Services: Offers annual reports, brochures/pamphlets and placement on mailing list. Can provide extensive publications list.

How to Contact: Write.

Harris Bank, 111 W. Monroe St., Chicago IL 60690. (312)461-6624. Press Relations Manager: Brace Pattou.

Purpose: "Harris Bank is the 24th largest bank in the United States. Its economic research office generates economic reports and studies. Through newsletters, its

experts offer advice on personal investments." Information covers economics.
Services: Offers aid in arranging interviews, annual reports and brochures/pamphlets.
How to Contact: Write or call.

Household Financial Corp., Money Management Institute, 2700 Sanders Rd., Prospect Heights IL 60070. (312)564-5000.
Purpose: Financial corporation. Information covers money management.
Services: Offers annual reports, brochures/pamphlets, placement on mailing list and statistics.
How to Contact: Write.

INA Corp., 1600 Arch St., Philadelphia PA 19101. Manager of Press Relations: Gloria McNaught.
Purpose: "INA Corp. is one of the nation's largest diversified financial institutions with major interests in insurance, insurance related services, health care management and investment banking." Information covers business.
How to Contact: Write or call. "We will try to help answer questions, but very little printed information is available."

MGIC Investment Corp., MGIC Plaza, Box 488, Milwaukee WI 53201. (414)347-6820. Contact: Marketing Communications Department.
Purpose: "To insure low down payment mortgage loans; to insure municipal bonds against loss of principal or interest; and to provide directors' and officers' liability insurance for financial institutions." Information covers business, economics and technical data.
Services: Offers aid in arranging interviews, annual reports, biographies, statistics, brochures/pamphlets and newsletter.
How to Contact: Write or call.

Manufacturers Hanover Corp., 350 Park Ave., New York NY 10022. (212)350-5254. Assistant Secretary: Michael O'Brien.
Purpose:"Manufacturers Hanover Corporation is a multi-bank holding company whose flagship bank, Manufacturers Hanover Trust Company, is the fourth largest in the US with assets at year-end of more than $39 billion. The corporation has achieved an average 13.8x compound annual rate of growth in earnings in the past five years. It serves domestic and international customers through banks and bank—related subsidiaries in mortgage banking, factoring, leasing, consumer finance and merchant banking."
Services: Offers annual reports, bibliographies, biographies, statistics, brochures/pamphlets, placement on mailing list, newsletter, photos and press kits.
How to Contact: Write or call.

The St. Paul Companies, Inc., 385 Washington, St. Paul MN 55102. (612)221-7911. Communication Office-Public Relations: David G. McDonnell.
Purpose: "The St. Paul Companies, Inc. is the management company for a group of subsidiaries that provide diversified financial services in the areas of property-liability insurance, life insurance, title insurance, consumer finance, investment banking, leasing, and mutual funds. Information covers business.
Services: Offers aid in arranging interviews, annual reports, biographies, statistics, brochures/pamphlets, and press kits.
How to Contact: Write or call.

Food

Associated Milk Producers, Inc., Box 32287, San Antonio TX 78284.
Purpose: Dairy marketing cooperative organized into three regions. Information cov-

ers agriculture.

Services: Offers placement on mailing list. Publications include *Dairymen's Digest*, monthly.

How to Contact: "Contact region in which information is needed." For mid-states region, write 8550 Bryn Mawr, Chicago IL 60631. For Southern region, write Box 5040, Arlington TX 76010. For North Central region, write Box 455. New Ulm MN 56073. "We're limited in personnel to handle extensive research. Try USDA first—they specialize in many dairy research items."

C. Brewer—Kilauea Agronomics, Box 1826, Honolulu HI 96805. (808)536-4461. Publicity Manager: C.E. Olcott.

Purpose: "Producers, processors and marketers of tropical products, including a Malaysian-type prawn. The parent company produces sugar and macadamia nuts." Information covers agriculture, business and new products.

Services: Offers aid in arranging interviews, annual reports and brochures/pamphlets. Publications include *Hawaiian Crown Prawns* (information and recipes).

How to Contact: Write.

Campbell Soup Co., Campbell Place, Camden NJ 08101. (609)964-4000. Manager of Information Services: C. Scott Rombach.

Purpose: The manufacture of "prepared convenience foods." Information covers agriculture, business, food and new products.

Services: Offers aid in arranging interviews, annual reports, biographies, photos and press kits. Publications include *The Eleventh Decade*, and material covering company history and chronology.

How To Contact: Write.

Castle and Cooke Foods, 50 California St., San Francisco CA 94111. (415)986-3000. Food Publicity Specialist: Carol Franz.

Purpose: "Castle and Cooke markets food under the Dole and Bumble Bee brands, including bananas, pineapple, coconut, mushrooms, tuna, salmon, crab, lobster and shrimp at retail and industrial markets. The food publicity specialist's job is to give in-depth information about the nutrition and home usage of each of these products. We provide recipes and photos for publication and free cookbooklets." Information covers agriculture, food and technical data.

Services: Offers brochures/pamphlets, placement on mailing list and newsletter. Publications include a 4-page fact sheet for each product and many recipe booklets.

How to Contact: Write.

Champagne News & Information Bureau, 522 5th Ave., New York NY 10036. (212)354-2232. Director: Irving Smith Kogan.

Purpose: "We are the educational arm in the US for the champagne industry of France. We serve as a resource for press, writers, commentators and the public. We maintain a library, photo file and staff to answer specific requests for information concerning champagne (both the wine and the region where it is produced). We will also assist writers in developing angles and material for articles." Information covers agriculture, business, celebrities, economics, entertainment, food, health/medicine, history, how-to, industry, law, new products, technical data and travel.

Services: Offers aid in arranging interviews, statistics, brochures/pamphlets, information searches, photos and press kits. Publications include *Entertaining with Champagne, There it is . . . but . . . Wait . . .*, *Champagne-Wine of France*, a brand sheet, route map and schedule of visiting hours in the cellars.

How to Contact: Write or call. "Our cooperation is limited to authentic champagne, i.e., the wine made only in the limited area in northern France. We have no information on other sparkling wines."

Peter Eckrich and Sons, Inc., Box 388, Fort Wayne IN 46801. (219)481-2443. Adminis-

trator, Public Affairs and Communications: Jack Yaggy.
Purpose: "Meat processing company with a line of sausage, frankfurters and luncheon meats that are distributed mainly in the Midwest, but also market by market from Baltimore to Phoenix." Information covers business, food, industry and science.
Services: Offers aid in arranging interviews, brochures/pamphlets, information searches, photos and press kits. "We can provide information on meat processing, meat research and consumer issues."
How to Contact: "We prefer an initial written contact and promise a quick follow-up. For urgent matters, phone calls are welcome."

General Foods Corp., 250 North St., White Plains NY 10625. (914)683-2429. Contact: Joanne Robinson.
Purpose: Foods manufacturer. Also manufactures dry goods and pet foods. Subsidiaries include Burger Chef Restaurants and Burpee Seeds Company. Information covers agriculture, business, economics, food, health, history, how-to, new products, self-help and technical data.
Services: Offers aid in arranging interviews, annual reports, biographies, statistics, brochures/pamphlets, information searches, placement on mailing list, photos and press kits. Publications include an annual report.
How to Contact: Write or call. "Freelancers must be writing for a bonafide publication."

General Mills, Inc., 9200 Wayzata Blvd., Box 1113, Minneapolis MN 55440. (612)540-2439. Contact: External Communications Department.
Purpose: Manufacturer of consumer goods. Products include Gold Medal Flour, Wheaties, Cheerios, and Betty Crocker mixes. Affiliates include Red Lobster Inns, David Crystal Fashions, Kimberly Fashions, Kenner and Parker Brothers. Information covers agriculture, art, business, celebrities, economics, food, health/medicine, how-to, industry, new products, recreation, sports, technical data and travel.
Services: Offers aid in arranging interviews, annual reports, bibliographies, biographies, statistics, brochures/pamphlets, information searches, placement on mailing list, photos, press kits and news releases.
How to Contact: Write. "Sometimes, a writer will be referred to an industry trade organization."

The Grand Union, 100 Broadway, Elmwood Park NJ 07407. (201)796-4800. Director, Corporate Communications: D.C. Vaillancourt.
Purpose: Retail supermarket chain.
Services: Offers aid in arranging interviews, biographies, placement on mailing list and photos.
How to Contact: Write or call.

Kahn's and Co., 3241 Spring Grove Ave., Cincinnati OH 45225. (513)541-4000. Consumer Affairs Coordinator: Mariann Feldmann.
Purpose: "We are a processed meats manufacturer owned by Consolidated Foods Corp. in Chicago. We can provide or put a writer in contact with someone who can provide information on Rudy's Farm and Hillshire Farm (brand names)." Information covers: food, health/medicine (relates to meat). "We also have information on Hillshire Farm, Rudy's Farm, the food service trade (restaurants, schools, etc.), and government regulation in regards to meat."
Services: Offers annual reports, biographies, statistics and brochures/pamphlets.
How to Contact: Write. "We will help in any way we can, but we like to know what kind of article is being written, what type of tone/theme/angle will be used, and something about the writer."

Knudsen Corp., 231 E. 23rd St., Los Angeles CA 90011. (213)747-6471. Manager of Public Relations: Richard N. Zwern.

Purpose: "Knudsen is the largest independent manufacturer of dairy products in California. The company is also engaged in agricultural management and fast food/convenience store operations. Our information relates to dairy products processing, nutrition and dairy farming." Information covers agriculture, food and new products.
Services: Offers aid in arranging interviews, annual reports and placement on mailing list.
How to Contact: Write.

Kraft, Inc., Kraft Court, Glenview IL 60025. Public Relations Manager: John J. Cameron.
Purpose: Manufacturer of prepared foods.
Services: Offers annual reports and brochures/pamphlets.
How to Contact: Write.

The Kroger Co., 1014 Vine St., Cincinnati OH 45201. (513)762-4440. Manager, Public Information: Audrey McCafferty.
Purpose: Activities include food processing and operation of supermarkets and drug stores.
Services: Offers aid in arranging interviews, annual reports, biographies, statistics, brochures/pamphlets, and "general information about the food and supermarket industry."
How to Contact: Write.

Mauna Loa Macadamia Nuts, Box 1826, Honolulu HI 96805. (808)544-6137. Marketing and Public Relations: Candice Olcott.
Purpose: "Macadamia nut processing, packaging and marketing. Also, the parent company (C. Brewer) markets prawns and guava." Information covers agriculture and new products.
Services: Offers aid in arranging interviews, annual reports, statistics, brochures/pamphlets, photos and press kits. Publications include *The Story of Macadamia Nuts* and *Macadamia Nut Recipes*.
How to Contact: Write. "Mauna Loa name credit must be given."

Pepsico, Inc., Anderson Hill Rd., Purchase NY 10577. (914)253-3294. Consumer Affairs: Daria Sheehan.
Purpose: Manufacturer of food and beverages. Products include Mountain Dew, Pepsi—Cola, Diet Pepsi and Pepsi Light. Subsidiaries include Taco Bell Foods and Pizza Hut Restaurants. Special programs of interest for ages 8 to 18 include Hot Shot Basketball, Run America Run, Pepsi Skate, and mobile tennis vans. Information covers agriculture, art, business, celebrities, entertainment, food, history, how-to, industry, law, new products, politics, recreation, science, sports, technical data, travel and education.
Services: Offers aid in arranging interviews, annual reports, bibliographies, biographies, statistics, brochures/pamphlets, clipping services, information searches and photos. Publications include *Pepsi World* (bimonthly) and *Vanguard* (quarterly).
How to Contact: Write.

Forestry, Lumber & Wood Products

Champion International Corp., 1 Landmark Square, Stanford CT 06921. (203)357-8611. Manager, Press Relations: Larry Miller.
Purpose: "Forest products industry. Our products are paper, packaging and building material." Information covers business, how-to, industry, new products and technical data.
Services: Offers aid in arranging interviews, annual reports, biographies, brochures/

pamphlets, information searches, placement on mailing list, statistics, newsletter, photos and press kits.
How to Contact: Write.

Crown Zellerbach, 1 Bush St., San Francisco CA 94119. (415)823-5522. Assistant Director, Corporation Communications: Charles Denton.
Purpose: "Internal and external corporate communications for the corporation and its business units: timber and wood products, pulp and paper, containers, packaging and wholesale distribution."
Services: Offers aid in arranging interviews, annual reports, biographies, statistics, brochures/pamphlets, placement on mailing list, newsletter and photos.
How to Contact: Write or call. "Give a minimum of 10 working days prior notice."

Georgia-Pacific Corp., 900 SW 5th Ave., Portland OR 97204. (503)222-5561. Information Manager, Building Products: Cathy Howard.
Purpose: "Georgia-Pacific manufactures and distributes a wide variety of building products—lumber, plywood, sidings, gypsum products, prefinished panelings, hardboard, particleboard, metal products, insulation, roofing and doors. Product information for both the consumer and trade is available, including photographs." Information covers how-to, new products and technical data.
Services: Offers brochures/pamphlets, placement on mailing list, photos, press kits, product catalogs and do-it-yourself information. Publications include *How to Install Wall Paneling*, *How to Make Beautiful Things Happen with Walls*, *Great Possibilities for Your Home*, 3 do-it-yourself booklets on gypsum wallboard installation, *Indoor Help* and *Plan Ahead for Winter*.
How to Contact: "Please write for information, being specific about the product or project in which you are interested. We suggest that a writer inquire first about literature then make a selection of photograph requests from what he sees in the literature. Photo credit must be given. Return transparencies promptly after use!"

St. Regis Paper, 150 E. 42nd St., New York NY 10017. (212)573-6440. Manager of Public Relations: Edgar C. Grimm.
Purpose: "We are a $2 billion paper packaging, construction and forest products company with 160 facilities in 33 states and nine foreign countries and investments in 76 plants in 23 countries."
Services: Offers aid in arranging interviews, annual reports, biographies, brochures/pamphlets, placement on mailing list and photos.
How to Contact: Write or call.

Weyerhauser Co., Tacoma WA 98401. (206)924-2345.
Purpose: "We are a forestry manufacturer and research company." Information covers business, economics, history, how-to, industry, nature, new products, politics (forestry issues), recreation, science, technical data, travel and forestry.
Services: Offers aid in arranging interviews, annual reports, bibliographies, biographies, statistics, brochures/pamphlets, information searches, placement on mailing list, photos and press kits.
How to Contact: Write or call.

Manufacturing

American Chain and Cable Co., Inc. (ACCO), 929 Connecticut Ave., Bridgeport CT 06602. (203)335-2511. Publications Services Manager: Robert B. Morgan.
Purpose: "American Chain and Cable Co., Inc. (ACCO) manufactures cranes, overhead conveyors, hoists, monorails, storage/retrieval systems, sorters, lifting devices, chain (except roller chain), load binders, slings, automatic cable controls, fence fabric, welding wire, hardness and tensile testing machines, abrasive cut-off wheels, alumi-

num casting machines and process control instruments." Information covers new products and technical data.

Services: Offers aid in arranging interviews, annual reports, brochures/pamphlets and photos.

How to Contact: Write or call.

American Olean Tile Co., 1000 Cannon Ave., Lansdale PA 19446. (215)855-1111. Director, Public Relations: Louise T. Brennan.

Purpose: "American Olean Tile Company is the largest producer of ceramic tile in the US. We have seven manufacturing plants across the country and make a wide variety of ceramic tile. As director of public relations, I work closely with a number of magazines and supply photographic material, resource information and articles." Information covers how-to, new products and technical data.

Services: Offers brochures/pamphlets, photos and press kits.

How to Contact: Write or call. "I would suggest that a telephone conversation would be more helpful than a letter, because we could have a better exchange of material needed and services available."

American Optical Corp., 14 Mechanic St., Southbridge MA 01550. (617)765-9711. Director, Corporate Communications: Wade W. Cloyd. Manager, Public Relations Services: Francis J. Doherty Jr. Supervisor, Publicity Services: Linda Burger.

Purpose: "The American Optical Corporation manufactures and distributes more than 2,000 products that help people live more naturally and healthfully in their environment. Information covers the corporation as a whole, the parent Warner-Lambert Co., and the products of American Optical's six line divisions: optical products, scientific instruments, safety products, soft contact lenses, and medical and fiber optics." Information covers new products and technical data.

Services: Offers aid in arranging interviews, biographies, brochures/pamphlets, placement on mailing list, photos and press kits. Publications include *This is American Optical*.

How to Contact: Write or call the corporate communications department.

The Ansul Co., 1 Stanton St., Marinette WI 54143. (715)735-7411. Public Relations Manager: Sara Lambrecht.

Purpose: "The Ansul Company manufactures fire protection products for high hazard, high risk industries such as petroleum, petrochemicals, mining, and other energy-related industries. The company carries on a large fire training program and has been the source of many innovations in such training. Ansul also manufactures specialty chemicals and pressure vessels, although these businesses are not as large as its fire protection business." Information covers how-to and new products related to fire protection and fire fighting training.

Services: Offers aid in arranging interviews, annual reports, brochures/pamphlets, placement on mailing list, newsletter, photos and press kits. Publications include material on fire protection.

How to Contact: Write. "Plan ahead. It's hard to get information for someone at the last minute, but if we have enough notice we can work it into our schedule."

Cannon Mills Co., Box 107, Kannapolis NC 28081. (704)933-1221. Public Relations Director: Edward L. Rankin.

Purpose: "We manufacture household textile products: towels, sheets, bedspreads, draperies, etc. We sell decorative fabrics to furniture manufactures for upholstery and fabrics for draperies. Information covers business, health/medicine (employee only), history, how-to, new products, technical data and travel (visitors center and plant tours).

How to Contact: Write."

Clairol, Inc., 345 Park Ave., New York NY 10022. (212)644-3100. Publicity Director: Phyllis Klein.

Purpose: "Leading manufacturer of hair coloring and hair care products." Information covers health, how-to (beauty/grooming) and new products.
Services: Offers aid in arranging interviews, brochures/pamphlets, photos and press kits.
How to Contact: Write or call. "No charge to the press."

Coils of tubing are depicted in this shot supplied by the American Chain and Cable Company (ACCO). ACCO publications services manager Robert B. Morgan envisions the photo used as illustrating a particular industry or type of product. "No charge is made for a reasonable number of photos," says Morgan, "but ACCO should be credited as the supplier of the photo if it's used with an article." Writers seeking photos "should be as specific as possible when requesting the photo," and should mention the type of product the writer's interested in, as well as its application."

Coats & Clark Inc., 75 Rockefeller Plaza, New York NY 10019. (212)265-7827. Public Relations: June King.
Purpose: "We are a privately owned company that manufactures thread, yarn and zippers." Information covers business, how-to, new products and technical data.
Services: Offers aid in arranging interviews, bibliographies, biographies, brochures/pamphlets, information searches, placement on mailing list, photos and press kits. Publications available.
How to Contact: Write.

Crane Carrier Co., 1925 N Sheridan Rd., Tulsa OK 74151. (918)836-1651. Advertising Manager: Jay R. Truk.
Purpose: "Manufacturer of heavy-duty carrier chassis (engines, frames and cabs) for the petroleum, refuse, construction, mining and logging industries." Information

covers technical data.
Services: Offers annual reports, brochures/pamphlets, placement on mailing list, and photos. Publications available.
How to Contact: Write.

Envirotech Corp., 3000 Sand Hill Rd., Menlo Park CA 94025. (415)854-2000. Corporate Communications Manager: A. W. ("Bill") Stewart.
Purpose: Products include "air pollution control equipment for removing particulates and gaseous contaminants from flue gas and other air streams; also equipment to control quality of in-plant (work environment) air; water/wastewater treatment equipment (liquid/solid separation, thermal waste processing, and specialized pumping equipment, plus instruments and controls); and underground mining equipment (drilling, hauling, etc.) for both coal and hardrock mining." Major markets served include "municipal sewage and water treatment, electrical utilities, coal and minerals mining/processing, steel, petroleum/chemical/petrochemical, pulp and paper, textiles, food processing and pharmaceutical processing." Information covers business, industry, new products, technical data and "government lelglislation related to our markets and products."
Services: Offers aid in arranging interviews, annual reports, brochures/pamphlets, placement on mailing list, photos and press kits. Publications include "four-page condensed fact sheet on the company, its divisions, and its markets/products; plus corporate annual report to shareholders; and technical brochures on individual product lines."
How to Contact: Write or call.

Fleetwood Enterprises, Inc., 3125 Myers St., Riverside, CA 92523. (714)785-3529. Advertising Assistant: Sue Allen.
Purpose: "The major manufacturer of recreational vehicles (motor homes, travel trailers, van conversions, and manufactured housing." Information covers entertainment, recreation and travel.
Services: Offers annual reports, brochures/pamphlets, placement on mailing list, photos and press kits.
How to Contact: Write or call. "Generally, the publications we deal with write their own evaluations or use freelance writers. We generally work with freelance writers after they have sold the story to the publication."

The Getzen Co., Inc., 211 W. Centralia, Elkhorn WI 53121. (414)723-4221. Vice President of Sales: Charles A. Ford.
Purpose: "We manufacture brasswind musical instruments and publish educational pamphlets on different phases of brasswind musical instrument playing." Information covers music.
Services: Offers brochures/pamphlets.

Glidden Coatings and Resins, Division of SCM Corp., 900 Union Commerce Bldg., Cleveland OH 44115. (216)771-5121. Manager, Public Relations: Bernice Bolek.
Purpose: "We are an industrial firm specializing in paint, coatings and resins." Information covers home improvement how-to and new products.
Services: Offers SCM annual reports, brochures/pamphlets and placement on mailing list.
How to Contact: Write or call.

M. Hohner, Inc., Andrews Rd., Hicksville NY 11802. (516)935-8500. Director of Advertising: Jack C. Kavoukian.
Purpose: "Sole distributors of Hohner and Sonor products in the US. Product line includes harmonicas, keyboards, diatonic and piano accordions, fretted instruments, recorders, melodicas, instruments for music education, sound modifiers, amplifiers, microphones and musical instrument accessories." Information covers music.

Services: Offers brochures/pamphlets. "We have product literature for each of our product lines."
How to Contact: "Contact the advertising department. Single copies of our literature will be supplied at no charge. For multiple copies, there will be a small handling and service charge."

International Harvester Co., 401 N. Michigan Ave., Chicago IL 60611. Public Relations Manager: Harry Conner.
Purpose: "One of the world's largest producers of farm equipment, commercial trucks, construction equipment and industrial gas turbines. We have been overseas since 1861 and currently do business in 168 countries. We can provide historical and current information." Information covers business, economics, industry, new products and technical data.
Services: Offers aid in arranging interviews, annual reports, brochures/pamphlets, placement on mailing list, statistics, photos and press kits.
How to Contact: Write or call. "We prefer written requests. Writers who contact us should be accredited.

McCulloch Corp., Box 92180, Los Angeles CA 90009. (213)390-8711. Director, Public Relations: David Kirby.
Purpose: "Manufacturer of gasoline-powered chain saws, portable electric generators, and other small engine products." Information covers industry, new products and technical data.
Services: Offers brochures/pamphlets, placement on mailing list, photos and press kits. Photos are of "chain saw and portable electric generator product lines, including in-use situations."
How to Contact: Write or call.

The Maytag Co., 403 W. 4th St. N., Newton IA 50208. Manager, Public Information: Ronald L. Froehlich.
Purpose: Manufacturer of laundry and kitchen appliances.
Services: Offers b&w and color photos color transparencies of home laundry settings; kitchens; anything in the area of laundry appliances, laundering, kitchen appliances, use of dishwashers, disposers; laundering procedures. Also available are industrial shots, in-factory assembly line photos.
How to Contact: Credit line and return of color transparencies required.

Mercury Marine, 1939 Pioneer Rd., Fond du Lac WI 54935. (414)921-8220. Publicity Manager: Greg Kissela.
Purpose: "We manufacture marine propulsion products." Information covers new products, recreation, technical data, boating, fishing and other water related activities.
Services: Offers aid in arranging interviews, placement on mailing list, photos and press kits.
How to Contact: Write or call, but a letter is preferred.

Lee Norse Co., Box 2863, Pittsburgh PA 15230. (412)787-7500. Advertising and Communications Coordinator: H. Mark Jones.
Purpose: "Underground coal mining equipment supplier." Information covers new products.
Services: Offers brochures/pamphlets and placement on mailing list.
How to Contact: Write.

Pitney Bowes, Walnut & Pacific Sts., Stamford CT 06904. (203)356-5090. Manager of Public Relations: Ralph H. Major Jr.
Purpose: "Pitney Bowes produces, markets and services business systems and retail systems. Business systems include postage meters, parcel registers, mailing machines, mailing scales, mail openers, mailroom furniture, folders and inserters, collators,

sorters, counters and imprinters, addresser-printers, cigarette tax-stamping machines and meters, post office facing and cancelling machines, and copiers and supplies. Retail systems include price-marking equipment and merchandise tags and labels." Information covers business and industry.
Services: Offers annual reports, biographies, statistics, placement on mailing list and photos. Publications include annual reports, biographies of officers, product information and sales promotion brochures.
How to Contact: Write. For strictly product information, write Richard Muniz, Manager of Product Publicity.

The Singer Co., 30 Rockefeller Plaza, New York NY 10020. (212)581-4800. Manager of Publications: Chuck Petty.
Purpose: "We manufacture sewing products; products for consumers including power tools, vacuum cleaners, automotive controls, and products and services for government." Information covers business, economics, industry, new products and technical data.
Services: Offers aid in arranging interviews, annual reports, brochures/pamphlets, placement on mailing list, statistics and press kits.
How to Contact: Write.

Soiltest, Inc., 2205 Lee St., Evanston IL 60202. (312)869-5500. Director of Public Relations/Advertising: Kenneth M. Wylie Jr.
Purpose: "We market and promote our engineering test equipment." Information covers agriculture, new products, science and technical data.
Services: Offers brochures/pamphlets. Publications include *The Testing World* (annual).
How to Contact: Write. "We welcome inquiries from writers who need information on quality control testing for construction. In some instances, we can supply photos."

Stone Container Corp., 360 N. Michigan Ave., Chicago IL 60601. (312)346-6600. Public Relations Manager: Elizabeth F. Goyak.
Purpose: "Stone Container Corporation is one of the leaders in the integrated paperboard packaging industry. From new materials to advanced packaging machinery, Stone Container has a broad product line backed by services and technical knowledge of all phases of packaging. Stone has 16 corrugated container manufacturing operations serving the East, North Central, South and Midwest US, and also two boxboard mills, a corrugated medium mill, and a draft lineboard mill." Information covers industry and new products.
Services: Offers aid in arranging interviews, annual reports, biographies, brochures/pamphlets, photos and press kits. Publications include brochures on products, and annual and quarterly reports.
How to Contact: Write or call. "We do not give out pricing information. We will be happy to assist writers."

Whirlpool Corp., Public and Government Relations, Administrative Center, Benton Harbor MI 19022. Public Information Managers: Carol Zerler, Steve Sizer.
Purpose: Manufacturer of major home appliances. Information covers food, how-to, new products and technical data.
Services: Offers aid in arranging interviews, annual reports, biographies, statistics, brochures/pamphlets, information searches, placement on mailing list, photos and press kits.
How to Contact: Written requests preferred. May charge for some publications.

Mining, Metals & Minerals

Aluminum Company of America (ALCOA), Alcoa Bldg., Pittsburgh PA 15219. Manager, Financial Communication: A.T. Post.
Services: Offers photos in "color and b&w on practically everything concerning aluminum—mining, refining, smelting, fabricating, products, uses, etc."
How to Contact: Write. Offers world rights.

Bethlehem Steel Corp., 8th and Eaton Aves., Martin Tower, Bethlehem PA 18016. Manager, News Media Divison: Marshall D. Post.
Purpose: "We are the nation's second largest steel producer." Information covers business (steel), economics, history, industry, new products, science, technical data and research.
Services: Offers aid in arranging interviews, annual reports, biographies, brochures/pamphlets, information searches, placement on mailing list and photos. "We have a library at our headquarters for serious researchers." Publications available.
How to Contact: Write. Charges for color photos.

Freeport Minerals Co., 200 Park Ave., New York NY 10017. (212)578-9200. Public Relations Director: E.C.K. Read.
Purpose: "The production of sulphur, phosphate rock, phosphoric acid, kaolin, potash, copper, gold, silver, oil and gas, nickel, cobalt and uranium oxide." Information covers mining, natural resources and energy.
Services: Offers aid in arranging interviews, annual reports, biographies, statistics, brochures/pamphlets, placement on mailing list and photos. Publications include "general booklets on sulphur and phosphoric acid, and numerous reprints on Indonesian copper, offshore sulphur mining, etc."
How to Contact: Write.

Reynolds Metals Co., 6601 W. Broad St., Richmond VA 23261. Director of Information: David M. Clinger.
Purpose: "Reynolds is a primary aluminum producer. Our activities cover the full range of mineral processing, from bauxite mining to fabrication of finished products and recycling." Information covers new products and technical data.
Services: Offers aid in arranging interviews, annual reports, biographies, brochures/pamphlets and photos. Publications include *Literature, Movie and Product Index*, which lists product information literature, general nontechnical information about Reynolds and the aluminum industry, Aluminum Association publications, technical handbooks, and movies.
How to Contact: Write. "Most literature listed in the above booklet may be obtained by writing on a business letterhead to Reynolds Metals Co., Advertising Distribution Center, Box 27003, Richmond 23261."

Miscellaneous

A&M Records, Inc., 1416 N. LaBrea Ave., Hollywood CA 90028. (213)469-2411.
Purpose: "Manufacturing and distributing records and promoting recording artists." Information covers entertainment and music.
Services: Offers aid in arranging interviews, clipping services, biographies, newsletter and press kits.
How to Contact: Write or call. Charges for services. "We deal with trade writers or known freelance writers."

ABC Records, 8255 Beverly Blvd., Los Angeles CA 90048. (213)651-5530. National Publicity Director: Peter Starr.

Purpose: "Manufacturing and merchandising records, doing publicity for artists, and coordinating press releases and publicity." Information covers entertainment and music.
Services: Offers aid in arranging interviews, biographies, brochures/pamphlets, clipping services, photos and press kits.
How to Contact: Write or call.
Tips: "Writers of far-reaching publications are preferred. Writers doing stories on specific artists should be familiar with the artist's work before going into detail with publicity."

ABC Records, Nashville Operation, 2409 21st Ave. S., Nashville TN 37212. (615)385-0840. Director, Press and Artist Relations: Jerry Bailey.
Purpose: "To manufacture phonograph records and to develop careers of recording artists. The director of press and artist relations acts as a liaison between recording artists and the press." Information covers art, business, celebrities and music.
Services: Offers aid in arranging interviews, biographies, statistics, placement on mailing list, newsletter, photos and press kits. "We can provide press kits on any ABC Records artist, including country, pop, jazz and rhythm and blues. We specialize in information on country artists."
How to Contact: Write or call. "Freelance or staff writers should show sufficient activity and circulation to merit receiving regular mailings of free records. We will supply individual records and press kits to any legitimate writer working on a specific article for any significant publication."

Adventours—Wet & Wild, Inc., Box B, Woodland CA 95695. (916)662-6824. President: Loren L. Smith.
Purpose: "Wet & Wild is an outdoor recreation business that conducts whitewater river trips, combination whitewater trips on horse trails or backpacking trips, and international nontourist type personal encounters, such as hostel bike-train trips and exploratory waterways adventures." Information covers nature, recreation and travel.
Services: Offers brochures/pamphlets.
How to Contact: Write or call. "Writers must identify how the material will be used. They must authenticate the publishing date and that our correct name, address and telephone number will be associated with the final published material. We would appreciate a prepublication copy."

Affiliated Warehouse Companies, Inc., 3507 N. Bosworth, Chicago IL 60657. (219)924-3800. Treasurer: Walter P. Taylor.
Purpose: "We do the national sales work and advertising for the 75 public merchandise warehouses that employ our service on a retainer basis." Information covers "data regarding the warehouses we represent."
Services: Offers brochures/pamphlets. Publications include an annual directory and direct mail advertising pieces.
How to Contact: Write or call.

Allright Auto Parks, Inc., 1625 Esperson Bldg., Houston TX 77002. (713)222-2505. National Director, Public Relations: H.M. Sinclair.
Purpose: "We are the world's largest auto parking company (United States and Canada). We offer all types of services, including consulting services, garages, open lots, etc. As the leader in the parking industry, we cover national information on parking and the history of parking. Our company occupies more downtown property than any other company and owns over 85 properties." Information covers business, history, industry and new products.
Services: Offers aid in arranging interviews, annual reports, biographies, statistical information, brochures/pamphlets, placement on mailing list, newsletter and photos. Publications include *Parking News Quarterly* and individual sheets on specific areas of parking.
How to Contact: Write or call.

Ariola Records, 8671 Wilshire Blvd., Beverly Hills CA 90211. (213)657-8143. National Publicity: Pam Turbov, Joanne Russo.
Purpose: "We are an international record company. American offices are based in Beverly Hills." Information covers music.
Services: Offers aid in arranging interviews, biographies, and services with promotional, publicity, and merchandise departments for writer's needs. Publications include contact publicity for artist roster.
How to Contact: Write or call. "Get in touch, and we can discuss all possibilities."

ATV Music Corp., 6255 Sunset Blvd., Hollywood CA 90028. (213)462-6933. Director of Writer/Artist Relations: Harry Shannon.
Purpose: "Record publisher/recording company." Information covers entertainment and music.
Services: Offers aid in arranging interviews and biographies.
How to Contact: Write or call. Charges for services. "Writers must be established or represent established companies."

Dallas/Ft. Worth Regional Airport, Drawer DFW, Dallas/Ft. Worth Airport TX 75261. (214)574-6701. Public Information Officer: Jim Street.
Purpose: "This is a major commercial airport handling nearly 20 million passengers per year. It is publicly owned and operated under a contract and agreement between the cities of Dallas and Ft. Worth. The public information officer assists news media in getting whatever kind of stories they need." Information covers business, economics, industry, technical data and travel.
Services: Offers aid in arranging interviews, annual reports, biographies, statistics, brochures/pamphlets, placement on mailing list, photos and press kits. Publications include guide and blue book.
How to Contact: Write.

The Delta Queen Steamboat Co., 511 Main St., Cincinnati OH 45202. (513)621-1445. Public Relations Director: Russell Barnes.
Purpose: "We are a steamboat cruise company with a one-of-a-kind product. *The Delta Queen* and *The Mississippi Queen*, the only overnight steamboats sailing America's rivers. These are full cruise vessels, not just excursion boats, and run all year, docking at Cincinnati, New Orleans, St. Louis, St. Paul/Minneapolis and Pittsburgh. We promote not just a product, but the tradition of steamboats as well." Information covers celebrities, entertainment, food, new products, recreation and travel.
Services: Offers aid in arranging interviews, biographies, statistics, brochures/pamphlets, photos and press kits.
How to Contact: Write.

Gallery of Prehistoric Paintings, 20 E. 12th St., New York NY 10003. (212)674-5389. Director/Owner: Douglas Mazonowicz.
Purpose: "We are specialists in prehistoric art. We make accurate silkscreened editions of cave art. We sell to France, Spain, Italy, North America and the United States." Information covers art, history, science, and prehistoric art.
Services: Offers brochures/pamphlets, regular informational newsletter, photos (cave art), films, slides, and books. Publications include *Voices From the Stone Age*.
How to Contact: Write or call. "We charge for slides, photographs and films." Charges $12.95/copy for *Voices from the Stone Age*.

Goodwill Industries of Southern California, 342 San Fernando Rd., Los Angeles CA 90031. Director of Community Relations: Craige Le Breton.
Purpose: "To train, employ and rehabilitate disabled/disadvantaged persons in the southern California area so that they can be gainfully employed by private business and industry. These physically, mentally, or socially disadvantaged persons are taught to live within the limits of their disabilities, trained to be self-sufficient, and

enabled to lead independent, satisfying and productive lives." Information covers health/medicine, history, industry, and rehabilitation techniques for the disabled and disadvantaged.

Services: Offers aid in arranging interviews, annual reports, biographies, statistics, brochures/pamphlets, photos and press kits. Publications available.

How to Contact: Write or call. "A Goodwill facility must be seen to be understood. Those interested in Goodwill programs would do well to personally visit their local plant to see them in action. At Goodwill Industries of Southern California, a telephone call would be all that is necessary to arrange a complete tour. Everyone is welcome."

Tips: "With regard to Goodwill Industries—and in dealing with disabled people in general—writers should remember that they are confronting individuals with only one thing in common: a need for 'a help up, not a handout.' To a disabled person, his/her disability is a unique factor in a personal way of life—not a social problem. It is a difficult form of courtesy to remember this."

Hanna-Barbera Productions, 3400 Cahuenga Blvd., Hollywood CA 90068. (213)851-5000. Vice President of Communications: John Michaeli.

Purpose: "We are a production studio involved in animated and live-action series, specials, telemovies and full-length features. We are also connected with amusement parks across the country and produce educational, industrial and commercial films. Merchandising for shows and characters is another important dimension of the company." Information covers celebrities, entertainment and recreation.

Services: Offers aid in arranging interviews, annual reports, biographies, brochures/pamphlets, information searches, photos and press kits. Publications include "press releases and artwork available on all shows produced here, celebrities involved plus historical information on the studio and animation process."

How to Contact: Write, "specifying materials needed and intended use. Send requests well in advance. Artwork must be credited with copyright."

Pacific Architects and Engineers, Inc., 600 S. Harvard Blvd., Los Angeles CA 90005. (213)381-5731. Public Relations Director: Natilee D. Johnson.

Purpose: Architectural and engineering design; operations and maintenance of technical services and vocational training overseas. Information covers technical data.

Services: Offers brochures/pamphlets, placement on mailing list and newsletter.

How to Contact: Write or call.

Philadelphia International Records, 309 S. Broad St., Philadelphia PA 19107. (215)985-0900. Publicity Manager: Becki Butler.

Purpose: "Philadelphia International Records (PIR) artists include Lou Rawls, Teddy Pendergrass, the O'Jays, Jerry Butler, Jean Carn, Billy Paul, MFSB Orchestra, Dexter Wansel, Dee Dee Sharp Gamble, Bobby Rush, the Jones Girls and the Futures. Kenneth Gamble and Leon Huff are writers, producers and company heads." Information covers entertainment.

Services: Offers aid in arranging interviews, biographies, clipping services, placement on mailing list and an occasional newsletter.

How to Contact: Write or call.

Princeton Antiques Bookshop, 2915-17 Atlantic Ave., Atlantic City NJ 08401. (609)344-1943. President: Robert E. Ruffolo II.

Purpose: "We are a library of architectural and historical photos on post cards dating from 1900 to 1940. We have a price and identification library of 12,000 volumes on art and antiques from 1900 to the present." Information covers 150,000 volumes of indexed out-of-print stock covering all subject areas from 1900 to 1970.

Services: Offers brochures/pamphlets and information searches.

How to Contact: Make an appointment or write, requesting author, title or subject area. Charges for services.

RCA Records, Nashville, 30 Music Square W., Nashville TN 37203. (615)244-9880. Manager, Artist Development: Jerry Flowers.
Purpose: "The promotion and development of careers of artists signed to RCA Records, Nashville Operations." Information covers music.
Services: Offers aid in arranging interviews, biographies, placement on mailing list, newsletter, photos and press kits.
How to Contact: Write or call.

Regina Exhibition Association, Ltd., Box 167, Regina, Saskatchewan, Canada S4P 2Z6. (306)527-2674. Information Officer: Malcolm Cunningham.
Purpose: "To provide programs and/or facilities for the enrichment of agriculture, business, sport, recreation and culture in Regina and in our larger community of Saskatchewan."
Services: Offers aid in arranging interviews, annual reports, statistics, brochures/pamphlets, placement on mailing list, newsletter, photos and press kits. Publications include press kit of facilities.
How to Contact: Write or call. "Copies of photos can require considerable lead time. Information other than that already in print form can also require considerable lead time, depending upon the nature of the information requested."

Richard Owen Roberts, Booksellers, 205 E. Kehoe Blvd., Wheaton IL 60187. (312)668-1025. Contact: Sales Department.
Purpose: "We stock and make available to the public approximately 100,000 volumes of rare and out-of-print religious and theological books in all the theological disciplines." Information covers history, music, religion and theology.
Services: Offers "catalogs of out-of-print religious and theological material."
How to Contact: Write or call. Request catalogs or specific information on authors and titles.

RSR Corp., 1111 W. Mockingbird Lane, Dallas TX 75247. (214)631-6070. Communications Coordinator: Peggy Jones.
Purpose: "We recycle lead by purchasing lead-bearing scrap and smelting and refining it to very stringent specifications. The primary market is battery manufacturers and primary competition is lead miners/refiners." Information covers history, industry, new products, financial and technical data.
Services: Offers aid in arranging interviews and annual reports. Publications include a technical industrial catalog of bulk lead alloys, and financial reports (annuals and quarterlies).
How to Contact: Write or call. "We are wary of releasing certain types of information."

Selame Design Associates, 2330 Washington St., Newton Lower Falls MA 02162. Executive Vice President: Elinor Selame.
Purpose: Creates graphic design concepts for businesses to use in advertising, on stationery, etc. Information covers business.
Services: Offers aid in arranging interviews, brochures/pamphlets, placement on mailing list, newsletter, photos and press kits.
How to Contact: Write.

San Francisco International Airport, San Francisco CA 94128. (415)761-0800. Public Relations Officer: Warren D. Hanson.
Purpose: "The operation and management of San Francisco International Airport." Information covers economics, history and technical data.
Services: Offers aid in arranging interviews, annual reports, statistics and brochures/pamphlets.
How to Contact: Write or call. "Telephone is OK for simple queries. Write for anything requiring research."

Sun City Center, Box 5698-Public Relations, Sun City Center FL 33570. (813)634-3311.
Purpose: "This is a retirement community which is self-sufficient, with its own recreation, entertainment, sports, arts and crafts, club activities and shopping areas."
Services: Offers aid in arranging interviews, annual reports, biographies, brochures/pamphlets, clipping services, information searches, placement on mailing list, newsletter and photos. Publications available.
How to Contact: Write or call.

Windjammer "Barefoot" Cruises, Box 120, Miami Beach FL 33139. (305)373-2466.
Public Relations Director: Toni Brodax Tuttle.
Purpose: "We provide six-day adventure-cruises aboard famous schooners in the Caribbean to over 400,000 passengers, who help sail, learn seamanship, learn to scuba dive, snorkel and explore islands." Information covers entertainment, recreation, sports and travel.
Services: Offers brochures/pamphlets, placement on mailing list, photos and press kits. Publications include *Great Adventure Book* and *Round-the-World Cruise*.
How to Contact: Write or call. "Supply a list of credentials."

World Wide Pictures, 2520 W. Olive, Burbank CA 91505. (213)843-1300. Public Relations Secretary: Twila Knaack.
Purpose: "Produces religious films for theaters, television and churches." Information covers religious subjects.
Services: Offers aid in arranging interviews, biographies, photos and press kits.
How to Contact: Write or call.

Pharmaceuticals

Brystol-Myers Co., 345 Park Ave., New York NY 10022. Public Relations Director: Ann Wyant.
Purpose: Pharmaceutical company.
Services: Offers annual reports. Publications include *Guide to Consumer Product Information*, edited by Bess Myerson.
How to Contact: Write.

Eli Lilly & Co., Box 618, Indianapolis IN 46206. (317)261-3570. Media Relations Director: Russ Durbin.
Purpose: "Eli Lilly & Company is a manufacturer of pharmaceutical products, agricultural products and cosmetics." Information covers agriculture, business, economics, health/medicine, industry, new products, science, technical data, travel and cosmetics."
Services: Offers aid in arranging interviews, annual reports, bibliographies, statistics, brochures/pamphlets, placement on mailing list, photos and press kits.
How to Contact: Write or call.

Pfizer, Inc., 235 E. 42nd St., 25th Floor, New York NY 11432. (212)573-2595. Manager, Corporate Press Relations: Joseph P. Callahan.
Purpose: Pharmaceutical company. Information covers agriculture, business, economics, food, health/medicine, industry and science.
Services: Offers aid in arranging interviews, annual reports, bibliographies, statistics, placement on mailing list and photos.
How to Contact: Write or call, but a letter is preferred.

Squibb Corp., 40 W. 57th St., New York NY 10019. (212)489-2000. Manager of Corporate Communications: Joan Berkley.
Purpose: "We are a diversified pharmaceutical company composed of four wholly-owned subsidaries: E.R. Squibb, Inc. (largest subsidiary); Life Savers, Inc. (confec-

tionary subsidiary); Dobb House, Inc. (food services for restaurants and airlines); and Charles of the Ritz Group, Ltd. (fragrances and cosmetics)." Information covers business, economics, new products and technical data.
Services: Offers aid in arranging interviews, annual reports, brochures/pamphlets, placement on mailing list, statistics and photos.
How to Contact: Write. Charges for photos if they have to be made.

Warner-Lambert, 201 Tarbor Rd., Morris Plains NJ 07950. (201)540-2000. Vice President, Public Relations: R.E. Zier. Manager, Corporation Information: Thorn Kuhl.
Purpose: "We do research, development, manufacturing and marketing of pharmaceuticals, optical products and consumer items."
Services: Offers aid in arranging interviews, annual reports and placement on mailing list.
How to Contact: Write or call.

Real Estate

CBL & Associates, Inc., 1 Northgate Park, Chattanooga TN 48400. (615)877-1151. Director of Public Relations: John R. Martin Jr.
Purpose: "We are a shopping center development firm specializing in leasing, building and managing shopping centers with major emphasis on the Southeastern, Midwestern and Western areas of the country. We primarily develop regional malls but, when appropriate, we also develop strip shopping centers." Information covers business, announcements of new sites for shopping centers and announcements of new store openings.
Services: Offers aid in arranging interviews, statistics, brochures/pamphlets, placement on mailing list, photos and press kits.
How to Contact: Write or call. "We are directly responsible for all news releases, press conferences and personal interviews involving representatives of our firm. Inquiries must go through our office first. Any direct inquiries are automatically referred to us initially."

Century 21, 18872 MacArthur Blvd., Irvine CA 92715. (714)752-7521. Advertising and Public Relations Director: Bruce Oseland.
Purpose: "We provide services to real estate brokers who are independently owned and franchised to operate under the name 'Century 21.' We are the largest franchise organization in the world, as of now, with about 7,000 offices in the US and Canada." Information covers business, economics, how-to, industry, law, new products, politics, recreation, technical data, travel and home construction.
Services: Offers aid in arranging interviews, annual reports, bibliographies, biographies, statistics, brochures/pamphlets, information searches, placement on mailing list, newsletter, photos and press kits. Publications include *Century 21 News Roundup* (monthly).
How to Contact: Write.

Electronic Realty Associates (ERA), Box 2974, Shawnee Mission KS 66201. (913)341-8400; toll-free (800)255-6623. Public Affairs Director: Harvey Bergren. Accounting Manager: Barry Sigale, (800)621-4315.
Purpose: "We are the second-largest real estate franchise and America's largest marketer of home warranty programs. We operate through 2,700 offices in 50 states. We do not buy or sell properties. All offices are independently owned. We are also the exclusive sponsor of the Muscular Dystrophy Association for the entire real estate industry." Information covers business, economics, industry, law, nature, politics, self-help and travel.
Services: Offers aid in arranging interviews, bibliographies, biographies, statistics, brochures/pamphlets, information searches, placement on mailing list, newsletter,

photos, and audiovisual materials. Publications include *ERA News* (bimonthly).
How to Contact: Write or call.
Tips: "Our press kits contain some story ideas on moving, etc. They could be of great source of ideas on the industry." Researchers may also contact Golin Communication Service in Chicago, (800)621-4315.

The Gallery of Homes, Inc., 1001 International Blvd., Atlanta GA 30354. (404)768-2460. Contact: Advertising and Public Relations Director.
Purpose: "The Gallery of Homes is a real estate franchising organization." Information covers business, economics, entertainment, food, health/medicine, history, how-to, industry, law, new products, recreation, sports and travel.
Services: Offers aid in arranging interviews, bibliographies, biographies, statistics, brochures/pamphlets, clipping services, information searches, placement on mailing list and newsletter. Publications include *Keynote* (monthly).
How to Contact: Write or call.

Resort Condominiums International, 3901 W. 86th St., Indianapolis IN 46268. (317)248-8531. Publications Director: Geri Cisco.
Purpose: "Resort Condominiums International (RCI) is a reciprocal exchange program. It is used primarily by owners of timeshares in condominimums in vacation resorts. Our members 'spacebank' their timeshare and exchange it for another time and place. It is an exchange service, not a direct barter. The resorts are in the US, Canada, Mexico, the Caribbean, Europe and Australia." Information covers resort timeshare exchanges.
Services: Offers press kits. Publications include *Exchange Listing*, the magazine *The Endless Vacation*, and article reprints.
How to Contact: "Call or write RCI publications department and explain the purpose of the information desired."

United Farm Agency, Inc., 612 W. 47th St., Kansas City MO 64112. (816)753-4212. Director of Corporate Information: Jack R. Waln.
Purpose: "The marketing of farms, ranches, town and country homes; recreational, business and commercial real estate in 42 states through 552 sales offices and customer service centers in 16 cities. Except for business and commercial properties, our activities are mainly in rural communities." Information covers agriculture, business and recreation as they relate to real estate.
Services: Offers aid in arranging interviews, biographies, statistics, brochures/pamphlets, placement on mailing list and press kits. Publications include "our seasonal catalog, published three times a year to provide an idea of what is selling and where."
How to Contact: Write or call. "We will assist in researching articles pertaining to our business and will provide other leads for related information. We'd appreciate receiving as much advance notice as possible. Not all information is readily available, and special computer programs may have to be written to obtain some data."

Retail

Federated Department Stores, 222 W. 7th St., Cincinnati OH 45202. (513)852-3000, 852-3700. Director of Media Relations and Editorial Resources: William Best.
Purpose: "Corporate headquarters for Federated Department Stores. Our business consists of operating 16 department store divisions across the US, two mass merchandising divisions, and a chain of grocery supermarkets in California." Information covers business and economics.
Services: Offers aid in arranging interviews, annual reports, brochures/pamphlets, placement on mailing list, statistics and press kits.
How to Contact: Write.

K-Mart Corp., 3100 W. Big Beaver, Troy MI 48084. (313)643-1021. Contact: Publicity Director.
Purpose: "We are a retail discount department store." Information covers business and merchandising.
Services: Offers aid in arranging interviews, annual reports, biographies, information searches and placement on mailing list.
How to Contact: Write.

JC Penney Co., 1301 Avenue of the Americas, New York NY 10019. (212)957-8105. Director of Public Information: Sylvia Dresner.
Purpose: "JC Penney Company is a department store and catalog chain." Information covers business, economics, how-to and self-help.
Services: Offers aid in arranging interviews, annual reports, statistics, news releases, and quarterly and annual stockholder reports.
How to Contact: Write or call. Written request is preferred.

Sears Roebuck and Co., Sears Tower, Chicago IL 60684. (312)875-2500. National Director of Public Relations: Donald Deutsch.
Purpose: "We are a mass retailer and mail order company." Information covers general business.
Services: Offers aid in arranging interviews, annual reports, brochures/pamphlets, placement on mailing list, statistics, newsletter and press kits.
How to Contact: Write. "We will answer reasonable requests."

Sports

Baseball

American League Office, 280 Park Ave., New York NY 10017. (212)682-7000.
Purpose: "An administrative service to the 14 member baseball clubs of the American League."
Services: Offers statistics and placement on mailing list.
How to Contact: Write on media letterhead.

Atlanta Braves, Box 4064, Atlanta GA 30302. (404)522-7630. Publicity Manager: Randy Donaldson.
Purpose: Information covers celebrities, entertainment, recreation and sports.
Services: Offers biographies, statistics, brochures/pamphlets, newsletter, club history and baseball. Publications include a media guide which includes biographical and statistical information on the players.
How to Contact: Write. "Only writers from daily, weekly or periodical news media need write."

Baltimore Orioles, Memorial Stadium, Baltimore MD 21218. (301)243-9800. Public Relations Director: Robert Brown.
Services: Offers biographies and statistics. Publications include information guide.
How to Contact: Write or call. Charges $2.50/mail and $2/pick up for information guide. Requests for information must be approved by Brown.

Baseball Commissioner's Office, 75 Rockefeller Plaza, New York NY 10019. Contact: Bob Wirz.

Boston Red Sox, Fenway Park, 24 Yawkey Way, Boston MA 02215. (617)267-9440. Public Relations Director: Dick Bresciani.
Purpose: Professional baseball team. Information covers celebrities, entertainment, recreation and sports.

Services: Offers aid in arranging interviews, brochures/pamphlets, biographies and statistics. Publications include press guide.
How to Contact: Write.

California Angels, Anaheim Stadium, 2000 State College Blvd., Anaheim CA 92803. (714)634-2000, 625-1123. Public Relations Directors: Tom Seeberg, Mel Franks.
Purpose: "We offer publicity and promotional services to accredited writers." Information covers celebrities, entertainment, recreation and sports.
Services: Offers aid in arranging interviews, biographies, statistics, brochures/ pamphlets, clipping services, information searches placement on mailing list, photos and press kits. Publications include media guide, containing statistics and biographies of players.
How to Contact: Write or call. Written request preferable. Charges $2.50/media guide if requested by someone who isn't a member of the press. Request on letterhead to prove credentials.

Chicago Cubs, Wrigley Field, 1060 Addison St., Chicago IL 60613. (312)281-5050. Contact: Director of Information and Services.
Purpose: "Chicago's National League ball club." Information covers celebrities (team members).
Services: Offers aid in arranging interviews, biographies, placement on mailing list, statistics and photos. Publications include media guide.
How to Contact: Write.

Chicago White Sox, Comisky Park, Dan Ryan & 35th St., Chicago IL 60616. (312)924-1000. Contact: Publicity Department.
Purpose: "We are a member of the American League." Information covers celebrities and sports.
Services: Offers aid in arranging interviews, biographies, brochures/pamphlets, placement on mailing list and photos. Publications available.
How to Contact: Write. Charges $2/media guide and $1/photo.

Cincinnati Reds, 100 Riverfront Stadium, Cincinnati OH 45202. (513)421-4510. Publicity Director: Jim Ferguson.
Services: Offers aid in arranging interviews, biographies, brochures/pamphlets, clipping services, information searches, statistics, newsletter, photos, and press kits. Publications include media guide.
How to Contact: Write or call. Charges freelance writers and photographers. All services free to accredited writers, photographers and radio and TV writers.

Cleveland Indians, Cleveland Stadium, Bouldreau Blvd., Cleveland OH 44114. (216)861-1200. Contact: Public Relations Director.
Services: Offers statistics, brochures/pamphlets and newsletters.
How to Contact: Write or call.

Detroit Tigers, Tiger Stadium, Detroit MI 48216. (313)962-4000. Director of Public Relations: Hal Middlesworth. Assistant Director of Public Relations: Dan Ewald.
Purpose: "Detroit baseball club is a member of the American League." Information covers celebrities (team members).
Services: Offers aid in arranging interviews, biographies, brochures/pamphlets, placement on mailing list, statistics and photos. Publications and photos available.
How to Contact: Write. Charges for publications and photos. Press guide and yearbook free to legitimate writers. "Sample copy of magazine or newspaper should accompany a letter from editor on magazine or newspaper letterhead."

Houston Astros, The Astrodome, Box 288, Houston TX 77001. Contact: Publicity Director.

Purpose: Baseball team.
Services: Offers brochures/pamphlets, information searches, statistics and newsletter. Publications include media guide.
How to Contact: Write.

Kansas City Royals, Box 1969, Kansas City MO 64141. (816)921-8000. Contact:Public Relations Department.
Purpose: Professional baseball club. Public relations department provides media information covering celebrities and sports.
Services: Offers aid in arranging interviews, biographies, brochures/pamphlets, clipping services, information searches, placement on mailing list, statistics, newsletter, photos and press kits. Publications include media kits.
How to Contact: Write. "We will place all our resources at the writer's fingertips, but lack of manpower prevents us from assisting in the research."

Los Angeles Dodgers, Dodger Stadium, 1000 Elysian Park Ave., Los Angeles CA 90012. (213)224-1301 or 224-1500. Director of Publicity: Steve Brener.
Purpose: Baseball team. Information covers sports.
Services: Offers aid in arranging interviews, biographies, statistics, brochures/pamphlets, clipping services, information searches, placement on mailing list, newsletter, photos and press kits.
How to Contact: Write. "The writer must be a working press member."

Milwaukee Brewers, Milwaukee County Stadium, Milwaukee WI 53246.

Minnesota Twins, Metropolitan Stadium, 8001 Cedar Ave., Bloomington MN 55420. (612)854-4040. Assistant Director of Public Relations: Laurel Prieb.
Purpose: An American League baseball team. Information covers celebrities (team members) and sports.
Services: Offers aid in arranging interviews, biographies, placement on mailing list, statistics and photos.
How to Contact: Write. "It would be best if written request be on letterhead of newspaper or magazine."

Montreal Expos, Box 500, Station M, Montreal, Quebec, Canada H1V 3P2. (514)253-3434. Publicists: Richard Giffio, Monique Giroux.
Purpose: Professional baseball team. Information covers celebrities, entertainment, recreation and sports.
Services: Offers aid in arranging interviews, biographies, statistics, brochures/pamphlets, information searches, placement on mailing list, newsletter and photos. Publications include Baseball Round-Up (quarterly) and media guide, listing statistics and biographies of players.
How to Contact: Write. Request placement on mailing list.

National League of Professional Baseball, 1 Rockefeller Plaza, New York NY 10020. (212)582-4213.
Services: Offers annual reports, statistics, information searches ("if not lengthy") and placement on mailing list. Publications include media guide.
How to Contact: Write or call. Media guide is available to "qualified journalists."

New York Mets, Shea Stadium, Flushing NY 11368. (212)672-2000. Director of Public Relations: Arthur Richman.
Purpose: "The New York Mets team is a National League baseball team which plays in Shea Stadium. We have 81 regularly scheduled home games plus exhibitions." Information covers celebrities (team members) and sports.
Services: Offers aid in arranging interviews, biographies, placement on mailing list, statistics and photos. Publications include a media guide and yearbook.

How to Contact: Write. Charges for yearbook; 1 free media guide per letter. Letters should be on the letterhead of the writer's magazine or newspaper.

New York Yankees, Yankee Stadium, Bronx NY 10451.

Oakland Athletics, Oakland Alameda County Coliseum, Oakland CA 94621. (415)638-4900. Contact: Public Relations Department.
Purpose: "The Oakland Athletics is a professional baseball team in the American league."
Services: Offers information about the team.
How to Contact: Write. Requires written request from the writer's publisher.

Philadelphia Phillies, Veterans Stadium, Broad St. & Pattison Ave., Philadelphia PA 19101. (215)463-6000. Publicity Director: Larry Sheck.
Purpose: Baseball team.
Services: Offers aid in arranging interviews, biographies, brochures/pamphlets, clipping services, information searches, statistics, newsletter and photos. Publications include media guide.
How to Contact: Write or call. "A freelance writer must have a letter from his editor or publisher. We will not give information for a speculative piece."

Pittsburgh Pirates, Three Rivers Stadium, Pittsburgh PA 15212. (412)323-1000. Contact: Director of Public Relations.
Services: Offers aid in arranging interviews, biographies, statistics, brochures/pamphlets, information searches, photos and press kits.
How to Contact: Write or call.

St. Louis Cardinals, Busch Memorial Stadium, 250 Stadium Plaza, St. Louis MO 63102. (314)421-3060. Assistant Public Relations Director: Ken Daust.
Services: Offers aid in arranging interviews, statistics, placement on mailing list and press kits.
How to Contact: Write or call.

San Diego Padres, 9449 Friars Rd., Box B-2000, San Diego CA 92120. (714)283-4494. Public Relations Director: Bob Chandler.
Services: Offers aid in arranging interviews, biographies, statistics, information searches, placement on mailing list and photos.
How to Contact: Write.

San Francisco Giants, Candlestick Park, San Francisco CA 94124. Director of Publicity: Stu Smith.
Purpose: Sports organization. Information covers celebrities and sports.
Services: Offers aid in arranging interviews, biographies, statistics, brochures/pamphlets, placement on mailing list and photos.
How to Contact: Write. "The letter should be from your editor and on publication letterhead."

Seattle Mariners, Box 4100, Seattle WA 98401. (206)628-3555. Director of Public Relations: Randy Adamack.
Purpose: "Our organization is a member of the American League of Baseball Clubs and plays in the Western Division. The club plays 162 games a year from April through September in the Kingdome, one of the few indoor stadia in the country." Information covers sports.
Services: Offers aid in arranging interviews, biographies, statistics, brochures/pamphlets, information searches, placement on mailing list, photos and press kits. Publications include a media guide, published each spring.
How to Contact: Write or call. "Our public relations department provides information

on all facets of the club, including front office and player personnel, game statistics, historical and baseball related information. Financial statements are not available."

Texas Rangers, Arlington Stadium, Box 1111, Arlington TX 76010.

Toronto Blue Jays, Box 7777, Adelaide St. PO, Toronto, Ontario, Canada M5C 2K7. (416)595-0077. Public Relations Director: Howard Starkman.
Purpose: Information covers celebrities, entertainment, recreation and sports.
Services: Offers biographies, statistics, information searches, placement on mailing list, weekly newsletter and photos. Publications include a club scrapbook published 3 times/year.
How to Contact: Write. Use official letterhead stationery.

Basketball

Atlanta Hawks, 100 Techwood Dr. NW, Atlanta GA 30303. (404)681-3600. Director of Public Relations: Chet Wright.
Purpose: "We are members of the NBA professional sports organization." Information covers sports.
Services: Offers aid in arranging interviews, biographies, statistics, brochures/ pamphlets, newsletter, photos and press kits. Publications include *Tip-Off*, the Hawks newsletter; a media guide with statistics and brief bios; and a yearbook containing feature stories.
How to Contact: Write.

Boston Celtics, Boston Garden at North Station, Boston MA 02114. (617)523-6050. Director of Public Relations: Howie McHugh.
Services: Offers aid in arranging interviews, biographies, statistics, brochures/ pamphlets, information searches, placement on mailing list and photos.
How to Contact: Write or call.

Buffalo Braves, Memorial Auditorium, Main & Terrace Aves., Buffalo NY 14202.

Chicago Bulls, 333 N. Michigan Ave., Chicago IL 60601. (312)346-1122. Public Relations Director: Brian McIntyre.
Purpose: Professional basketball team." Information covers celebrities (team members) and sports.
Services: Offers aid in arranging interviews, biographies, statistics and photos. Publications include media guide.
How to Contact: Write or call. "We prefer written requests on editor's letterhead."

Cleveland Cavaliers, Box 355, Richfield OH 48286.

Denver Nuggets, Box 4286, Denver CO 80204. Contact: Bob King.

Detroit Pistons, Pontiac Silverdome, Pontiac MI 48057. (313)338-HOOP. Public Relations Director: Bill Kreifelot.
Purpose: NBA professional basketball team. Information covers celebrities, entertainment, history and sports.
Services: Offers aid in arranging interviews, biographies, statistics, brochures/ pamphlets, placement on mailing list, newsletter and photos. Publications include an annual media guide/yearbook.
How to Contact: Write. Charges service charge for brochures, guides, yearbooks and photos. "Contact us in off-season when possible (June-July-August). Allow us lead time."

Golden State Warriors, Oakland Coliseum Arena, Oakland CA 94621. (415)683-6000.
Publicity Director: Bob Bestor. Assistant Director: Rick Moxley.
Purpose: "Professional basketball team." Information covers celebrities (team members) and sports.
Services: Offers aid in arranging interviews, biographies, placement on mailing list, statistics and photos. Publications include media guide.
How to Contact: Write or call. "We prefer a written request on your editor's letterhead."

Houston Rockets, National Basketball Association, The Summit, 10 Greenway Plaza E., Houston TX 77046, (713)627-0600. Director of Public Relations: Jim Foley.
Purpose: Professional basketball team. Information covers sports.
How to Contact: Write.

Indiana Pacers, 151 N. Delaware, Market Square Center, Indianapolis IN 46204. (317)632-3636. Public Relations Director: Lee Daniel.
Services: Offers aid in arranging interviews, biographies, statistics, clipping services and placement on mailing list (in Indiana only).
How to Contact: Write.

Kansas City Kings, 1800 Genesee, Kansas City MO 64102. (816)421-3131.
Purpose: Professional basketball team. Information covers celebrities, recreation and sports.
Services: Offers aid in arranging interviews, biographies, statistics, placement on mailing list, photos and press kits.
How to Contact: Write. Charges $2/press kit.

Los Angeles Lakers, Box 10, Inglewood CA 90306. (213)674-6000. Director of Public Relations: Roy Inglebrecht.
Purpose: "To promote, publicize and sell tickets for the Los Angeles Lakers." Information covers entertainment, recreation and sports.
Services: Offers aid in arranging interviews, biographies, placement on mailing list, statistics, photos and press kits.
How to Contact: Write or call. "Our approval of printed matter must be secured before publication."

Milwaukee Bucks, 901 N. 4th St., Milwaukee WI 53203.

New Jersey Nets, 30 Park Ave., Rutherford NJ 07070. (201)935-8888. Director of Public Relations: Ted Pase.
Services: Offers biographies, brochures/pamphlets, statistics, placement on mailing list, and newspaper clippings.
How to Contact: Call.

New Orleans Jazz, Box 53213, New Orleans LA 70153. (504)587-4263. Public Relations Director: David Fredman.
Purpose: "We are a sports business, with entertainment in mind." Information covers entertainment and sports.
Services: Offers aid in arranging interviews, biographies, brochures/pamphlets, information searches, statistics and press kits.
How to Contact: Write or call.

New York Knickerbockers, Madison Square Garden, 4 Pennsylvania Plaza, New York NY 10001. Director of Public Relations: Frank Blautschild.
Purpose: Sports organization. Information covers celebrities and sports.
Services: Offers aid in arranging interviews, biographies, statistics, brochures/pamphlets, placement on mailing list, photos and media guide.

How to Contact: Write or call. "A written request is necessary for writers unknown to our public relations department."

Philadelphia 76ers, The Spectrum Board and Pattison Sts., Philadelphia PA 19148. (215)339-7676. Contact: Public Relations Director.
Services: Offers statistics and press kits.
How to Contact: Write or call.

Phoenix Suns, Box 1369, Phoenix AZ 85001. Public Relations Director: Tom Ambrose.
Purpose: Professional basketball team. Information covers business, celebrities, entertainment, history, how-to and sports.
Services: Offers aid in arranging interviews, bibliographies, biographies, statistics, brochures/pamphlets, information searches, placement on mailing list, photos and press kits.
How to Contact: Write or call.

Portland Trail Blazers, 700 NE Multnomah St., Suite 380, Lloyd Bldg., Portland OR 97232. (503)234-9291. Publicity Director: John White.
Purpose: Basketball team.
Services: Offers aid in arranging interviews, biographies, brochures/pamphlets, clipping services, information searches, statistics and photos. Publications include press guide.
How to Contact: Write or call.

San Antonio Spurs, Hemisfair Arena, Box 530, San Antonio TX 78298. (512)224-4611. Director of Public Relations: Wayne Witt.
Purpose: Professional basketball team.
Services: Offers aid in arranging interviews, biographies, statistics and newsletter.
How to Contact: Write or call. Charges $4/media guide and $2/game magazine.

Seattle Supersonics, 419 Occidental St., Seattle WA 98104. (206)281-3450. Director of Public Relations: Rick Welts.
Purpose: Professional basketball team.
Services: Offers aid in arranging interviews, biographies, clipping services, statistics and photos. Publications include press guide.
How to Contact: Write or call.

Washington Bullets, Capital Centre, Landover MD 20786. (301)350-3400. Director of Public Relations: Mark Pray.
Purpose: Professional basketball team. Information covers sports.
Services: Offers aid in arranging interviews, biographies, statistics, brochures/pamphlets and photos. Publications include a press guide and programs.
How to Contact: Write. "Request should be submitted on publication letterhead."

Football

Atlanta Falcons, 521 Capital Ave. SW, Atlanta GA 30312. (404)588-1111. Director of Public Relations: Charlie Dayton.
Services: Offers aid in arranging interviews, biographies, brochures/pamphlets, statistics, information searches, placement on mailing list, newsletter and photos.
How to Contact: Write or call.

Baltimore Colts, Executive Plaza, Hunt Valley MD 21031. Contact: Jim Husand.

Buffalo Bills, 1 Bill's Dr., Orchard Park NY 14127. (716)648-1800. Public Relations Director: Budd Thalman.

Services: Offers aid in arranging interviews, biographies, statistics, placement on mailing list and newsletter.
How to Contact: Write or call.

Chicago Bears, 55 E. Jackson Blvd., Chicago IL 60602. (312)663-5409.

Cincinnati Bengals, 200 Riverfront Stadium, Cincinnati OH 45202. (513)621-3550. Public Relations Director: Al Heim.
Purpose: Sports organization. Information covers celebrities and sports.
Services: Offers aid in arranging interviews, biographies, statistics, brochures/pamphlets, clipping services, placement on mailing list, photos and press kits.
How to Contact: Write.

Cleveland Browns, Tower B Cleveland Stadium, Cleveland OH 44114. (216)696-5555. Director of Public Relations: Nathan Wallack.
Purpose: Professional football team. Information covers celebrities (team members) and sports.
Services: Offers aid in arranging interviews, biographies, brochures/pamphlets, placement on mailing list, statistics and photos. Publications include media guide.
How to Contact: Write. "You must be an accredited writer."

Dallas Cowboys, 6116 N. Central Expressway, Dallas TX 75206. (214)369-8000. Director of Public Relations: Doug Todd.
Purpose: Professional football team. Information covers celebrities (team members) and sports.
Services: Offers aid in arranging interviews, biographies, brochures/pamphlets, placement on mailing list, statistics and photos.
How to Contact: Write. "We prefer a letter of introduction from the editor of your magazine or newspaper on company letterhead stating the information wanted and requesting placement on our mailing list."

Denver Broncos, 5700 Logan St., Denver CO 80216. (303)623-8778. Contact: Public Relations Director.
Services: Offers aid in arranging interviews, biographies and statistics. Publications available.
How to Contact: Write or call.

Detroit Lions, 1401 Michigan Ave., Detroit MI 48216. (313)335-4131. Contact: Public Relations Department.
Purpose: Professional football team. Information covers celebrities (team members) and sports.
Services: Offers aid in arranging interviews (accredited only, no freelancers), bibliographies, placement on mailing list, statistics and photos.
How to Contact: Write. "We prefer a written request on company letterhead. We will only send out general information."

Green Bay Packers, 1265 Lombardi Ave., Green Bay WI 54304. (414)494-2351. Publicity Director: Lee Remmel.
Services: Offers aid in arranging interviews, biographies, statistics, clipping services, information searches, placement on mailing list, newsletter and photos.
How to Contact: Write or call.

Houston Oilers, 6910 Fannin, Houston TX 77001. (713)797-9111. Public Relations Officers: Bob Heim, Jack Cherry.
Purpose: Professional football team." Information covers celebrities (team members) and sports.
Services: Offers aid in arranging interviews, biographies, brochures/pamphlets, place-

ment on mailing list, statistics and photos.
How to Contact: Write or call. "New writers need introduction from editor by phone or on company letterhead."

Kansas City Chiefs, 1 Arrowhead Dr., Arrowhead Stadium, Kansas City MO 64129. (816)924-9300. Public Relations Director: Bob Springer.
Purpose: Sports organization. Information covers celebrities and sports.
Services: Offers aid in arranging interviews, biographies, statistics, brochures/ pamphlets, placement on mailing list, photos and press kits.
How to Contact: "You may initiate your request by phone, but a written request is required to receive information."

Los Angeles Rams, 10271 W. Pico Blvd., Los Angeles CA 90064. (213)277-4700. Director of Promotions: Jack Geyer. Directors of Public Relations: Jerry Wilcox, Geno Efler.
Purpose: "To promote and publicize the Los Angeles Rams." Information covers sports.
Services: Offers aid in arranging interviews, annual reports, biographies, brochures/ pamphlets, clipping services, placement on mailing list, statistics, newsletter, photos and press kits. Publications include media guide.
How to Contact: Write or call.

Miami Dolphins, 330 Biscayne Blvd., Miami FL 33132. (305)379-1851. Public Relations Director: Bob Kearney.
Purpose: Football team.
Services: Offers aid in arranging interviews, biographies, information searches and statistics. Publications include media guide.
How to Contact: Write or call.

Minnesota Vikings, 7110 France Ave. S., Edina MN 55435. (612)920-4805. Contact: Public Relations Department.
Purpose: Football team. Information covers business, celebrities, economics, entertainment, health/medicine, history, recreation, self-help, sports, technical data and travel.
Services: Offers aid in arranging interviews, annual reports, biographies, statistics, brochures/pamphlets, placement on mailing list, newsletter and photos.
How to Contact: Write. Charges for media guides. Players don't charge for photos.

National Football League, 410 Park Ave., New York NY 10022. Contact: Jim Hefferdan.

New England Patriots, Schaefer Stadium, Rt. 1, Foxboro MA 02035. (617)543-7911. Director of Public Relations: Pat Horne.
Purpose: Professional football team. Information covers celebrities, entertainment, health/medicine, history, sports and travel.
Services: Offers aid in arranging interviews, annual reports, bibliographies, biographies, brochures/pamphlets, information searches, placement on mailing list and statistics.
How to Contact: Write.

New Orleans Saints, 944 St. Charles Ave., New Orleans LA 70130. (504)524-1421. Assistant Public Relations Director: Greg Suit.
Purpose: Football team.
Services: Offers aid in arranging interviews, biographies, brochures/pamphlets, information searches, statistics, newsletter and photos. Publications include media guide.
How to Contact: Write or call.

New York Giants, Giants Stadium, East Rutherford NJ 07073.

New York Jets, 598 Madison Ave., New York NY 10022. (212)421-6600. Public Relations Director: Susan Curino.
Services: Offers media guides.
How to Contact: Write.

Oakland Raiders, Oakland Coliseum Arena, Oakland CA 94621. Contact: Rick Morley.

Philadelphia Eagles, Veterans Stadium, Broad St. and Pattison Ave., Philadelphia PA 19148. (215)463-2500. Public Relations Director: Jim Gallager.
Purpose: Football team.
Services: Offers aid in arranging interviews, biographies, statistics, brochures/pamphlets, information searches, newsletter, photos and press kits. Publications include media guide.
How to Contact: Write or call.

Pittsburgh Steelers, Three Rivers Stadium, 300 Stadium Circle, Pittsburgh PA. (412)323-1200. Public Relations Director: Joe Gordon.
Services: Offers aid in arranging interviews, annual reports, bibliographies, biographies, information searches, photos and press kits. Publications available.
How to Contact: Write or call.

Saint Louis Cardinals, 200 Stadium Plaza, St. Louis MO. (314)421-0777. Public Relations Director: Kevin Byrne.
Services: Offers aid in arranging interviews, biographies, statistics, placement on mailing list, photos and press kits. Publications available.
How to Contact: Write or call. There is a charge for press releases.

San Diego Chargers, 9449 Friars Rd., San Diego CA 92108. (714)280-2111. Director of Public Relations: Rick Smith. Assistant Director of Public Relations: Rick Schless.
Purpose: Football team.
Services: Offers aid in arranging interviews, biographies, information searches, statistics and photos. Publications include media guide.
How to Contact: Write or call.

San Francisco 49ers, 1255 Post St., Suite 300, San Francisco CA 94109.

Seattle Seahawks, 5305 Lake Washington Blvd., Kirkland WA 98033. (206)827-9777. Contact: Public Relations Department.
Purpose: Professional football team.
Services: Offers aid in arranging interviews, biographies, statistics, information searches, placement on mailing list, newsletter, photos and clipping files. Publications include press guide.
How to Contact: Write or call.

Tampa Bay Buccaneers, 1 Buccaneer Pl., Tampa FL 33607. (813)870-2700. Contact: Public Relations Department.
Purpose: Football team.
Services: Offers aid in arranging interviews, biographies, statistics, information searches, placement on mailing list and newsletter. Publications include media guide.
How to Contact: Write or call. Requests a copy of the article for their files.

Washington Redskins, Box 17247, Dulles International Airport, Washington DC. 20041.

Hockey

American Hockey League, 31 Elm St., Springfield MA 01103. (413)781-2030. Vice President, Secretary: Gordon C. Anziano.
Purpose: Professional ice hockey league. "We have nine active franchises and two inactive, in North America, Nova Scotia and Canada. Schedule runs from October through April in regular season, playoffs in April and May each year. We have working agreements with many NHL teams." Information covers sports.
Services: Publications include *Annual Guide*, which contains current and all-time records of the league.
How to Contact: Write. Charges for *Annual Guide*; "last year, it was $2.50."

Atlanta Flames Hockey Team, 100 Techwood Dr. NW, Atlanta GA 30303. (404)681-2100. Public Relations Director: John Marshall.
Purpose: "We are a professional sports team." Information covers sports.
Services: Offers aid in arranging interviews, biographies, statistics, brochures/pamphlets, clipping services, placement on mailing list, newsletter, photos and press kits.
How to Contact: Write or call.

Birmingham Bulls, Birmingham Jefferson Civic Center Coliseum, 1 Civic Center Plaza, Birmingham AL 35203. (205)251-2855.
Purpose: World hockey league team.
Services: Offers aid in arranging interviews, biographies, statistics and placement on mailing list. Publications include media guide.
How to Contact: Write or call.

Boston Bruins, Boston Garden, 150 Causeway, Boston MA 02114. (617)227-3206. Director of Public Relations: Nat Greenberg.
Purpose: National Hockey League team.
Services: Offers aid in arranging interviews, biographies, statistics, placement on mailing list and photos. Publications include media guide.
How to Contact: Write.

Buffalo Sabres, Memorial Auditorium, Buffalo NY 14202. (716)856-7300. Public Relations Director: Paul Wieland.
Purpose: National Hockey League team.
Services: Offers aid in arranging interviews, biographies, statistics, information searches, placement on mailing list and photos. Publications include media guide.
How to Contact: Write or call.

Chicago Black Hawks, 1800 W. Madison St., Chicago IL 60612. (312)733-5300. Public Relations Director: Don Murphy.
Services: Offers aid in arranging interviews, biographies, brochures/pamphlets, information searches, statistics, photos and press kits. Publications include press guide, programs and schedules.
How to Contact: Write or call.

Cincinnati Stingers, Riverfront Coliseum, Cincinnati OH 45202. (513)241-1818. Media Relations Director: Robert C. Firestone.
Purpose: "Professional hockey team; a member of the National Hockey League." Information covers celebrities (team members), history (of club) and sports.
Services: Offers aid in arranging interviews, biographies, statistics and photos.
How to Contact: Write or call. "Prefer written request on letterhead of magazine or newspaper. Most accredited writers are already on our mailing list, but we will consider someone after written request comes in."

Cleveland Barons, The Coliseum, Richfield OH 44286.

Colorado Rockies Hockey Club, McNichols Sports Arena, Denver CO 80204. (303)573-1800. Public Relations Director: Kevin O'Brien.
Purpose: "To provide entertainment in the form of professional sports (hockey). Our department is responsible for the dissemination of information dealing with the team, individual players and statistics. We are also responsible for maintaining relationships with the various print and electronic media for the benefit of the club. Other functions include contributions to deserving charities and civic programs, public appearances and a high visibility for the club in front of the public." Information covers sports.
Services: Offers aid in arranging interviews, annual reports, biographies, statistics, brochures/pamphlets, placement on mailing list, newsletter, photos, press kits, movies and speakers for banquets. Publications include an annual media guide/yearbook, weekly press releases and the *NHL Annual Guide* with biographies on every player.
How to Contact: Write or call. "We are strictly a sports information office dealing in hockey but we will try to help/answer any serious inquiry."

Detroit Red Wings, Olympia Stadium, 5920 Grand River at McGraw, Detroit MI 48208. (313)895-7000. Public Relations Director: Budd Lynch.
Services: Offers aid in arranging interviews, biographies, brochures/pamphlets and statistics. Publications include media guide.
How to Contact: Write or call. Written request preferred. No interviews on day of game.

Edmunton Oilers, Edmunton Coliseum, Edmunton, Alberta, Canada T5B 4M9. Public Relations Director: John Short.
Purpose: World Hockey League team.
Services: Offers aid in arranging interviews, biographies, statistics, placement on mailing list and photos. Publications include media guide.
How to Contact: Write or call. Explain why information is needed.

Houston Aeros, The Summit, 10 Greenway Plaza, Houston TX 77046.

Indianapolis Racers, 137 E. Ohio St., Indianapolis IN 46204. (317)635-3131. Director of Hockey Operations: Bill Neal.
Purpose: World Hockey League team.
Services: Offers aid in arranging interviews, biographies, statistics, information searches, placement on mailing list and photos. Publications include press guide.
How to Contact: Call.

Los Angeles Kings, The Forum, 3900 W. Manchester Blvd., Box 10, Inglewood CA 90306. (213)674-6000. Director of Public Relations: John Wolf.
Purpose: "To promote and publicize hockey." Information covers entertainment.
Services: Offers aid in arranging interviews, biographies, brochures/pamphlets, placement on mailing list, statistics and newsletter.
How to Contact: Write or call.

Minnesota North Stars, Metropolitan Center, 7901 Cedar Ave. S, Bloomington MN 55420. (612)854-4411. Contact: Public Relations Director.
Services: Offers aid in arranging interviews, biographies, brochures/pamphlets, clipping services, placement on mailing list, statistics and photos. Publications include rule book and scoring and media guide.
How to Contact: Write or call.

Montreal Canadians, 2313 St. Catherine St. W. Montreal, Quebec, Canada H3H 1N2. Public Relations Director: Eyves Tremblay.
Purpose: World Hockey League team.

Services: Offers aid in arranging interviews, biographies, statistics, placement on mailing list and photos. Publications include yearbook.
How to Contact: Call.

National Hockey League, 1221 Avenue of the Americas, 14th Floor, New York, NY 10020. Director of Public Relations: Bob Casey.
Services: Offers aid in arranging interviews and biographies (will direct to individual teams); information searches (limited); and placement on mailing list (write to New York office). Publications available.
How to Contact: Write. No charge for accredited writers, but charges fee to the general public. For statistical information write to the Montreal Office, 920 Sun Life Bldg., Montreal, Quebec, Canada H3B 2W2.

National Hockey League, 920 Sun Life Bldg., Montreal, Quebec, Canada H3B 2W2. (514)871-9220. Director of Public Relations: Bob Casey.
Services: Offers statistics and placement on mailing list (write to New York office). Publications available.
How to Contact: Write.

New England Whalers, 1 Civic Center Plaza, Hartford CT 06103. (203)728-3366. Director of Public Relations: Dennis Randall.
Purpose: Hockey team.
Services: Offers aid in arranging interviews, biographies, brochures/pamphlets, placement on mailing list, statistics and photos. Publications include: *Yearbook & Offical Guide* and *Blueline Magazine*.
How to Contact: Write or call. Charges for publications.

New York Islanders, 1155 Conklin St., Farmingdale NY 11735. (516)694-5522. Public Relations Director: Jim Higgins.
Purpose: National hockey league team.
Services: Offers aid in arranging interviews, biographies, statistics, placement on mailing list and photos. Publications include media guide, yearbook and programs.
How to Contact: Write. Charges for publications.

New York Rangers, Madison Square Gardens, 4 Pennsylvania Plaza, New York NY 10001. (212)563-8000. Contact: Public Relations Director.
Services: Offers aid in arranging interviews, biographies, clipping services, information searches, statistics, placement on mailing list and photos. Publications include yearbook, training camp guide, newsletter and programs.
How to Contact: Write or call. Accredited writer may use any services listed, but freelance writers must have specific assignment.

Philadelphia Flyers, The Spectrum, Pattison Place, Philadelphia PA 19148. (215)465-4500. Contact: Director of Public Relations.
Services: Offers aid in arranging interviews, biographies, brochures/pamphlets, clipping services, information searches, statistics, placement on mailing list and photos. Publications include media guide.
How to Contact: Write or call. "Write if detailed information is needed."

Phoenix Roadrunners, 1826 W. McDowell Rd., Phoenix AZ 85007.

Pittsburgh Penguins, Civic Arena, Gate 7, Pittsburgh PA 15219. (412)434-8911. Public Relations Director: Terry Schiffhauer.
Purpose: Professional hockey team in the NHL.
Services: Offers aid in arranging interviews, biographies, statistics, placement on

mailing list, photos and press kits.
How to Contact: Write or call. Written request preferable.

Quebec Nordiques, 2025 Avenue DuColisee, Quebec, Canada G1L 4W7. (418)529-4161. Director of Public Relations: Dennis Caron.
Purpose: World Hockey League team.
Services: Offers aid in arranging interviews, biographies, statistics, information searches and photos. Publications include media guide.
How to Contact: Write or call.

Saint Louis Blues, The Checker Dome, 5700 Oakland, St. Louis MO 63110. (314)781-5300. Public Relations Director: Susie Mathieu.
Services: Offers aid in arranging interviews, biographies, brochures/pamphlets, clipping services, information searches and statistics. Publications available.
How to Contact: Write or call. "We would like a copy of the piece when finished."

San Diego Hawks, 3500 Sports Arena Blvd., San Diego CA 92110. (714)225-9633. Public Relations Department: Ron Oakes.
Purpose: Professional hockey team. Information covers celebrities (team members) and sports.
Services: Offers aid in arranging interviews, biographies, brochures/pamphlets, placement on mailing list, statistics and photos.
How to Contact: Write or call.

Toronto Maple Leafs, Maple Leaf Gardens, 60 Carlton St., Toronto, Ontario, Canada M5B 1L1. (416)368-1641. Public Relations Director: Stan Obodiac.
Purpose: National Hockey League team.
Services: Offers aid in arranging interviews, biographies, statistics, placement on mailing list and photos. Publications include fact book.
How to Contact: Write.

Vancouver Canucks, Pacific Coliseum, 100 N. Renfrez St., Vancouver, British Columbia V5K 3N7. (604)254-5141. Director of Public Relations: Norm Jewison.
Purpose: National Hockey League team.
Services: Offers aid in arranging interviews, biographies, statistics, information searches and photos. Publications include official yearbook and training camp guide.
How to Contact: Write or call.

Washington Capitals, Capital Center, Landover MD 20786. (301)350-3400, ext. 440. Director of Public Relations: Pierce Gardner.
Services: Offers aid in arranging interviews, biographies, brochures/pamphlets, clipping services, information searches, statistics, placement on mailing list and photos (limited). Publications include press guide and schedules.
How to Contact: Write or call. Prefers written request for information from accredited writers only.

Winnipeg Jets, 15-1430 Maroons Rd., Winnipeg, Manitoba, Canada R3G 0L1. (204)772-9491. Superivorsor of Minor Officials: Sam Sanregret.
Purpose: World Hockey League team.
Services: Offers aid in arranging interviews, biographies, statistics, placement on mailing list and photos. Publications include media guide.
How to Contact: Write or call.

World Hockey Association, 1 Financial Plaza, Hartford CT 06103. (203)278-4240. Director of Public Relations: John A. Hewig.
Purpose: "To determine rules and maintain harmony between teams. We are the governing body for seven teams." Information covers history and sports.

Services: Offers biographies, statistics, information searches and photos. Publications include media guide and media directory.
How to Contact: Write or call. Charges for publications.

Miscellaneous

Daytona International Speedway/Alabama International Speedway, 1801 Speedway Blvd., Daytona Beach Fl 32015. (904)253-6711. Contact: Ron Meade.
Purpose: "To promote motor sports at Daytona International Speedway and Alabama International Speedway." Information covers recreation and motor sports.
Services: Offers biographies, statistics, placement on mailing list, photos and press kits.
How to Contact: Write. Charges $3/8x10 print and $25/search fee "if the photos are over two years old."

Giants Stadium, 15 Columbus Circle, New York NY 10023. (212)935-8111. Director of Media Services: Ed Croake.
Purpose: Giants Stadium, with a seating capacity of 78,000, houses football and soccer events, concerts and expositions. It is the home of the New York Giants. Information covers art, business, celebrities, entertainment, food, health/medicine, how-to, industry, law, music, nature, new products, politics, recreation, science, self-help, sports, technical data and travel.
Services: Offers aid in arranging interviews, annual reports, biographies, statistics, brochures/pamphlets, information searches, placement on mailing list, newsletter, photos and press kits.
How to Contact: Write.

Madison Square Garden Boxing, Inc., 4 Pennsylvania Plaza, New York NY 10001. (212)563-8000. Vice President/Publicity Director: John F.X. Condon.
Services: Offers biographies, placement on mailing list, photos and press kits.
How to Contact: Write.

New York Racing Association, Aqueduct Race Track, Box 90, Jamaica NY 11417. Press Director: Sam Kanchuger.
How to Contact: "Write for information needed and we will screen mail and send what is available."

New York State Racing & Wagering Board, 2 World Trade Center, New York NY 10047. (212)488-4040. Public Relations Director: Ken Beh.
Purpose: "Regulation and supervision of parimutual racing and wagering systems in New York State."
Services: Offers annual reports and statistics.

Purolator Racing Operations, 3200 Natal St., Fayetteville NC 28306. (919)425-4181. Manager, Public Relations: Joe Kennedy.
Purpose: "To provide information about Purolator's participation in Winston Cup Grand National racing and about David Pearson, driver of the Purolator Mercury." Information covers sports.
Services: Offers aid in arranging interviews, placement on mailing list, newsletter, photos and press kits.
How to Contact: Write or call.

Soccer

American Soccer League, 770 Lexington Ave., New York NY 10021. (212)826-6710. Public Relations Director: Haskel Cohen.
Services: Offers placement on mailing list and statistics. Publications include press guides, media guides and press releases.
How to Contact: Write. An accredited writer may get information free. Charges to general public.

Chicago Stings, 1525 333 N. Michigan Ave., Chicago IL 60601. (312)558-5425. Director of Media Relations: Jerry Epstein.
Services: Offers aid in arranging interviews, biographies, brochures/pamphlets, information searches, placement on mailing list, statistics, photos and press kits. Publications include media guide.
How to Contact: Write or call.

Dallas Tornados, 6116 N. Central Expressway, Suite 333, Dallas TX 75206. (214)750-0900. Public Relations Director: Paul Ridings.
Services: Offers aid in arranging interviews, biographies, brochures/pamphlets, information searches, placement on mailing list, statistics, photos and press kits. Publications include media guide.
How to Contact: Write or call.

New York Apollos, 125 Jericho Turnpike, Jericho NY 11753. (516)997-5113. Contact: Public Relations Director.
Purpose: Soccer team.
How to Contact: Write.

New York Cosmos, 75 Rockefeller Plaza, New York NY 10019. (212)265-7315. Public Relations Director: Chuck Adams.
Purpose: "We are a professional soccer team." Information covers sports.
Services: Offers biographies, statistics, brochures/pamphlets, placement on mailing list, and press kits. Publications include *Cosmos Media Guide*, annual club information and player biographies.
How to Contact: "A letter on a publication's letterhead will usually suffice. However, in order to be placed on our mailing list, a writer must be covering soccer with some regularity."

North American Soccer League, 1133 Avenue of Americas, New York NY 10036. (212)575-0066. Public Relations Director: James Trecker.
Services: Offers aid in arranging interviews (will direct to commissioner of league and public relations director of individual teams); biographies (select); information searches (limited); placement on mailing list; newsletter, statistics and photos. Publications include media guide "available to qualified writers."
How to Contact: Write or call. Charges for photos if they are to be used in a commercial book.

Portland Timbers, 10151 SW Barbur Blvd., S-101D, Portland OR 97219. (503)246-9926. Director of Public Relations: John F. Hahn.
Purpose: "To deal in all media relations for the professional soccer club." Information covers entertainment and sports.
Services: Offers aid in arranging interviews, biographies, statistics, brochures/pamphlets, photos and press kits.
How to Contact: Write or call.

Tennis

World Championship Tennis, Inc., 1990 1st National Bank Bldg., Dallas TX 75202. (214)748-5828. Public Relations Director: Bob Yates.

Services: Offers aid in arranging interviews, biographies, clipping services and information searches.
How to Contact: Write or call.

World Team Tennis Commissioners Office, 9300 Dielman Dr., St. Louis MO 63132. (314)727-7211. Contact: Public Relations Department.
Services: Offers biographies and statistics. Publications include media guide.
How to Contact: Write or call.

Tire & Rubber Products

Firestone Tire and Rubber Co., 1200 Firestone Pkwy., Akron OH 44317. (216)379-6000. Director of Public Relations Department: B.W. Frazier.
Purpose: "We are an industrial firm specializing in tire, rubber, plastics and diversified products." Information covers agriculture, economics, health/medicine, history, how-to (tire care), industry, nature, new products, recreation, science, sports, technical data and travel. "All of these relate to the rubber industry."
Services: Offers aid in arranging interviews, annual reports, bibliographies, biographies, statistics, brochures/pamphlets, information searches, placement on mailing list, photos and press kits.
How to Contact: Write or call.

General Tire and Rubber Co., 1 General St., Akron OH 44329. (216)798-2192. Director of Public Relations/Advertising: Jack Marshall.
Purpose: "General Tire and Rubber Company is a rubber manufacturer." Information covers entertainment, health/medicine, industry, new products, recreation, sports and technical data.
Services: Offers aid in arranging interviews, annual reports, bibliographies, biographies, statistics, brochures/pamphlets, information searches, placement on mailing list, newsletter, photos and press kits.
How to Contact: Write.

Uniroyal, Inc., 1230 Avenue of the Americas, New York NY 10020. (212)489-4000. Contact: Public Relations Department.
Purpose: "Uniroyal is an international developer and distributor of chemical, plastic and rubber products." Information covers agriculture, business, history, how-to, industry, new products, technical data and travel.
Services: Offers aid in arranging interviews, annual reports, bibliographies, biographies, statistics, brochures/pamphlets, information searches, placement on mailing list, newsletter, photos, press kits, and use of the corporate library (by request).
How to Contact: Write.

Transportation

Alco Historic Photos, American Locomotive Co., Box 655, Schenectady NY 12301. (518)374-0153. Chairman, Board of Trustees: Joseph D. Thompson.
Purpose: "Alco Historic Photos is the curator/custodian of photographic negatives of railroad locomotives built by Alco Products (American Locomotive Co.) and its predecessors. These are the so-called builder's photos taken by the company photographer. Our organization has published a catalog of the negatives and supplies prints to order (a mail order activity)." Information covers technical data and railroad locomotives.
Services: Offers information searches, photos, catalogs, photocopies of data and prints of engineering drawings. A publications and price list is available.
How to Contact: Write. Visits to research the photo collection are by appointment only. No charge for minor research; extensive research is by negotiation, subject to manpower limitations. Charges $3 postpaid/8x10 photo; prices for larger sizes on request. Charges $5/print published. Credit line and a copy of the publication required.

Allegheny Airlines, Inc., Washington National Airport, Washington DC 20001. (703)892-7000.
Purpose: "Our main activities are passenger and cargo transportation." Information covers economics, food, history, technical data, travel and finance.
Services: Offers annual reports, bibliographies, biographies, brochures/pamphlets, placement on mailing list, statistics, photos and press kits. Publications available.
How to Contact: Write or call.

Delta Air Lines, Inc., Harstfield Atlanta International Airport, Atlanta GA 30320. (404)762-2531. Contact: Public Relations Office.
Purpose: "Our main activities are cargo or passenger transportation." Information covers business, economics, history, how-to, industry, recreation, technical data and travel.
Services: Offers aid in arranging interviews, annual reports, bibliographies, biographies, statistics, brochures/pamphlets, placement on mailing list, photos and press kits.
How to Contact: Write. "Allow two weeks for delivery of requested information."

Eastern Airlines, Inc., Miami International Airport, Miami FL 33148. (305)873-6325. Public Relations Officer: Tom Meyers.
Purpose: Eastern is a major airline; information covers business, industry and travel.
Services: Offers aid in arranging interviews, annual reports, statistics, brochures/pamphlets, placement on mailing list and photos.
How to Contact: Write or call. "Because we are a small department, we don't do research. We will provide available information."

East Texas Motor Freight, Box 10125, Dallas TX 75207. (214)638-2280. Director of Public Relations/Advertising: Joel H. Mathis.
Purpose: "We are a motor freight/common carrier company." Information covers agriculture, art, business, celebrities, economics, entertainment, food, health/medicine, history, industry, music, nature, new products, politics, recreation, science, sports, technical data and travel.
Services: Offers statistics, brochures/pamphlets, placement on mailing list, newsletter and photos.
How to Contact: Write or call.

Federal Express Corp., 2850 Director's Cove, Memphis TN 38138. (901)369-3613. Manager, Media Relations: Armand Schneider.
Purpose: "The nation's only airline specializing in door-to-door, nationwide overnight transportation of high-priority shipments. Federal Express serves 135 major markets and more than 10,000 communities with 60 aircraft and more than 1,000 radio-equipped vans. The company handles more than 40,000 shipments nightly through its system. Federal Express has applied to CAB for permission to go into passenger service. It will use quick-change 727s and 737s to carry cargo at night and passengers during the daytime."
Services: Offers aid in arranging interviews, annual reports, biographies, placement on mailing list, photos and press kits.
How to Contact: Write or call. "Prearrange through PR department for interviews of top-level management."

The Greyhound Corp., 111 W. Clarendon Ave., Phoenix AZ 85077. (602)248-5276. Director, Public Relations: Lee Whitehead.
Purpose: "Greyhound Lines, Inc., is the nation's largest passenger transportation company. We have regular route service, charter service and group travel."
Services: Offers aid in arranging interviews, annual reports, bibliographies, biographies, statistics, brochures/pamphlets, placement on mailing list, photos and press kits.
How to Contact: Write or call.

Lykes Brothers Steamship Co., Lykes Center, New Orleans LA 70130. (504)523-6611.
Assistant Vice President, Public Relations: Larry Guerin.
Purpose: Global ocean freight transportation.
Services: Offers aid in arranging interviews, biographies, brochures/pamphlets and photos.
How to Contact: Write or call.

National Railroad Passenger Corporation, 400 N. Capital St., Washington DC 20001.
(202)484-7220. Director of Public Information: Brian Duff.
Purpose: "We are a nationwide intercity rail passenger service. We serve over 500 communities on a 27,000-mile network."
Services: Offers statistics, brochures/pamphlets, press releases, background material, photographs, 35mm slides and ridership. Publishes an annual report in February, a five year plan in October and a monthly ridership/one-time performance report.
How to Contact: Write or call. "Writers who regularly cover transportation or travel may request to be added to the mailing list for the above publications."

National Trailways Bus Systems, Box 3343, Harrisburg PA 17105.
Purpose: "We are an intercity bus system, and our activities include regular line passenger service and package express, charter buses for groups and tour busses." Information covers entertainment, how-to, industry, recreation, sports and travel.
Services: Offers aid in arranging interviews, annual reports, brochures/pamphlets, information searches, placement on mailing list, photos and press kits.
How to Contact: Write.

Pan American World Airways, Pan Am Building, New York NY 10017.
(212)880-1234. Contact: Director of Public Relations. Film Manager: Ruth Keary.
Purpose: "Pan Am is a commercial air transportation company, primarily serving international route network to some 19 cities in the United States and to some 70 cities in 58 foreign countries and territories around the world. Pan Am also engages in hotel operations through its unconsolidated subsidiary intercontinental hotel corporation. It maintains an airline service division, providing management and technical assistance to aviation interests abroad, and has an aerospace services division, providing managing and technical support to the US Air Force space program. The metropolitan air facilities division serves general aviation interests. Pan Am also holds 50% interest in the Falcon Jet Corp., which markets business jet aircraft worldwide." Information covers business, economics and technical data.
Services: Offers aid in arranging interviews, annual reports, brochures/pamphlets, placement on mailing list, statistics, photos and press kits.
How to Contact: Write. "Must be accredited member of the press. Photos supplied for use within travel context. Charges variable reproduction fee (lab costs) to supply duplicates."

Transport International Pool, 2 Bala Cynwyd Plaza, Bala Cynwyd PA 19004.
(215)667-7100. Director of Communications: Joseph J. O'Donnell Jr.
Purpose: "Transport International Pool rents and leases over 50 different types of semitrailers at over 120 branches in the US, Canada, UK and western Europe." Information covers industry and new products.
Services: Offers aid in arranging interviews, brochures/pamphlets, newsletter, photos and press kits. Publications include "yearly promotional calendar, which lists truck trailer weight, length, height restrictions in 50 states; and other leasing information."
How to Contact: Write or call.

Trans World Airlines, 605 3rd Ave., New York NY 10016. (212)557-6107. Vice President, Communications: Jerry Cosley.
Purpose: Trans World Airlines (TWA) is an airline, and a subsidiary of Trans World Corporation. Information covers business, economics, lodging and travel.

Services: Offers annual reports, statistics, brochures/pamphlets, placement on mailing list and press kits.
How to Contact: Written request is preferable. Write for a list of regional office locations.

Union Pacific Railroad, 1416 Dodge St., Omaha NE 68179. Director of Public Relations: Barry B. Combs.
Purpose: To promote Union Pacific Railroad and railroads in general.
Services: Offers 15,000 color transparencies and many b&w prints on national parks and monuments, cities and regions covered by the railroad. Also photos on railroad equipment and operations, and western agriculture and industry.
How to Contact: Write or call. Credit line required.

United Airlines, Inc., 1200 Algonquin Rd., Mt. Prospect IL 60056. Corporate Public Relations Director: James A. Kennedy, Box 66100, Chicago IL 60666. (312)952-4324.
Purpose: Information covers business, economics, food, health/medicine, history. how-to, industry, sports, technical data and travel.
Services: Offers aid in arranging interviews, annual reports, bibliographies, biographies, brochures/pamphlets, information searches ("to a limited degree") and newsletter (restricted to "qualified writers and somebody who will be writing on a steady basis"). Publications include *Inside United Airlines.*
How to Contact: Write.

Libraries & Archives

"Virtually any library has more information than most writers realize, and it's all just sitting there: public property," freelance writer Ron Frederick is quoted as saying in John Brady's *The Craft of Interviewing*. "I think that writers should use libraries the same way that truckers use public roads—that is, as public resources for creating private income."

Not all libraries, of course, are public property. Most are, but some are owned by and operated to serve companies or organizations. Yet, even privately owned libraries are willing to help writers and researchers.

Included in this list are specialized libraries, public and private, that cover particular subjects. Also listed here are archives—institutions that house documents, manuscripts, personal papers and other material, in addition to the usual complement of books and magazines. General public libraries, because of their broad coverage, are not included unless they contain special collections.

For information about using libraries in general, see "Getting Cozy in Public (Libraries)" in the introductory material of this book. For locations and brief descriptions of additional libraries, consult the *American Library Directory* (R.R. Bowker), available in, of course, most public libraries.

Libraries

Akron-Summit County Public Library, 55 S. Main St., Akron OH 44326. (216)762-7621. Community Relations Director: Patricia H. Latshaw.
Purpose: "To provide information services and programs to the general public and specialized reference services to those needing them. The Lighter Than Air Society collection is available for use in the library. It is one of the most extensive collections on this subject in the world. Special genealogical materials, as well as materials on the growth of the trucking industry (which largely began in Akron) are available." Information covers agriculture, art, business, celebrities, economics, entertainment, food, health/medicine, history, how-to, industry, law, music, nature, new products, politics, recreation, science, self-help, sports, technical information and travel.
Services: Offers brochures/pamphlets and newsletter.
How to Contact: "Visit the library any Monday through Thursday, 9 a.m. to 9 p.m.; Friday, 9 a.m. to 6 p.m.; or Saturday, 9 a.m. to 5 p.m. Many of the materials that we have can be photocopied at the writer's expense (single copy for reference use of a given page or item), but special collections such as the Lighter Than Air Collection cannot be used outside the library." Charges for reproduction of materials.

American Museum of Natural History Library, Photographic Collection, Central Park W. at 79th St., New York NY 10024. (212)873-1300, ext. 346. Collection Librarian: Pamela Haas. Associate Manager: Dorothy Fulton.

Purpose: "The photographic collection, which has been growing since the museum's opening in 1870, now consists of close to a half million b&w prints and almost 50,000 color transparencies. Many of these images are from museum expeditions to locations previously unseen through the lens of a camera. Examples of human beings, scenery, animals, plants, and minerals from all over the world are to be found in the files, as well as visual documentation of scientific phenomena." Information covers art, health/medicine and nature.

Services: Offers annual reports, bibliographies, brochures/pamphlets and photos.

How to Contact: Write or call. "Open Monday through Friday, 11 a.m. to 4 p.m. No appointment is needed, and guidance with files is provided. Prints may be ordered on a prepayment basis. Transparencies may be rented for preview or purchased for personal use." Charges for prints and transparencies.

American Precision Museum Association, Inc., 196 Main St., Windsor VT 05089. (802)674-5781. Director: Edwin A. Battison.

Purpose: "We have thousands of catalogs on pre-1930 mechanized industries, everything from stockyards to energy development. In addition, we have biographies, portraits, company histories and pictures of many industrial buildings and complexes." Information covers mechanical technology.

Services: Offers photos. "10,000-12,000 photos are contained in our library."

How to Contact: Write or call. Charges according to work done. "We do not lend material."

Architecture and Fine Arts Library, University of Southern California, Ray and Nadine Watt Hall, Los Angeles CA 90007. (213)741-2798. Librarian: Alson Clark.

Purpose: A collection of 25,000 monographs on architecture, urban design, art history, painting, sculpture, drawing, printmaking and the decorative arts. The collection of historic architecture periodicals, many in foreign languages, is the most extensive in southern California. The library houses a rare book collection of some 1,500 volumes; 5,000 bound volumes of periodicals; 90,000 slides and 10,000 art and architecture reproductions. Information covers art, history and architecture.

Services: Offers research facilities.

How to Contact: Write or call. Library hours are determined by class schedule. The collection is mostly noncirculating; student demand has priority.

Architecture and Urban Planning Library, University of California at Los Angeles, Room 1302, Architecture Bldg., Westwood CA 90024. (213)825-2747. Librarian: Jon S. Greene.

Purpose: Largely a teaching and reference collection serving the school of architecture and urban planning, the library includes the Library of Architecture and Allied Arts, and a collection of rare books and folios of architectural design. Information covers architecture.

How to Contact: Use of this library may be restricted during exam periods. Nonstudents must register and pay a fee of $24/year to remove books from the library. Charges 25¢/photocopy and 10¢/microform copy.

Arizona State Department of Library, Archives & Public Records, State Capitol, 3rd Floor, Phoenix AZ 85007. Director: Marguerite Cooley.

Purpose: "A research library with an extensive collection of Arizona materials including newspapers and state department publications. It is a law library containing the statutes and codes of all states and the federal government and is a federal regional depository. Other divisions of the library include records management, a library extension service and the library for the blind and handicapped." Information covers history and law.

Services: Offers bibliographies and information searches.

How to Contact: Write or call. Charges 15¢/photocopy and microfiche copy; 50¢-1.75/microfilm hand copy, depending on size.

Art Library, University of California at Los Angeles, Floor 2, Dickson Art Center, Los Angeles CA 90024. (213)825-3817. Librarian: Joyce Pellerano Ludmer.
Purpose: "A noncirculating collection in art history, architectural history, design, studio art and related areas." Information covers art and art history.
How to Contact: Hours are by appointment only. Research sources include the *Elmer Belt Library of Vinciana*, a special collection of materials on the Renaissance, with emphasis on Leonardo da Vinci, and the Princeton *Index of Christian Art*, an iconographic index of all media before 1400. During exam periods, the use of this library may be restricted.

Asian Collection, General Libraries, University of Texas at Austin, Ausin TX 78712. **(512)471-3135. Head Librarian: Kevin F. Lin.**
Purpose: "The collection contains approximately 40,000 volumes and 250 periodical subscriptions in Chinese and Japanese, along with selected English-language South Asian materials. It supports the teaching and research programs for Asian studies with humanities and social sciences of the university, and provides information to the general public." Information covers art, business, economics, entertainment, history, politics, language and literature.
Services: Offers bibliographies and statistics. Publications include *The Asian Collection*, a pamphlet describing the services and regulations of the library.
How to Contact: Write or call. Anyone has access to materials, "but to check out materials, one must be a University of Texas student."
Tips: "A long-range program of cataloging materials in Hindi, Sanskrit and Urdu for the Asian collection is underway."

Athenaeum of Philadelphia, 219 S. 6th St., Philadelphia PA 19106. (215)925-2688. Librarian: Roger W. Moss.
Purpose: "The Athenaeum is an independent research library founded in 1814 with a specialization in 19th century social and cultural history, especially architecture and decorative arts." Information covers art, history and travel.
Services: Offers bibliographies. Publications include books on of Victorian culture.
How to Contact: Write or visit. Publications and price list are available. "Ours is a rare book library with the usual restrictions."

Austin-Travis County Collection, Austin Public Library, Box 2287, Austin TX 78768. (512)472-5433. Curator: Audray Bateman.
Purpose: "The Austin-Travis County Collection serves the local historical information needs of the public by collecting and preserving noncirculating books, photographs, manuscripts, city/county governmental reports, maps and other informational material that document the history of Austin and Travis County." Information covers agriculture, art, business, celebrities, economics, entertainment, food, health/medicine, history, how-to, industry, law, music, nature, politics, recreation, sports, technical data and travel.
Services: Offers bibliographies, biographies, statistics, information searches and photos. "We offer to the researchers who visit the collection a detailed index to some 35,000 photographs, a newspaper index for the *American Statesman* (Austin) for the last 20 years, plus many other finding aids. We offer limited information searches requested by letter or telephone."
How to Contact: Write or call. "To receive the best information, visit the library." Credit for reproduction of photographs must be given to the Austin-Travis County Collection, Austin Public Library.

Francis Bacon Library, 655 Dartmouth Ave., Claremont CA 91711. (714)624-6305. Director: E.S. Wrigley.
Purpose: "To promote study in science, literature, religion, history and philosophy with special reference to the works of Francis Bacon, his character and life, and his influence on his own and succeeding times; maintenance of a rare book library for

research and reference; grants to the six Claremont colleges and their affiliates for lectureships and visiting professors; and occasional publications of brochures and bibliographies." Information covers art, economics, food, health/medicine, history, law, policics, and science (all on the 16th and 17th centuries, and on early America).
Services: Offers bibliographies, brochures/pamphlets and information searches.
How to Contact: Write or call or visit. Charges 10¢/photocopy.

Baltimore Museum of Art Library, Art Museum Dr., Baltimore MD 21218. (301)396-6317. Librarian: Joan Settle Robison.
Purpose: "The library provides reference and resource materials for the Museum staff, scholars and interested public. The collection encompasses 19th- and 20th-century art, American decorative arts and Primitive art. The public is admitted to the library by appointment only." Information covers art and history.
Services: Offers biographies, statistics, information searches, photos and slides.
How to Contact: "Reference questions requiring only a quick answer will be handled by phone or letter. In-depth reference and literature searches will be handled only in person. An appointment with the librarian is required before one may be admitted to the library. To obtain photos or slides, contact Nancy Press. There is a nominal charge for photos and slides, which varies with the intended use."

The Bancroft Library, University of California, Berkeley CA 94720. Contact: Curator of Pictorial Collections.
Services: Offers portraits, photographs, original paintings and drawings, prints and other materials illustrating the history of California, western North America and Mexico.
How to Contact: Researchers must consult card indexes and book catalogs to the collection. "The library cannot make selections." Photographic reference copies are available for purchase; negatives and transparencies are available on a loan basis only. "Commercial users of our pictorial resources are asked to make a donation comparable to the per-unit prices charged by commercial picture agencies for similar materials." Credit line required.

The Berkshire Athenaeum Local History and Literature Services, 1 Wendell Ave., Pittsfield MA 01201. Supervisor: Denis J. Lesieur.
Purpose: "Specialized research department of a public library devoted to providing free access to scholars and interested individuals in the following areas: local and family history of New England and New York State; Herman Melville—his life and work; literary development and production of significant authors in the Berkshires, including Oliver Wendell Holmes, William Cullen Bryant and others; and American Shaker communities." Information covers history and American literature.
Services: Offers bibliographies, brochures/pamphlets, and information searches. Publications include descriptive brochures of the Herman Melville collection and of the local history and literature services.
How to Contact: Write or call. "When requesting information searches, please be as specific as possible and provide as much relevant information as possible. There is a charge for duplication of material, depending on the type and amount of duplication."

Biomedical Library, University of California at Los Angeles, Center for Health Sciences, Los Angeles CA 90024. (213)825-6098. Librarian: Louise Darling.
Purpose: Collections serve the schools of medicine, dentistry, nursing, and public health and the departments of bacteriology and biology. The library houses the Pacific Southwest Regional Medical Library Service and the Brain Information Service. Special collections include literature and prints on the history of medicine and biology. Collections of early medical rarities, the writings of S. Weir Mitchell and Florence Nightingale, the classics of ornithology and mammalogy, and the history of ophthalmology are here, as well as the John A. Benjamin Collection, which includes works on the history of medicine. Information covers health/medicine, history and biology.

Services: Offers bibliographies, brochures/pamphlets, and information searches.
How to Contact: For descriptions of collections, services, and circulation regulation, see *Brief Guide to the Biomedical Library*. Computer search services, utilizing commercial data bases in the life and health sciences fields, are provided on a partial cost-recovery basis. A fee of $24/year is charged for nonstudents wishing to take books from the library. Charges 25¢/photocopy; 10¢/microform copy. During exam periods, the use of this library may be restricted.

Broadcast Pioneers Library, 1771 N St. NW, Washington DC 20036. (202)223-0088. Director: Catharine Heinz.
Purpose: "A research library dedicated to the history of broadcasting. The library contains photos, oral histories and runs of old broadcasting journals, as well as books, pamphlets and vertical file holdings." Information covers entertainment, history and broadcasting.
Services: Offers "limited" information searches and "occasional" informational newsletters.
How to Contact: "Make an appointment to use the library; write or phone for information requests. Do not ask general questions—be specific as to what you want."

Brooklyn Collection, Brooklyn Public Library, History Division, Grand Army Plaza, Brooklyn NY 11238. (212)636-3178. Librarians: Elizabeth L. White, Marie Spina.
Services: Offers about 5,000 b&w photos of Brooklyn buildings and neighborhoods. Also has the photograph file of the *Brooklyn Daily Eagle*. Includes thousands of national and local subjects.
How to Contact: Charges $5-50/photo for one-time editorial use; $5-15 print fee. "The photographs cannot be borrowed, but appointments can be made (with at least a week's notice) for the user to bring his own equipment to photograph prints. Permission to use the wire service photos must be obtained from that service." Credit line required.

California State Library, Library and Courts Bldg., Box 2037, Sacramento CA 95809. California Section Head Librarian: Kenneth I. Pettitt.
Services: Offers b&w California historical photos and portraits of Californians (mostly early residents).
How to Contact: Write or visit. "Photocopies of specific pictures may be ordered by mail. Selection should be done at the library by the researcher. Names of private researchers who work on a fee basis are available. Fees for photocopies vary according to the type and size of the print. Credit line required."

Chemistry Library, University of California at Los Angeles, Room 4238, Young Hall, Los Angeles CA 90024. (213)825-3342. Librarian: Marion Peters.
Purpose: A research collection in chemistry, biochemistry and molecular biology. Information covers chemical history and chemistry.
Services: Offers information searches. Special holdings include departmental theses, Sadtler spectra, *Morgan Memorial Collection* on the history of chemistry, and US Chemical Patents from 1952.
How to Contact: Open Monday through Thursday, 8 a.m. to 10 p.m.; Friday, 8 a.m. to 5 p.m.; Saturday, 9 a.m. to 5 p.m.; Sunday, 1 p.m. to 9 p.m. Computer search services utilizing commercial data bases in chemistry are provided on a partial cost-recovery basis. Charges: photocopies, 25¢; microform copies, 10¢. Material does not circulate. During exam periods, the use of this library may be restricted.

Circus World Museum Library & Research Center, 415 Lynn St., Baraboo WI 53913. (608)356-8341. Chief Librarian and Historian: Robert L. Parkinson.
Purpose: "To preserve the records, materials, history and nostalgia of the circus, and to make some materials available to researchers and inquirers under the protected facili-

ties of our library, which includes circus lithographs, photographs, negatives, programs, route books, personnel records, heralds and couriers." Information covers history the circus and the Wild West.

Services: Offers aid in arranging interviews, annual reports, bibliographies, biographies, statistics, brochures/pamphlets, limited information searches, photos, photo services, book lending service and reproduction service (of collection pieces).Publications include booklets on holdings and services.

How to Contact: Write or call. "We will do research on an inquiry for up to one hour as a public service. Research time beyond one hour is done for a fee. Persons calling at out premises and doing their own research may do so without charge. There is a charge for having photo prints or reproductions made, and a service charge for book and movie rentals. A publication fee is charged for images published. The inquirer should not, however, expect replies by return mail. Inquiries requiring research must allow time to be scheduled by limited staff to undertake research."

Tips: "Do not ask general questions that defy answering in the confines of one letter. We will not write your epistle for you, but will answer precise and direct questions which have answers. We are an open, free public library and research center to which researchers are invited to come, utilize our resources and do their own in-depth research."

Citizens Savings Athletic Foundation Sports Library, 9800 S. Sepulveda Blvd., Los Angeles CA 90045. Managing Director: W. R. "Bill" Schroeder.

Purpose: "The Citizens Savings Athletic Foundation's sports library, covering all sports, is considered to be the most complete in existence. The Olympic Games library is unsurpassed. The Athletic Foundation also maintains an extensive sports film library, as well as photograph files. Some films are available for special showings, on loan basis." Information covers sports.

Services: Offers bibliographies, biographies, statistics and information searches. Publications include press and media releases.

How to Contact: "The sports library is open for special research by members of the media, sports historians and researchers, authors and students, Monday through Friday, 9 a.m. to 5 p.m. All research must be conducted in the library; no book loans."

William Andrews Clark Memorial Library, 2520 Cimarron St., Los Angeles CA 90018. (213)731-8529. Librarian: Thomas Wright.

Purpose: "The volumes in the library are principally representative of English culture of the 17th and 18th centuries, certain aspects of 19th-century English literature, and fine printing of the 19th and 20th centuries. It also includes English books published 1640-1750; the publications of modern fine presses; and volumes of music books and songs, musical scores, and musicology printed before 1750." Information covers history (Montana and theWest); music (17th and 18th century); politics (1640-1750); and science (1640-1750).

Services: Offers brochures/pamphlets, information searches and photos.

How to Contact: Write or visit.

Ray P. Crocker Library of Business Administration, USC, Business Library, Hoffman Hall, Los Angeles CA 90007. Librarian: Judith Truelson.

Purpose: We house over 60,000 volumes and regularly receives ,more than 1,300 trade, financial, economic, labor and general business periodicals and newspapers. The library also has strong collections of annual reports and loose-leaf services in investment, taxation, and international business. It also has a food marketing management file. Information covers business.

Services: Offers research facilities. Hours vary with class schedule; call for appointment. Student demands are met first.

Dental Library, University of Southern California, Norris Dental Science Center, Los Angeles CA 90007. Librarian: Frank Mason.

Purpose: Houses one of the major collections in dentistry on the West Coast. The library has a book and journal collection of more than 29,000 volumes, and subscribes to more than 340 current periodicals. Information covers health/medicine (dental).
Services: Offers bibliographies and information searches. "Access to MEDLINE and other computer-generated bibliographies prepared by the Norris Medical Library staff is available through the dental library at a minimal fee."
How to Contact: Hours vary; call to arrange an appointment. "The library is mainly for the use of students and professionals in the field of dentistry. Use is very restricted."

Denver Public Library, Western History Dept., 1357 Broadway, Denver CO 80203. (303)573-5152, ext. 246. Contact: Eleanor M. Gehres.
Purpose: To preserve materials on the social, economic, political and historical developments of the US west of the Mississippi River, especially the Rocky Mountain states.
Services: Offers photos. Large holdings of photos (about 280,000 items) of Indians, railroads, towns, outlaws, irrigation, livestock, and forts. "The department is continually adding to the collection, increasing the holdings by several thousand annually."
How to Contact: Write or call. "Prints are not available to lend for consideration purposes. The department is willing to make selections on the subjects needed. Fee structure is based on the planned use of the photographs obtained from us."

Detroit Public Library, E. Azalia Hackley Collection, 5201 Woodward Ave., Detroit MI 48202. (313)833-1000. Curator: Jean Currie.
Purpose: "The Hackley Collection seeks to document the achievements of blacks in the performing arts: music, dance, radio, TV, theater and moving pictures." Information covers celebrities, entertainment, music and dance.
Services: Offers bibliographies, biographies, brochures/pamphlets, clipping services, information searches and photos. Publications include a brochure that provides descriptive information about the collection and services.
How to Contact: Write or call. "Materials do not circulate but many may be photocopied." Charges 10¢/photocopy plus 35¢ postage. Charges 50¢/photo plus 35¢ postage. "Extensive information searches are limited due to staffing limitations. If you will be visiting in person and need a tour or special assistance, call for an appointment. Identification is required for visits to do research in the collection."

Douglas County Museum History Research Library, Box 1550, Roseburg OR 97470. Research Director: Lavola Bakken.
Purpose: "Our purpose is to collect and preserve the history of Douglas County, Oregon. The bulk of our library and vertical files covers the period 1850-1910." Information covers history.
Services: Offers biographies and information on industry and the Indians of Douglas County.
How to Contact: Write. Charges 10¢/photocopy. Charges "cost" for photos. "We do not charge for research unless it entails more than four hours to complete."
Tips: "Writers should ask specific questions, not 'send me all the material you have on Indians, Douglas County, logging, etc.' It would be helpful if we could know to what use the writer intends to put the material, whether fact or fiction, publication or reference."

Education Library, University of Southern California, Los Angeles CA 90007. Librarian: Janet Harvey.
Purpose: Library and depository for the State of California curriculum materials. Information covers education.
Services: Offers books and periodicals in the areas of general education; educational psychology; sociology of education; international education; and instructional technology. Specialized collections include a juvenile and textbook collection; a psychological test file; the Chen Collection in Asian Studies; all theses and dissertations that have been written at USC in education; and an ERIC microfiche collection in education.

How to Contact: Call to make appointment. Charges for microfiche printings. Nonstudent loan card, $60 for 6 months. "Student use comes first. Open to anyone, but one must do research on campus."

Educational Film Library Association, Research Library, 43 W. 61st St., New York NY 10023. (212)246-4533. Contact: Reference Librarian.
Purpose: "Among its many activities, the Educational Film Library Association (EFLA) maintains a research library containing over 1,200 books, 150 periodicals, film distributors' catalogs, subject files and other reference materials. As a national information center for nontheatrical film, EFLA provides reference and advisory services to members by mail or phone. The staff is prepared to assist film users to locate sources of films, suggest films for particular needs, supply information about film library administration, advise about film distribution, and assist researchers with special projects." Information covers film, video, ·filmmakers and film festivals.
Services: Offers bibliographies, brochures/pamphlets, information searches, placement on mailing list and newsletter. Publications include a quarterly magazine, *Sightlines*, and a quarterly newsletter, *EFLA Bulletin*. "We also publish and sell specialized pamphlets and books on the 16mm nontheatrical field. A publications list is available on request."
How to Contact: "Make an appointment with our reference librarian to use our library, which is open to the public Monday through Friday, 9 a.m. to 5 p.m. Materials may not be removed from the premises. EFLA publications may be purchased by mail or at the office. EFLA is a membership organization; membership is preferred for intensive searches and preferred treatment, and especially important if phoning for reference aid. Materials not published by EFLA do not leave the library. We have a full library of books and periodicals and files on film and video, but they may not be removed from the library.
Tips: "Do not expect librarians to do your research for you. Our librarian will guide you to all the resources; you'll have to do the work of compiling the information that will best help your project."

Dwight D. Eisenhower Library, Abilene KS 67410. (913)263-4751. Director: John E. Wickman.
Purpose: "We provide research and education on the life and times of Dwight D. Eisenhower, 34th President. We have 18.5 million pages of manuscripts, 24,000 books, 300,000 still photographs and 300 oral history interviews." Information covers celebrities, history and politics.
Services: Offers brochures/pamphlets and information searches.
How to Contact: Write. Charges for photos and photocopies; write for current rates. "Be as specific as possible in requests. Searches are limited to manuscript resources. Please check out printed sources first."

Engineering & Mathematical Sciences Library, University of California at Los Angeles, Room 8270, Boelter Hall, Los Angeles CA 90024. (213)825-4951. Librarian: Rosalee Wright.
Purpose: The Engineering & Mathematical Sciences Library is largely a circulating collection. Information covers engineering and mathematics.
Services: Offers statistics and information searches.
How to Contact: Open Monday through Thursday, 8 a.m. to 10 p.m.; Friday, 8 a.m. to 5 p.m.; Saturday, 9 a.m. to 5 p.m.; Sunday 2 p.m. to 9 p.m. Printed indexing and abstracting tools to the journal and report literature of engineering and the physical sciences and technology fields, are provided on a partial cost-recovery basis to provide rapid access to abstracting and indexing publications. A special multidisciplinary collection of technical reports serves research interests in engineering and the life, physical and social sciences. The report collection includes the National Technical Information Service; the Department of Energy and NASA; and selected publications of the Rand Corporation. Computer researches are done on a partial cost-recovery

basis. Charges: photocopies, 25¢; microform copies, 10¢. Nonstudents must pay a fee of $24/year to use the facilities of the UCLA Libraries if they inted to take the material from the premises. During exam periods the use of this library may be restricted.

Florida Photographic Archives, Room 66, Strozier Library, Florida State University, Tallahassee FL 32306. (904)644-1222. Curator: Mrs. Allen Morris.
Purpose: "To preserve, and make available to the public, images of Florida. We search files for requested images." Information covers agriculture, art, business, celebrities, entertainment, food, health/medicine, Florida history, industry, law, music, nature, politics, recreation, science, sports and travel.
Services: Offers photos.
How to Contact: Write or call. Charges 6¢/photocopy; $2/8x10 b&w print; $4/11x14 print; and $6/16x20 print. Charges for postage. "Mounted copies are loaned for publication, if the collection is guaranteed that they will be carefully handled and promptly returned after use. A credit line is expected. We cannot do extensive image research. Normal hours are Monday through Friday, 9 a.m. to 1 p.m., but we will open the collection for out-of-town researchers on request."

Free Library of Philadelphia, Print and Picture Dept./Films Dept., Logan Square, Philadelphia PA 19103. (215)686-5367. Curator: Robert F. Looney. Films Department Head: Steven Mayover.
Services: The print and picture department offers a collection of portraits (300,000 items), Philadelphia history (9,000 items), Napoleonica (3,400 items) and fine prints (1,000 items). The films department offers a 16mm film collection and 35mm filmstrips. Subjects include agriculture, art, business, celebrities, economics, entertainment, food, health/medicine, history, how-to, industry, music, nature, politics, recreation, science, self-help, sports and travel.
How to Contact: Write. "Unfortunately, we can't send out samples of literature or groups of pictures from which selections may be made." Charges $3.50/photocopy. Credit line required for original material.

Freedom Center Collection, California State University Library, 800 N. St. College Blvd., Fullerton CA 92631. (714)773-3186. Librarian: Lynn M. Coppel.
Purpose: "To collect controversial political literature—mostly ephemeral. We have more than 7,000 pamphlets, 200 periodical titles, 90 linear feet of folders. Material covers the extreme right to the extreme left." Information covers economics, history and politics.
How to Contact: Visit. "Material can be used in library only; because of its value and ephemeral nature, the material does not circulate."

Geology/Geophysics Library, University of California at Los Angeles, Room 4697 Geology Bldg., Los Angeles CA 90024. (213)825-1055. Librarian: Nancy Pruett.
Purpose: Primarily a research library. Information covers geology, paleontology, geophysics, geochemistry, planetary physics, space science, hydrology, economic geology and geomorphology.
Services: Offers information searches.
How to Contact: Write or visit. Computer search services utilizing commercial data bases in geology or geophysics are provided on a partial cost-recovery basis. Charges 25¢/photocopy and 10¢/microform copy. During exam periods, use of this library may be restricted.

Billy Graham Center Library, Wheaton College, Wheaton IL 60187. (312)682-5194. Director: Richard Owen Roberts.
Purpose: "To assemble and make available to the public for research definitive collections on evangelism, revivalism and missions." Information covers history, music, religion and theology.

Services: Offers bibliographies, biographies and information searches.
How to Contact: Write. Charges for services.

The Rutherford B. Hayes Library and Museum, 1337 Hayes Ave., Fremont OH 43420. (419)332-2081. Director: Watt P. Marchman. Manuscripts Librarian: Thomas A. Smith. Books Librarian: Linda C. Hauck.
Purpose: "The Hayes Library and Museum contains the 19th President's personal library of 10,000 volumes, as well as his correspondence, papers, diaries, scrapbook, photographs and memorabilia. There is also a research library of 19th-century America with 100,000 books and over a million manuscripts." Information covers American history.
Services: Offers publications. Publications include *Hayes Historical Journal* (semiannual) and *The Rutherford B. Hayes State Memorial* (brochure).
How to Contact: "The reference library is open freely to the public for research and study between regular hours Monday through Friday, 9 a.m. to 5 p.m.; closed Saturday afternoons, Sundays and holidays. Library regulations apply." Charges $5/year for subscription to the journal, $1/brochure.

Holt-Atherton Pacific Center for Western Studies, University of the Pacific, Stockton CA 95211. (209)946-2404. Contact: Martha Seffer O'Bryon.
Purpose: "The center collects and organizes material on western History." Information covers history and travel.
Services: Offers bibliographies, biographies, brochures/pamphlets, information searches, newsletters and photos. Publications available.
How to Contact: Write. Charges for publications, research and photos. "Writers must apply to the center for research use of the archives and the Stuart Library. Do not expect the staff to do your research."

Hoose Philosophy Library, University of Southern California, Mudd Memorial Hall, Los Angeles CA 90007. Librarian: Bridget Molloy.
Purpose: Library. Information covers philosophy.
Services: Offers 45,000 volumes ranging from medieval manuscripts and incunabula to the latest works of today's philosophers and scholars. Its general strength is in metaphysics; epistemology; logic; ethics; and the philosophy of religion in various languages. Its holdings distinctively reflect the contributions of German philosophy. The *Gomperz Collection*, 3,500 volumes, concerns the Enlightenment and Romanticism periods. It's especially useful for the study of European philosophy from about 1700-1850. Complete, or nearly complete, runs of first editions of Kant; Schelling; Hegae; Schopenhauer; Wolff; Fichte; La Mettrie; and John Stuart Mill.
How to Contact: Call for appointment. Nonstudents may not take material from facility. Student demand comes first.

Humanities Research Center (HRC), The University of Texas at Austin, Box 7219, Austin TX 78712. (512)471-1833. Research Librarian: Ellen S. Dunlap.
Purpose: "The HRC is a major research library housing numerous rare book, manuscript, and other special collections. Special areas of interest include 19th- and 20th-century British, American and French literature and art, the history of science, photography, theater arts, and bibliography and book arts. The major units of the Humanities Research Center include the reading room, the photography collection, the Hoblitzell Theatre Arts Library, the iconography collection and the academic center collections." Information covers art, entertainment, history, law, music, science and literature.
Services: Offers brochures/pamphlets.
How to Contact: Write or call. "Address all inquiries to the Research Librarian." Charges for photocopies.
Tips: "This is a researach library. Unfortunately, we rarely have the staff or time to provide extensive searching and research services for commercial ventures. Each

researcher should be aware of the size of the collection: 800,000 printed volumes, 8 million manuscripts, 1,300,000 photographs, 50,000 art items, and several miles of clippings and ephemeral materials."

Illinois State Historical Library, Old State Capitol, Springfield IL 62706. (217)782-4836. State Historian: William K. Alderfer. Curator of Photographs and Prints: Janice Petterchak.
Purpose: "Department of the state historical society whose purpose is collecting, preserving and disseminating information about the history of Illinois." Information covers agriculture, how-to, politics, genelogy and state history.
Services: Offers aid in arranging interviews, annual reports, bibliographies, biographies, brochures/pamphlets, information searches, newsletter and 100,000 photos.
How to Contact: Write, call or visit. Charges $5-7.50/8x10 b&w glossy and 20¢/photocopy.

Indian and Colonial Research Center, Main St., Old Mystic CT 06372. President: Mary Virginia Goodman.
Purpose: "We are a research library housing the collection of Eva L. Butler—2,000 notebooks containing her vast research in colonial and Indian history, from old town records, deeds, diaries and letters." Information covers history.
Services: Offers brochures/pamphlets and information searches. Publications available.
How to Contact: Write or call. "We are only open on Tuesday, Thursday and Saturday. We do not lend books; they must be read in the library."

Indiana State Library, 140 N. Senate Ave., Indianapolis IN 46204. (317)633-4912. Library Director: Charles Ray Ewick.
Purpose: Houses general collection, Indiana collection, genealogical information and the archives of the state. Is also a depository of federal documents. Information covers agriculture, art, business, economics, entertainment, food, history, industry, music, nature, politics, recreation, science, self-help and sports.
Services: Offers aid in arranging interviews, annual reports, bibliographies, biographies, statistics, brochures/pamphlets, information searches, placement on mailing list, newsletter and photos. Publications include *Occurrent* (quarterly).
How to Contact: Visit and do research on premises. "We will attempt to handle out-of-state requests." Charges for photocopies. Open Monday through Friday, 8:15 a.m. to 5 p.m.; Saturday, 8:15 a.m. to noon—May through September.

Dorothy Vena Johnson Black History Collection, Vernon Branch Library, Leon H. Washington Jr. Memorial, 4504 S. Central Ave., Los Angeles CA 90011.(213)234-9106. Branch Librarian: Hortense E. Woods.
Purpose: "The purpose and general objectives of the Vernon Branch Library are, broadly, to provide the people in the community with the opportunity of lifelong educational growth and stimulation; to assemble, preserve and administer in organized collections the library's print and nonprint materials; and to support the cultural and recreational program of the community. A part of the Vernon Branch Library collection is the Dorothy Vena Johnson Black History Collection". Information covers art, business, celebrities, entertainment, health/medicine, history, music and sports.
Services: Offers bibliographies. Publications include a *Bibliography of the Negro History Collection of the Vernon Branch Library*.
How to Contact: Write or visit. "Hours vary. Some materials are reference only and will have to be used in the library."

Law Library, University of Southern California, Musick Law Center, Los Angeles CA 90007. (213)741-6487. Librarian: Albert O. Brecht.
Purpose: Primarily a research collection. Information covers law.

Services: Offers more than 150,000 volumes, 20,000 microform volume equivalents, 1,900 serial titles and various other forms of material.
How to Contact: Call for appointment. Because of limited seating, book resources and staff, use of the collection and circulation priveleges are limited. Members of the public may obtain permission to use the collection for research purposes if circumstances permit.

Bryon R. Lewis Historical Collections Library, Vincennes University, Vincennes IN 47591. (812)882-3350, ext. 330. Director: Robert R. Stevens.
Purpose: "To collect and preserve historical documents, archives and manuscripts." Information covers history and genealogy.
Services: Offers bibliographies, biographies and information searches. Indexes and a list of indexes are available.
How to Contact: Write or call.

Library of Congress, 1st and Independence Aves. SE, Washington DC 20540. (202)426-5108. Contact: Information Office.
Purpose: "The Library of Congress, the research arm of the US Congress, also serves as the national library of the United States. It acquires resources in all forms—books, periodicals, maps, music, manuscripts, prints and photographs, motion picture and television film, records and discs, and microform—and makes them available for research. Collections number over 74 million items (more than 18 million books) available on the premises. The Library of Congress is not a circulating library, but does make material available to serious investigators in their own libraries available on interlibrary loan." Information covers "every subject but agriculture and clinical medicine, which are covered by two other national libraries."
Services: Offers aid in arranging interviews, annual reports, bibliographies, biographies, statistics, brochures/pamphlets, placement on mailing list, newsletter, photos and press kits. "The information office can provide brochures about various activities and holdings of the library. *A List of Library of Congress Publications in Print*, revised annually, includes both free and priced publications. Review copies of library publications may be requested by book reviewers and review journals."
How to Contact: "Writers interested in covering the Library of Congress, its services, activities and events may write, call or visit the information office, Room G-107, Library of Congress Bldg. The office will provide information, arrange interviews and facilitate photographing or filming on library premises. Writers may also contact this office for guidance in using the collections of the library. The library cannot undertake research on behalf of any of its patrons. Reference questions that can be answered in 15 minutes are accepted; inquirers with more difficult problems are invited to do their own research." Charges for photocopies services and duplication of sound recordings.

Library Science Library, University of Southern California, Montgomery Ross Fisher Building, Los Angeles CA 90007. Librarian: Mae Furbeyre.
Purpose: Library. Information covers library science.
Services: Offers basic reference sources in the humanities, social sciences, and science and technology; essential runs of periodicals in the field of library and information science; cataloging and classification aids; juvenile books; literature on children's reading; monographs on libraries and related professional areas; and audiovisual software.
How to Contact: Call for appointment. Student demand comes first.

Los Angeles County Museum of Natural History Research Library, 900 Exposition Blvd., Los Angeles CA 90007. Librarians: Kathryn King, Katharine Donahue.
Purpose: "To assist museum staff in their research and assist the public." Information covers history, nature, science, earth science, new world archeology, Southwest Indians and California history.
Services: Offers bibliographies and biographies. Biannual reports available.

How to Contact: Write, call or visit. Charges 15¢/photocopy. "We do not lend out material; writers must fill out a request-to-do-research form."

Louisiana State Library, Box 131, Baton Rouge LA 70821. (504)342-4914. Contact: Harriet Callahan.
Purpose: A noncirculating historical photo collection pertaining to the state of Louisiana and people prominent in Louisiana history.
Services: Offers photos. Most are b&w; some are color.
How to Contact: Write. Credit line and return of pictures required.

M.G.M. Research Library, 10202 W. Washington Blvd., Culver City CA 90230. (213)836-3000, ext. 1474. Head of Research: Bob Rodgers.
Purpose: "We offer research facilities on all aspects of the M.G.M. Studios, the stars and the films, as well as information for and about pictures." Information covers entertainment and technical information.
Services: Offers biographies and statistics.
How to Contact: Write or call. Charges $20/hour depending on time and type of materials taken out. "We are not open to the public; to use our facilities, you must be an established writer or writing a screenplay for an established film company."

M.G.M. Studios Film Library, 10202 W. Washington Blvd., Culver City CA 90230. (213)836-3000. Head of Film Service: Mel Ridel.
Purpose: "We restore and store all M.G.M. films." Information covers entertainment and technical data.
Services: Offers information searches and films (for studios, like United Artists).
How to Contact: Write or call. "You must be approved for clearance to enter the lot."

Maine State Library, Cultural Bldg., Augusta ME 04333. Specialist in Maine Materials: Shirley Thayer.
Purpose: "We are the back-up resource center for all libraries in the central regional district. We are also a research library containing genealogical and state agency documents." Information covers agriculture, art, business ("very little"), entertainment, history, industry, music, nature, recreation, technical data, travel, lumbering, biography, archeology and religion.
Services: Offers biannual reports, bibliographies, biographies, brochures/pamphlets, information searches, statistics and photos. "We also have old glass slides, manuscripts, a map collection and poetry." Publications available.
How to Contact: Write, call or visit. Charges 10¢/page for photocopies. "We love to work with writers."

Management Library, University of California at Los Angeles, Rooms 1400-2400, GSM Bldg., Los Angeles CA 90024. (213)825-4021. Librarian: Charlotte Georgi.
Purpose: Library. Information covers accounting information systems; business economics; business history; comprehensive health planning; computers and information systems; finance and investments; general management; management theory; industrial relations; international and comparative management; management in the arts; marketing; operations research; socio-technical systems; and urban planning.
Services: Offers the *The Robert E. Gross Collection* of rare books in business and economics; the *Authur Young Accounting Collection*; the *Neil H. Jacoby Collection*; the *James R. Pattillo Banking and Finance Collection*; business histories; international business materials; and a collection of annual reports of major American and foreign corporations.
How to Contact: Write or visit. Charges 25¢/photocopy and 10¢/microform copy. During exam periods use of library may be restricted. Nonstudents must pay a fee of $25/year to take books from the library.

Map Library, University of California at Los Angeles, Room A 253, Bunche Hall, Los

Angeles CA 90024. (213)825-3526. Librarian: Carlos B. Hagen.
Purpose: The UCLA Map Library is a depository for the publications of many mapping agencies throughout the world. Information covers maps of all kinds.
Services: Offers modern maps of all areas of the world; gazetteers; and many other cartographic reference tools. Collections in the annex include atlases, guidebooks, aerial photographs, historical maps, periodicals and almost all cataloged volumes.
How to Contact: Nonstudents must pay $24/year to take material out. Charges 25¢/photocopy and 10¢/microform copy.

Music Library, University of California at Los Angeles, Room 1102, Schoenberg Hall, Los Angeles CA 90024. (213)825-4881. Librarian: Stephen M. Fry.
Purpose: Music library. Information covers music.
Services: Offers special music collections including the *Ernst Toch Archive*; the *John Vincent Archive*; music of film and television composers; the *Archive of Popular American Music* (noncirculating sheet music); and a collection of early Venetian opera librettos. The *Ethnomusicology Archive* (Room B 414), is a noncirculating research collection of phonograph and tape recordings principally of non-Western music.
How to Contact: Write or visit. Nonstudents must pay $24/year to take books out of the Library.

National Library of Medicine, 8600 Rockville Pike, Bethesda MD 20014. Contact: Chief, History of Medicine Division.
Purpose: Medical library.
Services: Offers b&w and color photos on the history of medicine (portraits, scenes and pictures of institutions); photos are not related to current personalities, events or medical science.
How to Contact: Write. Charges according to service provided; prices are subject to change without notice. Charges $3 minimum/copy print. No pictures sent on approval. Credit line required.

New Mexico State Library, Box 1629, Santa Fe NM 87501. (505)872-2033, ext. 54. Southwest Librarian: Rorlando Ronero.
Purpose: "Historical reference area for the state of New Mexico. A good place for the writer to start if he is looking for historical information on New Mexico. If we don't have it, we will refer him to other places that do." Information covers history.
Services: Offers aid in arranging interviews, bibliographies, biographies, brochures/pamphlets and information searches.
How to Contact: Write, call or visit. "We will do some specific Southwest research for writers. When requesting information, come prepared with dates and people involved, if possible."

The New York Botanical Garden Library, Bronx Park, New York NY 10458. (212)220-8749. Associate Librarian: Mrs. L. Lynos.
Purpose: Botany, horticulture, portraits of botanists and horticulturists; pictures from seed catalogs.
Services: Offers b&w photos (original and copy), glass negatives, film negatives, clippings, postcards, old prints, original drawings and paintings. "The collection is being reorganized; researchers are granted limited access."
How to Contact: Charges $35/b&w photo; $100/35mm color transparency. Offers one-time rights. Credit line required.

Norris Medical Library, University of Southern California, 2025 Zonal Ave., Los Angeles CA 90033. (213)226-2400. Public Services Librarian: Terry Ann Jankowski.
Purpose: "The Norris Medical Library serves primarily the schools of medicine and pharmacy, the Los Angeles County/USC Medical Center and USC students from other schools and colleges. Norris extends courtesy privileges to southern California health professionals and helps to meet community needs as a resource library for the region.

The Norris book and journal collection covers the basic biomedical sciences with an in-depth pharmacy collection." Information covers health/medicine, new drugs, psychology and psychiatry.
Services: Offers bibliographies, biographies, statistics, brochures/pamphlets, information searches and computerized bibliography search services in the biomedical sciences.
How to Contact: Write, call or visit. Charges for bibliographic computer search services. Materials are normally restricted to use in the library.

Northern Arizona University Library, Special Collections, Flagstaff AZ 86011. (602)523-4730.
Purpose: "Special Collections collects, preserves and makes available to researchers publications and archival materials concerning Arizona (past and present), primarily northern Arizona. Special Collections also includes an extensive collection of 20th-Century radical American social and political publications, primarily right wing; a collection of hundreds of books and pamphlets relatd to the game of checkers and draughts; and a large collection of fine press books from Elbert Hubbard's Roycroft Press." Information covers art, history, politics and recreation.
Services: Offers bibliographies, biographies, statistics, brochures/pamphlets, information searches and photos. Publications include *Grand Canyon and the Colorado Plateau, A Bibliography of Selected Titles in the NAU Libraries* ($2), *The Spanish Southwest 1519-1776 and After* and *A Guide to the NAU Libraries.*
How to Contact: Write, call or visit. Charges 5¢/photocopy; photographic charges vary.

Oriental Library, University of California at Los Angeles, Room 21617, Research Library, Los Angeles CA 90024. (213)825-4836. Acting Librarian: Ik-Sam Kim.
Purpose: Primarily a research facility. Information covers art, premodern history, politics, religion, anthropology, linguistics, political science and sociology.
Services: Offers information in archeology, art, Buddhism, premodern history, and the literature of China and Japan. The collection is mainly in Chinese and Japanese languages, with some in Korean.
How to Contact: Write or visit. Nonstudents must pay $24/year to remove books from the library.

Perkin Library/American Museum—Hayden Planetarium, 81st St. and Central Park W., New York NY 10024. (212)873-1300, ext. 478. Librarian: Sandra Kitt.
Purpose: "We are a department of astronomy, affiliated with a natural history museum. We are a public department which offers a major planetarium, with topical sky shows, to the public. We have two floors of exhibits, two multimedia theaters, classrooms, a research library and a gift shop. Our library (and the department) specializes in astronomy, astrophysics, meteorology, navigation and space technology. Our research library is considered the best available to the general public in this field." Information covers history, how-to, new products, science and technical data, all related to astronomy; also offers NASA technical information and mission reports.
Services: Offers bibliographies, information searches and photos for research only.
How to Contact: "The planetarium is open daily except Thanksgiving and Christmas. The library is open by appointment, Monday through Friday, 1 to 5 p.m. We charge for photocopies."
Tips: "Research must be done in-house; books and materials cannot be loaned."

Physics Library, University of California at Los Angeles, Room 213, Kinsey Hall, Los Angeles CA 90024. (213)825-4791. Librarian: J. Wally Pegram.
Purpose: "Primarily a research collection of books, periodicals and departmental theses. Information covers specialized subjects: solid state electronics, elementary particles, mathematics, nuclear physics, acoustics, spectroscopy and astrophysics. Smaller collections are maintained in closely related fields such as biophysics, chemistry, astronomy, geophysics and physical geology. Special files include an up-to-date

collection of high energy preprints and a physics conference information file."
Services: Offers information searches.
How to Contact: Write or visit. Computer search services utilizing commercial data bases in physics are provided on a partial cost-recovery basis. Charges 25¢ for photocopies. During exam periods, use of this Library may be restricted.

Enoch Pratt Free Library, 400 Cathedral St., Baltimore MD 21201. Contact: Maryland Department.
Purpose: Contains materials on Maryland and Baltimore.
Services: Offers b&w 8x10 glossies of Maryland and Baltimore: persons, scenes, buildings and monuments.
How to Contact: Write. Charges for copy prints. Credit line required.

Public Affairs Service Library, University of California at Los Angeles, Floor A, Research Library Building, Los Angeles CA 90024. (214)825-3135. Acting Head: Eugenia Eaton.
Purpose: The Public Affairs Service supplements the Library's more traditional resources by providing a coordinated information service to meet the needs of scholars working in the broadly defined area of public affairs. The University Library is a depository for the offical publications of California cities and counties; the state of California; the United States government; the United Nations and some of its specialized agencies (including the Food and Agriculture Organization and UNESCO); and such regional organizations as the European Communities and the Organization of American States. It also receives selected publications of other American cities and counties; of the other states and possessions of the United States; of interstate organizations; and of foreign governments and intergovernmental organizations. Information covers economics, history, politics and government.
Services: Offers government documents and pamphlet collections. The pamphlet collection focuses on such areas as ethnic materials; industrial relations; politics and political parties; public administration; public issues; social and economic problems; and social welfare. Certain parts of the 1970 census in machine readable form are owned by the Library. The *John Randolph Haynes and Dora Haynes Collection*; the *Franklin Hichborn Collection*; and the *Carey McWilliams Collection* contain important holdings on local government, urban problems and social conditions, and are kept in this department.
How to Contact: Write or visit. Charges 25¢/photocopy and 10¢/microform copy.

Queens Borough Public Library, Long Island Division, 89-11 Merrick Blvd., Jamaica NY 11432. (212)990-0770. Contact: Davis Erhardt.
Purpose: The preservation of all phases of Long Island history.
Services: Offers 20,000 b&w original photos, glass negatives, clippings, post cards, old prints. "Many are historical in nature, dating back to the 1890-1920 period."
How to Contact: Charges for prints and reproductions. Credit line required.

Renascence Library, 3611 Walnut, Kansas City MO 64111. (816)753-4120. President: Susan Carpenter.
Purpose: Private library, open to stockholder/members. Plans are being made to open it to the public. Information covers art, economics, food, health/medicine, history, how-to, science and self-help.
Services: Offers biographies, brochures/pamphlets, placement on mailing list and newsletter.
How to Contact: Write.

Research Library, University of California at Los Angeles, Research Library Bldg., Los Angeles CA 90024. (213)825-1201. University Librarian: Russell Shank.
Purpose: "The university library at UCLA comprises a campus-wide system of libraries serving programs of study and research in many fields."

Services: Offers bibliographies, brochures/pamphlets, and on-line computer search services. The total collections number more than 4,000,000 volumes. More than 56,000 serials are received regularly, and the libraries also hold collections of manuscripts, government publications, maps, microfilms and other scholarly resources. An international collection of selected current newspapers is available in the periodicals room for library use, as is a collection of current domestic college catalogs. *UCLA Library Guide* available in the lobby.

How to Contact: "Come into the University Research Library." Charges 25¢/photocopy and 10¢/microform copy. Nonstudents wishing to take books out of the library must register and pay a fee of $24/year. Those wishing to use the material on the premises must sign a card for the material and check it when they are through.

The Rhode Island Historical Society Library, 121 Hope St., Providence RI 02906. (401)331-0448. Reference Librarian: Charles A. McNeil.

Purpose: "To collect, preserve and make available information on Rhode Island history and genealogy." Information covers history.

Services: Offers bibliographies, limited information searches and photos.

How to Contact: Write or visit. Charges $3 for genealogical searches "limited to vital statistics for one surname"; 25¢/photocopy. Write for rates for photo reproductions.

Tips: "Writers requiring extensive information should visit in person. Staff can make only brief searches and supply limited information by mail."

St. Bonaventure University Library and Resource Center, St. Bonaventure University Art Collection, St. Bonaventure NY 14778. Librarian Emeritus: Fr. Irenaeus Herscher, O.F.M.

Purpose: "We are a university library with an art collection, stamp collection and coin collection. We specialize in Franciscan history, philosophy and theology. We have a Franciscan Institute and archival material of St. Bonaventure University." Information covers art, economics, history, law, music, nature, politics, recreation, science, sports and technical data.

Services: Offers bibliographies and biographies.

How to Contact: Write. Charges 5¢/photocopy, plus postage.

Seaver Science Library, University of Southern California, Los Angeles CA 90007. Librarian: John Vandermolen.

Purpose: Library. Information covers science.

Services: Offers major collections in astronomy; biological science; chemistry; engineering; geology; mathematics; and physics. Houses 140,000 volumes, most of which are bound periodicals.

How to Contact: Call for appointment. Nonstudents may not remove books from the library. Student demand comes first.

Social Work Library, University of Southern California, Los Angeles CA 90007. Librarian: Ruth Britton.

Purpose: Library. Information covers social science.

Services: Offers books and periodicals in the social welfare field. Special collections include the *Trabajadores de la Raza Collection of Chicano Materials*; uncataloged master's papers done in the School of Social Work since 1966; and a pamphlet file with timely information on relevant subjects.

How to Contact: Call for appointment. Nonstudents may not take material from the library. Student use comes first.

Sport Information Resource Center (SIRC), Coaching Association of Canada (CAC), 333 River Rd. Vanier, Ottawa, Ontario, Canada K1L 8B9. (613)746-5693. Executive Director: Lyle Makosky.

Purpose: "The Coaching Association of Canada is a national nonprofit organization. Its major aims are to increase coaching effectiveness in all sports and to encourage the development of coaching by providing programs and services to coaches at all levels." Information covers health/medicine, how-to, recreation, science, sports and technical data.

Services: Offers annual reports, brochures/pamphlets and information searches. "SIRC is a unique sport libarary and documentation center and its services are accessible to all CAC members as well as the sport community at large." Publications include a CAC pamphlet and a SIRC pamphlet in English and French.

How to Contact: Write or call. Charges for computerized reference service. "Our library doesn't lend books."

Stockbridge Library Historical Room, Main St., Stockbridge MA 01262. (413)298-5501. Curator: Pauline D. Pierce.

Purpose: "The Historical Room is a research center for the area. We have genealogical information on local families, books by and about local residents, church records, Mohican Indian records, manuscripts and memorabilia." Information covers history.

Services: Offers biographies and information searches.

How to Contact: Write or call.

Tennessee Department of Public Health Library, Cordell Hull Bldg., Nashville TN 37219. (615)741-3226. Librarian: Mary Wester-House.

Purpose: "To provide information services primarily health resources and human service resources, through print media and limited nonprint media to state and local health professionals, management, state agencies, health- related organizations, employees and the public in Tennessee." Information covers health/medicine.

Services: Offers brochures/pamphlets and information searches. Publications available in limited quantities to Tennesseans.

How to Contact: Write, call or visit. "Materials are loaned to department personnel only."

Texas State Library, Box 12927, Capital Station TX 78711. (512)475-2166.

Purpose: "Official depository of state historical records and library for state government." Information covers history, politics and genealogy.

Services: Offers annual reports, bibliographies, biographies, statistics, information searches, placement on mailing list, newsletter and photos.

How to Contact: "Write. Be specific."

Theater Arts Library, University of California at Los Angeles, Room 22478, Research Library, Los Angeles CA 90024. (213)825-4880. Librarian: Audree Malkin.

Purpose: A research and reference collection serving the Department of Theater Arts, the university community and the entertainment industry. Information covers entertainment.

Services: Offers materials primarily devoted to motion pictures and television. In addition to books, reference works, and periodicals, the collection includes such specialized materials as screenplays; television scripts; production stills; portraits of personalities; clipping files; film festival programs; motion picture programs; art work; the 20th Century Fox Collection; and the *Star Trek* papers.

How to Contact: Write or visit. Charges 25¢ for photocopies. During exam periods or other periods of high demand, use of this library may be restricted.

Tracor Technical Library, 6500 Tracor Lane, Austin TX 78721. (512)926-2800, ext. 139. Librarian: N.P. McCandless.

Purpose: "We are a business research library specializing in acoustics, aerospace, medical instruments, navigation and telecommunications." Information covers science, technical data and military specifications. Information is on film for reading and notetaking only; no prints allowed.

How to Contact: Call. Charges cost of time search for information, plus 50¢.
Tips: "Use United States documents for basic information. Remember that state libraries have lots of good information, too. Know a librarian who works in your field of interest."

University of Judaism Library, 15600 Mulholland Dr., West Los Angeles CA 90024. (213)472-0578. Director: Dr. Louis Shub.
Purpose: "To provide information on Hebrew, Bible studies, Hebrew studies and rabbinic studies." Information covers history and theology philosophy literature.
Services: Offers aid in arranging interviews, annual reports and university reports.
How to Contact: Write or visit. Charges $15 deposit to check out books, deposit returned when books are returned.

University of Washington Libraries, Photography Collection, Special Collections Division, Seattle WA 98195. (206)543-0742. Contact: Curator of Photography.
Services: Offers collection of 200,000 images devoted to the history of photography in the Pacific Northwest and Alaska from 1860 to 1920. Most early photographers of the two regions are represented, including Eric A. Hegg (Gold Rush), Wilhelm Hester (maritime), and George T. Emmons (anthropology). Special topical assemblies are maintained for localities, industries and occupations of Washington (territory and state), Seattle history, Indian peoples and totem culture, ships, whaling and regional architects and architecture.
How to Contact: Write or call. Will provide photocopies of selected views upon receipt of specific statements of needs. Charges 10¢/photocopies by arrangement. Credits required for publication and television uses.

Vancouver Public Library—Historical Photograph Section, 750 Burrard St., Vancouver, British Columbia, Canada V6Z 1X5. Photographic Curator: A.R. D'Altroy.
Purpose: "Collection of historical photographs and negatives of British Columbia and the Yukon from the 1860s to the present." Information covers agriculture, art, business, celebrities, economics, entertainment, food, health/medicine, history, how-to, industry, law, music, nature, politics, recreation, science, self-help, sports and technical data.
Services: Offers photos.
How to Contact: Write or call. Will send price list on request. Charges permission fees.

Von Kleinsmid Library (World Affairs), University of Southern California, Von Kleinsmid Center, Los Angeles CA 90007. (213)741-7347. Librarian: Lynn Sipe.
Purpose: Library. Information covers world affairs.
Services: Offers over 150,000 volumes housing the University's major collections in international relations; political science; public administration; and urban and regional planning. This library attempts to collect all publications of the United Nations; the Organization for Economic Cooperation and Development; the International Labor Organization, UNESCO; the Council of Europe; the Food and Agriculture Organization of the UN, the various international financial agencies; and is a depository of documents of the European Communities and the Organization of American States. The separately cataloged *Planning Documents Collection* contains over 2000 planning documents and reports from local, regional, and state planning agencies.
How to Contact: Call for appointment. Nonstudents may not take material from library. Student demand comes first.

Warner Research, Burbank Public Library, 110 N. Glenoaks Blvd., Burbank CA 91501. (213)847-9743. Research Librarian: Mary Ann Grasso.
Purpose: "To provide research to the entertainment industry's creative people; writers, art directors, set designers, etc. Our library allows us to provide visual (in the form of photographs, diagrams and magazine articles) and written documentation in a variety of areas and time periods. Our collection strengths include excellent period

information on all subjects; architecture; costume; transportation; all major wars; and United States military information. We have numerous catalogs and regulation manuals on all subjects." Information covers art, entertainment, food, health/medicine, history, industry, politics, recreation, sports and travel.

Services: Offers bibliographies, clipping services and information searches.

How to Contact: Call for an appointment. "At this time, state the research needed; we will then prepare the request in advance of the appointment, and the material will be ready.

Washington State Historical Society Library, 315 N. Stadium Way, Tacoma WA 98403. (206)593-2830. Librarian: Frank L. Green.

Purpose: "We are a resource library for the society museum as well as for anyone interested in research on the Pacific Northwest." Information covers history.

Services: Offers bibliographies, information searches and photos.

How to Contact: Write, call or visit. "Nothing we have can be sent out. Spot questions can be answered by phone or mail. Restrictions have been placed on some collections by the donors."

Western Jewish History Center, 2911 Russell St., Berkeley CA 94705. (415)849-2710. Archivist: Ruth Rafael. Assistant Archivist: Libby Fleischmann.

Purpose: "We are a manuscript and archival research library concentrating on the contributions of Jews and their institutions to the American West. The center is on the top floor of the Judah L. Magnes Memorial Museum, Berkeley, and includes the Jesse C. Colman Library."

Services: Offers bibliographies, biographies, brochures/pamphlets and information searches.

How to Contact: Write. Charges $25/roll for microfilm reproduction plus $10; $5/hour for any prolonged search; $1/photo plus $5 service charge; for documents photographed on the premises, $10 set-up, $4/print plus $1, $8/per roll (shooting time) plus tax; 15¢/photocopy if done at photocopier, 15¢/photocopy plus $5/hour if done by researcher. Only museums or institutions with museum-like protection may borrow original material for display. If a staff member needs to stay with the material, charges $5/hour time and labor charge plus cost.

Yarmouth County Historical Society Museum and Research Library, 22 Collins St., Yarmouth, Nova Scotia, Canada B5A 3C8. (902)742-5539. Curator: Eric Ruff. Librarian: Helen Hall.

Purpose: Provides materials on Yarmouth's history, shipping and Yarmouth genealogies. Information covers history and shipping.

Services: Offers photos and limited information searches. Publications include newspapers, manuscripts, documents and logs "which can be used on our premises."

How to Contact: Write. "We charge for photocopying, photo reproduction and searches. We insist on a credit line for photos, information, etc. from our sources."

Archives

Archives & History Bureau, New Jersey State Library, 185 W. State St., Trenton NJ 08625. (609)292-6260. Head, Archives and History Bureau: William C. Wright.
Purpose: "Depository of New Jersey governmental records." Information covers history, law and politics.
Services: Offers information searches.
How to Contact: Write or visit.

Baltimore City Archives, 211 E. Pleasant St., Baltimore MD 21201. (301)396-4861. City Archivist/Records Management Officer: Richard J. Cox.
Purpose: "The Baltimore City Archives (BCA) is the official repository for the historical records of the municipal government. These records extend back to 1729—the founding of the city—and to the present. The BCA is actively involved in taking inventory, microfilming and preparing guides to these records." Information covers history.
Services: Offers bibliographies and information searches.
How to Contact: Write. "There is a $2 charge for searching indexes for names. Detailed research requests are not undertaken, but written advice will be offered."

The Bettmann Archive, Inc., 136 E. 57th St., New York NY 10022. (212)758-0362. Picture Research: Diane Cook, Carol Fox or Victoria Schumacher.
Purpose: Collection of historical and editorial photos. Information covers agriculture, art, business, celebrities, economics, entertainment, food, health/medicine, history, how-to, industry, law, music, nature, new products, politics, recreation, science, self-help, sports, technical data and travel.
Services: Offers 5 million blank and white photos and 150,000 color photos. Offers one-time rights, editorial rights, advertising rights, reproduction rights or all rights.
How to Contact: Write or call. Charges $35 minimum/use. Will send free brochure or the *Bettmann Portable Archive* for $25.

California State Archives, 1020 O St., Room 130, Sacramento CA 95814. (916)445-4293. Archivist II: Chuck Wilson.
Purpose: "The California State Archives preserves and provides for research the basic historic and archival records of the state agencies. We maintain this material for researchers, but do not have a research staff capable of doing extensive research upon request. Areas of information are as broad as the functions of the state." Information covers history and politics.
Services: Offers brochures/pamphlets. Publications include *The California State Archives*, "an information pamphlet briefly relating the scope of our program and some of the major portions of our collection"; and *Genealogical Research in the California State Archives*, "a description of the records within our collection that contain genealogical information or that could be used to further genealogical research."
How to Contact: Write, call or visit. "Our materials are open to the public, but must be respected, as original documents must not leave this facility. We charge for copy services only."

Camden Archives, 1314 Broad St., Camden SC 29020. (803)432-3242. Manager/Archivist: Clyde I. Williams Jr.
Purpose: City archives covering the history of Camden, Kershaw County, South Carolina, "and the US as a whole to a limited extent." Information covers health/medicine, history, genealogy and "some insurance records."
Services: Offers brochures/pamphlets and "aid in doing historical (primarily local) and genealogical research." Publications include tour guides to historic buildings (50¢), city and county maps (25¢), tour guide to Liberty Hill homes (free), *Memories of Mulberry* ($1).
How to Contact: Visit. Hours are Monday through Friday, 8 a.m. to noon and 1 p.m. to 5

p.m.; Saturday and Sunday, 1 p.m. to 5 p.m. "Old newspapers and old documents must be used on the premises; access is restricted to persons doing serious research. The privilege may be denied if the materials are mishandled. Persons using our facilities should know the full names of persons as much as possible, and the approximate dates of births, deaths, marriages, etc." The staff will answer some questions by mail, but "the small size of our staff prohibits us from doing research for people."

Catholic Archives of Texas, Box 13327, Capitol Station, Austin TX 78711. (512)476-4888. Archivist: Sister M. Dolores Kasner, O.P.
Purpose: "Our institution is a depository for collections related to the Catholic Church in Texas. Holdings consist of some 70,000 pages of photostat copies of Spanish and Mexican documents; correspondence of early French missionaries in Texas (1842-1860s); official Catholic directories (1886-1978); Texas diocesan newspapers; books and periodicals related to the Church and State." Information covers history.
Services: Offers information searches.
How to Contact: Write or visit. "If a request comes through the mail, it will be honored if it is not too time-consuming." Charges 10¢/photocopy."

Commission on Archives and History, Central Illinois Conference of the United Methodist Church, Box 2050, 1211 N. Park St., Bloomington IL 61701. (309)828-5092. Archivist/Historian: Lynn W. Turner.
Purpose: "We are responsible for storing and cataloging historical church records pertaining to the activities of the Methodist and related churches, such as the United Brethren, in central Illinois: local church records, conference records, personal papers of ministers and members, church histories, biographies, photographs and artifacts." Information covers celebrities, history and religion.
Services: Offers biographies, information searches and photos. Also "limited help in genealogical search, location of baptismal and church membership records, use of the library and documentary collection for research." Publications include *The Historical Messenger* (quarterly).
How to Contact: Write or call for information and for appointment to do research in library. Charges $3/hour for simple research; "for complicated or lengthy research projects, individual negotiation will be necessary. We have no fixed hours for opening the archives and being available for help. Those who want to use our facilities would therefore have to make appointments beforehand."

Concordia Historical Institute, 801 De Mun Ave., St. Louis MO 63105. (314)721-5934, ext. 320. Director: August R. Suelflow.
Purpose: "To promote interest in Lutheran history; to collect and preserve historical articles; to stimulate and publish history and research; to serve as an official depository for the Lutheran church and other agencies; and especially to encourage students from all over the world in historical research." Information covers history and Lutheran pastors and teachers.
Services: Offers bibliographies, biographies, brochures/pamphlets and information searches. Publications include series of bulletins on such topics as developing an archives, writing congregational histories, restoring historic sites.
How to Contact: Write, requesting specific information. Charges for some services; write for summary of costs.

Georgia Department of Archives and History, 330 Capitol Ave. SE, Atlanta GA 30334. (404)656-2358. Director: Carroll Hart. Historical Research Advisor: Mike Llewellyn.
Purpose: Repository of primary information sources on Georgia; county and genealogical information; service agency to state institution. Information covers agriculture, art, business, celebrities, economics, health/medicine, history, law, nature, politics, recreation, science and technical data.
Services: Offers annual reports, biographies, statistics, information searches, placement on mailing list, newsletter and photos. Also maintains microfilm collection of

Georgia county records, deeds, marriage records, bills, state records and minutes of superior courts. Publications include quarterly newsletter.
How to Contact: Write.

INA Corp. Archives, 1600 Arch St., Philadelphia PA 19103. (215)241-3293. Archivist: N. Claudette John.
Purpose: "INA Corporation is one of the nation's largest diversified financial institutions, with major interests in insurance and insurance-related services, health care management and investment banking. The archive's collection is composed primarily of documents generated by the Insurance Company of North America, founded in 1792 to write marine, fire and life insurance. Documents relating to the history of INA Corporation and other INA subsidiaries are also held by the archives." Information covers business and history.
Services: Offers answers to questions. "The archives staff will research specific questions or make available material for the researcher to use in the archives." Publications include company histories, *Biography of a Business*, and *Perils: Named and Unnamed*, which may be requested when visiting the archives. "These volumes are available at many libraries. A guide to the materials in the archives is also available upon request."
How to Contact: "The writer may telephone or address written inquiries to the archivist. An appointment is needed to visit the archives." No charge unless extensive photocopying services are required. "Appropriate restrictions will be made at the discretion of the archivist."

Iowa Division of Historical Museums & Archives, E. 12th and Grand Aves., Des Moines IA 50319. (515)281-5111.
Purpose: "We have information on genealogy; and legal, administrative and historical material on Iowa. We also have a newspaper collection of state material." Information covers agriculture, art, business, celebrities, economics, entertainment, food, health/medicine, history, industry, law, politics, sports, archeology and genealogy.
Services: Offers aid in arranging interviews, annual reports, bibliographies, biographies, statistics, information searches and photos.
How to Contact: Write, call or visit. Charges for copies and photocopies. "We do not loan material."

C.G. Jung Institute, ARAS, 10349 W. Pico, Los Angeles CA 90064. (213)556-1193. Curator: Claire Oksner.
Purpose: "ARAS is an Archive for Research in Archetypal Symbolism—a comprehensive resource consisting of photographs, slides and descriptive material selected for their symbolic content. Born with the support of the Bollingen Foundation and later the C.G. Jung Foundation of New York, ARAS has developed into a collection of 13,000 photographs and slides. The projected number of items in the ARAS collection will be over 25,000. ARAS presents a body of research material selected for its symbolic importance and human meaning from the art works of man throughout the ages. It is a collection of photographs and slides, each with an accompanying catalog sheet presenting art-historical information, iconographical descriptions, and interpretations by noted scholars. All pictures are cross-referenced by historical period, subject, proper name, artist, material and technique, and source and location." Information covers art, food and health/medicine.
Services: Offers bibliographies and brochures/pamphlets.
How to Contact: Write or call. The information center is open weekdays, 10 a.m. to 5 p.m., and Saturday, 11 a.m. to 2 p.m.

James A. Kelly Institute for Local Historical Studies, St. Francis College, 180 Remsen St., Brooklyn NY 11201. (212)522-2300, ext. 202. Director: Arthur Konop.
Purpose: "Kelly Institute contains a collection of documents pertaining to Brooklyn (circa 1640 to present). The institute also has the papers of Congressman J.J. Rooney,

E.J. Keogh and the Brooklyn Democratic Party. We service scholars, genealogists and the local community." Information covers history.
Services: Offers information searches. Publications include a brochure describing the institute and its holdings.
How to Contact: Write. Charges for reproduction and duplication.

Los Angeles Photo Archives, 6300 Wilshire Blvd., Los Angeles CA 90048.
Services: Offers photos. "Photos are mainly based on the history of Los Angeles and southern California."
How to Contact: Write or visit.

Maine State Archives, Cultural Bldg., Search Room, Augusta MA 04333. (207)289-2451.
Purpose: "Repository for state agency records." Information covers agriculture, business, celebrities, economics, health/medicine, history, industry, law and genealogy.
Services: Offers annual reports, bibliographies, information searches, brochures/pamphlets, statistics and photos.
How to Contact: Write or visit. Charges 25¢/photocopy (first three are free); $2 for certification of records. "We do not loan material."

Mississippi Department of Archives and History, Box 571, Jackson MS 39205. (601)354-6218. Contact: Library.
Purpose: "The care and custody of official state archives, a collection of materials relating to Mississippi. We encourage preservation of historical structures and publication of related books, brochures and guides. We operate museums and historic sites." Information covers agriculture, art, business, celebrities, economics, entertainment, food, health/medicine, history, industry, law, music, nature, politics, recreation, science, sports and anything else that relates to Mississippi history.
Services: Offers annual reports, biographies, statistics, brochures/pamphlets and information searches.
How to Contact: Write or call. Charges 15¢/photocopy, $1.75/ photostat negative, $3.50/photostat positive, and $6.50/roll for microfilm (for existing film of all lengths or for 15 feet of copy for material previously unfilmed). "We do not have adequate staffing to handle research of material that isn't indexed."

North Carolina Division of Archives and History, 109 E. Jones St., Raleigh NC 27611. (919)733-3952. Contact: Archives Branch.
Purpose: "Most of the photographs in our custody pertain to North Carolina history and culture. Holdings include an extensive number of pictures depicting buildings and places in North Carolina that have been nominated for or placed on the National Register of Historic Places."
Services: Offers 300,000 photographs on file. Most are in the public domain.
How to Contact: No photographs are available for sale or loan, but prints can be made to order. Charges $2-8/b&w photo; charges cost, plus 15¢/ color photo. "Orders should be placed at least 2 weeks in advance. Detailed research cannot be done by mail or by telephone."

Public Archives of Canada, National Photography Collection, 395 Wellington St., Ottawa, Canada K1A 0N3. (613)992-3884, 995-1300. Chief, Picture Division: George Delisle.
Purpose: Provides photographic record of Canadian history and culture.
Services: Offers b&w prints and 35mm color transparencies of Canada: historical views, events, portraits, posters, cartoons, costumes, heraldry and medals. Material is in the public domain. "Photos of all Canadian subjects, documenting the political, economic, industrial, military, social and cultural life of Canada from 1850 to the present."
How to Contact: "On unrestricted or noncopyright material, reproduction rights are

normally granted upon request after examination of a statement of purpose, or legitimate use in publication, film or television production, exhibition or research." Charges $3/8x10 b&w print.

Simcoe County Archives, Rt. 2, Minesing, Barrie, Ontario, Canada L0L 1Y0. (705)726-9300. Archivist: Peter Moran.
Purpose: "To document the history of Simcoe County, Ontario, through collection of government records, maps, photographs, newspapers and manuscript material, and to make it available to researchers." Information covers agriculture, art, business, celebrities, economics, entertainment, food, health/medicine, history, industry, law, music, nature, politics, recreation, science, sports and technical data.
Services: Offers annual reports, biographies, statistics, brochures/pamphlets, information searches, photos, research aids and catalogs. Publications include a brochure on the hours and services of the archives.
How to Contact: Write or visit. "Mail inquiries will be answered in brief. Detailed research requires a personal visit." Charges $5 for mail inquiries.

South Dakota Archives Resource Center, State Capitol, Pierre SD 57501. (605)773-3173. State Archivist: Dennis F. Walle.
Purpose: "To assemble, preserve and make available the historically valuable records of the state government. The archives also has the responsibility for records of county and town government agencies when they are in danger of loss, deterioration or destruction." Information covers business, economics, health/medicine, history, industry and politics.
Services: Offers bibliographies and information searches. Publications include 1978 Annual Report, Archives Resource Center and Checklist of Record Series: South Dakota.
How to Contact: Write or call. "Genealogical requests should include full names, dates and locations (town and county). Government research requests should include department, agency and dates."

Vanderbilt Television News Archive, Joint University Libraries, Nashville TN 37203. (615)322-2927. Administrator: James P. Pilkington.
Purpose: Has "videotape collection, network evening news broadcasts and related specials, from August 5, 1968, to the present. Purpose: for reference, research and study; not for productions, rebroadcast, etc. Tapes may be viewed at the archive, or borrowed to use for study or instruction elsewhere." Information covers agriculture, art, business, celebrities, economics, entertainment, food, health/medicine, history, how-to, industry, law, music, nature, new products, politics, recreation, science, self-help, sports, technical data and travel.
Services: Offers "source material for research. We publish a monthly index to network evening news broadcasts titled Television News Index and Abstracts. In short, it is a videotape collection of the network evening newscasts for use for the same purposes newspaper collections are used."
How to Contact: Write or call. Charges $2/hour for viewing of tapes in archive; $15/tape hour of duplication; $30/tape hour of compilations; $5/tape hour of audio-only duplication. "Researchers must promise not to rebroadcast in any manner material borrowed; promise not to duplicate in any manner tapes lent; give an explanation of any public showings; and use material in accordance with copyright provisions."
Tips: "Research in television news generally is more time-consuming than comparable research in print media. Tailor research as specifically as possible."

West Virginia Archives and History Division, Cultural Center, Capitol Complex, Charleston WV 25305. (304)348-0230. Director: Rodney A. Pyles.
Purpose: "A research library of West Virginia history and genealogy and a depository for state records and documents. The division acts as secretariat for the West Virginia Historical Society." Information covers agriculture, art, business, celebrities, econom-

ics, entertainment, food, health/medicine, history, how-to, industry, law, music, nature, new products, politics, recreation, science, self-help, sports and technical data. **Services:** Offers aid in arranging interviews, annual reports, bibliographies, biographies, brochures/pamphlets, clipping services, information searches, placement on mailing list, newsletter, photos and press kits. Publications include publications list. **How to Contact:** Write. Charges for copying.

Women's History Archive, Sophia Smith Collection, Smith College, Northampton MA 01060. Director: Mary-Elizabeth Murdock, Ph.D.
Services: Offers millions of manuscripts and about 5,000 photos emphasizing women's history and general subjects: abolition and slavery, American Indians, outstanding men and women, countries (culture, scenes), US military history, social reform, suffrage and women's rights. Mainly b&w or sepia. Publications include *Picture Catalog*, which includes a free schedule.
How to Contact: Write. Offers US rights, one-time use only. Print fee based on cost of reproduction of print plus intended use. Charges $6 for *Picture Catalog*.

Regional Depository Libraries

The following libraries have been designated as regional depository libraries by the federal government. These libraries serve as valuable sources of government publications, since they are required to receive and retain a copy of every US government publication, which is made available in either print or microfacsimile form. Libraries here are listed alphabetically according to the states in which they are located.

Auburn University at Montgomery Library, Montgomery, Alabama

University of Alabama Library, University, Alabama

Department of Library and Archives, Phoenix, Arizona

University of Arizona Library, Tucson, Arizona

California State Library, Sacramento, California

University of Colorado Libraries, Boulder, Colorado

Denver Public Library, Denver, Colorado

Connecticut State Library, Hartford, Connecticut

University of Florida Libraries, Gainesville, Florida

University of Idaho Library, Moscow, Idaho

Illinois State Library, Springfield, Illinois

Indiana State Library, Indianapolis, Indiana

University of Iowa Library, Iowa City, Iowa

Watson Library, University of Kansas, Lawrence, Kansas

Margaret I. King Library, University of Kentucky, Lexington, Kentucky

Louisiana State University Library, Baton Rouge, Louisiana

Louisiana Technical University Library, Ruston, Louisiana

Raymond H. Fogler Library, University of Maine, Portland, Maine

McKeldin Library, University of Maryland, College Park, Maryland

Boston Public Library, Boston, Massachusetts

Detroit Public Library, Detroit, Michigan

Michigan State Library, Lansing, Michigan

Wilson Library, University of Minnesota, Moorhead, Minnesota

University of Mississippi Library, University, Mississippi

University of Montana Library, Missoula, Montana

Nebraska Publications Clearinghouse, Nebraska Publications Commission, Lincoln, Nebraska

University of Nevada Library, Reno, Nevada

Newark Public Library, Newark, New Jersey

Zimmerman Library, University of New Mexico, Albuquerque, New Mexico

New Mexico State Library, Santa Fe, New Mexico

New York State Library, Albany, New York

University of North Carolina Library, Chapel Hill, North Carolina

North Dakota State Library, Fargo, North Dakota

Ohio State Library, Columbus, Ohio

Oklahoma Department of Libraries, Oklahoma City, Oklahoma

Portland State University Library, Portland, Oregon

State Library of Pennsylvania, Harrisburg, Pennsylvania

Texas State Library, Austin, Texas

Texas Tech University Library, Lubbock, Texas

Merrill Library and Learning Resources Center, Utah State University Library, Logan, Utah

Alderman Library, University of Virginia, Charlottesville, Virginia

Washington State Library, Olympia, Washington

West Virginia University Library, Morgantown, West Virginia

State Historical Society Library, Madison, Wisconsin

Milwaukee Public Library, Milwaukee, Wisconsin

Wyoming State Library, Laramie, Wyoming

Museums

Museums, almost by their titles alone, seem intimidating, but with rare exceptions are willing sources of help to writers searching for original or pictorial material. Institutions with "Fine Arts" or "Art" in their titles tend to be the most difficult to work with because of the high value of individual pieces in their collections. If researchers pay a little attention to titles and organizations, however, they can be friends, instead of adversaries.

Museums are fascinating mother lodes of information waiting for the patient writer. Consulting them can add depth to writing. For example, one article I worked on made reference to fire trucks; had the piece called for it, I could have drawn on information from 11 fire-fighting history museums.

The top administrative officer of a museum is its "director." Forced to spend most of their time seeking funds from private or government sources, directors are likely to forward information requests to "curators." Curators are creative people with specialized fields of knowledge. As protective as the title implies (in England they're called "keepers"), they preserve the museum's holdings from physical harm and intellectual abuse. Read the entries in the following listings carefully, and you'll find the following types of curators:

Chief Curator indicates the curator of a large institution, with lesser curators who may have time to handle research requests.

Curator of Collections is often a grab-bag title suggesting that the holder may be the only staff member qualified to answer questions outside of the director. Allow ample time for a reply.

Curator of Ancient Egyptian Art or *Curator of European Decorative Arts* (as examples) indicates a person so highly trained as to be all but inaccessible to "amateurs." In cases like this, collections are often open only to qualified scholars and graduate students. Unless you have an overwhelming and provable need to see "curators of" in the larger art museums, try some other source. Historical societies use similar titles, but are friendlier.

Art museums, or museums containing art for whatever purpose, share common attitudes that are helpful to know before asking for help:

• Security has become increasingly tight at art museums, especially if you intend to physically be in storage areas or print rooms. Prior appointments are usually required; identification certainly is, and you will encounter escorts and searches. For your own protection, report immediately any damage you find—be they chips, smudges or tiny tears—to the curator in charge.

• Art museums view their holdings from an aesthetic, more than from a content point of view. Don't ask for haystack or lily pond pictures and expect to see Monet. Ask yourself if you really need to see the original—or will photos, or even photocopies, serve for the moment?

• Many museums—art or otherwise—will not let you take your own pictures of their holdings because electronic flash ages original works much faster than museum lights or daylight. You must often, therefore, request photographs to be made. The fee for this will include photographic services and a reproduction fee, which varies somewhat according to the planned use of the photo and the institution's policy.

Government museums generally charge less than private ones. Art museum curators tend to be more stuffy about nonscholarly use of their holdings (for example, to illustrate a travel piece or a calendar other than their own), though this isn't always true.

The way around all these potential problems is *preparation*. Read all available published sources on your subject, such as exhibition catalogs or museum quarterlies, as well as magazines having an art history orientation. Try to learn something about the curator you're asking to visit from the museum's public relations department or from local newspaper reports often published when a new man comes in.

If possible, visit the museum first as a tourist and see what's in plain sight. Nothing irritates a busy curator more than your asking to see something that's already on display.

After all that, if you still feel that only the original will do, write a good, tight letter explaining your project, follow the museum's rules, and enjoy the special pleasure and insight that comes only from confronting original works in person.

The person to whom you should direct your request is indicated in each of the following listings, as is precisely how to contact that person. A valuable source for more data on museums of all descriptions is *The Official Museum Directory*, published annually by the American Association of Museums. Many historical societies, historic sites, libraries and other organizations listed in other sections of *The Writer's Resource Guide* maintain museums as parts of their operations. Check these sections for additional information. (*The above introduction was written by William B. Stevens Jr., a freelance writer who has sold a number of articles based on his prowling through museums.*)

Alaska State Museum, 10 Whittier, Juneau AK 99801. (907)586-1224.
Purpose: "Preservation, collection and conservation; unique collection of Northwest Coast Indian art and Alaskan native art." Information covers art, history, how-to (collections), nature, and technical data (on native Alaskans).
Services: Offers brochures/pamphlets, information searches and placement on mailing list. Publications include pamphlet on the museum.
How to Contact: Write. Open Monday through Friday, 9 a.m. to 5 p.m.; Saturday and Sunday, 1 p.m. to 5 p.m.
Tips: "Writers might also wish to contact the Alaska Historical Library, State Office Blvd., Juneau 99811."

Allegany County Museum, Wells Lane, Belmont NY 14813. (716)268-7612. Historian: Bill Greene.
Purpose: "To record and research the history of Allegany County and to supply local genealogical information." Information covers agriculture, economics, history, industry, politics, recreation and travel.
Services: Offers aid in arranging interviews, biographies, statistics, information searches and genealogical searches.
How to Contact: Write to Bill Greene. Enclose SASE. "Though we strive for same-day service, replies may take one or two months, because of other activities."

American Museum of Immigration, National Park Service, Dept. of the Interior, Liberty Island NY 10004. (212)732-1236. Contact: Superintendent.
Purpose: "To tell the story of immigration." Information covers library, films and slides.
Services: Offers bibliographies, biographies, brochures/pamphlets, statistics and photos.
How to Contact: Write or visit.

The American Museum of Natural History, Library—Photographic Collection, Central Park W. at 79th St., New York NY 10024.

Purpose: Information covers anthropology, archeology, primitive art, botany, geology, mineralogy, paleontology, zoology and some astronomy.
Services: "The collection has about 16,000 color transparencies and 500,000 b&w negatives available for reproduction."
How to Contact: Write. Fees and other information will be supplied on request.

American Museum of Science & Energy, Box 117, Oak Ridge TN 37830. (615)576-3219. Director of Public Information: Judy Statzer. Assistant Director of Public Information: Tim Barlow.
Purpose: "The American Museum of Science & Energy is operated for the United States Department of Energy (DOE) by Oak Ridge Associated Universities (ORAU). ORAU also operates the DOE national traveling energy exhibits program. Photos and information are available on these exhibits." Information covers health/medicine, travel and science and energy information.
Services: Offers photos.
How to Contact: Write or call. Free catalog or brochure to writer on request. "We reserve rights to edit copy before publication. Some of the photographs will require a credit line for the photographer. No rights can be given to the writer."

American Museum—Hayden Planetarium, Perlun Library, 81st St. and Central Park W., New York NY 10024. (212)873-1300, ext. 478. Librarian: Sandra Kitt.
Purpose: "We are a department of astronomy, affiliated with a natural history museum. We are a public department which offers a major planetarium, with topical sky shows, to the public. We have two floors of exhibits, two multimedia theaters, classrooms, a research library and a gift shop. Our library (and the department) specializes in astronomy, astrophysics, meteorology, navigation and space technology. Our research library is considered the best available to the general public in this field." Information covers history, how-to, new products, astronomy and technical data, all relating to astronomy. Also offers NASA technical information and mission reports.
Services: Offers bibliographies, information searches and photos for research only.
How to Contact: "The planetarium is open daily except Thanksgiving and Christmas. The library is open by appointment Monday through Friday, 1 p.m. to 5 p.m. We charge for photocopies."
Tips: "Research must be done in-house; books and materials cannot be loaned."

Archives-Museum, The Citadel, Charleston SC 29409. (803)792-6846. Director: Mal J. Collet.
Purpose: "The purpose of the Archives-Museum is to function as a historical research and cultural center on The Citadel campus. The museum portrays the history of The Citadel, the military college of South Carolina. Special exhibits, lectures, film and slide series on a wide variety of subjects are held in the museum. The archives is the second largest college or university archives in the state of South Carolina. The nucleus of the collections pertains to the history of The Citadel (founded in 1842) and national recognized figures, e.g., Gen. Mark W. Clark, L. Mendel Rivers, Gen. W.C. Westmoreland, etc." Information covers history.
Services: Offers aid in arranging interviews, annual reports, bibliographies and photos. Publications include "Archives-Museum brochure and assorted brochures relating to The Citadel."
How to Contact: Write or call. Charges only for reproduction.
Tips: "Researchers are advised to consult the *National Union Catalogue of Manuscript Collections* on archives and museum holdings. Included in the permanent collection. "Fees vary according to subject."

Arizona State Museum, Photographic Collections, University of Arizona, Tucson AZ 85721. (602)626-2445. Assistant Curator: Ellen Horn.
Purpose: "The photographic collections are open for research purposes. Primary subject matter includes prehistoric and historic Southwestern archeology, ethnology

of the Indians of the American Southwest and northwestern Mexico, museum artifacts, specimens, displays, exhibits and additional materials." Information covers agriculture, art, food, history, how-to, nature, science, self-help, technical data, archeology, anthropology, museum exhibits and education.
Services: Offers information searches and photos of artifacts/specimens in the museum's collections.
How to Contact: Write or call for information on fees, availability of specific subject areas for research and appointments to view the collections.

Arkansas Post County Museum, Box 32, Gillett AR 72055. (501)548-2634. Curator: Myrtle Bergschneider.
Purpose: "To provide information on the first settlers in Arkansas, The Arkansas Post (the first settlement in the Louisiana Purchase), the Colbert Incident, and the encounter at the Arkansas Post (1783)." Information covers history and travel.
Services: Offers brochures/pamphlets. Publications include *Arkansas Post County Museum, Arkansas Post, Dates in Arkansas History, Information on the Colbert Incident, Information on Locks and Dams*, and *Information on the Early Settlers in Arkansas.*
How to Contact: Write.

Atikokan Centennial Museum, Box 1330, Atikokan, Ontario, Canada P0T 1C0. (807)597-6585. Curator: Diane Labelle Davey.
Purpose: "To collect, catalog, prepare and display items of interest related to lumbering, mining and the history of the Atikokan area; to acquire a permanent collection of relevant materials and to maintain an ongoing record of life in Atikokan through the use of memoirs and artifacts; to acquire current important records, articles, etc.; to give the community the best possible exhibits." Information covers art (local), history, science, technical data, and mining and lumbering pertaining to the Atikokan area.
Services: Offers biographies, brochures/pamphlets and newsletter.
How to Contact: Write or call. "Be as specific as possible in your request. Most of the material may be photocopied, but a portion of it must be used on the premises."

Bakken Museum of Electricity in Life, 3537 Zenith Ave. S., Minneapolis MN 55416. Education Coordinator: Nancy Roth.
Purpose: "Museum/library devoted to the history of electricity, particularly in its relation to medicine." Information covers health/medicine, history and science.
Services: Offers bibliographies, brochures/pamphlets, information searches and photos. Publications available.
How to Contact: Write or call. "Our topics are really very restricted—electricity in the life sciences only. For more general information on the history of medicine/electricity/technology, another library would be more helpful."

Balzekas Museum of Lithuanian Culture, 4012 S. Archer Ave., Chicago IL 60632. (312)847-2441. President: Stanley Balzekas Jr.
Purpose: "To present an outstanding and diverse collection of Lithuanian antiquities, artifacts, memorabilia and literature spanning 800 years in the history of Lithuania. Our information would cover exhibits, classes, lectures and slide programs."
Services: Offers publications. Publications include *Lithuanian Museum Review* (bimonthly).
How to Contact: Call or write. "Contact us for placement on our mailing list." Charges $1 general admission fee.

General Phineas Banning Residence Museum, 401 E. M St., Wilmington CA 90744. (213)549-2920. Director: Beverly Bubar.
Purpose: "The Banning House tells of the history, lifestyles and decorative arts of the West during the late 19th century." Information covers art and history.
Services: Offers brochures/pamphlets.

How to Contact: Write or call. "It is suggested that interested persons first get basic information on a public tour prior to contacting the office, which serves at this time primarily as a referral to pertinent resources."

Barbed Wire Hall of Fame, Box 327, Blockton IA 50836. (515)788-3641. President: Gene Troncin.
Purpose: "The collection of barbed wire and its history, which is displayed for the public to see." Information covers history.
Services: Offers newsletters. "We also hold shows and meets to further acquaint the public with one of the most important inventions that tamed the Wild West."
How to Contact: Write or call.

In the 1920s, R. Chapman Andrews lead three expeditions to Asia, where he located important paleontological information. Among his discoveries were dinosaur eggs, a find that helped scientists develop theories about the lives of dinosaurs. Andrews took this photo of his camel caravan traveling through the Mongolian desert on one of these expeditions. Andrews' photo is now part of the photographic collection of the American Museum of Natural History. "The collection is composed of historical material like this, as well as up-to-date data," says collection librarian Pamela Haas. She advises writers interested in photos to be specific in their requests. "The more information we receive in a request, the more closely we can fill it." A visit to the museum is also recommended. (Photo©American Museum of Natural History.)

Bath Marine Museum/Maine Maritime Museum, 963 Washington St., Bath ME 04530. (207)443-6311. Administrative Assistant: Bette Bugler.
Purpose: "The Bath Marine Museum and The Apprenticeshop are parts of the Maine Maritime Museum, a nonprofit educational corporation. The museum maintains four

historic sites throughout Bath to preserve Maine's maritime heritage. The Apprenticeshop is a training program in traditional small wooden boatbuilding." Information covers Maine maritime history.

Services: Offers aid in arranging interviews, brochures/pamphlets, information searches, newsletter, photos of sailing vessels and press kits.

How to Contact: "Services are best requested by letter, addressed 'Attention of Curatorial Services.' Specify the information desired. Appointments for personal on-site research may also be arranged."

Boys Town PhilaMatic Center, Box 1, Boys Town NE 68010. (402)498-1360. Curator: Melvin D. Stark.

Purpose: "We are a stamp, coin and currency museum exhibiting the collections donated to Boys Town over the years. The main thrust of the subject matter is philatelic and numismatic; however, we show artwork, artifacts, old newspapers (related to historic figures and events), documents, memorabilia and miscellaneous flat 'collectibles.' We also have a supportive library, which has been built through donations rather than on a constructive basis. We are reputed to exhibit more bank notes than anyone else in the world. Our purpose is to support the boys of Boys Town in their numismatic and philatelic hobbies, as well as to offer for exhibit the collections of Boys Town to philatelists, numismatists and general tourists." Information covers history and memorabilia.

Services: Offers "background material along historical and documentary lines about the exhibits here, research material for books authored on subject matter relating to our exhibits, and documentation of authentic bank notes for the purposes of prospective numismatic authors." Publications include a brochure on the PhilaMatic Center.

How to Contact: Write. "We suggest that requests be tentative and explicit. We might charge a nominal fee if the volume of requests and time warrant it."

Tips: "Try us. We may have something you will find nowhere else."

Branford Trolley Museum, 17 River St., East Haven CT 06512. (203)467-6927. Publicity Director: John Dumblis.

Purpose: "We are dedicated to the preservation, restoration and operation of antique electric railway cars (trolleys, interurbans and rapid transit cars). Trolleys are run over a three-mile ride for visiting tourists. Tours of cars in our car barns and restoration shops are provided." Information covers business, history, industry, recreation, technical data, travel and electric railway items.

Services: Offers aid in arranging interviews, brochures/pamphlets, information searches, photos and press kits. Publications include a museum color brochure, special events flyer and *Ride Down Memory Lane*, a museum guidebook about trolley cars. Has about 500 b&w and 100 color photos. Offers all rights, at cost. "We particularly appreciate any publicity value and exposure that the publication of our photos may generate."

How to Contact: Write John Dumblis, Publicity Director, 238-10 115 Terrace, Elmont NY 11003. "We capitalize on nostalgia, tourism and our scenic New England location. The historic line was built in 1901."

Brigham City Museum-Gallery, Box 583, Brigham City UT 84302. (801)723-6769. Director: Frederick M. Huchel.

Purpose: "Museum-repository of historical artifacts and resource center concerning art, history and natural resources as they pertain to and as they originate from the Brigham City and Box Elder County areas. Specialties: Utah history, Mormon history, history of the transcontinental railroad, the Utah pioneer period, and Utah natural history." Information covers history and nature.

Services: Offers placement on mailing list and newsletter. "We have a lot of printed material on the history of the transcontinental railroad and the 'Golden Spike' ceremony."

How to Contact: Write. Charges for extensive research and/or copying, depending on what is involved in each situation.

British Columbia Forest Museum, Rt. 4, Trans-Canada Hwy., Duncan, British Columbia, Canada V9L 3W8. (606)748-9389. Curator: Mr. R. Crittin.
Purpose: "To preserve and to demonstrate the relationship of man to the forest environment." Information covers history and the forest industry.
Services: Offers brochures/pamphlets.
How to Contact: Write. Charges $2/adult entrance fee.

Brockton Art Center/Fuller Memorial, Oak St., Brockton MA 02401. (617)588-6000. Executive Director: Marilyn Hoffman.
Purpose: "The only art museum and art workshop center between Boston and Cape Cod in southeastern Massachusetts. We offer college-level studio courses, lectures, and a library of art books. Permanent collection is primarily late 19th and early 20th century American. Visiting collections are of a wide variety." Information covers art and recreation.
Services: Offers aid in arranging interviews, brochures/pamphlets, information searches, newsletter, photos and press kits. Publications include periodic newsletter and art catalogs.
How to Contact: Contact public information officer via executive director. Requires special permission to photograph in galleries.

Pearl S. Buck Birthplace Foundation, Inc., Box 126, Hillsboro WV 24946. (304)653-4430. Executive Director: David C. Hyer.
Purpose: "To operate the Historic House Museum of 1892 (Pearl S. Buck birthplace), to establish a national and international center for arts and humanities, and to contribute to educational and cultural development of the region, state and nation. We conduct daily tours of the museum and restored barn seven days a week, all year long. Also, we have an annual Pearl S. Buck birthday celebration (June 26th); an author's day in August; and St. Nicholas Day (a Dutch celebration of Pearl S. Buck's ancestors) in December." Information covers entertainment and history.
Services: Offers aid in arranging interviews, bibliographies, brochures/pamphlets, information searches and newsletters (to members). Publications include *The Works of Pearl S. Buck* (a bibliography); *Birthplace Foundation Bibliography* tentatively scheduled for publication in late 1979 in the *Bulletin of Bibliography*.
How to Contact: Write or call.

Buffalo Bill Museum of LeClaire, Iowa, Inc., Box 284, LeClaire IA 52753. Curator: Esther M. Kenned.
Purpose: Local history museum. Information covers history.
Services: Offers information searches. Publications include a history of LeClaire, Iowa.
How to Contact: Write or visit. "We have heretofore cooperated with all legitimate requests for information when possible, and when they don't conflict with our normal routine."

Burnham Tavern Museum, Main St., Machias ME 04654. (207)255-4432. Chairperson: Mrs. John R. Atwood.
Purpose: "Historic preservation, and education and promotion of patriotic endeavors. Our material is about the history of the Machias River Valley area." Information covers history.
Services: Offers brochures/pamphlets. Publications include a brochure about the museum, a biography of Hannah Weston (Revolutionary War heroine), and numerous materials on the first naval battle of the American Revolution on June 12, 1775.
How to Contact: Write or call. Charges for photocopies and postage. "Appointments must be made for information or study."

California Museum of Science & Industry, 700 State Dr., Los Angeles CA 90037. (213)749-0101. Contact: Bud Hopps.
Purpose: "To present to people of all ages technical and science exhibits of a sensory

nature and to explain the most recent findings of science and technology to the public." Information covers agriculture, art, entertainment, health/medicine, how-to, nature, science and technical data.
Services: Offers aid in arranging interviews, brochures/pamphlets, information searches, placement on mailing list, statistics, newsletter, photos and press kits.
How to Contact: Write.

Canal Museum, Weighlock Bldg., Erie Blvd. E., Syracuse NY 13202. (315)471-0593. Librarian: Todd S. Weseloh.
Purpose: "Our museum and library seek to inform and educate the public through exhibits, tours, lectures and the dissemination of information on the history of canals in America and abroad. We cover information on all canals, but the real strength of our collections is on the construction and finance of the New York state canal system." Information covers history, technical data, transportation (canals) and engineering.
Services: Offers bibliographies, newsletter, photos and reference center. Publications include a general descriptive brochure on the museum."
How to Contact: "Call or write to ask questions about canals; the more specific the questions, the better." Charges cost plus postage for duplication of maps and plans; 10¢/photocopy of documents or book pages; $5-10/8x10 b&w photo.

Canal Museum, 200 S. Delaware Dr., Box 877, Easton PA 18042. (215)258-7155. Executive Director: J. Steven Humphrey.
Purpose: Information covers history.
Services: Offers brochures/pamphlets and photos. Publications include Canal Museum brochure.
How to Contact: Write. "Services open to seriously minded canal and history people."

Carnegie Museum of Natural History, 4400 Forbes Ave., Pittsburgh PA 15213. (412)622-3328. Publicity: Leda Hanin.
Purpose: "To collect and exhibit art and national history objects for the general public. We are noted worldwide for our dinosaur collection." Information covers art, health/medicine, history, nature, science and technical data.
Services: Offers aid in arranging interviews, annual reports, biographies, brochures/pamphlets, placement on mailing list, statistics, newsletter, photos and press kits.
How to Contact: Write.

Amon Carter Museum, 3501 Camp Bowie, Fort Worth TX 76107. (817)738-1933. Director of Public Relations: Michael Duty.
Purpose: "The Amon Carter Museum is devoted to the westering of North America. The program consists of special exhibitions, collections of American paintings, sculpture and photography, and special programs such as film series and seminars. Represented in the collection are such artists as Winslow Homer, Frederic Remington, Thomas Moran, Martin Johnson Heade, Georgia O'Keeffe, Charlie Russell, Albert Bierdstadt and Ben Shahn. The photographic collection includes works by W.H. Jackson, Edward Weston and Laura Gilpin." Information covers art and history.
Services: Offers bibliographies, biographies, statistics and photos. "We have an extensive library devoted chiefly to Western history, plus nearly 6,000 microfilm rolls of 19th century newspapers."
How to Contact: "Call or write for an appointment. The research library is open by appointment only. Interested writers who wish to do research in the photographic collections should contact Marjorie Morey, curator of the photographic collection. We have frequently been used as a research source by writers throughout the country and are happy to cooperate. We only ask that interested parties make appointments in advance and have specific requests. We require a credit line for any published reproduction of any item in the permanent collection." Charges for reproduction of art in the permanent collection. "Fees vary according to subject."

Cherokee Strip Living Museum, Box 230, Arkansas City KS 67005. (316)442-6750. Director: Herbert Marshall.
Purpose: "We house photos, documents, newspapers and other artifacts pertaining to the Cherokee 'Outlet' Run of 1893." Information covers art, history and travel.
Services: Offers aid in arranging interviews, bibliographies, statistics, brochures/pamphlets, clipping services and photos. Publications include a pamphlet on the Cherokee Strip land run. "Antique post cards dating from 1907, printed by the Cornish, are also available."
How to Contact: Write. Charges for pamphlet and post cards.

Chickasaw Council House Historic Site and Museum, Court House Square, Tishomingo OK 73460. (405)371-3351. Site Director: Beverly J. Wyatt.
Purpose: "The purpose of the organization is to display and promote the high culture of the Chickasaw Indians. We do research on various Indian families and assist many people to establish the quantum of Indian blood. The Chickasaws are one of the Five Civilized Tribes. Tishomingo was their capital during the days of the Indian Territory." Information covers history.
Services: Offers biographies, brochures/pamphlets, information searches and photos. "We do have a small library. The majority of the material we have is about the state of Oklahoma, the Indian Territory and the Chickasaws. We have brochures on the various historical sites of Oklahoma (one on the council house), and maps and other items of information about our state."
How to Contact: Write or call the office, visit the museum, or make an appointment with a member of the staff for help. "We are not open on Monday. Saturday and Sunday, the hours are 2 to 5 p.m., and during the remainder of the week we're open 9 a.m. to 5 p.m."

The Children's Museum, 30th and Meridian Sts., Indianapolis IN 46208. (317)924-5431. Public Information Director: Pat Chappell.
Purpose: "The Children's Museum is a 53-year-old museum devoted to the education of children of all ages through participatory programs and exhibits encompassing a wide range of topics. General areas on information include toy trains, firefighting, the Victorian era, pioneer history, toys and dolls, ancient Egypt and natural science, American Indians, and Eskimo and Alaskan cultures." Information covers agriculture, art, food, health/medicine, history, music, nature, recreation and science.
Services: Offers aid in arranging interviews, annual reports, brochures/pamphlets, placement on mailing list, newsletter, photos and press kits. Publications include *The Children's Newseum*, a monthly newsletter detailing a calendar of events, special programs and classes, etc.; *Looklet*, an annual publication giving the floor plan and layout of the museum; an annual report published in March of each year, giving an overview of tha past year; and monthly news releases covering general stories about monthly programs.
How to Contact: Write or call. "The Children's Museum maintains a 24-hour automatic information line—(317)924-KIDS—with information on current activities and special events."

Cincinnati Art Museum, Eden Park, Cincinnati OH 45202. (513)721-5204. Assistant Director: Betty L. Zimmerman.
Purpose: "We are a general art museum with collections that range over 5,000 years and offer a world review in all media—paintings; sculpture; decorative arts; costumes and textiles; tribal arts; prints; drawings; photographs; ancient arts of Egypt, Greece, Rome and the Near and Far East; and musical instruments dating up to the mid-19th century." Information covers art.
Services: Offers observation of original art objects, art reference library (materials circulate only to museum members), publications, brochures, postcards and slides. Publications brochure is available on request.
How to Contact: "A call or letter in advance to describe the research or information

needed can save time and confusion and give assurance that a special visit can produce the needed material. The museum is open Tuesday through Saturday, 10 a.m. to 5 p.m.; Sunday, 1 to 5 p.m. Admission is $1 (free on Saturdays). The library is open for research Tuesday through Friday, l0 a.m. to 4:45 p.m. Appointment with curators for specialized research must be made in advance. Standard charges are made for publication purchases. Charges for photographs and reproduction rights are available on request. Permission to take your own photographs must be arranged through the assistant Director. The right to reproduce photographs of art objects in the collections must be cleared well in advance of publication. Permission is needed for quotations taken from Cincinnati Art Museum publications which appear in print. Be sure that any illustrative material is used in correct context with exact identification of title, subject and place of origin. We have had Chinese art confused with Japanese, Persian art confused with Turkish, and the like."

Circus World Museum, 426 Water St., Baraboo WI 53913. (608)356-8341. Director: William L. Schultz. Business Manager: Dale Williams.
Purpose: To collect and disseminate circus history. Information covers entertainment, history, recreation and travel.
Services: Offers aid in arranging interviews, annual reports, brochures/pamphlets, information searches, placement on mailing list, photos and press kits. Publications include a guide to collections and library services, a booklet on summer operations, and a a schedule of events.
How to Contact: Write or call. Charges for library research involving pictures.

Citizens Savings Athletic Foundation Sports Museum, 9800 S. Sepulveda Blvd., Los Angeles CA 90045. (213)670-7550. Managing Director: W.R. Bill Schroeder.
Purpose: Displays awards (trophies and medallions) entrusted by famous athletes, coaches and sportsmen; uniforms and equipment worn and used by noted athletes; photographs; and other sports artifacts and memorabilia. "The Olympic Games section is one of the finest in existence." Information covers sports.
Services: Offers bibliographies, biographies, statistics and information searches. Publications include press and media releases.
How to Contact: "The museum is open for visitation, without charge, Monday through Friday, 9 a.m. to 5 p.m, and on Saturday, 9 a.m. to 3 p.m."

Clark County Historical Society Fine Arts Museum, Rt. 2, Loyal WI 54446. (715)255-8968. President: Florence Garbush.
Purpose: "Our society is for the preservation of area history, with a rural museum at Colby (home of Colby cheese) and a fine arts museum at Neillsville (in the 1897 Clark County jail). The residence of the sheriff is basically the museum and the jail is the research library. Our initial donation was 500 books of biographies and furniture identification; several hundred more were added since. The music library includes leather-bound conductor's scores, first printings of the European masters, and several copies of Japanese, Russian and German vocal selections. At the present time it is being cataloged and indexed." Information covers history, music and politics.
Services: Offers assistance.
How to Contact: Write, sending SASE, or call. Plans to charge for research. "I receive at least six requests of one kind or another every week. About two of the six send a stamped envelope, and most expect hundreds of hours of free research, which is impossible when time is donated to operate the museum."

Cloud County Museum, 7th and Broadway, Concordia KS 66901. (913)243-2866. Curator: Thelma Schroth.
Purpose: "An institution organized to care for all tangible inanimate objects related to Cloud County history, and to exhibit them to the public on a daily basis." Information covers agriculture, business, celebrities, entertainment, health/medicine, history, industry, law, music, nature, politics, recreation and science.

How to Contact: "Until we have the equipment for copying old books and papers, we are not offering these sources to the public for research. Our historian, Mildred Barber, does research for individuals."

Collier State Park Logging Museum, Box 428, Klamath Falls OR 97601. Curator: Alfred Collier.
Purpose: "The museum's theme is the evolution of logging equipment from the days of brute strength to the present day of modern equipment." Information covers logging.
How to Contact: "Come and see us."

Conneaut Railroad Museum, 324 Depot St., Box 643, Conneaut OH 44030. (216)599-7878. Treasurer: William S. Brandy.
Purpose: "An educational organization featuring historic artifacts and equipment of the steam railroad era as it relates to the development of the US. A haven for historic items dating back to the mid-19th century, including authentic railroad artifacts. This is considered by most railroad buffs to be the most complete steam railroad museum in the country. It features the #755 Berkshire engine that can be boarded." Information covers business, history, industry, recreation and travel.
Services: Offers brochures/pamphlets and newsletter. Publications include *Conneaut Railroad Museum*, *Semaphore* (monthly) and a book on the founding of the museum.
How to Contact: Write. Enclose SASE. "This is a free museum, open Decoration Day through Labor Day, 11 a.m. to 6 p.m. It is all volunteer."

Conner Prairie Pioneer Settlement, 30 Conner Lane, Noblesville IN 46060. (317)773-3633. Public Relations Associate: Sharon Frickey.
Purpose: "Conner Prairie is a living museum of some 25 buildings located on 55 acres. Since 1975, lives of ordinary people of central Indiana in the 1830s have been portrayed through historical buildings, artifacts of the period and craft demonstrations, and through first-person historic role interpretation. This role-playing allows the visitor to participate in the site interpretation on more than one level. By being involved in the recreated environment and treated as a drop-in visitor in the lives of the 1836 villagers, the visitor can hopefully gain insight into the past." Information covers agriculture, food, history, blacksmithing, spinning and dyeing, weaving and log cabin construction in 1836.
Services: Offers aid in arranging interviews, placement on mailing list, newsletter, photos and press kits. Publications include *Conner Prairie Peddler*, *Conner Prairie Pioneer Settlement* and other material.
How to Contact: "Our season runs from April 3 through December 17, closed on Mondays. The activities in the recreated village are dictated by the seasons, and special events are planned accordingly."

Cooper-Hewitt Museum, Smithsonian Institution, 2 E. 91st St., New York NY 10028. (212)860-6868. Public Information Officer: Isabelle S. Silverman.
Purpose: "Cooper-Hewitt Museum is the Smithsonian Institution's national museum of design. It serves as a reference center for designers, scholars and students in all fields of design and the decorative arts." Information covers art, interior design and the decorative arts.
Services: Offers placement on mailing list, photos and press kits. "We maintain a library of over 30,000 volumes and a picture reference library of over 1,500,000 illustrations relating to the arts and all aspects of design. In addition, there are archives of color, pattern, textiles, symbols and advertising." Publications include "folders describing the permanent collections of drawings, prints, textiles, wallpaper and all decorative arts; and information about the museum's home: the former Andrew Carnegie property, now a city and national landmark."
How to Contact: "Press information is obtained from the public information officer. Specific information about the museum's holdings is obtained by letter to the curator of the pertinent department. Anyone who wishes to use the museum's resources is

asked to make an appointment in advance with the curator of the department in which he wishes to work, or with the librarian."

Dacotah Prairie Museum, Box 395, Aberdeen SD 57401. (605)229-1608. Director: William Busta.
Purpose: "The Dakota prairie is a wide-open land of blue skies, broad horizons and climatic extremes. The museum is dedicated to telling the story of this land and the people who have lived on it. Information covers, primarily, the Dakota Prairie frontier from 1878 to 1910. The emphasis is on local history." Information covers agriculture, art, business, entertainment, food, health/medicine, how-to, industry, music, politics and sports.
Services: Offers information searches and photos.
How to Contact: Write or call. "There is no charge for use of photographs (approximately 5,000 pieces are in the collection). However, we request that researchers who want copies to send film. We will do photo-stand work at no charge, but the researcher is responsible for developing."

Debs Museum, 451 N. 8th St., Terre Haute IN 47807. (812)232-2163. Executive Vice President/Curator: Ned A. Bush Sr.
Purpose: "We are chiefly concerned about all phases of the life of Eugene V. Debs. We are nonprofit, nonpartisan and nonpolitical. We do have a library devoted to labor history, sociological problems, and the life of Debs as a labor leader and as a socialist candidate for president. We have a large amount of material regarding the socialist activities of Debs." Information covers history.
Services: Offers brochures/pamphlets.
How to Contact: Write or call. "We charge no fees. If our service has been valuable, we will gladly accept a free-will donation as we are dependent upon gifts and help from labor unions and other groups. Researchers are welcomed at the museum and we have a place for them to work. We do not loan out books or source materials. If photocopies are sought, we must charge for that service; we must get it done commercially. We have no copying facilities."

The Depot, Fortuna's Museum, Park St., Fortuna CA 95540. Secretary, Historical Commission: Debra Neuhaus.
Purpose: "The Fortuna Historical Commission operates the museum. Displays cover local and Western history." Information covers agriculture, business, history, and forest and fishing industries.
Services: Offers "written and oral information to be utilized by students, researchers, etc."
How to Contact: Write or visit. "All items and information are available for review, but can't be removed from the premises."

Detroit Historical Museum, 5401 Woodward, Detroit MI 48202. (313)833-1805.
Purpose: "The museum is funded by the city of Detroit and charged with the responsibility to collect, maintain and display artifacts relevant to the history of Detroit. Two branch museums are under its control: Historic Fort Wayne and the Dossin Great Lakes Museum." Information covers history.
Services: Offers brochures/pamphlets, newsletter and a limited number of photos. Most services are restricted to members of the Detroit Historical Society. Publications include the journal, *Detroit in Perspective; Walking Tour of Downtown Detroit; Historic Places around Detroit: A Guide to 330 Historic Sites in Wayne, Oakland and Macomb Counties; A Guide to Detroit's Historic Neighborhoods*; and brochures about the three museums mentioned above.
How to Contact: Call or write. "Where applicable, fees may be charged, or membership in the historical society required. We would appreciate receiving SASE with all requests."
Tips: "Be patient; we are extremely short-staffed."

Drake Well Museum, Rt. 3, Titusville PA 16354. (814)827-2797. Curator: Alan W. Perkins. Assistant Librarian, Photos: M. Jane Elder.
Purpose: "The Drake Well Museum, owned and operated by the Commonwealth of Pennsylvania, has a research library and numerous exhibits commemorating the growth of the petroleum industry, with special emphasis on the 19th century and Pennsylvania's role in these developments. We have an extensive collection of photographs." Information covers history and industry.
Services: Offers aid in arranging interviews, information searches and photos.
How to Contact: Visit. "Call for an appointment first so that we can schedule someone to help you."

Edward-Dean Museum of Decorative Arts, Riverside County Art & Culture Center, 9401 Oak Glen Rd., Cherry Valley CA 92223. (714)845-2626. Director: Mary Jo O'Neill.
Purpose: "The museum is a study environment for interior decorators and students of 17th and 18th century European and Chinese antiquities." Information covers art, history, how-to and travel.
Services: Offers study environment.

Essex Institute, 132 Essex St., Salem MA 01970. (617)744-3390. Community Relations Coordinator: Phyllis Shutzer.
Purpose: "One of the oldest and largest privately endowed regional historical societies in the US. The collections include material associated with the civil history of Essex County, Massachusetts, and adjacent areas since the early 17th century. The institute owns 13 buildings, all of which are listed in the National Register of Historic Places. It maintains a research library of extensive printed and manuscript materials, a museum collection of approximately 39,000 objects, and a publications department. The institute offers special exhibits, public lectures, guided period house tours, publications and library facilities." Information covers art, history and educational programs.
Services: Offers annual reports, brochures/pamphlets, placement on mailing list, newsletter, photos and press kits. Publications include descriptive brochures, booklets on historic houses and collections, a quarterly newsletter and other materials.
How to Contact: "Freelance writers may use our materials for publicity purposes without a fee. We charge a fee for photo reprint service unless the writer is doing a publicity piece."

Field Museum of Natural History, Division of Photography, Roosevelt Rd. at Lake Shore Dr., Chicago IL 60605.
Services: Offers photos.
How to Contact: No catalog of photos is available. It is necessary in ordering photos either to inspect the museum albums or to write, giving precise specifications of what's wanted. Prices and requirements for permission to reproduce are available on request.

Foothill Electronics Museum of the Perham Foundation, 12345 El Monte Rd., Los Altos Hills CA 94022. (415)948-8590, ext. 381. Curator: Jack H. Eddy.
Purpose: "The museum tells the story of electronics in the San Francisco Bay area from 1900 to the present. The deForest Memorial Archives house all of Dr. Lee deForest's papers and other early references on electronics." Information covers history and technical data.
Services: Offers brochures/pamphlets and photos. "Research may be done in the archives." Publications include *Guide to Foothill Electronics Museum* and *The Lee deForest Story*.
How to Contact: Write or call. Charges $10/b&w 8x10 photo.

Fort Lewis Military Museum, Bldg. 4320, Fort Lewis WA 98406. (206)967-4796. Contact: Barbara Dierking.
Purpose: "To preserve, interpret and exhibit the military history of the Northwest."

Information covers military history.
How to Contact: "Visit on appointment. If you can find it, you can use it."
Tips: "We are only a new research library with no archivist or librarian."

Fort Morgan Museum, Box 184, Fort Morgan CO 80701. (303)867-6331. Director: Stafford Crossland.
Purpose: "The museum serving northeastern Colorado. We deal in history, art, etc., and maintain a historical collection of artifacts, photographs, etc." Information covers agriculture, art, history and industry.
Services: Offers aid in arranging interviews, placement on mailing list, and newsletters.
How to Contact: Write. Charges for photocopies.

45th Infantry Division Museum and Library, 2145 NE 36th St., Oklahoma City OK 73111. (405)424-5313. Director: R.W. Jones.
Purpose: "The museum was created to tell the history of the citizen/soldier in Oklahoma. Funded by the state legislature and operated by the Oklahoma military department, its exhibits begin with the Choctaw (Indian tribal) Light Horsemen (tribal police) in the 1850s and continue through to modern training. The 45th Division spent more time in combat during World War II than any other division in Europe, and spent 426 days in combat in Korea. The library houses 2,600 volumes, as well as archives, maps, photographs, biographies, awards/decorations, unit histories, etc., for use on the premises." Information covers art (limited to graphics by 45th Division members) and history.
Services: Offers aid in arranging interviews, biographies, brochures/pamphlets, newsletter and photos. "We are in the process of updating individual unit histories and are planning to produce pamphlets regarding various aspects of the Oklahoma National Guard's history."
How to Contact: "Write for information and be specific. We, of course, prefer that researchers visit our installation and make use of the available material on these premises. The library is available to any interested party. Collections in the museum are also available for research; weapons research is permitted provided the researcher meets security requirements. Generally, research for writers is not performed unless the effort is directed at the history of the 45th Division or one of its components, or the Oklahoma National Guard." Charges for copies of photos.

The Franklin Institute Science Museum and Planetarium, 20th St. and Benjamin Franklin Pkwy., Philadelphia PA 19103. (215)448-1116. Editor, Public Affairs/Publications: Eric T. Rosenthal.
Purpose: "To further public understanding of science and technology and to find solutions to current socio-technological problems through basic and applied research, education and related cultural activities." Information covers economics, health/medicine, history, how-to, science and technical data.
Services: Offers aid in arranging interviews, annual reports, bibliographies, biographies, statistics, brochures/pamphlets, information searches, placement on mailing list, newsletter, photos and press kits.
How to Contact: Write or call. Certain areas of the facilities are open to members only; restrictions may be waived on an individual basis.

Geronimo Springs Museum, 325 Main St., Box 1029, Truth or Consequences NM 87901. (505)894-6600. Manager: Carolyn Elkins.
Purpose: "To preserve the history of Sierra County and New Mexico and to disseminate information about the area when requested." Information covers history.
How to Contact: Write or call. "We have no printed material to distribute, but we will try to research and reply to any specific inquiry about they history of our area. We are now completing a hardbound county history volume."

Great Plains Black Museum/Archives & Interpretive Center, 2213 Lake St., Omaha NE 68110. (402)344-0350. Director: Mrs. Bertha Calloway.
Purpose: "Our museum is the only black history museum in the Great Plains area which serves Nebraska, Iowa, South Dakota, North Dakota, Wyoming, Kansas, Missouri, Wyoming, Montana and Colorado. We are interested in documenting old information and seeking new information on the history of blacks in this area. Our original research has led us to new information on the Underground Railroad, the black settlers-homesteaders, the black cowboy and other people who came early to the Great Plains area. We also have a collection of old, rare books, photographs and artifacts relating to the Great Plains area. Much of the history of blacks in the Great Plains area has been lost, but our museum continues to find new materials such as magazines, letters, diaries and photographs that would excite anyone looking for new sources and new information pertaining to blacks from the end of the Civil War to the present time." Information covers art, business, celebrities, entertainment, food, history, music and politics.
Services: Offers information searches and photos. "The information available to writers would pertain more to original artifacts, letters and other information about blacks that would make interesting material for stories, scripts and plays."
How to Contact: Write or visit. "Charges depend on the amount of work we have to do and/or the reproduction of photographs and other work, i.e. both rare and out-of-print and original manuscripts that could lead to more information. All original research done at the museum should be credited to The Great Plains Black Museum. All photographs used should also be credited. If photographs are from a private collection, arrangements should be make to pay a fee and credit the collection."

Greeley Municipal Museum, 919 7th St., Greeley CO 80631. (303)353-6123, ext. 299. Museum Supervisor: Florence Clark.
Purpose: "We are a full-scale museum with a research library. We have a number of local and family histories. We also have 28 indexed and carded scrapbooks covering the families and history of this area. We also have a large assortment of ledgers, minutes, books, etc., as well as a large collection of miscellaneous information regarding the history of this area." Information covers history.
Services: Offers information searches and photos.
How to Contact: Write or call. "We will supply information on our holdings, but we will not do detailed research." Charges "cost plus postage" for services.

Greenfield Village/Henry Ford Museum, Dearborn MI 48121. (313)271-1620, ext. 362. Manager, Print Media Services: G. Donald Adams.
Purpose: "The village and museum compose the world's largest indoor-outdoor museum of Americana. The village contains more than 85 historic structures. The museum offers 14 acres of Americana, from 600-ton locomotives to silver spoons. The archives contain 8,000 cubic feet of records and 40,000 negatives. The research library includes primary sources in all of the collection areas. The education area has more than a dozen programs. The crafts program offers up to 30 different operating crafts." Information covers agriculture, art, business, celebrities, entertainment, food, history, how-to, industry, music, politics, recreation, science, travel, and "all areas relating to collection items."
Services: Offers aid in arranging interviews with the museum staff, annual reports, brochures/pamphlets, information searches, placement on mailing list, newsletter, photos and press kits. Publications include *Writer's Guide* (annual), as well as special information and general releases. "A look through the *Writer's Guide* indicates the historical material of the village and museum is virtually untapped.
How to Contact: Call or write. "Some historical photographs are available from our archives at about $8 a photograph. Other material is available at no charge for regular media and education sources. No material is available for advertising or commercial use."
Tips: "1979 is the 50th anniversary of Greenfield Village and the Henry Ford Museum,

as well as the 100th anniversary of Edison's light bulb. The village and museum compose the center spot for the centennial celebration in October. December 1978 is the 75th anniversary of the Wright Brothers' flight, and the village has the Wrights' cycle shop and home. Story potentials here and elsewhere are phenomenal."

Hall of Fame of the Trotter, 240 Main St., Goshen NY 10924. (914)294-6330. Director: Philip A. Pines.
Purpose: "The presentation of the history of harness racing in art, oils, sculpture, photos and prints." Information covers the history of the harness horse and the sport of harness racing.
Services: Offers photos.
How to Contact: Write or call. "We have thousands of b&w photos in our collection. We offer all rights. Charges depend on current costs. Free catalog on request."

Hanford Mills Museum, East Meredith NY 13757. (607)278-5744. Director: Richard Kathmann.
Purpose: "To restore and interpret a water- and steam-powered rural industrial complex. We research motive power, wood processing, technology, building construction technology, and industrial history." Information covers history and industry.
Services: Offers bibliographies, statistics and information searches. Publications include *Historic Structures Report*.
How to Contact: Write. Charges 50¢/page for manuscript bibliographies and statistics; $12.50/8x10 photo.

Rutherford B. Hayes Museum, 1337 Hayes Ave., Fremont OH 43420. (419)332-2081. Director: Watt P. Marchman. Manuscripts Librarian: Thomas A. Smith. Books Librarian: Linda C. Hauck.
Purpose: "The museum of the nineteenth president of the US contains Hayes family memorabilia, including several of Mrs. Hayes' gowns, including her wedding dress (1852) and reception gowns worn at White House functions; the President's carriage used at the White House; his Civil War relics as an officer in the war; a large sideboard from the White House dining room, carved in Cincinnati; White House china; Fanny Hayes' doll houses; Indian relics given to President Hayes; a weapons room; and souvenirs from all over the world collected by the President's second son." Information covers history.
Services: Offers publications. Publications include *Hayes Historical Journal* (semi-annual) and *The Rutherford B. Hayes State Memorial*.
How to Contact: Write, call or visit. Charges admission fee. Museum is open weekdays, 9 a.m. to 5 p.m.; Sundays and holidays, 1:30 to 5:30 p.m. Closed on Thanksgiving, Christmas and New Year's Day.

Hayward Area Historical Society Museum, 22701 Main St., Hayward CA 94541. (415)581-0223. Curator: Beulah E. Linnell.
Purpose: "To collect information about the Hayward area, including as much information as possible on the Alameda Bay area." Information covers agriculture, art, and history.
Services: Offers brochures/pamphlets, information searches, newsletter and photos.
How to Contact: Write or call. "There is no charge, but donations are gladly received."

Heckscher Museum, Prime Ave. and Rt. 25A, Huntington NY 11743. (516)271-4440. Public Information Officer: Barbara Press.
Purpose: "The Heckscher Museum is a small fine arts museum. Its collection includes some 400 works, primarily painting and sculpture, both European and American, from the 16th to the 20th centuries. The strength and quality is generally thought to be in the American area. The museum undertakes ten exhibitions annually. All are designed to appeal to scholars and the general public. In addition to exhibitions, we offer educational lectures, workshops and classes." Information covers art and artists.

Services: Offers newsletter and "information about Long Island artists through our artists registry. We publish catalogs for our exhibitions."
How to Contact: Write for a publications list. "We charge a shipping and handling charge, in addition to the cost of the catalog."

Hershey Museum of American Life, 1 Chocolate Ave., Hershey PA 17033. (717)534-3439. Curator: Mrs. E. Harrison.
Purpose: "The Museum of American Life has extensive collections of artifacts illustrating the life of German settlers in Pennsylvania in the 18th and 19th centuries. Also, it has fine collections of American Indian and Eskimo objects; military objects, especially Pennsylvania rifles; china; etc." Information covers agriculture, art, history, how-to and music.
Services: Offers aid in arranging interviews, brochures/pamphlets and photos. "We try to aid in all requests for information about our collections, individual objects, pictures, loans, etc."
How to Contact: Write or call. Charges for photos; "rates vary according to what is required. Credit must be given. Permission is generally given for one-time use."

Hinckley Foundation Museum, 410 E. Seneca St., Ithaca NY 14850. (607)273-7053. Curator: Janet Mara. Registrar: Margaret Hobbie.
Purpose: Museum devoted to local art and history. Information covers agriculture, art, business, economics, entertainment, history, how-to, industry, recreation and technical data.
Services: Offers annual reports, bibliographies, brochures/pamphlets and newsletter. Publications include *A Catalog of Ithaca and Related Imprints, 1820-1870*; *The Spirit of Enterprise: Nineteenth Century in Tompkins County*; and *Free Hollow to Forest Home*.
How to Contact: "Call the museum on Tuesday or Thursday afternoons between 1 and 4:30 p.m., or write. We do not have on-premises duplicating facilities and do not circulate our imprint holdings."

The Historic New Orleans Collection, 533 Royal St., New Orleans LA 70130. (504)523-7146. Assistant Curator: Roseanne McCaffrey.
Purpose: "The manuscripts division contains family papers and other original manuscripts and supporting materials (broadsides, sheet music, newspapers); extensive library of rare books, pamphlets, and major Louisiana studies. The pictorial division consists of engravings, lithographs, photographs, paintings, maps, original framings and artifacts. These materials cover almost every facet of New Orleans history, including architecture, culture, people, and river life, from the 17th to 20th century (largely 19th century)." Information covers agriculture, art, business, celebrities, economics, entertainment, food, health/medicine, history, how-to, industry, music, nature, politics, recreation, science and sports.
Services: Offers over 25,000 pictorial items on a loan basis to sister institutions with necessary insurance and professional staff. Reproduction rights available.
How to Contact: Write or call. Offers one-time rights, advertising rights and reproduction rights. Some material is in the public domain. Charges $30/item, $6/8x10 b&w print, $15/color print, and $3/color transparency (prints made to order).

Homestead Antique Museum, Box 700, Drumheller, Alberta, Canada T0J 0Y0. (403)823-2214. Secretary: Tom Kempling.
Purpose: "Our museum has a collection of items used by the pioneers of Alberta. We could supply information pertaining to the history of this part of the province." Information covers agriculture, business, history, how-to and industry.
How to Contact: Write.

Howard County Historical Museum, 1200 W. Sycamore St., Kokomo IN 46901. (317)452-4314. Curator: Richard A. Kastl.

Purpose: "To provide educational exhibits teaching our visitors about Howard County's past. We have information (documents, manuscripts, etc.) and/or objects relating to agriculture; industrial development (especially glass and automobile manufacturing); and the social, economic, archeological, anthropological and general history of our area. We also have information on our building, which is a restored, late-Victorian mansion."

Services: "We try to answer all inquiries, but can't conduct searches due to a lack of personnel. We can, however, provide someone with enough background information and possible source materials to conduct their own search." Publications include *Monroe Seiberling's Mansion.*

How to Contact: "The best approach is for a writer to contact the museum in writing. Those wishing to make use of the facilities should make arrangements prior to visiting the museum so that the materials are accessible. Often, specific requests have already been researched by us, and can be answered if the information is readily available. No materials may be taken from the museum. No photocopying equipment is available; one my bring a portable copying machine, but any materials being copied must be cleared through the curator, as some manuscripts can be damaged through photocopying."

Tips: "A research proposal giving specific information and a well-defined problem is essential."

Huntington Galleries, 2033 McCoy Rd., Huntington WV 25701. (304)529-2701. Program Coordinator: Janet Dooley.

Purpose: "To provide a cultural and entertainment outlet to the tri-state region through various art exhibitions which may be from our permanent collection, traveling exhibitions or exhibitions we originate, art and art related classes, theater, films, nature and observatory." Information covers art, entertainment, how-to, music, nature, recreation and science.

Services: Offers annual reports, statistics, brochures/pamphlets, placement on mailing list, newsletter, photos and press kits. Publications include catalogs, bulletin and calendar of events, and related brochures.

How to Contact: Write or call.

Indian Museum of the Carolinas, 607 Turnpike Rd., Laurinburg NC 28352. (919)276-5880. Director: Michael R. Sellon.

Purpose: "To preserve and display artifacts from American Indian groups, especially those relating to the southeastern United States, and to the Carolinas in particular. We are a research center for American Indian archeology and ethnology." Information covers agriculture, art, economics, entertainment, food, health/medicine, history and recreation, relating to Native Americans only.

Services: Offers annual reports, brochures/pamphlets, placement on mailing list and newsletter; also answers requests for information on Indians. Brochure describing the museum available.

How to Contact: "Write or telephone (no collect calls accepted). We will attempt to find the requisite information, or we will suggest alternative sources."

Tips: "We will not research information that is readily available in any good public library. We make no promises on results, and we will not research extensive problems."

Institute of American Indian Arts Museum, Cerrillos Rd., Santa Fe NM 87501. (505)988-6281. Museum Director: Charles A. Dailey.

Purpose: "We are a museum, but also offer the Native American Videotape Archives for research. This is comprised of some 350 ½-inch b&w tapes, 50 1-inch edited master tapes, and 100 ¾-inch color cassettes on various aspects of native American culture." Information covers art, history and native American arts, crafts and ethnology.

Services: Offers annual reports, brochures/pamphlets, placement on mailing list, and museum training and museum problem-solving information. Publication available.

How to Contact: Write.

Institute of Texan Cultures, Box 1226, San Antonio TX 78294. (512)226-7651. Director of Library Services: Judy G. Ranney.
Purpose: "Our purpose as stated by the legislature: 'To serve as the center of a statewide communications system which will interpret the history and folklife of Texas to the public.' We are basically a museum. We give tours and perform live demonstrations of various types of folk crafts. However, we also publish several items a year that are primarily in the realm of Texas history. The library houses photographs and support material in the way of research files and books." Information covers food (local and ethnic), history and music.
Services: Offers bibliographies, brochures/pamphlets and photos. "The institute has published a series of pamphlets dealing with specific ethnic groups that settled the state, e.g., *The Mexican Texans, The German Texans*, etc. In addition, we have published several books on various subjects ranging from sunken treasure to ethnic cooking."
How to Contact: Write or call. Charges $5 search fee for photos; hourly contract rate for extensive research inquiries; 20¢/photocopy of library material.
Tips: "Many photographs are 'restricted,' meaning that the writer must contact the individual who loaned the photo to us to secure a release for it."

International Museum of Photography, George Eastman House, 900 East Ave., Rochester NY 14607. Archives: Martha Jenks. Print Service: Michael Kamins.
Purpose: Photo collection. Collection spans the history of photography from 1839 to present day.
Services: Offers photos.
How to Contact: Write. Original prints do not leave the museum, except for approved traveling exhibitions. Reproduction prints must be returned, and a credit line is required. Work is listed by photographer, not subject. "Rates are determined by the circulation" of the publication in which the photo will appear. Charges $15-200 for one-time reproduction.

International Tennis Hall of Fame and Tennis Museum, Newport Casino, Newport RI 02840. (401)846-4567. Executive Director: Robert S. Day.
Purpose: Contains exhibits of tennis trophies and memorabilia; commemorates outstanding players from the past. Information covers sports (tennis).
Services: Offers brochures/pamphlets, placement on mailing list, photos and press kits for tournaments.
How to Contact: Write or call. Charges $12/photo. The library is open weekdays.

Irving House Historical Centre and New Westminster Museum, 302 Royal Ave., New Westminster, British Columbia V3L 1H7. (604)521-7656. Curator: Archie W. Miller.
Purpose: "We handle requests for historical information on the local area. We have a historical center where we maintain a 14-room home (1864-1890) and a museum, which contains an archival collection and photo collections on the local area." Information covers agriculture, art, business, celebrities, health/medicine, history, industry, music, politics and sports.
Services: Offers bibliographies and biographies. Publications available.
How to Contact: Write. Charges for photographs if needed; these are handled on an individual basis. "Donations are welcomed as we are a nonprofit group."

The Jewish Museum, 1109 5th Ave., New York NY 10028. (212)860-1888. Director, Public Information: Joan M. Hartman.
Purpose: "The museum is under the auspices of the Jewish Theological Seminary. It is dedicated to the presentation of Jewish culture, past and present, through exhibitions and education programs. Our permanent collections of Judaica contain over 15,000 ceremonial objects, paintings, graphics, sculpture and textiles. We have the largest collection of Judaica in the United States (in a museum) and the most comprehensive collection in the world." Information covers art, history and facets of Jewish culture.

Services: Offers brochures/pamphlets, placement on mailing list, newsletter and photos. "We offer information to the press about our permanent collections and current exhibitions—photographs, press releases, etc. Photographs for book reproduction and individual research are available on a rental and purchase basis." Publications include an information booklet, a membership flyer, press releases and brochure on traveling exhibitions.

How to Contact: "A writer interested in covering subject matter at The Jewish Museum should contact the director of public information for newspaper and magazine publications, or the curator of Judaica for book material and photographs. Please do not call. Write if at all possible. Of course, if you are meeting an editorial deadline, call and we'll do what we can to be of assistance." Charges for photographs reproduced in books.

Tips: "We do not have library facilities at the museum, nor does our staff have the time to spend hours researching your material for you. We can suggest library sources elsewhere which may meet your needs or generally offer advice in the area of Judaica. Occasionally we will refer you to another organization or source for the kind of information you seek. We have a small staff and cannot devote too much time to outside projects, but we are anxious to encourage your interest in our collections and general purposes."

Johnson County Historical Museum, 6305 Lackman, Shawnee KS 66217. (313)631-6709. President: Mrs. John Barkley.
Purpose: Museum preserves items from the mid-1800s to the present. Information covers history.
Services: Offers aid in arranging interviews, statistics, brochures/pamphlets and information searches.
How to Contact: Write.

Herbert F. Johnson Museum of Art, Cornell University, Ithaca NY 14853. (607)256-6464. Director: Thomas W. Leavitt.
Purpose: "The Johnson Museum serves as an exhibition, education and research source for upstate New York. Although many of its exhibitions and activities relate quite directly to academic programs of the university, the museum works to attract an audience from a larger geographic community. With a strong and varied art collection (including European and American paintings, drawings, sculpture, graphic arts and photographs, and arts of Asia and primitive societies) and a continuous series of high quality exhibitions, it fills a valuable mission as a center for the visual arts in the Northeast." Information covers art, history, library and archival materials.
Services: Offers artists' biographies, brochures/pamphlets, photos, "exhibitions of art objects from our collections and on loan from other sources," exhibition catalogs, and events such as concerts, lectures, films, tours of the galleries, and art classes. "We have a publications list."
How to Contact: "Write or visit the museum; apply in advance for our current quarterly calendar of events." List of publication prices available. Charges $4/8x10 b&w glossy print, plus postage and handling; 75¢/color transparency plus postage and handling. Appointments to study the achival material and art objects in storage (not on exhibition in the galleries) must be made in advance. "Permission for publication of facts on or photographs of objects in our collections must be officially requested in advance in writing."

Kendall Whaling Museum, Box 297, Sharon MA 02067. (617)784-5642. Director: Kenneth R. Martin.
Purpose: "The Kendall Whaling Museum collects, organizes and exhibits art, artifacts, books and manuscripts on whaling, whales, sealing and seals. Its primary dedication is the promotion of research publication and greater understanding in these areas." Information covers art, economics, history, industry, nature and science.
Services: Offers bibliographies, brochures/pamphlets and photos. Publications in-

clude *Whaling Books and Journals in the KWM Collection, Kendall Whaling Museum Paintings, Kendall Whaling Museum Prints,* and *And the Whale Is Ours, Creative Writing of American Whalemen.*
How to Contact: Write or call. Charges $7.50/b&w glossy print; $45/color transparency rental ($75 if published).
Tips: "Credit required in all cases. Writers are advised to have staff members screen their work before publication."

Koochiching County Historical Museum, Box 1147, Smokey Bear Park, International Falls MN 56649. (218)283-4316. Executive Secretary/Curator: Mary Hilke.
Purpose: "To preserve and interpret the history of Koochiching County and, more generally, the state of Minnesota." Information covers history and industry.
Services: Offers biographies and newsletter. "We have a large photo collection, including many pictures from the former Minnesota and Ontario Pulp and Paper Company (now Boise Cascade). We also have a manuscript collection and library, and a large collection of artifacts on exhibit."
How to Contact: Write or visit. "The museum is closed during the winter months, and is open to researchers only on Mondays and Tuesdays. For general visits, it's open every day, Memorial Day through Labor Day."

Lane County Museum, 740 W. 13th Ave., Eugene OR 97402. (503)687-4239. Archivist: E. Nolan.
Purpose: "To collect, preserve and interpret the history of Lane County, Oregon. All phases of Lane County history, 1840 to the present, are covered." Information covers agriculture, business, history, industry, politics, sports and logging.
Services: Offers photos. "We cannot provide extensive research by mail. A visit is recommended. Researchers should have well-defined needs."
How to Contact: Write or call first to discuss needs and set up appointment if a visit would be profitable. Charges for photos and copying fees. Photos are $3.50 per 20.3x25.4-centimeter print, plus $10/print for one-time use.

Le Centre Culturel, Université De Sherbrooke, Pavillon Central, Sherbrooke, Canada J1K 2R1. (819)565-5446. Director Artistique: Graham Cantieni.
Purpose: "Art gallery and cultural center offering exhibitions, conferences, discussions, seminars and films on and about art." Information covers art.
Services: Offers brochures/pamphlets, placement on mailing list, and newsletter. "We can also supply a traveling exhibition of Quebec printmakers."
How to Contact: Write or call.

The Little Brick House, 621 St. Clair St., Vandalia IL 62471. (618)283-0024. Museum Curator: Josephine Burtschi. Publisher: Mary Burtschi.
Purpose: "This organization disseminates knowledge about Illinois, collects and preserves materials related to state history, and assists in historical research, primarily during the 1820-1840 period. The James Hall Library specializes in material relating to the author James Hall (1793-1868) and to Abraham Lincoln as a legislator in Vandalia (1834-1839)." Information covers history.
Services: Offers brochures/pamphlets. Publications include *Port Folio for James Hall.*
How to Contact: Write or call Josephine Burtschi to make an appointment to use the library or to tour historic sites of Vandalia. "The fee is $3/hour for the use of rare book materials. These services are offered in June, July and August. Unless the writer shows that he is really interested, we do not send pamphlets or brochures."

MacArthur Memorial, MacArthur Square, Norfolk VA 23510. (804)441-2256. Acting Chief Administrator: Edward J. Boone Jr.
Purpose: "To perpetuate the deeds and thoughts of Gen. Douglas MacArthur by, among other things, making available to scholars, writers and students the general's

letters, reports, messages, manuscripts and library." Information covers economics, history, politics and military and foreign affairs.

Services: Offers photos. Publications include list of archive and library holdings and record inventories and location aids.

How to Contact: Write, call or visit. Charges for photos and 10¢/photocopy."We use a commercial photo firm and pass the cost on to the researcher." Requires security clearance from Adjutant General of the Army for classified material. "We are not staffed to do research for others. We can assist the researcher, we can photocopy requested material, we can have specific photos printed, but we cannot do your research." Museum, theater and gift shop are open 10 a.m. to 5 p.m., Monday through Saturday; 11 a.m. to 5 p.m., Sunday (except New Year's Day, Thanksgiving and Christmas). Library and arctives are open 8:30 a.m. to 5 p.m., Monday through Friday (except on national holidays).

McIntosh Gallery, The University of Western Ontario, London, Ontario, Canada N6A 3K7. (519)679-6027. University Art Curator: Maurice Stubbs.
Services: Offers newsletter, photos and press kits.
How to Contact: Write or call.

Madison Art Center, 720 E. Gorham St., Madison WI 53703. (608)257-0158. Publicity Director: Michael Bonesteel.
Purpose: "A certified museum dealing with contemporary art exhibitions. We have a permanent collection composed of 19th century Japanese prints and other historical works of art. We offer classes for children and adults, workshops, films, travel outreach programs and a gallery shop." Information covers art and entertainment.
Services: Offers annual reports, brochures/pamphlets and newsletter.
How to Contact: "To receive brochures and pamphlets, simply request them. To receive our newsletter, one must join the art center. Most services are available free or at a lower cost to members. Our museum is free and open to the public." Charges $15 (individual membership) to join the art center.

Maine State Museum, State House Complex, Augusta ME 04333. (207)289-2301. Director: Paul E. Rivard.
Purpose: "To interpret and exhibit Maine history and to organize historical resource material. Our archives include holdings of government state papers. We possess a large archeological collection and have holdings of adjutant general records from the Civil War." Information covers agriculture, business, celebrities, entertainment, history, industry, music, nature, politics, recreation, sports, technical data, travel, archeology and the conservation of the fine arts.
Services: Offers bibliographies about Maine and the American Revolution, brochures/pamphlets, placement on mailing list, newsletter, photos and press kits. Publications include *Broadside* (quarterly).
How to Contact: Write. Charges for photos and photoduplication. Credit line required.

Marine Corps Museum, Marine Corps Historical Center, Headquarters, US Marine Corps (Code H.D.), Washington DC 20380. (202)433-3840. Director: Brig. Gen. Edwin H. Simons, U.S.M.C., Ret.
Purpose: To make history available to the public. The focus is on amphibious warfare. Contains most of John Philip Sousa's collection. Information covers history, music and technical data.
Services: Offers aid in arranging interviews, bibliographies, statistics and newsletter. Publications include catalogs of collections and publications.
How to Contact: Write. Charges "for extensive copying and reproduction of motion picture footage, as determined by the Department of Defense."

The Mariners Museum, 1 Museum Dr., Newport News VA 23606. (804)595-0368. Public Relations Officer: Bruce N. Parker.

Purpose: "To preserve our maritime heritage. The Mariners Museum is international in scope, covering man's relationship with the sea around the world. We have ship models, small craft, artifacts, paintings and photographs, as well as a 60,000-volume reference library and a photo library." Information covers art, history, how-to, industry, recreation and technical data.
Services: Offers brochures/pamphlets, placement on mailing list, newsletter, photos and press kits.
How to Contact: Write or call.

The Metropolitan Museum of Art, 5th Ave. at 82nd St., New York NY 10028. Contact: Photograph and Slide Library.
Purpose: Information covers the history of art from ancient times to the present.
Services: Offers 4x5 and 8x10 b&w photos for sale; color transparencies for publication only (mostly 8x10). These cover only objects in the museum's collections. Publications include *Color Transparencies for Rental* ($3 plus tax).
How to Contact: Research must be done by the user. Charges $5-10/8x10 photo. Credit line required. Return required on color transparencies only; photographs made to special order are sold outright with one-time reproduction rights included.

Missouri Historical Society, Jefferson Memorial Bldg., Lindell and Debaliviere, St. Louis MO 63112. (314)361-1424. Contact: Gail R. Guidry.
Purpose: To preserve the history of Missouri.
Services: Offers 100,000 photos on Missouri and western life, the World's Fair, early St. Louis, early aviation; the Lindbergh Collection and Steamboat Collection.
How to Contact: Write or call. Reproduction rights on photos are available. Charges $15/photo reproduction fee. Charges $10/8x10 b&w print fee; $40/4x5 color transparency print fee. "Always write if you are out of state and you request prints. No telephone orders will be processed. Our collection can be seen by appointment."

Morton Museum of Cooke County, Box 150, Gainesville TX 76240. (817)668-8900. President: Mary McCain. Vice President: Margaret P. Hays.
Purpose: "In 1968 the Cooke County Heritage Society restored Gainesville's 1884 fire station/city hall and converted it into a county historical museum known as Morton Museum of Cooke County. The society continues to operate this museum, which has a collection of three-dimensional and archival materials. Archival material consists of essays and other material about early Cooke County. We also have a collection of photographs from the area, including many of the Gainesville Community Circus." Information covers history.
Services: Offers brochures/pamphlets and photos. Publications include material on the history of Cooke County.
How to Contact: Write or visit. Charges for publications, including shipping and handling. "Items for sale may be ordered from the museum. Archival material may be examined by visiting the museum at the corner of Dixon and Pecan Streets, Gainesville, Texas. Materials must be used on the premises of the museum."

Museum of African Art, Eliot Elisofon Archives, 316-318 A St. NW, Washington DC 20002. (202)547-6222. Archivist: Edward Lifschitz.
Purpose: "The Elisofon Archives is a collection of photographs of African art and culture (modern and traditional) and of the African diaspora in the New World." Information covers agriculture, art, celebrities, entertainment, food, health/medicine, history, how-to, industry, music, nature, politics, recreation, sports, travel, architecture, domestic activities and "scenes of everyday African life."
Services: Offers 35,000 b&w and 45,000 color photos; "a portion of the total number of color photographs is in the form of film outtakes and work prints." Offers one-time rights, editorial rights, advertising rights or reproduction rights. Publications include a free informational brochure.
How to Contact: "Selection of photographs is best made in person; if this is impossible,

we would be happy to make a selection for the writer. A fee is charged only if the photographs are published. Discounts are available for educational and other non-profit institutions."

Museum of Afro American History, Smith Court, Box 322, Boston MA 02114. (617)445-7400. President: Byron Rushing.
Purpose: "Research and exhibit Afro-American history in New England, including photography and film collections, historic preservation and walking tours." Information covers history.
Services: Offers aid in arranging interviews, brochures/pamphlets, information searches and photos. "We also have tours of black communities, historic and present, in New England.
How to Contact: Write or call. Charges for tours.

Museum of Anthropology, University of Missouri, 104 Swallow Hall, Columbia MO 65211. (314)882-3764. Director: Dr. Lawrence H. Feldman.
Purpose: "The exhibit and study of artifacts made by man in different cultures. Emphasis is on the American Indian and the aspects of anthropology emphasized are ethnography, archeology, linguistics and physical anthropology. We have a large collection of 19th century Euro-American agricultural tools and household equipment. The museum staff is small and the collections limited in size. Areas of special interest (because of particularly outstanding holdings) are Guatemalan ceramics and textiles and Missourian archaelogical artifacts. In general, we have a few items from most areas of the world rather than an enormous number of artifacts from one locality." Information covers agriculture, history, science and anthropology.
Services: Offers annual reports and brochures/pamphlets. Publications include publications list, annual reports, museum briefs, *Monographs in Anthropology* and miscellaneous publications.
How to Contact: Write to Office of Publications for information on publications. Charges for publications.

Museum of Cultural History at UCLA, 55A Haines Hall, University of California, Los Angeles CA 90024. (213)825-4361. Museum Assistant/Public Relations: Anne Bomeisler.
Purpose: "The Museum of Cultural History is a university museum whose purposes include exhibition, teaching, research and publication. Our collections, now numbering approximately 120,000 objects, incorporate non-Western and ethnic cultures—Africa, Oceania, Asia, the Americas, Indonesia and the Near East." Information covers art, history, anthropology and archeology.
Services: Offers brochures/pamphlets, photos, scholarly catalogs, monographs, research papers, etc. on topics related to museum collections. "The museum sponsors an active publications program, producing numerous catalogs, monographs, occasional brochures, etc. We also have a program whereby interested researchers can obtain photographs of objects in the collection."
How to Contact: For photographs, write Nancy Ellis, registrar. For publications and other information on museum collections, write Anne Bomeisler, public relations. "A complete list of available publications can be obtained free by writing Anne Bomeisler." Charges for photographic services vary according to project.

Museum of Modern Art, 11 W. 53rd St., New York NY 10019. (212)956-6100. Contact: Public Information Department.
Purpose: "The museum was founded in 1929 to establish a permanent, public museum to acquire, from time to time, collections of the best works of modern art." Information covers art, history and technical data.
Services: Offers aid in arranging interviews, annual reports, bibliographies, biographies, statistics, brochures/pamphlets, information searches, newsletter, photos and press kits. Has a reference library of articles written about the library, open by

appointment. Publications include *Monthly Calendar*.
How to Contact: Write or call. Give credentials.

The Museum of Modern Art, Film Stills Archive, 11 W. 53rd St., New York NY 10019. (212)956-4209. Contact: Mary Corliss.
Services: Offers approximately 3,000,000 b&w stills on foreign and American productions, film personalities and directors. Duplicates of original stills are sold at a cost of $8/still. Credit line required.

Museum of Modern Art of Latin America, Organization of American States (OAS), 201 18th St. NW, Washington DC 20006. (201)381-8261. Assistant Specialist: Jane Ayoroa. Director: Jose Gomez Sicre.
Purpose: "To promote the visual arts of the Latin American countries in the hemisphere and elsewhere." Information covers art.
Services: Offers aid in arranging interviews, bibliographies, biographies, brochures/ pamphlets and photos. Publications include exhibit catalogs.
How to Contact: Write or visit. Charges only to make copies of photographs or documents.
Tips: "We own the most complete archive on all the periods of the visual arts of Latin America." Material cannot be taken off the premises. "Scholars, professors, lecturers and researchers in general are welcome."

Museum of New Mexico, Photo Archives, Box 2087, Santa Fe NM 87503. (505)827-2087. Photographic Archivist: Arthur L. Olives.
Purpose: Museum. Information covers New Mexico; western and southwestern America; southwestern Indians; mining; railroads; agriculture; Latin America; anthropology; and the archeology of North, Central and South America.
Services: Offers 90,000 b&w and 500 color photos. Some 19th-century foreign holdings include material on Oceania, Japan and the Middle East. Publications include catalogs, photographer indexes and a fee schedule.
How to Contact: Write, and request fee schedule. Charges $3 minimum/print, plus reproduction/publication fees. Offers one-time and reproduction rights on photos. Credit lines required.

Museum of Northern British Columbia, Box 669, Prince Rupert, British Columbia, Canada V8J 3S1. (604)624-3207. Curator: M.J. Patterson.
Purpose: "The collection, preservation, and display of information relating to the history of the northwest coast of British Columbia. The museum receives thousands of tourists, runs an active school program, presents occasional lectures and other special events, houses an art gallery which displays local and regional arts, and carries out other activities normal to a community museum." Information covers history, nature and ethnology.
Services: Offers research facilities.
How to Contact: Write or call.

Museum of Repertorie Americana, Rt. 1, Mt. Pleasant IA 52353. (319)385-8937. Curator: Mrs. Neil Schaffner.
Purpose: "The museum houses a collection of pictures, posters, programs and memorabilia from the repertory theater companies that toured the opera house circuits or tent theaters throughout the United States. We have a great deal of material on an important yet overlooked phase of American theater history." Information covers entertainment, history, music and old theatrical scripts.
Services: Offers aid in arranging interviews.

How to Contact: Write or call. "Use of material must be cleared through head office of Midwest Old Theaters (parent organization)."

Museum of Science, Science Park, Boston MA 02114. Contact: Bradford Washburn.
Services: Offers b&w contact prints of Alaskan and Alpine mountains and glaciers.
How to Contact: Charges minimum $5/print and one-time reproduction fees based on use: $25/½-page or less, $50/1-page use, and $75/double-page spread. Credit line required.

Museum of Science and Industry, 57th St. and Lake Shore Dr., Chicago IL 60637. (312)684-1414. Public Relations Manager: Irving Paley.
Purpose: "Open to the public in 1933, the museum is the largest and most popular museum of science and technology, and is Chicago's number one tourist attraction. We have 600,000 square feet of exhibition space." Information covers agriculture, business, economics, food, health/medicine, history, how-to, industry, music, nature, new products, recreation, science, self-help, sports and technical data.
Services: Offers aid in arranging interviews, brochures/pamphlets, information searches, placement on mailing list, newsletter, photos and press kits. Publications Include *Progress*, a bimonthly in-house publication.
How to Contact: Write or call.

Museum of Science and Natural History, Oak Knoll Park, St. Louis MO 63105. (314)726-2888. Curator of Collections: James Houser.
Purpose: "A public museum with exhibits, collections and service activities. Collections include antique radios, pre-Columbian Indian artifacts, sea shells, rocks and minerals, antique lighting equipment, herpetology, lepidoptera, birds and bird eggs." Information covers nature, science, museum techniques and education.
Services: Offers photographs and slides. Publications include *The Great Ice Age*, *Transaction of the Academy of Science* and descriptive materials about the museum itself.
How to Contact: Write or call; "letter preferred." Access to information and collections is arranged by appointment. Charges $2/8x10 b&w print of existing negative; 75¢/copy of existing color slide or negative.
Tips: "Any photo taken of exhibits or collection material must be credited to the museum, if published."

Museum of South Texas, Corpus Christi Art Foundation, Inc., 1902 N. Shoreline, Box 1010, Corpus Christi TX 78403. (512)884-3844. Administrative Assistant: Marilyn Smith.
Purpose: "To increase art awareness in the southern Texas area by presenting exhibitions of the visual arts of the highest quality and to provide supplemental educational information on those exhibitions." Information covers art.
Services: Offers schedule of exhibitions held at the Art Museum of South Texas and supportive information when available. Publications include a general informational brochure that contains background information on the museum, its structure, programs and hours.
How to Contact: Write or call.

Museum of the American China Trade, 215 Adams St., Milton MA 02186. (617)696-1815.
Purpose: "Art and artifacts of the period of the American China trade. Archive of 100,000 documents related to the trade." Information covers art and history.
Services: Offers brochures/pamphlets and newsletter. Publications include descriptive brochure.
How to Contact: Call or write. "An appointment is necessary for use of archives/library."

Museum of the American Indian, Broadway at 155th St., New York NY   10032. Contact: Carmelo Guadagno.
Purpose: The photographic archives of the museum include negatives, b&w prints, and color transparencies from Indian cultures throughout the Western Hemisphere. The various categories present a selection of everyday customs, ceremonial paraphernalia, costumes and accessories, dwellings and physical types from various areas. Offers b&w photos and 35mm and 4x5 color transparencies (2,200 Kodachrome slides).
How to Contact: List available for $1. Send stamp. Charges one-time reproduction fee of $20/b&w, $40/color. Credit line required.

Museum of the City of New York, 5th Ave. at 103rd St., New York NY 10029. (212)534-1672. Photo Archives: Esther Brumberg.
Purpose: "To preserve the history of New York City. Collection includes all aspects of New York City history, including photographs, lithographs, engravings, costume, decorative arts and theater material." Information covers celebrities and history.
Services: Offers 22,000 photos; one-time rights or all rights.
How to Contact: "Write, requesting specific topics. Research is free of charge. We charge for b&w glossies, for permission to reproduce, and for rental of color transparencies of material from our collection." Charges $10/one-time use, $6-11/print fee and 25¢/photocopy.
Tips: "Allow several weeks for orders to be processed. Be as specific as possible with requests. Our collection includes very little material after 1940."

Museum of the Confederacy, 1201 E. Clay St., Richmond VA 23219. (804)649-1861. Librarian: Eleanor S. Brockenbrough.
Purpose: "To serve as a museum of Confederate history and a depository of manuscripts related to the period." Information covers economics, health/medicine, history, law and politics.
Services: Offers biographies, information searches, newsletter and photos.
How to Contact: Write or call. Special arrangements are made for the reproduction of photos and other pictorial material. Services, except for duplication, are without charge. Written requests must be made for material to be used in any publication, recognition made to the museum's assistance, and, if pictures are used, copies and the original negative must be deposited in the library.

Museum of the Fur Trade, Rt. 2, Box 18, Chadron NE 69337. (308)432-3843. Director: Charles E. Hanson Jr.
Purpose: "Museum devoted to the materials and methods of the North American fur trade." Information covers history—accurate details of Indian trade goods, clothing and equipment of traders and trappers.
Services: Offers brochures/pamphlets, information searches and professional services in reviewing manuscripts and artists' sketches for historical accuracy (fur trade period only, 1600-1900).
How to Contact: "Write or call, outlining in specific detail what help is needed. There is a standard professional consulting fee of $150 per day plus any travel or reproduction expenses. Normal searches for data are $10 per hour for an assistant with supervision. Photos and copies at regular commercial rates."

Museum of Transportation, 300 Congress St., Boston MA 02110. (617)426-7997. Public Relations/Special Projects: William T.G. Litant.
Purpose: "To chronicle the history of transportation as it relates to changes in American social history. We have an extensive collection of autos, buses, carriages, bicycles, watercraft and related artifacts. Library materials include information on these, as well as on industrial machinery, steam, rail, etc." Information covers art, business, celebrities, economics, entertainment, history, how-to, industry, law, music, recreation, science, technical data and travel.

Services: Offers bibliographies, biographies, statistics, brochures/pamphlets, information searches, placement on mailing list, photos and press kits. "Extremely varied services; virtually anything relating to transportation history and its social impact. We maintain large referral lists."
How to Contact: Write or call to make appointment. Charges for photocopies and photo reproduction.

Museum of Western Colorado, 4th and Ute St., Grand Junction CO 81501. (303)242-0971. Archivist: Michael J. Menard.
Purpose: "To preserve and protect all areas of social and scientific history of western Colorado." Information covers agriculture, art, economics, health/medicine, history, industry, nature, politics, science and sports.
Services: Offers brochures/pamphlets and photos.
How to Contact: Write or call.

Museums of the City of Mobile, 355 Government St., Mobile AL 36602. (205)438-7569. Museum Director: Caldwell Delaney.
Purpose: Museums and a reference library covering the history of Mobile and its area since 1702. Information covers art and history.
Services: Offers reference library, available for use by scholars doing research on subjects related to the history of Mobile by appointment.
How to Contact: Write or call. "Library is available to those doing serious research Tuesday through Friday, 10 a.m. to 5 p.m., by appointment. Material may not be removed from the library. Limited copying facilities are available."

The Musical Museum, S. Main St., Deansboro NY 13328. (315)841-8774. Curator: Arthur H. Sanders.
Purpose: "We have a large collection of early musical instruments and early complicated automatic musical instruments. We have a few photos on hand for purchase. We do not have a staff photographer, but welcome photographers, writers and recorders who may want to use our material as part of a story or for research. We prefer to be mentioned as a source. We will answer all letters and questions if return postage is provided." Also has antique oil lamps. Information covers entertainment, history, how-to, music, science and technical data.
Services: Offers brochures/pamphlets, information searches and photos.
How to Contact: Write or call. "Send good, clear questions, with payment for estimated time involved or we cannot answer. Postage must accompany request." Charges $5/hour average.
Tips: "We expect credit to be given for the source of the information. We suggest a visit with a camera and recorder."

Musquodoboit Railway Museum, Box 99, Musquodoboit Harbour, Nova Scotia, Canada B0J 2L0. Director/Curator: David E. Stephens.
Purpose: "While the main function of the Musquodoboit Railway Museum (MRM) is to provide public displays on material related to Nova Scotian railways, the museum also has a small library of reference material on Nova Scotia, Canada, America and some other foreign countries, related to railways. The material is in the form of books, booklets and vertical files." Information covers history of transportation.
Services: Offers brochures/pamphlets, clipping services, information searches, newsletter and photos. "MRM, through Yagar Book Services (same address), publishes a number of booklets and information sheets (as well as a quarterly newsletter) dealing mainly with railways in Atlantic Canada, although some material is available related to American railways. Information sheets and booklets are in the planning stages for other countries."
How to Contact: "It would be best if writers contact the director by mail, outlining their requests." Charges 10¢/photocopy of clippings, $1/8x10 b&w photo, 10¢/information sheet ("usually") and 50¢-$1/booklet. "There is no charge for search services to

qualified researchers/writers. Writers are asked to outline their requests with as much detail as possible; the more exact their requests for assistance, the better we can serve them."

National Air and Space Museum, 6th and Independence Ave. SW, Washington DC 20560. (202)381-4222. Public Affairs: Louise Hull.
Purpose: "National center for the collection, preservation, exhibition and study of the history of flight." Information covers history, science and technical data.
Services: Offers aid in arranging interviews, bibliographies, biographies, brochures/pamphlets, placement on mailing list, statistics, photos and press kits. Publications available.
How to Contact: Write or call.

National Baseball Hall of Fame and Museum, Inc., Box 590, Cooperstown NY 13326. (607)547-9988. Director: Howard Talbot. Historian: Clifford S. Kachline.
Purpose: Baseball museum and library. Features memorabilia displays, films, and library, which is open only for serious baseball research. Information covers history, recreation and sports (baseball).
Services: Offers bibliographies, biographies, statistics, brochures/pamphlets, information searches and photos. Publications include hall of fame booklet and brochure.
How to Contact: Write or call; describe needed subject matter. Library is open 9 a.m. to 5 p.m. weekdays, by appointment on weekends.

National Colonial Farm, Rt. 1, Box 697, Accokeek MD 20607. (301)283-2113. Assistant Director: David O. Percy.
Purpose: "The National Colonial Farm is a living historical farm museum. Its purposes are to educate the public through a re-creation of an 18th century, middle-class tobacco plantation. It also conducts research into historical agriculture. The farm is involved in genetic research into crops and is attempting to develop a blight-free American chestnut." Information covers agriculture, food, history and nature.
Services: Offers annual reports, brochures/pamphlets and newsletter. Publications include *A Companion Planting Dictionary*; *Herbs*; *Tobacco: The Cash Crop Along the Colonial Potomac*; *Corn: The Production of a Subsistence Crop Along the Colonial Potomac*; *An Update on Maize*; and *English Grains*.
How to Contact: "Write, requesting specific title or information. Some materials are restricted to use on the site of the National Colonial Farm." Charges $1.30-3/publication, including postage and handling.

National Cowboy Hall of Fame, 1700 NE 63rd St., Oklahoma City OK 73111. (405)478-2250. Director of Public Relations: Marsi Thompson.
Purpose: Information covers agriculture (ranching), celebrities (great Western performers), history and sports (rodeo).
Services: Offers brochures/pamphlets, photos and press kits. "Literature and a general information sheet on the museum library are available for in-person research."
How to Contact: Write, stating needs and intended use of material. "Charges will be made individually on the basis on use. Restrictions are placed on all photography of the museum."

National Gallery of Art, Constitution Ave. at 6th St. NW, Washington DC 20007. (202)737-4215. Information Officer: Katherine Warwick.
Purpose: "The National Gallery contains one of the world's finest collections of western European painting, sculpture and graphic arts from the 13th century to the present, and American art from the colonial period to contemporary times. In addition to its permanent collections, the gallery also offers major international loan exhibitions. Regular activities include tours, films, lectures and concerts. The gallery's extension service runs free films and slide programs devoted to the collections and selected exhibitions to schools and civic groups throughout the nation. Information

covers the gallery as an institution, its permanent collections, special exhibitions and other activities." Information covers art, business, celebrities, entertainment, history, industry, music, recreation, self-help and travel.
Services: Offers aid in arranging interviews, annual reports, bibliographies, biographies, statistics, brochures/pamphlets, placement on mailing list, newsletter, photos and press kits. Publications include *Brief Guide to the National Gallery of Art*, *Invitation to the National Gallery of Art*, *A Profile of the National Gallery of Art*, and the annual report.
How to Contact: Write or call. "Writers with assignments will be given priority. Please read all the literature the gallery distributes or is available on the gallery before conducting interviews. We're really glad to help anyone we can." Photographs of objects in the gallery's collection may be obtained from Ira Bartfield, National Gallery of Art Photographic Services, Washington DC 20565. (202)737-4215. Charges for reproduction or rental of color transparencies, depending on use.

National Museum of History and Technology, Smithsonian Institution, 14th St. and Constitution Ave., Washington DC 20560. (202)381-6218. Acting Public Affairs Director: Alvin Rosenfeld.
Purpose: "The Smithsonian is an independent trust establishment which conducts scientific and scholarly research and administers the national collections in numerous museums with exhibits representative of the arts, American history and technology, natural history, and aeronautics and space exploration."
Services: Offers aid in arranging interviews, annual reports, biographies, statistics, brochures/pamphlets, information searches, placement on mailing list, newsletter, photos and press kits. Publications include *Smithsonian Torch*.
How to Contact: Write or call public affairs office.

National Museum of Natural History, Smithsonian Institution, 10th and Constitution Ave. NW, Washington DC 20560. (202)381-6218. Acting Director of Public Affairs: Alvin Rosenfield.
Purpose: "To administer the national collection of natural history." Information covers nature, science and technical data.
Services: Offers aid in arranging interviews, annual reports, statistics, brochures/pamphlets, information searches, placement on mailing list, newsletter, photos and press kits. Publications include *Smithsonian Torch* (monthly) and a series in zoology, anthropology, botany, earth sciences, paleobiology and marine sciences.
How to Contact: Write or call.

Neville Public Museum, 129 S. Jefferson, Green Bay WI 54301. Director: James L. Quinn.
Services: Offers historical photos available pertinent to northeastern Wisconsin, especially the Green Bay area; most are in b&w, but some are color shots of modern-day subjects.
How to Contact: Photos available at cost only for educational purposes. Museum credit line required.

New Britain Museum of American Art, 56 Lexington St., New Britain CT 06052. (203)229-0257. Assistant to the Director: Lois L. Blomstrann.
Purpose: "The New Britain Museum is a museum of American art dating from 1741 to the present. The collection numbers approximately 3,000 works of art, including paintings, sculpture and graphics. In addition to work from the colonial period by Copley, Smibert, Stuart, etc., the collection encompasses the Hudson River and Ashcan Schools of art, murals by Thomas Hart Benton, and paintings by the Wyeth family." Information covers art.
Services: Offers annual reports, brochures/pamphlets, placement on mailing list, newsletter and photos. Publications include several catalogs.

How to Contact: Write. "We charge for catalogs, and there is a reproduction fee for the use of photographs. Permission in writing must be given for the use of photos."

Newark Museum, 49 Washington St., Newark NJ 07101. Contact: W.T. Bartle.
Purpose: Photos available on American art (18th, 19th and 20th centuries; painting and sculpture); Oriental art (especially of Tibet, Japan and India); and the decorative arts (furniture, jewelry and costumes).
Services: Offers 8x10 b&w photos.
How to Contact: Write. Charges for photos. Credit line required.

Illustrations available from information sources aren't limited to photographs. For example, Renoir's "The Luncheon of the Boating Party" is the most requested photo in the Phillips Collection, according to Kevin Grogan, assistant curator. "The photo collection is made up of black and white glossies, 35mm Ektachromes and color transparencies in various sizes, all of which depict works of art from the collection." Grogan's recommendation to writers seeking photos is, "Allow ample lead time, on the chance that a particular work is not represented in the photo collection."

North Carolina Museum of Art, 107 E. Morgan St., Raleigh NC 27611. (919)733-7568. Public Information Coordinator: Linda S. Hyatt.
Purpose: "To make available to the public, especially the citizens of North Carolina, the works of art in the collection and the information concerning them. Information concerning the collection is available in our publications and through the art reference library operated by the museum, as well as through staff service." Information covers art.
Services: Offers annual reports, brochures/pamphlets, placement on press mailing list,

regular informational newsletter, photos and press kits. Offers 8x10 b&w glossy prints and 2¼x2¼ and 4x5 color transparencies on permanent collections. Publications include "a general information pamphlet serving as an introduction to the North Carolina Museum of Art; a monthly informational publication, the *Calendar*, which describes current exhibitions and programs of the museum; and collection and exhibition catalogs available through the museum store. (A complete listing may be obtained on request.)"

How to Contact: "Requests for information, particularly appointments with museum administrative staff, should be made in writing prior to visiting the museum. Publications and photographs are available on a cost basis unless the writer is using these materials as part of museum news coverage; art reference library services are free to the public." Charges $1.50/glossy print, 75¢/original slide, 50¢/ duplicate slide, and $15 for 3-month rental of transparencies. Permission to publish is required. "Please note: Press information is made available to those writers dealing specifically with the museum and its programs. Confirmation of intent is required before inclusion on any press list. No photograph of a work of art in the museum may be reproduced without the prior consent of the museum. All copyrighted publications are subject to copyright restrictions. Individuals desiring permission to reproduce material should address inquiries to Head, Collections Research and Publication.

North Museum, Franklin and Marshall College, Lancaster PA 17604. (717)291-3943. Director: W. Fred Kinsey.
Purpose: Natural history museum.
Services: Offers exhibits and research. Publications include material pertaining to the museum and its programs.
How to Contact: Write, call or visit.

Northeastern Nevada Museum, Box 503, 1515 Idaho St., Elko NV 89801. (702)738-3418. Director: Howard Hickson.
Purpose: "To collect, preserve and exhibit history of northeastern Nevada. Our concentration is on northeastern Nevada, with general information on Nevada, ranching, railroading and mining." Information covers agriculture, business, celebrities, entertainment, history, industry and politics.
Services: Offers aid in arranging interviews, bibliographies, biographies, statistics, clipping services, information searches and photos. "We have excellent files on most of the newspapers (bound volumes and microfilm) of the area since mid-1869. Files are complete through the present. Our slide, photo and negative collection contains several thousand pieces dealing specifically with northeastern Nevada communities, industries and nature. Copies are available. Our director is a professional photographer and capable of selecting representative photographs of excellent quality for printing."
How to Contact: Write or call. Charges $4/hour for research of files and newspapers; 50¢/article, $1/page for copies of newspaper articles; $2/5x7 photo; $1/35mm slide; and 25¢/photocopy of manuscripts, books and quarterlies. "Research charges can be most economical if the specific dates or years are known."

Northwest Seaport, Inc., Box 395, 218-B Kirkland Ave., Kirkland WA 98033. (206)828-6685. Executive Director: Mary Stiles Kline.
Purpose: "The preservation of historic ships of the Pacific Northwest and the collection and research of maritime materials pertaining to the maritime trades of the Northwest, and ships." Information covers maritime history.
Services: Offers brochures/pamphlets, newsletter, photos, and "information searches in brief form or guidelines for seeking the related information." Publications include histories of the sailing schooner *Wawona*, tugboat *Arthur Foss*, lightship *Relief* and steam ferry *San Mateo*.
How to Contact: Write, call or visit by appointment. Charges for photocopies according to size and usage.

Notman Photographic Archives/McCord Museum, 690 Sherbrooke St. W., Montreal, Quebec, Canada. (514)392-4781. Contact: Stanley Triggs.
Services: Offers 600,000 photos: "portraits, landscapes, city views, street scenes, lumbering, railroad construction, trains, Indians, fishing, etc. Covers Canada, coast to coast. Mostly 19th century, some 20th."
How to Contact: Offers one-time non-exclusive publication rights. Charges $25 for most publications. "Photographs on loan only—to be returned after use."

Oglebay Institute's Mansion Museum, Oglebay Park, Wheeling WV 26003. (304)242-7272. Curator: Gary E. Baker.
Purpose: "To collect and preserve the artifacts of the Wheeling area and to interpret life in the upper Ohio Valley during the 19th century. The museum's collection of Wheeling glass is unrivaled." Information covers art and history.
Services: Offers brochures/pamphlets. Publications available include *Mansion Museum*.
How to Contact: "Write, requesting the brochure; it will be sent free of charge. Usually there is no charge for information, but someone needing photocopies or a reproduction of a photograph in the collection is expected to cover our expenses. If research is long and involved, we may recommend the hiring of a professional."
Tips: "We do not have extensive files of genealogical information. Anyone desiring information on an ancestor believed to have lived in Wheeling at one time should ask for a listing of the Wheeling city directories in which the name appears. Please be very specific in requesting material. A listing of the sources consulted will keep us from repeating material which you already have."

Oheary Library and Museum Association, Oheary, Prince Edward Island, Canada C0B 1C0. President: L.G. Dewar.
Purpose: "We are a public library and local museum, and we provide tourist information."Information covers history and travel.
Services: Offers annual reports, brochures/pamphlets and information searches.
How to Contact: Write.

Orchard House Historical Museum, Louisa May Alcott Memorial Association, Box 343, Concord MA 01742. (617)369-4118. Director: Jayne Gordon.
Purpose: "This is the home of the Alcott family where *Little Women* was written in 1868 by Louisa May. The family lived here from 1858 to 1877 and Louisa May's father, Amos Bronson Alcott, prominent transcendentalist, founded the Concord School of Philosophy here." Information covers history and literature.
Services: Offers brochures/pamphlets and "help in finding documents for historical research. Most of the manuscripts have been deposited by the Louisa May Alcott Memorial Association at the Houghton Library, Harvard University." Publications include *Story of the Alcotts*.
How to Contact: "Write well in advance to arrange to do research in the house. The house is often crowded with tourists in summer and fall, so writers need to make an appointment with the director so that we can be of assistance. The museum is closed from mid-November to mid-April. Plan any on-site visits for seasons when we are open and let us know you are coming."

W.H. Over Museum, Office of Cultural Preservation, University of South Dakota, Vermillion SD 57069. (605)677-5228. Director: June Sampson.
Purpose: "To collect, preserve and study the specimens and artifacts of the natural history of South Dakota and the cultural heritage of its people. We aim to interpret these collections as well as the similarities and diversity of people through exhibits, publications and educational programs for the benefit of the public and the educational institutions of South Dakota." Information covers history, nature and ethnology.
Services: Offers aid in arranging interviews, brochures/pamphlets and photos. Publications include *The South Dakota Museum* and *Old Style Plains Indians Dolls*.

How to Contact: "Please write, stating specific need or to set up an appointment. Fees are charged for photo reproductions and copies."
Tips: "Please give credit to the W.H. Over Museum for all material used. Please allow plenty of time for us to search out the information requested—up to three weeks, plus mailing time."

Owensboro Area Museum, 2829 S. Griffith Ave., Owensboro KY 42301. (502)683-0297. Director: Joe Ford.
Purpose: "Included in our collection are many specimens of archeological, geological and biological interest. We have living reptiles on display, a small art gallery, and a study room in which students may research topics of interest. For example, the last public hanging in the US occurred here in 1936. Many persons research details of this execution." Information covers art, history, nature and science.
Services: Offers researcher the opportunity to use facility.
How to Contact: Visit facility. "Any serious student may use our documents for study. All materials must be used in the building. Any item may be photographed. Copyright laws apply to printed material."

Oxford Museum, Free Public Library, Oxford MA 01540. (617)987-5837. Museum Director: Robert J. Shedd.
Purpose: "The care, preservation and display of artifacts and records pertaining to the history of the town of Oxford." Information covers history.
Services: Offers list of publications upon request.
How to Contact: Write, call or visit. Charges 10¢/photocopy, plus postage and handling. "Material must be used on the premises."

Paine Art Center and Arboretum, 1410 Algoma Blvd., Box 1097, Oshkosh WI 54902. (414)235-4530. Administrative Assistant: Jean L. Peters.
Purpose: "We have tours; display a permanent collection of a wide variety of English, French and Chinese artifacts; and hold temporary exhibitions and educational activities such as field trips, lectures and music programs." Information covers art.
Services: Offers brochures/pamphlets and photos. "Numerous catalogs pertaining to temporary exhibitions are available."
How to Contact: Call or write. "Enclose a large SASE if writing to request catalogs. We charge different rates for catalogs and pictures."

The Park County Museum, 118 W. Chinook, Livingston MT 59047. (406)222-3506. Caretaker: Doris Whithorn.
Purpose: "To collect and preserve for safekeeping articles of history, including published and unpublished articles on the history of the area, artifacts and memorabilia. We hope to be an inspiration to young people. Anyone may photograph our artifacts." Information covers history.
Services: Offers brochures/pamphlets.
How to Contact: Write or call.

Peabody Museum of Archaeology and Ethnology, Harvard University, 11 Divinity Ave., Cambridge MA 02138. (617)495-2248. Staff Assistant/Public Information Officer: Trish Lawry.
Purpose: "We are a university anthropological museum." Information covers primitive art and archeological and ethnological disciplines.
Services: Offers brochures/pamphlets and newsletter (to members only).
How to Contact: Write or call.

Peabody Museum of Natural History, Yale University, 170 Whitney Ave., New Haven CT 06520. (203)432-4478, 432-4044. Staff Assistant: Sara R. Martin.
Purpose: "The Peabody Museum of Natural History is one of the oldest of its kind in the United States and is known throughout the world. It serves as a valuable research

facility for scholars and as an educational resource for area schools. Approximately 40,000 people visit the museum each year to study the dinosaur hall, the outstanding anthropological exhibits, the third-floor dioramas, the bird hall and the many other fascinating and informative displays. The museum also mounts several temporary exhibits each year." Information covers agriculture, art, history, nature, recreation, technical data and travel.

Services: Offers bibliographies, brochures/pamphlets, placement on mailing list, photos and press kits. Publications include "a guidebook and a succinct brochure. The museum also publishes *Discovery*, a magazine which presents museum and natural scientific activities in layman's terms. Some special exhibitions will include catalogs. The curators of various departments of the museum can individually provide bibliographies of their publications."

How to Contact: Write to Sara Martin, staff assistant, or Zelda Edelson, editor, publications office. Charges for *Discovery* and museum bulletins.

Philadelphia Museum of Art, Rights and Reproduction Dept., Box 7646, Philadelphia PA 19101.

Purpose: "The preservation and exhibition of paintings, prints, furniture, silver, sculpture, ceramics, arms and armor, coffers, jades, glass, metal objects, ivory objects, textiles, tapestries, costumes and period rooms."

Services: Offers 250,000 5x7 and 8x10 b&w prints and 4x5 color transparencies "of works of art in our museum."

How to Contact: Charges $5/8x10 b&w print; $30 rental fee for color transparencies. Reproduction fees are based on usage.

The Phillips Collection, Office of Public Affairs, 1600-1612 21st St. NW, Washington DC 20009. (202)387-2151. Assistant Curator: Kevin Grogan.

Purpose: "The Phillips Collection, the oldest museum of modern art in the United States, collects, exhibits and interprets works of art from the last quarter of the 19th century through the present. Included in the permanent collection are isolated examples of the work of such masters from the more distant past as El Greco and Giorgione." Information covers art and music.

Services: Offers aid in arranging interviews, bibliographies, biographies, brochures/pamphlets, placement on mailing list, photos and press kits. Publications include an introductory handbook on the collection, the collection catalog, monographs, exhibition catalogs, checklists of individual exhibitions, and *Duncan Phillips and His Collection*.

How to Contact: Write or call.

Phoenix Art Museum, 1625 N. Central Ave., Phoenix AZ 85004. (602)257-1222. Public Relations Director: Cheryl Rexford.

Purpose: "We are one of the leading art museums in the Southwest. Our collection includes paintings, sculpture and decorative arts from the 15th through the 20th centuries. Among its major strengths are 18th century French painting, Western American, contemporary and Oriental art. We also have a comprehensive art reference library." Information covers art.

Services: Offers annual reports, brochures/pamphlets, placement on mailing list, newsletter, photos and press kits. Publications include membership brochures, annual reports, monthly newsletters and exhibition catalogs. "Any use of photographs must give credit to the museum. Approval must be obtained from the curatorial staff and/or public relations for use of museum material (explain where it is to be used, how, for what purpose, etc.)."

How to Contact: Write or call the public relations department or the development department. "Give us plenty of time to obtain the material you are requesting. Don't call the day before you need the information." Charges for exhibition catalogs.

Placer County Museum, 175 Fulweiler Ave., Auburn CA 95603. Curator: Cevera Ingraham.

Purpose: "The museum assembles, studies, interprets, exhibits and preserves artifacts, specimens, documents and records of educational and cultural value that illustrate Placer County's history and development." Information covers agriculture, art, business, economics, entertainment, history, industry, music, politics, recreation, science and sports.
Services: Offers aid in arranging interviews, bibliographies, biographies, statistics, information searches and photos.
How to Contact: Write. Charges 10¢/photocopy, plus postage. Enclose SASE. "Researchers are not permitted to photograph our rare books, documents or records."

Plymouth Historical Museum, 155 S. Main St., Plymouth MI 48170. (313)455-8940. Director: Barbara Saunders.
Purpose: Archives of Plymouth history and the Civil War. Information covers history.
Services: Offers genealogical records of the people of Plymouth, microfilm of Plymouth newspapers from 1885 to 1935, and pictures.
How to Contact: Call for an appointment.

Ponca City Indian Museum, 1000 E. Grand Ave., Ponca City OK 74601. (405)762-6123. Chairman, Museum Committee: Mrs. Paul T. Powell.
Purpose: "To collect, preserve, display and provide an educational program explaining the American Indians, with special emphasis on the tribes of our area: Ponca, Kaw, Otoe, Osage and Tonkawa." Information covers art, history, and music. "We also cover American Indian ethnology, archeology, crafts, clothing, costumes and pottery."
Services: "Our special library includes current news clippings, Indian rolls and current events of the tribes of the area." Publications include *Tribes of Oklahoma* and *Oklahoma Indians*.
How to Contact: Write for permission to use special library or to study the exhibits. The only charge is postage for brochures or cost of copy machine. Special permission must be obtained for the use of photographic equipment.

Presidio of Monterey (US Army) Museum, Presidio Bldg.,#5-113,Monterey CA 93940. (408)242-8414. Chief Curator: Margaret B. Adams.
Purpose: Museum "outlines the history of Presidio ('Old Fort') Hill during the Indian, Spanish, Mexican and American eras to the contemporary US Army language school of today. California history unfolded on this hill (Monterey was a principal Indian site and the first capital city of California in the Spanish, Mexican and early American periods of history); there are several historic sites close to the museum." Information covers history of the US Army in Monterey.
Services: Offers brochures/pamphlets and limited information searches. Publications include a tour pamphlet of Presidio Hill and a map of historic Monterey.
How to Contact: Write.
Tips: "Limited museum personnel (one to two persons, seasonally) means that only limited research can be done on behalf of authors and other scholars. The museum files are open to researchers who wish to come to the museum. The museum also has a limited library that is available for on-premise use."

Pro Football Hall of Fame, 2121 Harrison Ave. NW, Canton OH 44708. (216)456-8207. Vice President, Public Relations: Don Smith.
Purpose: "Historical repository and showplace of information on professional football greats of the past." Information covers sports.
Services: Offers aid in arranging interviews, biographies, placement on mailing list, statistics, photos and press kits.
How to Contact: Write or call.

The Quadrangle Art Museums, 49 Chestnut St., Springfield MA 01103. (413)732-6092. Publicist: Mike Brault.
Purpose: "To provide the citizens of Springfield with high quality art exhibits and to

educate them about their significance." Two art museums are maintained. Information covers art, history, how-to and music.
Services: Offers aid in arranging interviews, placement on mailing list and photos.
How to Contact: "Call museum publicist. Photos sought for permanent use must be paid for. If return is guaranteed, there is no charge for photos. There is a fee for museum catalogs. All press releases have unrestricted use."

Josephine D. Randall Junior Museum, 199 Museum Way, San Francisco CA 94114. (415)863-1399. Director: A. Kirk Conragan.
Purpose: "A children's museum—classes are offered in sciences, arts, crafts, shops and animal care. We have a live animal collection, exhibits and special educational lectures for groups. The museum stresses fun in education and environmental awareness." Information covers art, history, how-to, nature, recreation, science and crafts.
Services: Offers brochures/pamphlets.
How to Contact: Write or call. Classes and rental fees vary ($1.50-20). Call or write for specific information.

Regimental Museum, Governor General's Foot Guards, Drill Hall, Cartier Square, Ottawa, Ontario, Canada K1A 0K2. Curator: W.L. Gault.
Purpose: To "maintain a visual record of the history of the regiment in the form of artifacts, photos, records, uniforms, weapons, etc." Information covers history.
Services: Offers exhibits.
How to Contact: Write or visit. "We are a very small operation plagued with the common complaint of lack of space. We are fortunate to have good cooperation with the Archives of Canada and the Canadian War Museum, which are close by."

Remington Art Museum, 303 Washington St., Ogdensburg NY 13669. (315)393-2425. Director: Mildred B. Dillenbeck.
Services: Offers b&w prints and color transparencies of Frederic Remington paintings, watercolors, drawings and bronzes. Maintains "the largest and most complete collection of works by Remington."
How to Contact: Write or call. Charges rental and one-time reproduction fee of $6/b&w print and $35/color transparency. Credit line and return of pictures required.

Remington Gun Museum, Remington Arms Co., Inc., Ilion NY 13357. (315)894-9961. Curator: Laurence Goodstal.
Purpose: "We are a firearms manufacturer with an in-plant gun museum." Information covers history and technical data.
Services: Offers information searches.
How to Contact: Write or call.

Rice County Historical Society Museum, 221 E Ave. S., Lyons KS 67554. Curator: Clyde Ernst.
Purpose: To preserve the history of Rice County, including artifacts of the Quivira Indians and historical artifacts of Rice County. Information covers celebrities and history.
Services: Offers "a few" biographies. Publications include *History of Coronado Expedition, 1541*; *Up From the Sod*; *Coronado & Quivira*; and *Coronado*.
How to Contact: Write or visit.

John and Mable Ringling Museum of Art/Ringling Museum of the Circus, Ringling Museums, Information Dept., Box 1838, 5401 Bayshore Rd., Sarasota FL 33578. (813)355-5101. Chief, Information Department: Robert L. Ardren.
Purpose: "The newly renovated galleries of the Ringling Museum of Art house one of the largest collections of baroque art in the United States and a growing collection of contemporary art. The Museum of the Circus is one of two authentic circus museums in the country, and offers a brilliant collection of parade wagons, posters and circus

memorabilia." Information covers art, the circus and John Ringling.
Services: Offers aid in arranging interviews, annual reports, brochures/pamphlets, placement on mailing list, newsletter, photos and press kits. Publications include *Souvenir Book*, *Fifty Masterpieces in the Ringling Museum of Art* and *Ringling Museum of the Circus.*
How to Contact: Write, call or visit.

Will Rogers Memorial, Box 157, Claremore OK 74017. (918)341-0719. Curator/Director: Dr. Reba Collins.
Purpose: "To preserve the memory and promote the spirit of Will Rogers." Information covers Will Rogers and related material only.
Services: Offers brochures/pamphlets and personal aid as time permits to the serious researcher of Will Rogers. Publications include a biographical brochure and a list of books in print and those available from the Will Rogers Memorial.
How to Contact: "Write or call for an appointment. Please let us know in advance. We have half a million tourists a year here, and we cannot be of service to drop-ins who wish to do serious research without some notice. The staff is limited and we must make arrangements for someone to work with the researcher. We have the most complete collection of Will Rogers memorabilia and his writings in existence; some are rare originals, and we work closely with those doing research. No charge is made for academic research and most other serious research. We do, however, charge for pictures that have to be copied. We are not a lending library, and it is necessary for a serious student or researcher to come here to see the massive amount of material on Will Rogers. We can answer brief questions by mail or phone. We will be glad to explain further to anyone wanting more details. We are open every day of the year, 8 a.m. to 5 p.m."
Tips: "Only a few masters theses and doctoral dissertations have been done on Will Rogers, but there is plenty of material for many more. We have only begun to scratch the surface in that sort of research. Also, since Will Rogers was a Cherokee, he qualifies as a 'minority' person in textbooks, etc. There is a real need for more books for young people on this Indian-Cowboy."

Rosenbach Foundation, 2010 Delancey Place, Philadephia PA 19103. (215)732-1600. Contact: Arline Segal.
Purpose: "We function as a museum of decorative and fine arts, as well as a library of rare materials in British and American literature." Information covers art, history, and American and English literature.
Services: Offers bibliographies and biographies. Publications include a brochure, a flyer and a list of museum publications. "Most publications concern English literature. We also have information on the history of the museum and the history of its founders, the Rosenbach brothers."
How to Contact: Write or call. Charges for photocopies of manuscripts and books.

Rutgers University Art Gallery, Voorhees Hall, Hamilton St., New Brunswick NJ 08903. (201)932-7096; 932-7237. Curator of Education: Stephanie Grunberg.
Purpose: "We are a nonprofit institution, offering changing exhibitions and related activities and programs for the general public." Information covers art.
Services: Offers brochures/pamphlets, newsletter and photos. "Press releases are issued through the Rutgers University news service." Publications include newsletter and exhibition schedule.
How to Contact: Call or write.

San Francisco Maritime Museum, Foot of Polk St., San Francisco CA 94109. Contact: Isabel Bullen.
Purpose: Museum of West Coast shipping.
Services: Offers b&w and some color photos of West Coast shipping, deep-water sail,

steamships and contemporary ships.
How to Contact: Charges $4/8x10 glossy print and $7.50/textbook reproduction. Credit line required.

Schiele Museum of Natural History and Planetarium, Inc., Box 953, 1500 E. Garrison Blvd., Gastonia NC 28052. (704)864-3962. Contact: Director.
Purpose: "We are a nonprofit, educational, natural history/science museum housing the South's largest habitat collection of North American land mammals. We have formal Earth and space science education programs for students in kindergarten through college. We have a 23-acre outdoor learning area, a trail, and a 1754 restored pioneer homestead. We are currently the most visited museum in North Carolina and the most heavily visited regional museum in our category in the South." Information covers history, nature, recreation, science, technical data and outdoor education.
Services: Offers annual reports, statistics, brochures/pamphlets, clipping services, information searches, newsletter and photos. "We are listed in Gale reference/research publications, serve as one of the environmental reference centers for the state, and are listed as a southeastern reference center for the Library of Congress in matters relating to ecology, natural history, local history and space education in planetarium settings. We mail all in-house brochures (general museum, trail, environmant, planetarium, annual report, teacher's manuals, sample class sheets, etc.) on request if mailing costs are provided. We have extensive pamphlet and clipping files that can be photocopied. We have a small research library specializing in natural history that can be used on site. We have extensive photo files, 35mm slides, films, and 4x5 color transparencies that are often used in publications for nominal fees or publication credit."
How to Contact: Write or call. "Charges, if any, would depend on the extent of services requested and the intended use." Charges 10¢/photocopy.

Schoellkopf Geological Museum, Niagara Reservation, Niagara Falls NY 14303. (716)278-1780. Geologist: Jack Krajewski.
Purpose: "Interpretation of the natural history of Niagara Falls and the state park around them, and their use as educational tools. Reference material covers the natural history of Niagara, their use by man and many rare historical volumes." Information covers history, nature and science.
Services: Offers aid in arranging interviews, statistics and placement on mailing list.
How to Contact: Write or call. Charges 25¢/photocopy. Material must be used in the museum.

The Shaker Museum, Shaker Museum Rd., Old Chatham NY 12136. (518)794-9100. Director: Peter Laskovski.
Purpose: To preserve the history and artifacts of the Shakers. "Since 1950, the museum has gathered together what is now the finest collection of Shaker-made artifacts in the world. In addition, the museum sponsors a wide range of exhibition, education and research programs." Information covers agriculture, food, health/medicine, history, how-to and music.
Services: Offers bibliographies, brochures/pamphlets, information searches, placement on mailing list, newsletter, photos and press kits. Publications include books on all aspects of the Shaker community and philosophy, booklets, gallery guides and reprints of old Shaker materials. Photos, in b&w only, depict Shaker buildings and members, museum galleries, some furniture and other artifacts.
How to Contact: Write or call. Charges $10/hour for research (first 15 minutes are free). Special rates for members. Charges $25-50/one-time use for photos; $5 print fee; $10/print made to order; 10¢/photocopy; $5/copy negative. Charges $1 for making selection. Complete photo price list available. Credit line required.

Shakertown at Pleasant Hill, Kentucky, Inc., Rt. 4, Harrodsburg KY 40330. (606)734-5411. Coordinator of Communications: Jane Brown.
Purpose: "Shakertown at Pleasant Hill was incorporated as a living outdoor history

museum to preserve 27 original Shaker buildings and to interpret the way of life of this unusual 19th century religious sect. We provide visitors with an exhibition tour, dining, lodging, craft shops and a conference facility, all housed in original buildings on 2,200 acres. We would be happy to supply writers with historical information about our Shaker heritage—architecture, furniture, music and advanced ecological and social concepts, or information on the restoration and adaptive uses of our buildings, or information on our year-round visitor services." Information covers agriculture, art (Shaker architecture, cabinetmaking, spirit drawings), food, health/medicine (historic herb uses), history, industry (e.g., Shaker seed and broom industries), music and travel.

Services: Offers annual reports, brochures/pamphlets, placement on mailing list, photos and press kits. Publications include color brochure, calendar of events, hours and rates sheet, and *Writer's Fact Packet*, which covers the history of the Shakers and the restoration. "We canot make available our original source documents. They are not kept at Pleasant Hill, but are in a university library under climate control."

How to Contact: Write.

Shelburne Museum, Box 39, Shelburne, Nova Scotia, Canada B0T 1W0. Chairman of the Board: Mary Archibald.

Purpose: "Besides hosting national exhibits, we have much information on the Loyalists of the American Revolution who came to Shelburne. Our historic Coss-Thomson House has been in operation (summer only) for ten years. Our museum will open early in the spring and remain open 12 months." Information covers history.

Services: Offers annual reports, biographies, brochures/pamphlets, statistics, newsletter and photos. Publications available.

How to Contact: Write. Charges 5¢/page for information, plus mailing fee.

The Sheldon Art Museum, Archaeological and Historical Society, Inc., Box 126, Middlebury VT 05753. (802)388-2117. Curator: Nina R. Mudge. Librarian: Polly Darnell.

Purpose: "The museum is a three-story brick house, built in 1829, with furnishings of the 19th century. It features collections of Staffordshire, pewter, pianos, tools, furniture, quilts, sewing machines, dolls and doll house furniture, clocks and more than 62 oil paintings. The library and research center is housed in a separate building. The collection includes local newspapers from 1801 through the present, scrapbooks, books, pamphlets, letters and manuscripts; most pertain to local history." Information covers history and the 19th century.

Services: Offers annual reports, brochures/pamphlets and information searches.

How to Contact: Write, call or visit. "From June 1 to Oct. 15, we are open daily except Sundays and holidays, 10 a.m. to 5 p.m. Guided tours last about one hour." Charges $1/visit and $5/hour for research done by the museum or library staff. Requires museum membership ($5 minimum) for use of the library.

The Sheldon Museum, Box 236, Haines AK 99827. (907)766-2128. Curator: Elisabeth S. Hakkinen.

Purpose: "To preserve and teach local history." Information covers local and Alaskan history, and the Tlingit Indians. "We're quite a small museum, but interesting."

Services: Offers research facilities and brochure.

How to Contact: Write. Enclose SASE. Materials must be used on the premises.

The Shrine to Music Museum, Box 194, Vermillion SD 57069. (605)677-5306. Director: Dr. Andre P. Larson.

Purpose: "The Shrine to Music Museum holds the Arne B. Larson Collection of Musical Instruments and Library, which consists of more than 2,500 antique musical instruments and a large supporting library of music, books, sound recordings, photographs and related musical memorabilia." Information covers art, entertainment, history and music.

Services: Offers aid in arranging interviews, brochures/pamphlets, information searches and photos.
How to Contact: Write. Charges for photos, reproductions of printed materials and extensive research searches.

South Carolina Confederate Relic Room, 920 Sumter St., Columbia SC 29201. (803)758-2144. Director: LaVerne H. Watson.
Purpose: "We provide museum services. We collect, preserve and display items of historical value from all periods of South Carolina history." Information covers history.
Services: Offers research facilities.
How to Contact: Write or call. Charges for photocopies and pictures. "Research books may be used in the museum but cannot be checked out."

Spertus Museum of Judaica, 618 S. Michigan Ave., Chicago IL 60605. Curator: Grace Cohen Grossman.
Purpose: "The museum houses a collection of Judaica from many parts of the world, containing ceremonial objects, a pertinent collection of sculpture, paintings, and graphic arts, and ethnographic materials spanning centuries of Jewish experience." Information covers art.
Services: Offers biographies and photos. Publications include catalogs and price list.
How to Contact: Write or call. "We charge for photographic reproduction. Appropriate credit must be given."

Strawbery Banke, Inc., Box 300, Portsmouth NH 03801. (603)436-8010. Promotion Supervisor: Janet E. Story.
Purpose: "Strawbery Banke's purpose is to preserve the history of Portsmouth and New Hampshire, including buildings, furnishings and documents. The Banke's 10-acre area includes 35 buildings dating from 1698 to the mid-1800s, thus giving the visitor a chance to see how lifestyles and architecture changed over a 150-year period. Information we are able to provide dates from this same period." Information covers agriculture, art, economics, food, health/medicine, history, industry and technical data.
Services: Offers aid in arranging interviews, bibliographies (limited), brochures/pamphlets, information searches, placement on mailing list, photos and press kits. Publications include *Official Guide Book to Strawbery Banke*, *Herb Garden Booklet*, *Portsmouth and the Piscataqua: Social History and Material Culture* and *Portsmouth: An Architectural Evolution 1664-1890*.
How to Contact: Write. "Enclose check to cover expenses, including postage." Charges $4/print for some photos from collections. Charges for staff time, electricity, maintenance costs (if any), etc. for interior photography of historic houses.
Tips: "As an educational institution, we are deeply concerned with and committed to accuracy of facts and prefer to work closely with writers in these areas. We offer to proof an article for accuracy in these areas only and will do nothing to change style or content. Due to severe staff limitations, please allow for a great deal of lead time, if possible."

Swigart Museum, Box 214, Museum Park, Huntington PA 16652. (814)643-0885 or 634-3000. Owner: William E. Swigart Jr.
Purpose: "To preserve, renew and display the American antique automobile (classic and vintage) for the enjoyment of the private individual and groups. Research material is limited to the history and development of the American car." Information covers history and technical data.
Services: Offers statistics and photos.
How to Contact: Write or call. Charges for "the time spent in research and development of the topics." Charges up to $10/hour. "Materials must be researched by our staff. Not open to the public."

Temple Mound Museum, 139 Miraclestrip Pkwy., Box 1449, Fort Walton Beach FL 32548. (904)243-6521. Curator: Mrs. Yulee W. Lazarus.
Purpose: "To preserve early local Indian history." Information covers history.
Services: Offers brochures/pamphlets. Publications include reprints of archeological/anthropological papers published in *Florida Anthropologist* related to the area (lists provided on request), *Indians of the Florida Panhandle*, *Pottery of the Fort Walton Period* and *Indian Plant Foods*.
How to Contact: Write or call.

Tioca Point Museum, S. Main St., Box 143, Athens PA 18810. (717)888-7225. Museum Director: Loreita M. Jackson.
Purpose: "We are a museum association with a library and we have exhibits on Indian lore, local history, the Revolutionary War, Sullivan's Campaign, French Azilum, Stephen C. Foster, the Civil War, early canals and steam railroads, foreign culture, natural history, literature and fine arts. We also have a collection of rare books. Information covers history and nature.
Services: Offers brochures/pamphlets.
How to Contact: Write or call. Charges for genealogy services.

Toledo Museum of Health and Natural History, 2700 Broadway, Toledo OH 43620. (419)255-1073. Curator: Joseph F. Beckler. Director of Programs: Michael D. Crader.
Purpose: "Research in anthropology, archeology, entomology, mineralogy, paleontology and zoology, with related collections and exhibits." Information covers health/medicine, history, nature and science.
Services: Offers newsletter and literature about the museum and the Toledo Zoo. Publications include *Safari*, newsmagazine of the Toledo Zoo.
How to Contact: Write. "The museum and the Toledo Zoo are happy to cooperate with any individual and/or organization in supplying information and services. Write or call anytime!"

Tuck Memorial Museum, Hampton Historical Society, 40 Park Ave., Hampton NH 03842. Museum Curator: John M. Holman.
Purpose: "The Tuck Memorial Museum serves as a repository for the many historical artifacts of Hampton. It is open daily to the public during the months of July and August; open by appointment during the remainder of the year. It is staffed by volunteers. Admission is free. The museum library contains genealogies and books on the history of Hampton." Information covers history.
Services: Offers information searches. Publications include Tuck Memorial Museum brochure, 1938 tercentenary booklet, 1938 historic map of Hampton, and historic notepaper and post cards.
How to Contact: Write. Charges for photocopies.

United States Air Force Museum, Wright-Patterson Air Force Base, Dayton OH 45433. (513)255-3284. Chief, Information Division: R.E. Baughman.
Purpose: "To portray the history of the United States Air Force and its predecessor organizations." Information covers history of military aviation.
Services: Offers aid in arranging interviews, brochures/pamphlets and press kits.
How to Contact: "Call to discuss requirements, or preferably write to the museum explaining what is desired. We charge 10¢/per copy for documents from the research files.
Tips: "We prefer writers to visit and do their own research/photography because of our limited staff, but we do provide minimum service where possible to qualified writers with credentials. We do not provide complete research services for writers. We can generally provide a picture or stock news release, but writers cannot expect the museum to provide them a complete package of stories, pictures, etc. Our volume of requests does not permit this service."

United States Hockey Hall of Fame, Box 657, Eveleth MN 55734. (218)749-5167. Executive Director: Roger A. Godin.
Purpose: Sports hall of fame. Information covers sports.
Services: Offers 200 b&w and 25 color photos of players and teams, primarily of US origin.
How to Contact: Write or call. Offers one-time rights. Charges $3/print.

United States Tobacco Museum, 100 W. Putnam Ave., Greenwich CT 06830. (203)661-1100. Curator: Jane Brennan.
Purpose: "Public relations, collecting antiques related to tobacco, and research." Information covers art, business, economics, history and new products.
Services: Offers annual reports, bibliographies, biographies, statistics, brochures/ pamphlets, information searches, placement on mailing list, photos and press kits. Has 2,000 b&w and "several thousand" color photos: "prints, paintings, old advertising art, slides of our collection, transparencies and glossy prints of a variety of objects. Photographs can be taken with permission of the museum curator."
How to Contact: Write or call (203)869-5531 and a private tour or conference with the curator can be arranged.

University Art Museum, Berkeley, 2626 Bancroft Way, Berkeley CA 94720. (415)642-1207. Public Affairs Coordinator: Ruth Anderson.
Purpose: "All the activities an art museum engages in: collection, preservation and exhibition of art works." Information covers art.
Services: Offers placement on mailing list for art critics and others interested in reviewing museum exhibitions and events.
How to Contact: Write, explaining how press information will be used.

University Museum of the University of Pennsylvania, 33rd and Spruce Sts., Philadelphia PA 19104. (215)386-7400, ext. 213. Contact: Caroline G. Dosker.
Purpose: Information covers anthropology, archeology and ethnology.
Services: Offers over 100,000 photos for purchase or loan basis.
How to Contact: Reproduction rights offered. Charges $15/first print, $7.50/each additional print made to order. Credit line required.

Vancouver Art Gallery, 1145 W. Georgia St., Vancouver, British Columbia, Canada V6E 3H2. Information Officer: Dorothy Metcalfe.
Purpose: Provides "a regularly changing program of contemporary and historical exhibitions of national and international interest, with special emphasis on Canadian contemporary art." Information covers art.
Services: Offers aid in arranging interviews, annual reports and placement on mailing list.
How to Contact: Write.

Lurleen Burns Wallace Museum, 725 Monroe, Montgomery AL 36130. (205)832-6621. Guide: Charlotte Turnipseed.
Purpose: Memorial to Lurleen Wallace; contains memorabilia and photos. Information covers history, politics and self-help.
Services: Offers annual reports, bibliographies, brochures/pamphlets, information searches, newsletter and photos.
How to Contact: Write or call.

War Memorial Museum of Virginia, 9285 Warwick Blvd., Huntington Park, Newport News VA 23607. (804)247-8523. Curator: John Quarstein.
Purpose: "The War Memorial Museum of Virginia exists to reveal the military history of the United States from the Revolutionary War to the present. Exhibits include World War I and II posters, weapons, uniforms and insignia from all over the world. The library (which includes books, periodicals, historical files, tapes, photos and films)

contains information covering the US and world military history, especially concerning World War I and II." Information covers military history.

Services: Offers brochures/pamphlets and information searches. "We are presently preparing pamphlets about our collection of posters, weapons and local military history. We will assist a qualified researcher, as best as possible, in using our library, historical films and tapes when he is researching at the museum or through written correspondence." Publications include *Excavated Artifacts from Battlefields and Campsites of the Civil War; Bullets Used in the Civil War; German Medals and Decorations of World War II; Officers and Men at the Battle of Manila Bay; Shoulder Patch Insignia of the United States Armed Forces; Aviation Badges and Insignia of the United States Army, 1913-1946;* and *British Cut and Thrust Weapons.*

How to Contact: Write or call. Charges 50¢ entrance fee to the museum. "No materials of any form can leave the museum. By June 1979, the whole library, including films, historical files, tapes, books and name books, will be cataloged and located in a central position to ease research at the museum. However, until this is completed the museum will have a member of its staff available to aid a researcher in locating material."

Washington County Historical Museum, Washington County Historical Association, Fort Calhoun NE 68023. (402)468-5740. Curator: Genevieve Slader.
Purpose: "To preserve and display articles representative of the early history of Washington County, to serve in an educational capacity; to preserve and interpret documents for the use of those in search of family or historical information or who take pleasure in reading of the past." Information covers agriculture and history. "Our information touches on all subjects as applies to the history of the county."
Services: Offers brochures/pamphlets. Publications include *Fort Atkinson Story, Steamboat Bertrand, Portal to the Plains* (a history of the county), and a brochure describing the museum.
How to Contact: Write or call. Charges for photocopies and postage. "All materials must be used on the premises."

Mary Ball Washington Museum and Library, Inc., Box 97, Lancaster VA 22503. (804)462-7280. Executive Director: Ann Lewis Burrows.
Purpose: "A nonprofit, charitable foundation dedicated to the preservation and exhibition of articles of historic importance for the benefit of the general public. The historic heritage of Virginia's Northern Neck is a rich one. We have museum exhibitions, programs for the general public, a historical lending library, a genealogical library and research service, workshops, a film series, and departments of archeology and archives." Information covers history.
Services: Offers aid in arranging interviews, bibliographies, biographies, statistics, brochures/pamphlets, information searches, newsletter and photos.
How to Contact: Write or call. Charges $10 for genealogical research.

West Point Museum, US Military Academy, West Point NY 10996. (914)938-2203.
Purpose: "Military museum open to the public since 1854." Information covers "exhibits from the American Revolution until now, including uniforms, flags, arms, art, history and technical information."
Services: Offers aid in arranging interviews, biographies, brochures/pamphlets, placement on mailing list, photos and press kits. Publications include a portrait catalog.
How to Contact: Write.

Western Heritage Museum, Old Union Station, 801 S. 10th St., Omaha NE 68108. (402)444-5071. Director: Michael L. Kinsel.
Purpose: "A regional history museum covering westward expansion from the 1800s to the present. We have a research library, and exhibits, history education and oral history programs, with heavy emphasis on photography, utilizing KMTV's (local NBC affiliate) Bostwick-Frohardt Collection of historical photographs from the 1860s to 1950s." Information covers agriculture, business, celebrities, economics, entertain-

ment, food, history, industry, politics, recreation, sports and travel.
Services: Offers aid in arranging interviews, brochures/pamphlets, information searches and photos.
How to Contact: Write or call. Rates vary according to purpose. Charges $5/print for educational use to $150/print for publication for commercial purposes.

Whaling Museum, 18 Johnny Cake Hill, New Bedford MA 02740. Director: Richard C. Kugler.
Purpose: To preserve the history of whaling.
Services: Offers photos.
How to Contact: Write. "This museum adheres to the fee schedules recommended by the Association of Art Museum Directors. Permission to reproduce Whaling Museum material will be granted only to publications protected by copyright. Such copyright, where it applies to museum material, is understood to be waived in favor of the Whaling Museum. Credit line and return of pictures required."

The Wheelwright Museum, Box 5153, Santa Fe NM 87502. Contact: Director.
Services: Offers b&w and color photos.
How to Contact: Charges $1-15/copy print; $5-35/original photo; and $25/b&w print and $75/color photo for one-time reproduction. Credit line required.

Whitney Museum of American Art, 945 Madison Ave., New York NY 10021. Contact: Rights and Permissions.
Services: Offers color transparencies and b&w photographs for reproduction and reference purposes.
How to Contact: Credit line and return of slides required. Price schedule available by written request.

The Wine Museum of San Francisco, 633 Beach St., San Francisco CA 94109. (415)673-6990. Director: Ernest G. Mittelberger.
Purpose: Funded by Fromm & Sichel, distributors of Christian Brothers wine and brandy, this is "a free museum presenting Christian Brothers collection of wine in the arts. We offer a traveling exhibition of wine-related artworks—a 1,000-volume library of rare wine books (dating from 1550 to the present), a glass collection, and a 150-volume library on glass drinking-vessels." Information covers art, history and wine.
Services: Offers brochures/pamphlets and photo reproductions of all artworks in the collection. Publications include a fact sheet on the museum and its collection, *Thomas Jefferson and Wine in Early America* ($1), *Wine and Poetry* ($2), and *In Celebration of Wine and Life* ($14.95), and a catalog ($1.50 plus postage).
How to Contact: Visit. Charges $5-10/photo. Credit must be given to the collection and the museum when quoting materials or reproducing the photographs.

The Henry Francis du Pont Winterthur Museum, Winterthur DE 19735. (302)656-8591. Head of Public Relations: Catherine Wheeler.
Purpose: "Museum, gardens and research library in American decorative arts to early 20th century and their European antecedents. The museum of American decorative arts covers the period from 1650 to 1850, displayed in more than 200 rooms and small area settings. Graduate education programs in connoisseurship and conservation of decorative arts are offered in conjunction with the University of Delaware." Information covers art, history and nature (gardens).
Services: Offers annual reports, bibliographies, brochures/pamphlets, information searches, placement on mailing list, newsletter, photos and press kits. Offers b&w photos and color transparencies of furniture, silver, ceramics, prints, paintings, textiles, and other decorative art objects made or used in America from 1640 to 1840. Publications available.
How to Contact: Write or call. Charges vary for photography and filmmaking, and may

include overtime and utility costs. Articles should be written for a specific publication with a committment from that publication. Submit the request in writing, but make the initial inquiry by telephone. Selection of photos should be made from Winterthur publications or from photo files in registrar's office at the museum. Charges $10/b&w print (which includes print and one-time use). Credit line required.

Wyoming State Art Gallery, Barrett Building, Cheyenne WY 82002. (307)777-7519. Curator: Laura Hayes.
Purpose: "To collect biographical information on Wyoming's artists—some on artists outside of Wyoming. We exhibit the work of Wyoming artists, historical art and/or Western art." Information covers art and history.
Services: Offers a limited number of biographies.
How to Contact: Write. Charges 15¢/photocopy.
Tips: "Some artists have requested that their files not be open to the public at this time; only limited information will be available from these."

Wyoming State Museum, Photo Section, Barrett Bldg., Cheyenne WY 82002. (307)777-7518. Photographic Technician: Paula West.
Services: Offers 80,000 b&w photos relating to Western history in general and Wyoming history, including ranching, rodeos, railroads, towns, scenics, industry, mining, people, forts and the military.
How to Contact: Offers all rights. Charges $25-100 for one-time editorial or advertising use; $4-10/print. Credit line required.

Yale University Collection of Musical Instruments, 15 Hillhouse Ave., New Haven CT 06511. (203)436-4935. Assistant Curator: Nicholas Renouf.
Purpose: "The Yale University Collection of Musical Instruments is an independent member of the Yale community of museums devoted to the documentation and exposition of the history of music through historical instruments." Information covers history of music, organology and construction of musical instruments.
Services: Offers brochures/pamphlets and photos. "We handle specific research problems." Publications include publications list.
How to Contact: Write or call. "We prefer written requests. We charge for our publications, and also for publication rights for the photographs."

Yarmouth County Museum, 22 Collins St., Yarmouth, Nova Scotia, Canada B5A 3C8. (902)742-5539. Curator: Eric Ruff. Librarian: Helen Hall.
Purpose: "Yarmouth's history, shipping and genealogies." Information covers history and shipping.
Services: Offers photos and limited information searches. Publications include newspapers, manuscripts, documents, logs, etc., which can be used on the premises.
How to Contact: Write. Charges for photocopies, photo reproduction and searches. "Rates vary, but are minimal. We insist on a credit line for photo information from our sources."

Yesteryear Museum, Box 1890M, Morristown NJ 07960. (201)386-1920, 334-1877. Director: Lee R. Munsick.
Purpose: "Specializing in history of mechanical and automatic music in all fields: music boxes, nickelodeons, player pianos, phonographs, records and ragtime (especially Edison and Victor). The shop offers items related to these fields." Information covers celebrities, entertainment, history, industry, music, science and technical data.
Services: Offers photos.
How to Contact: Write or call.

John Young Museum and Planetarium (JYMP), 810 E. Rollins St., Orlando FL 32803. (305)896-7151. Public Affairs Manager: Nancy A. Thigpen.
Purpose: "JYMP is a 'hands-on' science museum that features exhibits on natural

history, anatomy, space and technology.'' Information covers nature and science.
Services: Offers exhibits.
How to Contact: Write or call.

Organizations & Associations

Every sport, vocation, hobby and field of interest has people rallying around it in the form of an organization or association. Thousands of these groups, ranging from nonprofit trade associations to fraternal organizations, exist today. The *Encyclopedia of Associations*, a directory that's kept track of such groups since 1956, lists more than 13,000 associations in the US alone.

Organizations and associations have myriad purposes: to serve as forums for information and idea exchange; to represent members or a particular field of endeavor in a favorable light; to effect change favorable to members, or to the public as a whole; to provide services to members; to conduct research. These functions make organizations and associations valuable resources for the writer/researcher. Disseminating information is an important aspect of most organizations. For example, the Council for Agricultural Science and Technology (CAST) serves "as a resource group to which the public and government can turn for information," says the council's executive vice president, Dr. Charles A. Black. CAST's other function, says Black, is "to disseminate this information in a usable form to the public, news media and the government."

Arthur Johnson, public information officer of the National Association of Black Manufacturers, concurs. "Associations have a lot of information that (writers/researchers) might need." Johnson mentions an additional value of consulting associations: "Usually, there is no cost."

Most organizations and associations are willing to help with information searches, but writers/researchers should realize the limitations of these groups. For example, "the 'small' organizations are more member-oriented, as it is *the members* who pay the bills, and they are generally served first," explains Lowell H. Rott, secretary-treasurer of the Morocco Spotted Horse Co-operative Association. "Most of us try to help, but it can be difficult at times, due to the lack of time, funds and resources at our disposal." Rott notes that costs like postage are a larger burden on the small organization than on the large one.

Many associations' public information offices are staffed by only a few people. Writers/researchers should, therefore, make information requests easy to handle. "Plan ahead," is Mike Segel's advice about accomplishing that. Segel, director of public information of Edison Electric Institute (an association of electric companies), adds, "Allow sufficient lead time to track down needed information."

No matter how much time you give the organization to dig up material, however, don't expect the organization to do all your work for you. You are the researcher; the organization is the source. Public information people expect both parties to fill those roles, and no others. "Researchers, including writers," says a representative of the American Music Center, should "be prepared to do their own legwork. We will work with them to provide the best information available, but can't transcribe and ingest that information." Keep information requests specific, as well. "For questions such as 'What is advertising?', consult your dictionary," says Anthon C. Lunt, director of public relations for the Association of National Advertisers. Such broad-based questions should be answered *before* you approach these sources. Inquiries that are too general will probably be disregarded, as will those that demonstrate lackadaisical research prior to approaching the organization. "Study the industry for general back-

ground so your questions are reasonably intelligent and *specific*, even on a lay basis,"
recommends Donald H. Watson of the Air Transport Association of Canada."

What's more, don't rely on a single organization for all your answers. Go to similar
organizations (and to other types of sources) with your questions. This will assure a
variety of information from which to choose if all inquiries are answered, and will
guarantee a response even if some of the sources can't answer your questions. Organizations and associations here are categorized according to their field of interest; if you
know the name of a specific organization you'd like to consult, check the index at the
back of the book. Names and addresses of additional organizations can be found in the
Encyclopedia of Associations (Gale Research Co.), edited by Margaret Fisk; and
National Trade & Professional Associations of the United States & Canada (Columbia
Books, Inc.), edited by Craig Colgate. Both directories should be available at your local
library.

Finally, realize that organizations and associations are sources of more than
information. Ideas are abundant here, too. Says Julie Brooks, director of communications of the United States Student Association: "We always have a million potential
leads and stories for interested reporters."

Accounting

American Institute of Certified Public Accountants, 1211 Avenue of the Americas,
New York NY 10036. (212)575-3878. Director, Public and State Society Relations
Division: Bradford E. Smith.
Purpose: "To organize the body of accounting knowledge; to conduct research; to
enforce the profession's technical and ethical standards; to guide the profession's
overall development along lines serving the broadest public interest; to encourage
cooperation betwen CPAs and professional accountants in other countries." Information covers business and industry and how accounting and auditing standards affect
them.
Services: Offers aid in arranging interviews, annual reports, biographies, statistics,
brochures/pamphlets, information searches, placement on mailing list and press kits.
"We have the most comprehensive US collection of published materials on accounting
and related subjects." Numerous publications available.
How to Contact: Write, call or visit. Prefers written request. "We can set a writer up to
do research in our library."

The Canadian Institute of Chartered Accountants, 250 Bloor St. E., Toronto, Ontario,
Canada M4W 1G5. (416)962-1242. Public Relations Officer: Helen Guest.
Purpose: "The Canadian Institute of Chartered Assountants (CICA) is a professional
organization to which all of Canada's chartered accountants belong. CICA's research
department and committees issue generally accepted accounting principles and auditing standards for Canadian business. CICA also produces professional development
courses for chartered accountants, a monthly professional magazine, and keeps records of the membership." Information covers business and accounting standards
and research.
Services: Offers aid in arranging interviews, annual reports, placement on mailing list,
newsletter and photos.
How to Contact: Write.

Society of California Accountants, 2131 Capitol Ave., Sacramento CA 95816.
(916)443-2057. Executive Director: T.B.O. Fertig.
Purpose: An association of professional public accountants. Information covers business and economics.

Services: Offers aid in arranging interviews, statistics, information searches, placement on mailing list and newsletter. Publications include *The California Accountant* (monthly) and *Guide For Accountants Engagement Letters.*
How to Contact: Write Society of California Accountants (SCA) Readers' Service, Box 160067, Sacramento CA 95816.

Advertising

The Advertising Council, Inc., 825 3rd Ave., New York NY 10022. Director of Public Affairs: Benjamin S. Greenberg.
Purpose: "The Advertising Council was founded in 1942 to produce public service advertising campaigns for the war effort. Since the end of World War II, it has continued its good work, now producing 30 public service campaigns annually in all media—TV, radio, press, magazines, business press, transit and outdoor advertising." Information covers art, economics, food, health/medicine, self-help, fundraising causes and government campaigns.
Services: Offers annual reports, brochures/pamphlets, placement on mailing list, newsletter, photos and press kits.
How to Contact: Write.

American Advertising Federation, 1225 Connecticut Ave., NW, Washington DC. 20036. Manager, Information and Education: Kathy Denk.
Purpose: "We are the only organization in the United States that relates to all aspects of the advertising community and seeks to improve advertising and the climate in which it functions through constructive programs in areas of government and public information, education, public service and self—regulation. Our headquarters are in Washington, but we also maintain a Western regional office in San Francisco."
Services: Offers brochures/pamphlets.
How to Contact: Write. Charges for publications.

Association of National Advertisers, 155 E. 44th St., New York NY 10017. (212)697-5950. Director of Press Relations: Anthon C. Lunt.
Purpose: "The Association of National Advertisers (ANA) is a nonprofit organization founded in 1910. We represent the interests of over 400 companies that use advertising regionally or nationally to provide information on their products and services to the public. Through workshops, surveys, reports and books, ANA has developed an extensive library which includes material on all aspects of advertising and other forms of marketing communications (audiovisuals, trade shows, etc.). It does not provide industry statistics other than in areas of management practice in which members have been surveyed." Information covers business and advertising.
Services: Offers assistance in developing accurate information on advertising and promotional activities: their management, execution and evaluation. Publications include a publications list.
How to Contact: Write or call. Charges for some publications. "An appointment to visit the ANA library for research may be arranged. We are willing to work with writers and researchers whenever called upon."

Aeronautics & Aviation

Aerospace Industry Association of America, 1725 De Sales St. NW, Washington DC 20036. (202)347-2315. Vice President/Public Affairs: Julian Levine.
Purpose: "Aerospace Industry Association of America is a national trade association which represents major manufacturers of aerospace equipment. We deal with commercial, military, civil and private aviation and space activities as they relate to the

design, development and manufacture of such equipment. We maintain statistical, historical and other information relative to the industry and are a spokesman on issues of industry wide significance."

Services: Offers aid in arranging interviews, statistics, brochures/pamphlets, placement on mailing list and newsletter. Publications include an annual report and *Aerospace*, quarterly magazine.

How to Contact: Write or call.

Aircraft Owners and Pilots Association (AOPA), 7315 Wisconsin Ave., Bethesda MD 20014. (301)654-0500. Vice President Public Relations: Charles Spence.

Purpose: "AOPA serves the interest of individuals who own and fly general aviation (nonairline, nonmilitary) aircraft. It offers services to members, plus representation of interests with the Federal Aviation Administration and Congress."Information covers industry and technical data.

Services: Offers aid in arranging interviews, statistics, brochures/pamphlets, placement on mailing list and press kits. Publications include aviation fact cards, safety fact sheets and reference articles.

How to Contact: Write or call. "Reasonable assistance can be given, but detailed research cannot be provided."

Antique Airplane Association, Rt. 2, Antique Airfield, Ottumwa IA 52501. (515)938-2773. President: Robert L.Taylor.

Purpose: "Formed in 1953 to save, restore, and fly antique and classic airplanes. We publish three quarterly magazines. We have 40 chapters and hold numerous fly-ins, meetings, and dinners." Information covers history (aviation), how-to, recreation and technical data.

Services: Offers brochures/pamphlets, placement on mailing list, photos and press kits. "We also provide consulting services to the TV and movie industry, air museums, and writers and publishers dealing in historical aviation subjects."

How to Contact: Write, indicating specific information required. "Historical aviation research is a time-consuming subject and fees depend on commercial applications by those requesting such data."

General Aviation Manufacturers Association, Suite 517, 1025 Connecticut Ave. NW, Washington DC 20036. (202)296-8848. Director of Communications: John Meyer.

Purpose: "The General Aviation Manufacturers Association (GAMA) represents US manufacturers of general aviation aircraft, avionics and accessories. It provides the general aviation industry with a Washington base and operations staff for dealing in international and national regulatory affairs, technical affairs and public affairs." Information covers business, economics, industry, new products and technical data.

Services: Offers aid in arranging interviews, annual reports, statistics, brochures/pamphlets, placement on mailing list, photos, and press kits; also, motion picture, slide and tape material. Publications include *The General Aviation Story*.

How to Contact: Write.

National Aeronautics Association, 821 15th St. NW, Suite 430, Washington DC 20005. (202)347-2808. Secretary, Contest and Records Board: Everett Langworthy.

Purpose: "To sanction and certify all aviation record attempts in the United States, both civil and military, including space; and to represent the United States in the Federation Aeronautique Internationale, the world governing body for sport aviation. We declare national records for all aircraft attempting official records in the US." Information covers aviaition record attempts.

Services: Offers listings of all official aviation records in the US and the world. Publications include *This Is NAA*, a brochure about the general activities of the association.

How to Contact: Write. Charges $35/copy for record book. "Credit must be given the National Aeronautics Association for material used from record book."

National Pilots Association, 805 15th St., NW, Washington DC 20005. (202)737-0773. Director of Communications: Marilyn Zimmer.
Purpose: "We are a division of the National Aeronautic Association and the official pilot representative of the Federation Aeronautique Internationale in the United States. It is the nation's largest member-controlled, nonprofit pilot organization. We maintain a Washington staff to represent individual and affiliate members for general aviation in Congress, FAA and elsewhere in the aviation community. We also sponsor the United States Precision Flight Team Competition, where basic aeronautical training and skills are tested. It is the sport of safe flying."
Services: Offers newsletter.
How to Contact: Write or call.

Agriculture

American Farm Bureau Federation, 225 Touhy Ave., Park Ridge IL 60068. (312)399-5700. Chief Economist: W.E. (Gene) Hamilton.
Purpose: "The American Farm Bureau Federation (AFBF) is local, statewide, national and international in scope and influence and is nonpartisan, nonsectarian, nonsecret in character. AFBF is a free, independent nongovernmental and voluntary organization of farm and ranch families united for the purpose of analyzing problems and formulating action programs to achieve educational improvement, economic opportunity and social advancement, thereby promoting the national well-being." Information covers agriculture.
Services: Offers annual reports, brochures/pamphlets and statistics.
How to Contact: Write or call.

Canada Grains Council, 500-177 Lombard Ave., Winnipeg, Manitoba Canada R3B 0W5. (204)942-2254. Communications Officer: Peggy Williams.
Purpose: "We provide a forum for discussion for the grains industry in Canada, as well as a liaison with government. We work toward increasing markets for Canadian grains overseas and at home. We seek general improvements for the grains industry, coordinate grain research and disseminate information." Information covers agriculture (grain only) and economics.
Services: Offers statistics, brochures/pamphlets and placement on mailing list. Publications include *Statistical Handbook 1978* ($5), *Open Door* (6 copies of a marketing newsletter available for $1) and reports on many specific subjects (free).
How to Contact: Write.

Council for Agricultural Science and Technology, Agronomy Bldg., Iowa State University, Ames IA 50011. (515)294-2036. Executive Vice President: Dr. Charles A. Black.
Purpose: The Council for Agricultural Science and Technology (CAST) advances the understanding and use of food and agricultural science and technology in the public interest. It serves as a resource group to which the public and government may turn for information on food and agicultural issues; organizes task forces of agricultural scientists and technologists to assemble and interpret factual information on these issues; and disseminates this information in a usable form to the public, news media and the government." Information covers agriculture, food and science.
Services: Offers aid in arranging interviews, brochures/pamphlets, reports on the scientific facts of curent issues, and newsletters. Publications include *News from CAST* (bimonthly newsletter) and *Directory of Environmental Scientists in Agriculture*.
How to Contact: Write or call. "CAST services are available to assist writers in making contact with responsible scientists, thus providing them with accurate information in developing stories."

Farmwoman News Service, 930 National Press Bldg., Washington DC 20045. (202)347-2776.
Purpose: "Information clearinghouse for the activities of women involved in natural resources and agriculture." Information covers agriculture, food and politics.
Services: Offers brochures/pamphlets and newsletter. Publications include *Congress Defined* (glossary) and *Guide to Legislative Tracking.*
How to Contact: Write, specifying research division. "List your specific need on outside of envelope—photo inquiry, etc." Charges vary for services; charges $5/pamphlet, $1.50/copy of newsletter ($28.50/year subscription), and varying fees for speakers.

Independent Livestock Marketing Association, 138 S. Main, Tipton IN 46072. (317)675-4680. Executive Director: Paul Juday.
Purpose: "Independent Livestock Marketing Association is a trade association of privately owned livestock marketing firms and their facilities in a Midwestern regional area covering 10-12 states. This office monitors legislation and regulation, provides general educational programs and strives to promote an understanding of our business activities to the general public." Information covers agriculture, economics, food, history, politics and technical data.
Services: Offers aid in arranging interviews, statistics, brochures/pamphlets, and newsletters. Publications include a catalog of member firms and branch locations.
How to Contact: Write or call. "We can not release financial data because it involves private enterprise."

National Cotton Council, Box 12285, Memphis TN 38112. (901)274-9030. PR Director: Emmett Robinson.
Purpose: "To increase use of cotton, cottonseed and their products." Information covers agriculture, economics, history and technical data.
Services: Offers aid in arranging interviews, statistics, brochures/pamphlets, photos and press kits. Publications include *Cotton, the First Fiber...Yesterday, Today, and Tomorrow; Cotton From Field to Fabric; The Story of Cotton;* and *Cotton: The Perennial Patriot.*
How to Contact: "Write or call. Be specific in requesting information." Most literature is available free for single copies; charges for quantity orders.

National Grange, 1616 H St. NW, Washington DC 20006. (202)628-3507. Director of Information/Public Relations: Judy Massabny.
Purpose: "We are the oldest and second largest farm organization. There are 500,000 members in this fraternal organization." Information covers agriculture and history of the Grange.
Services: Offers aid in arranging interviews and brochures/pamphlets. Publications include *Blue Book*, a summary of Grange history and structure, and legislative policies and programs.
How to Contact: Write or call. "We do not provide information on how to become a farmer or on methods of farming, etc."

Palliser Wheat Growers Association, 219-3806 Albert St., Regina, Saskatchawan, Canada S4S 3R2. (306)586-5866. Research Director: Doug Campbell.
Purpose: "Palliser is a producer organization—a commodity group founded in April 1970 to promote and safeguard interests in the production, handling and marketing of wheat. Palliser is noncommercial and nonpolitical. Palliser speaks for wheat growers only." Information covers agriculture.
Services: Offers annual report and newsletter.
How to Contact: Write or call.

Tobacco Growers Information Committee, Box 12046, Raleigh NC 27605. Managing Director: Billy Yeargin.

Purpose: "Tobacco Information and public relations/promotion." Information covers agriculture and tobacco.
Services: Offers aid in arranging interviews, clipping services, information searches, placement on mailing list, statistics and newsletter.
How to Contact: Write or call.

The Tobacco Institute, 1776 K St. NW, Washington DC 20006. Contact: George Yenowind, Jeannette Cohen.
Purpose: "The Tobacco Institute is a nonprofit, noncommercial organization that fosters public understanding of the smoking and health controversy, and public knowledge of the historic role of tobacco and its place in the national economy. It is a communicator of information and viewpoints on such matters to the public, news media and government bodies at local, state and federal levels." Information covers tobacco.
Services: Offers brochures/pamphlets.
How to Contact: Write. "The library is not open to the general public and publications are limited to no more than 10 copies."

U.S. Feed Grains Council, 1030 15th St. NW, Washington DC 20005. (202)659-1640. Director of Communications: Robert J. Brown.
Purpose: "We seek to increase the export of US grain (corn, sorghum and barley) to overseas countries, particularly lesser-developed nations, by teaching them how to improve their diets through more efficient animal (meat) production systems." Information covers agriculture, food and self-help.
Services: Offers aid in arranging interviews, annual reports, biographies, brochures/pamphlets, clipping services, information searches, placement on mailing list, newsletter, photos and press kits. Publications include *An Introduction to the U.S. Feed Grains Council and Its Foreign Market Development Programs.*
How to Contact: Write or call.

Animal

American Angus Association, 3201 Frederick Blvd., St. Joseph MO 64501. (816)233-3101. Director of Communications and Public Relations: Keith E. Evans.
Purpose: "We record ancestral and production records on purebred Angus cattle. We have a complete advertising and promotion program, a junior activities program involving some 11,000 young cattle breeders, and 30,000 active life members who produce registered beef cattle as seedstock for the commercial cattle industry. We are the largest beef cattle registry association in the world, as determined by annual registrations." Information covers agriculture, food, history, self-help and technical data.
Services: Offers aid in arranging interviews, annual reports, biographies, statistics, brochures/pamphlets, placement on mailing list and photos. Publications include *How To Be Successful With Your Small Angus Herd, History of the Angus Breed, Crossbreeding, Tool for Profit or Financial Disaster, Angus Sire Evaluation* and *Production Records.*
How to Contact: Write or call. "There is no fee for services except for special requests that would involve a great deal of time or research."

American Association of Owners & Breeders of Peruvian Paso Horses, Box 2035, California City CA 93505. (415)531-5082. President: Verne R. Albright.
Purpose: "To register Peruvian paso horses (pure bloods only); to keep a stud book; to promote the Peruvian horses and to foster good relations between our organization and the ANCPCPPC, Peru's Association." Information covers Peruvian Paso Horses.
Services: Offers brochures/pamphlets, newsletter and magazine.
How to Contact: Write. Charges for publications.

American Bashkir Curly Registry, Box 453, Ely NV 89301. (702)289-4228. Secretary: Mrs. Sunny Martin.
Purpose: "Registry for registering, promoting and propagating curly-coated horses. Besides registering curly-coated horses, we also encourage research on them, as they are so highly unusual. We offer yearly trophies to the top performance horse (arena), top trail horse (endurance or competitive), top youth showing a Curly, and breed promotion. We also have an annual convention, and sponser horse show classes for Bashkir Curly horses." Information covers horses.
Services: Offers brochures/pamphlets, newsletter and photos. "Our information, newsletter and photos apply to our Bashkir Curly horses exclusively."
How to Contact: Write or call. "We do charge for photos at cost, and have both black and white and color. We ask for constructive and positive research and articles, and naturally do not want derogatory articles about our horses, as they are indeed a highly unusual breed and still need much research done on them. Bashkir Curly horses do not seem to fit the norm for other breeds. Their blood, respiration, temperature and hair differ greatly from what is considered normal for other breeds and should be of great interest to researchers who study horses."

American Bullmastiff Association, Inc., Nabby Hill, Mohegan Lake NY 10547. Secretary: Tami Raider.
Purpose: "The preservation, protection and improvement of purebred bullmastiffs. We are a source of information on anything regarding the breed."
Services: Offers aid in arranging interviews, annual reports, brochures/pamphlets, information searches and newsletter. Publications include informational brochures, breeders' directory and *The Bullmastiff Bulletin* (triannual magazine).
How to Contact: Write or call. Charges $2/copy for magazine; "no charge for informational services other than the magazine."

American Cavy Breeders Association, 6560 Upham St., Arvada CO 80003. (303)421-1024. Secretary/Treasurer: Robert Leishman.
Purpose: "To promote the breeding and advancement of the Cavy and to secure the utmost publicity as exhibition and laboratory animals. We also seek to help all breeders to secure the utmost for their stock by providing information as to markets and show animals, afford membership to persons interested in breeding and marketing Cavies, investigate markets, and assist in legislation and publicity beneficial to this association." Information covers raising and showing Cavies.
Services: Offers statistics, brochures/pamphlets, information searches, newsletter and photos.
How to Contact: Write or call.

American Connemara Pony Society, HoshieKon Farm Rt. 1, Goshen CT 06756. (203)491-3521. Executive Secretary: Mrs. John E. O'Brien.
Purpose: "Maintenance of the registry, promotion of the breed, publication of all Connemara literature in North America and liason with Connemara societies in other countries." Information covers history (of the breed), recreation and sports.
Services: Offers brochures/pamphlets, statistics, newsletter and photos. Publications available.
How to Contact: Write. Charges for publications. "We would appreciate the source being credited. Request should be as specific as possible in asking for information or material."

American Gotland Horse Association, Rt. 2, Box 181, Elkland MO 65644. (417)345-7004.
Purpose: "The promotion and registration of the Gotland Horse breed." Information covers horses.
Services: Offers aid in arranging interviews, statistics, newsletter and photos.
How to Contact: Write or call. Charges for pictures and newsletter.

American International Charolais Association, 1610 Old Spanish Trail, Houston TX 77054. (713)797-9211. Director of Communications: Fred Wortham Jr.
Purpose: "To maintain the registry for Charolais cattle in the United States. We have members in Canada, Mexico, and Central and South America, as well as the United States. We also coordinate promotion of the Charolais breed on a national scale. We provide certain member services in the area of performance testing, group insurance and other functions." Information covers agriculture and Charolais cattle (beef).
Services: Offers aid in arranging interviews, biographies, brochures/pamphlets, placement on mailing list, statistics, photos and press kits. Publications available.
How to Contact: Write or call. "Under certain circumstances we would charge a fee for materials and on occasion might ask for a fee if the research done by our staff is extensive or unusual."

American Milking Shorthorn Society, 1722-JJ S. Glenstone, Springfield MO 65804. (417)887-6525. Executive Secretary: Harry Clampitt.
Purpose: "We are a registry office and a service to members and interested breeders. We promote Milking Shorthorn dairy cattle. We publish a monthly magazine available to members and subscribers." Information covers agriculture.
Services: Offers annual reports, statistics and brochures/pamphlets.
How to Contact: "Write this office. We do not charge to send leaflets or to answer letters, but we charge for the magazine, for animal registry, etc., and for statistics that require research."

The American Morgan Horse Association, Inc., Box 1, Westmoreland NY 13490. (315)736-8306. Executive Secretary: Avo Kiviranna.
Purpose: "Our mission is guidance, assistance and encouragement in the breeding, care and development of the Morgan Horse as America's most versatile and desirable breed."
Services: Offers statistics, brochures/pamphlets, information searches and photos. Publications include *The Morgan Horse* (monthly).
How to Contact: Write or call.

Animal Protection Institute of America, Box 22505, Sacramento CA 95822. (916)422-1921.
Purpose: "We educate the public on animal issues. Our goal is to alleviate or eliminate all pain and suffering of animals. We are involved in major campaigns to save the harp seal, the whale, wildlife, etc." Information covers animal.
Services: Offers statistics, brochures/pamphlets, information searches, newsletter, press kits, and a quarterly magazine.
How to Contact: Write or call.

American Society for the Prevention of Cruelty to Animals, 441 E. 92nd St., New York NY 10028. Director of Communication: Joan Weich.
Purpose: "An agency that handles animal control 24 hours a day, seven days a week; receives unwanted or stray animals; and operates an adoption agency."Services: Offers aid in arranging interviews, brochures/pamphlets, placement on mailing list, statistics, newsletter and news releases.
How to Contact: Write or call.

Beauty Without Cruelty International, 175 W. 12th St., New York NY 10011. Contact: Dr. Ethel Thurston.
Purpose: "A humane society that provides information on cruelties imposed on animals by the fashion and cosmetic industries, and how to obtain cruelty-free garments. This is the only animal welfare society of its kind. It has a field director who travels worldwide to investigate cruelties in the production of garments and toiletries. This includes the production of civet musk used in perfumes, methods of capture and slaughter of snakes and crocodiles for leather and the poaching of elephants and other

animals on the endangered species list. This information is passed onto members in 25 countries throughout the world. A line of cruelty-free cosmetics is also produced." Information covers agriculture and business.

Services: Offers annual reports, brochures/pamphlets, placement on mailing list, newsletter and press kits.

How to Contact: Write.

California Thoroughbred Breeders Association, 201 Colorado Place, Arcadia CA 91006. (213)445-7800. Librarian: Janet Sporleder.

Purpose: "The organization, a nonprofit corporation, is dedicated to the production of better thoroughbred horses for better thoroughbred racing. The library's collection includes general works on the horse, but the emphasis is on thoroughbreds: breeding and racing records date back 200 years."Information covers horses in general; thoroughbreds in particular.

Services: Offers biographies and statistics.

How to Contact: Write, call or visit. "The collection is for reference only—none of the books or periodicals circulate."

Canadian Maine-Anjou Association, 2424C 2nd Ave., Calgary, Alberta, Canada T2W 1P4. (403)273-8219. Executive Manager: John Russell. Promotion Director: Sue Siddall.

Purpose: "The major responsibilities of the Canadian Maine-Anjou Association (CMAA) are: maintenance of pedigree records and issuance of certificates on purebred and domestic recorded Maine-Anjou cattle, promotion of breeding, raising of purebred and up-graded Maine-Anjou cattle throughout Canada and assisting farmers, ranchers and cattle breeders with importing, exporting, breeding, raising and marketing purebred and percentage Maine-Anjou cattle." Information covers livestock.

Services: Offers statistics, brochures/pamphlets, placement on mailing list, newsletters and photos. Publications include *Information for Maine-Anjou Breeders, Maine-Anjou Breeder's Handbook, Maine-Anjou–The Performance Breed, Maine-Anjou Message* (monthly newsletter), *Maine-Anjou–Canadian Herd Reference Issue* and *Maine-Anjou Herd Sire Directory*.

How to Contact: Write or call.

Devon Cattle Association, Inc., Drawer 628, Uvalde TX 78801. Executive Secretary: Dr. Stewart H. Fowler.

Purpose: "We maintain the registry for the registration and transfer of purebred Devons in the United States; promote the breed; provide technical advice to aid prospective cattlemen get started in the cattle business; and assist active cattle breeders with selecting breeding stock, planning matings and herd improvement programs." Information covers agriculture, history, how-to and technical data.

Services: Offers annual reports, statistics, brochures/pamphlets, placement on mailing list, newsletter, photos, brochures translated into Spanish, an annual yearbook and color slides of Devon cattle.

How to Contact: Write or call.

Friends of Animals and the Committee for Humane Legislation, 11 W. 60th St., New York NY 10023. (212) 247-8120. Vice President: Bill Clark.

Purpose: "Both Friends of Animals (FOA) and Committee for Humane Legislation (CHL) are engaged in protecting both domestic and wild animals from human exploitation. FOA is essentially a public information organization and CHL is a lobbying organization." Information covers health/medicine, law, nature, science, self-help, technical data, humane education and wildlife.

Services: Offers aid in arranging interviews, statistics, brochures/pamphlets, information searches, placement on mailing list, photos and press kits.

How to Contact: Write or call. "We will be glad to accommodate any writer who is researching work in relationships between the human and nonhuman species."

Galiceno Horse Breeders Association, 111 East Elm St., Tyler TX 75702. (214)593-7341. Secretary: Mary Stubblefield.
Purpose: "Our association is to collect, record and preserve the pedigrees of Galiceno horses. We also help publicize and maintain the purity of the breed. The association promotes horse shows for the breeders and exhibitors. The promotional material that we have available explains the origin of the breed, the uses of the Galiceno and information about the association." Information covers Galiceno horses.
Services: Offers brochures/pamphlets.
How to Contact: Write. "We charge 30¢ for our larger brochure, if ordered in quantities of more than one."

International Atlantic Salmon Foundation, Box 429, St. Andrews, New Brunswick, Canada E0G 2X0. (506)529-3818. I/E Coordinator: Mrs. Lee Sochasky.
Purpose: "A nonprofit research and educational organization dedicated to the conservation and wise management of the Atlantic salmon and its environment. Directs and supports many vital programs in the areas of education, public information, research and international cooperation." Information covers catch statistics and world news.
Services: Offers annual reports, statistics, brochures/pamphlets, information searches, placement on mailing list and newsletter.
How to Contact: Write or call.

International Crane Foundation, City View Rd., Baraboo WI 53913. (608)356-3553. Education Coordinator: John Wiessinger.
Purpose: "We are working to preserve the world's cranes from extinction. Our information covers agricultural practices, conservation and research programs, environmental education, science and conservation."
Services: Offers aid in arranging interviews, annual reports, brochures/pamphlets, newsletter, and tours of the facilities (by appointment only). Publications include a general International Crane Foundation brochure, a slide presentation flier and a school program flier.
How to Contact: Write.

International Illawarra Association, 1722-JJ S. Glenstone, Springfield MO 65804. (417)887-6526. Executive Secretary: Harry Clampitt.
Purpose: "To promote Illawarra cattle, to service members and to publish a monthly magazine." Information covers agriculture.
Services: Offers annual reports, brochures/pamphlets and statistics. Publications available.
How to Contact: Write. Charges for membership, registration, research and magazine.

Morab Horse Registry of America, Box 143, Clovis CA 93613. (209)439-5437. Registrar: Alana Miller.
Purpose: "To collect, verify, record and preserve the pedigrees of a specific breed of horse, the American Morab, and to publish a Stud Book and Registry. We also promote and further the cause of Morab horses and regulate any and all other matters which pertain to history, breeding, exhibition, publicity or improvement of the breed known as Morab." Information covers agriculture.
Services: Offers annual reports, brochures/pamphlets, statistics, newsletter and photos.
How to Contact: Write or call.

Morocco Spotted Horse Co-operative Association of America, Inc., Rt. 1, Ridott IL 61067. (815)449-2659. Secretary Treasurer: Lowell H. Rott.
Purpose: "To register and record pedigrees and ancestries of a specific horse breed and its descendants in several related breed divisions dating as far back as the 1840s in England. We provide the official record of the breeding of these animals and their

ownership. We also provide genetic research data and materials relating to their breeding. We carry some genetic data on livestock diseases and inherited defects in equines." Information covers agriculture and history.

Services: Offers statistics, brochures/pamphlets, information searches on pedigrees, newsletter and photos. Publications include publicity brochures and *Official Rule Book.*

How to Contact: Write or call. "At present we offer material free, unless the request requires extensive research work, photocopies, nonreturnable photos, etc. Here we charge only our actual costs. Our association is strictly volunteer operated, and our budget is strictly break-even right now. Requests that require a lot of research, expense and detailed response will get delayed, or perhaps not be answered at all."

Tips: "Please be specific, giving us detailed questions that can be answered briefly. Questions requiring specific data on the varied activities of members and their operations in this field are just about impossible to answer, as we simply do not require such detailed data to be filed with the business office."

Morris Animal Foundation, 45 Inverness Dr. E., Englewood CO 80112. Executive Director: Claude Ramsey.

Purpose: "Grant-making organization in the area of health of dogs, cats, horses and zoo animals." Information covers animals health and science.

Services: Offers aid in arranging interviews, brochures/pamphlets and information searches. Publications include *Great People Doing Great Things for Animals.*

How to Contact: Write. "If reporting on scientific findings, clear the information with the scientific investigator."

National Association of Animal Breeders, Box 1033, Columbia MO 65205. (314)445-4406. Circulation Manager: Carol Buckley.

Purpose: "The National Association of Animal Breeders (NAAB) is the trade association for the artificial insemination (AI) industry. Our information covers AI and reproductive physiology of beef and dairy cattle, primarily." Information covers agriculture, industry, science and technical data.

Services: Offers statistics about semen sales, brochures/pamphlets and magazine. Publications include *The Advanced Animal Breeder*, magazine published 9 times/year (subscription, $4); *Beef Proceedings*, covering the annual Beef Artificial Insemination Conference ($2); *Annual Convention Proceedings*, covering the annual NAAB convention (50¢); *Technical Proceedings*, covering the biennial Artificial Insemination Technical Conference ($6); *Better Beef With AI* (50¢); *AI Industry of the U.S.A.* (15¢); *Dairy Sire Evaluation in the U.S.A.* (9¢); *Career Opportunities in Artificial Insemination* (free); *Recommended Standards for Health of Bulls Producing Semen for Artificial Insemination* (free); *Recommended Minimum Standards for Training Artificial Insemination Technicians and Herdsman Inseminators* (8¢ and postage); *Beef Artificial Insemination Regulations* (20¢ each; minimum order—$1); *Artificial Insemination Requirements of Members of PDCA* (4¢ and postage); and *CSS Serving the Livestock Industry* (free).

How to Contact: "Write and ask. Prices are subject to change. Most of our material is copyrighted. Written permission must be obtained to use it."

National Board of Fur Farm Organizations, Inc., 3055 N. Brookfield Rd., Brookfield WI 53005. (414)786-4242. Administative Officer: Bruce W. Smith.

Purpose: To educate and inform people about US farm-raised mink and foxes, excluding the promotion and marketing of mink and fox furs. Information covers agriculture, business, celebrities, economics, food, nature and technical data.

Services: Offers aid in arranging interviews, bibliographies, statistics and brochures/pamphlets. Publications include *Mink Farming in the United States* and *Research References on Mink and Foxes.*

How to Contact: Write. "We do not do literature searches or other work which writers themselves can do. Tell us exactly why you want the information and how you propose to use it." Charges $2 ($3 outside of the US) for *Research References on Mink and Foxes.*

National Buffalo Association, Box 706, Custer SD 57720. (605)683-2073. Executive Director: Judi Hebbring.
Purpose: "To promote buffalo and buffalo products; to encourage the raising of buffalo; to distribute information on buffalo breeding, health, etc.; to monitor legislation that affects buffalo and to promote research on buffalo nutrition and immunity to cancer." Information covers business, economics, food, history, how-to and technical data.
Services: Offers brochures/pamphlets and newsletter. Publications include *American Buffalo*, information on the association, a buffalo cookbook ($2) each, and *Buffalo!* (bimonthly magazine).
How to Contact: Write. Charges $7/year for *Buffalo!*.

National Reining Horse Association, 28881 SR 83, Coshocton OH 43812. (614)622-5611. Contact: Secretary.
Purpose: "The National Reining Horse Association is a nonprofit association dedicated to the promotion of the reining horse. The association was formed in 1966 to encourage the showing of reining horses by providing worthwhile purses for which they can compete, by developing a standard method under which all reining contests can be conducted, and by acting as a forum for their breeders and trainers."
Services: Offers newsletter.
How to Contact: Write or call.

North American Police Work Dog Association, 410 W. Locust, Springfield MO 65803. (417)736-3060. President: Richard Warner.
Purpose: "We have a working standard for all police dogs, handlers and trainers and test and certify them through our accreditation program. We provide educational material relating to court decisions, training procedures, budgets, etc." Information covers how-to, law, new produts and technical data.
Services: Offers statistics, brochures/pamphlets and newsletter.
How to Contact: Write or call. "Fees for services are being established." Requires permission of national headquarters to use services.

Palomino Horse Association, Inc., Box 324, Jefferson City MO 65102. (314)635-1923. Secretary/Treasurer: Robert E. Dallmeyer.
Purpose: The registration and promotion of palomino horses.
Services: Offers brochures/pamphlets.
How to Contact: Write. The first copy of any publication is free, but additional copies cost 25¢.

Percheron Horse Association of America, Rt. 1, Belmont OH 43718. (714)782-1624. Seretary: Dale Cossett.
Purpose: "The association was organized for the purpose and with the object of the preservation, recording and certifying of pedigrees of the Percheron Horse and for promoting and maintaining the purity of the Percheron breed." Information covers horse registrations.
Services: Offers brochures/pamphlets. Publications include brochures giving the history and characteristics of the Percheron horse.
How to Contact: Write.

Pet Information Bureau, 666 5th Ave., Suite 1200, New York NY 10019. (212)399-4422. Assistant Director: Joanne Delaney.
Purpose: "We are a consumer service of the American Pet Products Manufacturers Association. We act as a central clearinghouse for consumer information on pets." Information covers pets, statistics, industry trends and pet care.

Services: Offers writers with story lines, backgrounders, releases and photographs. "We can also put the writer in touch with American Pet Products Manufacturers Association spokespersons, members and pet shop owners."
How to Contact: Write or call.

Pony of the Americas Club, Inc., Box 1447, 1452 N. Federal, Mason City IA 50401. (515)424-1586. Executive Secretary: George B. LaLonde.
Purpose: "We are a nonprofit organization involved with a breed of horses developed for youth. We put on horse shows and sales throughout the country. Our office registers horses and keeps their records up to date, puts out a monthly national publication, and keeps track of show points on all Pony of the Americas Club (POA) shows across the country for our several awards programs." Information covers history.
Services: Offers brochures/pamphlets and photos.
How to Contact: Write. "There are no service charges unless more than 200 brochures are requested; we then charge 3¢ a piece after 200. We ask that a credit line be given on photos. As a youth organization, we are not in a position to reimburse writers who do stories for our magazine. They are given full credit for articles."

Society for Animal Rights, Inc., 421 S. State St., Clarks Summit PA 18411. (717)586-2200. President: Helen Jones.
Purpose: "To prevent the exploitation and abuse of animals and to promote the concept of animal rights. We collect, research and disseminate documentary material on the various forms of exploitation and abuse of animals and recommend appropriate action." Information covers animals and their need for protection.
Services: Offers bibliographies, brochures/pamphlets, information searches, placement on mailing list, statistics, newsletter and photos. "We maintain extensive subject files containing documentary material on animals. We also maintain a small but excellent library."
How to Contact: Write or call. "We are listed with the Library of Congress as an information resource and we in turn sometimes call upon the Library of Congress for information."

Texas Longhorn Breeders Association of America, Box 659, San Antonio TX 78293. (512)225-3444. Executive Director: David G. Sweet.
Purpose: "Registration and record maintenance of Texas Longhorn cattle."
Services: Offers aid in arranging interviews, brochures/pamphlets, placement on mailing list and newsletter.
How to Contact: Write or call.

U.S. Trotting Association, Publicity Dept., 750 Michigan Ave., Columbus OH 43215. (614)224-2291. Vice President of Publicity and Public Relations: Donald P. Evans. Publicity Director: Philip Pikelny.
Purpose: "U.S. Trotting Association (USTA) is a breed organization for standardbred horses. It is the rulesmaking and recordkeeping body for the sport of harness racing in the US and Canadian maritimes. The publicity department coordinates all national press and generally anything and everything connected with the sulky sport." Information covers business, celebrities, economics, entertainment, history, industry, rules, recreation, sports, technical data and breeding facts.
Services: Offers aid in arranging interviews, bibliographies, biographies, statistics, brochures/pamphlets, placement on mailing list, regular informational newsletter, photos and press kits. Publications include *Trotting and Pacing Guide*, a statistical publication designed for sportswriters and sportscasters to assist their reporting; *Harness Handbook*, biographies and statistics on the sport's leading horses and horsemen; *Hoof Beats*, a monthly magazine of USTA featuring information pieces to industry and feature ideas for writers; *Year Book*; *Sires and Dams Book*; and *Microfiche Stats*, industry publications listing racing and breeding performances.

How to Contact: Write or call. "Requests must be of a specific nature; we are not interested in fishing expeditions. Information is free except for large orders for photos; these are filled at cost."

Wyandotte Bantam Club of America, Box 100, 10 Lincolnway W., New Oxford PA 17350. (717)624-2347. Secretary-Treasurer: W.L. "Bill" Zeigler.
Purpose: "Members breed Wyandotte bantams, and attend club shows and meets."
Services: Offers placement on mailing list. Publications include quarterly newsletter and yearbook.
How to Contact: Write or call. "We would be glad to answer any questions or give any specific information at any time."

The Arts

American Council for the Arts, 570 7th Ave., New York NY 10018. (212)354-6655. Contact: Katharine Hoblitzelle.
Purpose: "American Council for the Arts (ACA), a nonprofit membership organization that functions as a national spokesman for the arts and as a service organization, addressing the management and policy needs of all the arts. Through its Washington office, ACA monitors developments at the federal level that affect artists and nonprofit cultural organizations." Information covers art, business and politics "as they apply to arts management and policy making."
Services: Offers annual reports, statistics, placement on press mailing list and regular informational newsletter. "ACA's news publication, *ACA Reports*, is a benefit of membership and is issued ten times a year. Other ACA services include books and informational packets, technical assistance, a research library and at least six management training or issue-oriented seminars/conferences a year. ACA publishes a variety of books, such as *A Guide to Corporate Giving in the Arts, Local Government and the Arts, Issues in Public Policy and the Arts: A Summary of Hearings on a White House Conference on the Arts* and *Americans and the Arts: A Louis Harris Opinion Poll*. These serve as resources for researchers, writers and members of the press. ACA conducts statistical research on such topics as state legislative appropriations for the arts, United Fund-raising for the arts, art administrators' salaries and benefits, etc."
How to Contact: "Call or write ACA. At the discretion of the publicity director, someone may be added to ACA's news release list at no cost. The published results of ACA statistical research are sometimes free and sometimes priced at $5 or less."

American Theatre Association, 1000 Vermont Ave. NW, Washington DC 20005. (202)628-4634. Director of Publication: Roxanne Rhodes.
Purpose: "The American Theatre Association is a nonprofit association that brings together individuals and organizations with an interest in and a concern for the growth and development of noncommercial theater."
Services: Offers aid in arranging interviews, brochures/pamphlets and newsletter. Publications include annual directory of colleges with theater programs and four magazines, *Theatre New, Theatre Journal, Children's Theatre Review* and *Secondary School Theatre Journal*.
How to Contact: Write or call. "We prefer written requests for detailed information." Charges for publications.

Canadian Conference of the Arts, 3 Church St., Suite 47, Toronto, Ontario, Canada M5E 1M2. (416)364-6351. Executive Director: John Hobday.
Purpose: "We are a nonprofit national association linking together over 400 organizations as well as over 700 artists and arts supporters from across Canada. Established in 1945, Canadian Conference of the Arts' (CCA) objectives are to promote public interest and concern for the arts; to foster a sense of community within the arts; to encourage cultural policies and programs and to ensure adequate levels of support for the arts.

Individual membership is available for $20 and organizational for $35, $75 and $100."
Information covers art, entertainment and music.
Services: Offers brochures/pamphlets, placement on mailing list, newsletter, reports,
and studies. Publications include *Arts Bulletin*, reports on a wide variety of arts
subjects (arts and municipalities, arts and education, etc.) and a series of handbooks
(*Who We Are*, *Who's Who* and *Who's Got the Money?*).
How to Contact: Write or call. "Minimal fees are charged to cover the cost of photocopying or printing report. Back issues of *Arts Bulletin* are available for $2.50. Hand-
books vary in price—approximately $3 each. We insist on payment in advance for all
reports, handbooks and bulletins."

The Crayon, Water Color and Craft Institute, Inc., 60 Rock Harbor Rd., Orleans MA
02653.
Purpose: Information covers art and health/medicine.
Services: Offers brochures/pamphlets.
How to Contact: Write.

International Foundation for Art Research, Inc., 46 E. 70th St., New York NY 10021.
Executive Director: Bonnie Burnham.
Purpose: "We examine works of art to determine authenticity and maintain an index of
stolen works and files on art forgeries." Information covers art.
Services: Offers statistics, brochures/pamphlets, placement on mailing list and newsletter; also "an archive of clippings and news items on the subjects we research. Our
publications include an annual index of stolen art, a monthly newsletter, a detailed
report on art theft, and reports on the specific works we have examined."
How to Contact: Write.

National Association of Women Artists, 41 Union Square W., New York NY 10003.
(212)675-1616. Secretary: Connie Costa.
Purpose: "To give professional women artists the opportunity to exhibit their works in
creditable shows." Information covers art.
Services: Offers brochures/pamphlets. Publications include synopsis of the
organization's services and purpose.
How to Contact: Write or call.

The New Dramatists, 424 W. 44th St., New York NY 10036. (212)757-6960. Executive
Director: Kathleen Norris.
Purpose: "To facilitate the development of writers for the theater through a series of
programs." Information covers art.
Services: Offers annual reports, brochures/pamphlets, placement on mailing list and
newsletter.
How to Contact: Write. "Most services are available to members only."

The Religious Arts Guild, 25 Beacon St., Boston MA 02108. (617)742-2100. Executive
Secretary: Barbara M. Hutchins.
Purpose: "To create and foster interest in the fine arts within the life of churches; to
increase appreciation of beauty in the lives of religious people and to provide materials
and resource contacts in all the arts for liberal churches." Affiliate of the Unitarian
Universalist Association. Information covers art, music and architecture.
Services: Offers brochures/pamphlets. Publications include an awards folder describing three biannual competitions in poetry, playwriting and service; a catalog listing
loan anthems; resources listing of worship services; and a listing of Unitarian Universalist performing artists.
How to Contact: Write.

Southern Humanities Conference, c/o Dennis Hall, University of Louisville, Department of English, Louisville KY 40208. President: Donald Kay.

Purpose: "To further the humanities; to increase and develop public and professional interests in the humanities; to preserve and protect those aspects of the humanities often neglected; and to act as liaison between the humanities and businesses."
Services: Offers newsletter. Publications include *Southern Humanities Review* (quarterly) and *Humanities in the South* (semiannual). (The latter publication is available from the Center for the Humanities, Converse College, Spartanburg SC 29301.)
How to Contact: Write.

Theatre Communications Group, Inc. (TCG), 355 Lexington Ave., New York NY 10017. (212)697-5230. Associate Director: Lindy Zesch.
Purpose: "Theatre Communications Group (TGG) is the national service organization for the noncommercial professional theatre, established to provide a national forum and communications network for the profession and to respond to the needs of its constituents for a variety of artistic, administrative and informational programs and services aimed specifically at assisting noncommercial professional theater organizations, professional theater training institutions and individual theater artists, administrators and technicians. TCG also acts as the central national clearing house of information about the nonprofit professional theaters and publishes a number of theater publications. TCG's goal is to encourage thoughtful coverage of the noncommercial professional theater field nationwide in order to raise the consciousness of the American people about the revolution that has occurred in the theater in the past 10 to 20 years."
Services: Offers aid in arranging interviews, annual reports, bibliographies, statistics, brochures/pamphlets, information searches, placement on mailing list, newsletter and photos. "Publications include a guide to theater nationwide and an annual financial and statistical survey of approximately 150 to 160 theater institutions. We also offer advice, consultation and information."
How to Contact: Write or call. "Information is free. There is a charge for purchase of some publications. Our ability to fulfill requests for information depends on the nature of the request, the amount of lead time allowed, the availability of the required information and the importance of the story and coverage to the nonprofit professional theater. TCG does not have available information on the commercial theater or the purely avocational theater. Try to identify the universe of theaters you are interested in writing about—the field is incredibly diverse."

Wolf Trap Farm Park for the Performing Arts, 1624 Trap Rd., Vienna VA 22180. (703)938-3810. Associate Director, Office of Public Affairs: Larisa Wanserski.
Purpose: "Wolf Trap Foundation operates to provide the Wolf Trap Farm Park for the Performing Arts, which is maintained by the park service, with performances in opera, symphony, jazz, pop, ballet, musicals, country and western, and bluegrass during the summer months (June through August)." Information covers art, celebrities, history, music, nature, recreation, technical information and education in the performing arts programs.
Services: Offers aid in arranging interviews, brochures/pamphlets, biographies, placement on mailing list, photos and press kits.
How to Contact: Write or call. Writers desiring to tour the Filene Center Theater at Wolf Trap or interview performers should first contact the Office of Public Affairs.

Automobile

Action for Child Transportation Safety, Box 266, Bothell WA 98011. (206)522-4766. Chairman: Deborah Richards.
Purpose: "Action for Child Transportation Safety (ACTS) is an organization of citizens, health, and safety educators and administrators dedicated to educating the public about the need for child safety restraints to protect young children in automobiles, and working to upgrade school bus transportation safety levels. It is entirely

member supported, and was the first citizens' group to specifically devote itself to these aspects of highway safety." Information covers health/medicine and travel.
Services: Offers brochures/pamphlets and newsletter. Publications available.
How to Contact: Write. Enclose SASE. Charges for publications and other specific materials (order form on request).

Automotive Information Council, 18850 Telegraph Rd., Southfield MI 48034. (313)358-0290. Contact: Library.
Purpose: "The Automotive Information Council is a voice for the motor vehicle industry. Its business is information—both to collect pertinent information from other sources, and more importantly to digest, analyze and disseminate this information in useful form. It is our purpose to provide useful information that will help people in government, in all forms of media and in education. Our purpose, simply, is to create and sustain an image of honesty, reliability, quality and fair play where automotive products and services are concerned." Information covers automotive subjects.
Services: Offers aid in arranging interviews, bibliographies and statistics. Publications include *The Automotive Information Council*.
How to Contact: "Write or, if a simple question, call. Ask for specific information, not 'Send me the material you have on the automobile.' " Charges "if request requires that we bring in an outside researcher."

Cadillac Convertible Owners of America, Inc., Box 920, Thiells NY 10984. (914)947-1109. President: James Brachfeld.
Purpose: "To promote consumer interest in the Cadillac convertible, especially since the 1976 model is the last domestic convertible produced, and to share our interest with owners of Cadillac convertibles." Information covers economics (price of car), entertainment (use of car), new products and travel.
Services: Offers aid in arranging interviews, annual reports, statistics, newsletters and photos. Publications include a quarterly magazine.
How to Contact: Write.

Motorists Information, Inc., 519 New Center Bldg., Detroit MI 48202. (313)872-4242. Executive Director: Robert M. Hanson.
Purpose: "To conduct informational and educational programs on issues of interest to the motoring public, such as safety belts." Information covers auto issues for the public.
Services: Offers aid in arranging interviews and brochures/pamphlets. "We also have reports and results on campaigns, and information on issues addressed by companies." Publications include *Program Summary Report* (results of safety belt advertising campaign) and a brochure on safety items.
How to Contact: Write or call.

National Automobile Dealers Association, 8400 Westpark Dr., McLean WV 22102. (703)821-7100.
Purpose: "To facilitate and represent dealers." Information covers economics, industry, law, new product information, politics, self-help and technical information.
Services: Offers aid in arranging interviews, brochures/pamphlets, information searches, placement on mailing list and newsletter. Publications include *Your Career in Retailing*.
How to Contact: Write or call.

National Automobile Theft Bureau, PR Dept., 390 N. Broadway, Jericho NY 11753. (516)935-7272. Director of Public Relations: Alan J. Herbert.
Purpose: "The National Automobile Theft Bureau (NATB) assists in the location of stolen vehicles and investigates auto fire and theft losses which may be fraudulent. It maintains a computerized record system which aids law enforcement agencies and the insurance industry, and it promotes programs to prevent or reduce auto theft losses."

Information covers business, law and self-help.
Services: Offers aid in arranging interviews, annual reports, statistics, brochures/ pamphlets, placement on mailing list, newsletter and press kits. Publications include annual report and *Your Car Could Be Stolen This Year.*
How to Contact: Call or write.

Broadcasting

Action for Children's Television, 46 Austin St., Newtonville MA 02146. (617)527-7870. Editorial Director: Maureen Harmonay.
Purpose: "Action for Children's Television is a nonprofit consumer organization which works to increase diversity and eliminate commercial abuses for chidren's television." Information covers health/medicine.
Services: Offers aid in arranging interviews, biographies, brochures/pamphlets, clipping services, placement on mailing list, statistics and newsletter. Publications available.
How to Contact: Write or call.

American Council for Better Broadcasts, 120 E. Wilson St., Madison WI 53703. (608)257-7712. Executive Director: Marieli Rowe.
Purpose: "To promote quality programming in broadcasting via educational means to help the teaching of critical viewing." Information covers broadcasting.
Services: Offers brochures/pamphlets and newsletter. "We also participate in annual look-listen opinion polls." Publications available.
How to Contact: Write or call. Charges for some publications. "We will not write a student's paper for him/her and we will not do his/her research. However, we can often suggest resources where the needed material can be found and can supply addresses."

National Association of Broadcasters, 1771 N St. NW, Washington DC 20036. (202)293-3520. Secretary/Treasurer: Michael Harwood.
Purpose: The National Association of Broadcasters (NAB) represents radio and television stations and networks, and is involved in program and advertising codes and legislation affecting broadcasters.
How to Contact: Write.

National Academy of Television Arts & Sciences, Inc., 110 W. 57th St., New York NY 10019.

National Citizens Committee for Broadcasting, 1028 Connecticut Ave. NW, Washington DC 20036. (202)466-8407. Director: Sam Simon.
Purpose: "Media reform, especially broadcasting and telecommunications." Information covers art, entertainment, law, music and politics.
Services: Offers aid in arranging interviews, brochures/pamphlets, placement on mailing list, statistics and newsletter. Publications price list available.
How to Contact: Write or call.

National Association of Educational Broadcasters, 1346 Connecticut Ave. NW, Washington DC 20036. (202)785-1100. Assistant to the President: Wayne Jackson. Director of Marketing and Development: Lori Evans.
Purpose: "The National Association of Educational Broadcasters (NAEB) is the only professional association of individuals either employed in, or seeking to further the growth of public and educational telecommunications. The goal of the NAEB is to promote and maintain a high quality of professionalism and to foster new ideas by

facilitating formal and informal professional communication and education." Information covers any material relating to public or educational telecommunications.
Services: Offers newsletter. Publications include bimonthly magazine, professional training and development seminars (EBI), job/personnel matching and referral service (PACT), and a directory listing (NAEB) members in all fields of public/education telecommunications.
How to Contact: Write or call. "If the NAEB cannot provide the informtion required, we can usually rcommend someone who can provide it." Charges $35/year for membership, "but it is not necessary to be a member to take advantage of the other services." Charges $10/directory for nonmembers; $18/*Public Telecommunications Review*.

National Citizens Communications Lobby, Box 19101, Washington DC 20036. Executive Director: Townes L. Osborn.
Purpose: "The National Citizens Communications Lobby (NCCL) ensures that the public interests in media are represented before Congress and government agencies. Such interests include communications legislation in Congress and the issues of children's televison, public affairs programming, the Fairness Doctrine, cable television, minority ownership and employment, and others." Information covers industry, law, politics and self-help
Services: Offers aid in arranging interviews, brochures/pamphlets, placement on mailing list and newsletter. Publications include articles, commentaries and legislative briefings.
How to Contact: Write.

Telocator Network of America, 2301 E St. NW, Washington DC 20036. (202)659-6446. Editor/Publisher: Alan Arthur Reiter.
Purpose: "The Telocator Network of America (TNA) is the national association of Radio Common Carriers (RCCs). RCCs provide radiotelephone (car), portable telephone and pager (beeper) service to thousands of individuals and companies across the country. TNA promotes land mobile communications through its *Telocator* magazine, news *Bulletin*, and *Filings & Grants* license fact sheet. We sponsor three regional meetings and one national convention every year where hundreds of people interested in communications gather for seminars and exhibitions." Information covers business, new products, science, technical data and FCC regulations and communications information.
Services: Offers annual reports, biographies, statistics, brochures/pamphlets, placement on mailing list and newsletter. Publications available.
How to Contact: Write or call. Charges for membership and some publications. "There are no restrictions, however, the researcher usually visits our offices to obtain the information since our function is not primarily as a research organization."

Business Administration & Management

American Society for Personnel Administration, 30 Park Dr., Berea OH 44017. (216)826-4790. Director, Communications: Ray Vladar.
Purpose: "To provide international leadership in establishing and supporting standards of excellence in the personnel administration/industrial relations profession. Through publications, professional development seminars, problem-solving channels, conferences, Washington representation and sponsored research, the society works with its members to improve the quality of human resource management." Information covers new developments and legislation affecting personnel administration/industrial relations.
Services: Offers aid in arranging interviews, bibliographies, statistics and placement on mailing list. Publications are available.
How to Contact: "Write or call the office with reference to a specific area of interest and appropriate direction will be provided." Charges for some materials.

Association of Executive Recruiting Consultants, 30 Rockefeller Plaza, New York NY 10020. (212)541-7580. Executive Director: John F. Schlueter.
Purpose: "We are the only association of the kind in the world comprising the leading executive recruiting firms, large and small. Members work solely for client companies to locate executives in the $25,000 and higher salary range. Resumes from individuals seeking executive employment are accepted by Association of Executive Recruiting Consultants (AERC) members, but there is no guarantee of employment as the firms never work for individuals seeking employment. AERC provides a list, brochure and code of ethics to anyone." Information covers business.
Services: Offers statistics, brochures/pamphlets, placement on mailing list, and a list of member firms. Publications include *A Company's Guide to Executive Recruiting*, the AERC code of ethics and professional practice guidelines.
How to Contact: Write or call.

Association for Systems Management, 24587 Bagley Rd., Cleveland OH 44138. Technical Director: R.B. McCaffrey.
Purpose: "We are the one professional association serving the business systems field, i.e., office and paperwork management." Information covers business.
Services: Offers statistics and information searches. Publications include "a monthly journal and 35 publications in the field."
How to Contact: Write.

The Cooperative League of the USA, Suite 1100, 1828 L St. NW, Washington DC 20036. (202)872-0550. Director of Public Affairs: S.E. Southard.
Purpose: "The league is a national federation of all types of customer-owned businesses. It is the US member of International Cooperative Alliance." Information covers agriculture, business, food and health/medicine.
Services: Offers cooperative news service for co-op publications. Publications include publications list.
How to Contact: Write.

International Entrepreneurs' Association, 631 Wilshire Blvd., Santa Monica CA 90401. (213)394-3787. Vice President, Communications: Ron Tepper.
Purpose: "We provide in-depth start-up information on new and unique small businesses and conduct monthly seminars on same." Information covers business, how-to, and new products.
Services: Offers biographies, photos and press kits. Publications include magazine and 140 how-to manuals on business.
How to Contact: Write. "We charge consumers for our service."

International Executives Association, 122 E. 42nd St., Suite 1014, New York NY 10017. (212)661-4610. Contact: Mildred Herschler.
Services: Offers aid in arranging interviews, statistics, brochures/pamphlets and press releases for special events. Publications include *Sale Executive*.
How to Contact: "Written request from editor or writer. Interviews must be reviewed before being granted." Charges $15/year for nonmembers and $5/year for members for *Sale Executive*.

Medical Group Management Association, 4101 E. Louisiana Ave., Denver CO 80222. (303)753-1111. Associate Director: Fred E. Graham II.
Purpose: "To improve management in medical groups, thereby serving members of the association, the organizations they represent, the patients they serve, and the group practice of medicine." Information covers business, economics, health/medicine, how-to, law, new products, politics and technical data.
Services: Offers bibliographies, statistics, brochures/pamphlets, information searches and newsletter. Publications include a bimonthly journal. "A publications list is available upon request, as is a 'guidelines' information sheet for those interested in

writing articles for our journal."
How to Contact: Write or call the Medical Group Management Association Library Reference Service. Charge depends on amount and type of service required. "Be specific in stating request for assistance."

Meeting Planners International, 3201 Barbara Dr., Middletown OH 45042. (513)424-6827. Manager, Communications: James L. Horvath.
Purpose: Meeting Planners International (MPI) is an educational association serving all who plan meetings and those who supply goods and services to the planner. We conduct national conferences, seminars and training sessions for those engaged in producing meetings in business, industry, government and the private sector— unions, trade associations, societies, etc."
Services: Offers biographies, statistics, brochures/pamphlets and newsletter. Publications include *Tax Facts for Meeting Planners*, *Tipping and Gratuities*, *Convention Checklist and Meeting Plan*, *Hotel Negotiations*, *Group Travel*, membership brochure and application, trade journal reprints as available, and copies of monthly newsletter as available. Membership directory is available to MPI members only.
How to Contact: Write or call. "With a limited staff capability we must be the judges in granting time if the request comes at a time when we are busy. Phone or personal interviews must be cleared through the MPI." Charges $2 for some publications.

National Association of Church Business Administrators, Box 7181, Kansas City MO 64113. (913)236-9571. Executive Director: Floyd Barnes.
Purpose: "To extend the kingdom of God through a program of study, service, fellowship, exchange of information and problem discussion." Information covers matters pertaining to the management of the business of the church or religious institution.
Services: Offers brochures/pamphlets and newsletter to members.
How to Contact: Write or call.

National Small Business Association, 1604 K St. NW, Washington DC 20006. (202)296-7400. Communications Coordinator: David Kramarsky.
Purpose: "To communicate with the federal government on issues affecting small business and to advance and protect small businesses." Information covers business, economics, law, politics and technical data.
Services: Offers aid in arranging interviews, statistics, placement on mailing list, newsletter and photos.
How to Contact: Write or call.

Office Technology Research Group, c/o Simon Public Relations, 11661 San Vicente, Suite 903, Los Angeles CA 90049. (213)820-2606. Account Executive: Frank L. Pollare.
Purpose: "Office Technology Research Group (OTRG) is a national association of corporate executives interested in staying abreast of, understanding the ramifications of, and implementing 'office of the future' developments into their company's operations. The office of the future concept, also known as office automation, is an area of growing concern for executives, especially in the light of developing office technologies/systems." Information covers business.
Services: Offers aid in arranging interviews, biographies, statistics, placement on mailing list, newsletter, photos and press kits. "Our material covers an executive's view on future office operations from an overview perspective, not as a how-to approach." Publications include brochure on capabilities.
How to Contact: Write or call.

SCORE—Service Corps of Retired Executives, 1441 L St. NW, Room 100, Washington DC 20416. (202)653-6725. Director of Public Relations: Bryson Randolph.
Purpose: "SCORE is an organization of more than 8,200 business executive volunteers who offer free business management counseling to the American small business community. SCORE is sponsored by the Small Business Administration. SCORE also

offers pre-business workshops and problem clinics covering the major fundamental aspects of business—marketing and advertising, planning, merchandising, accounting, legal considerations, business insurance and taxes." Information covers business.
Services: Offers aid in arranging interviews, statistics and brochures/pamphlets. Publications include "free publications on nearly ever subject of business management and operation."
How to Contact: "Contact the SCORE organization in your local area, or write the Washington office. SCORE can't undertake any research projects, but will endeavor to supply answers to specific questions."

Small Business Legislative Council, 1604 K St. NW, Washington DC 20006. (202)296-7400. Communications Coordinator: David Kramarsky.
Purpose: "To communicate with the federal government on issues affecting small business and to advance and protect small businesses." Information covers business, economics, law, politics and technical data.
Services: Offers aid in arranging interviews, statistics, placement on mailing list, newsletter and photos.
How to Contact: Write or call.

Colleges & Universities

American Association of University Professors (AAUP), 1 Dupont Circle, Suite 500, Washington DC 20036. (202)466-8050. Director of Communication: James Trulove.
Purpose: "The American Association of University Professors is an association of college and university teachers, graduate students, college presidents and deans. We promote academic freedom and tenure and sound institutional government, and we represent faculty as a bargaining agent." Information covers economics.
Services: Offers annual reports, statistics, brochures/pamphlets, placement on mailing list and news releases. Publications include *Academe* (published 8 times/year).
How to Contact: Write or call.

Association for the Coordination of University Religious Affairs, Box 5118, Southern Station, Hattiesburg MS 39401. (601)266-7139. President: Dr. Graham Hales.
Purpose: "Organization of religious affairs administrators in higher education. The work of the Association for the Coordination of University Religious Affairs (ACURA) includes professional conferences and study sessions to apprise its members and others of current developments in religious affairs and student development. It serves as a liaison and conducts activities in conjunction with the major professional associations engaged in religious affairs, and also those in student personnel work. ACURA works as a consultant with colleges and universities, especially those seeking to redesign the institutional form of religious presence on campus." Information covers religion.
Services: Offers brochures/pamphlets and newsletter. Publications include *Dialogue on Campus* (quarterly newsletter) and *The Public University and Religious Practice: an Inquiry Into University Provision for Campus Religious Life*.
How to Contact: Write. Charges "for cost of materials only."

Association of College Honor Societies, 1411 Lafayette Pkwy., Williamsport PA 17701. (717)323-7641. Executive Secretary: Dr. Dorothy I. Mitstifer.
Purpose: "Coordinating agency for college and university honor societies. Provides facilities for the consideration of matters of mutual interest, defines honor societies and classifies existing societies, and assists college administrators in maintaining standards and useful functions." Information covers description of member societies and minimum requirements for members.

Services: Offers brochures/pamphlets. Publications include *ACHS Booklet of Informa-tion.*
How to Contact: Write.

College Sports Information Directors of America (CoSIDA), c/o Don Kopriva, Univer-sity of Wisconsin—Parkside, Kenosha WI 53141. (414)553-2404. Secretary: Don Ko-priva.
Purpose: "College Sports Information Directors of America (CoSIDA) was founded in 1975. Previously, sports information directors as a group were a part of the American College Public Relations Association, but most SIDs at those ACPRA meetings felt that a separate organization was needed. There were 102 members at the original meeting; since that time, CoSIDA has grown to nearly 700 members in the United States and Canada. Our association is designed to help the SID at all three NCAA and both NAIA levels. We want our profession to take its rightful place on the decision-making levels of college athletics. Everything we do is geared to this objective." Information covers college sports publicity and promotion.
Services: Offers newsletter. Publications include CoSIDA telephone directory of col-lege sports publicity directors and *CoSIDA Digest*, a newsletter.
How to Contact: Write. Charges $10/subscription to *CoSIDA Digest*, $3/copy of *CoSIDA Directory*.

United States Student Association, 1028 Connecticut Ave. NW, Suite 300, Washing-ton DC 20036. (202)667-6000. Director of Communications: Julie Brooks.
Purpose: "The United States Student Association (USSA) is the only nationally and internationally recognized representative of college and university students in the US. Representing students in all 50 states through 360 student government members, we lobby on issues such as federal financial aid, department of education, affirmative action and abortion rights, on Capitol Hill and at the White House. Our information service collects data on 100 subjects from collective bargaining to drug abuse and student fees." Information covers history, how-to, law, politics, self-help, technical data and higher education.
Services: Offers annual reports, statistics, brochures/pamphlets, information searches, placement on mailing list, newsletter, photos, press kits, press releases, "legislative alerts," mailing lists, conferences and conventions, and manuals. Publications in-clude *Student Fee Law Reporter, Sub-Minimum Wage and College—Work Study Stu-dents, Proposition 13 and Its Effects on Higher Education, CIA on Campus, Mandatory Fees and Student Rights."
How to Contact: Write or call. Charges for publications, mailing lists, conference registration, copying costs and postage. "We prefer that freelance writers tell us where stories are going to be published. Our archives materials on 32 years of student association history is restricted and requires USSA permission for reporters or resear-chers to look at documents."
Tips: "We always have a million potential leads and stories for interested reporters on subjects as vast as South Africa and financial aid."

University and College Placement Association, 133 Richmond St. W., Suite 303, Toronto, Ontario, Canada M5H 2L3. (416)862-1837. Executive Director: Wayne Gartley.
Purpose: "To promote selection of courses and careers based on interests, abilities and knowledge of the labor market (supply and demand). Services and activities support job functions of members—career planning and placement officers at Canadian col-leges and universities as well as employers of post-secondary graduates." Information covers "career planning, placement and recruitment of post-secondary graduates in Canada."
Services: Offers aid in arranging interviews, annual reports, bibliographies, statistics, brochures/pamphlets, clipping services, information searches, placement on mailing

list, newsletter, photos and press kits.
How to Contact: Write or call. "Have a specific request."

Consumer

Consumers' Association of Canada, Suite 100, 200 1st Ave., Ottawa, Ontario, Canada
K1S 5J3. (613)233-9383, 233-4840. Director of Testing and Publications: Cam Sec-
combe.
Purpose: "We test consumer products and publish results in *Canadian Consumer*
magazine." Information covers agriculture, business, economics, food, health/
medicine, industry, law and self-help.
Services: Offers aid in arranging interviews, bibliographies, brochures/pamphlets,
placement on mailing list and newsletter.
How to Contact: Write or call.

Consumer Federation of America, 1012 14th St. NW, #901, Washington DC 20005.
(202)737-3732. Executive Director: Kathleen F. O'Reilly.
Purpose: "Consumer Federation of America is a nonprofit public interest organization." Information covers agriculture, business, food, health/medicine, law, new products, politics and technical data.
Services: Offers annual reports, biographies, brochures/pamphlets, clipping services,
information searches, placement on mailing list, newsletter and photos.
How to Contact: Write or call.

Consumers Union, 256 Washington St., Mt. Vernon NY 10550. Contact: Office of
Public Information.
Purpose: "To provide consumers with information and counsel on consumer goods
and services, to give information on all matters relating to the expenditure of the
family income, and to initiate and cooperate with individuals and group efforts
seeking to create and maintain decent living standards." Information covers business,
economics, entertainment, food, health/medicine, industry, law, new products and
self-help.
Services: Offers publications.
How to Contact: Write. Charges for publications and books. "Because of all the
incredible number of unsolicited requests for information from all sectors of the
domestic and international media, resources are severly strained. Therefore, we will
do our best to try to help only writers who can verify that they are on a definite
assignment. Please do your homework before you write us."

Education

American Montessori Society, 150 5th Ave., New York NY 10011. (212)924-3209.
National Director: Bretta Weiss. Assistant: Judith Delman.
Purpose: "A national, nonprofit, nondiscriminatory, tax-exempt organization dedicated to promoting better education for all children through teaching strategies consistent with the Montessori system, and the incorporation of the Montessori approach
into the framework of education." Information covers early childhood and elementary
education.
Services: Offers aid in arranging interviews, annual reports, bibliographies, biographies, statistics, brochures/pamphlets, information searches and photos. Publications include *Montessori Education*; *Montessori Philosophy*; *Basic Characteristics of
a Montessori Program*; "The Montessori Infant," reprint from *American Baby Magazine*; "What is the Montessori Method," reprint from *Town and Country*; and "Make
Mine Montessori" and "Big on Promises, Short on Delivery," reprints from *Parents*

Magazine.
How to Contact: Write or call. "Give specifics on the nature of the kind of writing you do. Written requests should be accompanied by a 6x9 envelope and $1 to cover mailing costs. Any specific bulletins cost 65¢ presently. Costs of photostating any additional materials must be paid. We should like to check for accuracy any articles for which we have supplied data and assistance."

Association of American Library Schools, Inc., 471 Park Lane, State College PA 16801. (814)238-0254. Executive Secretary: Janet Phillips.
Purpose: "To promote excellence in education for library and information science as a means of increasing the effectiveness of library and information service; to provide a forum for the active interchange of ideas and information among library educators; to promote research related to teaching and to library and information science; to formulate and promulgate positions on matters related to library and information science education; and to cooperate with other organizations in matters of mutual interest." Information covers library science education.
Services: Offers statistics and information searches. "We provide on-line searches of the Association of American Library Schools (AALS) Dissertations in Progress computerized data base, and offer research grants in the area of library and information science education." Publications include *Journal of Education for Librarianship* ($12 annually) and an annual directory listing of AALS members and the faculty (and their specialties) in institutional member schools.
How to Contact: Write or call.

Canadian Association of Schools of Social Work, 151 Slater St., Ottawa, Ontario, Canada K1P 5H3. (613)563-3554. Executive Director: Dennis Kimberley.
Purpose: "We provide coordination and consultation assistance in facilitating the development of, and ensuring the ongoing improvement of, social work education in Canada."
Services: Offers brochures/pamphlets, and newsletters.
How to Contact: Write or call.

College and University Personnel Association, 11 Dupont Circle, Suite 120, Washington DC 20036. (202)462-1038. Executive Director: Frank Mensel.
Purpose: "Professional organization for human resources management in colleges and universities." Information covers human resources and personnel management.
Services: Offers bibliographies, brochures/pamphlets, placement on mailing list, statistics (salary and wages) and newsletter.
How to Contact: Write or call.

Conference of Executives for American Schools for the Deaf/Convention of American Instructors for the Deaf, 5034 Wisconsin Ave. NW, Suite 11, Washington DC 20016. (202)363-1327. Executive Director: Hubert D. Summers.
Purpose: "This is the national office for the Conference of Executives for American Schools for the Deaf (CEASD) and the Convention of American Instructors for the Deaf. This office also houses the publishing offices of the *American Annals for the Deaf*, a bimonthly educational journal for the deaf." Information covers technical data and deaf education.
Services: Offers bibliographies, statistics and brochures/pamphlets. Publications include bibliographies and *American Annals for the Deaf*. "The April issue of the *Annals* gives a compehensive listing of statistics, schools, programs, clinics, members, etc. as relating to deaf education."
How to Contact: Write or call. "Some services have a fee connected with request. Public information requests are generally handled free of charge and referrals are often made."

End Violence Against the Next Generation, Inc. 977 Keeler Ave., Berkeley CA 94708. (415)527-0454. Executive Director: Adah Maurer.
Purpose: "To abolish corporal punishment in schools and institutions that educate or care for children. Our newsletter covers legal cases, local regulations, protests of parents, opinion, attitude surveys, nostalgia, book reviews, etc. concerning physical punishments in schools and suggests local actions that can mitigate the damage." Information covers health/medicine, law, technical data and education.
Services: Offers bibliographies, statistics, brochures/pamphlets and newsletter.
How to Contact: Write or call.

Forum for the Advancement of Students in Science and Technology, 2030 M St., NW, Suite 402, Washington DC 20036. (202)466-3860. President: Alan Ladwig. Program Director: Leonard David.
Purpose: "The forum is a national network of organizations and individuals working to increase student opportunities in the discussion of science and technology issues. We serve individual students with science education materials and serve organizations as a clearinghouse for student opportunities." Information covers industry, science and technical data.
Services: Offers aid in arranging interviews, bibliographies, information searches, placement on mailing list and newsletters. "We also sponsor conferences and conduct studies." Publications include a news magazine (quarterly) and press releases (to campus and educational publications).
How to Contact: Write or call. Charges $10/year for subscription to *FASST NEWS*. News service is free to writers who subscribe to the *News*. Other charges depend upon nature of request and cost to the forum to relay information to the writer. "The forum is interested in receiving increased visibility and identification as a source for science information and programs for students. We will go to great lengths to cooperate with writers and help them with information searches, if they will give the forum appropriate credit and recognition. While the forum has an extensive library of science information, there is no card catalog system for retrieval. Searches will take a little longer than at a regular library,"

International Reading Association, 800 Barksdale Rd., Box 8139, Newark DE 19711. (302)731-1600. Public Information Officer: Drew Cassidy.
Purpose: "The International Reading Association has three general goals: to improve the quality of reading instruction through the study of the reading process and teaching techniques; to promote the lifetime reading habit and an awareness among all people of the impact of reading; and to promote the development of every reader's proficiency to the highest possible level." Information covers reading and education.
Services: Offers aid in arranging interviews, annual reports, statistics, brochures/ pamphlets, placement on mailing list, newsletter and press kits.
How to Contact: Write or call.

Kentucky Education Association, 101 W. Walnut St., Louisville KY 40202. (502)582-2273. Director of Public Relations and Research: Charles Whaley.
Purpose: "We are a membership organization of Kentucky teachers, mostly in public schools, organized for the purpose of improving public education and speaking for the members of the teaching profession." Information covers education.
Services: Offers statistics and brochures/pamphlets. Publications include *How Kentucky Ranks, Salary Schedules of Kentucky Public School Teachers,* and occasional reports.
How to Contact: Write.

National Affiliation for Literacy Advance (NALA), 1320 Jamesville Ave., Box 131, Syracuse NY 13210. (315)422-9121. Executive Secretry: Adelaide L. Silvia.
Purpose: "The National Affiliation for Literacy Advance is a membership organization of Laubach Literacy International, and exists to promote and coordinate volunteer

literacy programs for adults and undereducated teenagers throughout the United States and Canada. Certified trainers offer programs to help communities meet the literacy needs of undereducated teenagers and adults on a one-to-one or small-group basis. Training is offered in three workshop formats, each based on the Laubach principles of teaching." Information covers how-to, self-help and literacy.
Services: Offers annual reports, bibliographies, biographies, statistics, brochures/pamphlets, newsletter and press kits. Also gives "aid in contacting tutors and trainers in a network of programs for literacy in the United States and Canada." Publications include publications catalog, member directory, Literacy Advance and News for You (newspapers), and The Laubach Way to English.
How to Contact: Write or call.

National Association of Independent Schools (NAIS), 4 Liberty Square, Boston MA 02109. (617)542-1988. Director of Public Information: Thomas E. Wilcox.
Purpose: "The National Association of Independent Schools is a nonprofit, tax-exempt, voluntary membership organization which serves over 825 independent schools in the United States and abroad, as well as some 60 local, state, regional and special-purpose associations of independent schools." Information covers education.
Services: Offers aid in arranging interviews, annual reports, bibliographies, biographies, statistics, brochures/pamphlets, information searches, placement on mailing list and regular NAIS publications.
How to Contact: Write or call.

National Association for Creative Children and Adults, 8080 Springvalley Dr., Cincinnati OH 45236. (513)631-1777. Editor: Ann F. Isaacs.
Purpose: "We are dedicated to helping us become the best we can be through understanding and applying the research on creativity. When constructively expressed, this enables individuals and groups to achieve more with less time and energy and on higher levels." Information covers agriculture, business, celebrities, health/medicine, how-to, music, nature and new products.
Services: Offers biographies, brochures/pamphlets and newsletter. Also offers programs, projects, workshops, conferences, publications, in-service training, books and question and answer service for members. Publications include Creative Child and Adults (quarterly).
How to Contact: Write. Enclose SASE and 50¢ for more information.

National Association for Industry-Education Cooperation, 235 Hendricks Blvd., Buffalo NY 14226. (716)278-5726. President: Donald M. Clark.
Purpose: "To provide a national organization for representatives of business, industry, education, government and labor in order to promote increased levels of cooperation; to identify areas of mutual interest; to formulate programs and procedures which meet acceptable standards; and to communicate with any group concerned with education about cooperative programs and projects." Information covers educational programs.
Services: Offers brochures/pamphlets and newsletter. Publications include handbooks on industry education councils and community resources workshops.
How to Contact: Write.

National Association of Schools of Art, 11250 Roger Bacon Dr., #5, Reston VA 22090. (703)437-0700. Executive Secretary: Samuel Hope.
Purpose: "We are an accrediting agency for college and university programs in art and design." Information covers art.
Services: Offers annual reports and statistics. Publications include Directory, a list of art schools and departments accredited by National Association of Schools of Arts.
How to Contact: Write. Charges for publications.

National Association of Schools of Music, 11250 Roger Bacon Dr., #5, Reston VA 22090. (703)437-0700. Executive Director: Samuel Hope.

Purpose: "We are an accrediting agency for music schools and departments." Information covers music.
Services: Offers aid in arranging interviews, annual reports, statistics and newsletter. Publications include *Directory 1978*, which lists National Association of Schools of Music (NASM) members; and *Music in Higher Education*, a statistical report about music programs on college and university levels.
How to Contact: "Write to publications department." Charges for publications.

National Association of Training Schools and Juvenile Agencies, 5256 N. Central Ave., Indianapolis IN 46220. (317)257-3955. Contact: Windell W. Fewell.
Purpose: "To promote improvement and research for prevention and treatment of juvenile delinquency in the US and Canada. Information covers technical data. "We have professional presentations related to juvenile corrections."
Services: Offers brochures/pamphlets. Publications include *The Proceedings*.
How to Contact: Write or call.

National Center for Public Service Internship Programs, 1735 Eye St. NW, Washington DC 20006. (202)331-1516. Executive Director: Richard A. Ungerer.
Purpose: "We are a nonprofit organization dedicated to serving the needs of public service internship programs, students and institutions, by providing current information about experiential education. The center publishes three comprehensive internship directories, journals and reports examining key issues in the field of public service internships and a bimonthly newsletter. The center also offers technical assistance regarding the development of internship programs and funding sources." Information covers technical data.
Services: Offers brochures/pamphlets, newsletters and directories of internship programs.
How to Contact: Write. Charges $7/directory for nonmembers.

National Education Association, 1201 16th St. NW, Washington DC 20036. (202)833-4484. Manager, Public Information Office: Philip G. King.
Purpose: "Since 1857, the purpose of the National Education Association (NEA) has been to elevate the character and advance the interests of the profession of teaching, and to promote the cause of education in the United States. Goals include human and civil rights in education, leadership in solving social problems, an independent united teaching organization, professional excellence, economic and professional security for all educators, and significant legislative support for public education." Information covers education.
Services: Offers aid in arranging interviews, statistics, brochures/pamphlets, information searches, placement on mailing list, newsletter and photos. Publications include *Comprehensive Publications Catalog* (covers materials prepared for in-service teacher education).
How to Contact: Write or call NEA Communications Services. "NEA credit or mention required in material published or broadcast."

National Forum of Catholic Parent Organizations/NCEA, 1 Dupont Circle, Suite 350, Washington DC 20036. (202)293-5954. Executive Director: Elinor R. Ford.
Purpose: "Founded in 1976 as a commission of the National Catholic Educational Association, to support and promote the role of parents as primary educators of their children." Information covers how-to and self-help. "We also provide programs for Catholic parent organizations."
Services: Offers newsletters. Publications include *Parentcator* (newsletter), *Catholic Parent Organizations Handbook*, and *Catholic Parent Organizations Program Guide*.
How to Contact: Write. Charges for publications. "We charge for transportation and expenses for workshop appearances."

National School Boards Association, 1055 Thomas Jefferson St. NW, Washington DC

20007. (202)337-7666. Director, Public Information: Philip A. Smith.
Purpose: "We represent the nation's 95,000 school board members of public schools. We conduct training workshops for board members and school administrators, and we conduct an annual convention each April." Information covers major issues in public education and statistics."
Services: Offers aid in arranging interviews, annual reports, statistics and placement on mailing list.
How to Contact: Write or Call.

National Society of Hebrew Day Schools, 229 Park Ave. S., New York NY 10003. (212)674-6700. Associate Director: Rabbi Goldenberg.
Purpose: "Our purposes include establishing Hebrew day schools and servicing such schools. Principals, PTAs and teachers in this system have affiliated organizations in the US." Information covers education.
Services: Offers aid in arranging interviews, annual reports, statistics and brochures/pamphlets. Publications include annual reports, statistics and enrollment brochures.
How to Contact: Write or call.

Parent Cooperative Preschools, International, 20551 Lakeshore Rd., Baie D'urge, Quebec, Canada H9X 1R3. In US: 9111 Alton Pkwy., Silver Spring MD 20910. Executive Secretary: Linda Armitage.
Purpose: "Parent Cooperative Preschools, International (PCPI) is a service organization for member co-op preschools, teachers and parents." Information covers how-to cooperative preschools and parent participation preschools.
Services: Offers aid in arranging interviews, bibliographies, brochures/pamphlets and regular informational journal.
How to Contact: Write. Publication list available on request. "Members get first priority, except in processing orders of pamphlets, reprints and journals."
Tips: "Don't address letters to our organizations as 'Dear Sir'!"

Parents Rights in Education, 12571 Northwinds Dr., St. Louis MO 63141. (314)434-4171. President: Mae Duggan.
Purpose: "To disseminate information and research material in support of the parents' natural, human right to direct and control the education of their own children. Our special interest is to reform the present government controlled monopoly in education, in order to allow parents a free choice of schools and the type of education they desire for their own children. Such solutions as a tuition voucher, tax credits and exemption from public school taxation have been researched. Reform of compulsory attendance laws and minimum school standards are considered." Information covers history, law and education.
Services: Offers statistics, brochures/pamphlets, information searches and newsletter. Publications include *Parents Rights* (newsletter), *Legal Brief in Support of Parents Rights in Education*, *A Case for Liberty and Justice*, *Freedom in Education*, *Family Choice in Education*, *Secular Humanism and the Schools*, *How to Start Your Own School*, and *Educational Freedom*.
How to Contact: Write or call. "There is a charge for the materials we send. Prices are listed. To be placed on our mailing list, we require at least a $5 yearly donation."

Energy

American Association of Petroleum Geologists, 1444 S. Boulder Blvd., Tulsa OK 74101. Executive Director: Fred Dix.
Purpose: "The bulletin of the American Association of Petroleum Geologists (AAPG) and other special publications include scientific information relating to the geology of

petroleum resources worldwide." Information covers science.
Services: Offers statistics. Publications include a monthly bulletin—the November issue is an annual membership directory; the August and October issues contain North American and overseas drilling activity reports.
How to Contact: Write or call.

American Petroleum Institute, 2101 L St. NW, Washington DC 20037. Manager, Print Media: Earl A. Ross.
Services: Offers b&w glossy photos pertaining to petroleum for noncommercial, non-advertising use only.
How to Contact: Write. The American Petroleum Institute must be given a credit line.

Canadian Electrical Association, Suite 580, 1 Westmount Square, Montreal, Quebec, Canada H3Z 2P9. (514)937-6181. Public Affairs Officer: Robin Palin.
Purpose: "To represent the whole electric utility industry in Canada. Our information includes national data on electrical energy generation, transmission and distribution, especially in the areas of exports, generation by type, long range supply potential, rates, standards and research." Information covers business, economics, industry and technical data.
Services: Offers aid in arranging interviews, bibliographies, biographies, statistics, brochures/pamphlets, information searches, placement on mailing list, newsletter and press kits. Publications include *The Role of Electricity in a National Energy Policy*.
How to Contact: Write or call. "Writers using our services must have a press affiliation."

Citizens' Energy Project, 1413 K St. NW, 8th Floor, Washington DC 20005. (202)783-0452. Coordinator: Ken Bossong.
Purpose: "Citizens' Energy Project is a nonprofit research group that conducts research in the areas of energy policy (primarily pro-solar and anti-nuclear), environmental protection and consumer safety, and appropriate technologies. We are also an advocacy and organizing group working to promote alternative energy technologies and to help localities to become energy self-reliant through the development of indigenous renewable resources." Information covers politics, self-help and technical data.
Services: Offers bibliographies, brochures/pamphlets, placement on mailing list and newsletter.
How to Contact: Write. "Consulting is free if limited, charged for if extensive; the rate depends on the task."

Edison Electric Institute, 1140 Connecticut Ave. NW, Washington DC 20036. (202)862-3837. Director, Public Information: Mike Segel.
Purpose: "Edison Electric Institute (EEI) is the association of America's investor-owned electric utility companies. Organized in 1933 and incorporated in 1970, EEI provides a principal forum where electric utility people exchange information on developments in their business, and maintains a liaison between the industry and the federal government. Its officers act as spokesmen for investor-owned electric utility companies on subjects of national interest. EEI ascertains factual information, data and statistics relating to the electric industry, and makes them available to member companies, the public and government representatives." Information covers energy and the electric utility industry.
Services: Offers aid in arranging interviews, statistics, brochures/pamphlets, information searches, placement on mailing list, photos, press kits, and access to the research library. Publications include *Coal, Nuclear Power* and *Emerging Energy Technologies*.
How to Contact: Write, call or visit. "The library is accessible by appointment only."

Independent Petroleum Association of America, 1101 16th St. NW, Washington DC 20036. (202)857-4722. Director of Communications: Martin Reilly.

Purpose: "The Independent Petroleum Association of America (IPAA) is a Washington based association representing 5,000 independent producers of domestic crude oil and natural gas. IPAA is dedicated to the advancement of an aggressive, competitive domestic petroleum industry to assure increased production of oil and gas for an expanding economy and national security. Its functions include congressional relations, federal departmental and agency liaison, and public information. It is a nonprofit organization." Information covers economics, industry and energy.

Services: Offers aid in arranging interviews, annual reports, statistics, brochures/pamphlets and placement on mailing list. Publications include *Petroleum Independent* (bimonthly magazine), *America's Energy Dilemma: Facts vs. Fallacies* and *The Oil Producing Industry in Your State.*

How to Contact: "For statistical information, call (202)857-4760. For booklets and press information, call (202)857-4770."

The International Microwave Power Institute (IMPI), Box 634, Sub 11, University of Alberta, Edmonton, Alberta, Canada T6G 2E0. (403)433-6045. Administrator: R. P. Halpern.

Purpose: "The International Microwave Power Institute (IMPI) is the forum to foster the exchange of ideas in the science of microwave energy in the areas of domestic, industrial, scientific and medical applications. Activities organized by IMPI are short courses, workshops and its annual symposium." Information covers agriculture, food, health/medicine, industry, science and technical data.

Services: Offers brochures/pamphlets and newsletter. Publications include *The Journal of Microwave Power*, (a quarterly, referred, scientific journal relating to microwave energy for noncommunication purposes) and *Microwave Energy Applications Newsletter* (bimonthly).

How to Contact: Write.

National Coal Association, 1130 17th St. NW, Washington DC 20036. (202)628-4322. Contact: Herbert Foster.

Services: Offers 2,000 photos, "mostly b&w shots of bituminous coal production, transportation and use, and reclamation of mined land. Some color transparencies of coal production, many showing land reclamation. Most are modern—no historical pix."

How to Contact: Free editorial use. Credit line required.

National Petroleum Council, 1625 K St. NW, Washington DC 20006. (202)393-6100. Director of Information: Joan Walsh Cassedy.

Purpose: "The purpose of the National Petroleum Council is solely to advise, inform and make recommendations to the Secretary of the Interior on any matter relating to petroleum or the petroleum industry. Members of the National Petroleum Council are appointed by the Secretary of the Interior and represent all segments of petroleum interests." Information covers economics, industry and technical data.

Services: Offers placement on mailing list and publications. Publications include *US Energy Outlook*, task group reports, *Environmental Conservation* and others.

How to Contact: Write. Charges for publications.

Tips: "The council does not maintain any statistics on an ongoing basis. Several of the council's reports are statistically oriented, however."

National Stripper Well Association, 5902 S. 68th East Ave., Tulsa OK 74145. (918)627-7880. Executive Vice President: Frank B. Taylor.

Purpose: "To provide public information and meaningful data on stripper well activities nationally, stripper wells being those which produce 10 barrels of oil daily or less. Stripper wells are located in 28 oil-producing states." Information covers petroleum energy.

Services: Offers annual reports. Publications include releases and studies directly related to the stripper oil well division of the domestic petroleum industry.

How to Contact: Write or call.

Natural Gas Supply Committee, 1025 Connecticut Ave. NW, Washington DC 20036. (202)223-9575. Director of Public Information: Carl J. Suchocki.
Purpose: "A Washington-based national organization representing the major independent producers of domestic natural gas in the specific areas of federal regulation of their exploration and production activities. We provide educational and informational material about the natural gas-producing industry and its legislative and regulatory aspects." Information covers economics, industry and government regulation.
Services: Offers aid in arranging interviews, statistics, brochures/pamphlets, placement on mailing list and press kits. "Available printed information ranges from the role of natural gas in US energy policy, to statistical and economic analyses of the federal regulatory impact on domestic natural gas production."
How to Contact: Write or call.

Task Force Against Nuclear Pollution, Box 1817, Washington DC 20013. (202)547-6661. Coordinator: Franklin Gage.
Purpose: "To ban nuclear power and promote energy efficiency and solar energy." Information covers energy.
Services: Offers reports and brochures/pamphlets.
How to Contact: "We prefer that writers write to us. Call only if necessary."

Engineering

Abrasive Engineering Society, 1049 S. Main St., Plymouth MI 48170. Contact: Roy Denial.
Service: Information covers business, industry, new product information and technical data. Offers aid in arranging interviews, statistics, information searches and photos.
How to Contact: Write or call.

American Society for Quality Control, 161 W. Wisconsin Ave., Milwaukee WI 53203. (414)272-8575. Manager, Public Information Office: Darlene C. Schmidt.
Purpose: "American Society for Quality Control (ASQC) is the society of professionals engaged in the management, engineering and scientific aspects of quality and reliability. It creates, promotes and stimulates interest in advancing the science of quality control and its applications. ASQC holds courses and conferences to help educate quality control practitioners, so they can keep up-to-date on their chosen field. They thereby do a better job for their employers and for the general public. It also publishes technical literature to this same end, and is involved in publishing generic standards of quality control." Information covers "all industrial or product and service areas in regard to designing, measuring and assuring the quality and reliability of a product or service."
Services: Offers aid in arranging interviews, biographies, brochures/pamphlets, information searches, placement on mailing list and press kits "when applicable." Publications include *QC Contacts*, "a directory of some 80 members available to be interviewed regarding quality control in their industrial or service areas throughout the US"; *Quality Progress*, a monthly news magazine; *Careers in the Quality Sciences*; and other brochures detailing the background and activities of the society.
How to Contact: "Contact the manager of the public information office and specify what organization you write for or your purpose in requesting information. This will help us determine what additional materials might help you. We have access to some 25 years of articles on quality control that have been published in our periodicals. If the researcher has 'key words/phrases' that tie in with the technicality of this field, it's easier to find reference material for him. We will be glad to help any writer, broadcaster, magazine, newspaper or freelancer with a story in planning."

American Society of Civil Engineers, 345 E. 47th St., New York NY 10017. (212)644-

7496. Manager, Public Information Services: H. R. Hands.
Purpose: "The society's goal is to enhance the profession in its service to mankind. We have a membership of 75,000 individual civil engineers." Information covers agriculture, science, technical data and civil engineering.
Services: Offers aid in arranging interviews, bibliographies and a library.
How to Contact: Write or call.

Engineers' Council for Professional Development, 345 E. 47th St., New York NY 10017. (212)644-7685. Executive Director: D. Reyes-Guerra.
Purpose: "A federation of 19 professional societies in engineering. We promote professional development, guidance, education, ethics and areas of general professional interest to engineers." Information covers engineering.
Services: Offers aid in arranging interviews, annual reports and brochures/pamphlets.
How to Contact: Write. Charges for services "based on the cost of the research effort; other fees are charged as stated on publications list."

Engineers Joint Council, 345 E. 47th St., New York NY 10017. (212)644-7840. Publications Director: Ellie Barbarash.
Purpose: "Engineers Joint Council (EJC) is a professional society for engineers." Information covers business, industry and salary information.
Services: Offers annual reports, biographies, statistics, brochures/pamphlets and placement on mailing list.
How to Contact: Write or call. "Contact the Publications Office for a catalog that lists prices."

Society of Manufacturing Engineers, 1 SME Dr., Box 930, Dearborn MI 48128. (313)271-1500. Manager of Public Relations: Tom Akas.
Purpose: "Society of Manufacturing Engineers (SME) is a professional technical society dedicated to advancing manufacturing technology and productivity through the continuing education of manufacturing engineeers and managers. It sponsors tool and manufacturing expositions, conferences and clinics, programmed learning and home study courses and certification for manufacturing engineers. It publishes a monthly magazine and other technical publications. It confers annual awards for important technical contributions to manufacturing engineering and manufacturing engineering education." Information covers technical data.
Services: Offers aid in arranging interviews and placement on press mailing list if publication the writer works with is pertinent to an industrial readership.

Finance & Banking

American Bankers Association, 1120 Connecticut Ave. NW, Washington DC 20036. (202)467-4273. Director of Public Relations: Daniel S. Buser.
Purpose: "American Bankers Association (ABA) is the national trade association for America's full-service commercial banks. ABA's membership comprises 13,254 banks, 92%of the nation's total. ABA manages the largest private adult education program in the world and represents the banking industry on the federal government level. Information on all aspects of banking is available from the ABA Public Relations Division." Information covers business and banking.
Services: Offers aid in arranging interviews, annual reports, biographies, statistics, brochures/pamphlets, information searches, placement on mailing list, photos, press kits and a wide variety of information and publications.
How to Contact: Call. "If you are writing about banking, call us. We may very well have more current information, good interview contacts and, possibly, another point of view not yet considered. It doesn't matter if the questions are extremely specific or very general. If we have an answer, it's yours. If we don't know, we'll tell you that. If we know a better place to get the information we'll refer you to it."

American Commercial Collectors Association, Inc., 4040 W. 70th St., Minneapolis MN 55435. (612)929-9669. General Manager: Dottie Anderson.
Purpose: "To further and promote the general welfare of the commercial collection profession in the US and elsewhere; to regulate practices, prescribe ethics, and enforce proper conduct among its members; to encourage and promote the adoption of legislation in the various states and in the US favorable to the rights of commercial collectors and the credit-granting public, and to gather and disseminate material relative to the commercial collection profession which may be valuable to members of the association." Information covers commercial collection, credit granting, finance and recovery of monies because of nonpayments.
Services: Offers brochures/pamphlets, newsletter and press kits. Publications include *What ACCA Is*; *Collection Guidelines for Commercial Credit Grantors*; *Introducing the American Commercial Collectors Association, Inc.*; *Scope* (a newsletter); and *Blue Book* (a membership directory).
How to Contact: Write. Service fees vary.
Tips: "Clearance must be obtained on some purchases. If we cannot help you we will try to refer you to someone who may be able to assist."

Institute for Monetary Research, Inc., 1200 15th St. NW, Washington DC 20005. (202)223-9050. Secretary/Treasurer: F.J. Broderick.
Purpose: "Research on monetary questions." Information covers business, economics, industry and politics.
Services: Offers information searches.
How to Contact: Write or call. Charges for services.

National Association of Bank Women, Inc. (NABW), 111 E. Wacker Dr., Chicago IL 60601. (312)565-4100. Contact: Public Relations Director.
Purpose: "To bring together women executives engaged in the profession of banking for the interchange of experiences, ideas and interests; to further the meaningful profession or career of bank women; and to encourage young women to choose banking as a career and to advance the career opportunities for all women in banking." Information covers professional development for women.
Services: Offers aid in arranging interviews, annual reports, biographies, statistics, brochures/pamphlets, placement on mailing list, photos and press kits. Press kits cover regional conferences and convention. Publications include *NABW Fact Sheet*.
How to Contact: Write or call. "Detail what you're doing and what you'd like from us, as well as any information that would help us serve you in the future."

National Bankers Association, Suite 1120, 499 S. Capital St. SW, Washington DC 20003. (202)488-5550. Deputy Executive Director: Leon Hampton.
Purpose: Trade organization for minority banks.
Services: Offers brochures/pamphlets, newsletter and press kits.
How to Contact: Write or call.

Food

American Bakers Association, 2020 K St. NW, Suite 850, Washington DC 20006. (202)296-5800. Contact: Mr. French.
Purpose: Chief emphasis is legislative and regulatory issues affecting wholesale bakers, their suppliers and customers.
Services: Offers aid in arranging interviews, statistics, brochures/pamphlets, placement on mailing list, newsletter and speakers.
How to Contact: "Telephone contact is preferred, unless a great deal of information is needed."

American Spice Trade Association (ASTA), Box 1267, Englewood Cliffs NJ 07632.

(201)568-2163. Secretary-Director, Member Services: Edward J. McNeill.
Purpose: Organization for firms producing, trading or processing spices; using spices in industrial quantities; or selling products or services to the spice industry. "American Spice Trade Association's (ASTA) purpose is that of an aggressive trade association designed to protect the interests and promote the welfare of its industry and to assume as a group those functions which the individual member firm cannot perform as effectively itself." Information covers agriculture, business, food and history.
Services: Offers aid in arranging interviews, bibliographies, statistics and brochures/pamphlets. Publications include several booklets, brochures and article reprints. Publications guide available.
How to Contact: Write Mr. M. Neale, Lewis and Neale, Inc., 350 5th Ave., New York NY 10001. "This firm has handled our PR and has operated our test kitchens for over 30 years."
Tips: "Know what you want. Don't ask us to 'send me all your information about spices.' "

Calorie Control Council, 64 Perimeter Center E., Atlanta GA 30346. (404)393-1340. Public Relations Director: Frank Slover.
Purpose: "The Calorie Control Council is an association of manufacturers and suppliers of dietary foods and beverages." Information covers saccharin.
Services: Offers brochure on saccharin, *Saccharin: A Benefit to Millions.*
How to Contact: Write or call. Charges for brochure: $9/hundred (0-499); $8.25/hundred (500-999); and $7/hundred (1000-Over).

Corn Refiners Association, Inc., 1001 Connecticut Ave. NW, Washington DC 20036. (202)331-1634. Director, Public Affairs: K.D. Brenner.
Purpose: "Our organization represents the corn refining (wet milling) industry of the US, producers of starches, syrups, feeds and oil from corn. Primary areas of activity are research on corn products and processing, government relations and public relations." Information covers agriculture and food.
Services: Offers annual reports, brochures/pamphlets, placement on mailing list and press kits. Publications available.
How to Contact: Write. Small charge for some printed material.

Food Research and Action Center, Inc. (FRAC), 2011 Eye St. NW, Washington DC 20006. Deputy Director: Jeff Kirsch.
Purpose: "Food Research and Action Center (FRAC) operates as a law firm and advocacy center representing the interests of poor people who participate and who are entitled to participate in the federal food programs (food stamps, school lunch and breakfast, elderly nutrition, and other child nutrition programs). The staff is composed of lawyers, researchers, lobbyists and community organizers. They work with local and state antihunger groups to expand and improve the federal food programs, and to encourage the development of poor people's organizations. FRAC also works on welfare reform issues." Information covers food, law, politics, welfare and 'other poor people's issues.' "
Services: Offers aid in arranging interviews, bibliographies, statistics, brochures/pamphlets and placement on mailing list. Has "information on the governmental and private-sector efforts to end hunger in this country and reform the welfare system. There is also material on legislative matters affecting poverty issues."
How to Contact: Write or call.

The Kosher Wine Institute, 175 5th Ave., New York NY 10010. Executive Director: John L. Nanovic.
Purpose: "To inform the public about kosher wines—what they are, how they are made, etc., as differing from other wines." Information covers business, entertainment and history.

Services: Offers aid in arranging interviews, brochures/pamphlets and placement on mailing list. Publications include *What are Kosher Wines* and *Listing of Kosher Wines*. "Others to come."
How to Contact: Write.

National-American Wholesale Grocers' Association, 51 Madison Ave., New York NY 10010. (212)532-8899. Editor: Ellen Lusk.
Purpose: "To provide educational representational services to our members." Information covers wholesale food distribution.
Services: Offers aid in arranging interviews and placement on mailing list. Publications include pamphlets/brochures, available for specific projects only. Publications list available.
How to Contact: Write or call.

National Dairy Council, 6300 N. River Rd., Rosemont IL 60018. (312)696-1020. Manager, Nutrition Information: Robert E. Kowalski.
Purpose: "The National Dairy Council provides nutrition research, nutrition information dissemination and nutrition education materials and program." Information covers food, health/medicine and nutrition.
Services: Offers aid in arranging interviews, statistics, brochures/pamphlets, information searches, placement on mailing list and photos. "We provide specific information on the nutritional value of dairy foods as part of a balanced diet." Publications include consumer information sheets and *Nutrition Source Book*.
How to Contact: Write or call.
Tips: "We are very anxious to work with writers interested in food and nutrition in general and in dairy foods in particular."

National Food Processors Association, 1133 20th St. NW, Washington DC 20036. (202)331-5900. Vice President, Public Communications: Roger Coleman.
Purpose: "To provide laboratory services to member companies and to represent the interests of the food processing industry in Congress and before various regulatory agencies." Information covers food.
Services: Offers brochures/pamphlets. Publications include pamphlets on the food processing industry.
How to Contact: Write or call. "We will generally try to assist in a variety of ways anyone seeking information on the food processing industry."

National Hot Dog & Sausage Council, 400 W. Madison, Chicago IL 60606. (312)454-1242. Executive Secretary: Frances Altman.
Purpose: "We are a service to the meat industry. Our objective is encouraging the increased consumption of sausage products and furthering the consumer's knowledge of processed meats (sausage)." Information covers food, history and new products.
Services: Offers aid in arranging interviews, brochures/pamphlets, information searches, newsletter and photos. Publications include hot dog fact sheet.
How to Contact: Write or call.

National Peach Council, Box 1085, Martinsburg WV 25401. (304)267-6024. Executive Secretary: Robert K. Phillips.
Purpose: "The only national organization devoted solely to the interests of the peach industry." Information covers freestone peaches for the fresh fruit market.
Services: Offers aid in arranging interviews and information searches. Publications include *Peach Times*, a monthly newsletter; an annual publication detailing proceedings of their national convention; and folders concerning NPC and its overall operations.
How to Contact: Write or call. "Writers should try to be after reasonably specific informatioin, as volume of information available on some things concerning peaches can make giving full details by letter either difficult or impossible."

National Restaurant Association, 1 IBM Plaza, Suite 2600, Chicago IL 60611. (312)787-2525. Director of Communications: Jerry Q. Greenfield.
Purpose: "The association represents more than 125,000 food service units nationally, promoting and protecting their interests as business people. Information developed covers broad areas of legislation, consumer attitudes, market and economic research, as well as specific project areas." Information covers business and economics.
Services: Offers aid in arranging interviews, annual reports, statistics and press kits.
How to Contact: Write or call.
Tips: "We suggest inquiries be as specific as possible to assist in providing meaningful information."

Tea Council of the USA, Inc., 230 Park Ave., New York NY 10017. (212)986-6998. Director, Consumer Services: Beryl Walter.
Purpose: "The Tea Council of the USA is a nonprofit organization established in 1953 for the purpose of increasing US sales and consumption of tea. It is supported by the major firms of the US tea industry and the major tea producing countries. Its aim is to extend and increase the consumer's knowledge and awareness of the benefits of tea drinking. It uses all media in its educational, promotional, public relations and publicity programs. It prepares and sends material to a wide variety of individuals including food and women's page editors, radio and television commentators, program directors, news and business editors, sports editors and teachers." Information covers food (beverages) and sports.
Services: Offers brochures/pamphlets and photos. "We also offer food releases and background information of tea (its history, legends, growing, processing etc.). Publications include *The Story of Tea* (16 pages; the romance, history, growing and processing of tea shown in captioned drawings; preparation methods), *Two Leaves and a Bud* (16 pages; the legends and history connected with tea; how and where it is grown and processed; types of tea; preparation methods), and *What You Should Know About Tea* (16 pages; how to prepare hot tea; using loose tea; teabags; instant and iced tea mixes; and tea party serving suggestions and recipes. Illustrated).
How to Contact: Write or call.

US Feed Grains Council, 1030 15th St. NW, Washington DC 20005. (202)659-1640. Director of Communications: Robert J. Brown.
Purpose: "Through offices located around the world, the council works to develop overseas markets for US feed grains either as a direct source of food grain) or indirect source (livestock feed) for human consumption." Information covers agriculture.
Services: Offers aid in arranging interviews, annual reports, biographies, statistics, brochures/pamphlets, placement on mailing list, newsletter, photos and press kits.
How to Contact: Write or call. "We are currently developing a communications program."

Wine Institute, 165 Post, San Francisco CA 94108. (415)986-0878. Media Director: Brian St. Pierre.
Purpose: Information covers agriculture, business, economics, food, health/medicine, history, how-to, industry, law, politics, recreation, science, technical data and travel.
Services: Offers aid in arranging interviews, bibliographies, biographies, statistics, brochures/pamphlets, information searches, placement on mailing list and photos. Publications include a wine information course.
How to Contact: Write or call.

Foreign Affairs

Brazilian-American Cultural Institute, 4201 Connecticut Ave. NW S/211, Washington

DC 20008. (202)362-8334. Executive Director: Jose M. Neistein.
Purpose: "The Brazilian-American Cultural Institute promotes Brazilian cultural values in the US. We offer courses on the Portuguese language; Brazilian literature and history; Brazilian artists' shows (several of them travel to museums and university art galleries throughout the US); concerts of Brazilian music performed by Brazilian and American musicians; a library specialized in Brazilian studies; a tape library; and we also publish a book on Brazilian studies."
Services: Offers annual reports, biographies, brochures/pamphlets and press kits.
How to Contact: Write or call.

Center for Inter-American Relations, 680 Park Ave., New York NY 10021. (202)249-8950. Director, Public Information: Edna Phillips.
Purpose: "To promote and encourage better understanding within the US of our neighbors to the north and south." Information covers art, entertainment, history, music and politics.
Services: Offers aid in arranging interviews, placement on mailing list and newsletter.
How to Contact: Call.
Tips: "Before traveling to Latin America on a writing assignment, check in with us."

Council on Hemispheric Affairs (COHA), 1735 New Hampshire NW, Washington DC 20009. (202)332-8860. Director: Laurence R. Birns.
Purpose: "The Council on Hemispheric Affairs (COHA) monitors the full spectrum of the economic, political and social aspects of US-Latin American relations, including the human rights performances of nations in the hemisphere. COHA publishes an average of three research memoranda weekly on a variety of inter-American topics, as well as periodic in-depth analyses on current topics. COHA has been particularly active in encouraging and assisting research of newspaper, magazine and journal articles on regional topics and in aiding authors of hemispheric studies." Information covers agriculture, business, economics, history, law and politics.
Services: Offers aid in arranging interviews, bibliographies, biographies, statistics, clipping services, information searches and newsletter. Publications include descriptive brochures on COHA, "regular human rights reports on Latin American human rights violators, and updates on current developments in specific Latin American nations and in US-Latin American relations. Also, economic reports, diplomatic analyses and newsletters to Congress and Latin American specialists."
How to Contact: Write or call. "Specific requests will, in general, be handled free of charge. We will be pleased to work with any writer doing serious work on some inter-American theme." Charges $25/year for subscription to weekly COHA research memoranda.

Joint Baltic American National Committee, Box 432, Rockville MD 20850. (301)340-1954. Director of Public Relations: John Bolsteins.
Purpose: "The Joint Baltic American National Committee (JBANC) represents the central Estonian-, Latvian- and Lithuanian-American organizations in the US; coordinates the presentation of, and acts as spokesman for, issues which affect the Baltic states. JBANC information primarily deals with historical/current and political/sociological aspects of the Baltic States and peripherally the Soviet Union and eastern Europe." Information covers economics, history and politics.
Services: Offers bibliographies, brochures/pamphlets and newsletter.
How to Contact: Write or call. "Ethnic nationalism in the USSR is and has been increasing and could become a significant factor for US-USSR relations. For the Baltic area, JBANC can provide information complementary to that which, for example, foreign correspondents in the USSR might seek."

Washington Office on Latin America, 110 Maryland Ave. NE, Washington DC 20002.

Purpose: "Washington Office on Latin America (WOLA) was created by a board coalition of churchpersons and scholars to monitor events in Latin America and Washington (as they relate to Latin America) with emphasis on human rights and efforts to promote participation in government." Information covers politics, human rights and democratic opposition.
Services: Offers brochures/pamphlets, placement on mailing list and newsletter. "We are willing to do occasional briefings on current developments in US/Latin America for interested journalists." Publications include *Update*.
How to Contact: Write or call. "We respond better to phone calls; writing letters in response to inquiries requires too much time. Be as specific as possible about issues and countries of concern." Donations appreciated. Charges 10¢/photocopy, plus postage.

Fraternal & Community Service

Ancient Egyptian Arabic Order of the Mystic Shrine, 1308 Broadway, Tobin Bldg., Detroit MI 48226. (313)961-9148. Imperial Recorder: Booker T. Alexander.
Purpose: "We are a charitable and fraternal organization."
Services: Offers aid in arranging interviews and quarterly magazine for members.
How to Contact: Write or call. "Written requests preferred."

Federation of Junior Leagues of Canada, 366 Victoria Ave., Montreal, Quebec, Canada H3Z 2N4. Chairman: Shirley MacArthur.
Purpose: "To promote voluntarism, to develop the potential of its members for voluntary participation in community affairs, and to demonstrate effectiveness of the trained volunteer." Information covers "training for the community in career development."
Services: Offers brochures/pamphlets. Publications include informational brochures.
How to Contact: Write to Chairman, 4906 126th St., Edmonton, Alberta, Canada T6H 3W2. Charges $5-10 for materials.

Jaycees International, Box 340577, Coral Gables FL 33134. (305)446-7608. Contact: Public Relations Director.
Purpose: "To promote leadership training through community services." Information covers agriculture, art, business, celebrities, economics, entertainment, food, health/medicine, history, how-to, industry, law, music, nature, politics, recreation, science, self-help, sports and travel.
Services: Offers aid in arranging interviews, statistics, brochures/pamphlets, information searches, placement on mailing list, newsletter and press kits. Publication available.
How to Contact: Write. "Requests should be as specific as possible. Our material is available in English, Spanish and French."

Kiwanis International, 101 E. Erie St., Chicago IL 60611. (312)943-2300. Public Relations Director: John L. McGehee.
Purpose: "International service organization, providing fellowship and helping youth, community and nation."
Services: Offers aid in arranging interviews, biographies, statistics and brochures/pamphlets. "We also have service reports and a library." Publication available.
How to Contact: Write.

Lions Club International, 300 22nd St., Oak Brook IL 60570. (312)986-1700. Division Manager of Public Relations and Communications: Frank Brueske.
Purpose: "We are a world organization in 151 countries with volunteers in humanitarian services in these areas or countries."
Services: Offers brochures/pamphlets, placement on mailing list, statistics, photos and press kits. Publication available.
How to Contact: Write or call. "We would prefer that requests be in writing."

Loyal Order of Moose, Supreme Lodge, Mooseheart IL 60539. (312)859-2000. Director General: Herbert W. Heilman.
Purpose: "Men's fraternal society."
Services: Offers annual reports, brochures/pamphlets, statistics and press kits.
How to Contact: Write or call. "Prefer written request."

Optimist International, 4494 Lindell Blvd., St. Louis MO 63108. (314)371-6000. Publicity Director: John Altmansberger.
Purpose: Active in youth activities, community service and aid to the deaf.
Services: Offers aid in arranging interviews, brochures/pamphlets, statistics, newsletter, photos and press kits.
How to Contact: Write.

Rotary International, 1600 Ridge Ave., Evanston IL 60201. Public Relations Director: Jack Giles.
Purpose: "We are an organization of business and professional men, united and worldwide who are interested in humanitarian service, high ethical standards in all vocations and helping to build goodwill for peace in the world."
Services: Offers aid in arranging interviews (at headquarters only), annual reports, brochures/pamphlets, statistics and press kits. Publication available.
How to Contact: Write or call.

The United States Jaycees, Box 7, Tulsa OK 74121. (918)584-2481. Public Relations Manager: Bill Babb.
Purpose: "We are an organization for 18- to 35-year-old men. The three areas of primary concentration are personal development, management training and community involvement. Through a balanced program including all three, the Jaycees help develop leaders for communities, states and the nation, while improving the quality of life in the communities served. Two programs worthy of special mention are the Outstanding Young Farmer recognition program and the Congress of America's Ten Outstanding Young Men. We have programs in CPR, youth sports, governmental involvement and energy conservation, among others." Information covers agriculture, health/medicine, self-help and sports.
Services: Offers annual reports, information searches and press kits. Publications available.
How to Contact: Write. "Our materials and publications may not be reproduced without the express written permission of the US Jaycees, and not for profit under any circumstances. The Jaycees public relations department will cooperate in any way possible with writers who seek their assistance."

Health

Alcoholism National Council, 6155 Oak, Kansas City MO 64113. (816)361-5900. Director: James Eads.
Purpose: "To provide public information and education, crisis line and referral service." Information covers health/medicine and alcoholism related information.
Services: Offers statistics and research library. Publications available.
How to Contact: Write or call.

American Alliance for Health, Physical Education, and Recreation (AAHPER), 1201 16th St., NW, Washington DC 20036. (202)833-5554. Director of Information: Elinore M. Darland.

Purpose: "AAHPER is an alliance of voluntary professional associations totaling 50,000 individual members. Members share a common mission of educating and promoting the related areas of health education, safety, physical education, dance, sport, recreation and leisure services. Through its local, state, district and national membership networks, the alliance reaches into more than 16,000 school districts, more than 2,000 colleges and universities and over 10,000 community recreation units." Information covers health/medicine, recreation and sports.

Services: Offers aid in arranging interviews, bibliographies, biographies, brochures/pamphlets, information searches, placement on mailing list and information service dealing with physical education and recreation for the handicapped.

How to Contact: Write or call.

American Blood Commission, 1901 N. Ft. Myer Dr., Suite 300, Arlington VA 22209. (703)522-8414. Administrative Specialist for Policies and Programs: Robert C. Hubbell.

Purpose: "To implement the National Blood Policy by assuring that all Americans have ready access to an adequate supply of voluntarily donated blood at reasonable cost." Information covers health/medicine; "all areas pertaining to blood products and services."

Services: Offers aid in arranging interviews, annual reports, statistics, brochures/pamphlets, placement on mailing list, newsletter and photos. Publications include reports on American Blood Commission programs in: Donor Recruitment, National Blood Data Center, Regional Association of Blood Services, Utilization of Blood and Blood Components.

How to Contact: Write or call. "Nominal fees for the costs of reproduction and postage are charged for some reports requested in multiple copies."

Tips: "As a national agency consisting of over forty national associations, organizations, and professional societies representing consumers and providers of health care services (including the American Association of Blood Banks, American Red Cross, American Legion, American Medical Association, AFL-CIO, American Cancer Society, and Veterans Administration) the American Blood Commission is in a position to assist and refer inquiries to appropriate sources. Writers should understand that the American Blood commission is an agency coordinating the interests of a diverse set of member organizations, rather than a typical 'trade association.' As such, the Commission often tries to assist writers by referring them to these organizations rather than itself representing these groups' views."

American Cancer Society, Inc., 777 3rd Ave., New York NY 10017. (212)371-2900. Assistant Director, Magazine and Book Relations: Linda Schoenfeld.

Purpose: "Threefold program of research, education and service aimed at controlling and eliminating cancer. Service and rehabilitation programs include information, counseling and transportation. Volunteer visitors assist in rehabilitating laryngectomy and mastectomy patients. Other patient assistance programs, specific to each local division, are also available."

How to Contact: Write or call.

American Dental Association, 211 E. Chicago Ave., Chicago IL 60611. (312)440-2806. Manager of Media Relations: Lou Joseph.

Purpose: A voluntary national health organization with 130,000 members.

Services: Offers assistance.

How to Contact: Write or call.

American Diabetes Association, Inc., 600 5th Ave., New York NY 10020. (212)541-4310. Contact: Public Relations Department.

Purpose: "We are a voluntary nonprofit health organization serving 10 million diabetics through programs of research, patient and public education and community services. The New York headquarters works in conjunction with 68 affiliates in all states and locations in the United States, Alaska and Hawaii. Diabetics and the public in general are encouraged to contact local diabetes associations for assistance and information." Information covers health/medicine.
Services: Offers aid in arranging interviews, annual reports, brochures/pamphlets, placement on mailing list, statistics, newsletter and press kits.
How to Contact: Write or call. "We really stress use of local offices."

American Health Care Association, 1200 15th St. NW, Washington DC 20005. Director of Public Affairs: Michael Codel.
Purpose: "The American Health Care Association is the nation's largest federation of nursing homes and long-term health care facilities for the aged and the convalescent. It is composed of 48 state associations with more than 7,000 facility members providing over 600,000 long-term care beds, half of all such beds in America. AHCA was founded in 1949 to provide leadership in promoting high standards of professional operation and administration of long term and related convalescent health care facilities to ensure quality care for patients and residents in safe surroundings, on a basis of fair payment for services."
Services: Offers aid in arranging interviews, statistics, brochures/pamphlets, placement on mailing list, newsletter, and press kits for members only. Publications include *Weekly Note* and *Journal of the American Health Care Association*, (bimonthly).

American Heart Association, 7320 Greenville Ave., Dallas TX 75231. (214)750-5300. Public Relations Chief: Al Salerno.
Purpose: "To reduce death and disability from cardiovascular diseases through research, education and community service projects." Information covers health/medicine and science.
Services: Offers aid in arranging interviews, annual reports, biographies, statistics, brochures/pamphlets and press kits.
How to Contact: Write or call.

American Lung Association, 1740 Broadway, New York NY 10019. (212)245-8000. Public Relations Director: Helen Jones.
Purpose: "To fight for good lung health and to fight against lung disease. We have information on a number of lung diseases, anti-smoking and air pollution materials." Information covers health/medicine.
Services: Offers aid in arranging interviews and brochures/pamphlets. A publication list is available.
How to Contact: Write. "You may wish to contact your local lung association."

American Optometric Association, Communications Division, 243 N. Lindbergh Blvd., St. Louis MO 63141. (314)991-4100. Associate Director, News: Charlotte A. Rancilio.
Purpose: "The American Optometric Association represents 20,900 doctors and students of optometry. Its objectives are to improve the vision care and health of the public and to promote the art and science of the profession of optometry. Optometric care encompasses children's vision, vision care of children with learning problems, vision care of the aging, rehabilitation of the partially sighted, contact lenses, environmental vision in industry and agriculture, vision in sports and recreation and vision in driving." Information covers health/medicine, how-to, science and sports.
Services: Offers aid in arranging interviews, bibliographies, statistics, brochures/pamphlets, information searches, placement on mailing list and photos. Publications include "specially prepared news backgrounders and news features on various vision care topics available exclusively to the media. These cover a subject in more depth than brochures and pamphlets. For example, *Contact Lens News Backgrounder* and

Consumer Advice on Vision Care: A News Backgrounder."
How to Contact: Write. "Specify the vision care subject area in which you are interested, your audience, and, if known, the name of the publication for which you are writing. This helps us to pinpoint the exact background material you will find most useful and the exact interview subjects who will be most helpful to you. Writers should not abuse the privilege of receiving in-depth backgrounders from us by requesting them for their own personal use with no intention of passing the information in them along to others through their writing. After your article is published, please send tearsheets."

American Social Health Association, 260 Sheridan Ave., Palo Alto CA 94306. (415)321-5134. Program Directors: Sam Knox, Carla Hines.
Purpose: "A nonprofit research and development corporation spearheading new strategies and techniques for solving the venereal disease problem through programs of research, public awareness, information dissemination, professional education and public advocacy." Information covers health/medicine.
Services: Offers annual reports, statistics, brochures/pamphlets and newsletter. Publications include *The Sexually Active and VD, Some Questions and Answers About Penicillin Resistant Gonorrhea, Women and VD, Body Pollution* and other materials related to VD.
How to Contact: Write or call. "Single copies of pamphlets are given free with SASE. All materials are copyrighted. Permission must be requested before any items can be duplicated."

The Arthritis & Rheumatism Association of Metro Washington, 2424 Pennsylvania Ave. NW, Washington DC.(202)331-7395. Executive Director: Nancy Fields.
Purpose: "We are the only voluntary health agency seeking the total answer—cause, prevention and cure—to the crippling effects of arthritis. The chapter supports research, finances training for doctors studying to be rheumatologists, expands community services to patients and their families, seeks to improve treatment techniques, finances studies to develop new ways to prevent and correct disability and to develop and test new drugs. We provide free information service and a referral service of area rheumatologists." Information covers health/medicine, new products, science, self-help and technical data.
Services: Offers statistics, brochures/pamphlets, information searches and newsletters.
How to Contact: Write or call.

The Arthritis Society, 920 Yonge St., Suite 420, Toronto, Ontario, Canada M4W 3J7. (416)967-1414. Managing Director: Edward Dunlop.
Purpose: "The society aims to help in the acquisition and dissemination of knowledge about the cause, cure and prevention of arthritis. Also, it aims to assist the health professions, hospitals, medical schools and governments to bring about a rapid and continuous improvement in the quality of care for arthritis. Its principal mechanism for the attainment of these purposes is the provision of grants in aid of research, associateships and fellowships." Information covers health/medicine.
Services: Offers brochures/pamphlets. Publications include *About Arthritis* and *About the Arthritis Society*.
How to Contact: Write or call.

The Better Sleep Council, 1270 Avenue of the Americas, New York NY 10020. (212)265-0303. Contact: Karen Lane.
Purpose: "The Better Sleep Council seeks to help the consumer become better informed about sleep—overcoming problems and learning how to get more out of sleep. We offer information on everything from how to fight jet lag, get children to bed painlessly, whether rocking helps a baby sleep, 'beauty sleep' and what your dreams

tell you." Information covers health/medicine and technical data.
Services: Offers aid in arranging interviews and brochures/pamphlets. Publications include *How to Sleep Better* and *Twenty Ways to Fight Insomnia*.
How to Contact: Write or call.

Better Vision Institute, 230 Park Ave., New York NY 10017. (212)682-1731. Executive Secretary: Larry Aasen.
Purpose: "The Better Vision Institute is a nonprofit public relations association which uses all the media to urge Americans to have regular eye examinations and to tell the public the importance of vision care. BVI is supported by the optical companies, optometrists, ophthalmologists, opticians, and educational institutions. In our 50 years, we have gathered a lot of data on general vision subjects, eye care, eyeglasses, contact lenses, sunglasses, etc."
Services: Offers aid in arranging interviews, statistics, brochures/pamphlets and photos. Publications include *Facts You Should Know About Your Vision* and *A Home Guide to Better Vision*, plus 12 other vision pamphlets on general subjects.
How to Contact: Write or call.
Tips: "Our files, books, magazines, etc. are all open to writers at any time. As we have copies of many articles written on the vision field, we can save a writer or researcher a lot of time. We also know who the experts are in each vision field."

Canadian Heart Association, Suite 1200, 1 Nicholas St., Ottawa, Ontario, Canada K1N 7B7. (613)237-4361. Executive Director: Mr. E. McDonald.
Purpose: "This foundation is committed to the support of research and education in cardiovascular and cerebrovascular areas. We are a source of information on a mass of information in these fields." Information covers economics, health/medicine, science, technical data and statistics.
Services: Offers annual reports, statistics and brochures/pamphlets. Several publications available.
How to Contact: Write or call.

Cerebral Palsy Association, 3914 Washington, Kansas City MO 64111. (816)531-4189. Executive Director: Mr. Minter.
Purpose: "To promote the general welfare of persons with cerebral palsy." Information covers health/medicine and public information of cerebral palsy.
Services: Offers aid in arranging interviews, brochures/pamphlets, placement on mailing list, statistics and press kits.
How to Contact: Write or call. "For more extensive material contact the National Headquarters in New York."

Cystic Fibrosis Foundation, 6000 Executive Bldg., Rockville MD 30326. Contact: Public Relations Director.
Purpose: "Our main goal is to come up with a cure and control for cystic fibrosis." Information covers celebrities, food, health/medicine, how-to, new products, recreation, science, self-help, sports, technical data and travel.
Services: Offers aid in arranging interviews, annual reports, bibliographies, biographies, statistics, brochures/pamphlets, information searches, placement on mailing list, newsletter, press kits and films.
How to Contact: "Write or visit." Gives writing awards for the best story written by or about a cystic fibrosis patient. The winners are published and cash awards are offered.

Diabetes Association, 616 E. 63rd St., Kansas City MO 64110. (816)361-3361. Program Director: Rosemaree Fafu.
Purpose: "To provide public education, patient education, seminars and professional information." Information covers health/medicine, law, self-help and technical data.
Services: Offers aid in arranging interviews, brochures/pamphlets, clipping services, information searches, placement on mailing list, statistics, newsletter and films.

Publications available.
How to Contact: Write (enclose SASE), call or visit; prefers visit.

Easter Seal Research Foundation, 2023 W. Ogden Ave., Chicago IL 60612. (312)243-8400. Director: William Gellman.
Purpose: "The purpose of the Easter Seal Research Foundation is to support, stimulate and advance research." Information covers rehabilitation of physically disabled persons.
Services: Offers brochures/pamphlets and information on applying for grants.
How to Contact: Write or call.

Epilepsy Foundation of America (EFA), 1828 L St. NW, Washington DC 20036. (202)293-2930. Contact: Public Education Department.
Purpose: "EFA provides parent/patient information; counseling and referrals; employment assistance; medical services; advocacy; special programs such as day care, training grants and publications for physicians and other professionals; EEG training grants and programs; sponsorship of national conferences to train volunteer and staff members; education programs for teachers (School Alert); support of medical research; and public health education." Information covers celebrities, health/medicine, history, how-to, law, new products, recreation, science, self-help, sports and technical data.
Services: Offers aid in arranging interviews, annual reports, bibliographies, statistics, brochures/pamphlets, newsletter, photos and press kits. Publications include publications list. "Specialized information is also available from the EFA library."
How to Contact: Write or call.
Tips: "Much of the most current information is not widely disseminated. However, EFA is able to direct writers to most current and authoritative sources."

International Childbirth Education Association, 5636 W. Burleigh, Milwaukee WI 53210. (414)445-7470. Office Manager: Mrs. Hamilton.
Purpose: "To provide comprehensive preparation for pregnancy and childbirth. Classes for childbirth with a teaching staff of 50 instructors." Information covers food (nutrition), health/medicine, history, how-to, self-help, technical data and public service organization for consumer awareness.
Services: Offers aid in arranging interviews, annual reports, bibliographies, brochures/pamphlets, information searches, placement on mailing list, statistics and newsletter.
How to Contact: Write or call. Charges for people attending classes and some books.

Helen Keller International, Inc., 22 W. 17th St., New York NY 10011. (212)620-2100. Director of Public Relations: Margaret C. Bayldon.
Purpose: "Helen Keller International, Inc., is the oldest agency in the United States devoted to alleviating the problems of blindness in the developing countries. The organization works in the fields of prevention of blindness, education of blind children, and rehabilitation of blind adults. Helen Keller was a founder, staff member and trustee of the agency from 1915 until her death in 1968." Information covers health/medicine, technical data, education and rehabilitation.
Services: Offers aid in arranging interviews, annual reports, statistics, brochures/pamphlets, placement on mailing list and newsletter. Publications include *Sixty Years of Caring About Blindness* (general brochure) and *The Right to See* (brochure describing prevention program).
How to Contact: Write.

Leukemia Society of America, Inc., 211 E. 43rd St., New York NY 10017. (212)573-8484. Director of Publicity: Florence Phillips.
Purpose: "To raise funds for support of research aimed at finding a cure or control for leukemia and allied diseases, patient aid and professional/public information." Infor-

mation covers celebrities, health/medicine and science.
Services: Offers aid in arranging interviews, annual reports, biographies, statistics, brochures/pamphlets and placement on mailing list. Publications include *What Is Leukemia?*, *Nature of Leukemia* (with slides), *Hodgkin's Disease*, *Management of a Child With Leukemia*, *Fact Sheet*, and *Annual Report*.
How to Contact: Write or call.

Make Today Count, Inc., Box 303, Tama Bldg., Suite 514, Burlington IA 52601. (319)754-7266 or 754-8977. Founder: Orville E. Kelly. Executive Director: Rodney Wittkamp.
Purpose: "An international organization with 211 chapters, bringing together terminally ill persons (especially cancer patients), family members, members of the health care professions and other interested persons to help patients and family members cope with the emotional problems of depression, rejection, etc., associated with an illness such as cancer. Make Today Count sponsors seminars on Death and Dying and Living With a Life-Threatening Illness. Mr. Kelly also lectures in the United States and Canada, helping others cope with problems such as the fear of death and cancer. In addition, Make Today Count individual chapters are located in approximately 34 states. Most chapter members are willing to talk with writers and representatives of the news media." Information covers health/medicine, how-to and self-help.
Services: Offers brochures/pamphlets, information searches, newsletter and photos. Publications available.
How to Contact: Write or call.
Tips: "Contact Orville E. Kelly, founder of the organization, who is a cancer patient himself and a writer and lecturer. As a former newspaper editor, whose second book will be released in June, 1978, he will be able to put you in touch with patients, family members, doctors, nurses, etc."

Muscular Dystrophy Association, 810 7th Ave., New York NY 10019. Director, Public Health Education: Horst Petzall.
Purpose: "To find the cause of and cure for muscular dystrophy and related neuromuscular diseases, while providing the best available daily care to patients and their families free of charge." Information covers health/medicine.
Services: Offers annual reports, brochures/pamphlets and newsletter.
How to Contact: Write.

The National Foundation—March of Dimes, 1275 Mamaroneck Ave., White Plains NY 10605. (914)428-7100. Associate Public Information Director: Dorothy Davis.
Purpose: The prevention of birth defects through support of basic and clinical research, medical services, public and professional education in genetics, prenatology, human biology and environmental factors affecting prenatal health. Information covers food (prenatal nutrition), health/medicine, science (biomedical), self-help and technical data.
Services: Offers aid in arranging interviews, annual reports, bibliographies, biographies, statistics, brochures/pamphlets, information searches, placement on mailing list, photos and press kits. Publications include *Maternal/Newborn Advocate* (quarterly newsletter reporting on government activity in prenatal health care at federal, state and local levels). Catalog available on books, films, publications and exhibits.
How to Contact: Write or call Joseph Mori or Richard Leavitt, Science Information Division for scientific information; Dorothy Davis, associate director of public information; or Patricia O'Connell, news editor.
Tips: Information on anticipated publication or type of audience for articles in preparation is helpful to us in selecting appropriate background material.

National Kidney Foundation, 2 Park Ave., New York NY 10016. Public Information Director: Jim Warren.
Purpose: "Major voluntary organization seeking total answer to diseases of the

kidney—prevention, treatment and cure."
Services: Offers aid in arranging interviews, annual reports, bibliographies, brochures/pamphlets, placement on mailing list, statistics and quarterly newsletter.
How to Contact: Write or call. "Written requests will get prompt attention."

National Society to Prevent Blindness, 79 Madison Ave., New York NY 10016. (212)684-3505. Director of Public Relations: Lydia Maguire.
Purpose: "The National Society to Prevent Blindness, founded in 1908, is the oldest voluntary health agency nationally engaged in the prevention of blindness through comprehensive programs of community services, public and professional education and research. Materials are available on eye health and eye safety." Information covers health/medicine.
Services: Offers aid in arranging interviews, annual reports, bibliographies, statistics and brochures/pamphlets. *Catalog of Publications and Films* available.
How to Contact: Write or call. Charges handling fee for film loan.

National Sudden Infant Death Syndrome Foundation, 310 S. Michigan Ave., Chicago IL 60604. (312)663-0650. Assistant Executive Director: Edith McShane.
Purpose: "The easing of burdens on families who lose a child to SIDS or any other unexpected cause; educational and research programs; volunteer programs; public awareness campaigns; resource and referral mechanism; and the ultimate elimination of Sudden Infant Death Syndrome." Information covers health/medicine, science and self-help.
Services: Offers annual reports, bibliographies, statistics, brochures/pamphlets and newsletter.
How to Contact: Write or call. Publication price list available. "We suggest that writers have their work checked by a person knowledgeable about SIDS. Staff at the national office can assist directly or refer requests for such services. There is no charge for such consultation. Because of the sensitive nature of all issues relating to SIDS, it is imperative that a writer have a broad perspective and be willing to research the interdisciplinary aspects."

The People-to-People Health Foundation, Inc./Project HOPE, 2233 Wisconsin Ave. NW, Washington DC 20007. Director, Department of Information Services: Anson B. Campbell.
Purpose: "Medical education programs throughout developing world. Health sciences education and research projects centered at HOPE center. International symposia on health-related topics. Coordinate national committee investigating health and public policy. We have a growing collection of literature on the various countries with whom we work—state of health care delivery, cultural aspects, political climate, level of technological development, etc. Our large collection of medical education program reports, writen by staff, could be a valuable resource in various fields of inquiry." Information covers health/medicine and health education curricula.
Services: Offers annual reports, bibliographies, biographies, brochures/pamphlets, information searches, placement on mailing list, newsletters, photos and press kits. "We also have an educational monograph series, commissioned scholars' papers on the US health care system and a printed program summary series."
How to Contact: Direct inquiry to Department of Information Services or Learning Resources Center, The HOPE Center, Millwood VA 22646. "We usually ask for credit line where applicable. We have limited staff and can offer little individual research assistance."

Sickle Cell Disease Foundation of Greater New York, 209 W. 125th St., Suite 108, New York NY 10027. (212)865-1201. Executive Director: Dick Campbell.
Purpose: "We are a nonprofit, charitable, informational and educational organization." Information covers health/medicine, science and technical data.
Services: Offers aid in arranging interviews, statistics and brochures/pamphlets.

How to Contact: "Send check for $5 to cover mailing and preparation costs of a complete package on Sickle Cell Anemia."

History

Alabama Association of Historians, 17 Pinemont Dr., Tuscaloosa AL 35401. (205)345-8391. Contact: William D. Barnard.
Purpose: "The association provides a forum for those who teach history in the colleges and universities within the state of Alabama to address mutual interests in the teaching of history and in historical research." Information covers history.
How to Contact: Write or call.

American Association for State and Local History, 1400 8th Ave. S., Nashville TN 37203. (615)242-5583. Publications Director: Gary G. Gore.
Purpose: "Our organization has a membership of nearly 6,000 professional historians librarians and museologists. We have an active publishing program of books, technical leaflets and monthly *History News* aimed at professional development of members, including the researching and writing of local history. The American Association for State and Local History (AASLH) directory lists 4,442 state and local history agencies, which are an excellent source of local history records." Information covers art, history and how-to for history professionals, museologists and historians.
Services: Offers bibliographies, brochures/pamphlets, newsletter and books. Publications include *Researching, Writing, Publishing Local History* ($6), *Directory of Historical Societies in US and Canada* ($24), *Transcribing and Editing Oral History* ($6.75), and *Bibliography on Historical Organization Practices Volumes I, II, and III* ($10 each).
How to Contact: Write or call. Individual association membership (to receive newsletter) is $16. "The Director of Publications at AASLH will review unsolicited manuscripts aimed at history professionals, particularly how-to books for local historians, librarians and museologists."

American Historical Association, 400 A St. SE, Washington DC 20003.
Purpose: "Promotion of historical studies; collection and preservation of historical manuscripts and dissemination of historical research." Information covers history.
Services: Offers annual reports, brochures/pamphlets, statistics and newsletter.
How to Contact: Write.

National Trust for Historic Preservation in the United States, 740 Jackson Place NW, Washington DC 20006. (202)638-5200. Director of Media Services, Office of Public Affairs: Fletcher Cox Jr. Director of Planning, The Preservation Press: Diane Maddex. Librarian, Office of Preservation Services: Brigid Rapp.
Purpose: "The National Trust is a private, nonprofit organization chartered by Congress in 1949 with the responsibility to facilitate public participation in the preservation of sites, buildings and objects significant in American history and culture. Support for the National Trust is provided by membership dues, endowment funds and contributions and by federal grants, including matching grants from the Department of the Interior. The trust owns historic properties; publishes a monthly newsletter, quarterly magazine, books and newsletters; provides advisory services; awards matching grants; conducts conferences and workshops, and administers six regional offices in the areas of history, architecture, conservation, archaeology, planning, and preservation law." Information covers art/architecture, business, economics, history, how-to (restoration and adaptive use), law, nature/conservation and technical data on

restoration. "The National Trust serves as a clearinghouse for preservation groups and programs, financing, government programs, ordinances, aesthetic guidelines and restoration techniques."

Services: Offers aid in arranging interviews, annual reports, bibliographies, statistics, brochures/pamphlets, information searches, placement on mailing list, newsletter and press kits. "Preservation Press provides advisory services for publications. Media services provides assistance to press and other media. Library provides research assistance." Publications include *Preservation News*, *Historic Preservation*, *Historic Preservation and the National Trust*, *The Preservation Press*, *Preservation Services*, *Annual Report*, various press releases and brochures describing publications, and the *Information* series of technical advice. "The library is a major depository of preservation research materials in the US. A list of preservation periodicals and newsletters, both national and state, is available from the library also."

How to Contact: "Writers may contact one of our three offices and request information—the more specific, the more appropriate the response. The six regional offices will provide information on preservation groups and activities and issues in their areas. Library services must be in person. Send letter of inquiry for manuscript review and advice. Membership in the trust is encouraged; magazine and newspaper are available as benefits of membership." Charges $15/year for membership.

Tips: "Another source is the state historic preservation office of each state, as well as city historic district or landmarks commission in most US cities. Check with local historical societies. National Register of Historic Places has documentation of historic buildings, sites or objects of national, state and local significance. Historic American Buildings Survey has an excellent collection of architectural drawings and photographs (available through the Library of Congress.)"

Hospitals & Hospital Administration

American College of Hospital Administrators, 840 N. Lake Shore Dr., Chicago IL 60611. (312)943-0544. Editor: Lynn C. Wimmer.

Purpose: "The five primary objectives of the American College of Health Administrators (ACHA) are to elevate the standards of hospital administration; establish a standard of competence for hospital administration; develop and promote standards of education and training for hospital administrators; educate hospital trustees and the public to understand that the practice of hospital administration calls for special training and experience; and provide a method for conferring fellowships in hospital administration on those who have done or are doing noteworthy service in the field of hospital administration."

Services: Offers annual reports, statistics, brochures/pamphlets and newsletter. Publications include task force reports, proceedings of international seminars and miscellaneous publications related to hospital administration.

How to Contact: Write or call.

Tips: "We can put the writer on to appropriate persons on the staff or, if necessary, in the field (practitioners or academicians) who can be of most help. When writers are seeking documentation on specifics about who's doing what in a specialized area, we usually can be of help, since our membership includes the major CEO's and their top managerial staffs in the nation's leading health service facilities."

American Hospital Association 840 N. Lake Shore Dr., Chicago IL 60611. (312)280-6000. Contact: Division of Public Affairs.

Purpose: "The American Hospital Association is a membership organization for hospitals and hospital workers, whose purpose is education, research and statistical data."

Services: Offers aid in arranging interviews, bibliographies, statistics, brochures/

pamphlets, placement on mailing list, newsletter, press kits and press releases. Publications include *AHA Guide to Health Care*; *AHA Hospital Books*, and *Hospital Week*.
How to Contact: Write.

American Osteopathic Hospital Association, 930 Busse Hwy., Park Ridge IL 60068.
(312)692-2351. Director of Communications/Editor: Lin Fish.
Purpose: "The purpose of this organization is to promote the public health and welfare through effective hospital leadership; provide member hospitals a channel through which to act collectively in areas of common interest; collect and analyze appropriate data; and provide management services and programs that improve the ability of member hospitals to deliver quality osteopathic health care." Information covers health/medicine.
Services: Offers aid in arranging interviews, annual reports, statistics, brochures/pamphlets, placement on mailing list and newsletter. Publications include *More Important Now Than Ever Before*.
How to Contact: Write or call. "We represent hospitals and have only general information on physicians."

The Catholic Hospital Association, 1438 S. Grand Blvd., St. Louis MO 63104.
(314)773-0646. Director of Public Relations: Stephen M. Moldaver.
Purpose: "The purpose of the Catholic Hospital Association is to promote Christian community and enhance the dignity of man by assisting Catholic church—related health care organizations to provide optimal health care services and programs, which contribute to the physical, psychological, emotional and spiritual well being of the people and communities served." Information covers health/medicine.
Services: Offers aid in arranging interviews, annual reports, bibliographies, biographies, statistics and brochures/pamphlets.
How to Contact: Write or call.

Connecticut Hospital Association, Box 90, 10 Alexander Dr., Wallingford CT 06492.
(202)265-7611, ext. 22. Assistant Vice President, Public Affairs and Development: Thomas H. Ulfelder.
Purpose: "The Connecticut Hospital Association is a private, nonprofit hospital association acting as a representative for the Connecticut hospitals in planning, finance, shared services, public relations and government relations." Information covers economics, health/medicine and new products.
Services: Offers newsletter.
How to Contact: Write.

Hospital Association of Hawaii (HAH), 320 Ward, Suite 202, Honolulu HI 96822.
(808)521-8961. Public Relations Director: Kimi Mann.
Purpose: "The Hospital Association of Hawaii was founded in 1939 as a nonprofit organization to promote institutional excellence in health care, with the stress on care and human concern. The association serves as a forum for health care specialists to collectively deal with the complexities of health care. Information covers administration, fiscal management, legal liability, public information, cost containment strategies, and cooperates closely with national organizations in coordinating activities its members share."
Services: Offers aid in arranging interviews, annual reports, statistics, brochures/pamphlets and newsletter. Publications include *Containing Costs* and *Hawaii's Hospitals Care*.
How to Contact: Write. "Services are limited to other state hospital associations, national hospital/medical care associations, press and media, and hospitals. Requests from unaffiliated individuals will be considered as time and resources permit."

Hospital Association of New York State, Inc., 15 Computer Dr. W., Albany NY 12205.
(518)458-7940. Director of Communications: Andrew A. Foster.

Purpose: "The Hospital Association of New York State is a trade association representing more than 300 voluntary and public hospitals in New York state (including New York City). Information covers operation of health care facilities in New York state (services, finances, governmental regulation and monitoring, health planning, staffing patterns). Information covers health/medicine.
Services: Offers aid in arranging interviews, information searches, placement on mailing list, statistics and newsletter. Publications available.
How to Contact: Write or call. Charges for some reports; newsletter costs $25/year.
Tips: "The prospective hospital reimbursement system now being used in New York state is the oldest such system in the nation. Efforts now underway to correct inequities in the system should be of interest to everyone concerned with the effort to contain hospital costs and the effect of these efforts on hospital-based health care services."

Hospital Council of Western Pennsylvania, Box 412, Warrendale PA 15086. (412)367-1968. Public Relations Consultant: Betty Havryluk.
Purpose: "With members of over 100 hospitals in western Pennsylvania, this is a voluntary association whose members work cooperatively to improve patient services, meet manpower needs and initiate shared programs in cost containment, management and group purchasing. It has offices in Pittsburgh, Meadville and Altoona."
Services: Offers statistics and brochures/pamphlets. Publications include *PR* (newsletter for hospital public relations directors), *Emphasis* (newsletter for hospital administrators) and *Human Resources (newsletter for personnel directors)*.
How to Contact: Write or call.

Massachusetts Hospital Association, 5 NE Executive Park, Burlington MA 01803. (617)272-8000. Public Relations Director: Richard Pozniak.
Purpose: "The Massachusetts Hospital Association is concerned with health and hospital care in Massachusetts." Information covers health/medicine.
Services: Offers aid in arranging interviews, statistics, brochures/pamphlets, clipping services, information searches, newsletter and press kits. Publications include *Monday Report*, a weekly review of medical developments in Massachusetts; and *Legislative Update*, a review of legislative development concerning health care in Massachusetts.
How to Contact: Write or call.

North Carolina Hospital Association, Box 10937, Raleigh NC 27605. (919)834-8484. Director of Public Relations: Kaye Lasater.
Purpose: "The exchange of knowledge and ideas to improve efficiency in hospital management. Our objective is the improvement of the health and well-being of all North Carolinians through our work with member hospitals." Information covers health/medicine.
Services: Offers annual reports, brochures/pamphlets and newsletter.
How to Contact: Write or call.

Housing

Apartment Owners-Managers Association of America (AOMA), 65 Cherry Plaza, Box 232, Watertown CT 06795. Contact: Members Services Dept.
Purpose: Organization for apartment construction and management.
Services: Offers brochures/pamphlets. Publications include descriptions of association services.
How to Contact: Prefers written inquiries.

Building Owners and Managers Association International, 1221 Massachusetts Ave. NW, Washington DC 20005. (202)638-2929. Editor: Marc L. Intermaggio.

Purpose: "Building Owners and Managers Association International (BOMA) represents the high-rise office building industry. BOMA members own and/or manage over 500 million square feet of commercial office space in approximately 80 major US and Canadian cities, and others worldwide. Our newsletter contains information on legislative and regulatory decisions, both federal and local, which affect the high-rise industry. We also feature building operations articles on subjects such as renovation, maintenance, energy conservation, etc. We also have a research library—Information Central—to handle special topics." Information covers business, economics, how-to, industry, law and technical data.
Services: Offers bibliographies, statistics, brochures/pamphlets information searches, placement on mailing list and newsletter. Publications include semiannual survey of occupancy rates and *Building Owner and Manager* (newsletter).
How to Contact: Write or call. Charges $25/year for newsletter subscription, $95 for experience exchange reports, "which compare expense and income data from BOMA members. The reports are designed to be primary tools for ownership, management, mortgage, appraisal and investment."

National Association of Housing Cooperatives, 1828 L St. NW, Washington DC 20036. (202)872-0550. Writer/Editor: Claudia Conner.
Purpose: "We are a nonprofit, tax-exempt organization of more than 425 cooperatives and nine regional associations representing more than 100,000 families living in cooperative housing communities across the United States. Our major goals are to educate people about the advantages of housing co-ops, and to improve and make more efficient the organization and operation of housing cooperatives, especially those whose members are primarily low-, moderate- and middle-income families. We publish the monthly *Cooperative Housing Bulletin* and *Cooperative Housing Journal*, books, pamphlets and educational materials. We also sponsor conferences, seminars, education programs, research services, government relations programs and a cooperative housing information clearing house. Cooperatives are an excellent method of removing housing from the speculative market, of offering people control over where and how they live. Cooperatives are not for people who can buy their own home; they offer equity and ownership for those who cannot otherwise buy. Co-ops are not condominiums." Information covers business, economics, how-to, industry, law, politics, self-help, technical data, new products, insurance, safety and all aspects of co-op housing.
Services: Offers annual reports, bibliographies, brochures/pamphlets, information searches, statistics, newsletter and photos. Publications available.
How to Contact: Write or call. Charges for membership and publications.

The National Housing Partnership, 1133 15th St., NW Washington DC 20005. (202)857-5700. Director or Corporate Affairs: Edwin L. Stoll.
Purpose: "The largest private producer in the nation of housing for families of low and moderate income, The National Housing Partnership (NHP) enters into partnerships with builders, developers, and nonprofit and community groups at local levels for the construction of housing, either multifamily rental or single-family sales. Providing equal capital and joint venture funds, NHP supplies also guidance and assistance from its staff of professionals during the planning and building stages of a project, plus management responsibility upon completion. In its nationwide operations, NHP fulfills the objective of its Congressional charter by stimulating the production by private enterprise of low and moderate income housing and by assisting the building industry in general." Information covers business and how-to.
Services: Offers annual reports, brochures/pamphlets, placement on mailing list, and photos. Publications available.
How to Contact: Write. "Our information pertains primarily to the operations of the National Housing Partnership, and we are not a source for government statistics."

Human Services

American Association of Retired Persons (AARP), 1909 K St. NW, Washington DC 20049. (202)872-4700. Contact: Public Relations Department.
Purpose: "The nation's largest organization of older Americans. Legislation-oriented, nonprofit, nonpartisan. Activities include legislation, community service, education and information." Information covers business, economics, food, health/medicine, industry, law, recreation, science, self-help, technical data and travel.
Services: Offers aid in arranging interviews, bibliographies, statistics, brochures/pamphlets, information searches, placement on mailing list and newsletter.
How to Contact: Write.

American Red Cross, 17th and D Sts. NW, Washington DC 20006. (202)737-8300. Director, Office of Systems Analysis, Information and Statistics: Meyer Mathis.
Purpose: "The aims of the American Red Cross are to improve the quality of human life and to enhance individual self-reliance and concern for others. It works toward these aims through national and chapter services governed and directed by volunteers. American Red Cross services help people avoid emergencies, prepare for emergencies and cope with them when they occur. To accomplish its aims, the Red Cross provides volunteer blood services to a large segment of the nation, conducts community services, and, as mandated by its congressional charter, serves as an independent medium of voluntary relief and communication between the American people and their armed forces; maintains a system of local, national and international disaster preparedness and relief; and assists the government of the United States to meet humanitarian treaty commitments." Information covers health/medicine, history, disasters, and military welfare services.
Services: Offers annual reports, bibliographies, biographies, statistics, brochures/pamphlets, information searches and photos. Publications include *Publications of the American National Red Cross*, a catalog of materials available. Publications cover American Red Cross services, including safety programs (general information, first aid, small craft, water safety), nursing and health programs, international relations, Red Cross youth service programs, volunteer services opportunities, disaster services, blood program information (including studies of the functions and processing of blood), and general and historical information about the organization. Also publishes first aid and safety textbooks.
How to Contact: "Writers may query by letter, asking for information as specifically as possible. Or, they may visit our library. For library visits, researchers must advise us in advance of their date of visit." Red Cross publications are available from local American Red Cross chapters.

Aquarian Research Foundation, 5620 Morton St., Philadelphia PA 19144. (215)849-1259, 849-3237. Director: Art Rosenblum.
Purpose: "Research aimed at finding humanistic alternatives to competitive society. Information on natural birth control, new sciences, alternative lifestyles—especially alternative communities." Information covers health/medicine, new products, science, self-help, technical data and travel.
Services: Offers brochures/pamphlets and newsletters. Publications include *The Natural Birth Control Book*, *Unpopular Science*, and a newsletter published monthly in *Green Revolution Magazine*.
How to Contact: Write or call.

Association of Halfway House Alcoholism Programs of North American, Inc., 786 E. 7th St., St. Paul MN 55106. (612)771-0933. Executive Director: Diane Adams.
Purpose: "The association is a voluntary vehicle by which halfway house alcoholism programs have bound themselves together to promote the role of supportive residential facilities in the continuum of care and rehabilitation in the recovery process of those with alcoholism and other addictive disorders." Information covers how-to and

technical data.
Services: Offers statistics, brochures/pamphlets and newsletter.
How to Contact: Write or call. Charges nonmembers for services. "Our materials are, for the most part, descriptive, firsthand reports and experiences."

Candlelighters Foundation, 123 C St. SE, Washington DC 20003. (202)483-9100, 544-1696. President: Grace Powers Monaco. Executive Director: Julie Sullwan.
Purpose: "An international organization of parents groups (our children have or have had cancer). We have postal parent-to-parent and group-to-group buddy systems, parent-to-parent phone lines, a speakers bureau, promotion of quality educational materials, surveys of patient and family needs, and placement of parents on federal and state social services advisory." Information covers health/medicine, how-to, politics, science, and self-help.
Services: Offers bibliographies, brochures/pamphlets, placement on mailing list, and newsletter. Publications available.
How to Contact: Write or call.

CARE, Inc., 3600 Broadway, Kansas City MO 64111. Regional Director: Mary Ann Vaan Vooren. 660 1st Ave., New York NY 10016. Director of Public Information: Jack Thatcher.
Purpose: "To provide international aid and overseas information. We have 16 US offices, and our world headquarters in New York." Information covers agriculture, economics, food, health/medicine, history, law, nature, politics, science, travel and specific geographic/cultural information about countries using CARE.
Services: Offers aid in arranging interviews, annual reports, brochures/pamphlets, statistics, newsletter and photos.
How to Contact: Write or visit a regional office. "This office has only two staff people, so time is limited regarding aid in research."
Tips: "Research the subject well. There is a great deal of misinformation about overseas countries that is the result of superficial research. Much has been written that just does not make sense to someone who has actually been there."

Child Abuse Prevention Association, 1505 W. Truman Rd., Independence MO 64050. (816)252-8388. Director: Paula Davis.
Purpose: "We handle a crisis line, volunteer parent aid, 'parents anonymous,' discussion groups and public education— all related to child abuse." Information covers law, health/medicine and child abuse statistics.
Services: Offers aid in arranging interviews, bibliographies, statistics, brochures/pamphlets, placement on mailing list and newsletter.
How to Contact: Write.

Child Welfare League of America, Library/Information Service, 67 Irving Place, New York NY 10003. (212)254-7410. Information Specialist: Emily Gardiner. Adoption Information Specialist: Claire Berman.
Purpose: "To improve services for dependent and neglected children in the US and Canada. Child Welfare League of America (CWLA) sets standards, conducts research, publishes a journal and books, sponsors educational conferences, provides consultation and maintains a public affairs office in Washington." Information covers child welfare services.
Services: Offers bibliographies, statistics and brochures/pamphlets.
How to Contact: Write or call.

The Children's Foundation, 1028 Connecticut Ave. NW, #1112, Washington DC 20036. (202)296-4450. Deputy Director: Joanne Williams.
Purpose: "The Children's Foundation is a national, nonprofit, anti-hunger advocacy organization designed to monitor all the federally funded child nutrition programs: the national school lunch and breakfast programs; summer food and child care food

programs; the special supplemental food program for women, infants and children; and the food stamp program. Additionally, we provide training and technical assistance, and prepare resource materials for community groups, individuals, local elected officials and school administrators who either are interested in implementing the programs or want to expand and improve already existing ones. Headquarted in Washington, we maintain regional offices in: Santa Fe, New Mexico; Atlanta; and Pierre, South Dakota." Information covers food, how-to, self-help, training, and technical assistance in the area of community organizing in relation to access to the federal food programs.

Services: Offers aid in arranging interviews, annual reports, brochures/pamphlets, placement on mailing list, statistics and newsletter. Publications available.

How to Contact: Write or call. Charges for publications.

Day Care & Child Development Council of America, 520 Southern Bldg., 805 15th St. NW, Washington DC 20005. (202)638-2316. Administrative Assistant: Carolyn P. Jones.

Purpose: "To foster the improvement and expansion of child care services in the United States—providing information and assistance to organizations and individuals professionally caring for children—and informing the general public on needs and issues relevant to day care and child development." Information covers how-to, law, politics and technical data.

Services: Offers brochures/pamphlets, statistics and newsletter.

How to Contact: Write or call. Charges for publications. "As a small organization, the council can best respond to specific requests for information and can offer on-site use of a resource library in the central office in Washington."

Edna McConnell Clark Foundation, 250 Park Ave., New York NY 10017. (212)986-7050. Director of Communications: Barbara Radloff. Assistant to the Director: Suzanne Koblentz.

Purpose: "We fund organizations working in the following areas: adoption/foster care system reforms which advance the placement of parentless children into families; alternatives to incarceration and the protection of the rights of former and present prisoners and mental patients; schistosomiasis research regarding immunology, drug development and experimental field control; and job placement for the hard-to-employ. The specific focus of this last program is still being formulated." Information covers "background about the problem areas listed above and about organizations (specifically, our grantees), working to ameliorate these problems."

Services: Offers aid in arranging interviews, annual reports, brochures/pamphlets and placement on mailing list. Publications include *Current Goals and Interests, Edna McConnell Clark Foundation Annual Report* and various brochures from grantees.

How to Contact: "Call or write. Writers should realize that, while we are eager to help, our communications staff consists of only two people, so that the depth of support we can offer may be limited by other demands on our time."

Face Learning Center, Inc., 12945 Seminole Blvd., Largo FL 33706. (813)586-1110, 585-8155. Director, Community Development: Teri Rosati.

Purpose: "We are a nonprofit service through which women learn self-sufficiency, emotional stability and financial independence."

Services: Offers aid in arranging interviews, bibliographies, brochures/pamphlets, placement on mailing list, community programs and classes.

How to Contact: Write or call.

Family and Children Services, 3515 Broadway, #300, Kansas City MO 64111. Contact: J.R. Majors.

Purpose: "Provides counseling to people affected by divorce, adoption, alcoholism and problem pregnancies. We also have services for older adults, financial assistance for high school students, and family life education programs." Information covers

health/medicine and family life education.
Services: Offers aid in arranging interviews, statistics and newsletter.
How to Contact: "Interview staff members in person."

Family Planning, Inc., 2301 Locust, Kansas City MO 64108. (816)274-2211. Public Health Program and Community Development: Linda Herring.
Purpose: "Family planning counseling, education, examinations, fertility counseling and public information." Information covers health/medicine and sexuality.
Services: Offers aid in arranging interviews, brochures/pamphlets, information searches and statistics. Publications available.
How to Contact: Write or call.

First Sunday (Couples Whose Child Has Died), 1234 Washington Blvd., Detroit MI 48226. (313)327-5810. Advisor: The Rev. Russell E. Kohler.
Purpose: "First Sunday couples seek to make a healthy adjustment in the months following the death of their child. The couples contribute to in-service training in Detroit area hospitals. The couples originated the Pope John XXIII Hospitality Program, which houses relatives and chemotherapy from out-of-state who are in treatment, but ambulatory in the Detroit Medical Center Hospitals." Information covers art therapy, health/medicine and self-help.
Services: Offers reprints of articles on the group from the *Journal of Pediatrics* and related news articles. Publications available.
How to Contact: Write. Charges for postage and reprint fees (5¢/page). "A group advisor (chaplain or psychiatric social worker) will write to supply information or the name of a couple from the group. We are concerned about the possible detrimental effects on the terminally ill as well as the emotionally ill university student who is finding the death and dying literature an option to his stress and contributing to suicide factors. We prefer to recognize the threat of death as a life intensifier which heightens perception in the dying child and we link the artist and musician to the child so that the family may relate to the creativity and nonverbal communication of the child until the goal becomes primarily comfort of the body."

Goodwill Industries of America, 9200 Wisconsin Ave., Washington DC 20014. Public Relations Director: Matt Warren.
Purpose: "To provide leadership and assistance to organizational members in their efforts to help the handicapped, disabled and disadvantaged attain their fullest potential. The primary purpose of Goodwill is to provide rehabilitation services, training, employment and opportunities for personal growth for handicapped, disabled and disadvantaged persons who cannot fit into the competitive labor market or the usual facets of society."
Services: Offers aid in arranging interviews, annual reports, placement on mailing list, statistics and newsletter.
How to Contact: Write. "Material is available on a limited basis."

Homosexual Information Center, Inc., 6715 Hollywood Blvd., #210, Los Angeles CA 90028. (213)464-8431.
Purpose: "We have the most complete file and library on issues and aspects of homosexuality in the world. Our library contains the archives of the homosexual movement. We have early newsletters, etc., which are unavailable anywhere else in the world. We as a staff have over 25 years experience dealing with aspects of homosexuality, having cooperated with such people as Evelyn Hooker and Kinsey. A co-founder, Don Slater, is the foremost thinker on the subject in the world. We present a balanced view." Information covers history, law, politics and self-help.
Services: Offers aid in arranging interviews, bibliographies, brochures/pamphlets and newsletter. Publications available.
How to Contact: Write. "We are tax-deductible and we accept donations, but we do expect acknowledgment in the published article for use of our library, etc. We counsel

people, of course, who have problems in the field and then refer any major legal or psychological problems to properly qualified agencies. Not all agencies really are good at handling homosexuality.''

International Halfway House Association (IHHA), 2525 Victory Pkwy., Suite 101, Cincinnati OH 45206. (513)221-3250. Past President: Eb Henderson.
Purpose: ''The International Halfway House Association (IHHA) has been in the forefront of the movement to treat community problems in the community. The IHHA serves as a focal point where the public and private sectors may address issues related to social policies and programs. It provides a forum for its members to exchange ideas and information about treatment, research and administration.'' Information covers how-to and technical data.
Services: Offers brochures/pamphlets and newsletter.
How to Contact: Write or call.

La Leche League International, Inc., 9616 Minneapolis, Franklin Park IL 60131.
Purpose: ''To give help and encouragement primarily through personal instruction to those mothers who want to nurse their babies. We believe breastfeeding is the ideal way to initiate good mother-child relationships and strengthen family ties. The international office reaches out to mothers through 4,225 groups in which certified league leaders meet with women who want to know about the womanly art of breast-feeding. There are more than 11,000 league leaders who volunteer their time to help other mothers.''
Services: Offers annual reports, brochures/pamphlets, newsletter and press kits. Publications available.
How to Contact: Write. Charges for publications.

Methadone Maintenance Institute, 571 W. Jackson, Chicago IL 60606. (312)663-9224. Contact: Jeanne Anderson.
Purpose: Information covers health/medicine, drug and alcohol abuse and environmental issues.
Services: Offers brochures/pamphlets, newsletter, cassettes and movies. Publications include *Drug Health Alert!* (monthly newsletter) and approximately 30 other titles on drug abuse and other issues.
How to Contact: Call or write. Charges 25¢-$2/copy for brochures/pamphlets; $15/individual membership and subscription to newsletter.

Metropolitan Organization to Counter Sexual Assault, 2 W. 40th St., #104, Kansas City MO 64111. Administrative Assistant: Sue Symon.
Purpose: ''To provide sexual assault counseling, mental health and public education and legal aid on sexual assault.'' Information covers health/medicine, law and self-help.
Services: Offers aid in arranging interviews, bibliographies, brochures/pamphlets, placement on mailing list, statistics and newsletter. Publications available.
How to Contact: Write or call. ''The staff does not have the man power to aid in the actual research process.''

National Association of Social Workers (NASW), 1425 H St. NW, Suite 600, Washington DC 20005. (202)628-6800. Public Relations Coordinator: Sheila B. Healey.
Purpose: Membership association and lobbying organization. Information covers social work, social welfare and social services.
Services: Offers aid in arranging interviews, statistics, newsletter, photos and press kits. Publications include *NASW News* (monthly newspaper) and *The Advocate* (roundup of social service legislation); policy statements on such issues as immigration, racism, social services, housing, confidentiality; and standards booklets for social workers in schools, hospitals, personnel practices and social service manpower.

How to Contact: Call or write the public relations coordinator. Charges $6/year for *NASW News*, $20/year for *The Advocate*.

National Black United Fund, 3741 Stocker St., Suite 211-212, Los Angeles CA 90008. (213)295-6431. Communication Specialist: Regina Gordon.
Purpose: "The Black United Fund is a mechanism by which the black community can determine its own priorities and then fund organizations and agencies working on those priorities. We have affiliates in eleven cities to which we provide technical and administrative assistance; we do not provide allocations, but each local affiliate does." Information covers self-help and fund-raising expertise.
Services: Offers newsletter and assistance in setting up local Black United Funds.
How to Contact: Write or call.

National Conference on Social Welfare, 22 W. Gay St., Columbus OH 43215. (614)221-4469; 221-4460. Administrative Assistant: Joan Christman.
Purpose: "Our primary purpose is education and information. Through its meetings, publications and special events, the National Conference on Social Welfare builds knowledge and expertise. More specifically, it provides ideas and information on effective programs to serve people, standards and guidelines for the social services and human care, advocacy for organizations to help people, and a focus for the broad involvement of the American public in social policy. The National Conference on Social Welfare is a voluntary organization composed of individuals and agencies representing all aspects of the human services." Information covers economics, health/ medicine, social service industry, recreation, techincal data and "all aspects of social service and social service delivery."
Services: Offers bibliographies, brochures/pamphlets, information searches, placement on mailing list and newsletter (available through membership only). Publications include publications brochure, membership and service information, and SCAN listings by subject desired. "We have documented all material from *Social Welfare Forum* and related publications from 1873 to 1923 and from 1924 to 1962. The latter is published in our *KWIC Index*. Unpublished manuscripts selected by an editorial committee are published annually in our conference bulletin with a short abstract. These have been documented under various categories since 1964. A writer publishing any copyrighted material from our official proceedings (*Social Welfare Forum*) must secure permission from Columbia University Press, New York City, and give proper credit line. Any unpublished manuscripts must give proper identification in credit line."
How to Contact: Write or call. "There is never a charge for information; however, we do charge for our publications, with discounts to members on some publications. Our SCAN manuscripts are $3/manuscript to nonmembers, and *Social Welfare Forum* is a part of membership as well as for sale to individuals or agencies."

The National Council on the Aging, Inc., 1828 L St. NW, Washington DC 20036. (202)223-6250. Media Director: Michael Edgley.
Purpose: "We are a nonprofit organization that improves the lives of older Americans through a variety of programs administered by the National Council on the Aging (NCOA) and by providing technical assistance and training to other practitioners in the field of aging. Among others, NCOA is involved in senior centers, employment, preretirement, the arts and humanities. We also confer with the producers of prime time TV programming, provide information to other media and testify before Congress." Information covers art, business, economics, entertainment and politics.
Services: Offers bibliographies, statistics, brochures/pamphlets and placement on mailing list. Publications include *Facts and Myths About Aging*, a general information booklet developed for use in NCOA's advertising council all-media campaign; a brochure giving a brief overview of NCOA's activities; and *Senior Community Service Projects*, a description of the job program administered by NCOA.
How to Contact: Write or call. "We have a large publications list; some must be

purchased. Additionally, if we were asked to provide detailed lengthy services we would negotiate a fee."

National Safety Council, 444 N. Michigan Ave., Chicago IL 60657. (312)527-4800. Director, Public Relations: James G. Shaffer.
Purpose: "We are a voluntary public-service organization of people and organizations acting to increase the safety and improve the occupational health of the American people." Information covers agriculture/farming, business, economics, health/ medicine, how-to (safety), industry, new products, traffic and transportation, recreation, self-help, sports, technical data, travel, and anything related to safety in the public and private sectors.
Services: Offers aid in arranging interviews, annual reports, bibliographies, biographies, statistics, brochures/pamphlets, information searches, placement on mailing list, photos and press kits. Publications include complete catalogs available in areas of farming, recreation, industry, school/college and miscellaneous related subjects.
How to Contact: Write or call.
Tips: "Information excerpted from National Safety Council materials must be credited to the council. All National Safety Council programs and/or products also must be attributed to the council. The National Safety Council's *Accident Facts* magazine is available for quick reference with credit to the council where applicable. This service is a supplement to the council's research department which may be contacted for reference through the public relations department."

Negative Population Growth, Inc., 101 Park Ave., New York NY 10017. (212)683-5454. President: Donald Mann.
Purpose: Nonprofit organization advocating reduction of population growth.
Services: Offers annual reports, brochures/pamphlets, placement on mailing list and newsletter. Publications include position papers and newsletter, *Human Survival*.
How to Contact: Write or call.

Orphan Voyage, Rt. 1, Box 153A, Cedaredge CO 81413. (303)856-3937. Coordinator: Jean Paton.
Purpose: "Life history of members of the adoption population, particularly adopted individuals who desire to find kindred; as well as birthparents of adopted people wishing reunion."
Services: Offers aid in arranging interviews, annual reports, bibliographies, brochures/pamphlets, placement on mailing list and newsletter. Publications available.
How to Contact: Write and enclose SASE. Charges for publications, or, if in-depth assistance with research is needed, charges will be worked out individually. "We are busy here, and have to be motivated. Our focus is on giving service to members of the adoption population."
Tips: "When it comes to human affliction, statistics are not all that important. Each individual bears the truth within him. When repeated, it becomes very persuasive. But the language of the social orphan, one who has lost parents by a social decision, is difficult to hear. The meanings of our words are different from the meanings of words to standard people."

Parents Without Partners, Inc., 7910 Woodmont Ave., Washington DC 20014. (301)654-8850. Information Center: Ann Parks or Barbara Chase.
Purpose: "We are a volunteer national and international organization of single parents—the widowed, divorced, separated or never-married—who are bringing up children alone, or who, through not having custody, are still parents and concerned with the upbringing of their children. In 1978, Parents Without Partners (PWP) listed over 170,000 members in about 1,000 chapters and is growing steadily in the United States and Canada. Each chapter's volunteer leaders plan and conduct programs of help, with general guidelines and material provided by PWP, Inc. PWP is tax-exempt

under federal law as a nonprofit educational organization." Information covers self-help for single parents.

Services: Offers bibliographies, brochures/pamphlets, statistics and a research library with resources pertaining to single parents (some materials available on many subjects such as parenting, custody, divorce and child support).

How to Contact: Write. Charges for materials plus postage/handling.

SIECUS (Sex Information and Education Council of the United States), 84 5th Ave., New York NY 10011. (212)929-2300. Executive Officer: Barbara Whitney.

Purpose: "Our aim is to establish human sexuality as a health entity. Through our publications, our own programs (and those cosponsored as part of our affiliation with the department of health education, school of education, health, nursing, and arts professions of New York University) and the activities of our state affiliates, we try to serve as a clearinghouse for information on all aspects of human sexuality, with special emphasis on sex education." Information covers health and human sexuality.

Services: Offers biographies, brochures/pamphlets and newsletter. Publications available.

How to Contact: Write or call. "Our extensive library on human sexuality will be housed in the New York University department of health education and is available for use by persons obtaining special permission from SIECUS and NYU."

Society for the Right To Die, 250 W. 57th St., New York NY 10019. (212)246-6973. Executive Director: Alice V. Mehling.

Purpose: "To advance legislation enabling individuals, by means of a legally binding document, to limit the futile prolongation of dying." Information covers health/medicine and law.

Services: Offers aid in arranging interviews, annual reports, bibliographies, brochures/pamphlets, placement on mailing list and newsletter. Publications available.

How to Contact: Write or call. "We can provide information on right-to-die bills in any state, together with the names of legislative sponsors and supporters as well as background information nationwide or in an individual state."

Solo Center, 6514 35th Ave. NE, Seattle WA 98115. (206)522-7656. Executive Director: Margaret (Marge) Lueders.

Purpose: "We serve as a resource, information and referral program and growth center for adults (and their families) in transition by reason of separation, divorce, widowing or never having married. We offer a social/emotional support system during crisis caused by loss of marital or relationship partner. Programs are scheduled 365 evenings of the year, a monthly newspaper/program is published and distributed, and special programs and brochures are provided." Information covers how-to, self-help, human services and emotional stabilization.

Services: Offers annual reports, statistics, brochures/pamphlets, placement on mailing list, information and referral services and a "listening ear. We are neither a social club nor a mental health center." Publications include a monthly newsletter, various brochures and reprints.

How to Contact: Write or call.

Tips: "The entire subject of single adults, single-parent families, displaced homemakers—and all that goes with marital disruption—is an expanding concern across the country. This center and its affiliate in Portland, Oregon may be unique in providing the services and focus that we do."

Unitarian Universalist Service Committee, 78 Beacon St., Boston MA 01866. (617)742-2120. Communications Director: Rick Pozniak.

Purpose: "This organization is involved in revamping the criminal justice system in the US and bringing health care, economic development and human rights to Third World countries." Information covers agriculture, health/medicine, law and politics.

Services: Offers aid in arranging interviews, annual reports, statistics, brochures/ pamphlets, newsletter and photos.
How to Contact: Write or call.

United Way of America, 801 N. Fairfax St., Alexandria VA 22314. (703)836-7100. Manager, Media Relations: Steve Delfin.
Purpose: "United Way of America is a nonprofit association, providing a variety of services to independent local United Way organizations located in about 2,300 US communities. Information covers economics, health/medicine, history, industry, politics, recreation, technical information, local fundraising and financial support of local charities.
Services: Offers aid in arranging interviews, annual reports, statistics, brochures/ pamphlets, information searches and press kits.
How to Contact: Write. "United Way of America is an important resource for writers interested in gaining a better understanding of the local operations of United Way organizations—how funds are collected and disbursed in the community. Charitable groups funded by United Way contain the seeds of a multitude of human interest stories linked with the human care service agencies United Way supports."

Vocational Rehabilitation, Box 1118, Hato Rey PR 00919. (809)725-1792. Assistant Secretary: Luis A. Bonilla.
Purpose: "Through counseling, physical and/or mental restoration services, evaluations, vocational training, economic assistance, job placement and other services on an individualized, as-needed basis, we help handicapped people become productive and independent." Information covers rehabilitation of the handicapped.
Services: Offers aid in arranging interviews and answers to requests for specific information, when available. Publications inlcude *State Plan of Operations* (annual).
How to Contact: Write for information, stating for what purpose it will be used. Request an interview with a staff person knowledgeable in a certain area.

Volunteers of America, Box 1621, Houston TX 77001. (713)864-7375. Texas State Officer: J.H. Kehrberg.
Purpose: "To serve those in need regardless of race, creed or color, through child care centers, prison ministries, Christmas food baskets for the needy, school clothing for indigent youngsters, residential treatment for alcoholic women, and nonprofit housing for low- and moderate-income families." Information covers business, economics, food, history, how-to, politics, self-help and technical data.
Services: Offers annual reports, brochures/pamphlets and newsletter. Publications include *School Clothing Center, Rogers Street—For Alcoholic Women* and *Will You Help Santa This Christmas?*.
How to Contact: "Mail a detailed request to us."

Wider Opportunities for Women, 1649 K St. NW, Washington DC 20006. (202)638-4868. Public Relations Coordinator: Rhoda Glickman.
Purpose: "Job development and training for women (blue-collar work), job referral and support system for women reentering job market and information on career changing or upward mobility. We press for policy and social changes for equal employment." Information covers employment issues for women.
Services: Offers aid in arranging interviews, biographies, brochures/pamphlets, placement on mailing list, statistics and press kits.
How to Contact: Write.

Zero Population Growth, Inc., 1346 Connecticut Ave. NW, Washington DC 20036. (202)785-0100.
Purpose: "To promote public attitudes and policies favoring stabilization of US and world population size." Information covers economics, health/medicine, politics, environmental education and family planning.

Services: Offers aid in arranging interviews, statistics, brochures/pamphlets, place-ment on mailing list and newsletter. Publications include leaflets on US population policy, statistics, school curricula, immigration, effects on economy and environment-related topics.
How to Contact: Write or call.
Tips: "For a local angle, in many cities, we can give you the phone number for local ZPG activists or chapters. For specific population statistics and expert analysis, call the US Census Bureau, (301)763-5002. For perspective of a US group concerned about population growth, call ZPG."

Insurance

American Council of Life Insurance, 1850 K St. NW, Washington DC 20006. (202)862-4064. New York Office: 1270 Avenue of the Americas, New York NY 10020. (212)245-4198. Contact: Press and Editorial Services.
Purpose: "The public relations division of the council provides the public with information about the purpose of life insurance and pensions, maintains research facilities to record the performance of the business and measures attitudes of the public on issues relevant to the business." Information covers life insurance, pensions and related subjects.
Services: Offers aid in arranging interviews, statistics and brochures/pamphlets. "We can provide helpful booklets to meet appropriate requests."
How to Contact: Write to the appropriate regional office.

Consumer Credit Insurance Corp., 307 N. Michigan Ave., Chicago IL 60601. Director of Communications: Jim Kielty.
Purpose: "A credit insurance trade group representing 140 insurers which sell credit insurance. We provide information to our member companies regarding legislative and regulatory activities in the states regarding credit insurance. We also sponsor two yearly meetings. PR activities include publicizing favorable studies regarding the credit insurance product. We are not a credit rating bureau, and our dealings with credit itself are minimal. We are involved with credit insurance: credit life and credit auto and home insurance, as well as credit property insurance and its regulation." Information covers economics.
Services: Offers statistics, brochures/pamphlets and newsletter. Publications include various studies on the credit insurance field, as well as *Proceedings*, covering annual meetings and fall executive planning conferences.
How to Contact: "Write the association on letterhead stationery. Please have specific questions in mind."

Health Insurance Institute, 1850 K St. NW, Washington DC 20006. (202)862-4065. Contact: Press and Editorial Services.
Purpose: "The Institute is maintained by the nation's insurance companies as a central source of information for the public on health insurance." Information covers insur-ance.
Services: Offers aid in arranging interviews, statistics and brochures/pamphlets.
How to Contact: "If possible, write a letter to the institute, detailing needs. Allow sufficient time if request is detailed."

Insurance Information Institute, Suite 1039, 175 W. Jackson, Chicago IL 60604. (312)922-5584. Midwest Regional Manager: William Sirola.
Purpose: "The Insurance Information Institute (III) is the only national organization operating exclusively in the area of public relations and public education with respon-sibility for property, liability and marine lines and the related fields of surety and fidelity. It is supported directly or indirectly by several hundred property and liability insurance companies, both stock and mutual." Information covers insurance.

Services: Offers statistics, brochures/pamphlets and information searches. Publications include *Insurance Facts, Deductibles Can Stretch Your Insurance Dollar, At Your Own Risk* and *Every Ten Minutes.* "We also have a variety of filmstrips available on auto insurance, home insurance, and walking to school without getting hurt."
How to Contact: Write. Charges for publications.

Insurance Information Institute, 110 William St., New York NY 10038. (212)233-7650. Contact: Press Relations Department.
Purpose: "A public relations and educational organization for all lines of insurance except life and health insurance. It is sponsored by several hundred insurance companies, and provides services on a fee basis to major industry organizations. The institute has 10 field offices across the US. The headquarters in New York house an educational division, a research division, media relations branch and special projects branch; the last two specialize in insurance information and dissemination." Information covers property and casualty insurance.
Services: Offers aid in arranging interviews, statistics, brochures/pamphlets, information searches, press kits, and films related to property and casualty insurance. Publications include a general publications list, *Insurance Facts, What's Behind Rising Insurance Costs?* and *Wood Stove Safety.*
How to Contact: Write or call. Charges for publications. "Due to a limited staff, the institute will not conduct research projects for college and high school students. We will, however, be glad to provide any relevant data that has been requested. Also, the institute may be able to refer the person to the proper source of information."

National Association of Health Underwriters, 145 North Ave., Hartland WI 53029. (414)367-3248. Executive Vice President: John K. Pardee.
Purpose: "An association of disability and health insurance persons and companies who sell and service these products." Information covers health/medicine and disability income and health insurance.
Services: Offers aid in arranging interviews. Publications include *Health Insurance Underwriter* (magazine).
How to Contact: Write or call.

National Association of Life Underwriters, 1922 F St. NW, Washington DC 20006. (202)331-6030. Director of Public Relations: Marvin Kobel. Associate Director of Public Relations: John W. Galloway.
Purpose: Trade association of life insurance agents. Information covers business, economics, history, how-to, industry, law and self-help.
Services: Offers aid in arranging interviews, bibliographies, biographies, brochures/ pamphlets, information searches, placement on mailing list, newsletter, photos and press kits. Publications include *NALU, Your Life Insurance Agent and You, You and Your Life Insurance Agent* and *Why the Life Insurance You Already Own May Be Your Best Buy.*
How to Contact: Write or call. "We are a reference and resource body on life and health insurance sales and service. We'd be glad to make referrals to other organizations that may be able to help."

Teachers Insurance & Annuity Association, 730 3rd Ave., New York NY 10021. (212)490-9000. Corporate Communications Administrator: Claire M. Sheahan.
Purpose: "Teachers Insurance & Annuity Association (TIAA-CREF) was founded by the Carnegie Foundation for the Advancement of Teaching to provide pension and insurance programs for staff members of colleges, universities, independent schools, and related nonprofit educational and research organizations. Our brochures merely cover our own benefit programs." Information covers pension and insurance.
Services: Offers annual reports, brochures/pamphlets and placement on mailing list. Publications include *The Role of TIAA-CREF in Higher Education.*
How to Contact: Write.

Journalism

Academy of American Poets, 1078 Madison Ave., New York NY 10028. (212)988-6783.
Purpose: "Established in 1934 to encourage, stimulate, and foster the production of American poetry. Awards prizes and conducts poetry workshops, readings and other literary events."
Services: Offers placement on mailing list and newsletter. Publications available.
How to Contact: Write or call. "We do not ask for contributions and will serve writers if at all possible by answering questions."

American Society of Journalists & Authors, Inc. (ASJA), 1501 Broadway, New York NY 10036. (212)997-0947. Executive Director: Holly M. Redell.
Purpose: "We are the nation's foremost organization of professional writers of nonfiction articles and books. The purpose of the American Society of Journalists and Authors, Inc. (ASJA) is to assist writers/members in the pursuit of their careers. This is done through information about the craft and business of writing in the ASJA's monthly newsletter. We provide information on new markets, editorial changes, copyright protection and other matters affecting writers. Through our annual directory, we make information available to buying editors and publicists about the skills available from our members." Information covers agriculture, art, business, celebrities, economics, entertainment, food, health/medicine, history, how-to, industry, law, music, nature, new products, politics, recreation, science, self-help, sports, technical data and travel.
Services: Offers services to members. Publications include *ASJA Directory* and *ASJA Newsletter*.
How to Contact: Write or call. "Annual membership, upon acceptance, is $60 within 50 miles of New York City; $45 outside of New York City."

Associated Business Writers of America, 1450 S. Havana, Suite 620, Aurora CO 80012. (303)751-7844. Associate Director: Donald E. Bower.
Purpose: "To improve the image and working conditions of business writers. Associated Business Writers of America (ABWA) has a primary thrust of better communication between editors and freelance business writers for adherence to standards of good practice and our code of ethics." Information covers agriculture, business, economics, industry, new products and technical data.
Services: Offers aid in arranging interviews, annual reports, biographies, statistics, brochures/pamphlets, information searches, placement on mailing list, newsletter and photos. Publications include *Directory of Business Writers* (annual) and *Confidential Bulletin* (monthly to members only).
How to Contact: Charges $10/directory. Other services available at no charge

The Authors Guild, Inc., 234 W. 44th St., New York NY 10036. (212)398-0838. Executive Secretary: Peter Heggie.
Purpose: "To act and speak with the collective voice of 5,000 writers in matters of joint professional and business concern; to keep informed on market tendencies and practices, and to keep its membership informed; and to advise members on individual professional and business problems as far as possible. Those eligible for membership included any author who shall have had a book published by an established American publisher within 7 years prior to his application or any author who shall have had 3 works (fiction or nonfiction) published by a magazine of general circulation within 18 months prior to application."
How to Contact: Write or call. "We are not in a position to answer any questions from nonmembers." Charges $35/year for membership."

Authors League of America, Inc., 234 W. 44th St., New York NY 10036. (212)391-9198. Administrative Assistant: Fay W. Glover.

Purpose: "Established in 1912. The Authors League membership is restricted to authors and dramatists who are members of the Authors Guild, Inc., and the Dramatists Guild, Inc. Matters of joint concern to authors and dramatists, such as copyright and freedom of expression, are in the province of the league. Other matters, such as contract of terms and subsidiary rights, are in the province of the guilds."
Services: Offers written material on the leagues.
How to Contact: Write or call.

Aviation/Space Writers Association, Cliffwood Rd., Chester NJ 07930. (201)879-5667. Executive Secretary: William F. Kaiser.
Purpose: "To establish and maintain high standards of quality and veracity in the gathering, writing, editing and disseminating of aeronautical information; to advance the cause of aviation and space in the interest of progress, and by education, advance the status and efficiency of persons engaged in aviation/space writing and other allied pursuits." Information covers aviation/space.
Services: Offers brochures/pamphlets, placement on mailing list and newsletter. Publications available.
How to Contact: Write or call for membership application. "All materials for members only." Charges $35/year for membership, plus $10 initiation fee.

Canadian Authors Association, 18 St. Joseph St., Toronto, Ontario, Canada M4Y 1J9. (416)923-2362. Headquarters Chariman: Frankish Styles.
Purpose: "To foster and develop a climate favorable to the creative arts, and to promote recognition of Canadian writers and their work. We also work for protection of Canadian writers and other artists producing copyrightable material; act as a spokesman before royal commissions and offical inquiries; sponsor a system of awards, and otherwise encourage work of literary and artistic merit; and publish a quarterly magazine (*Canadian Author & Bookman*)."
Services: Offers brochures/pamphlets.
How to Contact: Write or call. Charges for membership and publications.

Garden Writers Association of America, 101 Park Ave., New York NY 10017. (212)685-5917. Executive Secretary: Margaret Herbst.
Purpose: "To be of service to garden writers." Information covers garden writers.
Services: Offers newsletter to members only.
How to Contact: Write or call for membership application. Charges $15/year for membership.

International Association of Business Communicators, 870 Market St., Suite 928, San Francisco CA 94102. (415)433-3400. Researach Director: Irene Piraino.
Purpose: "To provide information about internal communications and to help members do their jobs and advance in their fields. Members include more than 5,000 communication managers, publication editors and writers, audiovisual specialists and others in the business communications field." Information covers business, economics, industry and organizational communication.
Services: Offers annual reports, bibliographies, statistics, brochures/pamphlets, information searches and newsletter. Also has placement service, publications critique, awards program and extensive reference library. Publications include membership directory, *IABC News* (tabloid), and *Journal of Organizational Communication* (magazine).
How to Contact: Write. Charges $30 to nonmembers for membership directory; $55/year for membership. Some publications are restricted to member use. Applicants for membership "must be connected in some way with the field."

Mystery Writers of America, Inc., 105 E. 19th St., New York NY 10003. (212)473-8020. Executive Secretary: Gloria Amoury.

Purpose: "Established in 1945, the organization is dedicated to the proposition that the detective story is the noblest sport of man. Membership includes active members who have made at least one sale in mystery, crime, or suspense writing; associate members who are either novices in the mystery writing field or nonwriters allied to the field; editors, publishers and affiliate members who are interested in mysteries."
How to Contact: Write or call. Charges $35/year for United States membership and $10/year for Canadian and overseas membership.

National Association of Science Writers, Box 294, Greenlawn NY 11740. (516)757-5664. Executive Director: Wadsworth Likely. Administrative Secretary: Diane McGurgan.
Purpose: "This organization was established to foster the dissemination of accurate information regarding science through all media normally devoted to informing the public. In pursuit of this goal, The National Association of Science Writers (NASW) conducts a varied program to increase the flow of news from scientists, to improve the quality of its presentation, and to communicate its meaning and importance to the reading public."
Services: Offers annual reports, brochures/pamphlets and newsletter. Publications include *Newsletter of the National Association of Science Writers*.
How to Contact: Write or call. "We're not set up to answer queries from writers."

The National League of American Pen Women, Inc., 1300 17th St. NW, Washington DC 20036. (202)785-1997. National President: Wauneta Hackleman.
Purpose: "To provide workshops and contests for women in the creative arts of writing, art, and music composition. (Writing category includes poetry, journalism, short stories and authors; art category includes painting, drawing, sculpture and crafts.) We provide scholarships for students who show interest and ability in the creative arts." Information covers art, music and writing.
Services: Offers brochures/pamphlets.
How to Contact: Write.

National Poetry Day Committee, Inc./World Poetry Day Committee, Inc., 1110 N. Venetian Dr., Miami Beach FL 33139. (305)373-9790. National Director: Frances Clark Handler.
Purpose: "To keep interested writers informed as to what the market offers; where to obtain information; how to search for material of all kinds, including pictures and artwork relating to writing of poetry and prose; how to design/edit/publish your own books, etc. We keep members informed as to what is going on in the literary field, and provide information about contests and other pertinent subjects." Information covers art, business, celebrities, economics, entertainment, food, health/medicine, history, how-to, industry, law, music, nature, new products, politics, recreation, science, self-help, technical data and travel.
Services: Offers aid in arranging interviews, annual reports, biographies, brochures/pamphlets, clipping services, information searches, statistics, newsletter and photos. "We also have information about courses to aid in their work for members. Information about special meetings to attend other than our own. Information about other places that offer services to writers for fees and without fee."
How to Contact: Write or call. "All receivers of information from us must be members. It would not be fair to spend our members' money to send out free information to nonmembers. We assist our members in any way we can, but we area nonprofit organization. We supply anything that a writer wants in the way of information."

The National Writers Club, 1450 S. Havana, Suite 620, Aurora CO 80012. (303)751-7844. Director: Donald E. Bower.
Purpose: "To provide assistance for all freelance writers; to fight for the rights of freelancers; to seek out and try to remedy any unsatisfactory practice pertaining to writing; and to provide specific help in areas of marketing, manuscript criticism,

research and consultation on many writing problems." Information covers "any subject pertaining to writing."

Services: Offers bibliographies, brochures/pamphlets and newsletter. Publications include material covering the fields of writing and publishing.

How to Contact: Charges annual dues; services available to members only.

Outdoor Writers Association of America Inc., 4141 W. Bradley Rd., Milwaukee WI 53209. (414)354-9690.

Purpose: "Writing association aimed at the outdoor communicator (lecturer, photographer, etc.). To join, one must be a professional in the field." Information covers art (outdoor).

Services: Offers brochures/pamphlets.

How to Contact: Write or call.

Society of Children's Book Writers, Box 296, Los Angeles CA 90066. Executive Director: Lin Oliver.

Purpose: "To aid writers of children's books." Information covers writing.

Services: Offers brochures/pamphlets. Publications include market reports, publishing guide, research guide and guide to contracts.

How to Contact: Write. Charges $25/membership. Publications available only to members.

Society of Professional Journalists, Sigma Delta Chi, 35 E. Wacker Dr., Chicago IL 60601. (312)236-6577. Executive Officer: Russell Hurst.

Purpose: "The Society of Professional Journalists, Sigma Delta Chi is the largest, oldest and most representative organization serving journalism. Membership includes both students and those already working in the media. The membership is unique in that it extends horizontally to include all branches of print and broadcast media, and vertically to include all ranks of journalists." Information covers journalism and communications.

Services: Offers brochures/pamphlets. Publications include *The Big Story* (answers to most basic questions about entering the field of journalism) and "How to Apply for a Job in Media" (reprint from *The Quill*).

How to Contact: Write.

Women in Communications, Inc., Box 9561, Austin TX 78766. (512)345-8922. Executive Director: Mary Utting.

Purpose: "To work for a free and responsible press; to unite women engaged in all fields of communication; to recognize distinguished achievements of women journalists; to maintain high professional standards; and to encourage members to greater individual effort." Information covers business, history, industry, self-help and sports (reporting).

Services: Offers bibliographies, statistics, brochures/pamphlets, information searches, placement on mailing list, newsletter and press kits. Publications include professional papers, job and salary survey, careers pamphlet, monthly newsletter and *Matrix*, monthly magazine.

How to Contact: Write. Charges cost plus postage for publications.

The Word Guild, 119 Mt. Auburn St., Cambridge MA 02138. (617)492-4656. President: Zelda Fischer.

Purpose: "The Word Guild exists to provide services and support to freelancers involved in the communications business. We are a clearinghouse for assignments as well as a source of instruction. We hold monthly meetings, publish a monthly magazine, and offer group health insurance to members. We have a fulltime placement agency. We locate freelance assignments, when possible, for members and also offers job counseling on an informal, as well as a formal, basis." Information covers agricul-

ture, art, business, celebrities, economics, entertainment, food, health/medicine, history, how-to, industry, law, music, nature, new products, politics, recreation, science, self-help, sports, technical data and travel.
Services: Offers aid in arranging interviews and newsletter.
How to Contact: Write or call.

Writers Guild of America, East, 22 W. 48th St., New York NY 10036. (212)575-5060.
Purpose: "A labor organization representing all screen, television and radio writers."
How to Contact: Write or call. Charges dues: $12.50/quarter and $500 initiation fee.

Writers Guild of America, West, 8955 Beverly Blvd., Los Angeles CA 90048. (213)550-1000.
Purpose: "A labor organization representing all screen, television and radio writers."
How to Contact: Write or call. Charges dues: $10/quarter and $500 initiation fee.

Labor & Unions

AFL-CIO, 815 16th St. NW, Washington DC 20006. (202)637-5000. Public Relations Director: Al Zach.
Purpose: "We are a labor organization." Information covers statements and views, convention resolution every 2 years and reaction to government statements.
Services: Offers aid in arranging interviews, annual reports, bibliographies, biographies, statistics, brochures/pamphlets, clipping services, placement on mailing list, newsletter and photos (limited).
How to Contact: Write or call. Charges for photos and large books for conventions. "Written requests preferred, but we will answer simple questions on the phone. Placement on free mailing list depends on Mr. Zack's decision."

AFL-CIO Public Employee Department (PED), 815 16th St. NW, Room 308, Washington DC 20006. Director of Public Relations: Michael Grace.
Purpose: "PED is an autonomous department of the AFL-CIO, representing 31 international unions with a combined membership of nearly two million federal, state and local government and postal service workers. The department conducts legislative, research and public relations activities in support of affiliated unions. PED materials offer rationale, positions and supplemental information concerning the viewpoint of organized labor on various issues." Information covers economics, history, law (especially public sector labor regulations, laws and pending legislation) and politics.
Services: Offers aid in arranging interviews, biographies, statistics, brochures/pamphlets, placement on mailing list, newsletter, photos and press kits. Publications include brochures on the PED and various research reports, speeches and articles on public sector labor relations.
How to Contact: Write.

American Federation of Teachers (AFT), 11 DuPont Circle NW, Washington DC 20036. (202)797-4400. Public Information Officers: Larry Sibelman and Phyllis Franck.
Purpose: "Collective bargaining union for teachers (K-12) and health care professionals."
Services: Offers annual reports, bibliographies, biographies, statistics, brochures/pamphlets, placement on mailing list and press kits.
How to Contact: Write or call. "We would prefer written requests."

Association of Canadian Television and Radio Artists, 105 Carlton St., Toronto, Ontario, Canada M5B 1M2. (416)363-6335. Assistant General Secretary/Writers' Administrator: Margaret Collier.
Purpose: "The Association of Canadian Television and Radio Artists (ACTRA) negoti-

ates collective agreements for writers in film, TV, radio, etc. with Canadian film, TV and broadcasting companies."
Services: Offers brochures/pamphlets and newsletter.
How to Contact: Write or call.

Automobile, Aerospace and Agricultural Implement Workers of America, International Union/United Auto Workers, 8000 E. Jefferson Ave., Detroit MI 48214. (313)926-5291. Contact: Public Relations Department.
Purpose: "We are a labor union."
Services: Offers aid in arranging interviews, biographies, brochures/pamphlets, statistics, information searches, placement on mailing list and newsletter. Publications available.
How to Contact: Write or call. "Written requests preferred, but we will answer brief questions on the phone."

Coalition of American Public Employees (CAPE), 1126 16th St. NW, Washington DC 20036. (202)223-2267. Associate Director: Donovan McClure.
Purpose: "The Coalition of American Public Employees (CAPE) was formed in 1972 by public employee organizations in an effort to coordinate programs of political, legal and legislative action and public education at the national and state levels. Members include AFSCME, NEA, ANA, NASW and PNHA. Representing nearly four million workers, CAPE is the largest organization of public employees in the nation. Our information covers what's happening in public sector labor relations."
Services: Offers publications, including "a monthly newsletter called *CAPE Update* that presents an inside view of what's happening in the public sector."
How to Contact: Write.

Communications Workers of America, 1925 K St. NW, Washington DC 20006. (202)785-6740. Public Information Officer: Lee M. White.
Purpose: "Labor organization." Information covers telephone work and workers, communicators and technology from workers' point of view.
Services: Offers placement on mailing list. Publications available.
How to Contact: Write. "Written requests must state what the information will be used for. We are not interested in writing school reports."

Fraternal Order of Police, 3136 W Pasadena Ave., Flint MI 48504. (313)732-6330. National Secretary: William Bannister.
Purpose: "To improve the situation and working conditions of police." Information covers celebrities, economics, history, law, politics and labor relations.
Services: Offers aid in arranging interviews, biographies, statistics, information searches, placement on mailing list, newsletter and photos. Publications include *The Journal,* a tabloid newspaper published bimonthly and an annual survey of salaries and working conditions of police departments in the US.
How to Contact: Write. Charges $5 for the salary survey.

International Alliance of Theatrical Stage Employees and Moving Picture Machine Operators of the US and Canada, 1515 Broadway, New York NY 10036. (212)730-1770. Editor/Publicity Director: Mr. Rene L. Ash.
Purpose: Dissemination of news related to the union, and to the motion picture, television and stage industries. Information covers entertainment and technical data.
Services: Offers placement on mailing list.
How to Contact: Write.

International Association of Fire Fighters, 1750 New York Ave., NW, Washington DC 20006. (202)872-8484. Acting Director of Research: Mike Smith.
Purpose: "International union concerned with wages and working conditions of fire fighters."

Services: Offers statistics (information made available by fire fighters for public death and injury surveys). Publications available.
How to Contact: Write or call. "We can only answer questions about the international organization; for information about state or local groups, you must go through those groups."

International Brotherhood of Teamsters, Chauffeurs, Warehousemen, and Helpers of America, 25 Louisiana Ave. NW, Washington DC 20001. (202)624-6911. Press Secretary: Bernard Henderson.
Purpose: "The International Brotherhood of Teamsters represents members in matters regarding wages, working conditions and fringe benefits. We are the largest union in the world." Information covers agriculture, art, business, celebrities, economics, entertainment, food, health/medicine, history, how-to, industry, law, politics, recreation, science, self-help, sports, technical data and travel.
Services: Offers aid in arranging interviews, annual reports, bibliographies, biographies, statistics, brochures/pamphlets, information searches, placement on mailing list, newsletter, photos, press kits, library research department and audiovisual aids. Publications include *The Teamster* (monthly).
How to Contact: Write.

National Association of Letter Carriers, 100 Indiana Ave., NW, Washington DC 20001. Communications Officer: Gerald Cullinan.
Purpose: "Postal union for letter carriers." Information covers history.
Services: Offers bibliographies, brochures/pamphlets, placement on mailing list and press kits. Publications available for members.
How to Contact: Write.

National Maritime Union of America, 346 W. 17th St., New York NY 10011. (212)924-3900. Director of Public Relations: Samuel Thompson.
Purpose: "Labor union for unlicensed seamen."
Services: Offers statistics, placement on mailing list and newspaper.
How to Contact: Write. Requires written request from the publication a writer is working for. Charges for newspaper.

The Newspaper Guild, 1125 15th St. NW, Washington DC 20005. (202)296-2990. Contact: David J. Eisen.
Purpose: "The guild's jurisdiction is to advance the economic interests and improve the working conditions of its members, to raise the standards of journalism and ethics of the news industry, and to promote industrial unionism.To those ends, our activities consist principally of organizing and bargaining on behalf of news industry employees, and of legislative and other activity in areas of concern to journalism." Information covers economics, industry, law and journalism. "Our information covers the newspaper industry and related media, particularly those areas that are labor-related or of professional concern."
Services: Offers annual reports, statistics, brochures/pamphlets and placement on mailing list. Publications include *Thanks to the Guild* (a description of the Guild, its history and operations), "Gentlemen and Scholars of the Press" (an article by Judith Crist on charges wrought by the guild) and *The Newspaperman Who Founded a Union* (a biographical sketch of Heywood Broun).
How to Contact: Write or call. "Allow adequate time for reply."

Public Service Research Council, 8330 Old Courthouse Rd. #600, Vienna VA 22180. (703)790-0700. Director, Public Relations: George C. Bevel.
Purpose: "The Public Service Research Council is the nation's largest citizens' lobby concerned exclusively with curbing the abuses of public sector unions in the US." Information covers politics, union negotiations, trends and elections.
Services: Offers annual reports, statistics, brochures/pamphlets and newsletter. Publi-

cations include *Forewarned!* (monthly newsletter), *The Government Union Critique* (published 26 times/year), *The Effect of Collective Bargaining on Teacher Salaries*, *Civil Service Reform Aimed at Wrong Target*, *Compulsory Unionism in Government Employees*, *Compulsory Binding Arbitration and Public Sector Labor Disputes*, *Public Sector Supervisors-Should They Bargain Collectively?* and *Hatch Act Revision*.
How to Contact: Write or call.

Typographical Union, International, Box 157, Colorado Springs CO 80901. (303)471-2460. Contact: Public Relations Office.
Purpose: "The same as other labor unions—to pursue common interest of members, collective bargaining and negotiating." Information covers economics, history, industry, law, politics and technical information.
Services: Offers aid in arranging interviews, annual reports, biographies, statistics, brochures/pamphlets, information searches, newsletter, photos and press kits.
How to Contact: Write.

United Farm Workers of America, AFL-CIO, La Paz, Keene CA 93531. (805)822-5571. Press Secretary to the President: Marc Grossman.
Purpose: "To liberate farm workers from the exploitation and poverty that impoverishes so many people in the US through the process of collective bargaining." Information covers farm labor.
Services: Offers aid in arranging interviews, bibliographies, biographies, statistics, brochures/pamphlets, placement on mailing list and "occasionally" press kits. Publications include regularly updated bibliography on Cesar Chavez and United Farm Workers.
How to Contact: Write or call.

United Mine Workers of America, 900 15th St. NW, Washington DC 20005. (202)638-0530. International Press Aide: Eldon Callen.
Purpose: "Labor union."
Services: Offers aid in arranging interviews, brochures/pamphlets, placement on mailing list and press kits (for specific occasions).
How to Contact: Write or call. "We prefer written requests, but will answer simple questions on the phone."

United Steelworkers of America, 5 Gateway Center, Pittsburgh PA 15222. (412)562-2631. Director of Public Relations: Russell Gibbons.
Purpose: "We represent our members who are in the steel, aluminum, nonferrous metals, can, fabricating and chemical industries." Information covers business, economics, health/medicine, history, how-to, industry, law, politics, recreation, technical data and mining.
Services: Offers aid in arranging interviews, statistics, brochures/pamphlets, information searches, placement on mailing list, newsletter, photos and occasional press kits. Publications include *Steelabor* (monthly).
How to Contact: Write.

Law, Law Enforcement & Criminology

American Bar Association, 77 S. Wacker Dr., Chicago IL 60606. (312)621-9240. Contact: Mr. Glass, Ms. Taylor.
Purpose: "To improve the justice system and the practice of law." Information covers law.
Services: Offers aid in arranging interviews, brochures/pamphlets and information searches. Publications include *Story Lines*, *Law and the Courts*, *The American Lawyer: How to Choose and Use One*, fair trial and free press materials and other publica-

tions on specific legal issues.
How to Contact: Call or write. Charges for some publications. "If a writer wishes to use copyrighted material, he should contact us first."

Constitutional Rights Foundation, Box 2362, Texas City TX 77590. President: William D. Allen Sr.
Purpose: "To give people information on how to use their constitutional rights to stop harassment from government agencies including the IRS, to repeal income tax, end deficit spending by a constitutional amendment, and return the United States to a free market economy. Our primary goal is to provide a society that respects the right of all Americans to life, liberty and property." Information covers business, economics, history, how-to, industry, law and politics.
Services: Offers brochures/pamphlets, newsletter and lectures and speakers. Publications available.
How to Contact: Write. Charges for some publications. "Please describe your project and how you think we may be of assistance."

Federal Judicial Center, 1520 H St. NW, Washington DC 20005. (202)633-6365. Information Specialist: Sue Welsh.
Purpose: "To further the development and adoption of improved judicial administration in the courts of the US. Information service collection consists of books, articles, and periodicals in the field; especially court management, automation, and criminal justice." Information covers law (federal courts).
Services: Offers annual reports, bibliographies, clipping services and statistics. Publications available.
How to Contact: Write or call. Judicial personnel are given priority on requests. However, the information service is open to the public for viewing files.

International Common Law Exchange Society, 5 Palo Alto Square, Suite 283, Palo Alto CA 94304. (415)493-9248. President and Editor-in-Chief: Ira B. Marshall.
Purpose: "To foster and encourage the international exchange of law through symposia, meetings, transnational law journal publications and international colloquia in an effort to achieve equal access to justice through international exchange." Information covers business, celebrities, economics, health/medicine, history, law, politics, technical data and travel. "Our primary emphasis is on developments within comparative and international law."
Services: Offers annual reports, bibliographies, biographies, statistics, brochures/pamphlets, information searches, placement on mailing list and newsletter. Publications available.
How to Contact: Write. Charges for publications. "Services limited to subscribers and members of the society."
Tips: Concentrate on developments locally, nationally and internationally that affect or enhance the international practice of law or the comparative and/or transnational applications and developments of law and virtually every law subject."

London Club, 214 W. 6th St., Suite AA, Box 4527, Topeka KS 66604. Chairman: Dennis A. Baranski.
Purpose: "An organization serving as a clearinghouse for criminal research. Specializing in researching unsloved crime both past and present; ex. Jack the Ripper, Whitechappel Murders, and Lincoln and Kennedy assassinations as well as current unsolved crime in the US and abroad. Seeks to become a mass private sector for researching unsolved crime on a local level by bringing together experts from various fields." Information covers law (criminology).
Services: Offers aid in arranging interviews, brochures/pamphlets and press kits.
How to Contact: Membership in the organization is a prerequisite. Apply for membership ($20/year) by writing the chairman. "Services are available only to members in good standing. We expect members to contribute articles, essays and research to *The*

London Club Journal for consideration by the editors. If the article is sold to another publication as a reprint, the author will be paid a royalty on the sale. The London Club employs the same standard of accuracy as does any major news reporting service in the US. The London Club is seeking professionals in all fields who feel that they have something to contribute to the fields of criminology as researchers and investigative reporters. The organization is also open to individuals who feel they have an interest in criminology and something worthwhile to contribute."

National Association of Chiefs of Police, 2000 P St. NW, Room 615, Washington DC 20036. (202)293-9088. Executive Administrator: Col. Fred Pearson.
Purpose: "An association of chiefs of police, sheriffs, security directors and those who hold command positions above the rank of sergeant." Information covers business, history, how-to, law, new products and technical data.
Services: Offers aid in arranging interviews and brochures/pamphlets. Publications include *Terrorism*, *Hostage Taking*, *Drug Investigation*, *Public Relations* and *Police Chiefs Manual*.
How to Contact: Charges for publications and for services; "fees depend on the time involved and whether research is required. We do require appointments in advance and notice of the subject for any interview."

National Association of Women in Criminal Justice, 906 5th Ave., Pittsburgh PA 15213. (412)281-7380. Executive Director: Charlotte Ginsburg.
Purpose: "The National Association of Women in Criminal Justice is an organization of women and men who seek to improve the position and increase the numbers of women employed within the criminal justice system; to reduce the isolation of those women; and to increase the awareness within the system and the general public of the female as employee, offender and victim." Information covers law.
Services: Offers newsletter.
How to Contact: Write or call.

World Correctional Service Center, 2849 W. 71st., Chicago IL 60629. (312)925-6591. President: Harry Woodward Jr.
Purpose: "Our organization was founded to focus public attention to the field of criminal justice, particularly corrections. From time to time we hold seminars and conferences to that end. In addition we make certain publications available to the public." Information covers law and criminal justice.
Services: Offers brochures/pamphlets.
How to Contact: Write.

Libraries

American Library Association, 50 E. Huron St., Chicago IL 60611. (312)944-6780. Executive Director: Robert Wedgeworth.
Purpose: "Founded in 1876, the American Library Association has 35,000 members, 200 staff and 56 local groups. Members include libraries, librarians, trustees, friends of libraries and others interested in the responsibilities of libraries in the educational, social and cultural needs of society. We promote libraries and librarianship. We establish standards of service; support; promote adoption of standards; conduct liaison with federal agencies; promote popular understanding and public acceptance of the value of library services; maintain a special library and publish monographs, pamphlets and journals." Information covers libraries and library science.
Services: Offers bibliographies, brochures/pamphlets, placement on mailing list, newsletter and press information on libraries. Publications available.
How to Contact: Write or call. "Communication by mail is preferred."

Church and Synagogue Library Association, Box 1130, Bryn Mawr PA 19010. (215)853-2870. Executive Secretary: Dorothy Rodda.
Purpose: "The purpose of the Church and Synagogue Library Association is to provide educational guidance in the establishment and maintenance of library service in churches and synagogues. We hold an annual national conference and workshop and have 14 chapters throughout the country that hold regional meetings." Information covers history, how-to, new products, self-help and technical data.
Services: Offers aid in arranging interviews, annual reports, bibliographies, statistics, brochures/pamphlets, information searches and newsletter. "Our publications include *Church and Synagogue Libraries* (bimonthly), eight guides for congregational libraries, two tracts and two bibliographies. Our library services also distribute small publications designed to be of help to librarians. A number of graduate students have done research papers for their degrees on the subject of congregational libraries. We have a list of these, plus other publications by denominations, etc., which are available."
How to Contact: Write. Charges for some publications.

Lumber, Forestry & Wood Products

American Forest Institute, 1619 Massachusetts Ave. NW, Washington DC 20036. (202)797-4500. Public Information Director: Marvin G. Katz.
Purpose: "We are a communications organization serving the forest products industry." Information covers agriculture, business, economics, history, industry, nature, recreation, science, technical data and forest management."
Services: Offers aid in arranging interviews, statistics, brochures/pamphlets, photos, press kits, forest tours and briefings. Publications include *Green America* (issued three times/year), *Forest Facts and Figures*, *Managing The Great American Forest* and *Wood and Wilderness*.
How to Contact: Write or call.

American Wood Council, 1619 Massachusetts Ave. NW, Suite 500, Washington DC 20036. (202)265-7766. Communications Director: Venlo Wolfsohn.
Purpose: "To promote the use of wood products in new single-family houses built in metropolitan areas." Information covers wood product use in home building.
Services: Offers photos.
How to Contact: Write or call.

Fine Hardwoods/American Walnut Association, 5603 W. Raymond, Suite 0, Indianapolis IN 46241. (317)244-3312. Executive Director: Larry R. Frye.
Purpose: "We represent the hardwood lumber and face veneer industry. Our publications are basically educational, promoting hardwood lumber and veneer." Information covers how-to.
Services: Offers brochures/pamphlets, information searches and photos. "Let us help on all hardwood stories." Publications include *Fine Hardwoods Selectorama*, *Growing Walnut for Profit and Pleasure* and *Hardwood Dollars and Sense*.
How to Contact: "Write to us directly. Writers must give us proper publication credit." Charges $5/copy for *Fine Hardwoods Selectorama*.

Fir and Hemlock Door Association, 1500 Yeon Bldg., Portland OR 97204. (503)224-3930. Manager, Product Publicity: Raymond W. Moholt.
Purpose: "To provide technical and product literature and promotion for producers of carved panel wood doors and other doors manufactured from fir and hemlock lumber. Information covers selection, storage, care and handling, installation and finishing of these doors." Information covers how-to, new product information and technical data.
Services: Offers statistics, brochures/pamphlets and photos. Publications include *Care*

and Handling of Fir and Hemlock Doors.
How to Contact: Write or call. "We must be allowed to check technical text, and credit must be given to the Fir and Hemlock Door Association."

Hardwood Plywood Manufacturers Association, Box 6246, Arlington VA 22206. (703)671-6262. Administrative Assistant: Joseph Lomerson.
Purpose: "We concentrate in six major areas of member services: information clearing-house through publications; public relations/promotion in the form of news releases to the press; brochures and color slide presentations on the manufacture and uses of hardwood plywood to specifiers, purchasers and users of hardwood plywood; industry representation in various legislative issues affecting the hardwood plywood and veneer industry; semi-annual conventions as well as regional meetings providing a common forum for the industry to work toward solving common problems, exchanging information, and becoming better acquainted with other hardwood plywood manufacturers, prefinishers and suppliers to the industry; active committees on building codes, conventions, environment improvement, legislation, safety, technical, trade promotion and public relations; and technical activities featuring the most complete testing laboratory for hardwood plywood in the US." Information covers how-to, industry, new products and technical data.
Services: Offers statistics, brochures/pamphlets, placement on mailing list and photos. PUblication and price list available.
How to Contact: Write or call.

Interior Lumber Manufacturers Association, 333 Martin St., Suite 295, Penticton, British Columbia, Canada V2A 5K7. (604)492-5810. Manager: Alan D. Macdonald.
Purpose: "The objective of the Interior Lumber Manufacturers Association (ILMA) is to unite all who are engaged in the manufacture of forest products in southern British Columbia and to deal with matters of mutual concern. All problems, with the exception of labor relations and direct sales, are within the scope of the association. The ILMA publicizes matters of importance and interest to members. Our areas are the central and southeastern areas of British Columbia." Information covers lumber manufacturing.
Services: Offers statistics and brochures/pamphlets. Publications include *Member Mill Directory*, NLGA grade rule books and Canadian lumber grading manuals.
How to Contact: Write. Charges $3.50/member directory, $3.50/grade rule book and $2.50/grading manual.

Manufacturing, Miscellaneous

American Seat Belt Council, 1730 Pennsylvania Ave. NW, Suite 460, Washington DC 20006. (202)393-1300. President: Charles H. Pulley.
Purpose: "We are composed of manufacturers of active and automatic seat belts and webbing. The council was formed in 1961 to assist in the establishment of uniform production standards for seat belts. Since launching its first major nationwide buckle-up campaign 12 years ago, the American Seat Belt Council (ASBC) has worked with news media and other safety organizations to encourage greater use of seat belts. In addition to its public education campaigns, the council has cooperated with state legislatures to develop seat belt use laws. ASBC has information on both active and automatic seat belts, including pamplets, films, and studies." Information covers new products and technical data.
Services: Offers aid in arranging interviews, bibliographies, biographies, statistics, brochures/pamphlets, photos and press kits. Publications available.
How to Contact: Write or call. "We will put writers in contact with ASBC members, primarily spokesman Charles Pulley."

Canvas Products Association International, 350 Endicott Bldg., St. Paul MN 55101.

(612)222-2508. Director of Public Relations: Mary Burczyk.

Purpose: "We are a vertical trade association for the industrial textile industry. Membership includes mills, fabric coaters, distributors and product fabricators involved with industrial textiles. Our textiles are found in almost every existing industry, including the design and architectural markets. Our membership includes members in 13 European countries, Canada and the US (1100 members). Information covers agriculture, business, industry, new products, recreation, sports and technical data (textiles).

Services: Offers aid in arranging interviews, statistics, brochures/pamphlets, placement on mailing list, photos and press kits. Publications include various background information-type articles on the products of this industry (awnings, air structures, camping products, marine fabric products, sail making, industrial plant uses of fabric, etc.) "We publish a monthly magazine and brochures."

How to Contact: Write or call. "We can help define questions and ideas on related topics as well as distribute or provide specific information."

Carpet and Rug Institute, Box 2048, Dalton GA 30720. (404)278-3176. Director of Consumer Affairs: Richard Ned Hopper.

Purpose: "Trade association of carpet and rug manufacturers and those allied industries supplying services and products to the industry." Information covers economics, history, how-to and technical data.

Services: Offers annual reports, statistics, brochures/pamphlets and press kits. Publications include information to help consumers with carpet purchases and carpet care.

How to Contact: Write or call.

Contact Lens Manufacturers Association, 435 N. Michigan Ave., Chicago IL 60611. (312)644-0828. Executive Director: Glenn W. Bostrom. Administrative Director: Beth Perry.

Purpose: "To collect and disseminate information regarding contact lenses and accessories to the public (for the betterment of public health); to recommend standards for the improvement of the industry; to sponsor and promulgate research related to contact lenses and accessories; to provide information to the eye care field regarding contact lenses and accessories; to provide information to the contact lens industry." Information covers "activities of interest to contact lens manufacturers."

Services: Offers brochures/pamphlets and newsletter. Publications include *Living with Contact Lenses . . . And Enjoying Them, News and Views* and membership directory.

How to Contact: Write or call.

Cosmetic, Toiletry and Fragrance Association, Inc., 1133 15th St. NW, Washington DC 20005. (202)331-1770. Director of Public Information: Lorna C. Rhoads.

Purpose: "We are a leading US trade association for the cosmetic industry, representing manufacturers of roughly 90% of US sales in cosmetics, toiletries and fragrances. We are the industry voice on industry issues. We will handle inquiries on cosmetics in general, but not specific brands. We encourage consumers and press to contact the Cosmetic, Toiletry and Fragrance Association (CTFA) for information about cosmetics." Information covers business, health/medicine, science, self-help, technical data and general information about cosmetics.

Services: Offers aid in arranging interviews, annual reports, bibliographies, biographies, statistics, brochures/pamphlets, placement on mailing list, regular informational newsletter, photos, press kits, and in-depth background information on product categories or specific issues relating to the cosmetic industry. Publications include *Introducing The Cosmetic, Toiletry and Fragrance Industry Today, Who's Who In The Cosmetic Industry* ($15 charge), *CTFA Annual Report* and *CTFA Cosmetic Journal* ($12/year). Individual issues might be sent free if they contained material valuable to the writer's purpose."

How to Contact: Write or call. "We would be glad to talk to or correspond with any serious writer."
Tips: "Statistics on cosmetic industry sales are difficult to come by and are frequently out-of-date. When attempting to write an article about a cosmetic product or an issue affecting the cosmetic industry, the writer should be prepared to understand a wide variety of scientific information. Disciplines related to this industry include microbiology, chemistry and toxicology.

Embroidery Council of America, 500 5th Ave., #5801, New York NY 10036. (212)730-0685. Account Assistant: Jan Liverance.
Purpose: "We maintain a library of samples from different embroidery manufacturers which is open to designers and the press." Information covers fashions.
Services: Offers aid in arranging interviews, statistics, brochures/pamphlets, photos and fashion and trend information about present and future uses of embroidery, lace and eyelet in apparel and home furnishings. Publications include *This is Embroidery* ($1) and *Sewing with Lace and Embroidery* (35¢).
How to Contact: Write or call. Publications are available from the Embroidery Manufacturers Promotion Board, 513 23rd St., Union City NJ 07087.

Institute for Briquetting and Agglomeration, Box 794, Erie PA 16512. (814)456-2157. Executive Director: W. Eichenberger.
Purpose: "The Institute for Briquetting and Agglomeration is a group of business and technical people interested and involved in the research, development and production of briquets, agglomerates and other densified products." Information covers agriculture (fertilizers), industry, science and technical data.
Services: Offers newsletter.
How to Contact: Write or call.

National Association of Black Manufacturers, Inc., 1625 I St. NW, Suite 918, Washington DC 20006. (202)785-5133. Public Information Officer: Arthur Johnson.
Purpose: "The National Association of Black Manufacturers (NABM) is constantly at work on behalf of minority industry, advising legislators, marketing minority capabilities and providing needed information and statistics about the minority industry. NABM membership services provide increased corporate support; encouragement and support to minority people interested in pursuing manufacturing entrepreneurship; and marketing development and support to minority women penetrating the industrial sector." Information covers business, economics, industry and new products.
Services: Offers statistics, brochures/pamphlets and newsletter. Publications include *NABM News* (biweekly newsletter on current manufacturing and business-related items) and *NABM Legislative Review* (biweekly publication about relevant Congressional matters).
How to Contact: Write. "We require that we receive publication credit for information."

National Association of Manufacturers, 1776 F St. NW, Washington DC 20006. (202)331-3700. Public Relations: Paul Lockwood.
Purpose: "Trade association representing 75% of the nation's manufacturers. We represent members before Congress and regulatory agencies on national economics and business issues. We are nonprofit."
Services: Offers aid in arranging interviews, brochures/pamphlets, placement on mailing list, statistics, newsletter and press kits. Publications available.
How to Contact: Write or call.

National Association of Plastic Fabricators, 1701 N St. NW, Washington DC 20036. (202)223-2504. Executive Director: J. M. Wettrich. Meeting Planner: Linda Doneff.
Purpose: "To promote increased use and consumption of the products of the decora-

tive laminate industry." Information covers industry.

Services: Offers statistics and newsletter.

How to Contact: Write. "Nonmembers (other than press) are charged $25/hour for research with a $25 deposit required 'up-front.' Requests must be industry related."

National Association of Uniform Manufacturers, c/o Liss Public Relations, Inc., 250 E. Hartsdale Ave., Hartsdale NY 10530. (914)472-5900. President: Norman J. Liss.

Purpose: "Uniforms and their effect and usage in the US in every application." Information covers business, history, how-to, industry, new products and technical data.

Services: Offers aid in arranging interviews, statistics, brochures/pamphlets, placement on mailing list, photos and press kits.

How to Contact: Write or call.

The National Paint and Coatings Association, 1500 Rhode Island Ave. NW, Washington DC 20005. (202)462-6272. Manager, Editorial Services: Bonnie Benhayon.

Purpose: "We represent paint and coatings manufacturers." Information covers home maintenance and decorating with paint and coatings (such as roof coatings or driveway coatings).

Services: Offers brochures/pamphlets, information searches, placement on mailing list, photos, fact sheets on various products or techniques, and articles for use as background material. "All of our material deals with paint and coatings in generic terms; we never mention company names or product trade names in our material." Publications list is available.

How to Contact: Write or call. "For quick service ask for the manager of editorial services. All we require is a tear sheet of the published article so that we may keep it on file. We prefer that writers do not tell their readers to write to us for the same free materials we gave the writer—not all of these materials are free to consumers. If the writer wants to do something like this, he should discuss the matter with the manager of editorial services."

Recreation Vehicle Industry Association, Box 204, Chantilly VA 22021. (703)968-7722. Public Relations Administrator: Gary M. LaBella.

Purpose: "We represent the interests of the recreation vehicle industry before state, local and federal governments and the news media, and generally promote the use of recreation vehicles in outdoor recreation and travel. Our membership totals 500 manufactures and suppliers. Our manufacturer members produce motor homes, travel trailers, van conversions, truck campers and fold-down camping trailers (not mobile homes)." Information covers industry, recreation and outdoor life.

Services: Offers aid in arranging interviews, brochures/pamphlets, placement on mailing list, statistics, press kits and vehicle loans to writers with specific assignments from editors of reputable consumer publications. Publications available.

How to Contact: Write or call.

The Soap and Detergent Association, 475 Park Ave. S., New York NY 10016. (212)725-1262. Assistant Public Affairs Director: Mary C. Ansbro.

Purpose: "The Soap and Detergent Association (SDA) is a national trade group representing the manufacturers of well over 90% of the soap and detergents made in the US. Member companies include producers of consumer and industrial clearing products, raw materials suppliers, and producers of fatty acid and glycerine. Areas of information include general industry information; generic consumer and industrial/institutional information relating to cleanliness and washing/cleaning products; and statistical data (mostly from government or other public sources)." Information covers industry, technical data, and information on soaps, detergents and other cleaning products.

Services: Offers statistics and brochures/pamphlets. Publications list available.

How to Contact: Write or call. Charges for some brochures.

Writing Instrument Manufacturers Association, c/o Liss Public Relations, 250 E. Hartsdale Ave., Hartsdale NY 10530. (914)472-5900. President: Norman J. Liss.
Purpose: "Pens, markers, mechanical pencils, information in an effort to stamp out illegible handwriting in the United States." Information covers business, history, industry, new products, technical data and sales information.
Services: Offers aid in arranging interviews, biographies, statistics, brochures/ pamphlets, placement on mailing list, photos and press kits.
How to Contact: Write or call.

Marine & Marine Products

American Association of Port Authorities, 1612 K St. NW, #502, Washington DC 20006. (202)331-1263.
Purpose: "We are an information exchange for the port industry. Membership is basically port authorities in the Western Hemisphere with other classes of members also with an interest in the port industry." Information covers technical data and the port industry.
Services: Offers "for our *own* membership": annual reports, statistics, brochures/ pamphlets and newsletter.
How to Contact: "Outside sources are not usually placed on our mailing lists."

American Boat & Yacht Council, Inc., Box 806, 190 Ketcham Ave., Amityville NY 11701. (516)598-0550. Executive Director: G. James Lippmann.
Purpose: "The American Boat & Yacht Council is primarily an engineering and technical society devoted to the development and publication of safety standards and recommended practices covering the design and construction of boats and their equipment." Information covers recreational boats and technical data.
Services: Offers brochures/pamphlets and information searches. Publications include *AYBC Is for Safer Boating* (descriptive brochure) and Safety Standards for Small Craft (a compendium of standards and practices).
How to Contact: Charges $35/copy for *Safety Standards*. "All material is copyrighted and specific permission for its use is required. Suitable acknowledgment of source is appreciated."

Canadian Shipbuilding and Ship Repairing Association, Suite 701, 100 Sparks St., Ottawa, Ontario, Canada K1P 5B7. (613)232-7127. President: Henry M. Walsh.
Purpose: "The objectives of the association are the preservation, maintenance and development of the Canadian shipbuilding, ship repairing and allied industries for the advancement of the industrial, technological, economic, social, defense and sovereign interests of Canada. Our association consists of 25 shipbuilding and ship repairing companies and 50 allied manufacturing and consulting organizations." Information covers shipbuilding and allied industries.
Services: Offers aid in arranging interviews, annual reports, statistics and newsletter. Publications include annual reports, *Canadian Shipbuilding–Services, Products, Facilities* and *A National Strategy for the Shipbuilding, Ship Repairing and Allied Marine Industries*.
How to Contact: Write. "Our staff is very limited; therefore, detailed inquiries cannot normally be answered."

Institution of Navigation, 815 15th St. NW, Suite 832, Washington DC 20005. (202)783-4121. Executive Director: Emmett Deavies.
Purpose: "Scientific, nonprofit organization, dedicated to enhancement of all forms of navigation."
Services: Offers aid in arranging interviews, bibliographies, statistics, brochures/ pamphlets, newsletter and press releases as necessary.
How to Contact: Write or call.

International Oceanographic Foundation, 3979 Rickenbacker Causeway, Virginia Key, Miami FL 33149. (305)361-5786. Contact: Sea Secrets Department.
Purpose: "To encourage the extension of human knowledge by scientific study and exploration of the oceans and to educate the public concerning the marine sciences through publication of the periodicals *Sea Frontiers* and *Sea Secrets*, membership information service, film rentals, book discounts, etc., and the educational museum/exposition Planet Ocean, which is open to the public." Information covers marine science.
Services: Offers placement on mailing list and newsletter. Publications include *Sea Secrets* and *Sea Frontiers*.
How to Contact: Services free to members. "Answers to members' questions are primarily reference lists, but specific questions are answered, if possible."

Marine Technology Society, 1730 M St. NW, Room 412, Washington DC 20036. (202)659-3251. Executive Director: George K. Gowans.
Purpose: "Marine technology, sciences, resources and research." Information covers science and technical data.
Services: Offers biographies and brochures/pamphlets. Publications include membership brochures, career information booklets and publications list.
How to Contact: "Write, describing information needed. We will provide you with the information or try to direct you to the agency that can give you what you need." Charges postage and handling on publications orders.

National Association of Engine and Boat Manufacturers, Box 5555, Grand Central Station, New York NY 10017. (212)697-1100. PR Manager: Sandy Mills.
Purpose: "A trade association of the recreational boating industry, devoting energies and resources toward improving the lot of the recreational boatman. The National Association of Engine and Boat Manufacturers (NAEBM) supports boating safety through education and standards." Information covers industry and recreation.
Services: Offers statistics, brochures/pamphlets, newsletter and photos. Publications include annual boating information guide, *Sailing Is Fun, Boating Speakers Bureau* and *Where to Learn to Sail*.
How to Contact: "Boating writers may request to be put on news release mailing list free by writing to NAEBM." Charges for some publications.

National Safe Boating Council, Inc., Commandant G-BA-2, Washington DC 20590. (202)426-9716. Secretary: Neal Mahan.
Purpose: "To provide a setting for national or regional, nonprofit member organizations interested in boating education and safety, to advance and foster the safe enjoyment of recreational boating and to educate the growing boating public in the principles of safe boating with the goal of protecting life and property. Information covers recreation (boating).
Services: Offers aid in arranging interviews, statistics, brochures/pamphlets and photos. Publications available.
How to Contact: Write or call.

Sea Grant Marine Advisory Program, Extension Communication, Oregon State University, Corvallis OR 97331. (503)754-3311. Marine Extension Specialist: Charles Jackson.
Purpose: "The Sea Grant Marine Advisory Program is chartered to provide information and education on the uses of marine resources. It is the statewide educational arm of the state's Sea Grant college. As such, it teaches classes and short courses on the management of marine resources, interprets applied research for marine resource users, and publishes educational materials relating to vocational and recreational uses of marine resources. Its information resources cover the Pacific Northwest, Columbia River and Oregon natural resources and their uses." Information covers business, economics, food, how-to, industry, law, nature, recreation, science, technical data,

fisheries, aquaculture and economic development.
Services: Offers aid in arranging interviews, annual reports, bibliographies, statistics, brochures/pamphlets and photos. "The program maintains more than 50 educational publications."
How to Contact: Write or call.

Medicine

American Academy of Allergy, 611 E. Wells St., Milwaukee WI 53202. Executive Director: Donald McNeil. PR Contact: Ted Klein.
Purpose: "A medical specialty society." Information covers health/medicine.
Services: Offers statistics, brochures/pamphlets, placement on mailing list and press kits. Publications include an abstract book (papers presented at annual meeting), position statements and material on hymenoptera (insect) stings.
How to Contact: Write or call Ted Klein, Ted Klein & Co., 118 E. 61st St., New York NY 10021. (212)935-1290.

American Academy of Physician Assistants, 2341 Jefferson Davis Hwy., Suite 700, Arlington VA 22202. (703)920-5730. Director of Communications: Martha L. Wilson.
Purpose: "The American Academy of Physician Assistants (AAPA) is a nonprofit organization representing physician assistants. Its range of activities include many specific membership services, meetings and conferences, research on the profession, public relations, publications and legislative activity. The AAPA has the most complete demographic information on the PA profession and is dedicated to providing the public with a greater understanding of the role of PA's in the health care delivery system." Information covers health/medicine.
Services: Offers aid in arranging interviews, annual reports, bibliographies, statistics, brochures/pamphlets, placement on mailing list, newsletter and press kits. Publications include *The P.A. Profession...What You Should Know* and *AAPA National Health Practitioner Program Profile* (catalog of physician assistant programs).
How to Contact: Write. Charges $7/copy for programs catalog, 10¢/copy for pamphlets/brochures in quantities greater than 10.

American Association of Blood Banks, 1225 Connecticut Ave. NW, Washington DC 20036. (202)872-8333. Contact: Lorry Rose or Peggy Smith.
Purpose: "We are the largest association of blood banking professionals in the world. The membership is made up of hospitals and transfusion services and individual scientists, administrators, technicians and donor recruiters. Our areas of research include blood composition, diseases, transfusions and the need for blood." Information covers health/medicine.
Services: Offers aid in arranging interviews, annual reports, brochures/pamphlets, statistics and newsletter. Publications available.
How to Contact: Write or call Lorry Rose.

American Association of Poison Control Centers, Children's Orthopedic Hospital, Box C5371, Seattle WA 98105. (206)634-5072, 634-5171. Secretary/Treasurer: William O. Robertson.
Purpose: "To set up standards of operation for poison control centers; to encourage poison prevention programs at public and professional levels; to provide information to the public and develop information services concerning toxicology; to stimulate educational programs and scientific research on toxic substances; and to assist federal, state and local officials and voluntary agencies in the field of poison control." Information covers health/medicine.
Services: Offers annual reports, brochures/pamphlets and newsletter. Publications include *Poison Isn't Kid Stuff, Home Checklist, Syrup of Ipecac, When Times Get Hot, First Aid for Poisoning, Animal and Human Toxicology* (bimonthly journal), and

Standards, Including Recommended Antidotes, Supplies and References for Poison Control Centers.
How to Contact: Write. Copies of annual report and newsletter available to members only. For copy of *Standards*, write Irving Sunshine, M.D., Educational Committee, c/o Academy of Medicine, Cleveland Poison Information Center, 10525 Carnegie Ave., Cleveland OH 44106. Charges $2.50/copy for *Standards* to nonmembers, $15/year for subscription to *Animal and Human Toxicology*, $25/year individual membership.

American College of Emergency Physicians (ACEP), 3900 Capital City Blvd., Lansing MI 48906. (517)321-7911. Director of Public Relations: Philip Stoffan. EMSIC Director: Catherine Sleicher.
Purpose: "To improve the quality of emergency medical care through the educational association of practitioners of emergency medicine. We have available information about most aspects of emergency medical services." Information covers health/medicine and emergency health care.
Services: Offers aid in arranging interviews, annual reports, bibliographies, statistics, brochures/pamphlets, information searches, placement on mailing list, photos and press kits. "Mailing list placement of accredited media representatives only." Publications include a brochure on services to members; a brochure, *A User's Guide to Emergency Medical Services Information Center*; CME requirements; *1968-1978: ACEP's First Decade of Achievement* and general information about emergency medicine.
How to Contact: Write or call.
Tips: "Formulate your question clearly. The more specific the question, the easier it will be for us to search the appropriate file."

American Dance Therapy Association (ADTA), 2000 Century Plaza, Columbia MD 21044. (301)997-4040. Office Manager: Pat Latteri.
Purpose: "To establish and maintain high standards of professional education and competence in the field. ADTA stimulates communication among dance therapists and members of allied professions through publication of the *American Journal of Dance Therapy*, memographs, conference proceedings, bibiographies and a newsletter. ADTA holds an annual conference and supports formation of regional groups, conferences, seminars, workshops and meetings throughout the year." Information covers health/medicine, self-help, creative arts therapy and nonverbal communication.
Services: Offers aid in arranging interviews, bibliographies, brochures/pamphlets and newsletter. Publications available.
How to Contact: Write or call. "As most dance therapy is practiced in psychiatric hospitals, special schools, etc., releases must be obtained before taking photographs. If interviews with practitioners and dance therapy educators are desired, contact the communications chairperson for help in arranging them."

American Dental Hygienists' Association, 211 E. Chicago Ave., Chicago IL 60611. (312)440-8930. Director, Communications Division: JoEllyn Sangsland.
Purpose: "American Dental Hygienists' Association (ADHA) is an organization of dental hygiene professionals dedicated to promoting the oral health of the public. Two journals are published devoted to all aspects of this health care field; also, several brochures containing educational aspects." Information covers health/medicine.
Services: Offers aid in arranging interviews and brochures/pamphlets. Publications include two journals, *Dental Hygiene* and *Educational Directions*.
How to Contact: Write or call the communications division.

American Medical Association, 535 N. Dearborn St., Chicago IL 60610. Contact: Tom Carroll.
Purpose: "To inform physicians on progress in clinical medicine, pertinent research and landmark evolutions." Information covers medical economics, food/nutrition,

health/medicine, history, how-to, industry and environment, new pharmaceutical products, science and sports medicine.
Services: Offers statistics, brochures/pamphlets, clipping services, library searches, placement on mailing list and newsletter. Publications include a publications list.
How to Contact: Write or call. May charge for services.

American Medical Technologists, 710 Higgins Rd., Park Ridge IL 60068. (312)823-5169. Contact: Eleanore Bors.
Purpose: "American Medical Technologists (AMT) is a registry for medical laboratory personnel. It provides continuing education programs for these professionals." Information covers health/medicine.
Services: Offers aid in arranging interviews and brochures/pamphlets. Publications include *Information on a Career in Medical Technology.*
How to Contact: Write or call.
Tips: "We can provide interviews with working laboratorians on such topics as: Why the high cost of laboratory services in the hospital; What does modern technology offer the patient; What are career opportunities. Contact US Department of Labor's *Occupational Outlook Handbook* for background information on the medical lab occupation."

American Occupational Medical Association (AOMA), 150 N. Wacker Dr., Suite 2240, Chicago IL 60606. (312)782-2166. Director of Public Relations: Priscilla Campbell.
Purpose: "American Occupational Medical Association (AOMA) is the nation's largest professional society of physicians who provide employee health care. Approximately 4,000 members are engaged in the specialty of occupational medicine, both in the US and abroad. Most members work with business and industry, and others are affiliated with academic institutions or governmental agencies. The *Journal of Occupational Medicine*, internationally recognized as the foremost publication in the field, is AOMA's official scientific publication. The American Occupational Health Conference, one of the largest annual meetings dealing with occupational health issues, combines the annual scientific meetings of AOMA and the American Association of Occupational Health Nurses." Information covers health/medicine.
Services: Offers aid in arranging interviews, placement on mailing list, newsletter, photos and press kits; also list of reprints from *Journal of Occupational Medicine.* Publications also include *AOMA Report*, usually made available to members only, but which "can be sent to members of the press in some cases."
How to Contact: Write or call.

American Psychiatric Association, 1700 18th St. NW, Washington DC 20009. (202)797-4950. Assistant Director: Ron McMillen.
Purpose: "A professional medical society representing 24,000 US psychiatrists. Our goals are to improve treatment, rehabilitation and care of the mentally ill; to promote research; to advance standards of all psychiatric services and facilities; and to educate other medical professionals, scientists and the general public." Information covers health/medicine, science, social problems and human services.
Services: Offers aid in arranging interviews, bibliographies, biographies, statistics, brochures/pamphlets and placement on mailing list. Publications include "advance and post-convention articles and news releases each May concerning annual meetings and scientific proceedings; more than 400 individual papers on a wide range of topics are typically available each year. A wide range of publications on many aspects of human life are available, depending on the writer's specific interests."
How to Contact: Write or call. Charges $2/topic "for unusually large requests for scientific papers from the annual meeting."

American Society of Clinical Pathologists, 2100 W. Harrison St., Chicago IL 60612. (312)738-1336. Manager, Public Information: John L. Normoyle.
Purpose: "The American Society of Clinical Pathologists (ASCP) is a professional

society of clinical pathologists that conducts a year-round program of continuing medical education that is the largest of any medical organization in the world. The program is designed to enable pathologists and other medical laboratory personnel (medical technologists, technicians, microbiologists, etc.) to augment their professional knowledge with the latest advances in research and techniques of laboratory medicine." Information covers health/medicine.
Services: Offers aid in arranging interviews, biographies, statistics, placement on mailing list, photos and press kits. Publications include "a basic information kit on the field of pathology and laboratory medicine."
How to Contact: Write or call. "We are in the field of pathology and laboratory medicine and will be glad to assist in any research in that field. We will not comment on subjects outside our field. Please be definite in your questions."

Association of Existential Psychology and Psychiatry, 40 E. 89th St., New York NY 10028. Secretary: Louis De Rosis.
Purpose: "To disseminate new findings about existential thought and practice." Information covers health/medicine, science and technical data.
Services: Offers journal and newsletter.
How to Contact: Write.

Canadian Schizophrenia Foundation, 2231 Broad St., Regina, Saskatchewan, Canada S4P 1Y7. (306)527-7969. General Director: I.J. Kahan.
Purpose: "To improve diagnosis, treatment and prevention of children's and adults' disorders. Many brochures, books and two periodicals are distributed." Information covers health/medicine, self-help, psychology and sociology.
Services: Offers brochures/pamphlets and newsletter. Publications include *The Journal of Orthomolecular Psychiatry* plus several books and brochures. List of publications available.
How to Contact: Write or call.

Emergency Care Research Institute, 5200 Butler Pike, Plymouth Meeting PA 19462. (215)825-6000. Editor: Robert Mosenkis.
Purpose: "We conduct comparative evaluations of medical devices used by hospitals and publish a monthly journal, *Health Devices*. We investigate medical device hazards on behalf of hospitals and include many of our reports in our journal. Despite our name, we are involved in all medical devices, equipment and disposables. We are the hospitals' analog to Consumers Union, and accept no funds from medical device manufacturers for our evaluations. We also provide inspection and repair services to hospitals under contract and publish a semimonthly newsletter, *Health Devices Alerts*, that abstracts reported problems and hazards with medical devices." Information covers health/medicine and technical data.
Services: Offers placement on mailing list and response to telephone inquiries "for information in areas of our work."
How to Contact: Write or call.
Tips: "By 'services' we mean information to writers, not our technical services. While we do not charge for providing this information, understand that we are not offering any more than verbal statements on medical equipment, hospital regulation, device recalls, etc. We have no expertise in drugs or in personal health care; our interaction is primarily with hospitals."

Foundation for Naturopathic Education & Research, Inc., Box 7528, Marietta GA 30065. (404)425-1895 or 377-7110. Director: John Fenev. Chairman: James Berryhill.
Purpose: "To promote naturopathic medical research and education through information dissemination activities, including news releases, fact sheets and press packages. We give grants to qualified applicants (individual and institutional). We act as the accrediting agency for naturopathic medical schools in the United States." Information covers health/medicine and self-help.

Services: Offers aid in arranging interviews, annual reports, statistics, brochures/ pamphlets, placement on mailing list and press kits. Provides "general and specific information dealing with the naturopathic approach to health care through assistance to the natural healing powers of the body."
How to Contact: Write or call.
Tips: "Another currently popular term to describe naturopathic medicine is 'wholistic' or 'holistic' medicine or health care. We can provide information and assistance to writers dealing with these topics as well as the usual naturopathic specialities, such as homoeopathy, chromotherapy, etc."

International Chiropractors Association (ICA), 1901 L St. NW, Washington DC 20036. (202)659-6476. Editor: Jane Redicker.
Purpose: "International Chiropractors Association (ICA) is dedicated to the objective of preserving chiropractic as a separate philosophy, science and art in the health care field. Its membership is composed of chiropractors and students of chiropractic. ICA works to promote chiropractic research and to ensure the passage of legislation that is in the best interests of chiropractic. It provides malpractice insurance for its members. ICA has information about the history of chiropractic, the philosophy of chiropratic, chiropractic colleges, current developments and practice in the field, and current legislation affecting chiropractic."
Services: Offers brochures/pamphlets and placement on mailing list. Publications include *International Review of Chiropractic* (quarterly magazine), *ICA Newsletter* (quarterly newsletter) and *Washington Legislation Today* (monthly newsletter). "Researchers may request individual issues or copies of articles in issues."
How to Contact: Write. Charges 10¢/page for photocopying.

National League for Nursing, 10 Columbus Circle, New York NY 10019. (212)582-1022. Press Relations Manager: Barbara Snow.
Purpose: "Dedicated to improving the standards for nursing education and nursing service. Areas include education of nurses; nursing service in hospitals, long-term care institutions and home health agencies; public affairs; research; testing; and any other subject related to education or service." Information covers health/medicine.
Services: Offers aid in arranging interviews, annual reports, statistics, brochures/ pamphlets and placement on mailing list. "We have hundreds of publications dealing with a variety of subjects." Publications catalog available.
How to Contact: Write or call.

National Male Nurse Association, 2309 State St., West Office, Saginaw MI 48602. (517)799-8208. Secretary: Chester Retlewski.
Purpose: "To join together in order to help eliminate prejudice in nursing, to interest men in the nursing profession, to encourage education and promote further professional growth, to discuss common problems, to advise and assist in areas of professional inequities, to help develop sensitivities to various social needs and to promote the principles and practices of positive health care." Information covers health/ medicine, new products and technical data.
Services: Offers annual reports, statistics, brochures/pamphlets, information searches and newsletter. Publications include *Men in Nursing*, a bimonthly newsletter, and pamphlets and brochures.
How to Contact: Write.

National Society for Medical Research, 1000 Vermont Ave. NW, 1100, Washington DC 20005. (202)347-9565. Director of Public Relations: Bettie W. Payne.
Purpose: "The purpose of National Society for Medical Research (NSMR) is to generate public understanding of the benefits derived through responsible animal experimentation in biomedical research and teaching and to protect the rights of scientific investigators to use laboratory animals when appropriate for the betterment of man-

kind. Staff monitors state and federal legislation and regulations which might hinder animal research. Services rendered include a monthly bulletin, news service, journalism award, special publications, data bank, press relations and exhibits." Information covers health/medicine.

Services: Offers annual reports, brochures/pamphlets, placement on mailing list, newsletter and press kits. Also operates a "news service for the media describing the benefits of animal experimentation." Publications include several booklets and brochures; write for publications list.

How to Contact: Write or call.

The Psychology Society, 100 Beekman St., New York NY 10038. (212)285-1872. Director: Pierre C. Haber.

Purpose: "The society is an association of nearly 2,000 practicing psychologists (people who treat people) interested in the application of psychology to the solution of contemporary problems." Information covers health/medicine.

Services: Offers aid in arranging interviews and aid in securing specific data.

How to Contact: Write or call. "We are interested in disseminating our findings in psychology to an interested readership."

Southern Society of Orthodontists, 135 Professional Concourse, 3393 Peachtree Rd. NE, Atlanta GA 30326. (404)261-5528. Executive Director: John Ottley Jr.

Purpose: "To enhance professionalism of members through continuing scientific education and to educate the public about orthodontics in the area of adult orthodontics, when children should first see an orthodontist, long-range aspects of orthodontic treatment, noncosmetic aspects; orthodontic insurance coverage, other dental and physical problems that are related to a bad bite, the selection of an orthodontist and orthodontic training."

Services: Offers aid in arranging interviews, brochures/pamphlets and information searches. Publications include *Tell Your Fortune*; *Orthodontic Treatment Under Insurance Programs*; *Orthodontic Tooth Brushing*; *There's Still Time*; *Age 3, Age 7*; *It's Just a Habit* and *The Big Day*.

How to Contact: Write or call.

Tips: "Do not publicize orthodontist in his own town; ethics forbid. If you have time, ask interviewee to review technical portions of your story. It's a complex dental speciality. Don't hesitate to refer to the American Association of Orthodontists as well. We can help with regional stories."

The Military

American Legion, 700 N. Pennsylvania St., Indianapolis IN 46206. (317)635-8411. Public Relations: Mr. Anderson.

Purpose: "To uphold and defend the constitution of the United States; to maintain law and order; to foster and perpetuate 100% Americanism; to preserve memories incidents of our associations in the great wars; and to promote peace and goodwill on earth." Information covers business, economics, health/medicine, history, recreation and sports.

Services: Offers aid in arranging interviews, annual reports, bibliographies, biographies, brochures/pamphlets, statistics, information searches and placement on mailing list. Publications available.

How to Contact: Write.

Armed Forces Mail Call (formerly *Military Overseas Mail*), Box 1797, Baltimore MD 21203. (301)539-3497. Director: Lee Spencer.

Purpose: "Our organization exists to provide a link between the United States public and young members of the armed forces. In the past this has been primarily accomplished through collection of mail during the Christmas season. This mail is then

distributed to military members through USOs, armed forces hospitals, chaplains, etc."
Services: Offers publicity concerning our program. "We issue news releases at appropriate times."
How to Contact: Write or call.

Jewish War Veterans U.S.A., 1712 New Hampshire Ave. NW, Washington DC 20009. (202)265-6280. Executive Director: Col. Irwin R. Ziff.
Purpose: "A veterans association of Americans of Jewish faith who have served in US armed forces during periods of war."
Services: Offers newsletter.
How to Contact: Write.

P.T. Boats, Inc., Box 109, Memphis TN 38101. (901)272-9980. Founder and Director: J.M. "Boats" Newberry.
Purpose: "Compiling the operational histories of the 43 operating squadrons, 25 bases, and 20 tenders (mother ships); maintaining museum and library; publishing newspaper and roster for over 7,500 on list." Information covers history.
Services: Offers aid in arranging interviews, information searches, newsletter and photos. Publications include squadron histories.
How to Contact: Write, call or visit. "Any research or service is $10/hour or part of an hour; photos vary in price."

Veterans of Foreign Wars of the United States, 34th and Broadway, Kansas City MO 64111. (816)756-3390. Editor: James K. Anderson.
Purpose: "The purpose of this organization shall be fraternal, patriotic, historical and educational; to preserve and strengthen comradeship among its members; to assist worthy comrades; to perpetuate the memory of our dead and to assist widows and orphans; to maintain true allegiance to the government of the United States of America, and fidelity to its Constitution and laws; to foster true patriotism; to maintain and extend the institution of American freedom; and to preserve and defend the United States from all her enemies whomsoever." Information covers economics, history, law, science and national defense.
Services: Offers brochures/pamphlets and newsletter. Publications include *V.F.W. Magazine* (monthly), *Washington Action Reporter* (monthly), *Speak Up for Democracy* (monthly radio/TV script), *Post Exchange* (bimonthly newsletter).
How to Contact: Write or call.

Miscellaneous

Academy of Motion Picture Arts and Sciences: National Film Information Service, 8949 Wilshire Blvd., Beverly Hills CA 90211. (213)278-8990. Coordinator, National Film Information Service: Anthony Slide.
Purpose: National film information service. Information covers motion pictures.
Services: Offers film stills filed by personality and by film title.
How to Contact: Write or call. Charges $5/8x10 still. Larger sizes available on special order. "No catalog of the collection is available, but we will answer all research requests."

Afro-American Cultural Foundation, 255 Grove St., White Plains NY 10601. (914)761-4778. Chairman & Acting Director: Mr. John H. Harmon.
Purpose: Information covers art, business, celebrities, economics, history, music and self-help.
Services: Offers aid in arranging interviews, biographies, brochures/pamphlets, information searches, placement on mailing list, statistics and newsletter.
How to Contact: Write or call. Charges vary depending on services requested.

American Camping Association, Bradford Woods, Martinsville IN 46151. (317)342-8456. Editor: Glenn T. Job.
Purpose: "American Camping Association (ACA) is the sole accrediting agency of organized children's camps, both private and agency, in the US. ACA provides training, direction, legislative lobbying, workshops, publications and conventions aimed at continuous updating and improvement of organized camping and camp management." Information covers agriculture, art, entertainment, food, health/ medicine, history, how-to, music, nature, new products, recreation, science, sports, travel and experience pieces.
Services: Offers statistics, brochures/pamphlets, media releases and media kits. Publications include "camping magazine author's guide and general informational brochures on the subject of organized camping and ACA. Our services are generally restricted to the rather narrow field of organized, fixed children's camps. We can't help with Winnebagos and KOAs, etc., but if you're patient, we'll help all we can in our discipline."
How to Contact: Write or call.

American Divorce Association for Men (ADAM), 1008 White Oak St., Arlington Heights, IL 60005. (312)394-1040.
Purpose: "A men's rights group in domestic relations area affecting attitudinal and legal changes. Members' dues support the movement, and in return, they receive individualized legal and nonlegal counseling, as well as referral to competent attorneys, investigators and other professional services. We work mainly in the areas of pre- and post-divorce issues." Information covers economics, law and self-help.
Services: Offers brochures/pamphlets and information searches. "We will cooperate with writers or researchers for mutual considerations."
How to Contact: Write or call.

American Institute of Architects, 1735 New York Ave. NW, Washington DC 20006. Administrative Assistant, Public Relations Department: Linda Vasquez.
Purpose: "American Institute of Architects is a voluntary professional organization representing more than 31,000 registered architects. Its programs are addressed to improving professional competence, developing and supporting policies in the public interest on issues of national concern, and promoting public understanding of the architectural profession's role in shaping the built environment."
Services: Offers aid in arranging interviews, annual reports, bibliographies, statistics, brochures/pamphlets, placement on mailing list, newsletter and press kits.
How to Contact: Write. Many publications available. Charges for some.

American Movers Conference, 1117 N. 19th St., Arlington VA 22209. (703)524-5440. Director of Public Relations: James W. Mansfield.
Purpose: "National representative trade association of the interstate household goods moving industry, representing 1,400 moving companies and an underlying membership of over 8,000 movers worldwide. Each year, its member firms move interstate almost 1.7 million household goods shipments, 60% of which occur during the three heavy vacation months of June, July and August." Information covers business, economics, history, how-to, industry, self-help and technical data.
Services: Offers aid in arranging interviews, biographies, statistics, brochures/ pamphlets, placement on press mailing list and photos. Publications include *Tips on Moving*, "a how-to booklet on the intricacies of moving," and *Moving and Children*, "a companion piece to the above with emphasis on including children in plans for moving, psychological impact, etc."
How to Contact: Write or phone.

American Philatelic Society, Box 800, State College PA 16801. (814)237-3803. Editor: Richard L. Sine. Executive Secretary: Col. James T. DeVoss.
Purpose: "We are the largest organization of stamp collectors (45,000 plus) in this

country." Information covers how-to.
Services: Offers aid in arranging interviews, bibliographies, statistics, brochures/pamphlets and information searches. Publications include publications list.
How to Contact: Write or call.

American Recovery Association, Inc., 4040 W. 70th St., Minneapolis MN 55435. (612)929-9669. General Manager: Dottie Anderson.
Purpose: "To further and promote the general welfare of the repossession profession in the US and elsewhere; to regulate practices, prescribe ethics and to enforce proper conduct among its members; to promote the adoption of legislation in the various states and in the US favorable to the rights of repossessors and the credit-granting public; and to gather and disseminate material relative to the repossession profession which may be valuable to members of this association." Information covers finance recover of property in default.
Services: Offers brochures/pamphlets and newsletter. Publications include *News & Views*, a monthly newsletter; *Directory* lists members and territory covered and *Can't Collect*, a pamphlet for credit grantor.
How to Contact: Write. "Clearance may have to be obtained on some items."

Bald Headed Men of America, Box BALD, Dunn NC 28334. (919)726-1004, 892-7365. Founder/Executive Director: John T. Capps.
Purpose: "To eliminate the vanity that is associated with the loss of one's hair. To promote the fun of being baldheaded. If you don't have it, flaunt it or go topless."
Services: Offers aid in arranging interviews, brochures/pamphlets and press kits. Publications available.
How to Contact: Write or call.

Barre Granite Association, 51 Church St., Barre VT 05641. (802)476-4131. Manager, Retail Services: Thomas Riley.
Purpose: "To promote products of our members and upright memorialization. Our members are engaged in the manufacture of cemetery memorials." Information covers art, business and industry.
Services: Offers brochures/pamphlets, newsletter, press kits and motion pictures. Publications include *Story of Granite* and *Monuments Yesterday, Today and Tomorrow*.
How to Contact: Write or call.

Canadian Telecommunications Carriers Association (CTCA), 1 Nicholas, Suite 700, Ottawa, Ontario, Canada K1N 7B7. (613)238-3080. Supervisor, News and Information: Bonni Kilbrick-Evans.
Purpose: "We have 21 member companies, all of which represent any form of telecommunication carried in Canada. We develop policies and priorities and are the lobbying group for the telecommunications industry." Information covers business, economics, new products, politics, science and technical data.
Services: Offers aid in arranging interviews, annual reports, bibliographies, biographies, statistics, brochures/pamphlets, clipping services, information searches, placement on mailing list, newsletter, photos, press kits, and conference and museum exhibits. Publications include *Telenews, Televiews*, and a CTCA pamphlet.
How to Contact: Write or call.

Center for the History of American Needlework, Box 8162, Pittsburgh PA 15217. (412)422-8749. Contact: Rachel Maines.
Purpose: "We are a national study center for needlework and textiles offering information, research and referral services including library, photos and publication." Information covers art.
Services: Offers aid in arranging interviews, annual reports, bibliographies,

brochures/pamphlets, information searches, placement on mailing list, newsletter and photos. Publications available.

How to Contact: Write or call. "Our library includes some manuscript resources. We include not only general history in the needle arts, but also textiles, technology in the needlework industry, and sewing. We charge for exhibitions, photos (at cost), book publications and pattern portfolios. Bibliographies and many other publications are free for SASE."

Children's Book Council, 67 Irving Place, New York NY 10003. (212)254-2666. Publications Director: Christine Stawicki.

Purpose: "To encourage interest in children's books; in using and enjoying children's books; and the promotion of children's books in a general way." Information covers children's literature.

Services: Offers bibliographies, informational brochures and informational sheets. Publications available.

How to Contact: Write or call (no collect calls). Charges for publications.

Comics Magazine Association of America, Inc., 41 E. 42nd St., New York NY 10017. (212)697-6750. Administrator: Leonard Darvin.

Purpose: "We function as a trade association for the comics magazine industry; operate a comics library; and, chiefly, enforce a code of decency for editorial and advertising matter published in comic books." Information covers comic books.

Services: Offers brochures/pamphlets. Publications include *Code of the Comics Magazine Association of America* and *Americana in Four Colors*, a paperback of comic books and code enforcement. "We also have articles, newspaper clippings and books in our library about comics."

How to Contact: Write or visit.

Continental Association of Funeral and Memorial Societies, Inc., 1828 L St. NW, Suite 1100, Washington DC 20036. (202)293-4821. Executive Director: Elizabeth C. Clemmer.

Purpose: "Continental Association of Funeral and Memorial Societies (CAFMS) aims to aid consumers by providing information about funerals; by encouraging preplanning of funerals; and by helping people to join memorial societies which provide their members with assistance in obtaining less expensive, simple and dignified funerals." Information covers funerals.

Services: Offers bibliographies, statistics, brochures/pamphlets and newsletter. "We also frequently review TV and radio scripts and magazine articles on funerals. We check for accuracy and give leads in turning up stories, etc."

How to Contact: Write or call. "A publication list gives prices if writer wishes to order books. We may charge an hourly fee for review of scripts, etc. if the time spent is substantial. It is frequently difficult to obtain information on funeral laws in a particular state or to get funeral directors to give their costs and to explain them. This may be changing as the consumer movement grows. CAFMS regularly assists writers and is glad to do so."

Deltiologists of America, 3709 Gradyville Rd., Newtown Square PA 19073. (215)353-1689. Director: James L. Lowe.

Purpose: "To supply collectors with information about pre-1915 picture postcards, their artists and publishers." Information covers art, business, celebrities, entertainment, history, industry, music, nature, new products, politics, science, sports, technical data and travel.

Services: Offers bibliographies, brochures/pamphlets and placement on mailing list. Publications include *Deltiology*.

How to Contact: Write with SASE. Call only in emergency. There is a fee for publications and services.

Direct Selling Association, 1730 M St. SW, Suite 610, Washington DC 20036. (202)293-5760. Manager, Media Programs: Paula Auerbach.
Purpose: "We are a national trade association representing approximately 100 firms which manufacture and distribute goods and services directly to the consumer. The association acts as liaison between the direct selling industry and all levels of government. DSA works to help the public better understand the direct selling industry and form of retailing. Internationally, the association keeps in close contact with direct selling associations around the world." Information covers industry (facts and figures on the direct selling industry).
Services: Offers aid in arranging interviews, bibliographies, statistics, brochures/ pamphlets, placement on mailing list and press kits (available through the Direct Selling Educational Foundation, at the same address). Publications available.
How to Contact: Write. "Give the association as much lead time as possible."

Early American Industries Association, Old Economy, Ambridge PA 15003. (412)266-4500. Editor: Daniel B. Reibel.
Purpose: "The primary interests are in American tools and technology. Our members are primarily tool collectors and museums with large collections of tools. We have many members in the academic area. We publish a quarterly journal, *The Chronicle*, and an occasional newsletter, *The Shavings*. We have two meetings a year. We also have a scholarship fund in the area of American technology. We will help institutions with our expertise on tools, identify unknown tools, and furnish technical advice. We publish a number of books on tools and technology." Information covers agriculture, business, good, history, how-to, industry and technical data.
Services: Offers brochures/pamphlets, bibliographies, information searches and newsletter.
How to Contact: Write, but keep requests brief and specific.

Feather & Down Association, 1350 Broadway, New York NY 10018. (212)695-9280. Director, Marketing Committee: Ellen Stark.
Purpose: "To publicize and promote feather and down products, such as pillows, comforters, sleeping bags, garments, and furniture filled with feathers and down." Information covers business, economics, how-to, industry, new products and technical data.
Services: Offers aid in arranging interviews, statistics, photos and press kits.
How to Contact: Write or call.

The Ford Foundation, Office of Reports, 320 E. 43rd St., New York NY 10017. (212)573-5000.
Purpose: "The Ford Foundation is a private, philanthropic institution chartered to serve the public welfare. Under the policy guidance of its board of trustees, the foundation works mainly by giving funds for educational, developmental, research and experimental efforts designed to produce significant advances on selected problems of national and international importance. Through mid-1977, the foundation has expended more than $5 billion, including grants to 7,200 institutions and organizations in the US and in 96 foreign countries." Information covers agriculture, art, business, economics, law, music, nature, politics, science, self-help and technical data.
Services: Offers placement on mailing list and newsletter. Publications include publications list.
How to Contact: Write "Some publications are sold; most are free."

Foundation for Handgun Education, 100 N. Washington St., Falls Church VA 22046. (703)534-9099. President: David Gorin.
Purpose: "The Foundation for Handgun Education (FHE) is an educational organization devoted to the preparation, production and distribution of materials designed to

educate the American people about handgun violence and abuse. The FHE maintains files on all aspects of the handgun control controversy and files on handgun violence and abuse." Information covers handgun violence and crime.
Services: Offers aid in arranging interviews, bibliographies, statistics, brochures/pamphlets and photos. Publications include *FHE Program Statement* and *A Gun is Not a Toy*. Other materials now in process are a seminar program for high schools and teen clubs and a "National Handgun Awareness Tests", a film.
How to Contact: Write or call.
Tips: "The FHE offers a different perspective on handguns than any of the other anti- or pro-control groups. FHE is unrelated to any other existing organization. Available materials are often biased for or against gun control. It is very difficult to find facts/statistics which one side or the other will not dispute."

Free Beaches Documentation Center, Box 132, Oshkosh WI 54902. (414)231-9977. Information Coordinator: Lee Baxandall.
Purpose: "We exist to coordinate the efforts of persons and groups working to gain full recognition for clothing-optional sunbathing, swimming and other modes of recreation."
Services: Offers aid in arranging interviews, bibliographies, brochures/pamphlets, placement on mailing list, photos and press kits. Publications include pertinent legal documents and *Guide to Nude Beaches of the World* (annual).
How to Contact: Write. "We provide an overview of the current acceptance, the problems and historical origins of nude beaches and related activities. Writers are encouraged to contact local advocates and sources as well; we may or may not be able to facilitate such contacts."
Tips: " 'Participatory' practices by reporters and photographers going to skinny-dipping sites in their area will result in greater cooperation by sources."

The Fund for Investigative Journalism, 1346 Connecticut Ave. NW, Washington DC 20036. (202)462-1844. Executive Director: Howard Bray.
Purpose: "To increase public knowledge about the concealed, obscure or complex aspects of matters significantly affecting the public."
Services: Offers brochures/pamphlets.
How to Contact: Write or call.

Graphic Arts Technical Foundation, 4615 Forbes Ave., Pittsburgh PA 15213. (412)621-6941. Communications Manager: John N. Dutkovich.
Purpose: "The foundation is a nonprofit, scientific, technical and educational organization serving the international graphic communications community. GATF is the oldest, continuous organization of its kind in graphic communications. GATF is one of the world's leading centers for graphic communications research and education. GATF offers it membership and the industry a wide variety of educational programs, printing production quality and technical assistance services." Information covers technical data, graphic arts education and literature.
Services: Offers annual reports, statistics, brochures/pamphlets and information searches. Publications available.
How to Contact: Call. "All services are priced. Rates are too many and varied to list. We will provide information on specific questions when they are received."

Rene Guyon Society, 256 S. Robertson Blvd., Beverly Hills CA 90211. Spokesperson: Tim O'Hara.
Purpose: "World's leading authority on child sexuality. We work for child sex law easement and cooperates with worldwide child sexual freedom movements." Information covers health/medicine, history, law, politics, science and technical data.
Services: Offers aid in arranging interviews, bibliographies, and brochures/pamphlets. Publication available.

How to Contact: Write or call. "Please provide a #10 SASE with 28¢ postage. We provide free introductory data. For an extensive coverage of our field, we need co-author credit."

Handwriting Analysts Inc., 1504 W. 29th St., Davenport IA 52804. (319)391-7350. President: Robert Martin.
Purpose: "To bring together analysts, students and interested people in graphology to share information." Information covers graphology.
Services: Offers newsletter and informational programs and speakers three times a year. "We can usually recommend analysts in most geographical areas who are qualified to help writers/researchers." Publications include *Handwriting Analysts Journal*.
How to Contact: Write or call. Charges for subscription to *Handwriting Analysts Journal* (order from Box 42959, Chicago 60642).

Handy-Cap Horizons, Inc., 3250 E. Loretta Dr., Indianapolis IN 46227. President/Editor/Tour Sponsor: Dorothy S. Axsom.
Purpose: "Handy-Cap Horizons, Inc. is an organization which strives to bring the world to the door of handicapped and elderly, either by actual travel through the USA and other parts of the world—or by articles in its quarterly magazine of the same name. Nonhandicapped people also seem to enjoy the magazine (and libraries all over the country subscribe). All who become members are eligible for discounted tours, tours planned to fit the disabled and the older person who wishes a slower pace. For more along this line, read the history written by our quadriplegic vice president and associate editor. We are a nonprofit organization, chartered in Indiana, with tax-exempt status. We are completely volunteer. We're people-to-people, too! We visit with our own government offical in foreign countries, as well as the VIPs of the country visited, handicapped groups, families, etc. (being international, we have members in so many places to help with the planning. Our tours are group tours only; several have asked us to plan independent travel. We are not a travel agent, rather a travel club and we cannot plan independent touring for many reasons." Information covers art, celebrities, entertainment, food, health/medicine, history, how-to, new products, recreation, science, self-help, sports, technical data and travel.
Services: Offers aid in arranging interviews, annual reports (to members), brochures/pamphlets, regular informational magazine and press kits for members. Publications include *Horizons Handy-Cap History*.
How to Contact: Write or call. "We will help with information and articles only pertaining to handicapped activities and travel."

Humor Societies of America/National Laugh Enterprises, 74 Pullman Ave., Elberon NJ 07740. (201)229-9472. Executive Director: George Q. Lewis.
Purpose: "To discover, develop, encourage and showcase future funny men and women of America; to provide information and education about the art of laughmaking; to provide lecturers and coordinate special events that provide opportunity for humor exchange across the nation and to coordinate careers in comedy for both gag writers and comedy performers." Information covers art, business, celebrities, economics, entertainment, history, how-to, new products, recreation, science, self-help and technical data.
Services: Offers aid in arranging interviews and annual reports. "We coordinate special events in conjunction with the laughmakers' calendar of events, conduct a college of comedy, and lecture in colleges. We develop handouts that give how-to information on every aspect of the art of laughmaking."
How to Contact: Write or call. "We invite membership in the humor exchange network; the fee is $25/year."

Institute for Encyclopedia on Human Ideas of Ultimate Reality and Meaning, 15 Saint

Mary St., Toronto, Ontario, Canada M4W 1P3. (416)922-2476. General Editor: Tibor Horvath.
Purpose: To coordinate and publish interdisciplinary studies and research on man's effort to find meaning in his world. Information covers art, history, music, science, anthropology, philosophy and linguistics.
Services: Offers *Information for Contributors* (writer's guidelines) and *Ultimate Reality and Meaning* magazine.
How to Contact: Write.

The Inventors Association, Box 281, Swift Current, Saskatchewan, Canada S9H 3V6. (306)773-7762. Secretary-Treasurer/General Manager: Phyllis Z. R. Tengum.
Purpose: "The Inventors Association provides services and advisory assistance to inventors, such as the filing of a caveat to protect an invention, having a patent search conducted to find out if the invention is patentable and helping to find a market for an invention when it has been patented. Organized in 1955, there is a membership from all across Canada of around 300 members." Information covers material for inventors.
Services: Offers brochures/pamphlets and services to inventors. A publication list, including prices, is available.
How to Contact: Write. "There is a $5 service fee."

Jewelry Industry Council, 608 5th Ave., New York NY 10020. (212)757-3075. President: Morton R. Sarett.
Purpose: "We are the nationwide nonprofit public information organization of this entire industry which supplies generic facts about gems and jewelry of all kinds." Information covers diamonds, pearls and other gems; gold; silver; platinum; watches; jewelry of every price range; and consumer guidelines.
Services: Offers aid in arranging interviews, brochures/pamphlets, photos, generic facts, and related information about gems and jewelry products of all kinds, including history, lore, fashion trends, consumer guidelines, etc. Publications include leaflets and booklets on diamonds, pearls, watches, silver, gold, fashion tips for teenagers, jewelry for the woman of today, men's jewelry, birthstones, china, crystal, stainless, planning the wedding, gifts for the wedding party, the modern wedding anniversary list, fashion jewelry, the romance of rings and birthstones.
How to Contact: Write or call. "The Jewelry Industry Council does not publicize or promote individual companies or brand names."

Magazine Association of Canada, 1240 Bay St., Toronto Canada M5R 2A7. (416)922-3181. Research Director: Miss Jo Marney.
Purpose: "To help Canadian consumer magazines grow by developing advertising revenue. Data available on Canadian magazines size, frequency, cost, etc."
Services: Offers information searches, brochures/pamphlets and placement on mailing list.
How to Contact: Write or call.

National Association of Barber Schools, Inc., 304 S. 11th St., Lincoln NE 68508. Secretary/Treasurer: Albert D. Howard.
Purpose: "To promote and advance barber education and to promote and advance the barber industry." Information covers industry.
Services: Offers brochures/pamphlets. Publications include a description of the barber industry—history, educational requirements, opportunities, training and future.
How to Contact: Write.

National Association of Recycling Industries, 330 Madison Ave., New York NY 10017. (212)867-7330. Director, Public Relations: John R McBride.
Purpose: "We represent the processors and industrial consumers of recycled materials in the US, Canada and many countries overseas." Information covers business, eco-

nomics, recycling industry and technical data.
Services: Offers aid in arranging interviews, statistics and brochures/pamphlets. A publications and price list is available.
How to Contact: Write or call.

National Ballroom & Entertainment Association, Box 338, West Des Moines IA 50265. (515)223-1341. Secretary: Frances B. Archer.
Purpose: "To promote dancing to live music; to get dancers into the ballroom; to promote big band ballroom dancing." Information covers history.
Services: Offers brochures/pamphlets, newsletter, annual yearbook and an annual convention.
How to Contact: Write or call.

National Christmas Tree Association, Inc., 611 E. Wells St., Milwaukee WI 53202. (414)276-6410. Associate Editor: Mary Garity.
Purpose: "To aid producers and individuals involved in the Christmas tree industry; to provide information concerning natural Christmas trees and work in conjunction with the 31 affiliated state associations. A biennial convention is sponsored and includes technical sessions, farm tours and equipment and product demonstrations." Information covers information pertaining to Christmas trees.
Services: Offers bibliographies, statistics, brochures/pamphlets and press kits. Publications include *The American Christmas Tree Journal* (quarterly trade magazine) and the *Christmas Merchandiser* (annual retail magazine).
How to Contact: Write or call. Charges $2/copy for magazine.

National Costumers Association, 2616 Philadelphia Pike, Claymont DE 19703. Secretary/Treasurer: Mrs. Doris Jester.
Purpose: "To establish and maintain professional and ethical standards of business in the costume industry; to encourage and promote a greater and more diversified use of costumes in all fields of human activity; and to provide trade information, cooperation and friendship among its members, together with a sound public relations policy." Information covers business, economics, entertainment, history, how-to, new products and educational seminars.
Services: Offers annual reports, books, patterns, plots and placement. All services and publications are limited to the membership.
How to Contact: Write the Membership Chairman, Mr. Erin Wertenberger, 303 W. Federal St., Youngstown OH 44503. "Membership in the National Costumers Association is open to any qualified costumer who meets the membership requirements and is approved by the membership."

National Hearing Aid Society, 20361 Middlebelt Rd., Livonia MI 48152. (313)478-2610. Executive Secretary: Anthony DiRocco.
Purpose: "To promote welfare of hearing impaired; coordinate programs of society; provide communications among members in industry; improve methods of selling, fitting and using hearing aids; establish standards; examine qualifications of hearing aid specialists; create public education; and cooperate with medical professionals."Certifies qualified hearing aid specialists, sponsors and supports educational programs, enforces code of ethics, publishes information on hearing health care, cooperates with professional groups and government officials, ans sponsors consumer protection programs. Also publishes *Audecibel* and provides information packets. Information covers health/medicine and technical data.
Services: Offers statistics, brochures/pamphlets, information searches, placement on mailing list and newsletter. Publications available.
How to Contact: Write.

National Notary Association, 23012 Ventura Blvd., Woodland Hills CA 91364.

(213)347-2035. Publicity Director: Bill Cobert.
Purpose: "To serve and educate the nation's notaries public and to keep the general public and legislators informed and aware of the purpose and needs of notaries. We cover every area that affects or could affect the notary, usually changes in law or in business and economic conditions." Information covers business, economics, history, how-to, industry, law, new products and technical data.
Services: Offers aid in arranging interviews, annual reports, bibliographies, statistics, brochures/pamphlets, newsletter and press kits. Publications include *What is a Notary Public?*, *11 Questions about the NNA*, *The National Notary* magaine, *Viewpoint* newsletter, *Notary Digest* and uniform notary legislation.
How to Contact: Write or call.

National Pyrotechnic Distributors Association, Inc., Box 1922, Saginaw MI 48605. (517)752-6123. Executive Secretary-Treasurer: David Opperman.
Purpose: "To promote the continued growth of the fireworks industry." Information covers all aspects of fireworks.
Services: Offers aid in arranging interviews, statistics, photos and press kits.
How to Contact: Write.

National Rifle Association of America, 1600 Rhode Island Ave. NW, Washington DC 20036. (202)783-6505. Assistant Director, Public Affairs: R.W. Hunnicutt.
Purpose: "We are the national governing body of the shooting sports, the largest organization of shooting sportsmen in the nation, and a recognized authority on all firearms topics. We sponsor US Olympic and world championship teams and represents the interests of shooters, hunters and firearms collectors at all levels of govern-

The nonwear and tear of a tug-of-war is demonstrated by this shot from the Free Beaches Documentation Center. The photo, available free from the center, depicts activities at Black's Beach in San Diego. Lee Baxandall, information coordinator of the center, stresses that any use of photos from the center must be nonexploitive, a restriction all photo sources will impose on writers.

ment." Information covers how-to, law, nature, new products, politics, recreation, sports and technical data.

Services: Offers aid in arranging interviews, annual reports, statistics, brochures/pamphlets, placement on mailing list, photos and press kits.

How to Contact: For sports and general information, contact the NRA Office of Public Affairs. For political information, contact the NRA Institute for Legislative Action, Communications Division.

Package Designers Council, Box 3753, Grand Central Station, New York NY 10017. (212)682-1980. Assistant President: Lea S. Liu.

Purpose: "We are a professional organization of industrial design consultants who specialize in package design and other visual expressions of the corporate image." Information covers package design.

Services: Offers information searches.

How to Contact: Write or call.

Plastic Bottle Information Bureau, 99 Park Ave., 3rd Floor, New York NY 10016. (212)599-6929. Bureau Director: Hal Hart. Research Director: Tery Yacona.

Purpose: "The Plastic Bottle Information Bureau of the Plastic Bottle Institute disseminates information and handles media inquiries on all aspects of plastic bottles." Information covers business, economics, health/medicine, history, industry, science and technical data.

Services: Offers aid in arranging interviews, statistics and newsletter. Publications include *Energy Use and Resource Recovery*, *Municipal Solid Waste Management* and *Health and Safety Aspects of Plastic Bottles*.

How to Contact: Write.

Ski the Rockies News Bureau, 666 5th Ave., Suite 1500, New York NY 10019. (212)399-2772. Assistant Director: Terry Gabel.

Purpose: "To generate awareness of resort facilities within the association, including dissemination of current facts about ski business in general, ski lift operations and the resort/travel business." Information covers sports and travel.

Services: Offers aid in arranging interviews, statistics, brochures/pamphlets, information searches, photos and press kits. Publications include *1978 Ski*, *the Rockies Complete Travel Guide* and resort brochures from Aspen, Breckenridge, Copper Mountain, Crested Butte, Jackson Hole, Snowbird, Snowmass, Steamboat, Sun Valley, Taos, Vail and Winter Park.

How to Contact: Write or call. "Be specific. With as many aspects of skiing as there are at one resort multiplied by 12 resorts, writers should not ask that everything available be sent."

Tarot, International, Grand Lodge, Box 3254, Carbondale IL 62901. President: L.D. Worley.

Purpose: "Fraternal order open to men and women interested in the study and use of tarot cards." Information covers self-help.

Services: Offers brochures/pamphlets and complete training in tarot divination. Publications include information flyers.

How to Contact: Write.

Toastmasters International, 2200 N. Grand Ave., Santa Ana CA 92711. (714)542-6793. Membership and Public Relations Manager: Alan L. La Green.

Purpose: "Toastmasters International is the world's largest organization devoted to training individuals in public speaking, communication and leadership skills. The organization has 3,500 Toastmasters clubs in the US, Canada and 45 other countries. Founded in 1924, Toastmasters is one of the oldest self-help organizations in existance. Major emphasis today is on corporate public speaking programs through in-house Toastmasters clubs." Information covers business, how-to, industry, recreation, self-help and public speaking.

Services: Offers aid in arranging interviews, bibliographies, brochures/pamphlets, information searches, placement on mailing list and press kits. "Anyone preparing a story on public speaking, corporate communications, speech seminars, etc. should start by contacting Toastmasters." Publications include *All About Toastmasters*, *Communication—Your Success Depends On It!*, *The Toastmaster* (monthly), and *Annual Directory of Toastmasters Clubs*.

How to Contact: "Call or write the membership, club extension and public relations departments. We can then put writers in touch with local Toastmaster volunteer leaders."

Tips: "The recently published *Book of Lists* ranked speaking in public as the number one fear of most Americans (it outranked the fear of death by a two to one margin!)."

Uglies Unlimited, 1714 Merrimac Trail, Garland TX 75043. Founder: Danny McCoy.
Purpose: "To bring about the awareness of discrimination of human beings because of their unfavorable appearance." Information covers self-help.
Services: Offers aid in arranging interviews and information searches.
How to Contact: Write or call.

Women Make Movies, Inc, 257 W. 19th St., New York NY 10011. (212)929-6477. Executive Director: Janet Benn.
Purpose: "Women Make Movies is a nonprofit, tax-exempt educational women's membership organization of independent film and video makers and those interested in the production and distribution of social change media, particularly media that accurately reflect the lives and concerns of women. Activities encompass all aspects of filmmaking: teaching women the essential techniques of film, producing films, and distributing and showing films (both those produced by Women Make Movies, and outside productions). Our objectives are to encourage and support the production and proliferation of women-made media that emphasize and promote enlightened social change; to serve as a resource center through which a woman has the opportunity to gain technical skills, borrow and use production equipment at low or no cost, receive financial, technical and emotional support toward the realization of her completed work, have her completed film distributed by us, and share her skills and resources with other women. Information covers film and video making."
Services: Offers biographies, brochures/pamphlets, placement on mailing list and newsletter.
How to Contact: Write or call.

World Association of Detectives, Box 5068, San Mateo CA 94402. (415)341-0060. Vice President: Vance I. Morris.
Purpose: "For the professional upgrading and training of private investigators." Information covers law and private investigation.
Services: Offers aid in arranging interviews and information searches.
How to Contact: Write or call.

Music

American Music Center, Inc., 250 W. 57th St., New York NY 10019. (212)247-3121.
Purpose: "We are the best source for information on contemporary American music in the country, and are pleased to be of help to people looking for specific information." Information covers musical celebrities and music.
Services: Offers biographies, statistics, information searches and newsletter. Publications include a brochure describing the American Music Center's (AMC) activities, ongoing catalogs of the AMC library holdings (Volume I covers choral and vocal music and Volume II covers chamber music), *Contemporary Music Performance Directory*, and quarterly *Newsletter* (on subscription).

How to Contact: Write or call. "We charge for major reference services and, in some instances, we charge commercial organizations for all services rendered. Call to describe what you need and/or want to do. Facilities are open from 9:30 a.m. to 5:30 p.m. weekdays. We can provide reference and guidance in project research, but can rarely do the research itself."

American Old Time Fiddlers Association, 6141 Morrill Ave., Lincoln NE 68507. (402)466-5519. President: De DeRyke.
Purpose: "To preserve and promote old time fiddling and its related arts and skills." Information covers music, technical data, fiddling and violin.
Services: Offers newsletters.
How to Contact: Write or call. "We are one of the most complete sources of information of fiddling, especially traditional. Interviewing writers have to fit into our schedule and not bother the fiddling instruction classes."
Tips: "Just be persistent and figure out different approaches if the first fails. I have been researching fiddling for over 20 years, and it is harder now than when I started."

American Society of Composers, Authors and Publishers (ASCAP), 1 Lincoln Plaza, New York NY 10023. (212)595-3050. Contact: Public Relations Department.
Purpose: To collect and distribute royalties for composers and publishers of music. Information covers music.
Services: Offers aid in arranging interviews, annual reports, biographies, brochures/pamphlets, information searches, placement on mailing list and photos.
How to Contact: Write or call.

Louis Braille Foundation for Blind Musicians, Inc., 215 Park Ave. S., New York NY 10003. (212)982-7290. Executive Director: Shel Freund.
Purpose: Provides services for and promotes blind musicians. Information covers music.
Services: Offers aid in arranging interviews and placement on mailing list.
How to Contact: Write or call.

Broadcast Music, Inc. (BMI), 40 W. 57th St., New York NY 10019. (212)586-2000. Vice President of Public Relations: Russell Sanjeko.
Purpose: "Broadcast Music, Inc. (BMI) currently represents over 55,000 writers and publishers of music of all types in the licensing and collection of fees for the public performance of their music by users of all kinds. Through reciprocal agreements, we also represent writers and publishers associated with 39 similar societies all around the world. It is the largest organization of its kind in the world." Information covers music.
Services: Offers assistance to songwriters. Publications include *Handbook for BMI Writers and Publishers*, *You and the Music You Use*, *BMI–The World's Largest Licensing Organization* and *The Many Worlds of Music and You*.
How to Contact: Write.

Country Music Association, Inc., 7 Music Circle N., Nashville TN 37203. (615)244-2840. Editor: Marsha Gepner.
Purpose: "Country Music Association, Inc. (CMA) is a trade organization for the country music industry made up of approximately 5,000 members. We promote country music throughout the world and sponsor various activities during the year. CMA also produces an annual country music awards show which is televised over national TV every October." Information covers country music business, country music celebrities, country entertainment, country music industry and country music.
Services: Offers brochures/pamphlets, placement on mailing list, newsletter and press kits. "We also offer lists of country radio stations throughout the US, music publishing companies, record company personnel, clubs that feature country music entertainments, artists and managers and booking agents, and publication lists. However, these

are available to CMA members only." Publications include "two booklets (both are part of our press kit) which give statistical information about the country music industry, such as the dollar amount of country product sales in the US, the number of country radio stations, the number of hours country music is programmed, interesting facts about Nashville and the country music industry, etc. These brochures are entitled *Industry* and *Country Goes Uptown*."

How to Contact: Write or call. "We will, of course, help writers as much as we can. A freelance writer may get brochures or whatever information we have at CMA to help him. A writer assigned by a publication to do a story may get additional help from CMA in arranging interviews with celebrities, record company personnel, etc., depending upon the availability of CMA staff's time. In our busy seasons (May-June, September-October) we may not be as able to help as at other times."

Tips: "People wishing current information about country music in general should contact CMA first. People wishing historical information should contact the Country Music Foundation, 4 Music Square E., Nashville TN 37203. The Country Music Foundation has a complete library and archives housing information about virtually all phases of country music. People wishing information about a specific artist should contact the artist's booking agent or record label."

Lute Society of America, 1930 Cameron Ct., Concord CA 94518. (415)686-1828. Microfilm Librarian: Nancy Carlin.

Purpose: "We deal with 16th- and 17th-century music for lute and related instruments." Information covers music.

Services: Offers information searches and newsletter; also has one bibliography on lute construction sources. Publications include an annual journal, quarterly newsletters and an annual music edition.

How to Contact: Write or call. "Library users must be members." For bibliography and membership information, write Claire Handelman, 2395 Franasco, #203, San Fransisco 94123.

National Music Publishers' Association, 110 E. 59th St., New York NY 10022. (212)751-1930. President: Leonard Feist.

Purpose: "We protect the rights of music publishers and their authors and composers." Information covers music.

Services: Offers brochures/pamphlets and newsletter. Publications include *Bulletin*, a quarterly newsletter, and *The United States Copyright Law: A Guide For Music Educators*.

How to Contact: Write or call. "All other information is available to members only. Membership is strictly music publishers in the US; dues are $50 annually."

National Youth Orchestra Association of Canada, 76 Charles St. W., Toronto, Ontario, Canada M5S 1K8. (416)922-5031. General Director: John Brown.

Purpose: Brings distinguished teachers of music to Canada to teach Canadian youth.

Services: Offers aid in arranging interviews, biographies, statistics, brochures/pamphlets, information searches, and placement on mailing list. Publications include *National Youth Orchestra of Canada: Who We Are and What We Do*.

How to Contact: Write. Charges for reimbursement of costs incurred. Wants clearance of copy directly related to interviews with staff.

Percussive Arts Society, 130 Carol Dr., Terre Haute IN 47805. (812)466-2982, 232-6311, ext. 2276. Executive Secretary: Neal Fluegel.

Purpose: "To elevate the level of percussion performance and teaching; to expand understanding of the needs and responsibilities of the percussion student, teacher and performer; and to promote a greater communication among all areas of the percussion arts." Information covers celebrities, history, music, new products and technical data.

Services: Offers aid in arranging interviews, annual reports and brochures/pamphlets.

How to Contact: Write.

The Ragtime Society, Inc., Box 520, Station A, Weston, Ontario, Canada M9N 3N3. (416)489-1970. President: Idamay MacInnes.
Purpose: "To preserve and make available all information regarding ragtime music (1895-1915). Records and music available. Reprints of old music not available." Information covers music.
Services: Offers newsletter.
How to Contact: Write. Charges $8/year for membership.

Songwriters Resources and Services, 6381 Hollywood Blvd., Suite 503, Hollywood CA 90028. (213)463-7178, 463-5691. Project Coordinator: Kathy Gronau.
Purpose: "A nonprofit membership organization to educate and support songwriters. We're committed to the songwriter. We try to eliminate restrictions, whether in-house or in the world; to promote songwriting of all types and styles; to provide members with ongoing counseling about the business of songwriting; to teach and promote the craft of songwriting; and to act as an advocate for songwriters." Information covers entertainment, business, entertainment, how-to, law, music, self-help, technical data, workshops and forums on music.
Services: Offers aid in arranging interviews, annual reports, brochures/pamphlets, information searches, newsletter, registration of material, lead sheet service and evaluation of material. Publications include monthly newsletter, information brochure, collaborator's directory, artist directory, and the following pamphlets: *Songwriter Agreements*, *The Personal Manager* and *The New Copyright Law*.
How to Contact: Write or call. Charges $2 for pamphlets. "Ask for an information packet; we will mail one out. We register songs for members or nonmembers, but you must be a member for our other services, which are too numerous to mention. Membership fee is $30 per year."

Nature & the Environment

American Water Resources Association, St. Anthony Falls Lab, Mississippi River and 3rd Ave. SE, Minneapolis MN 55414. (612)376-5059. Executive Secretary: Mr. Dana C. Rhoads.
Purpose: "The American Water Resources Association is a nonprofit scientific organization devoted to the advancement of water resources research, planning, development, management and education. Additionally, the association presents annual meeting forums for persons in the field of water resources and disseminates ideas and information in the field of water resources science and technology through the publications of the association."
Services: Offers aid in arranging interviews, brochures/pamphlets and placement on mailing list. Publications include publications and membership brochures and news releases.
How to Contact: Write or call. Charges "if extensive time is required of staff personnel for assistance; however, we would attempt to provide information and limited services on a gratis basis if at all possible. Writers are restricted from using any copyrighted materials without permission of the organization. Additionally, services requested should be outlined in detail in order to keep assistance time to a minimum."

Association for Conservation Information (ACI), 458 Lowell Blvd., Denver CO 80204. (303)934-6734. Editor: George Feltner.
Purpose: "We are an organization which deals in keeping information and education personnel in state and provincial conservation agencies (mainly hunting, fishing and parks) informed on ways and means of keeping the public informed on the latest developments in hunting, fishing and other forms of outdoor activities (including hiking, backpacking, camping, bird-watching, nature hikes and studies, etc.). The ACI itself does not distribute this information to the public. The member agencies keep each other informed through our publication, *The Balance Wheel*, on what we are

doing in the form of publications or electronic media to keep the general public informed and educated." Information covers recreation.

Services: Offers information on where to get information. "As an organization, we have no leaflets, pamphlets, booklets or any other form of information. But our member states and provinces have informational material on a wide variety of subjects in the outdoor recreational field and the conservation of our wildlife resources. Interested parties can get information more quickly by contacting state or federal conservation (mainly hunting, fishing and parks departments) directly."

How to Contact: Write or call.

Concern, Inc., 2233 Wisconsin Ave. NW, Washington DC 20007. (202)965-0066. Office Manager: Barbara Roark.

Purpose: "To promote public awareness of envrionmental issues and to recommend appropriate citizen action. Guides called eco-tips cover energy, drinking water, food additives, land use, ozone, toxic substances, protection of wetlands and oceans."

Services: Offers brochures/pamphlets, information searches and newsletters. Write for publication price list.

How to Contact: Write. "All material is copyrighted and a credit line is required."

Conservation and Research Foundation, Inc., Box 1445, Connecticut College, New London CT 06320. (203)873-8514. President: Richard H. Goodwin.

Purpose: "To promote conservation of the earth's natural resources, to encourage research in the biological sciences, and to deepen understanding of the entire city relationship between man and the environment that supports him. We make research and facilitating grants."

Services: Offers brochures/pamphlets.

How to Contact: Write or call.

Conservation Education Association, University of Wisconsin, Green Bay WI 54302. Contact: Dr. Richard W. Presnell.

Purpose: "The Conservation Education Association (CEA) believes that a major goal of education must be the recognition by man of his interdependence with his environment. CEA members have a common interest in forwarding the broad aspects of environmental and conservation education to help people achieve this understanding. The CEA concept of conservation education includes formal classroom and outdoor education, adult education and education through public communications." Information covers conservation.

Services: Offers brochures/pamphlets and newsletter. Publications include *Conservation Education: A Selected Bibliography*, *Environmental Conservation Education Bibliography*, *Proceedings of the National Conservation Education Association Annual Conferences*, and bibliographic supplements.

How to Contact: Write. Charges for subscription to CEA packet service and newsletter.

The Conservation Foundation, 1717 Massachusetts Ave. NW, Washington DC 20036. (202)797-4300. Director of Communications: Jerry Kline.

Purpose: "Since its founding in 1948, the Conservation Foundation has attempted to provide intellectual leadership in the cause of wise management of the earth's resources—its land, air, water and energy." Information covers the environment.

Services: Offers annual reports, placement on mailing list and newsletter. "The Conservation Foundation regularly publishes books and issues reports on a number of environmental subjects."

How to Contact: Write or call. "We will try to put the writer in touch with the foundation staff members who can respond to their questions, or who would be available for interviews." Charges for books and the newsletter.

Tips: "The Conservation Foundation might be most useful to writers who are looking for a reaction, or expert response, to some environmental issue of the day. The foundation may not know the specifics of the issue—unless it's conducted research in that area—but may have helpful observations to make regarding the general issue involved."

Environmental Action Coalition, 156 5th Ave., Room 407, New York NY 10010. Librarian: Robert M. Guttentag.
Purpose: "Concerned with environmental self-help and education."
Services: Offers aid in arranging interviews, statistics, brochures/pamphlets, placement on mailing list, newsletter and press releases as needed. Publications include *Cycle*, membership newsletter; and *Echo*, children's newsletter.
How to Contact: Write or call. "Detailed information requires written request."

Environmental Law Institute, Suite 620, 1346 Connecticut Ave. NW, Washington DC 20036. (202)452-9600. Librarian: Barbara Rodes.
Purpose: To gather information in the area of environmental law.
Services: Offers bibliographies and information searches. Publications include several books and periodicals.
How to Contact: Write or visit.

Environmental Policy Center, 317 Pennsylvania Ave. SE, Washington DC 20003. (202)547-6500. Editor: Lynn Coddington.
Purpose: "Lobby organization influencing natural resource and energy issues in Congress and the federal government. Primarily work with citizen groups, farm organizations, consumer groups and others." Information covers agriculture, politics and natural resource and energy issues.
Services: Offers newsletter.
How to Contact: Write or call. Charges $25/year for newsletter.

Forest History Society, Inc., 109 Coral St., Santa Cruz CA 95060. Editor: Ronald J. Fahl.
Purpose: "To collect, interpret, publish and promote North American forest and conservation history." Information covers history and forestry, conservation and forest industries.
Services: Offers bibliographies and newsletter.
How to Contact: Write or call.

Keep America Beautiful, Inc., 99 Park Ave., New York NY 10016. (212)682-4564. Director of Public Information: Bob Mihen.
Purpose: "Founded in 1953. We are a national nonprofit, nonpartisan, service organization working with CIT groups, government agencies, private industry and academic institutions. To stimulate individual involvement in environment improvement. We are meeting our objectives thru the Clean Community System, the behavioral approach to waste handling now being implemented in more than 100 cities and countries in America."
Services: Offers aid in arranging interviews, annual reports, brochures/pamphlets, placement on mailing list, statistics, newsletter, photos and press kits.
How to Contact: Write or call.

National Parks and Conservation Association, 1701 18th St. NW, Washington DC 20008. (202)265-2717.
Purpose: "Preservation of national parks, wildlife history and collection of general conservation issues." Information covers nature, recreation, science and sports.
Services: Offers occasional reports.
How to Contact: Write and send SASE. Charges $1.50/copy of magazine.

National Wildlife Federation, 1412 16th St. NW, Washington DC 20036. Information Division: Diane Kelly.
Purpose: "A nonprofit, conservation education organization, dedicated to arousing public awareness of the wide use, proper management and conservation of the natural

resources upon which all life depend: air, water, soil, minerals, forest, plant life and wildlife."
Services: Offers aid in arranging interviews, bibliographies, statistics, brochures/pamphlets, placement on mailing list and several newsletters on different subjects.
How to Contact: Write or call. Charges for some materials. "To get listing of materials, write for bibliography."

Sierra Club, 530 Bush St., San Francisco CA 94108. Information Services: Rosie Goldenberg.
Purpose: "The purpose of the Sierra Club is to explore, enjoy and preserve the nation's forests, water, wildlife and wilderness."
Services: Offers aid in arranging interviews, annual reports, bibliographies, statistics, brochures/pamphlets, newsletter and press releases. Publications include *Sierra* (bi-monthly) and *National News Report* (35 issues/year).
How to Contact: Write. Charges for large quantities of printed material and $12/year for *National News Report*.

Izaak Walton League of America, Inc., 1800 N. Kent St., Suite 806, Arlington VA 22209. (703)528-1818. Editor: Fred Vallejo.
Purpose: "Promotes the wise use and conservation of America's natural resources and helps educate the public to effect these goals." Information covers how-to, nature and conservation/environmentalism.
Services: Offers publications.
How to Contact: Write or call.

Wilderness Society, 1901 Pennsylvania Ave. NW, Washington DC 20006. (202)293-2732. Information Specialist: Michelle Curtin.
Purpose: "National nonprofit citizens organization maintaining contact with Congress to work with public on issues concerning wilderness."
Services: Offers aid in arranging interviews, annual reports, statistics, brochures/pamphlets and newsletter. Publications include *Living Wilderness* (quarterly), *Wilderness Report* (monthly newsletter), and special mailing alerts.
How to Contact: Write, detailing information needed.

Photography

National Association for Photographic Art, 10 Shaneen Blvd., Scarborough, Ontario, Canada M2N 1X2. Secretary: Helen Hancock.
Purpose: "The National Association for Photographic Art (NAPA) is a nonprofit organization for Canadian photographers. The aims of NAPA are to promote good Canadian photography and to provide useful information for photographers in all parts of the country, and to inform the public about the medium." Information covers photography.
Services: Offers newsletter, slide sets, evaluation of photographs, competitions, technical service, brochures/pamphlets and travel aids. Publications include *Camera Canada* (quarterly) and *Foto Flash* (news bulletin published 5 times/year).
How to Contact: Write. "Services are available to all members automatically and to anyone wishing to use information. You must have written permission to use any material printed in our publications." List of services and charges available upon request.

Photo Marketing Association, 603 Lansing Ave., Jackson MI 49202. (517)783-2807. Managing Editor, Newsletters and Press Information: Monica Smiley.
Purpose: "Photo Marketing Association is an international trade association that caters to the needs of those businesses involved in selling, manufacturing and distri-

buting photographic equipment for the consumer market, and to businesses engaged in the photofinishing industry." Information covers photographic marketing.
Services: Offers biographies, statistics, brochures/pamphlets, information searches, placement on mailing list, newsletter, photos and press kits. Publications include *Photo Marketing* (monthly magazine with controlled circulation), nine in-house newsletters and various reports on the photographic industry.
How to Contact: Write or call. Some services are available only to members of Photo Marketing Association. "Rates for services vary. Most publications are free, and those with a fee are usually available only to members of the association."

Photographic Society of America, 2005 Walnut St., Philadelphia PA 19103. (215)563-1663. Executive Secretary: Harold Virmes.
Purpose: "To advance art of photography among amateurs."
Services: Offers aid in arranging interviews and brochures/pamphlets.
How to Contact: Write.

Professional Photographers of America, 1090 Executive Way, Des Plaines IL 60018. (312)299-8161. Contact: Public Relations Department.
Purpose: "We establish and maintain ethical standards as well as standards of performance. We try to expand the total market for pro photography."
Services: Offers aid in arranging interviews, annual reports, statistics, brochures/pamphlets, placement on mailing list, newsletter and press kits. "We also have a limited resource library."
How to Contact: Write or call.

Society of Photographers in Communications (ASMP), 205 Lexington Ave., New York NY 10016. (212)889-9144. Executive Director: Stuart Kahan.
Purpose: "To promote and further the interests of professional photographers in communications media such as journalism, corporate advertising, fashion and books. We act as a clearinghouse for photographic information on markets, rates, and business practices of magazines, advertising agencies, publishers and electronic media. Works for copyright law revisions; offers legal advice, through counsel, to members concerning questions of rights, ethics and payment."
Services: Offers bibliographies, brochures/pamphlets, placement on mailing list, statistics and newsletter.
How to Contact: Write or call. Charges for some information.

Politics, Government & Legislation

American Civil Liberties Union, 22 E. 20th St., New York NY 10016. (212)725-1222. Public Relations Director: Trudi Schutz.
Purpose: "The American Civil Liberties Union exists to make sure people get their rights as stated in the Bill of Rights. We strive to achieve our goal through litigation, legislation and public education."
Services: Offers aid in arranging interviews, annual reports, bibliographies, statistics, brochures/pamphlets, placement on mailing list, newsletter, photos and press releases. "We can arrange for people to go through our files." Publications include *Civil Liberties*.
How to Contact: Write or call.

American Conservative Union, 316 Pennsylvania Ave. SE, Washington DC 20003. (202)546-6555. Media Director: Fran Griffin.
Purpose: "We are a 300,000-member citizens lobby based in Washington, D.C. We have 42 state affiliates and 75 members of Congress on our advisory board. Major projects include tax limitation (we have a separate committee called Americans to Cut Taxes Now to work on this issue); defense (we have a Defense Task Force headed by

Sen. Jack Garn); and Stop OSHA (a project headed by US Rep. George Hansen to fight abuses of this federal agency). We are also involved in a variety of legislative issues in the US Congress and at the state and local levels." Information covers politics.
Services: Offers aid in arranging interviews, annual reports, brochures/pamphlets, placement on mailing list, newsletter, photos and press kits. Publications include *Battle Line,* a monthly magazine edited by syndicated columnist John Lafton, Jr.; *Public Monitor Report,* a bimonthly newsletter; and *Ratings of Congress,* "in which we score members of Congress on their voting records."
How to Contact: Write or call.

John Birch Society, 395 Concord Ave., Belmont MA 02178. (617)489-0600. Public Relations Director: John McManus.
Purpose: "Less government, more responsibility, and, with God's help, a better world." Information covers agriculture, business, economics, health/medicine, history, industry, law, politics, science and technical data.
Services: Offers aid in arranging interviews, bibliographies, statistics, brochures/ pamphlets, information searches, newsletter, photos and limited press mailing list. Publications include *The John Birch Society* (monthly bulletin), *The Review of the News* (weekly), and *American Opinion* (monthly).
How to Contact: Write or call. Charges for bibliographies. Placement on press mailing list "must benefit the society."

College Republican National Committee (CRNC), 310 1st St. SE, Washington DC 20003. (202)484-6527. Communications Director: Jim Merriam.
Purpose: "The College Republican National Committee is a national affiliate of the Republican National Committee. It attempts to organize college students into precinct-style campaign workers available to assist Republican candidates. The CRNC is the clearinghouse for such activity, and conducts training seminars, publishes newsletters and guides and assists local clubs. We also do research into student-related legislation before Congress." Information covers economics and politics.
Services: Offers aid in arranging interviews, bibliographies, biographies, statistics, brochures/pamphlets, placement on mailing list, newsletter, photos and press kits. Publications include brochures on the committee, history of the Republican party, media relations, producing a newsletter, starting a new club and current issues before Congress.
How to Contact: "In almost all cases, a person must be either a College Republican or affiliated with a newspaper, magazine, or the media. Contact the communications director by letter, phone or in person."

Citizens Committee for the Right to Keep and Bear Arms, 600 Pennsylvania Ave. SE, #205, Washington DC 20003. (202)543-3363. Public Affairs Director: John M. Snyder.
Purpose: "To defend the Second Amendment to the United States Constitution. We fight restrictive gun control legislation." Information covers history, law and politics.
Services: Offers aid in arranging interviews, annual reports, brochures/pamphlets, placement on mailing list and newsletter. Publications available.
How to Contact: Call.

Common Cause, 2030 M St. NW, Washington DC 20036. (202)833-1200. Issue Mail Coordinator: Erica Hunter. Field Organization: Melissa Howard.
Purpose: "Common Cause—the hard-hitting citizen movement of the 70s—is a proven new force in government. If was founded on the premise that only by banding together can citizens overcome the scandalous capacity of money to buy political outcomes and the old political habit of doing the public's business behind closed doors. Our purpose is to make the system work. Its targets are the politicans who ignore the people, unresponsive bureaucracies, and behind-the-scenes betrayals of the public trust." Information covers business, law and politics.
Services: Offers brochures/pamphlets, information searches, placement on mailing

list, statistics and newsletter. Publications available.
How to Contact: Write or call. Charges for publications. "There are limited quantities of material available. You may also contact the Common Cause office in each state, usually located in the state capitol."

Communist Party, 235 W. 23rd St., 7th Floor, New York NY 10011. (212)989-4994. Communications and Media Director: Betty Green.
Purpose: Political party.
Services: Offers aid in arranging interviews, bibliographies, brochures/pamphlets, placement on mailing list and press kits (irregularly).
How to Contact: Write.

Democratic National Committee, 1625 Massachusetts Ave. NW, Washington DC 20036. (202)797-5900. Contact: Director of Commmunication or Director of Research.
Purpose: "This is the national organization for the Democratic party, made up of three representatives of each state, the state chairman, a committeeman and a committee woman. The Washington office is headquarters of the national committee. Our purpose is to set up conventions, handle day-to-day press, and help with local campaigns. The chairman is spokesman for the party when there is no Democratic president." Information covers economics (fundraising) and politics.
Services: Offers aid in arranging interviews, bibliographies, biographies, statistics, clipping services, information searches, placement on mailing list, photos and press kits. Publications include the rules, bylaws and constitution of the party.
How to Contact: Write or call.

House of Representatives GOP Task Force on the Handicapped, 434 Cannon Bldg., Washington DC 20515. (202)225-3635. Staff Director: Ted Cormaney.
Purpose: "To get action on bills, laws and rules that affect the handicapped, including handicapped voting rights, handicapped employment rights, and transportation and travel rights of the handicapped." Information covers health/medicine and politics.
Services: Offers aid in arranging interviews, statistics, brochures/pamphlets, information searches, placement on mailing list, newsletter and photos. Publications include *A Few Things You Can Do to Help a Lot of People Who Are Trying Very Hard to Help Themselves.*
How to Contact: Call or write.

Initiative America, 606 3rd St. NW, Washington DC 20001. (202)347-5959. National Director: John Forster.
Purpose: "National advocate and clearinghouse for voter inititative and referendum processes. We are a public interest, voters advocate group that is funded by voluntary memberships." Information covers history, how-to, law and politics.
Services: Offers aid in arranging interviews, bibliographies, statistics, brochures/pamphlets, placement on mailing list, model constitutional amendments (state and national) to obtain voter initiative rights, how-to organizing plans for citizens who wish to place issues on the ballot by petition, up-to-date information on all issues on statewide ballots nationally and historical information about initiative and referendum processes. Publications include the *Hearing Record* on the voter initiative constitutional amendment and a question-and-answer pamphlet about Vote Initiative/Initiative America.
How to Contact: Write or call.
Tips: "If you are writing about voter turnout, referendums, initiatives, citizen participation, politics or organizing, contact us."

League of Conservation Voters, 317 Pennsylvania Ave. SE, Washington DC 20003. (202)547-7200. Executive Director: Marion Eddy.
Purpose: "National nonpartisan campaign committee formed in 1970 to support conservationists running in the House, Senate and gubernatorial elections." Informa-

tion covers environment and government.
Services: Offers wall chart of congressmen and senators, telling how they rate on environmental issues; and election analysis.
How to Contact: Write or call.

League of Women Voters of the U.S., 1730 M St. NW, Washington DC 20036. Contact: Public Relations Director.
Purpose: "We are a voluntary citizen education, public interest and lobbying organization whose aim is to involve people in the political process at all levels of government. Information covers current public policy issues: energy, environment, civil rights, urban crisis, and international relations."
Services: Offers bibliographies, statistics and newsletter. Publications include *Tell It To Washington*, *Federal Environmental Laws and You*, and newsletter and quarterly.
How to Contact: Write. "A nominal fee is charged for printed material."

Liberal Party, 165 W. 46th St., Suite 1400, New York NY 10036. (212)582-1100. Associate Executive Director: Patrick Gianacova.
Purpose: "The Liberal party is the political vehicle for independent candidacy and corrective mechanism to the major parties. We advocate progressive liberalism and run candidates for office."
Services: Offers biographies, statistics, brochures/pamphlets, placement on mailing list and press kits. Publications include *The Liberal Manifesto* and *History of the Liberal Party*.
How to Contact: Write or call. "A written request is preferred, and SASE is appreciated."

Libertarian Party, 1516 P St. NW, Washington DC 20005. (202)232-2003. National Director: Chris Hocker.
Purpose: "To elect libertarians to office, affect the existing political structure, and educate the public about our philosophy and programs." Information covers agriculture, business, economics, health/medicine and politics.
Services: Offers aid in arranging interviews, brochures/pamphlets, placement on mailing list, newsletter and press kits.
How to Contact: Write or call. "Booklets on local problems and environment will be sent upon assurance that an article, review, etc. will be based upon them."

National Abortion Rights Action League, 825 15th St. NW, Washington DC 20005. Public Information Director: Janet Beals.
Purpose: "The National Abortion Rights Action League (NARAL) is the largest national membership and lobby organization to defend the Supreme Court decision on legalizing abortion."
Services: Offers aid in arranging interviews, annual reports, statistics, brochures/pamphlets, placement on mailing list, newsletter, photos and press releases. Research library and slides also available. "New pamphlets coming out all the time."
How to Contact: Write or call. Charges for speakers/debaters notebook.

National Organization for Women (NOW), 425 13th St. NW, Suite 1048, Washington DC 20004. (202)347-2279.
Purpose: Attention to federal and state legislation that affects the area of women's rights. Also provides educational services in women's rights, literature and annual conferences.
Services: Offers aid in arranging interviews, statistics, brochures/pamphlets, placement on mailing list, newsletter, photos and press kits. Publications include *N.O.W. Times*.
How to Contact: "We prefer phone requests." Publications available by subscription or through membership.

National Right to Life Committee, Inc., 529 14th St. NW, #341, Washington DC 20045. (202)638-4396. Office Manager: Judie Brown.
Purpose: "The goal of the National Right to Life Committee is the attainment of a human life amendment to the US Constitution which will prohibit abortions except to prevent the death of the mother." Information covers health/medicine, how-to and law.
Services: Offers aid in arranging interviews, bibliographies, biographies, statistics, brochures/pamphlets, information searches, placement on mailing list, newsletter and press kits. Publications include *National Right to Life News*, monthly; books dealing with abortion, euthanasia, population, counseling, etc.; legislative updates and alerts; medical information; and reviews of literature available on subjects of interest to the pro-life movement.
How to Contact: Write or call. "Specify exactly what your area of interest is and we will accommodate with as much information as we have—an up to the minute accounting in most cases. If a writer has a specific area of interest which will require one-time use of our services, there is never a charge for this; we are more than happy to supply additional study material if needed." Charges for publications.
Tips: "Be prepared to search the libraries, especially the medical libraries, for statistics pertinent to the areas of medical concern with regard to abortion."

National Urban League, 500 E. 62nd St., New York NY 10021. (212)644-6600, 644-6601. Contact: Communications Department.
Purpose: "An interracial, nonprofit community service organization that uses the tools and methods of social work, economics, law, business management and other disciplines to secure equal opportunities in all sectors of our society for black Americans and other minorities."
Services: Offers aid in arranging interviews, annual reports, bibliographies, statistics, brochures/pamphlets, placement on mailing list and sometimes press kits. Publications include *Urban League Review*.
How to Contact: Write or call. "Request detailed information in writing. We will give interviews and place a writer on our mailing list only if we feel the project is worthwhile and the writer legitimate."

Public Citizen, Inc., 1346 Connecticut Ave. NW, Box 19404, Washington DC 20036. (202)293-9142. Executive Director: Ralph Nader. Director of Support Projects: Don Sodo.
Purpose: "Provides support to the following groups: Congress Watch; Critical Mass; Public Citizen Litigation Group; Freedom of Information Act Clearinghouse; Visitors Center; Center for Study of Responsive Law; Resident Utility Consumer Action Group; and health, tax reform, housing, public interest and corporate accountability research groups."
Services: Offers brochures/pamphlets and newsletter. Publications include *Public Information Forum*.
How to Contact: Write, call or visit.

Republican National Committee, 310 1st St. SE, Washington DC 20003. Contact: Director of Research or Director of Communication.
Purpose: "The Republican National Committee is the national organization for the Republican party. The chairman is spokesman for the party when there is no Republican president. The committee is made up of three representatives from each state: the state chairman, a committee man and a committee woman. This is the headquarters of the national committee." Information covers politics and fundraising.
Services: Offers aid in arranging interviews, statistics, brochures/pamphlets, placement on mailing list and press kits. Publications include *First Monday*, a monthly magazine to members; and a book about election results that is published after each election.
How to Contact: Write or call.

Socialist Labor Party, 914 Industrial Ave., Box 10018, Palo Alto CA 94303.
Purpose: "A political party formed 89 years ago to further the socialist view."
Services: Offers brochures/pamphlets and newsletter. Publications include *Weekly People*, a weekly newspaper.
How to Contact: Write.

Socialist Workers Party, 14 Charles Lane, New York NY 10014. (212)242-5530.
Purpose: "The Socialist Workers party was started in 1938. Our view is a four-day work week with no cut in pay; the use of military budget for public works programs; an end to racism and oppression of women and gays; and an end to military and economic intervention abroad." Information covers politics.
Services: Offers bibliographies, biographies, brochures/pamphlets, newsletter and press releases for specific occasions. Publications include *The Militant*, a newspaper with socialist editorial policy.
How to Contact: Write or call. "Written requests preferred. Catalog may be ordered from Pathfinders Press, 410 West St., New York, New York."

Taxation With Representation, 6830 N. Fairfax Dr., Arlington VA 22213. Contact: Thomas F. Field.
Purpose: "Appeal for money, lobby for tax reform and to monitor Congress."
Services: Offers publications. Publications include *Taxation With Representation*, $1/year, and *Tax Note*, $99/year, a weekly magazine for tax attorneys.
How to Contact: Write. "Requests must be written. Our staff is too small to respond by phone."

Women's Campaign Fund, 1521 New Hampshire Ave. NW, Washington DC 20036. (202)332-1000. Contact: Kimberley Gerol.
Purpose: "Women's Campaign Fund (WCF) raises money to donate to progressive women running for public office. While we concentrate on races at the federal level, we help pro-ERA women running against 'anti' opponents in key unratified states and help women in state and local races of special significance to women. In addition to dollar contributions, we provide our candidates with professional consulting and technical services." Information covers politics.
Services: Offers statistics, brochures/pamphlets, placement on mailing list and newsletter. Publications include a brochure describing the difficulty women face raising money for political campaigns.
How to Contact: Write or call.

Women's Lobby, Inc., 201 Massachusetts Ave. NE, Washington DC 20002.
Purpose: "Active legislative equality for women."
Services: Offers aid in arranging interviews, annual reports, statistics, brochures/pamphlets, placement on mailing list, newsletter and press kits. Publications include *Alerts*, to subscribers or individuals/organizations who contribute $25 or more; *Committee System*; *Voting Charts*, rating members of Congress; and special reports.
How to Contact: Write or call.

Religion

American Baptist Churches in the United States, Valley Forge PA 19481. (215)768-2000. Contact: Division of Communication.
Purpose: "National church body (6,000 congregations) located in 49 of the 50 states. We have three Boards and 37 regional divisions and are also involved in foreign mission programs." Information covers food (world hunger crisis), health/medicine and religion.
Services: Offers aid in arranging interviews, brochures/pamphlets and statistics.

Publications available.
How to Contact: Write or call.

American Jewish Committee, 165 E. 56th St., New York NY 10022. (212)751-4000.
Director of Public Relations: Morton Yarmon.
Purpose: "This a human relations agency, founded in 1906, mandated to protect the civil and religious rights of Jews in the US and abroad, and to advance the cause of improved human relations for all people. Our information covers issues of Jewish concern, human rights, intergroup activities generally." Information covers the following as they apply to the Jewish community: agriculture, art, business, celebrities, economics, entertainment, food, health/medicine, history, how-to, industry, law, music, nature, new product information, politics, recreation, science, self-help, sports, technical data and travel.
Services: Offers aid in arranging interviews, annual reports, bibliographies, statistics, brochures/pamphlets, information searches, placement on press mailing list, newsletters and press kits. "We have an excellent library given over to subject matter of our concern and acknowledged experts who can offer authoritative comment on such subject matter." Publications include *Publications of the American Jewish Committee Institute of Human Relations*, a catalog of materials available. "These materials are available free to writers, and we will send the catalog in response to serious inquiries from writers."

B'nai B'rith International, 1640 Rhode Island Ave. NW, Washington DC 20036. (202)857-6536. Director of Communications: Hank Siegel.
Purpose: "We are designed to foster Jewish unity and the future of Judaism in the world. Programs generally aimed at young people—education, cultural, religious orientation—nonsectarian programs are also offered the elderly." Information covers self-help, education, religion and youth activities.
Services: Offers aid in arranging interviews, brochures/pamphlets, placement on mailing list and photos.
How to Contact: Write or call.

Board of Church and Society of the United Methodist Church, 100 Maryland Ave. NE, Washington DC 20002. (202)488-5600. Contact: Office of Communications.
Purpose: "We are a religious organization." Information covers food and health/medicine and social issues (racism, environmental, population, drug, criminal justice) and economic issues.
Services: Offers annual reports, brochures/pamphlets, information searches, statistics and monthly publication.
How to Contact: Write or call. "We prefer written requests for information."

Catholic Information Center, 741 15th St. NW, Washington DC 20005. (202)783-2062.
Purpose: "Giving information, counseling and teaching. We are not governed by the archdiocese, but subject to it for 25% of funding." Information covers religious counceling.
Services: Offers aid in arranging interviews, information leads, statistics and a reference library. Publications available.
How to Contact: Write or call. Charges for paperbacks and magazines.

Church of the Nazarene, 6401 The Paseo, Kansas City MO 64121. Division of Christian Life: Mrs. Beagel.
Purpose: "The Paseo houses the offices of four divisions of the Church of the Nazarene. They are publishing, world mission colleges and training courses, and communication for the US and international churches. The offices of the executive directors are also housed here."
Services: Offers aid in arranging interviews, bibliographies, statistics and brochures/pamphlets. Publications include *Preacher*, a regular magazine.

How to Contact: "We prefer a written request so the letter can be forwarded to the proper office."

Episcopal Church Center, Office of Communication, 815 2nd Ave., New York NY 10017.
Purpose: National headquarters. Information covers religion.
How to Contact: "We prefer requests in writing so the office can evaluate the merit of the piece. State the specific information you wish to have."

The First Church of Christ, Scientist, Christian Science Center, Boston MA 02115. (617)262-2300. Manager of the Committee on Publication: A.W. Phinney.
Purpose: "Christianity in a sceintific age; restoration of Christian healing." Information covers history of Christian Scientist Church and religion (beliefs, theology and organizations).
Services: Offers aid in arranging interviews, bibliographies, and information searches. Publications available.
How to Contact: Write or call.

General Conference of Seventh-day Adventists, 6840 Eastern Ave. NW, Washington DC 20012. (202)723-0800. Assistant Director of Communication: James R. Gallagher.
Purpose: "We are the highest administrative body of the Seventh-day Adventist Church, with 550,000 members in North America, three million worldwide. We are especially active in health education, cancer research and operation of hospitals (over 200). We are involved with a large educational system (400,000 students in kindergarten through PhD programs worldwide). Our popular Five-Day Plan to Stop Smoking is conducted in cooperation with American Cancer Society. A heavy disaster relief program (SAWS—Seventh-day Adventist World Service), is also headquartered here." Information covers food, health/medicine and religion.
Services: Offers aid in arranging interviews, biographies, statistics, brochures/pamphlets, clipping services, information searches, placement on mailing list, photos and press kits. Publication available.
How to Contact: Write or call. Adventist headquarters are located in each state and province of the US and Canada (local conferences). These can provide localized information. Contact the communication director in each case; conference names are available in the *SDA Fact Book* available from General Conference.

Greek Orthodox Church in The Americas/Greek Orthodox Archdiocese of North and South America, 8-10 E. 79th St., New York NY 10021. (212)628-2500. Director of Public Affairs: Terry Kokas.
Purpose: "We are a Greek Orthodox church with over two million members." Information covers food, health/medicine and religion.
Services: Offers aid in arranging interviews, annual reports, bibliographies, biographies, brochures/pamphlets, information searches, placement on mailing list and press kits.
How to Contact: Write or call. "We prefer written requests but will answer urgent questions by phone."

Jehovah Witnesses, 124 Columbia Heights, Brooklyn NY 11201.
Purpose: Nonfundamentalist religious group.
Services: Offers annual reports, biographies, statistics on missionary work, brochures/pamphlets and newsletter. Publications include *20th Century*, *Watch Tower* and *Awake!*
How to Contact: Write. Charges 50¢ for yearbook, available from December through March. "Order ahead."

Lutheran Church—Missouri Synod, 500 N. Broadway, St. Louis MO 63102. (314)231-6969. Director of Public Relations: Victor W. Bryant.

Purpose: "We offer services, liaison and national organization membership to 6,100 congregations (with approximately 2.8 million members) who affiliate with the Lutheran Church—Missouri Synod (LCMS). Our national body operates 13 colleges and two seminaries and has a partnership relation to mission outreaches in over 20 foreign lands. LCMS congregations operate the largest system of Protestant schools in the nation." Information covers religion.

Services: Offers bibliographies, statistics, brochures/pamphlets, placement on mailing list and photos. Publications include *A Brief Historical Sketch of the LCMS*, *Blessed To Serve* (description of LCMS programs), *That We May Grow* (descriptive brochure), *The Lutheran Witness* (monthly magazine) and *The Reporter* (weekly newspaper). "A number of other regular publications are offered."

How to Contact: For brochures, write Department of Public Relations. For *Lutheran Witness* or *The Reporter*, write Concordia Publishing House, 3558 S. Jefferson Ave., St. Louis MO 63118. Charges $4/year subscription for *Witness*, $9/year for *Reporter*.

Mennonite Central Committee, 21 S. 12th St., Akron PA 17501. (717)859-1151. Director of Information: Tina Mast Burnett.

Purpose: "A service agency of the Mennonite Church—not a clearinghouse of information. The agency sends people out to places of service; we send volunteers all over the world." Information covers history and general information about the church.

Services: Offers aid in arranging interviews, annual reports, statistics, brochures/pamphlets, information searches and a limited number of photos. Publications include *Introducing MCC*, *Who Are the Mennonites?*, *We're a Little Peculiar* and *Peace Section* brochure.

How to Contact: Write.

Metropolitan Community Church, 110 Maryland Ave., NE, Suite 210, Washington DC 20002. (202)543-2260. Social Action Director: Adam DeDaugh.

Purpose: "Ecumenical Christian Church with a special outreach to those who have been excluded. Representative for more than 120 churches and a liaison between government and church."

Services: Offers aid in arranging interviews, brochures/pamphlets, information searches, statistics and newsletter. Publications available.

How to Contact: Write or call. Charges for publications.

National Association of Evangelicals, National Office, 350 S. Main Place, Box 28, Wheaton IL 60187. (312)665-0500. Director of Communications: Harold Smith.

Services: Offers statistics, brochures/pamphlets, information searches, newsletter and press kits.

How to Contact: Write.

National Baha'i Center, 112 Linden Ave., Wilmette IL 60090. (312)256-4400. Contact: Information Correspondent, National Information Office.

Purpose: "An independent, worldwide religion based on the teachings of Baha'u'llah. Some of the principles of the faith are the oneness of mankind, the independent investigation of truth, equality of men and women, the elimination of all forms of prejudice (racial, social, religious, class, etc.), the essential harmony of science and religion, a spiritual solution to the economic problem, universal education, a universal auxiliary language, and the need for a world government to maintain world peace." Information covers "all aspects of the Baha'i faith."

Services: Offers brochures/pamphlets "pertaining to the history and teachings of the faith. A number of topics are covered, from death to racial unity."

How to Contact: "Write to the national information office and specify the type of information desired."

National Conference of Christians and Jews, 1425 H St. NW, Suite 735, Washington

DC 20005. Director: Donald F. Sullivan.

Purpose: Nonprofit organization "concerned with human relations problems in metropolitan areas." Information covers human relations.

Services: Offers aid in arranging interviews, brochures/pamphlets, clipping services, information searches and newsletter.

How to Contact: Write.

News and Information Services of the National Council of Churches of Christ, 475 Riverside Dr., Room 805, New York NY 10027. Director of Special Services, News and Information: Faith Pomponio.

Purpose: "We are composed of 32 member denominations; we are an ecumenical organization seeking to unify activities of members of the church." Information covers domestic issues, overseas missionaries, education, justice, liberation, human fulfillment, theology, communication, church stewardship, region and local humanism and religion.

Services: Offers annual reports, bibliographies, placement on mailing list, newsletter and press kits. Publications available.

How to Contact: Write or call, (212)870-2227 for the general office, (212)870-2253 for the Director of Special Services or (212)870-2252 for the Director of Newspaper Information. "We would like the name of the newspaper or magazine the article will be published in."

Unitarian Universalist Association, 25 Beacon St., Boston MA 02108. (617)742-2100. Information Director: Carl Seaburg.

Purpose: "We are a central service organization for the Unitarian Universalist churches. We provide religious education material and strive for the ideals of brotherhood, justice and peace." Information covers agriculture, art, food, health/medicine, history, law, music, nature, politics, world hunger, pollution, camps and conference centers, poetry and social issues.

Services: Offers aid in arranging interviews, annual reports, bibliographies, biographies, statistics, brochures/pamphlets, information searches, newsletter, photos and placement on mailing list. Publications include *Unitarian Universalist World* ($3/year), *Unitarian Universalist Association Now* and an annual directory ($7.50).

How to Contact: Write or call. "Photocopies are made at the writer's expense. Tours are available."

United Church of Christ, 297 Park Ave. S., New York NY 10010. Secretary of United Church of Christ: The Rev. Joseph H. Evans.

Purpose: "Founded in 1957. This is the congregational evangelical church of the Protestant denomination."

Services: Offers brochures/pamphlets and statistics. Publications available.

How to Contact: Write.

United Presbyterian Church, United States of America, 475 Riverside Dr., Room 1935, New York NY 10027. (212)870-2005. Director, Office of Information: Vic Jameson.

Purpose: "We are a religious organization." Information covers religion mission work, social action, housing and economics.

Services: Offers information searches, placement on mailing list and press kits.

How to Contact: Write or call. "A written request for information is preferred, but we will answer simple questions on the phone."

World Community Al-Islam in the West, 7351 S. Stony Island Ave., Chicago IL 60649. (312)667-7200. Contact: James Abdul Aziz Sha Bazz.

Purpose: "The World Community Al-Islam in the West center is concerned with Islam in the United States." Information covers religion.

Services: Offers annual reports, brochures/pamphlets (historical) and statistics.

How to Contact: Write or call. "Write for specific information, call if there is a simple question that can be answered on the phone."

Research & Information

Governmental Research Association, Box 387, Ocean Gate NJ 08740. (201)269-3489. Assistant Secretary: Sandra Leibrick.
Purpose: "An organization of individuals professionally engaged in governmental research. It draws its membership from staffs of privately supported organizations; from college and university faculties and research bureaus; from local, state and federal governments; and from organizations of public officials."
Services: Offers newsletter. Publications include *GRA Reporter* (quarterly) and *GRA Directory*.
How to Contact: Write. Charges $20/copy for *Directory*.

Information Industry Association, 4720 Montgomery Lane, Suite 904, Bethesda MD 20014. (301)654-4150. Communications Director: Helena M. Strauch.
Purpose: "Information Industry Association (IIA) is a trade association of for-profit companies engaged in the business of information. This covers the creation, retrieval, publishing, marketing, distribution and use of data, documents and literature. Information may be produced in various media—hard copy, microfiche, computer tape, etc. Our industry includes library services, information on demand, business information, marketing management, document delivery, data processing and word processing, records management, looseleaf services, information technology, online services, publishing, management information systems, office of the future, and so on." Information covers business, history, industry, law, new products, politics, science and technical data.
Services: Offers aid in arranging interviews, statistics, brochures/pamphlets, placement on mailing list and newsletter. Publications include descriptive brochures.
How to Contact: Write or call. Charges for photocopies "and for other expenses that might be incurred when answering an inquiry. Within reasonable limits, we will not charge for our staff time."

Science

American Association for the Advancement of Science, 1776 Massachusetts Ave. NW, Washington DC 20036. (202)467-4400. Public Information Officer: Carol Rogers.
Purpose: The American Association for the Advancement of Science is a membership organization whose purpose is the advancement of science. Information covers science.
Services: Offers statistics, brochures/pamphlets, placement on mailing list and press releases. Publications include *Science*, a magazine free to members or available by subscription.
How to Contact: Write or call. Written request preferable.

Association of Systematics Collections, University of Kansas, Museum of Natural History, Lawrence KS 66045. (913)864-4867. Registry Coordinator: Carol J. Terry.
Purpose: "One of the Association of Systematics Collections' (ASC) projects is the Registry of Taxonomic Resources and Services. This is a referral service designed to provide the names of professional biologists and biological collections to anyone interested in obtaining taxonomically oriented information. The expertise of the persons listed in the registry is primarily systematic (i.e., identification of biological specimens) rather than behavioral, ecological or physiological. The ASC Registry is used mainly by professional biologists inquiring about the locations of collections of particular plants and animals, or persons involved in environmental surveys who need bioligical specialists to perform various tasks—for example, specimen collection or identification." Information covers biological law and biology.
Services: Offers aid in arranging interviews, brochures/pamphlets, information searches and newsletter. Publications include *Biological Reconnaissance*.

How to Contact: Call. "Most services are free. Exceptionally long queries of our computer data base may require a small fee. The registry is not an information service, but provides only references to biologists with taxonomic expertise."

Dividends from Space, 3228 N. 26th St., Milwaukee WI 53206. (414)873-0133. Chairman: Daniel M. Lentz.
Purpose: "To illustrate the benefits that have come to mankind through space exploration, and to look at possibilities for the future. This is done through publication, a speakers bureau and by confering honors upon those actively promoting space explorations." Information covers benefits of space exploration.
Services: Offers brochures/pamphlets and newsletter. Publications available.
How to Contact: Write or call. Charges printing cost, plus postage (50¢-$1.50).

Institute for Epidemiologic Studies of Violence, Box 21, Rt. 2, Carbondale IL 62901. Executive Director: Dr. David F. Duncan.
Purpose: "Research into the nature, frequency, distribution and causes of human violent behavior, applying epidemiologic rather than psychological or sociological methods and models." Information covers health/medicine, crime, child abuse, spouse abuse, etc.
Services: Offers aid in arranging interviews and reprints of published papers and research reports.
How to Contact: Write.

Laser Institute of America, 4100 Executive Park Dr., Cincinnati OH 45241. (513)662-2299. Secretary: D.C. Winburn.
Purpose: "Organized to disseminate laser technology by local chapter activities, short courses, publications, conferences and support of student chapters at schools offering laser training." Information covers health/medicine, how-to, industry, science and technical data.
Services: Offers aid in arranging interviews and brochures/pamphlets. Publications include publications list.
How to Contact: Call or write.

National Academy of Sciences, National Academy of Engineering, National Research Council, Institute of Medicine, 2101 Constitution Ave. NW, Washington DC 20418. (202)389-6511. Director of Media Relations, Office of Information: Barbara Jorgenson.
Purpose: "The National Academy of Sciences (NAS) is a private membership organization dedicated to furthering science and its use for the general welfare. The Academy of Engineering, established under the NAS charter, provides similar services on engineering questions. The National Research Council serves both academies in carrying out this responsibility. The Institute of Medicine studies and reports on problems associated with delivery of adequate health services to all sectors of society." Information covers agriculture, health/medicine and science.
Services: Offers aid in arranging interviews and annual reports. "We can often supply copies of reports of these organizations to members of the working press. Information is limited to material on the organization or its publications."
How to Contact: "Questions must deal specifically with the activities and/or reports of these organizations. We cannot provide individual reference or search services or respond to general queries."

National Geographic Society, 17th and M Sts. NW, Washington DC 20036. (202)857-7000. Secretary: Sharn Vanwie.
Purpose: "Nonprofit scientific and educational organization to diffuse knowledge."
Services: Offers information searches, photos and press kits. Publications include *History of the National Geographic Society*.
How to Contact: Write, and enclose resume.

Sports

Association for Intercollegiate Athletics for Women, 1201 16th St. NW, Washington DC 20036. (202)833-5485.
Purpose: "The Association for Intercollegiate Athletics for Women is the governing body for women's intercollegiate athletics. We conduct national championships in a variety of sports." Information covers sports.
Services: Offers aid in arranging interviews, biographies, statistics, brochures/pamphlets, placement on mailing list and press kits. Publications include handbook, directory and high school brochure.
How to Contact: Write or call.

Coaching Association of Canada, 333 River Rd. Vanier, Ottawa, Ontario, Canada K1L 8B9. (613)746-5693. Executive Director: Lyle Makosky.
Purpose: "The Coaching Association of Canada is a national nonprofit organization. Its major aims are to increase coaching effectiveness in all sports and to encourage the development of coaching by providing programs and services to coaches at all levels. We also operate the Sports Information Resource Center (SIRC). It is a unique sport library and documentation center, and its services are accessible to all CAC members as well as to the sports community at large." Information covers health/medicine, how-to, recreation, science, sports and technical data.
Services: Offers annual reports, brochures/pamphlets and information searches. Publications include *Coaching Review* (bimonthly magazine) and *Sport and Recreation Index.*
How to Contact: Write. Charges for publications.

Harness Tracks of America, Inc., 333 N. Michigan Ave., Chicago IL 60601. (312)782-5100. Executive Assistant: Thomas L. Aronson.
Purpose: "Harness Tracks of America is an association of North American race tracks, dedicated to the advancement and progress of the harness racing sport. Activities enter into all areas of the race track business, including economic information and statistics." Information covers business, economics, history, law, politics and sports.
Services: Offers statistics, brochures/pamphlets and newsletters.
How to Contact: Write or call.

International Golf Association, 1271 Avenue of Americas, New York NY 10020. Contact: Stephanie Jubert.

Little League Baseball, Inc., Box 3485, Williamsport PA 17701. (717)326-1921. Public Relations Director: Preston Hadley.
Purpose: "Little League Baseball, Inc., is a youth sports organization." Information covers health/medicine, how-to, recreation and sports.
Services: Offers aid in arranging interviews, bibliographies, statistics, brochures/pamphlets, information searches, placement on mailing list, photos, press kits and an organizational profile. Publications include *Where Little League Stands in Service to Youth* and *Little League Today: The Total Community Program.*
How to Contact: Write or call.

National Association of Intercollegiate Athletics, 1221 Baltimore St., Kansas City MO 64105. (816)842-5050. Director of Public Relations: Charles Eppler.
Purpose: "To promote interests of the colleges of moderate enrollment." Information covers sports.
Services: Offers statistics, brochures/pamphlets and newsletter.
How to Contact: Write or call.

National Association of Professional Baseball Leagues, Box A, St. Petersburg FL

33731. (813)822-6937. Assistant to President: Joan Dittrich.
Purpose: "We are the main governing body of minor league baseball and the central clearinghouse for all its paperwork and records." Information covers baseball.
Services: Offers statistics, information searches and newsletter. Publications include a monthly newsletter and *Baseball* (annual magazine).
How to Contact: Charges $2/year for membership in National Association of Baseball Writers for "qualified writers"; membership includes newsletter.

National Bowling Council, 1666 K St. NW, Washington DC 20006. (202)659-9070. Public Relations Director: Keith L. Saiter.
Purpose: "The National Bowling Council is the education and promotion arm of the sport, with a membership representing all facets of the game." Information covers business, celebrities, entertainment, health/medicine, history, how-to, industry, recreation, sports and technical data.
Services: Offers aid in arranging interviews, annual reports, biographies, statistics, brochures/pamphlets, information searches, placement on mailing list, photos and press kits. "We can supply or direct writer to every aspect of the sport, cutting down on the number of calls which must be made." Publications include *Bowling Factbook* (demographics on the sport).
How to Contact: Write or call.

National Collegiate Athletic Association, Box 1906, Shawnee Mission KS 66222. (913)384-3220. Director of Public Relations: David Cawood.
Purpose: "To promote sports in 13 colleges." Information covers sports.
Services: Offers aid in arranging interviews, brochures/pamphlets, information searches, placement on mailing list, statistics, newsletter and press kits.
How to Contact: Write or call.

National Football League Players Association, Suite 407, 1300 Connecticut Ave. NW, Washington DC 20036. (202)833-3310. Public Relations Director: Frank Woschitz.
Services: Offers statistics (limited).
How to Contact: Write or call.

National Junior College Athletic Association, 12 E. 2nd St., Hutchinson KS 67501. (316)663-5445. Executive Director: George Hillian.
Purpose: "To promote and foster junior college athletics on intersectional and national levels, so that results will be consistant with the total educational program of its members."
Services: Offers aid in arranging interviews, brochures/pamphlets, information searches and statistics (on national tournaments). Publications available.
How to Contact: Write. Charges for publications.

Professional Association of Diving Instructors, 2064 North Bush St., Santa Ana CA 92706. (714)547-6996. Information covers business, recreation, sports, technical data and scuba diving.
Services: Offers brochures/pamphlets and newsletters. Publications include *Undersea Journal* ($12/year), *Dive Manual and Dive Tabler* ($9.95), *Instructors Manual* ($20), and information bulletins ($1).
How to Contact: Write.

Professional Bowlers Association, 1720 Merriman Rd., Akron OH 44313. Contact: Bud Fisher.

Professional Golfers' Association of America (PGA), Box 12458, Lake Park FL 33403. (305)844-5000. News Director: James C. Warters.
Purpose: "The Professional Golfers' Association of America is an association of 16,000 members and apprentices. The organization carries out various administrative functions for members, including education; operation of various activities, such as profes-

sional golf tournaments; a credit union; membership processing; and annual business and executive meetings." Information covers business, celebrities, economics, entertainment, history, how-to, industry, new products, recreation, sports and technical data.

Services: Offers aid in arranging interviews, annual reports, bibliographies, biographies, statistics, brochures/pamphlets, information searches, placement on mailing list, newsletter, photos, press kits and films. Publications include *PGA Media Reference Guide* and *PGA Apprentice Program*.

How to Contact: Write or call. Charges $10/film, plus shipping costs.

United States Golf Association, Liberty Corner Rd., Far Hills NJ 07931. (201)234-2300. Public Information Representative: Patrick Leahy.

Purpose: "An association of 4,700 member golf clubs and courses. The governing body of golf in the US, the United States Golf Association (USGA) writes and interprets the rules of golf; conducts the ten national championships of golf, including the US Open; tests balls and equipment so that they conform to rules; maintains golf house library and museum; offers USGA green section and turfgrass advisory service to member clubs; and supports turfgrass research at universities." Information covers golf.

Services: Offers aid in arranging interviews, annual reports, bibliographies, biographies, statistics, brochures/pamphlets, placement on mailing list, photos and press kits. Publications include material on golf rules, golf course maintenance, handicapping and course rating, competitions and general golf literature.

How to Contact: Charges for publications. "USGA must be given proper credit when copyrighted material is used."

Youth

Boy Scouts of America, North Brunswick NJ 08902. (201)249-6000. Contact: Public Relations Division.

Purpose: "Boy Scouts of America is a youth-serving organization stressing citizenship training, character building and physical fitness." Information covers recreation, sports and youth.

Services: Offers aid in arranging interviews, annual reports, brochures/pamphlets and photos. Offers numerous publications.

How to Contact: Query the PR department of the national office, or check the local Boy Scout council or scout supply outlet, where much of the information is available. "Use mail order forms for literature, available from the local scout council."

Tips: "Much help can often be better provided by your local scout council rather than by the national office. Your needs should be specific. 'Send us information on kids who have done exciting projects' isn't of much help to us for you."

The Boys' Clubs of America, 771 1st Ave., New York NY 10017. (212)557-7755. Manager of Public Information: Evan McElroy.

Purpose: Maintains clubs; "a place of their own for youth, 6-18 years of age, where a professional, guidance-oriented staff is available full time, offering diversified programs in social recreation, health, education and leadership development. There are currently 1,100 Boys' Clubs in all 50 states, Puerto Rico and the Virgin Islands. They are predominantly located in urban and inner city areas. Most Boys' Clubs professionals are experts in child care and development." Information covers health/medicine, history, how-to, recreation, self-help, sports, travel, education and volunteerism.

Services: Offers aid in arranging interviews, annual reports, bibliographies, biographies, statistics, brochures/pamphlets, information searches, placement on mailing list, newsletter, photos and press kits. Publications include *The Bulletin* (quarterly).

How to Contact: Write. Will give regional referrals if writer needs local material.

Camp Fire Girls, Inc., 4601 Madison Ave., Kansas City MO 64112. (816)756-1950. Director, Public Relations: Shirley Montague.
Purpose: "Camp Fire Girls is a nationwide youth organization committed to providing a program of informal education and opportunities for youth to realize their potential in functioning effectively as caring, self-directed individuals responsible to themselves and to others. We seek to improve those conditions in society which affect youth." Information covers how-to and recreation.
Services: Offers aid in arranging interviews, annual reports, bibliographies, biographies, statistics, brochures/pamphlets, newsletter, photos and press kits. Publications include *Leadership* (quarterly magazine) and annual reports.
How to Contact: Write. "Writers must contact public relations director for permission to use services."

Girls Clubs of America, Inc., 205 Lexington Ave., New York NY 10016. (212)689-3700. Director of Public Relations: Susan L. Davis.
Purpose: "Girls Clubs of America is a national service and advocacy organization for girls age 6-18. More than 250 girls clubs serve nearly one-quarter of a million girls, regardless of race, creed or national origin. Clubs are located in urban areas and are open daily after school, weekends and during the summer. Programs in the arts, sports, education for sexuality, education/employment and juvenile delinquency prevention are featured." Information covers health/medicine, how-to, recreation and sports, as well as national issues and trends of concern to girls and those who work with them.
Services: Offers aid in arranging interviews, annual reports, bibliographies, biographies, brochures/pamphlets, placement on mailing list, statistics, newsletter, photos and press kits. Publications available.
How to Contact: Write or call.

Girl Scouts of the USA, 830 3rd Ave., New York NY 10022. (212)940-7500. Contact: Public Information Section, Public Relations Department.
Purpose: "The Girl Scouts of the USA is the largest voluntary organization for girls in the world. We are dedicated to helping girls find their place in today's world and giving them the skills and confidence to do their share in making tomorrow's world a better one." Information covers agriculture, art, business, celebrities, economics, entertainment, food, health/medicine, history, how-to, industry, law, music, nature, new products, politics, recreation, science, self-help, sports, technical data and travel.
Services: Offers aid in arranging interviews, annual reports, biographies, statistics, brochures/pamphlets, information searches, placement on mailing list, newsletter and press kits.
How to Contact: Write.

Junior Achievement (JA), 550 Summer St., Stamford CT 06901. (203)359-2970. Contact: Public Relations Department.
Purpose: "To further the understanding of the workings of the American business system to youth in particular, and the public in general." Conducts economic education and applied management programs in junior high and high schools, and economic awareness programs among 5th and 6th graders. Information covers business, celebrities, economics, history, how-to, industry, new products, self-help and education.
Services: Offers aid in arranging interviews, annual reports, bibliographies, biographies, statistics, brochures/pamphlets, information searches, placement on mailing list, photos, press kits and speakers bureau. Also maintains hall of fame for US business leaders. Publications include *The Achiever* (monthly).
How to Contact: Write or call.

INDEX

Books of Interest From Writer's Digest

The Beginning Writer's Answer Book, edited by Kirk Polking, Jean Chimsky, and Rose Adkins. "What is a query letter?" "If I use a pen name, how can I cash the check?" These are among 567 questions most frequently asked by beginning writers — and expertly answered in this down-to-earth handbook. Cross-indexed. 270 pp. $8.95.

The Cartoonist's and Gag Writer's Handbook, by Jack Markow. Longtime cartoonist with thousands of sales, reveals the secrets of successful cartooning — step by step. Richly illustrated. 157 pp. $9.95.

A Complete Guide to Marketing Magazine Articles, by Duane Newcomb. "Anyone who can write a clear sentence can learn to write and sell articles on a consistent basis," says Newcomb (who has published well over 3,000 articles). Here's how. 248 pp. $7.95.

The Confession Writer's Handbook, by Florence K. Palmer. A stylish and informative guide to getting started and getting ahead in the confessions. How to start a confession and carry it through. How to take an insignificant event and make it significant. 171 pp. $6.95.

The Craft of Interviewing, by John Brady. Everything you always wanted to know about asking questions, but were afraid to ask — from an experienced interviewer and editor of *Writer's Digest.* The most comprehensive guide to interviewing on the market. 244 pp. $9.95.

The Creative Writer, edited by Aron Mathieu. This book opens the door to the real world of publishing. Inspiration, techniques, and ideas, plus inside tips from Maugham, Caldwell, Purdy, others. 416 pp. $8.95.

The Greeting Card Writer's Handbook, by H. Joseph Chadwick. A former greeting card editor tells you what editors look for in inspirational verse . . . how to write humor . . . what to write about for conventional, studio and juvenile cards. Extra: a renewable list of greeting card markets. Will be greeted by any freelancer. 268 pp. $8.95.

A Guide to Writing History, by Doris Ricker Marston. How to track down Big Foot — or your family Civil War letters, or your hometown's last century — for publication and profit. A timely handbook for history buffs and writers. 258 pp. $8.50.

Handbook of Short Story Writing, edited by Frank A. Dickson and Sandra Smythe. You provide the pencil, paper, and sweat — and this book will provide the expert guidance. Features include James Hilton on creating a lovable character: R.V. Cassill on plotting a short story. 238 pp. $8.95.

How to be a Successful Outdoor Writer, by Jack Samson. Longtime editor of *Field & Stream* covers this market in depth. Illustrated. 288 pp. $10.95.

Law and the Writer, edited by Kirk Polking and Leonard S. Meranus. Don't let legal hassles slow down your progress as a writer. Now you can find good counsel on libel, invasion of privacy, fair use, plagiarism, taxes, contracts, social security, and more — all in one volume. 249 pp. $9.95.

Magazine Writing: The Inside Angle, by Art Spikol. Successful editor and writer reveals inside secrets of getting your mss. published. 288 pp. $9.95.

Magazine Writing Today, by Jerome E. Kelley. If you sometimes feel like a mouse in a maze of magazines, with a fat manuscript check at the end of the line, don't fret. Kelley tells you how to get a piece of the action. Covers ideas, research, interviewing organization, the writing process, and ways to get photos. Plus advice on getting started. 220 pp. $9.95.

Mystery Writer's Handbook, by the Mystery Writers of America. A howtheydunit to the whodunit, newly written and revised by members of the Mystery Writers of America. Includes the four elements essential to the classic mystery. A comprehensive handbook that takes the mystery out of mystery writing. 273 pp. $8.95.

Writing the Novel: From Plot to Print, by Lawrence Block. Practical advice on how to write any kind of novel. 256 pp. $9.95.

1001 Article Ideas, by Frank A. Dickson. A compendium of ideas plus formulas to generate more of your own! 256 pp. $9.95.

One Way to Write Your Novel, by Dick Perry. For Perry, a novel is 200 pages. Or, two pages a day for 100 days. You can start and finish your novel, with the help of this step-by-step guide taking you from blank sheet to polished page. 138 pp. $8.95.

Photographer's Market, edited by Melissa Milar and William Brohaugh. Contains what you need to know to be a successful freelance photographer. Names, addresses, photo requirements, and payment rates for 3,000 markets. 615 pp. $12.95.

The Poet and the Poem, by Judson Jerome. A rare journey into the night of the poem — the mechanics, the mystery, the craft and sullen art. Written by the most widely read authority on poetry in America, and a major contemporary poet in his own right. 482 pp. $9.95.

Songwriter's Market, edited by William Brohaugh. Lists 1,500 places where you can sell your songs. Included are the people and conpanies who work daily with songwriters and musicians. Features names and addresses, pay rates and other valuable information you need to sell your work. 349 pp. $9.95.

Stalking the Feature Story, by William Ruehlmann. Besides a nose for news, the newspaper feature writer needs an ear for dialog and an eye for detail. He must also be adept at handling off-the-record remarks, organization, grammar, and the investigative story. Here's the "scoop" on newspaper feature writing. 314 pp. $9.95.

A Treasury of Tips for Writers, edited by Marvin Weisbord. Everything from Vance Packard's system of organizing notes to tips on how to get research done free, by 86 magazine writers. 174 pp. $7.95.

Writer's Digest. The world's leading magazine for writers. Monthly issues include timely interviews, columns, tips to keep writers informed on where and how to sell their work. One year subscription, $15.

The Writer's Digest Diary. Plan your year in it, note appointments, log manuscript sales, be prepared for the IRS. With advice such as the reminder on March 21 to "plan your Christmas story today." It will become a permanent annual record of writing activity. Durable cloth cover. 144 pp. $8.95.

Writer's Market, edited by Bruce Joel Hillman. The freelancer's bible, containing 4,500 places to sell what you write. Includes the name, address and phone number of the buyer, a description of material wanted and rates of payment. 947 pp. $14.95.

The Writer's Resource Guide, edited by William Brohaugh. Over 2,000 research sources for information on anything you write about. 480 pp. $10.95.

Writer's Yearbook, edited by John Brady. This large annual magazine contains how-to articles, interviews and special features, along with analyses of 500 major markets for writers. $2.50.

Writing and Selling Non-Fiction, by Hayes B. Jacobs. Explores with style and know-how the book market, organization and research, finding new markets, interviewing, humor, agents, writer's fatigue and more. 317 pp. $9.95.

Writing and Selling Science Fiction, complied by the Science Fiction Writers of America. A comprehensive handbook to an exciting but oft-misunderstood genre. Eleven articles by top-flight sf writers on markets, characters, dialog. "crazy" ideas, world-building, alien-building, money and more. 197 pp. $8.95.

Writing for Children and Teen-agers, by Lee Wyndham. Author of over 50 children's books shares her secrets for selling to this large, lucrative market. Features: the 12-point recipe for plotting, and the Ten Commandments for Writers. 253 pp. $8.95.

Writing Popular Fiction, by Dean R. Koontz. How to write mysteries, suspense thrillers, science fiction, Gothic romances, adult fantasy, Westerns and erotica. Here's an inside guide to lively fiction, by a lively novelist. 232 pp. $8.95.

(1-2 books, add $1.00 postage and handling; 3 or more, additional 25¢ each. Allow 30 days for delivery. Prices subject to change without notice.)

Writer's Digest Books, Dept. B, 9933 Alliance Road, Cincinnati, Ohio 45242